VIZ GRAPHIC NOVEL
RANMA 1/2™

15

This volume contains
RANMA 1/2 PART EIGHT #1 through
#7 in their entirety.

Story & Art by Rumiko Takahashi

English Adaptation by Gerard Jones & Toshifumi Yoshida

*

Touch-Up Art & Lettering/Wayne Truman
Cover Design/Hidemi Sahara
Graphics & Layout/Sean Lee
Assistant Editor/Bill Flanagan
Editor/Trish Ledoux & Julie Davis
Managing Editor/Annette Roman

*

V.P. of Sales & Marketing/Rick Bauer
V.P. of Editorial/Hyoe Narita
Publisher/Seiji Horibuchi

*

First published by Shogakukan, Inc. in Japan

*

Printed in Canada

*

Published by Viz Communications, Inc.
P.O. Box 77010
San Francisco, CA 94107

www.viz.com • www.j-pop.com • www.animerica-mag.com

*

10 9 8 7 6 5 4 3
First printing, May 2000
Second printing, June 2001
Third printing, February 2003

VIZ GRAPHIC NOVEL

RANMA 1/2™

STORY & ART BY

RUMIKO TAKAHASHI

CONTENTS

Part 1
KUNG FU STEW

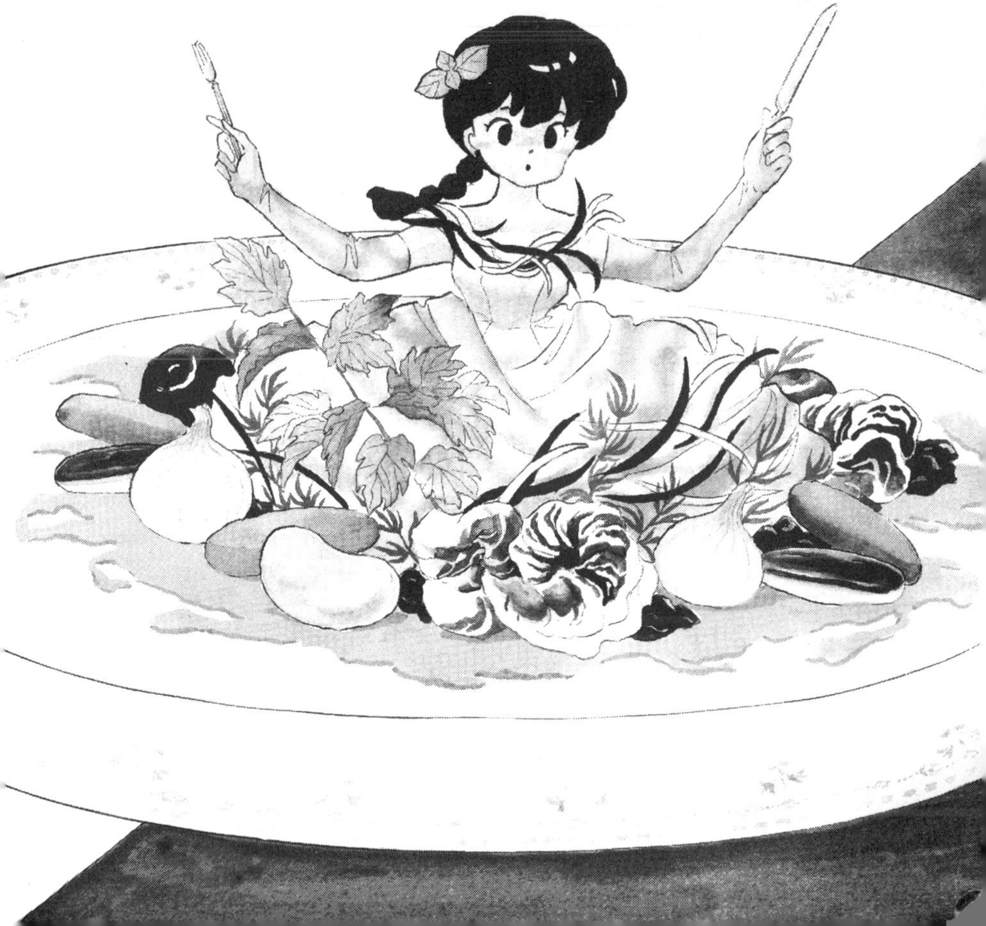

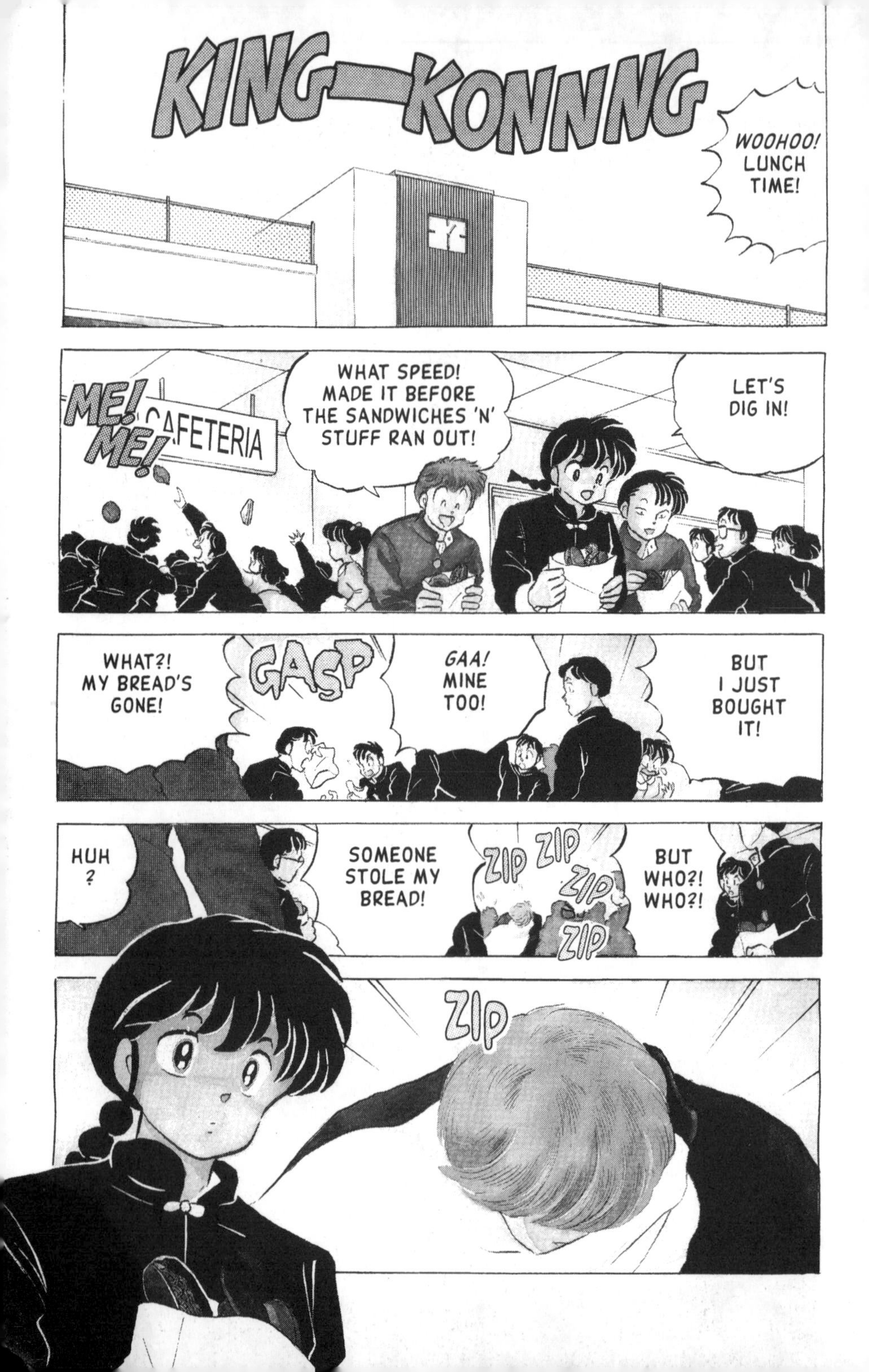
KING—KONNNG
WOOHOO! LUNCH TIME!
ME! ME!
CAFETERIA
WHAT SPEED! MADE IT BEFORE THE SANDWICHES 'N' STUFF RAN OUT!
LET'S DIG IN!
WHAT?! MY BREAD'S GONE!
GASP
GAA! MINE TOO!
BUT I JUST BOUGHT IT!
HUH ?
SOMEONE STOLE MY BREAD!
ZIP ZIP ZIP ZIP
BUT WHO?! WHO?!
ZIP

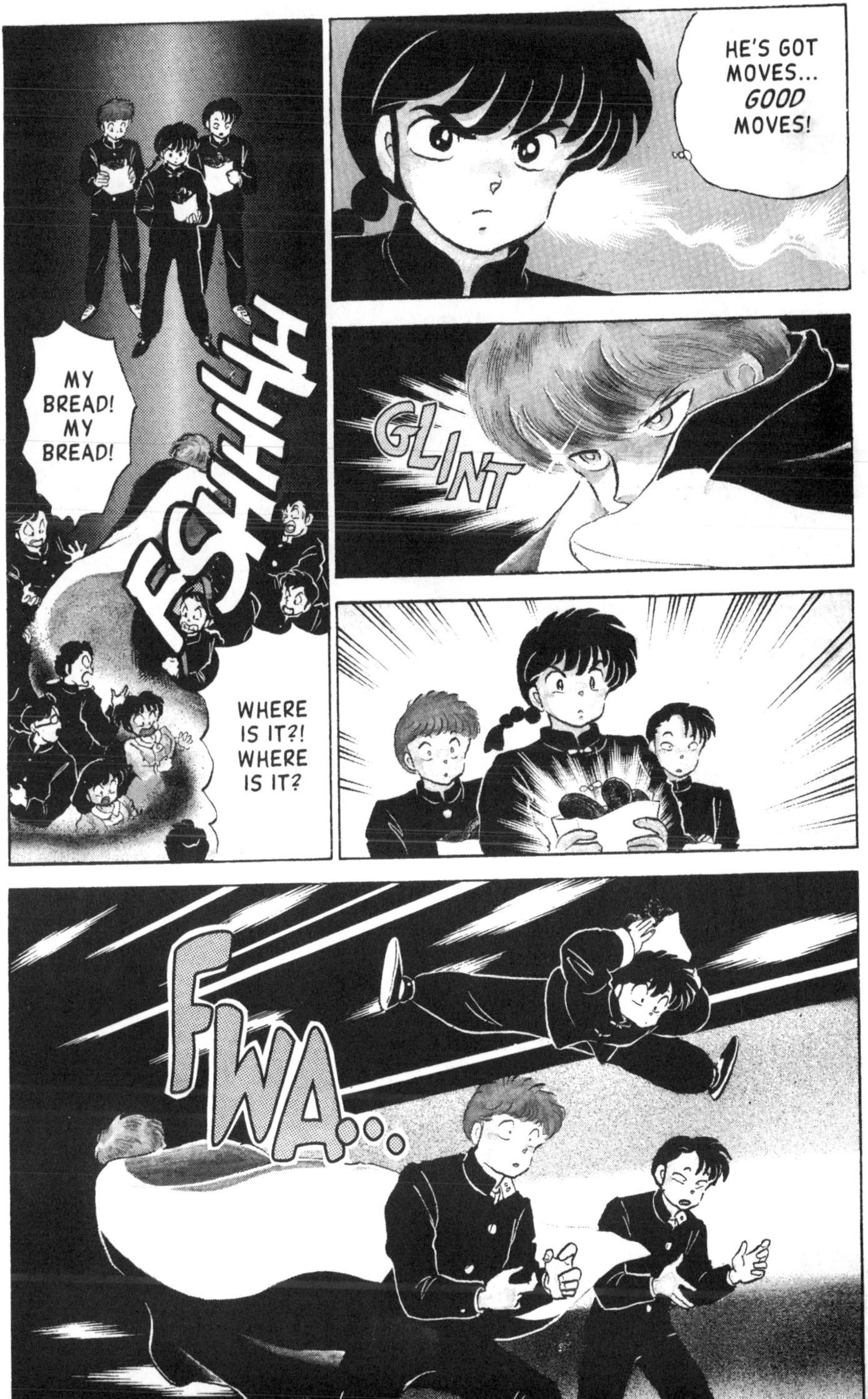
MY BREAD! MY BREAD!
FSHHHH
WHERE IS IT?! WHERE IS IT?
HE'S GOT MOVES... GOOD MOVES!
GLINT
FWA...

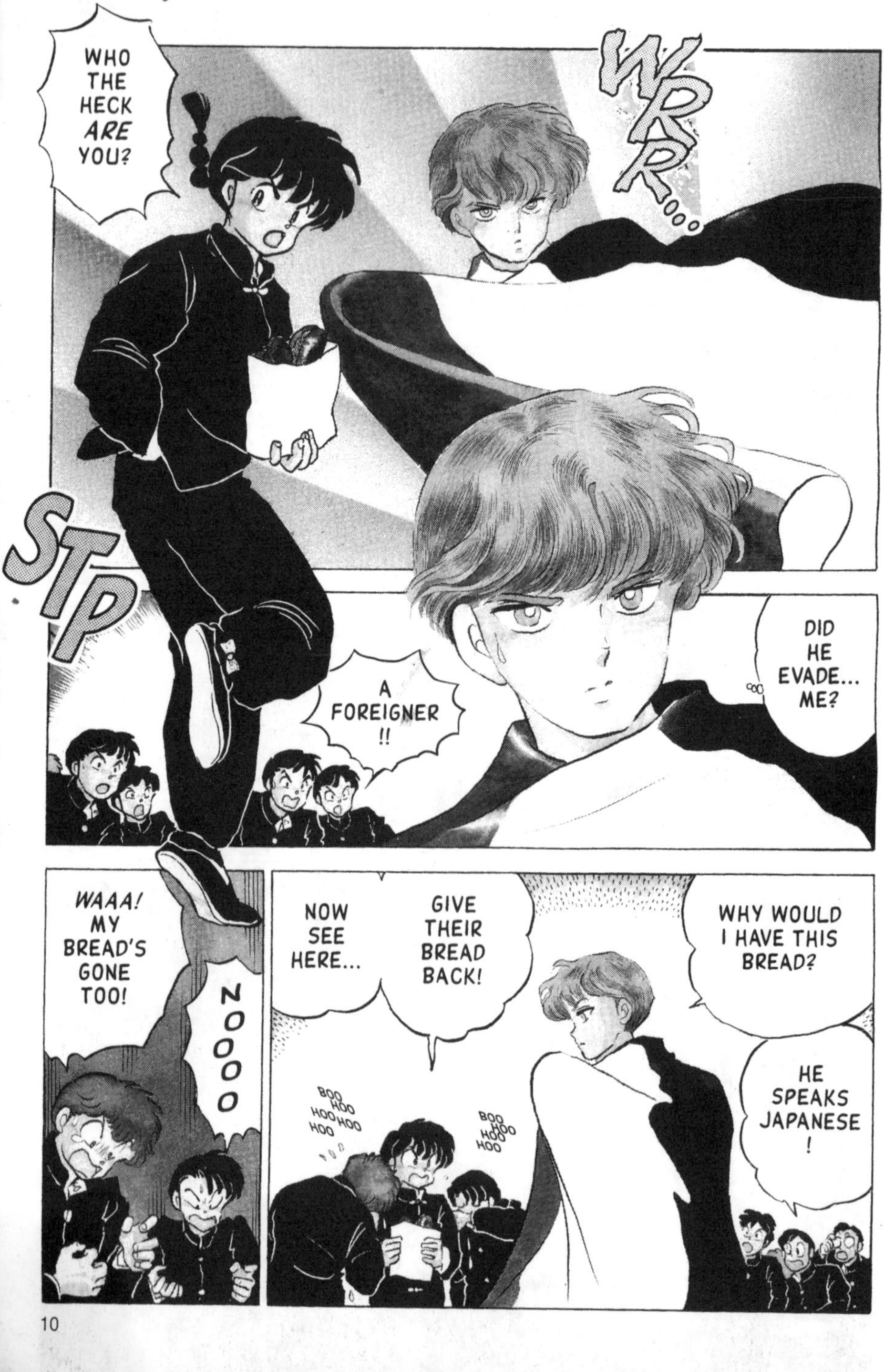
WHO THE HECK ARE YOU?
WRR...
STP
A FOREIGNER !!
DID HE EVADE... ME?
WAAA! MY BREAD'S GONE TOO!
NOOOO
NOW SEE HERE...
GIVE THEIR BREAD BACK!
BOO HOO HOO HOO HOO
BOO HOO HOO HOO
WHY WOULD I HAVE THIS BREAD?
HE SPEAKS JAPANESE !

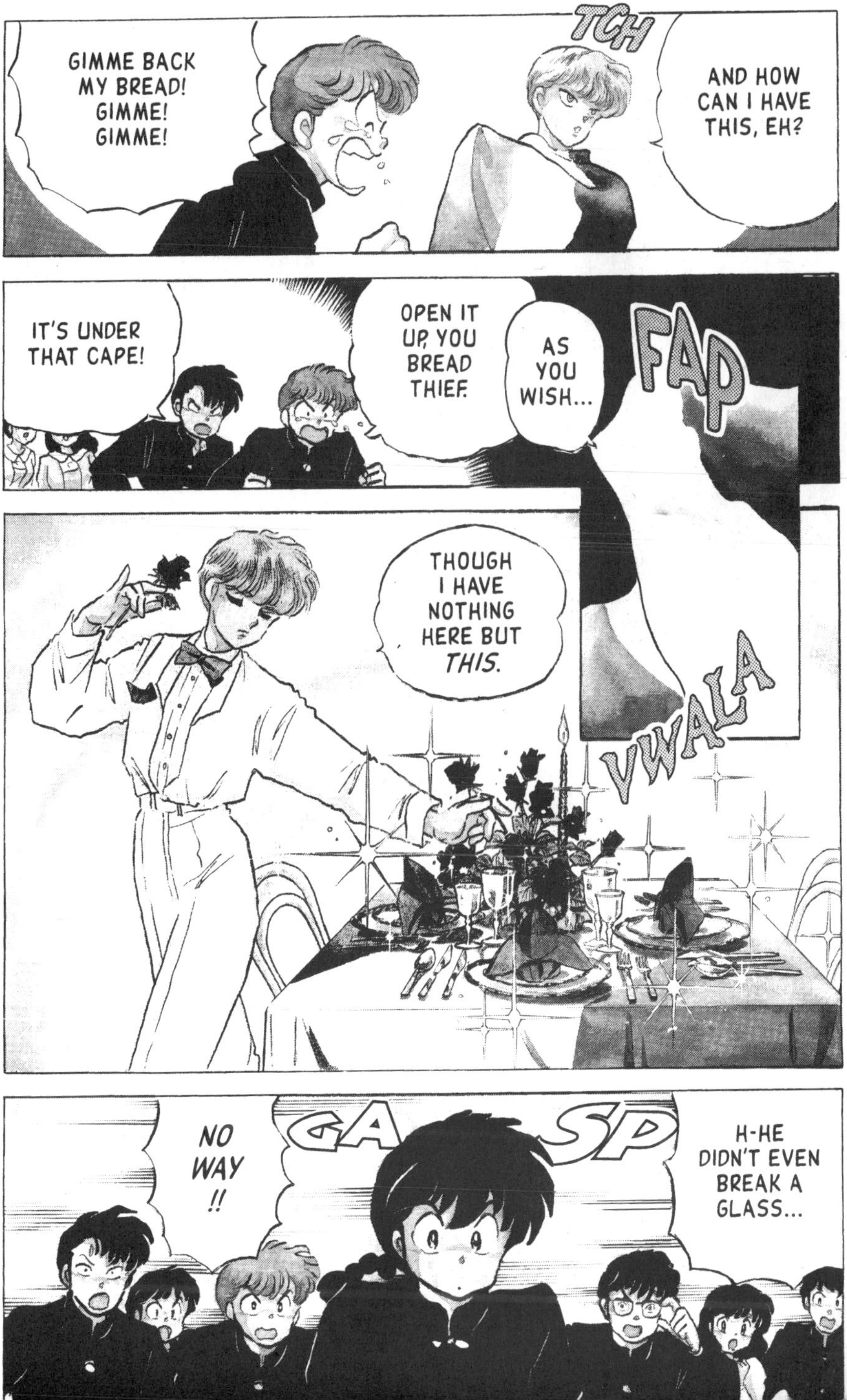
GIMME BACK MY BREAD! GIMME! GIMME!
TCH
AND HOW CAN I HAVE THIS, EH?
IT'S UNDER THAT CAPE!
OPEN IT UP, YOU BREAD THIEF.
AS YOU WISH...
FAP
THOUGH I HAVE NOTHING HERE BUT *THIS.*
VWALA
NO WAY !!
GASP
H-HE DIDN'T EVEN BREAK A GLASS...

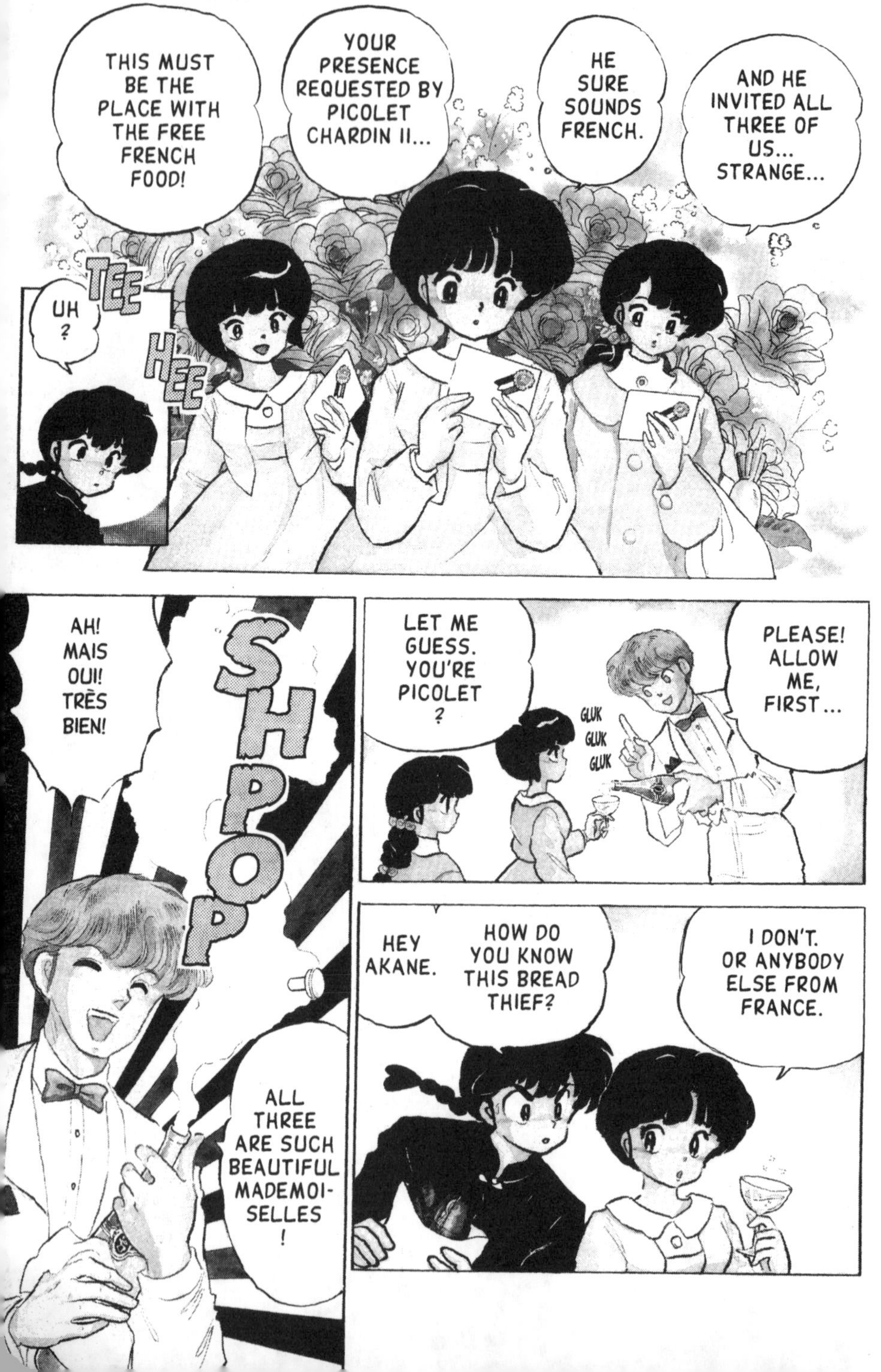

THIS MUST BE THE PLACE WITH THE FREE FRENCH FOOD!
YOUR PRESENCE REQUESTED BY PICOLET CHARDIN II...
HE SURE SOUNDS FRENCH.
AND HE INVITED ALL THREE OF US... STRANGE...
UH ?
TEE HEE
AH! MAIS OUI! TRÈS BIEN!
SHPOP
ALL THREE ARE SUCH BEAUTIFUL MADEMOI-SELLES !
LET ME GUESS. YOU'RE PICOLET ?
GLUK GLUK GLUK
PLEASE! ALLOW ME, FIRST...
HEY AKANE.
HOW DO YOU KNOW THIS BREAD THIEF?
I DON'T. OR ANYBODY ELSE FROM FRANCE.

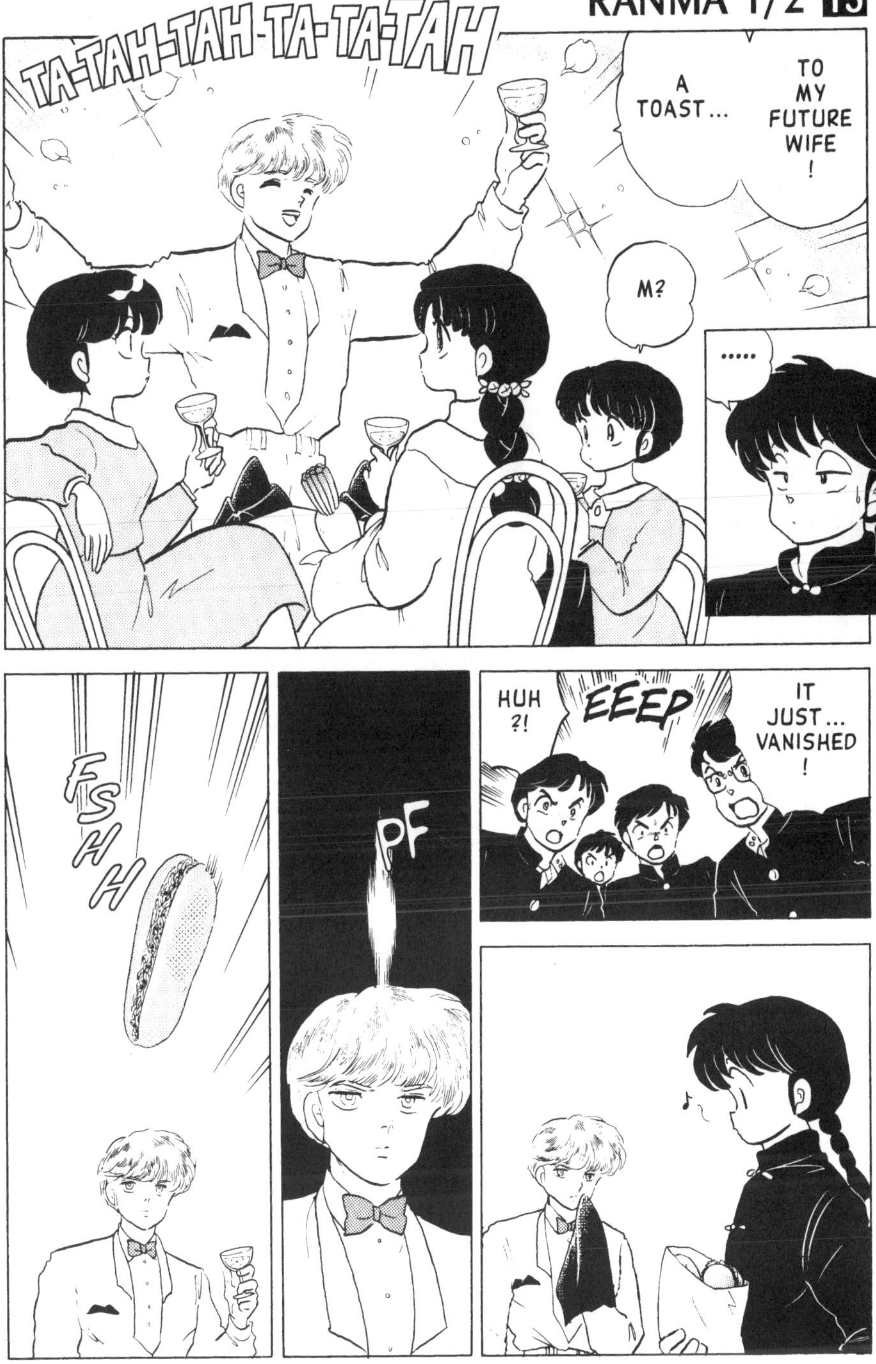
TA-TAH-TAH-TA-TA-TAH
A TOAST...
TO MY FUTURE WIFE !
M?
.....
FSHH
PF
HUH ?!
EEEP
IT JUST... VANISHED !

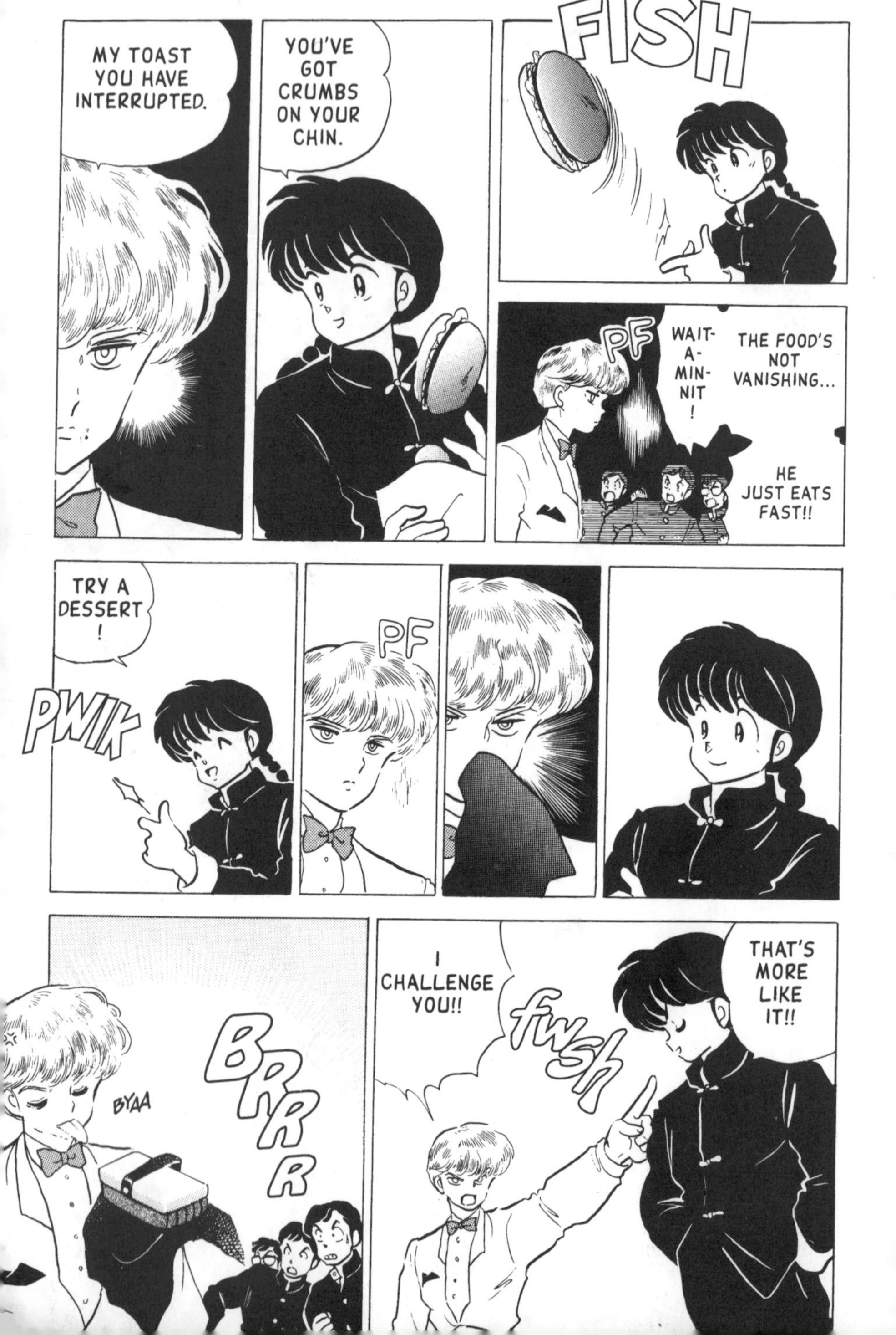
MY TOAST YOU HAVE INTERRUPTED.
YOU'VE GOT CRUMBS ON YOUR CHIN.
FISH
PF
WAIT-A-MIN-NIT!
THE FOOD'S NOT VANISHING...
HE JUST EATS FAST!!
TRY A DESSERT!
PWIK
PF
BYAA
BRRR
I CHALLENGE YOU!!
fwsh
THAT'S MORE LIKE IT!!

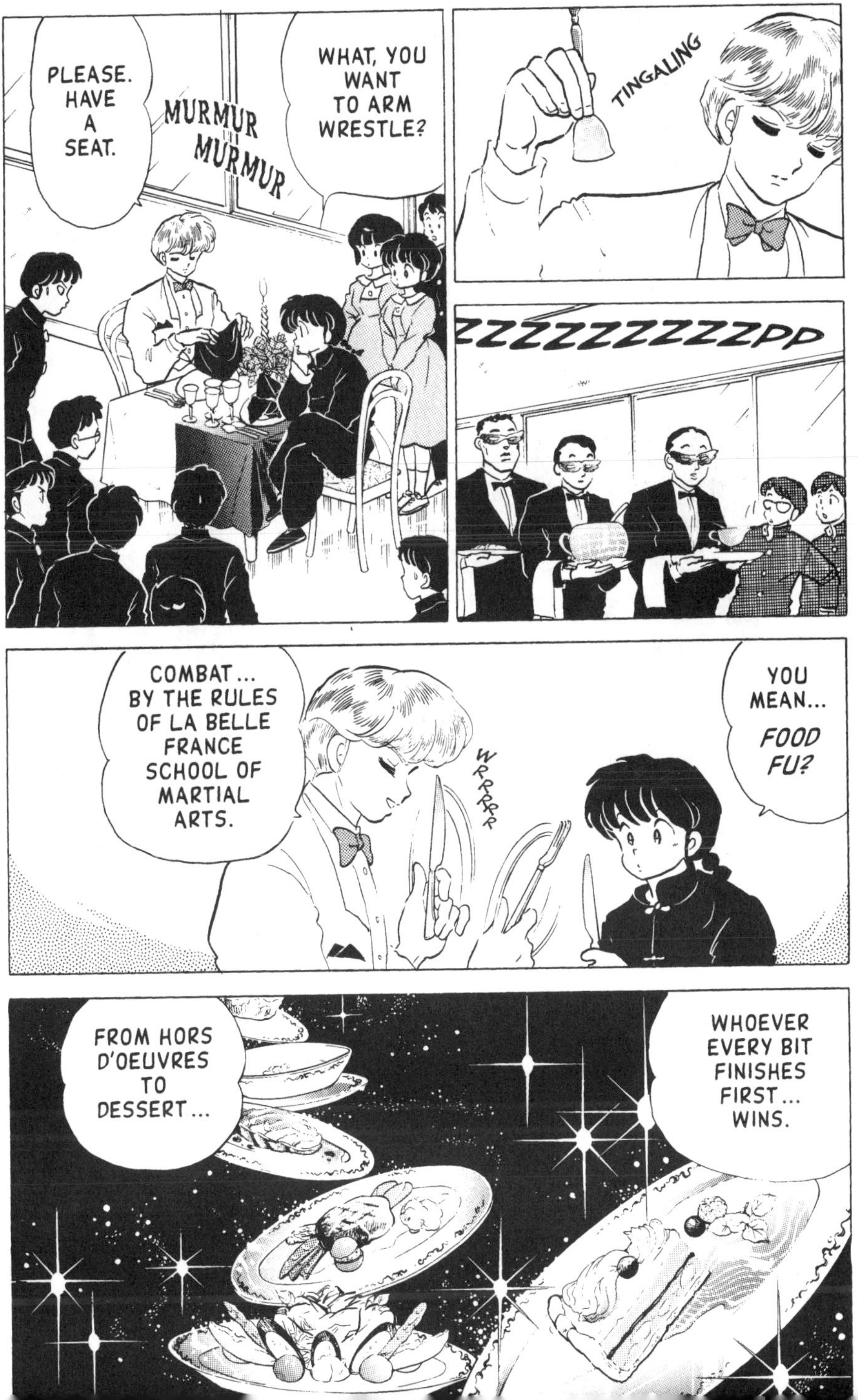
PLEASE. HAVE A SEAT.
MURMUR MURMUR
WHAT, YOU WANT TO ARM WRESTLE?
TINGALING
ZZZZZZZZZZZPP
COMBAT... BY THE RULES OF LA BELLE FRANCE SCHOOL OF MARTIAL ARTS.
WRRRRR
YOU MEAN... *FOOD FU?*
FROM HORS D'OEUVRES TO DESSERT...
WHOEVER EVERY BIT FINISHES FIRST... WINS.

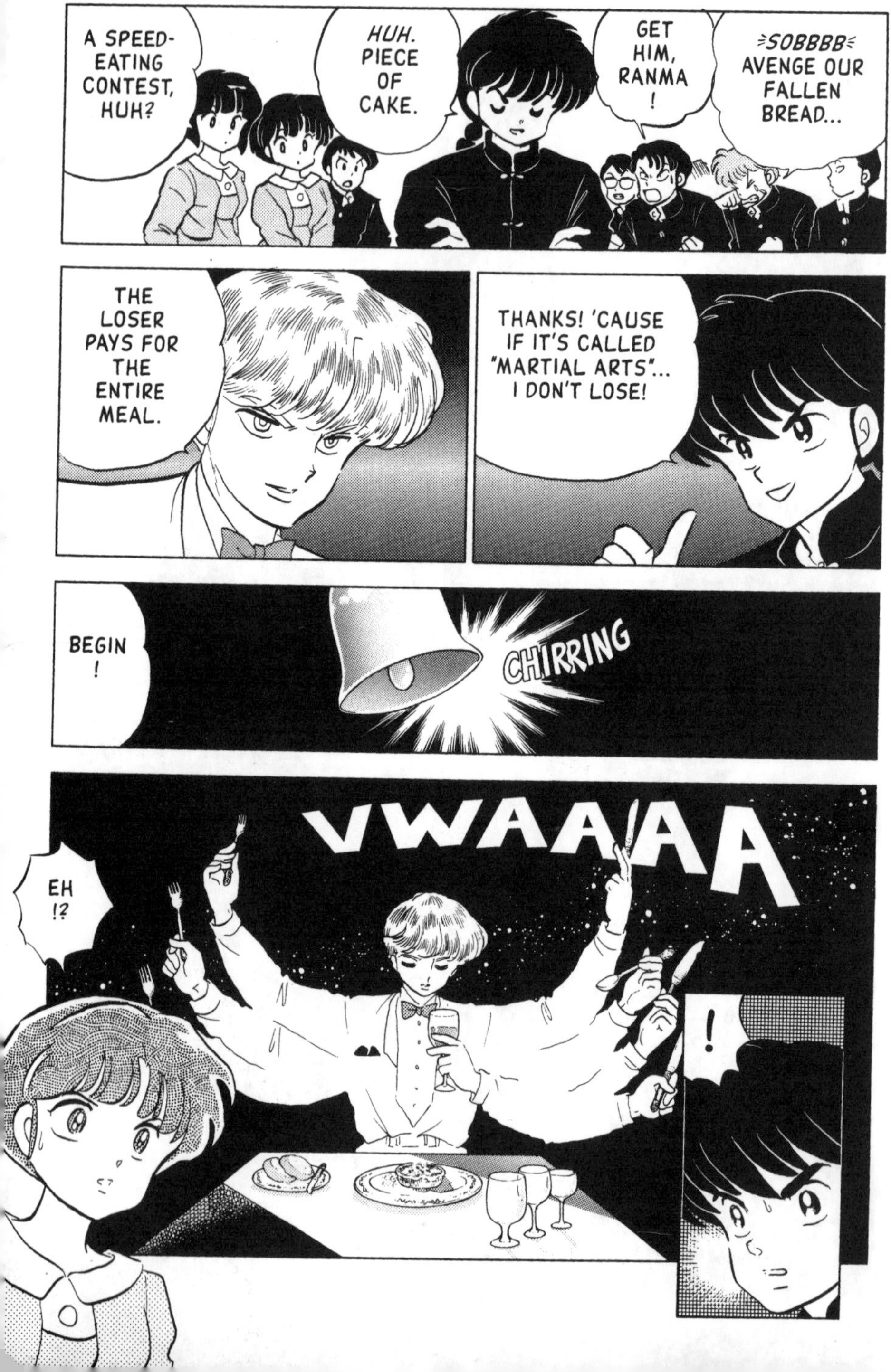
A SPEED-EATING CONTEST, HUH?
HUH. PIECE OF CAKE.
GET HIM, RANMA!
≈SOBBBB≈ AVENGE OUR FALLEN BREAD...
THE LOSER PAYS FOR THE ENTIRE MEAL.
THANKS! 'CAUSE IF IT'S CALLED "MARTIAL ARTS"... I DON'T LOSE!
BEGIN!
CHIRRING
VWAAAA
EH!?
!

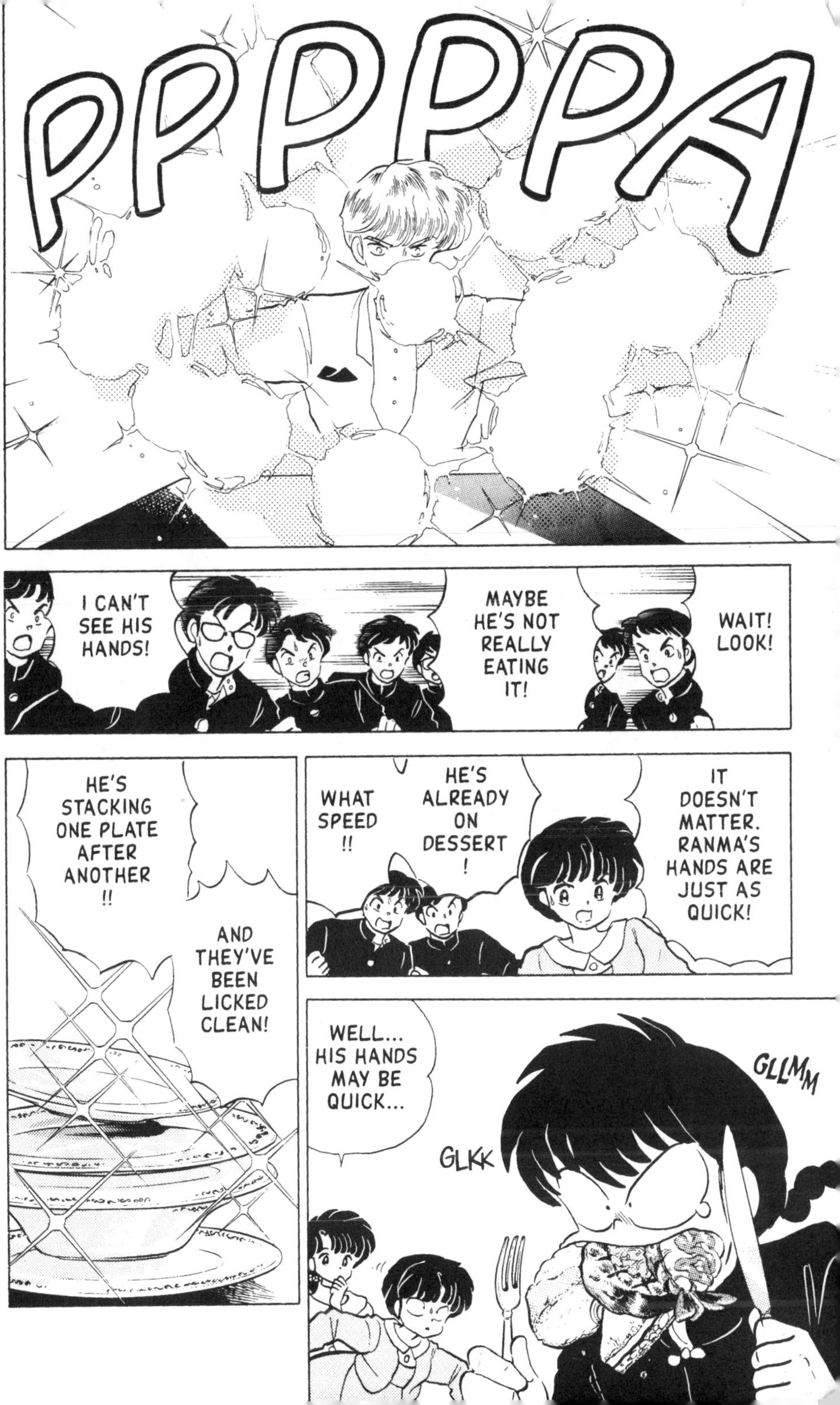
PPPPPA
I CAN'T SEE HIS HANDS!
MAYBE HE'S NOT REALLY EATING IT!
WAIT! LOOK!
HE'S STACKING ONE PLATE AFTER ANOTHER !!
AND THEY'VE BEEN LICKED CLEAN!
WHAT SPEED !!
HE'S ALREADY ON DESSERT !
IT DOESN'T MATTER. RANMA'S HANDS ARE JUST AS QUICK!
WELL... HIS HANDS MAY BE QUICK...
GLLMM
GLKK

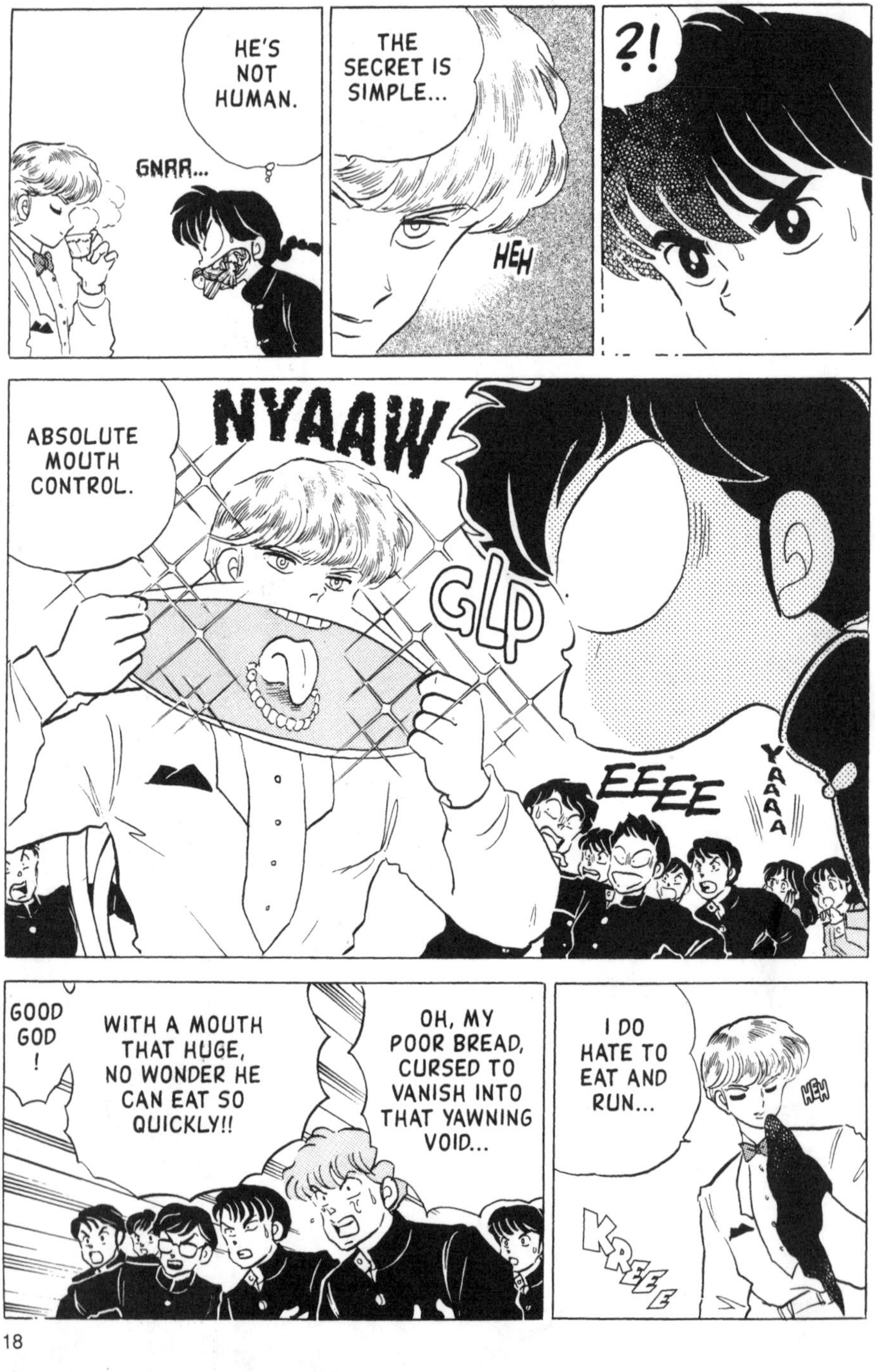

HE'S NOT HUMAN.
GNRR...
THE SECRET IS SIMPLE...
HEH
?!
ABSOLUTE MOUTH CONTROL.
NYAAW
GLP
EEEEE
YAAAA
GOOD GOD !
WITH A MOUTH THAT HUGE, NO WONDER HE CAN EAT SO QUICKLY!!
OH, MY POOR BREAD, CURSED TO VANISH INTO THAT YAWNING VOID...
I DO HATE TO EAT AND RUN...
HEH
KREEEE

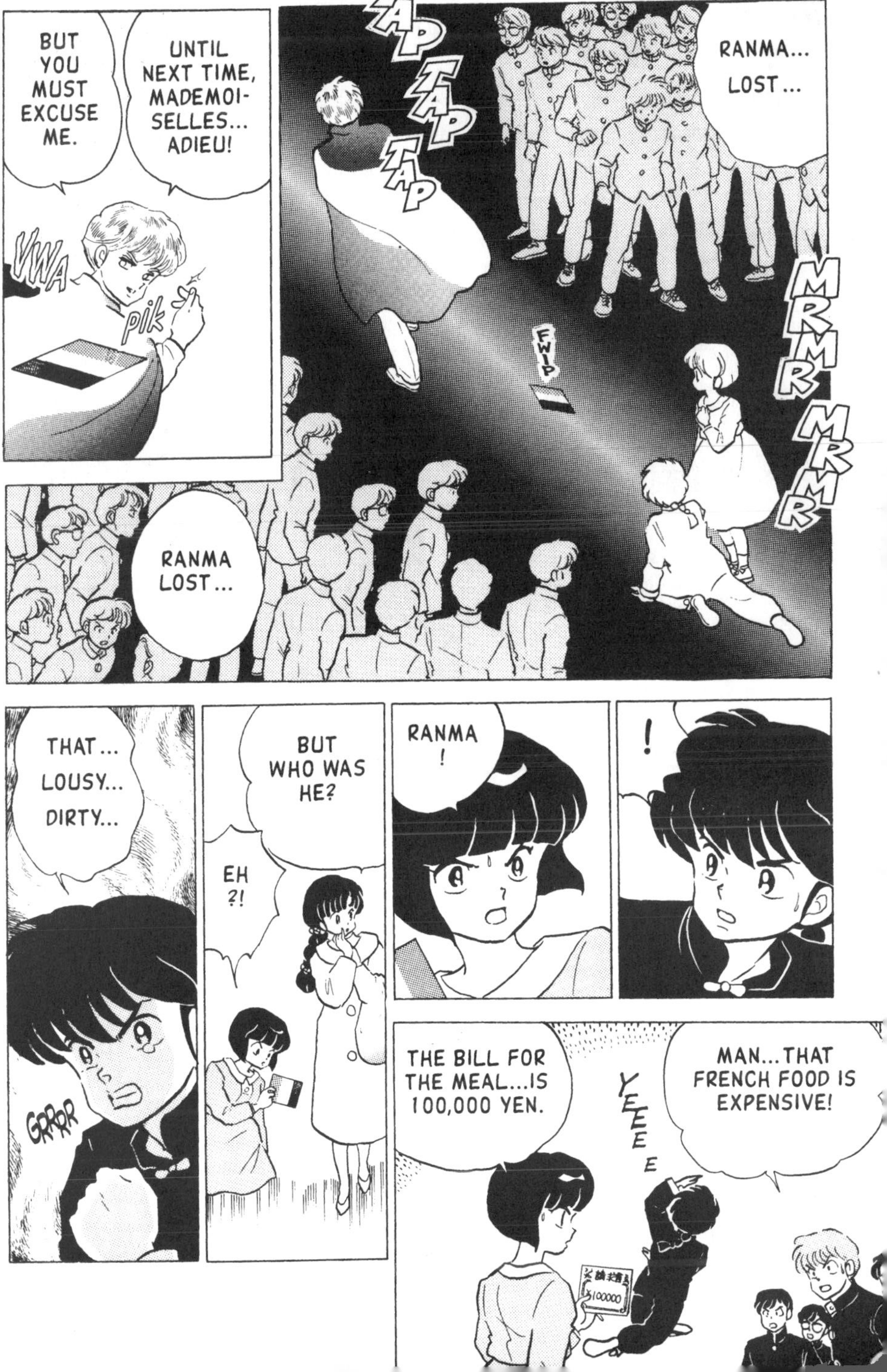
BUT YOU MUST EXCUSE ME.
UNTIL NEXT TIME, MADEMOISELLES... ADIEU!
VWA
pik
TAP TAP TAP
RANMA... LOST...
FWIP
MRMR MRMR
RANMA LOST...
THAT... LOUSY... DIRTY...
GRRRR
BUT WHO WAS HE?
EH ?!
RANMA !
!
THE BILL FOR THE MEAL...IS 100,000 YEN.
YEEEE
MAN...THAT FRENCH FOOD IS EXPENSIVE!
¥100000

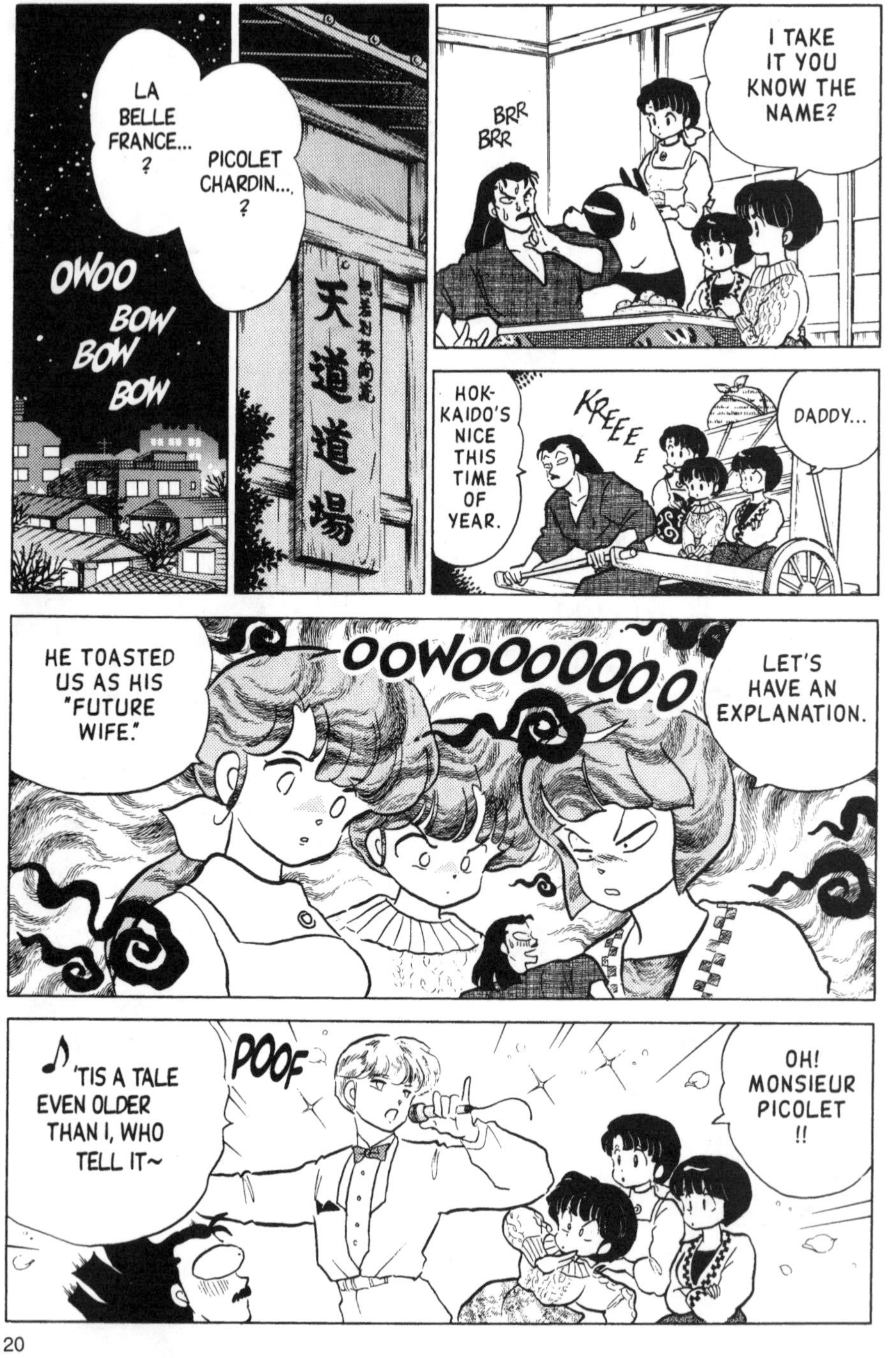
LA BELLE FRANCE... ?
PICOLET CHARDIN... ?
OWOO BOW BOW BOW
天道道場
BRR BRR
I TAKE IT YOU KNOW THE NAME?
HOK-KAIDO'S NICE THIS TIME OF YEAR.
KREEEEE
DADDY...
HE TOASTED US AS HIS "FUTURE WIFE."
OOWOOOOOOOO
LET'S HAVE AN EXPLANATION.
♪ 'TIS A TALE EVEN OLDER THAN I, WHO TELL IT~
POOF
OH! MONSIEUR PICOLET !!

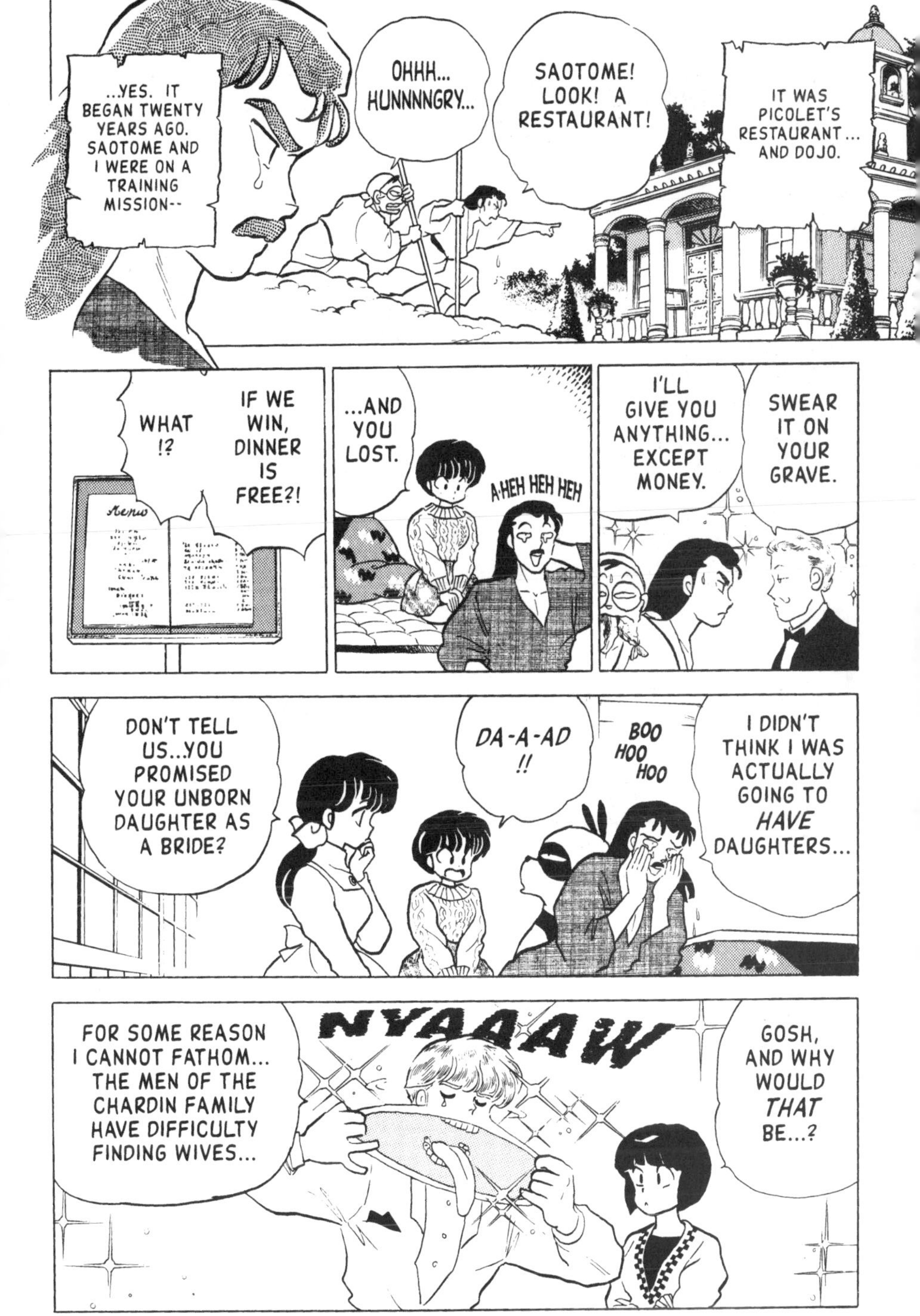
...YES. IT BEGAN TWENTY YEARS AGO. SAOTOME AND I WERE ON A TRAINING MISSION--
OHHH... HUNNNNGRY...
SAOTOME! LOOK! A RESTAURANT!
IT WAS PICOLET'S RESTAURANT... AND DOJO.
IF WE WIN, DINNER IS FREE?!
WHAT !?
...AND YOU LOST.
A-HEH HEH HEH
I'LL GIVE YOU ANYTHING... EXCEPT MONEY.
SWEAR IT ON YOUR GRAVE.
DON'T TELL US...YOU PROMISED YOUR UNBORN DAUGHTER AS A BRIDE?
DA-A-AD !!
BOO HOO HOO
I DIDN'T THINK I WAS ACTUALLY GOING TO *HAVE* DAUGHTERS...
FOR SOME REASON I CANNOT FATHOM... THE MEN OF THE CHARDIN FAMILY HAVE DIFFICULTY FINDING WIVES...
NYAAAW
GOSH, AND WHY WOULD *THAT* BE...?

BUT IT MATTERS NOT NOW, EH?

WHICHEVER MADEMOISELLE WOULD BE MY WIFE...SHALL COME TO THE CHARDIN ESTATE TO LEARN THE ART OF MARTIAL DINING!

WHAT SHALL WE DO...?

SNIFFLE

YEAH, DADDY. WHAT SHALL *YOU* DO?

DON'T FORGET THAT YOU HAVE ANOTHER DAUGHTER!

THIS MARTIAL ARTS DINING...

I COULD USE THE LESSONS.

BUT YOU ARE NOT "ANOTHER DAUGHTER"...

YOU ARE THE FINEST OF ALL!

SHPOP

TEE-HEE-HEE. I CAN'T WAIT.

DO YOU THINK RANMA'S HOLDING A GRUDGE...

OH, HEAVENS NO.

AND SO WERE THE GATES OF HELL OPENED.

Part 2
BAD MANORS

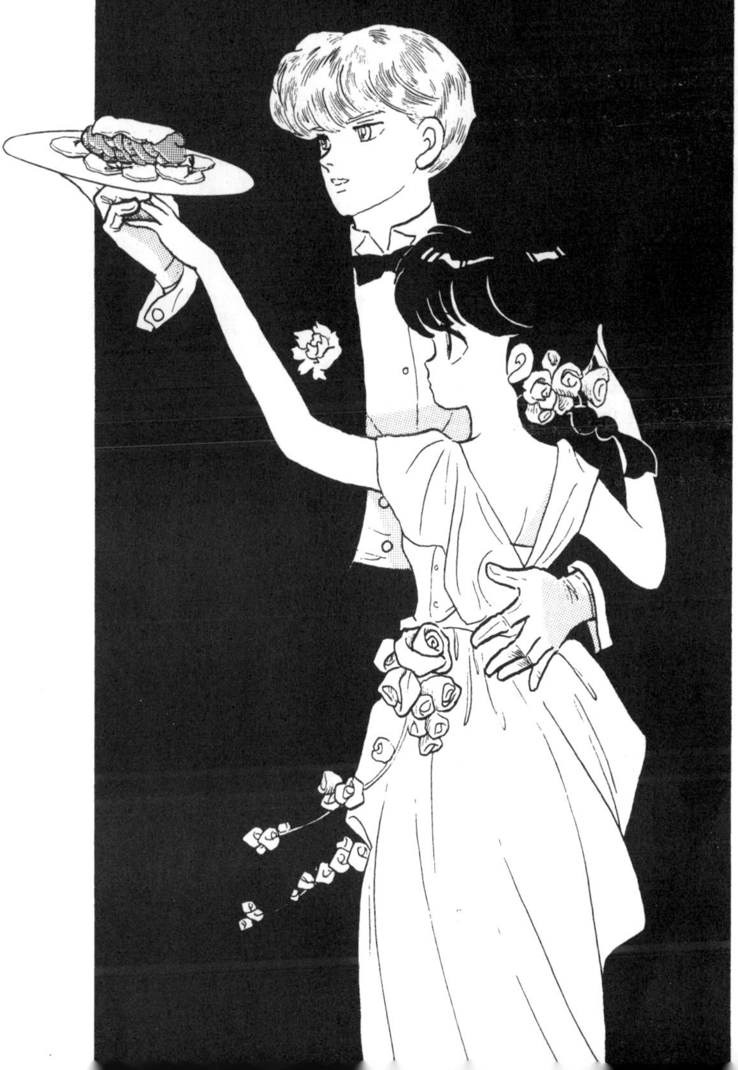

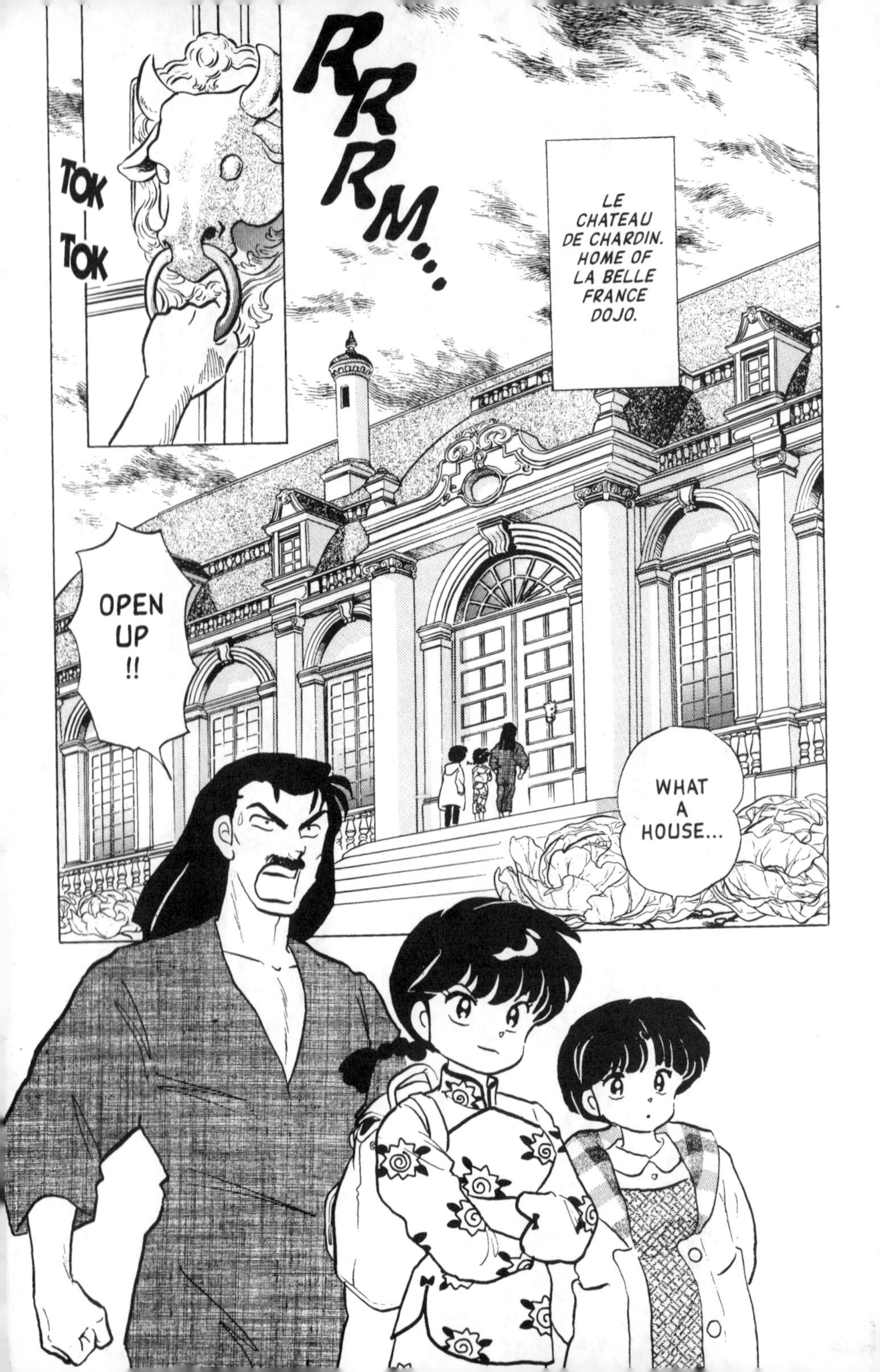
TOK
TOK
RRRM...
LE CHATEAU DE CHARDIN. HOME OF LA BELLE FRANCE DOJO.
OPEN UP !!
WHAT A HOUSE...

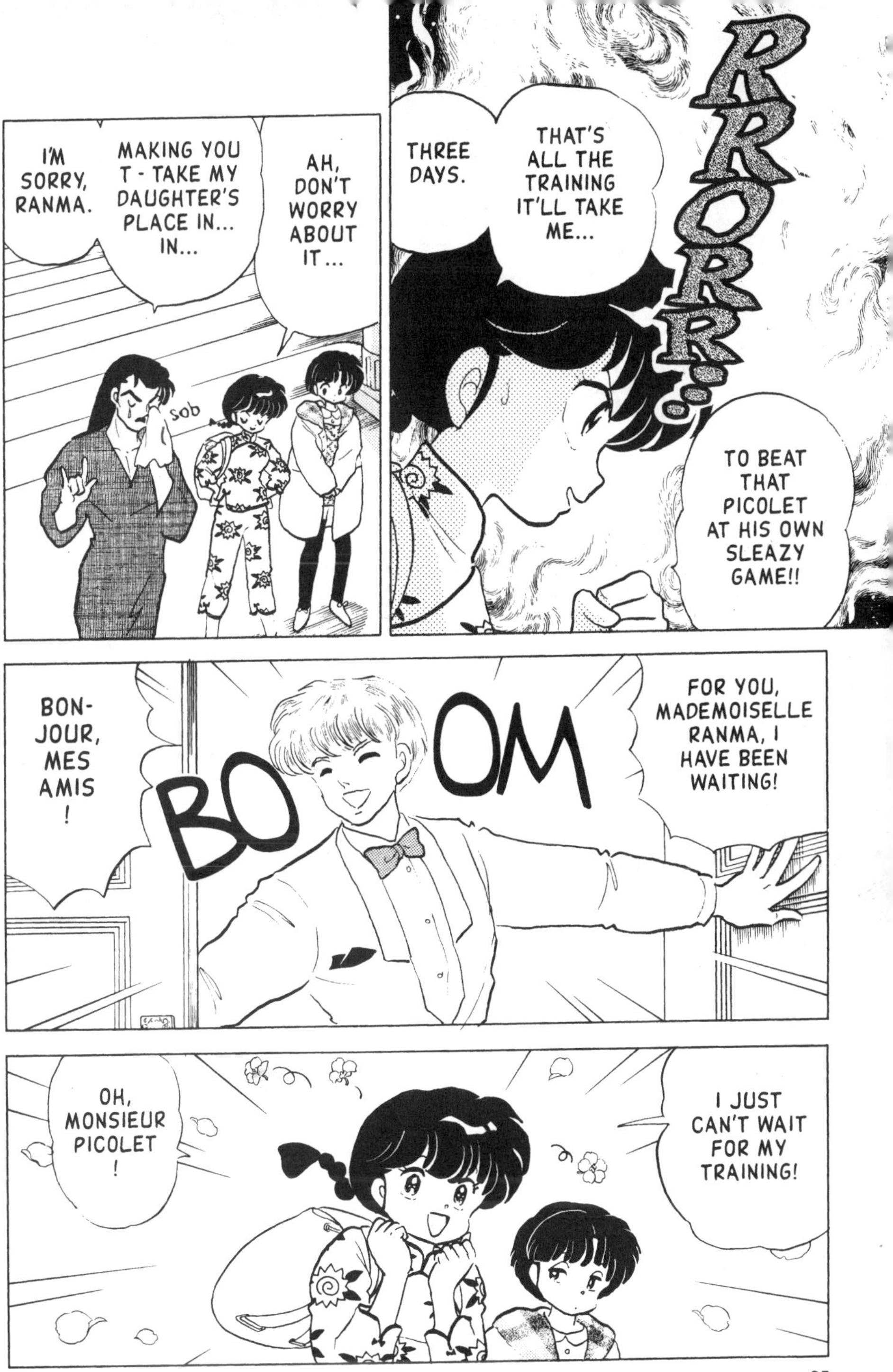
I'M SORRY, RANMA.
MAKING YOU T - TAKE MY DAUGHTER'S PLACE IN... IN...
AH, DON'T WORRY ABOUT IT...
sob
THREE DAYS.
THAT'S ALL THE TRAINING IT'LL TAKE ME...
RRORR..
TO BEAT THAT PICOLET AT HIS OWN SLEAZY GAME!!
BON-JOUR, MES AMIS!
BOOM
FOR YOU, MADEMOISELLE RANMA, I HAVE BEEN WAITING!
OH, MONSIEUR PICOLET!
I JUST CAN'T WAIT FOR MY TRAINING!

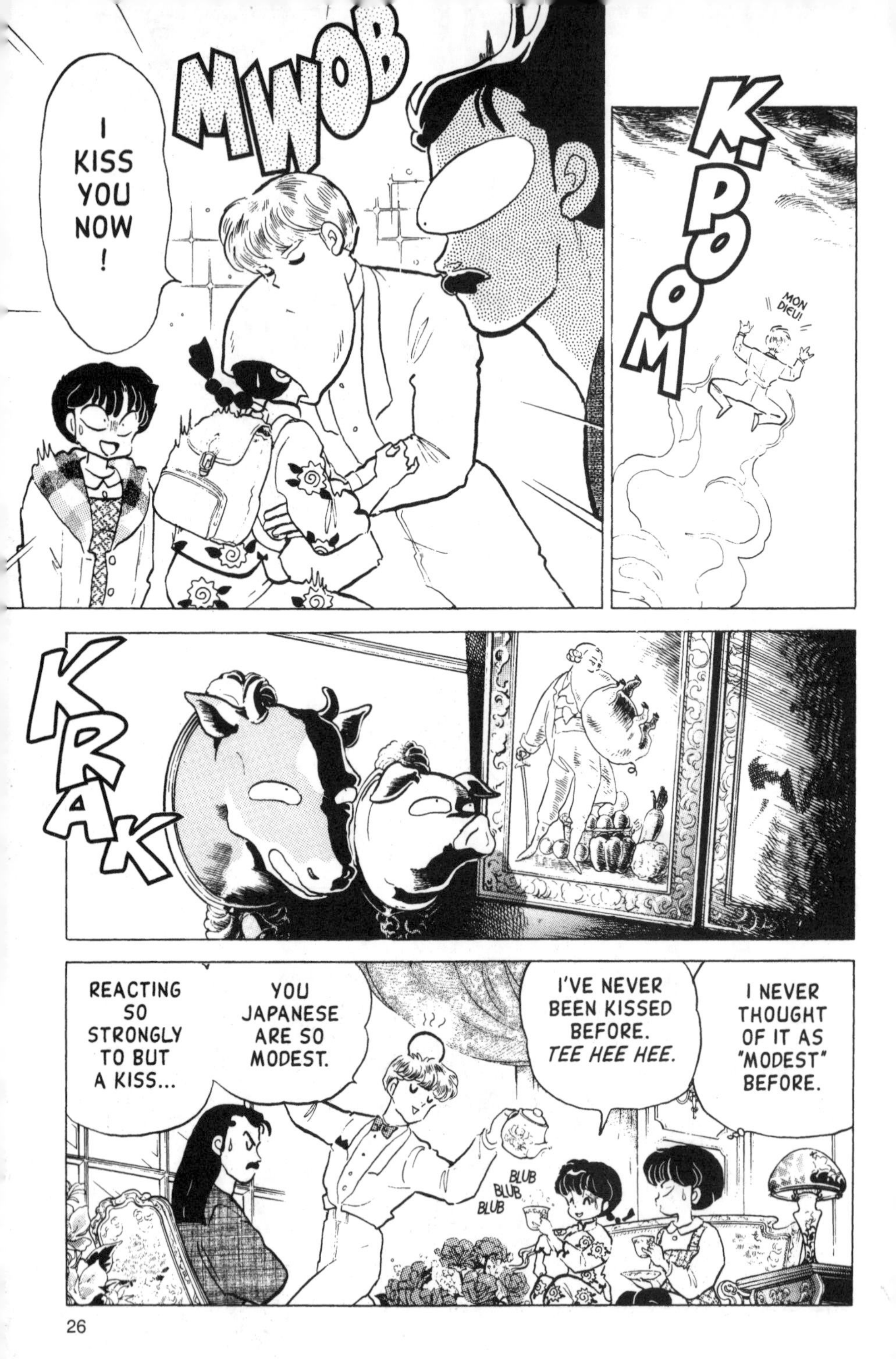
I KISS YOU NOW!
MWOB
K.POOOM
MON DIEU!
KRAK
REACTING SO STRONGLY TO BUT A KISS...
YOU JAPANESE ARE SO MODEST.
I'VE NEVER BEEN KISSED BEFORE. *TEE HEE HEE.*
BLUB BLUB BLUB
I NEVER THOUGHT OF IT AS "MODEST" BEFORE.

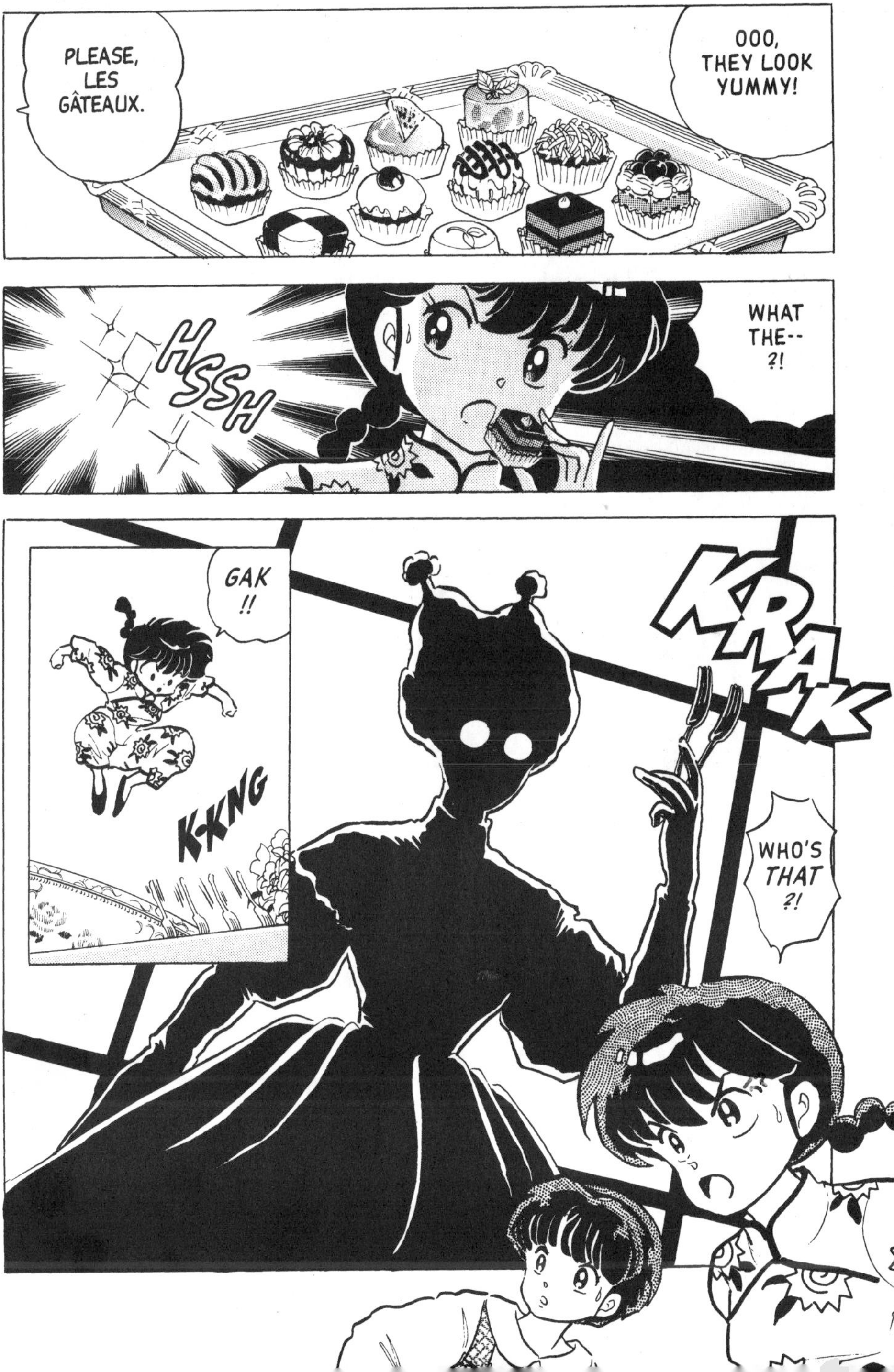
PLEASE, LES GÂTEAUX.
OOO, THEY LOOK YUMMY!
HSSH
WHAT THE--?!
GAK!!
K-KNG
KRAK
WHO'S THAT?!

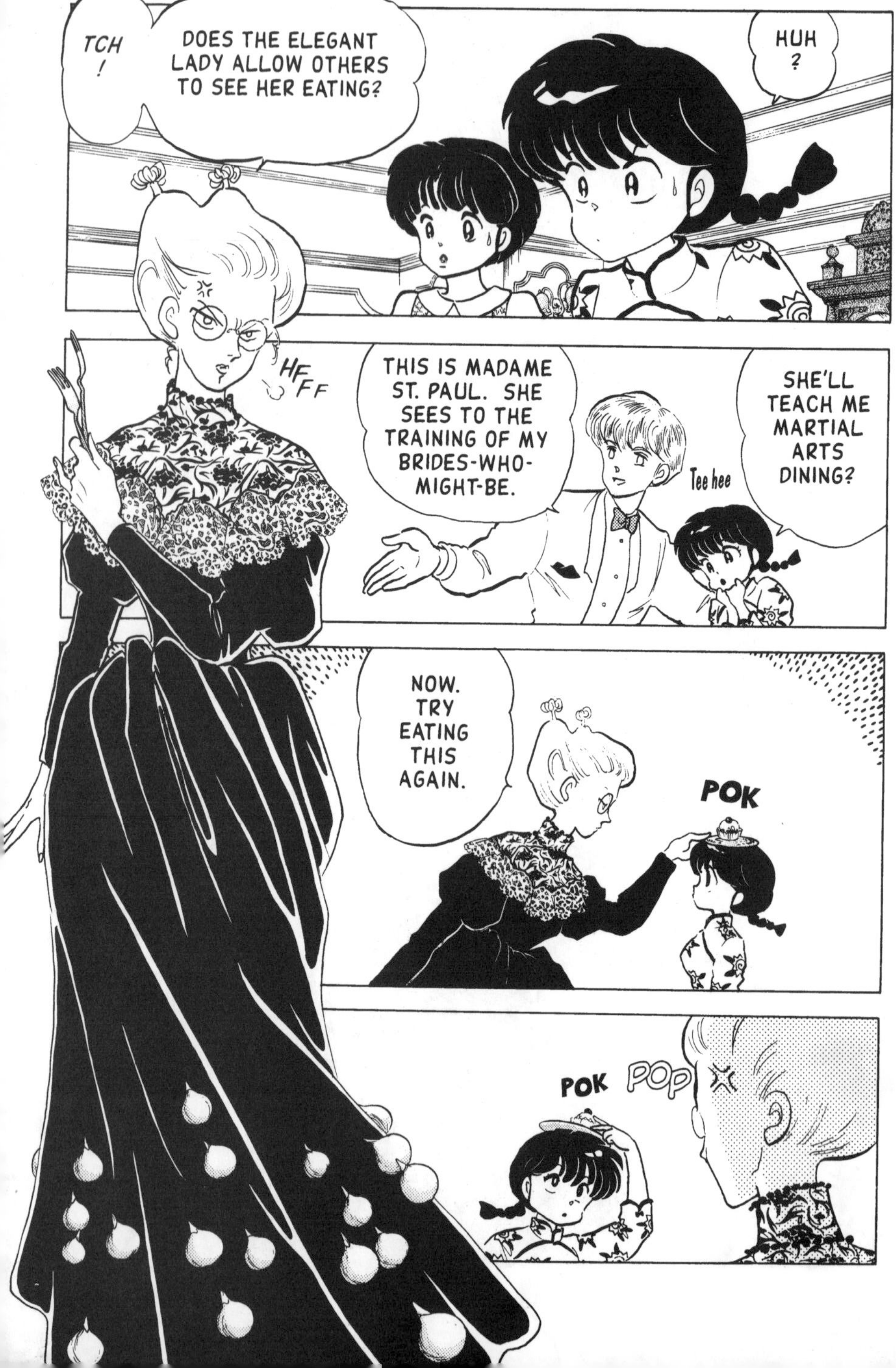
TCH!
DOES THE ELEGANT LADY ALLOW OTHERS TO SEE HER EATING?
HUH?
HFFF
THIS IS MADAME ST. PAUL. SHE SEES TO THE TRAINING OF MY BRIDES-WHO-MIGHT-BE.
Tee hee
SHE'LL TEACH ME MARTIAL ARTS DINING?
NOW. TRY EATING THIS AGAIN.
POK
POK
POP

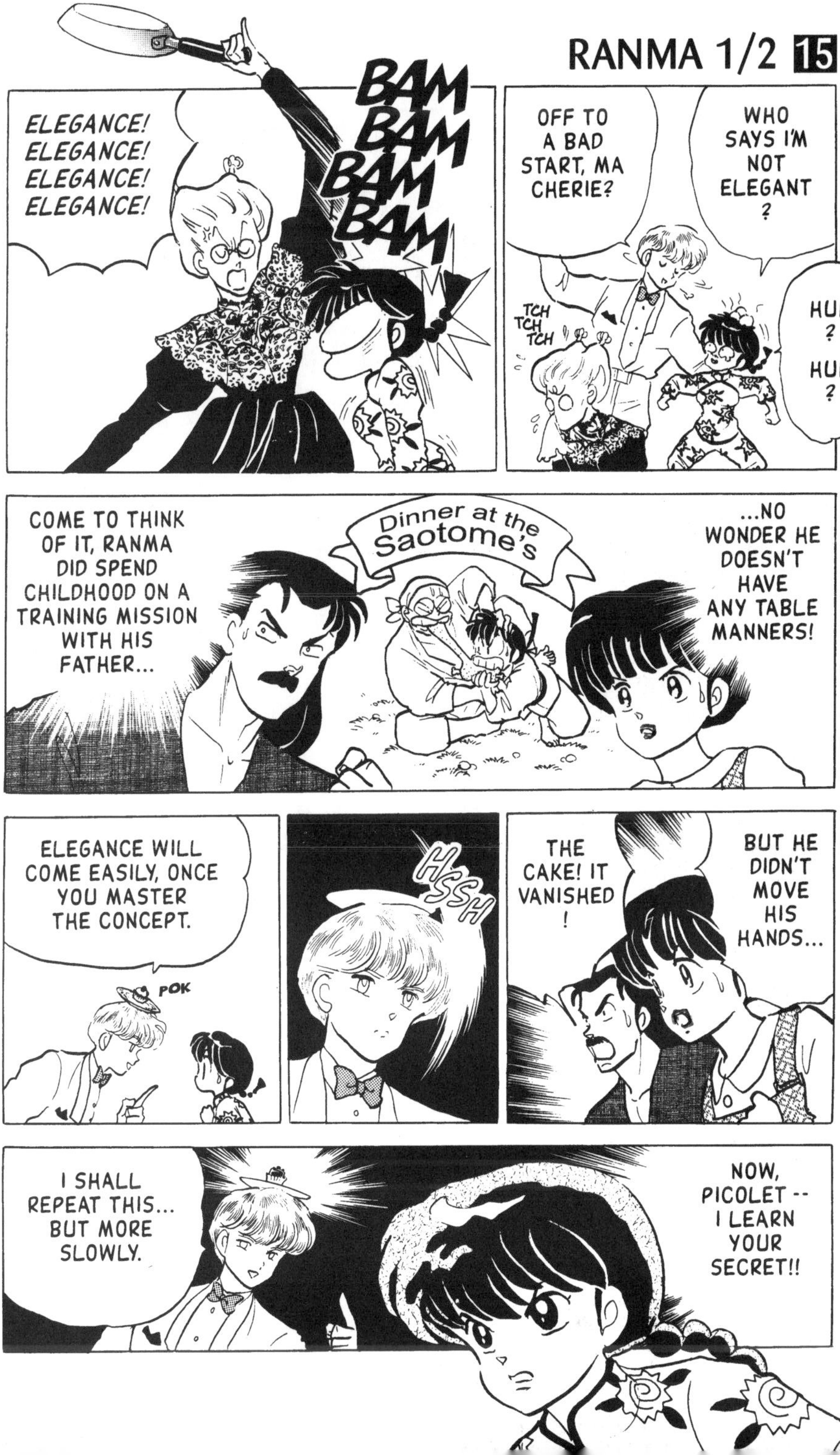
ELEGANCE! ELEGANCE! ELEGANCE! ELEGANCE!
BAM BAM BAM BAM
OFF TO A BAD START, MA CHERIE?
WHO SAYS I'M NOT ELEGANT?
TCH TCH TCH
HUH? HUH?
COME TO THINK OF IT, RANMA DID SPEND CHILDHOOD ON A TRAINING MISSION WITH HIS FATHER...
Dinner at the Saotome's
...NO WONDER HE DOESN'T HAVE ANY TABLE MANNERS!
ELEGANCE WILL COME EASILY, ONCE YOU MASTER THE CONCEPT.
POK
HSSH
THE CAKE! IT VANISHED!
BUT HE DIDN'T MOVE HIS HANDS...
I SHALL REPEAT THIS... BUT MORE SLOWLY.
NOW, PICOLET -- I LEARN YOUR SECRET!!

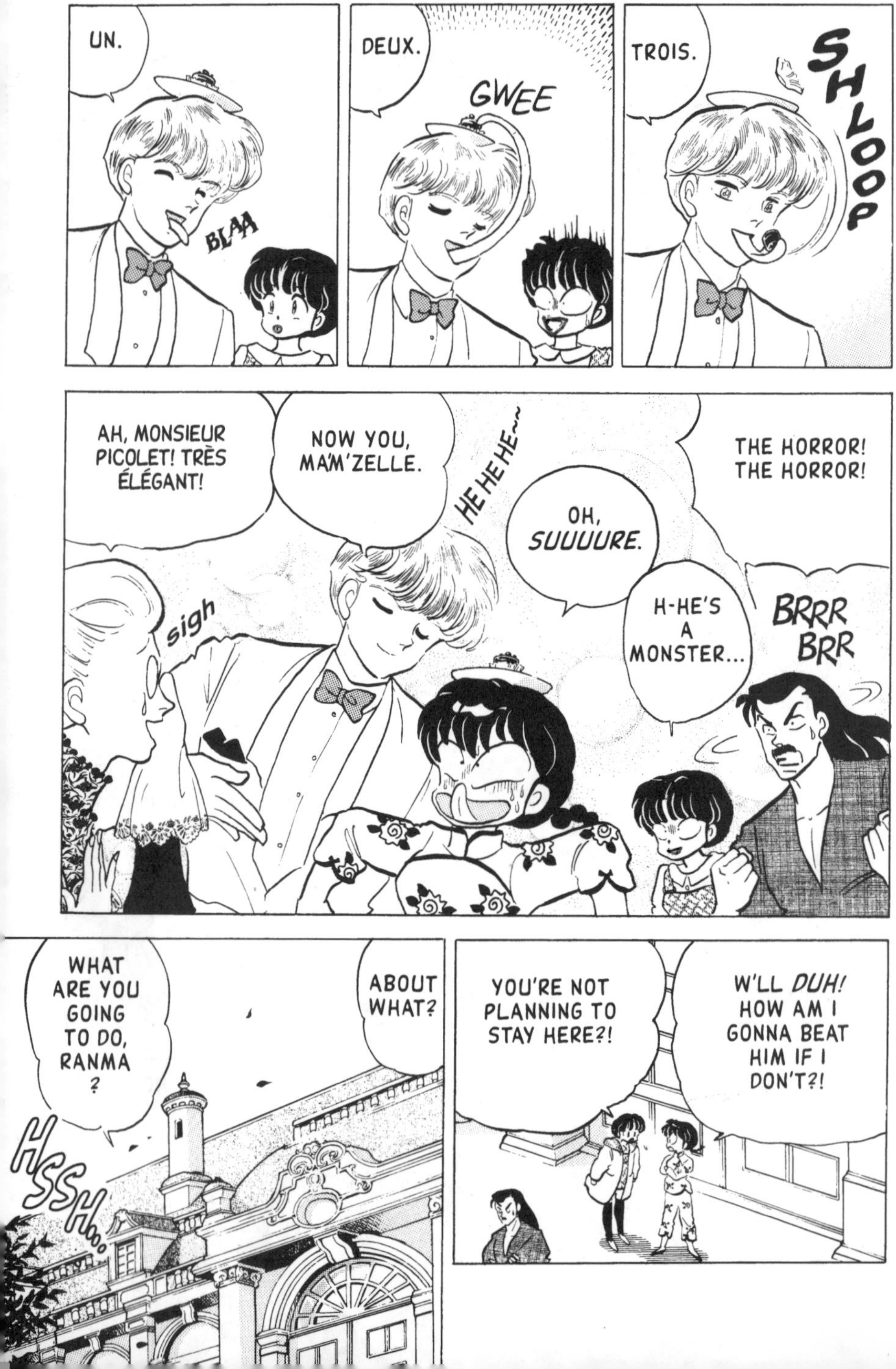
UN.
BLAA
DEUX.
GWEE
TROIS.
SHLOOP
AH, MONSIEUR PICOLET! TRÈS ÉLÉGANT!
NOW YOU, MA'M'ZELLE.
HEHEHE~~
sigh
OH, SUUUURE.
H-HE'S A MONSTER...
THE HORROR! THE HORROR!
BRRR BRR
WHAT ARE YOU GOING TO DO, RANMA?
ABOUT WHAT?
HSSH...
YOU'RE NOT PLANNING TO STAY HERE?!
W'LL DUH! HOW AM I GONNA BEAT HIM IF I DON'T?!

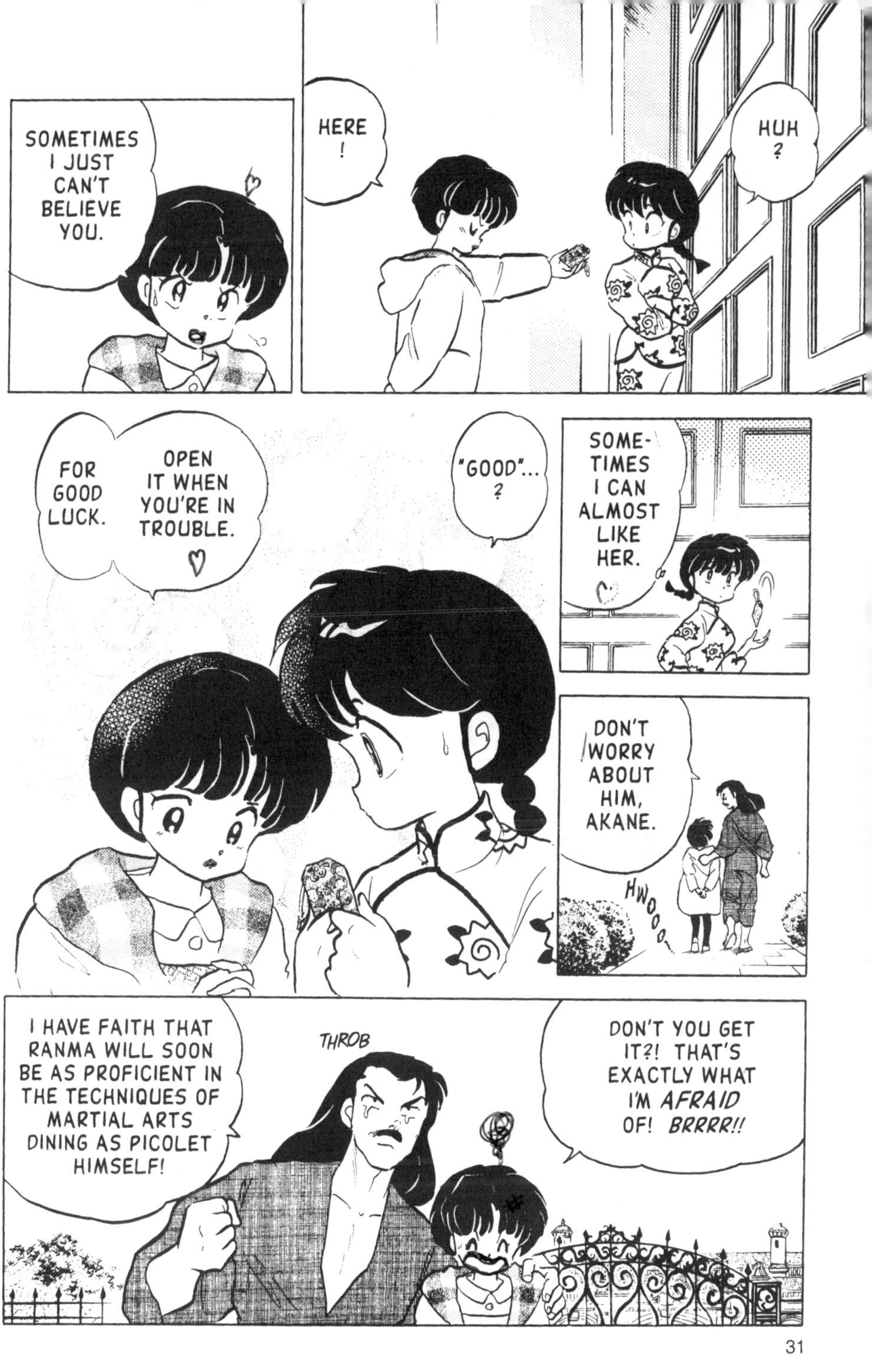
SOMETIMES I JUST CAN'T BELIEVE YOU.
HERE!
HUH?
FOR GOOD LUCK.
OPEN IT WHEN YOU'RE IN TROUBLE.
"GOOD"...?
SOME-TIMES I CAN ALMOST LIKE HER.
DON'T WORRY ABOUT HIM, AKANE.
HWOOOO...
I HAVE FAITH THAT RANMA WILL SOON BE AS PROFICIENT IN THE TECHNIQUES OF MARTIAL ARTS DINING AS PICOLET HIMSELF!
THROB
DON'T YOU GET IT?! THAT'S EXACTLY WHAT I'M *AFRAID* OF! *BRRRR!!*

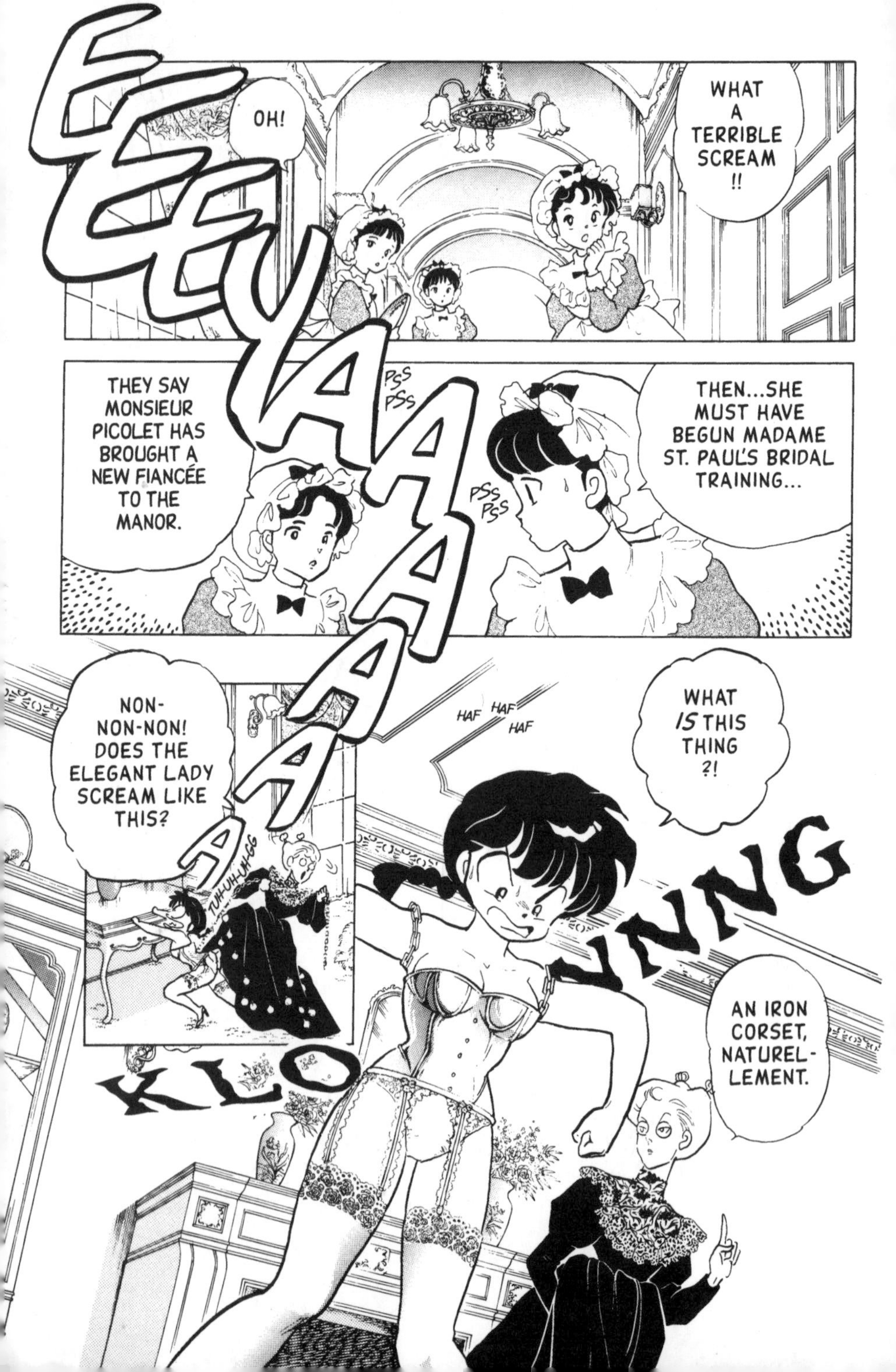
EEEYAAAAAAAA
OH!
WHAT A TERRIBLE SCREAM !!
THEY SAY MONSIEUR PICOLET HAS BROUGHT A NEW FIANCÉE TO THE MANOR.
PSS PSS
PSS PSS
THEN...SHE MUST HAVE BEGUN MADAME ST. PAUL'S BRIDAL TRAINING...
NON-NON-NON! DOES THE ELEGANT LADY SCREAM LIKE THIS?
TUH-UH-UH-GG
HAF HAF HAF
WHAT *IS* THIS THING ?!
KLO YNNG
AN IRON CORSET, NATUREL-LEMENT.

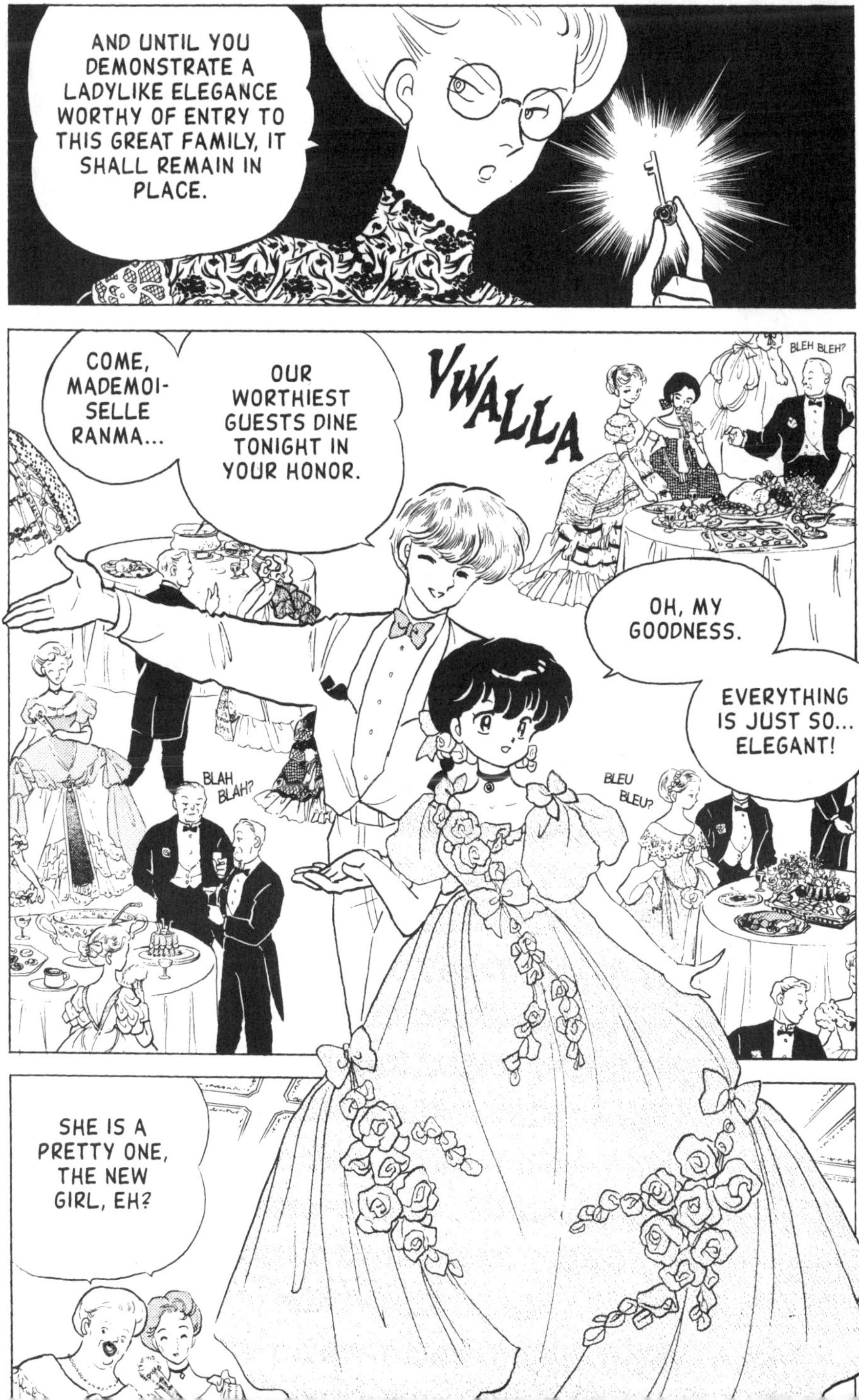
AND UNTIL YOU DEMONSTRATE A LADYLIKE ELEGANCE WORTHY OF ENTRY TO THIS GREAT FAMILY, IT SHALL REMAIN IN PLACE.
COME, MADEMOI-SELLE RANMA...
OUR WORTHIEST GUESTS DINE TONIGHT IN YOUR HONOR.
VWALLA
BLEH BLEH?
OH, MY GOODNESS.
EVERYTHING IS JUST SO... ELEGANT!
BLAH BLAH?
BLEU BLEU?
SHE IS A PRETTY ONE, THE NEW GIRL, EH?

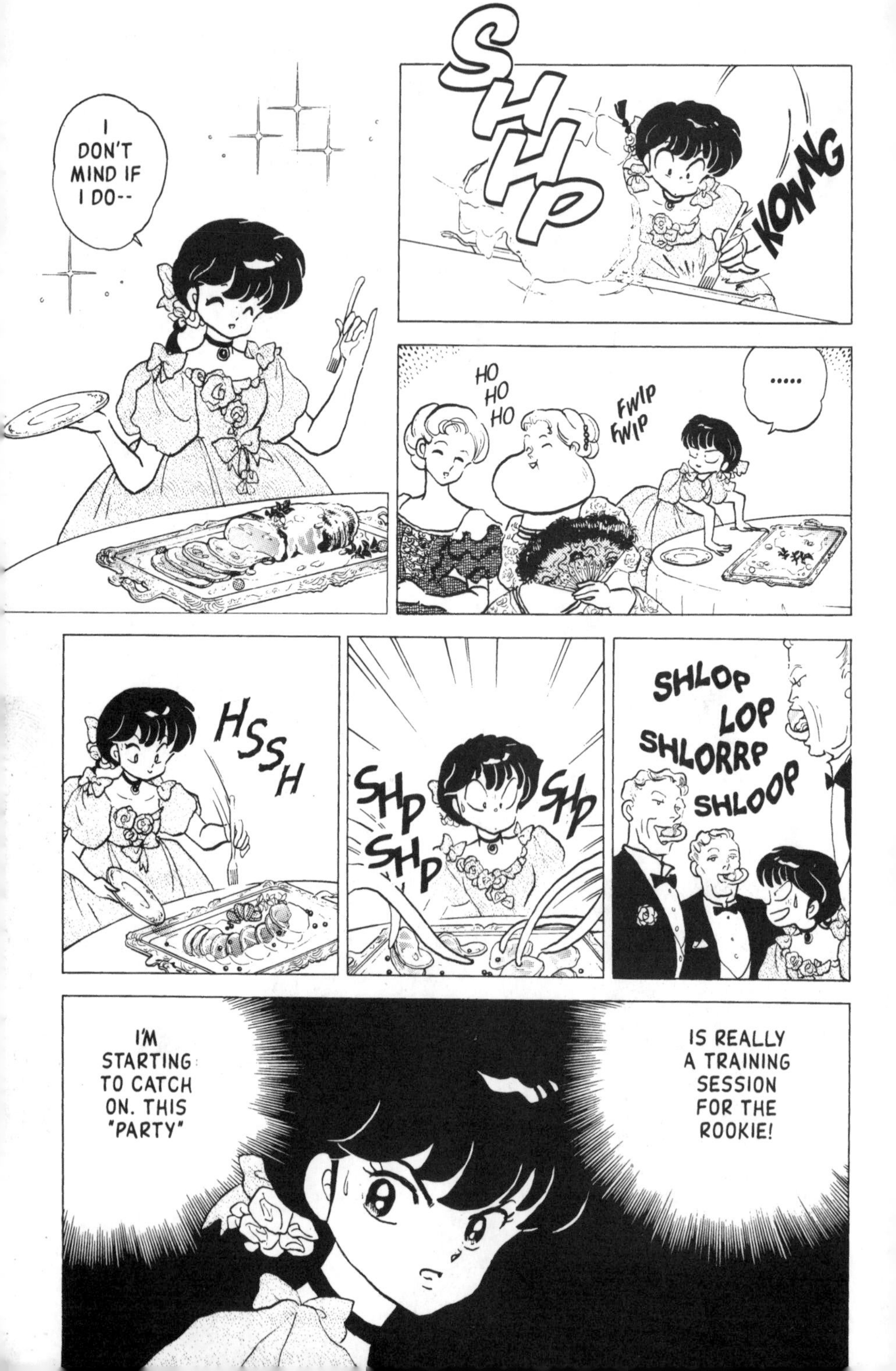
I DON'T MIND IF I DO--
SHHP
KONG
HO HO HO
FWIP FWIP
.....
HSSH
SHP SHP SHP SHP
SHLOP
LOP
SHLORRP
SHLOOP
I'M STARTING TO CATCH ON. THIS "PARTY"
IS REALLY A TRAINING SESSION FOR THE ROOKIE!

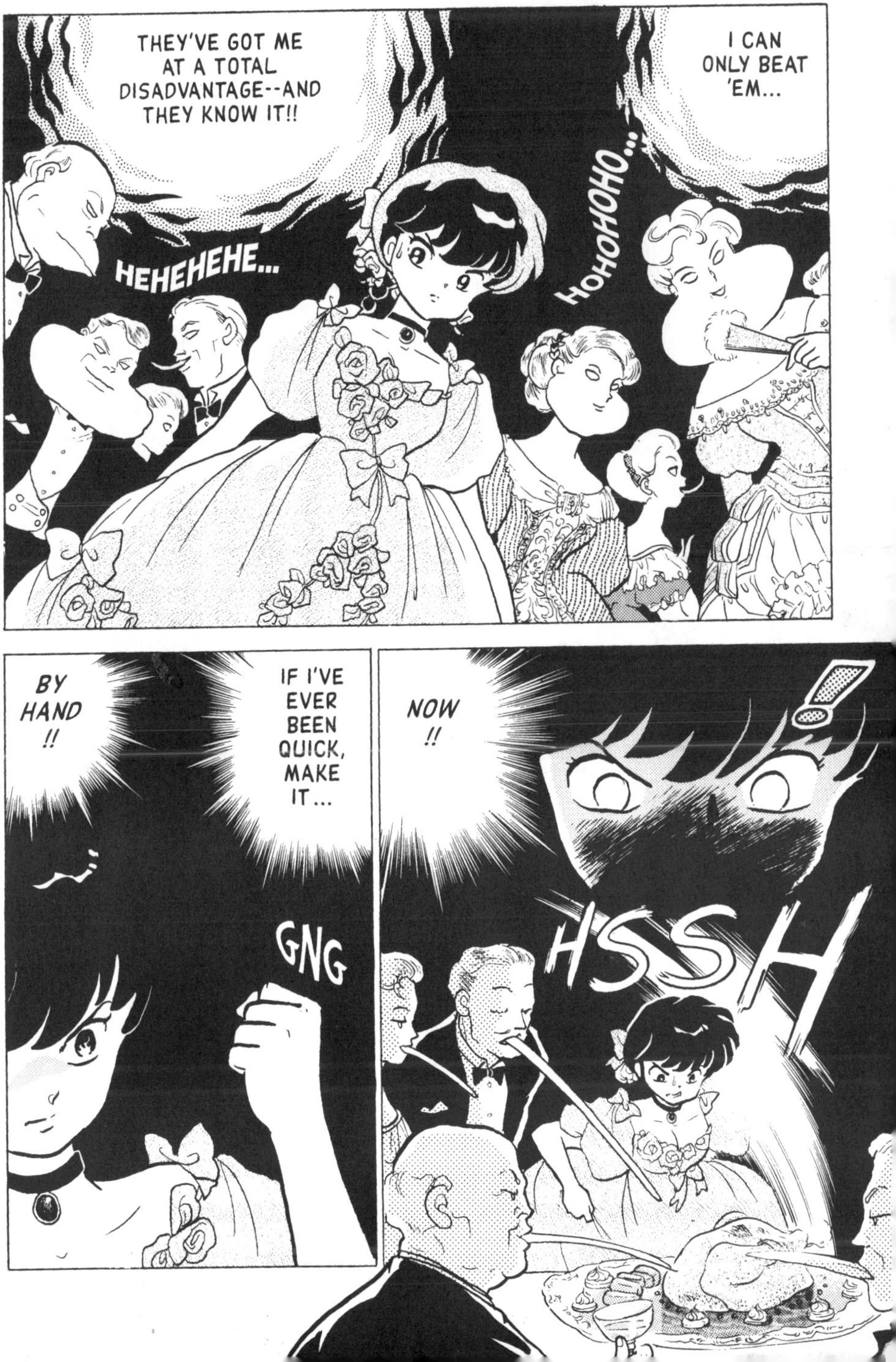
THEY'VE GOT ME AT A TOTAL DISADVANTAGE--AND THEY KNOW IT!!
I CAN ONLY BEAT 'EM...
HEHEHEHE...
HOHOHOHO...
BY HAND !!
IF I'VE EVER BEEN QUICK, MAKE IT...
GNG
NOW !!
!
HSSH

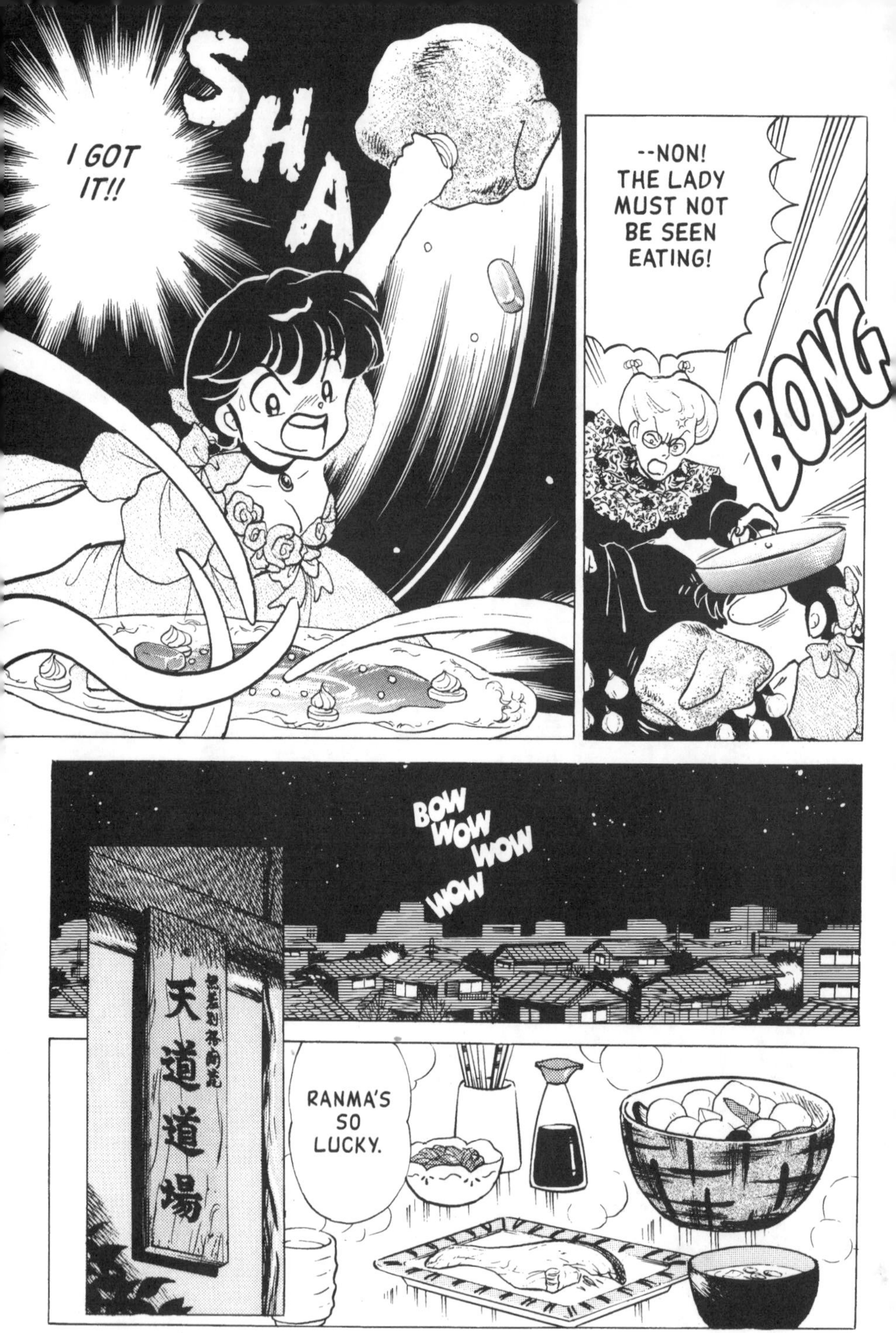
I GOT IT!!
SHA
--NON! THE LADY MUST NOT BE SEEN EATING!
BONG
BOW WOW WOW WOW
天道道場
RANMA'S SO LUCKY.

HE'S PROBABLY GORGING HIMSELF ON FRENCH CUISINE RIGHT NOW.

I HOPE HE DOESN'T UPSET HIS STOMACH.

HMPH. IF ONLY MY "TRAINING" WERE JUST A MATTER OF EATING...

.....

GROWWWL

SO HUNGRY...

IF YOU WISH TO EAT, YOU MUST MASTER OUR MARTIAL ART.

NOTHING~~~. NOT EVEN ONE CRUMMY CRUMB O' CRUMB CAKE...

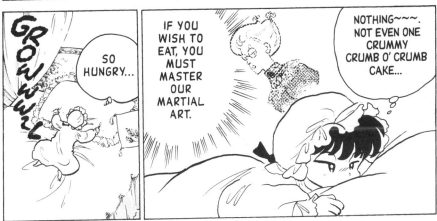

FOR GOOD LUCK...

OPEN IT WHEN YOU'RE IN TROUBLE!

.....

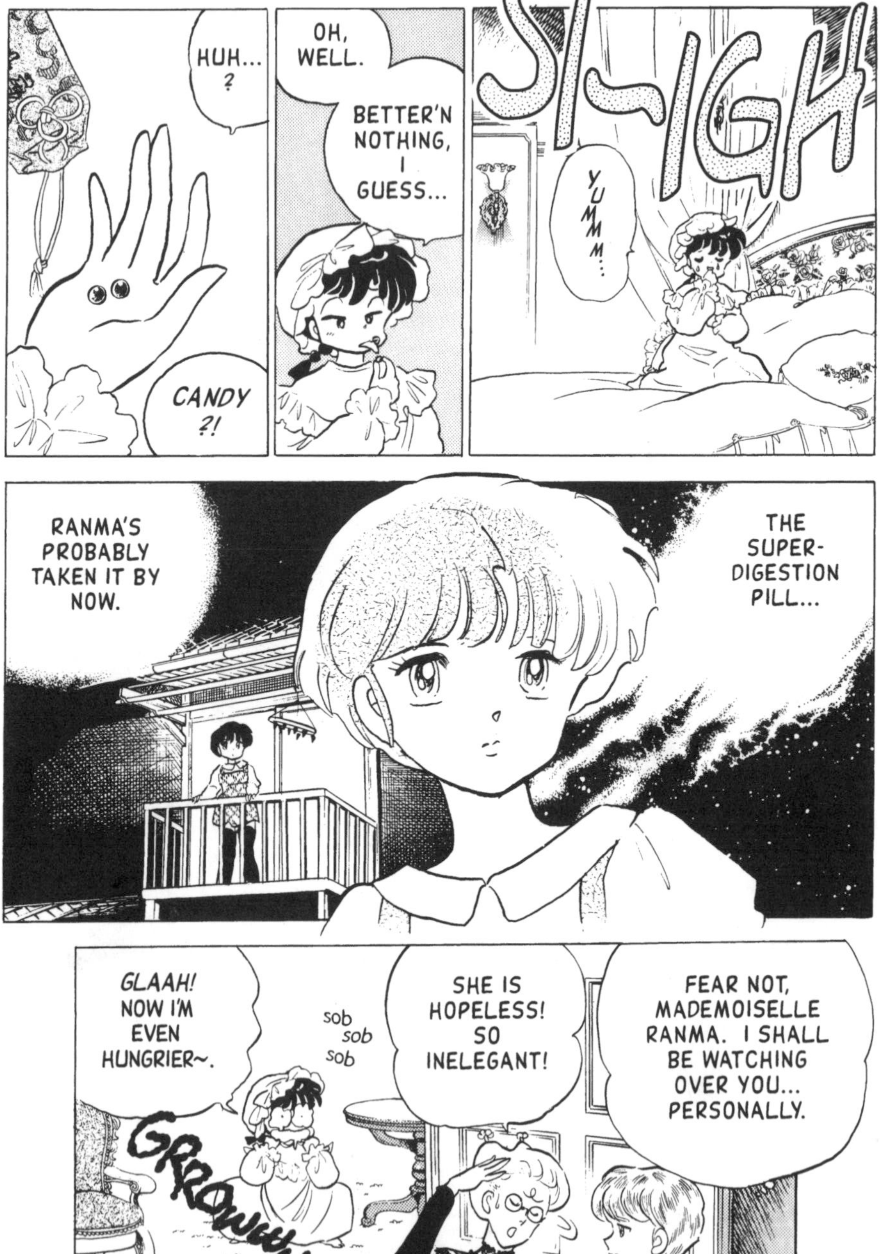
HUH...?
CANDY?!
OH, WELL.
BETTER'N NOTHING, I GUESS...
SI~IGH
YUMMM...
RANMA'S PROBABLY TAKEN IT BY NOW.
THE SUPER-DIGESTION PILL...
GLAAH! NOW I'M EVEN HUNGRIER~.
sob sob sob
SHE IS HOPELESS! SO INELEGANT!
FEAR NOT, MADEMOISELLE RANMA. I SHALL BE WATCHING OVER YOU... PERSONALLY.

Part 3
LA MISERABLE

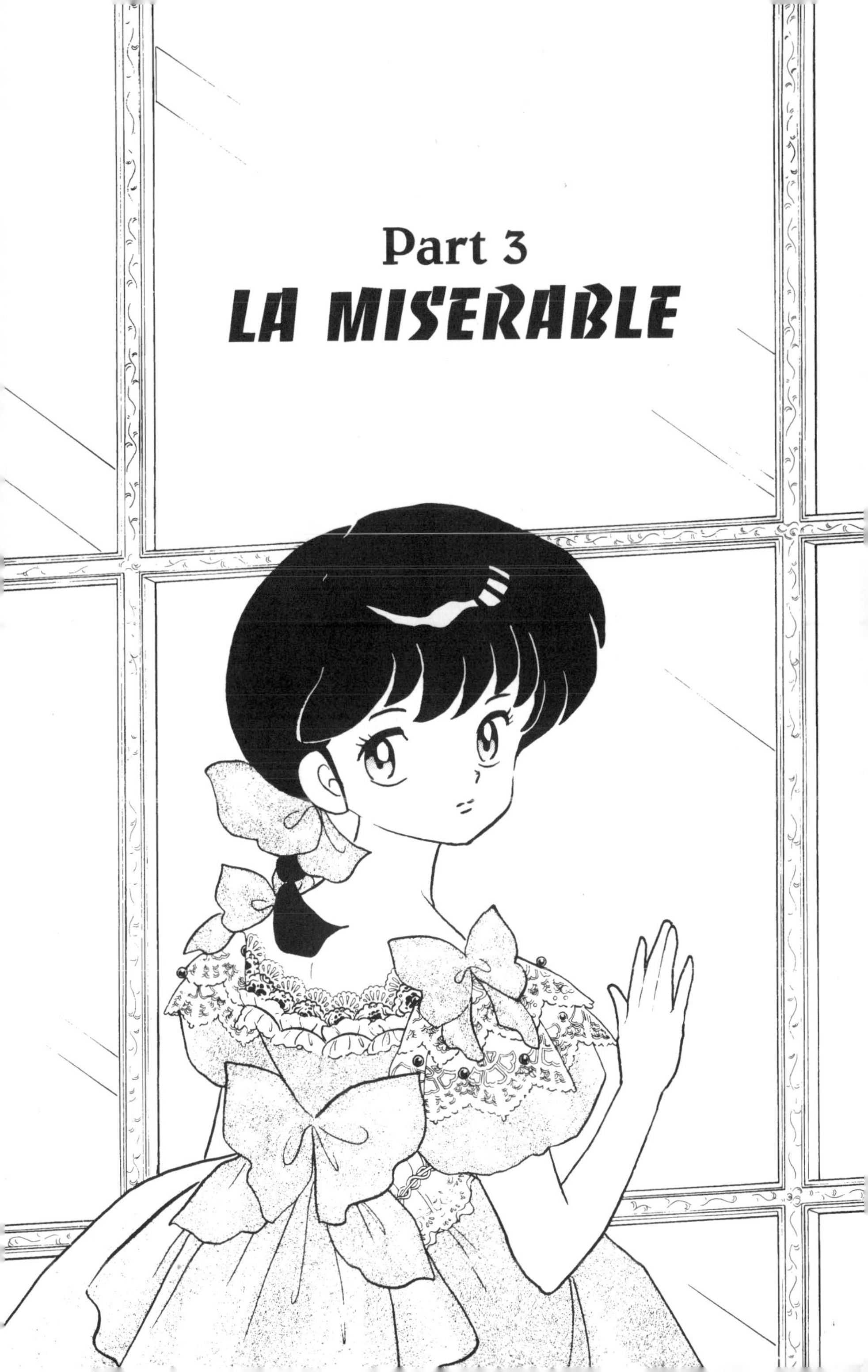

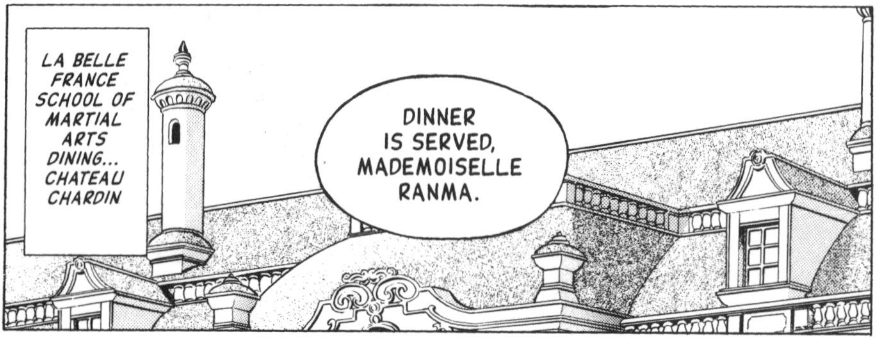
LA BELLE FRANCE SCHOOL OF MARTIAL ARTS DINING... CHATEAU CHARDIN
DINNER IS SERVED, MADEMOISELLE RANMA.

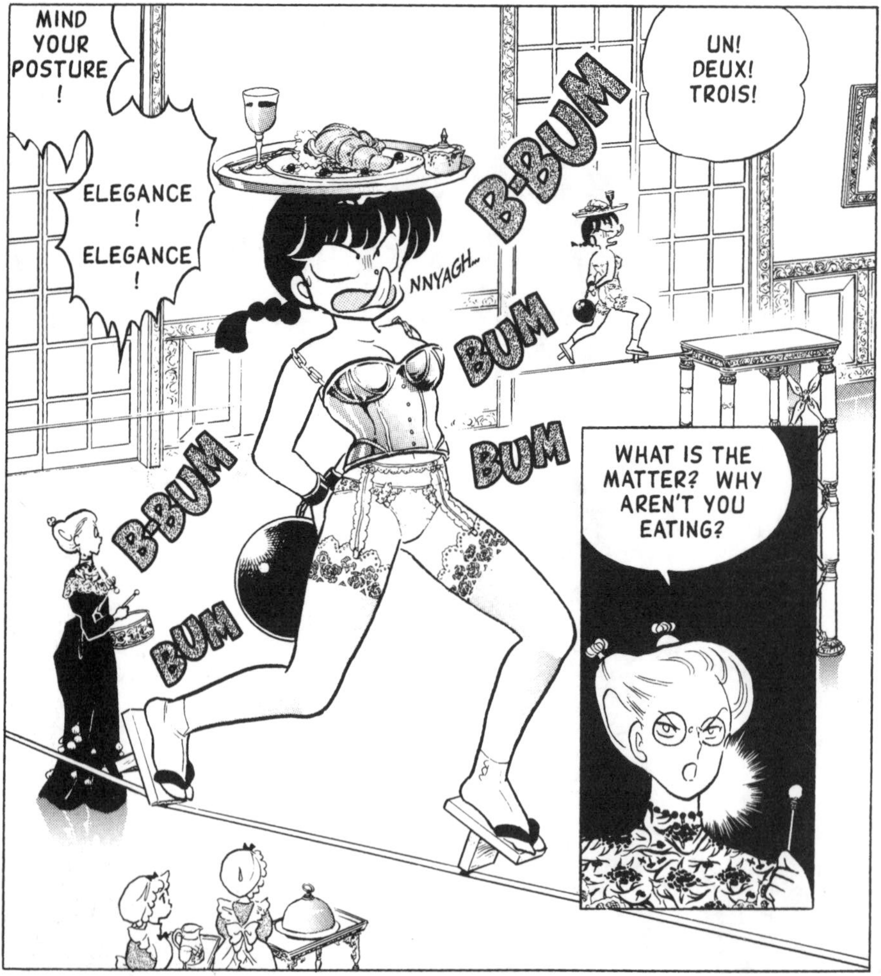
MIND YOUR POSTURE!
ELEGANCE! ELEGANCE!
B-BUM
NNYAGH...
UN! DEUX! TROIS!
BUM
B-BUM
BUM
BUM
WHAT IS THE MATTER? WHY AREN'T YOU EATING?

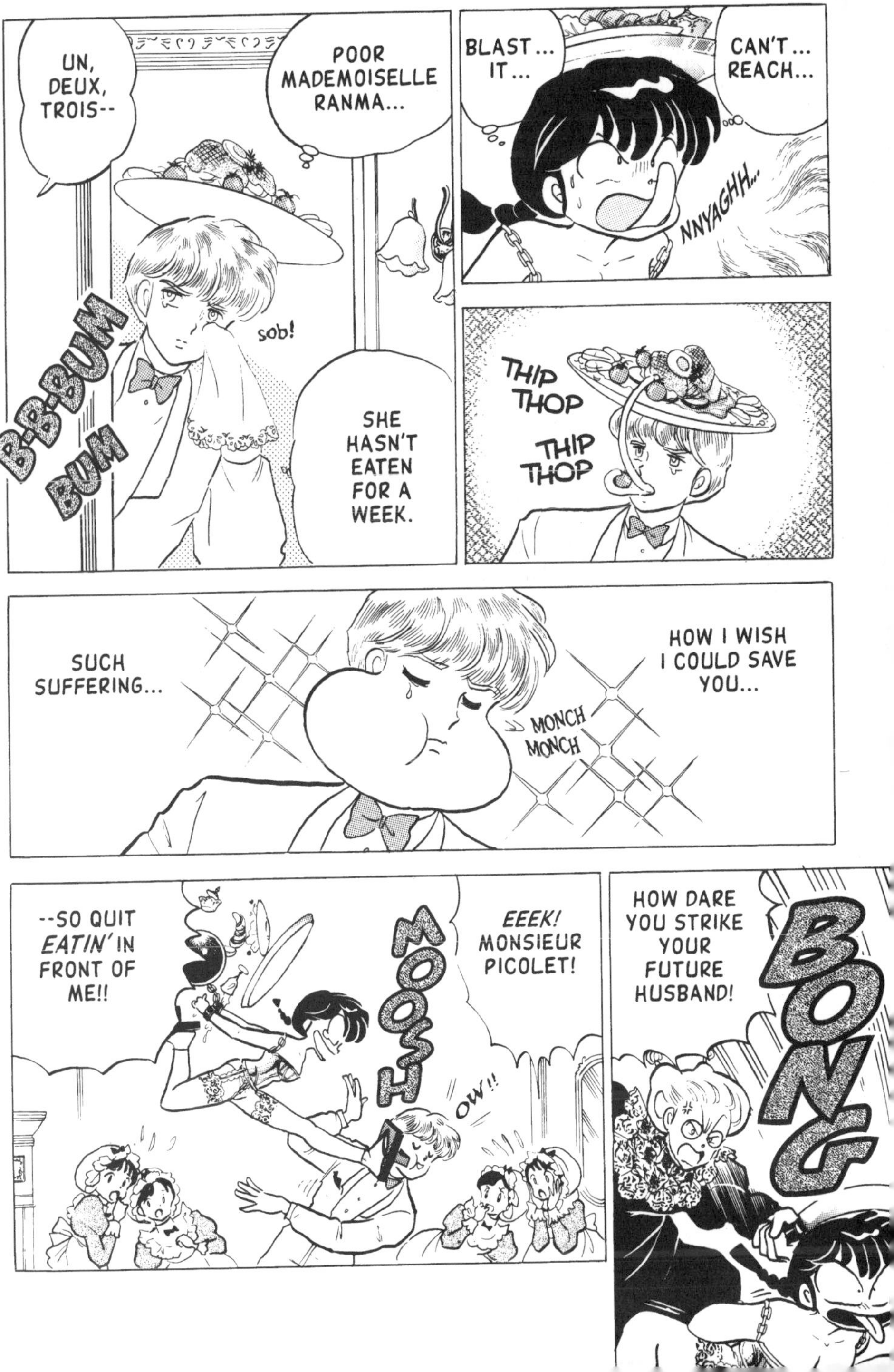
UN, DEUX, TROIS--
POOR MADEMOISELLE RANMA...
sob!
B-B-BUM BUM
SHE HASN'T EATEN FOR A WEEK.
BLAST... IT...
CAN'T... REACH...
NNYAGHH...
THIP THOP
THIP THOP
SUCH SUFFERING...
MONCH MONCH
HOW I WISH I COULD SAVE YOU...
--SO QUIT *EATIN'* IN FRONT OF ME!!
WOOOSH
EEEK! MONSIEUR PICOLET!
OW!!
HOW DARE YOU STRIKE YOUR FUTURE HUSBAND!
BONG

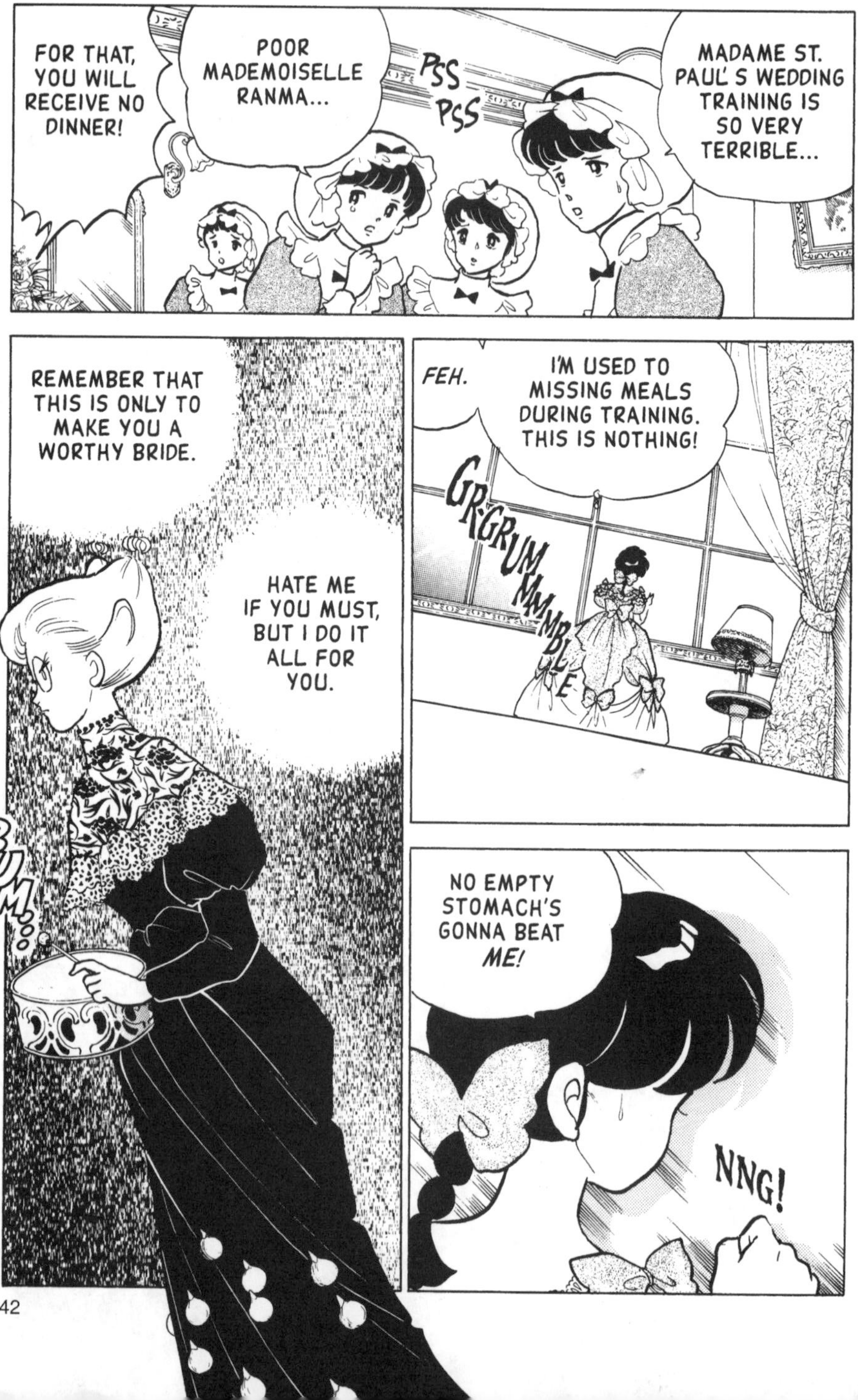
FOR THAT, YOU WILL RECEIVE NO DINNER!
POOR MADEMOISELLE RANMA...
PSS PSS
MADAME ST. PAUL'S WEDDING TRAINING IS SO VERY TERRIBLE...
REMEMBER THAT THIS IS ONLY TO MAKE YOU A WORTHY BRIDE.
HATE ME IF YOU MUST, BUT I DO IT ALL FOR YOU.
BUM...
FEH.
I'M USED TO MISSING MEALS DURING TRAINING. THIS IS NOTHING!
GR-GRUMMMMBLE
NO EMPTY STOMACH'S GONNA BEAT ME!
NNG!

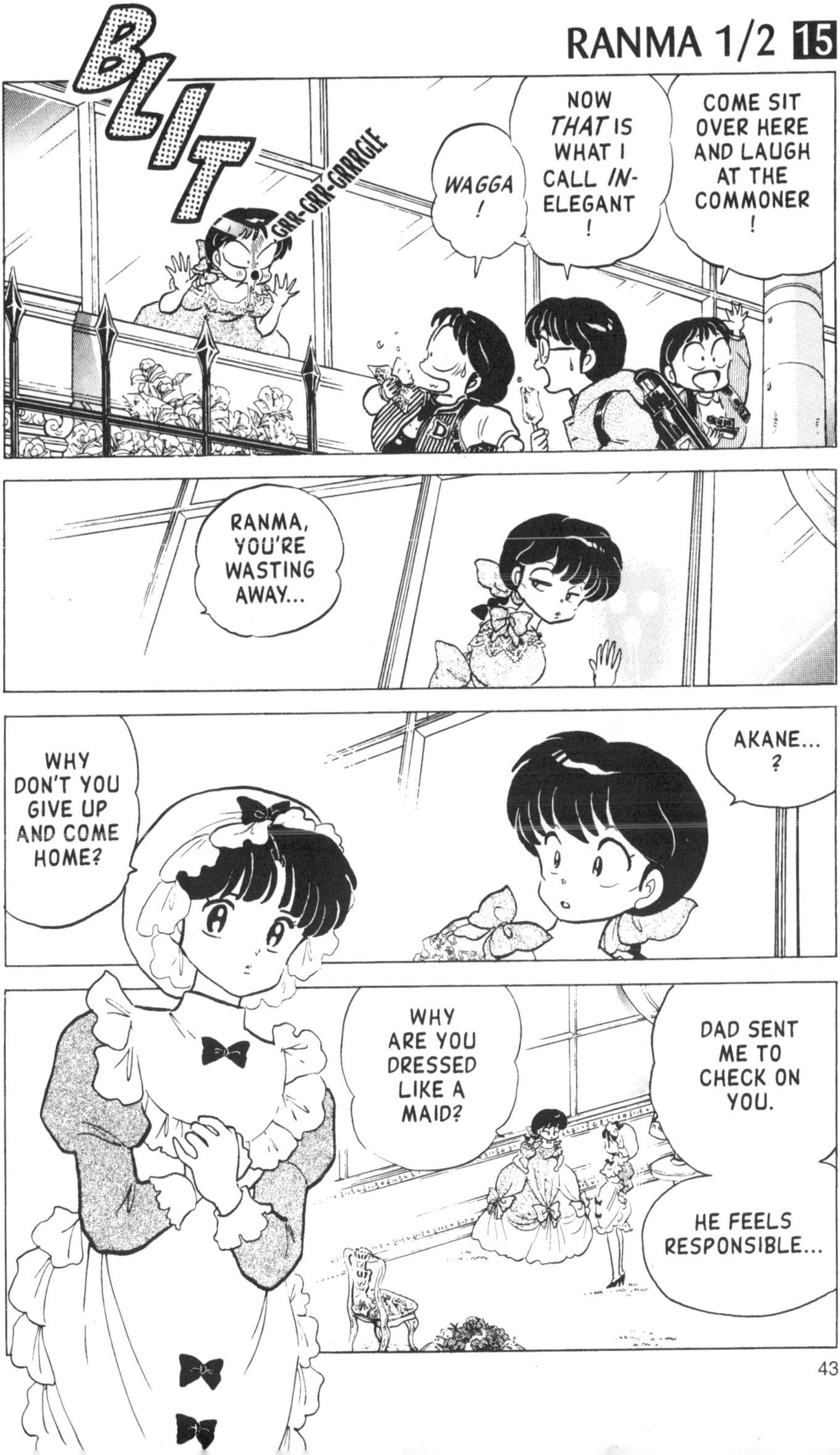
BLIT
GRR-GRR-GRRRGLE
WAGGA!
NOW *THAT* IS WHAT I CALL *IN-*ELEGANT!
COME SIT OVER HERE AND LAUGH AT THE COMMONER!
RANMA, YOU'RE WASTING AWAY...
WHY DON'T YOU GIVE UP AND COME HOME?
AKANE...?
WHY ARE YOU DRESSED LIKE A MAID?
DAD SENT ME TO CHECK ON YOU.
HE FEELS RESPONSIBLE...

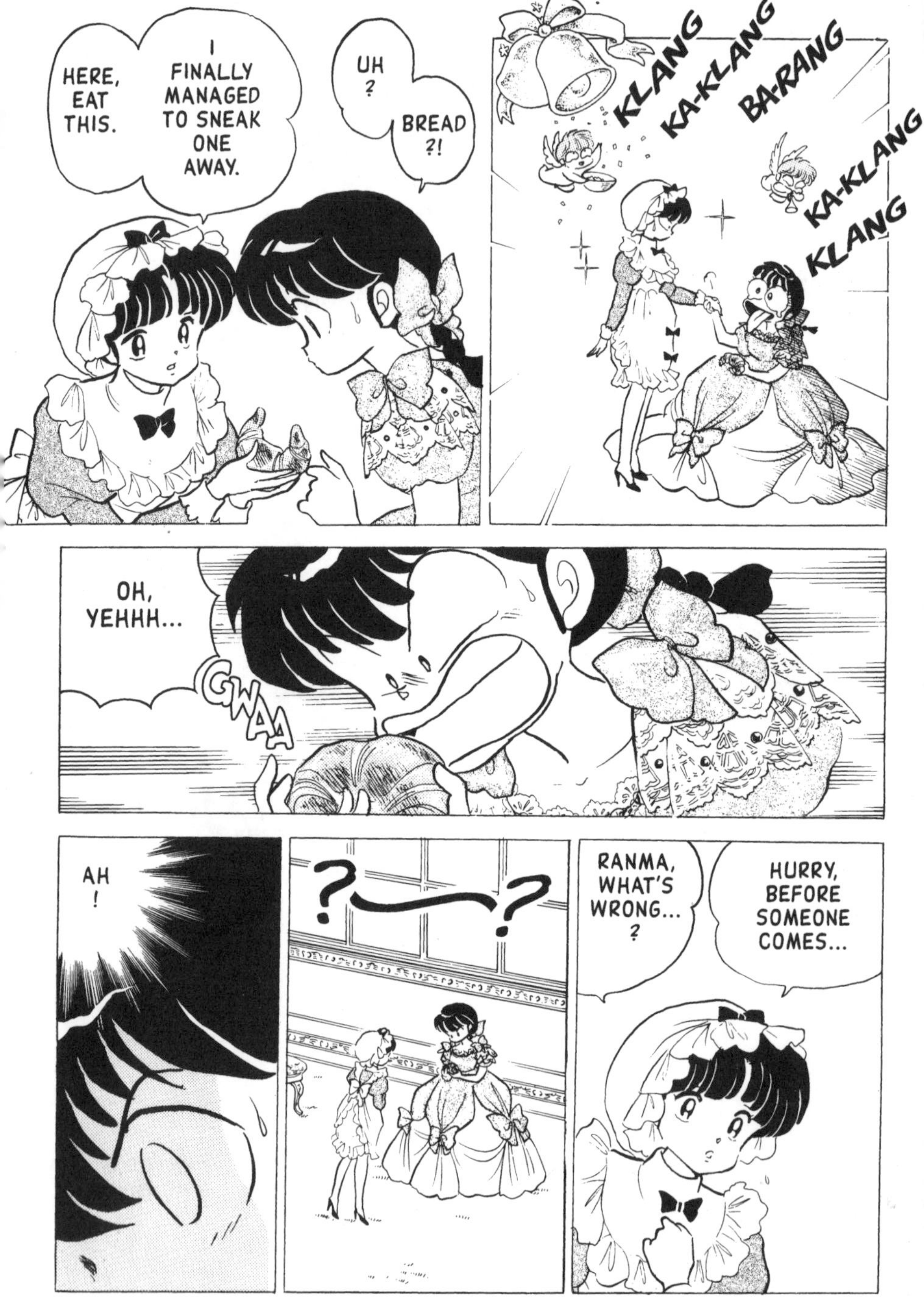
HERE, EAT THIS.
I FINALLY MANAGED TO SNEAK ONE AWAY.
UH ? BREAD ?!
KLANG
KA-KLANG
BA-RANG
KA-KLANG
KLANG
OH, YEHHH...
GWAA
AH !
?—?
RANMA, WHAT'S WRONG... ?
HURRY, BEFORE SOMEONE COMES...

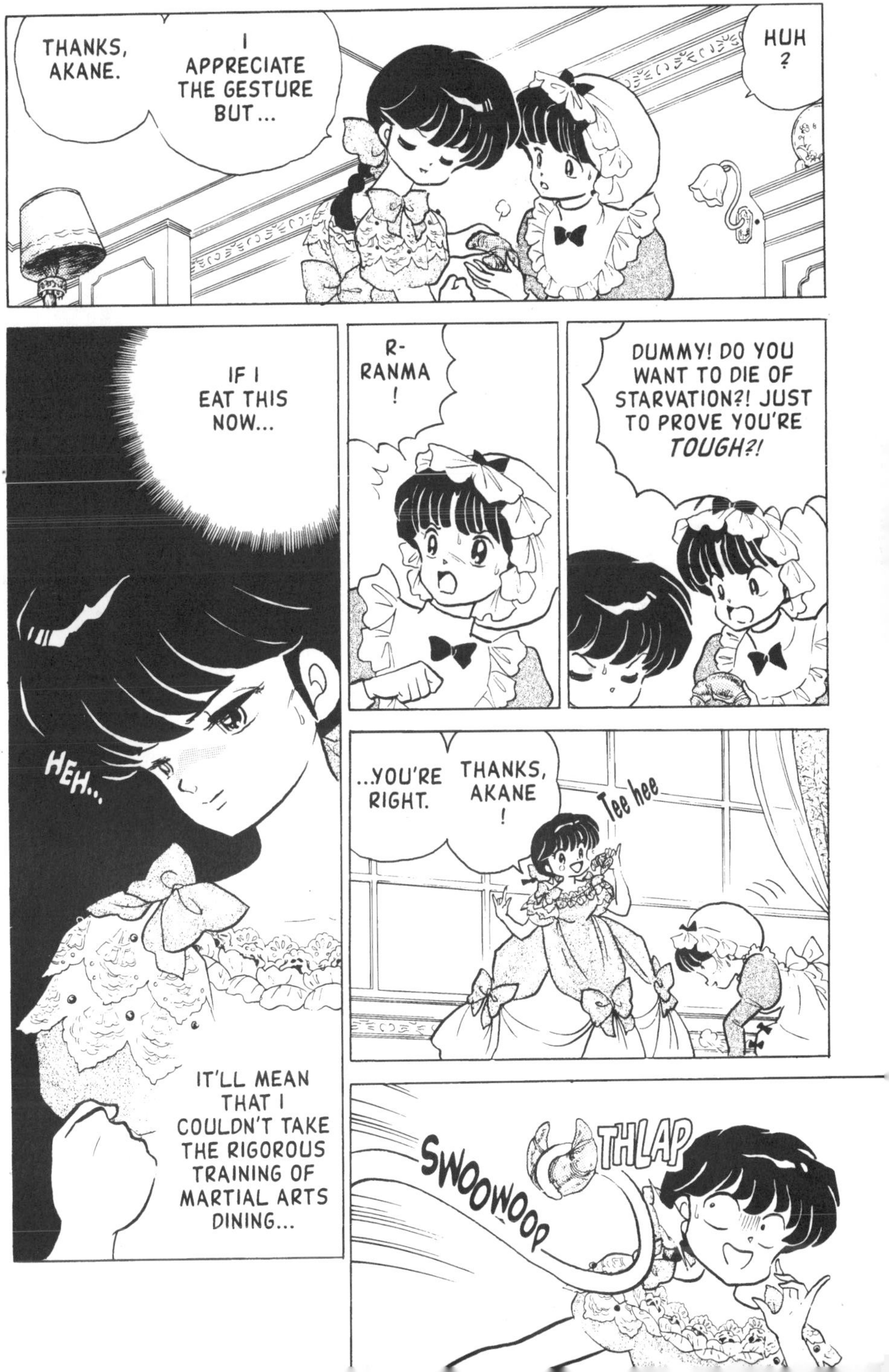
THANKS, AKANE.
I APPRECIATE THE GESTURE BUT...
HUH?
IF I EAT THIS NOW...
HEH...
IT'LL MEAN THAT I COULDN'T TAKE THE RIGOROUS TRAINING OF MARTIAL ARTS DINING...
R-RANMA!
DUMMY! DO YOU WANT TO DIE OF STARVATION?! JUST TO PROVE YOU'RE *TOUGH?!*
...YOU'RE RIGHT.
THANKS, AKANE!
Tee hee
SWOOWOOP
THLAP

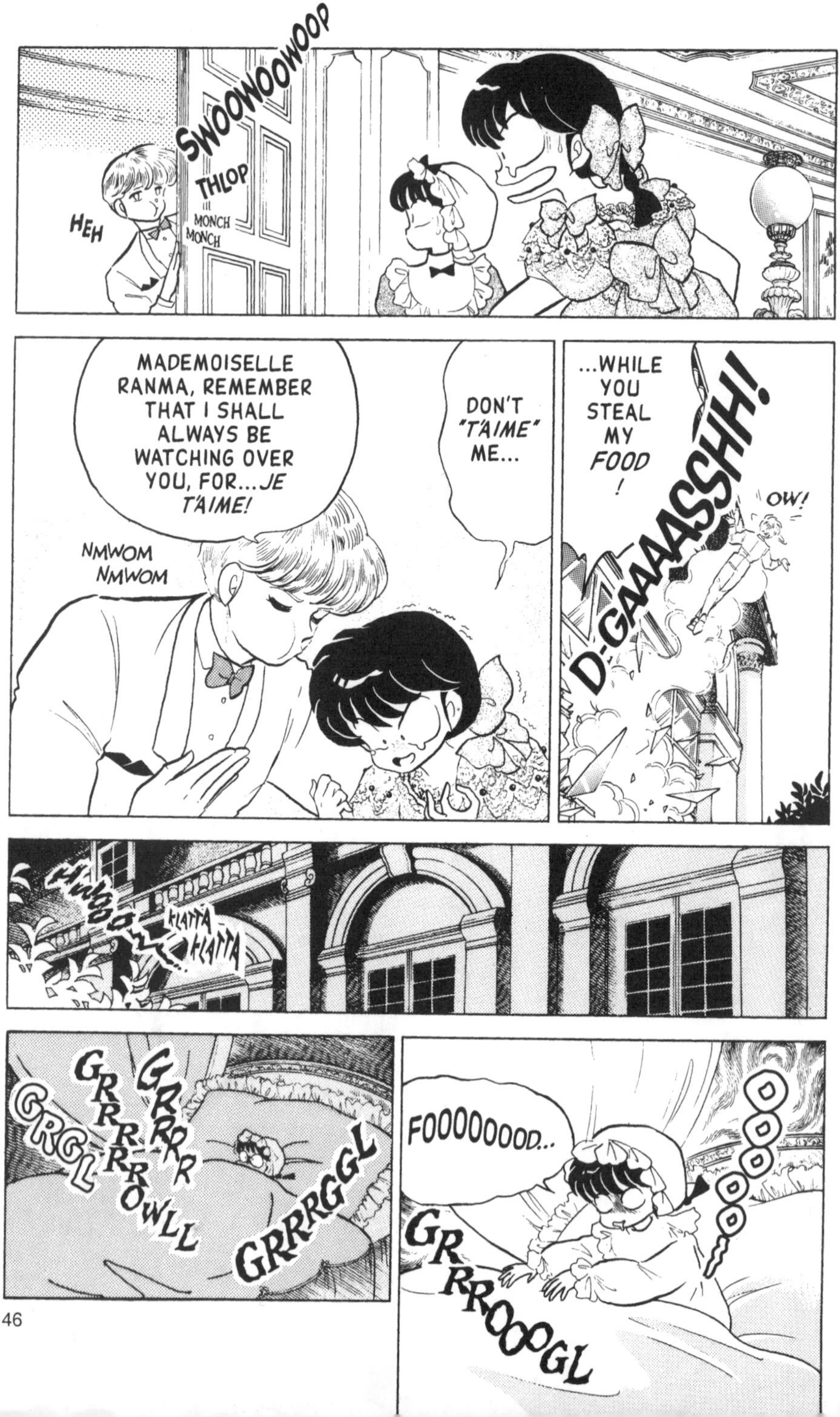
SWOOWOOWOOP
HEH
THLOP
MONCH MONCH
MADEMOISELLE RANMA, REMEMBER THAT I SHALL ALWAYS BE WATCHING OVER YOU, FOR... *JE T'AIME!*
NMWOM NMWOM
DON'T *"T'AIME"* ME...
...WHILE YOU STEAL MY *FOOD*!
D-GAAAASSHH!
OW!
KLATTA KLATTA
GRGL
GRRRRROWLL
GRRRR
GRRRGGL
FOOOOOOOD...
GRRROOOGL

HWOOOO...!

K-KLATA...!

RE... FRIG... ERATOR...

GRROWRR...

FOOOOD!

CHK

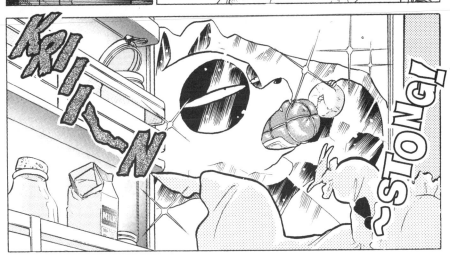

KRIIIIN

~STONG!

MILK

VROOOOM

HM ?

MR. SAOTOME ?

RRROOOMM

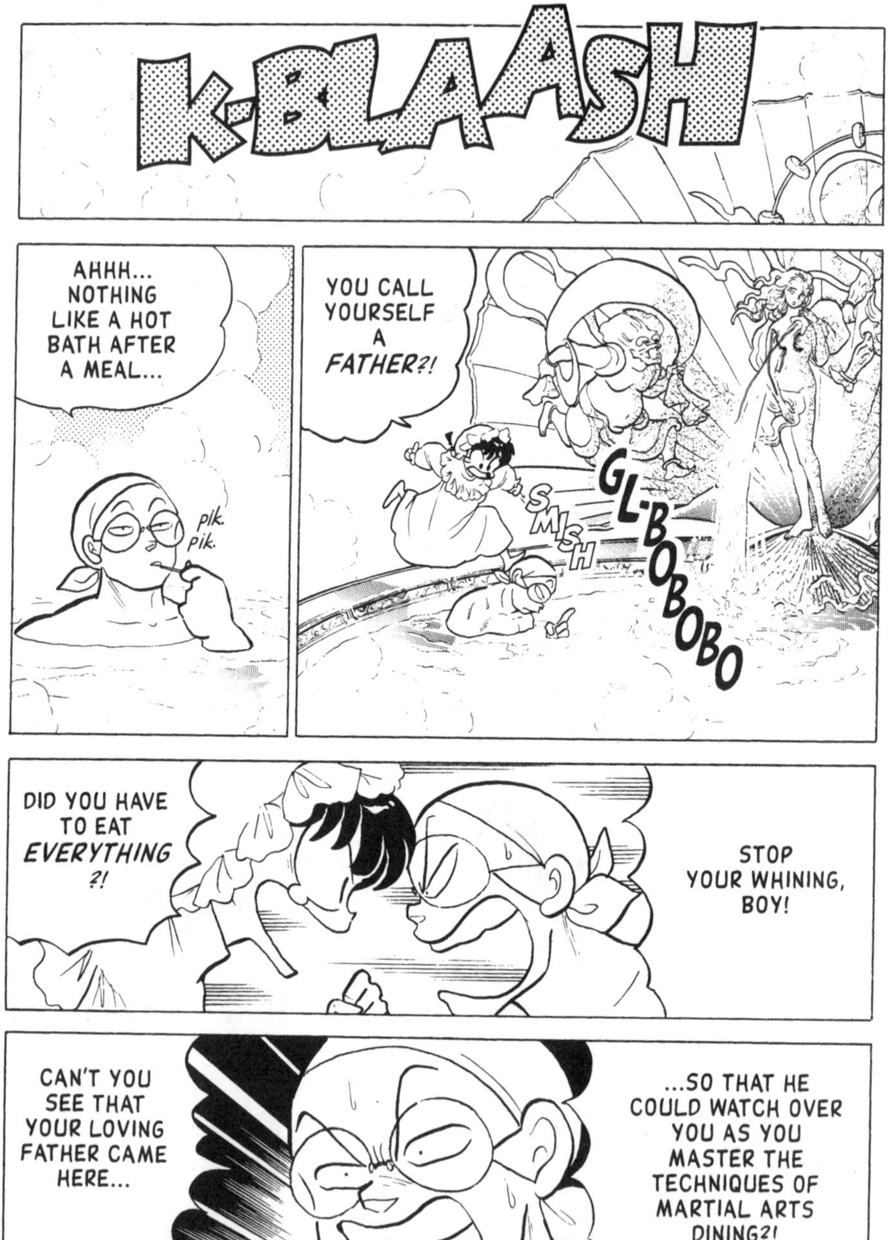
K-BLAASH
AHHH... NOTHING LIKE A HOT BATH AFTER A MEAL...
pik. pik.
YOU CALL YOURSELF A *FATHER*?!
SMISH
GL-BOBOBO
DID YOU HAVE TO EAT *EVERYTHING*?!
STOP YOUR WHINING, BOY!
CAN'T YOU SEE THAT YOUR LOVING FATHER CAME HERE...
...SO THAT HE COULD WATCH OVER YOU AS YOU MASTER THE TECHNIQUES OF MARTIAL ARTS DINING?!

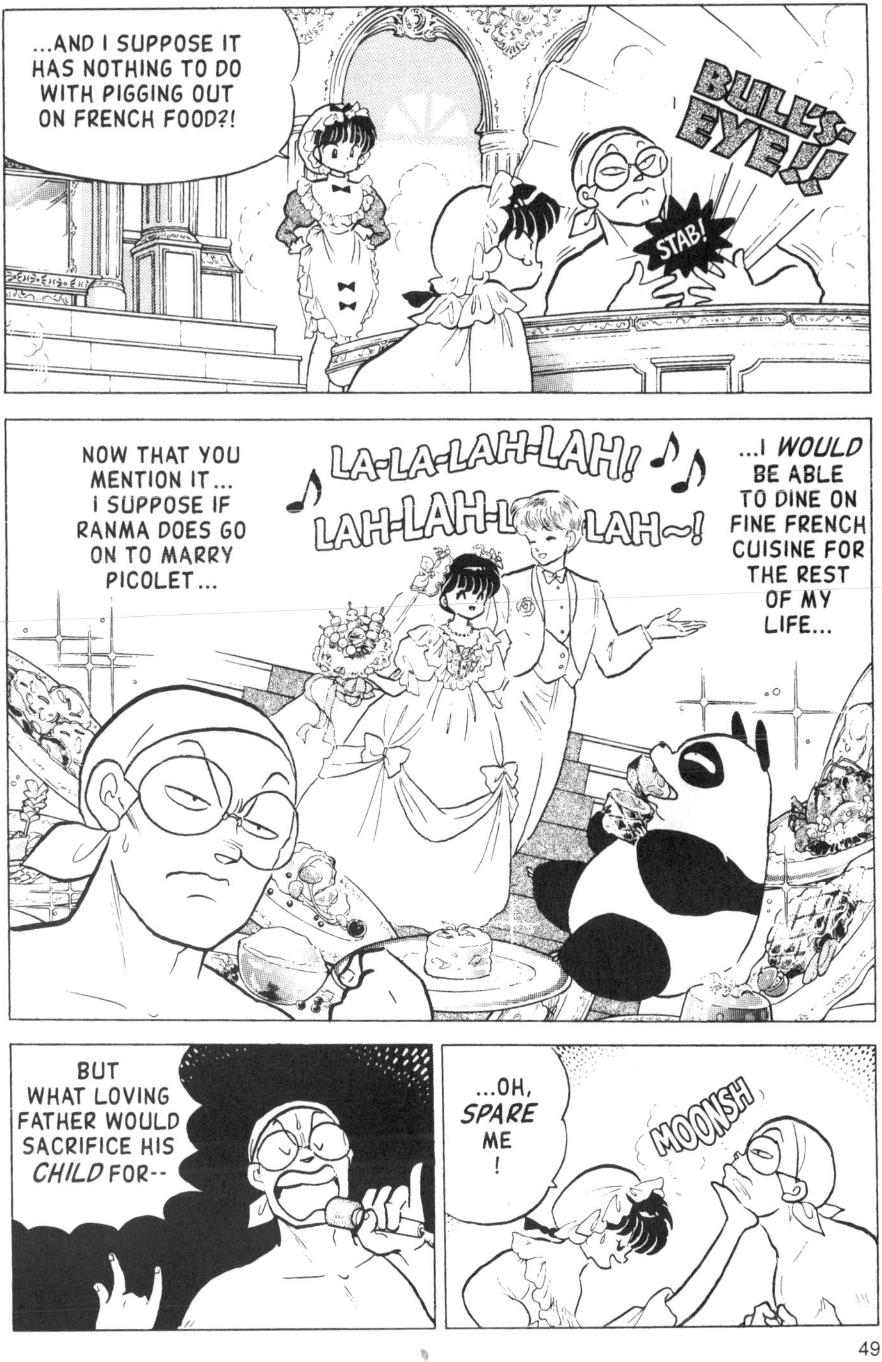
...AND I SUPPOSE IT HAS NOTHING TO DO WITH PIGGING OUT ON FRENCH FOOD?!
BULL'S-EYE!!
STAB!
NOW THAT YOU MENTION IT... I SUPPOSE IF RANMA DOES GO ON TO MARRY PICOLET...
LA-LA-LAH-LAH!
LAH-LAH-L
LAH~!
...I *WOULD* BE ABLE TO DINE ON FINE FRENCH CUISINE FOR THE REST OF MY LIFE...
BUT WHAT LOVING FATHER WOULD SACRIFICE HIS *CHILD* FOR--
...OH, *SPARE* ME!
MOONSH

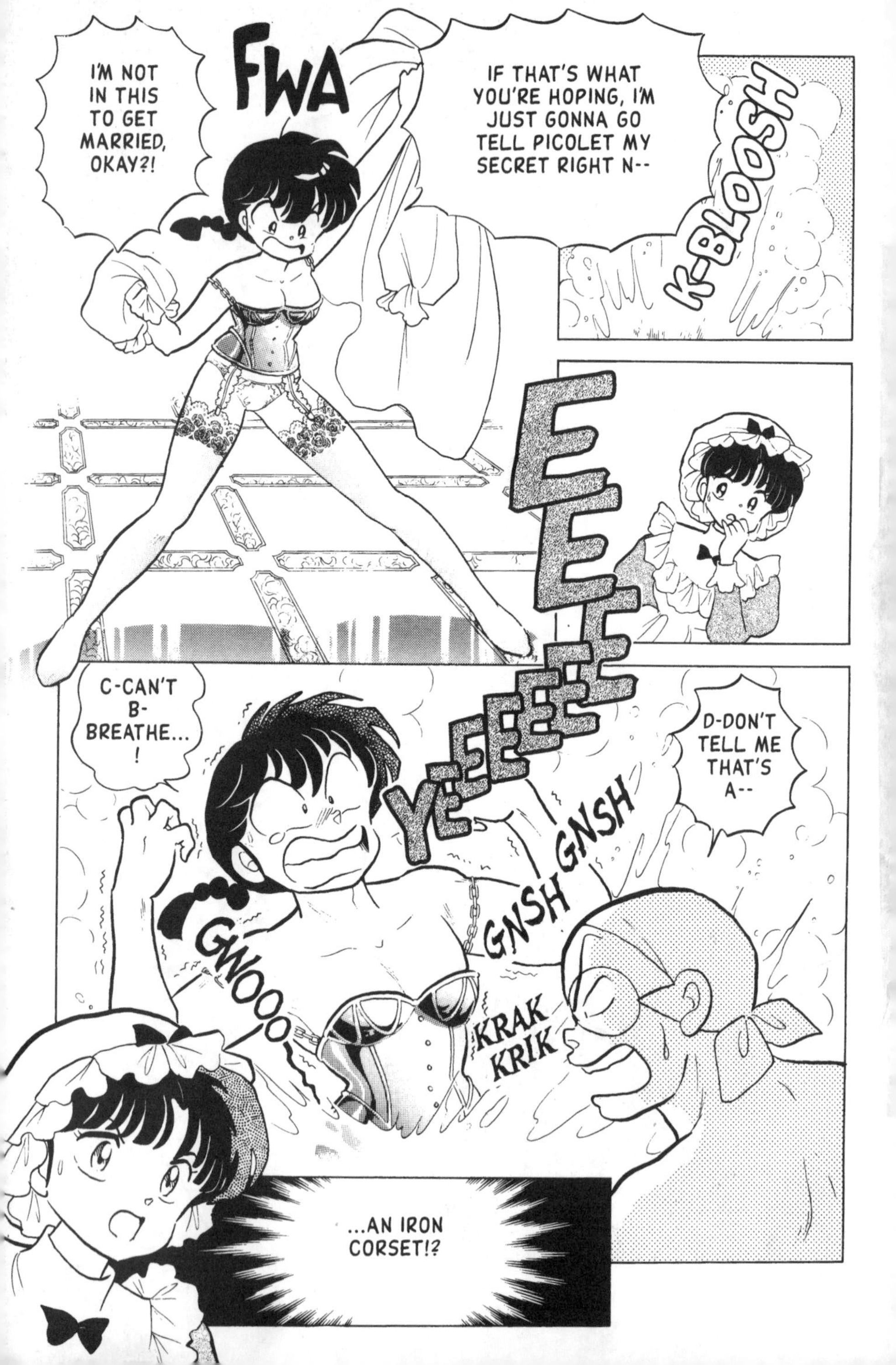
I'M NOT IN THIS TO GET MARRIED, OKAY?!
FWA
IF THAT'S WHAT YOU'RE HOPING, I'M JUST GONNA GO TELL PICOLET MY SECRET RIGHT N--
K-BLOOSH
EEEE
C-CAN'T B-BREATHE... !
YEEEEEE
D-DON'T TELL ME THAT'S A--
GNSH GNSH GNSH
GWOOO
KRAK KRIK
...AN IRON CORSET!?

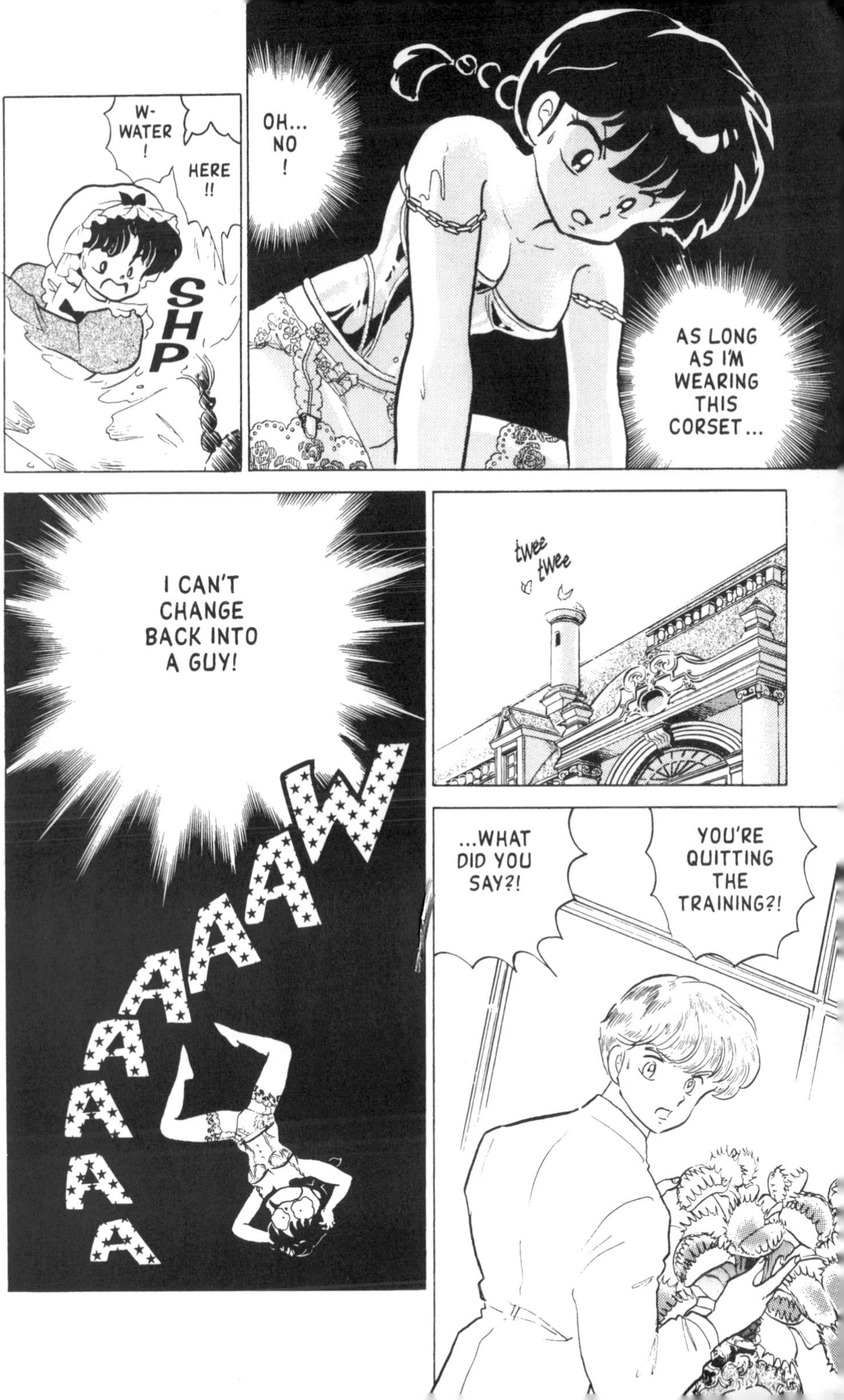
W-WATER!
HERE!!
SHP
OH... NO!
AS LONG AS I'M WEARING THIS CORSET...
I CAN'T CHANGE BACK INTO A GUY!
AAAAAAAAAW
twee twee
...WHAT DID YOU SAY?!
YOU'RE QUITTING THE TRAINING?!

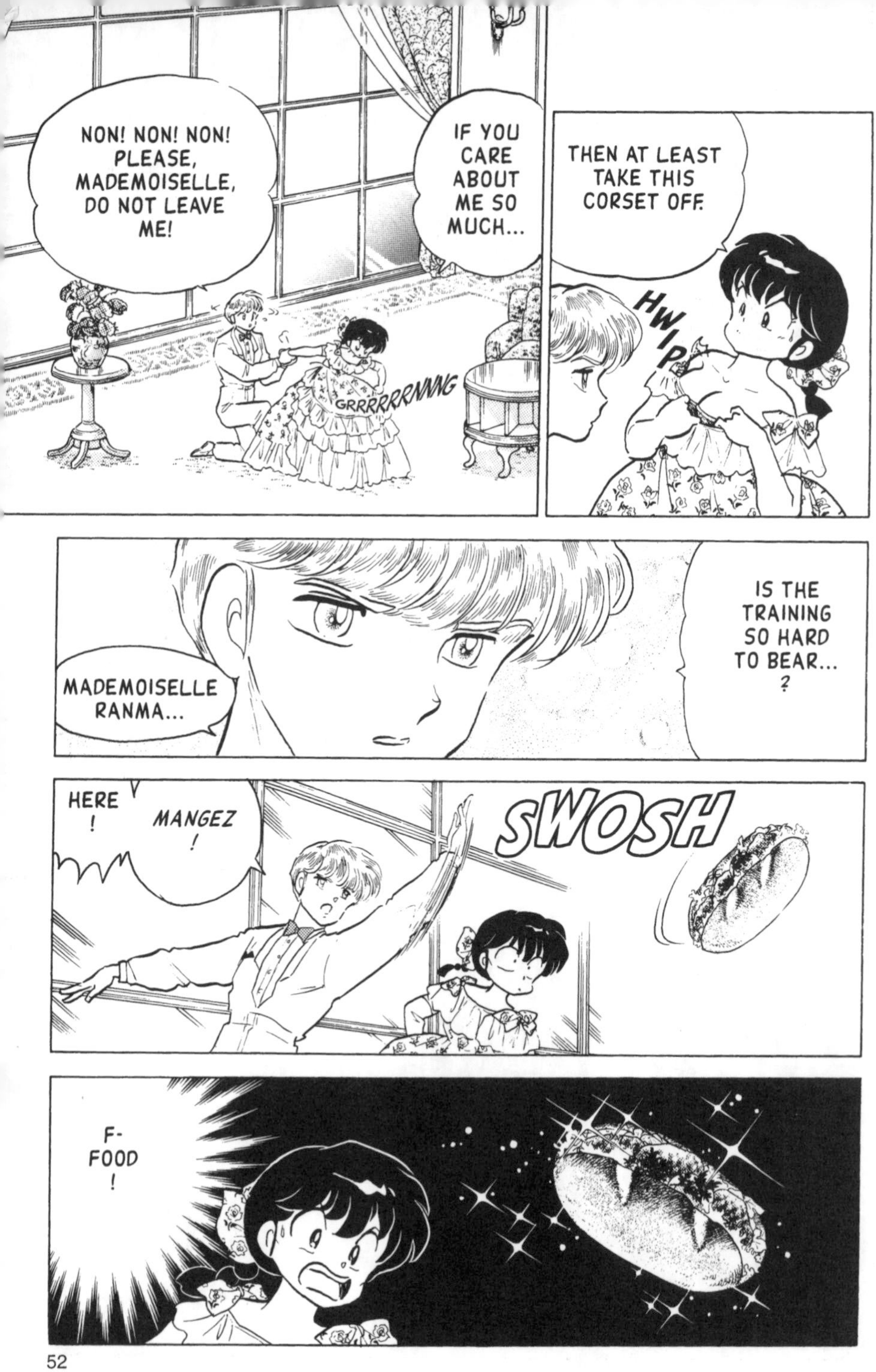
NON! NON! NON! PLEASE, MADEMOISELLE, DO NOT LEAVE ME!
IF YOU CARE ABOUT ME SO MUCH...
GRRRRRRNNNG
THEN AT LEAST TAKE THIS CORSET OFF.
HWIP
MADEMOISELLE RANMA...
IS THE TRAINING SO HARD TO BEAR...?
HERE!
MANGEZ!
SWOSH
F-FOOD!

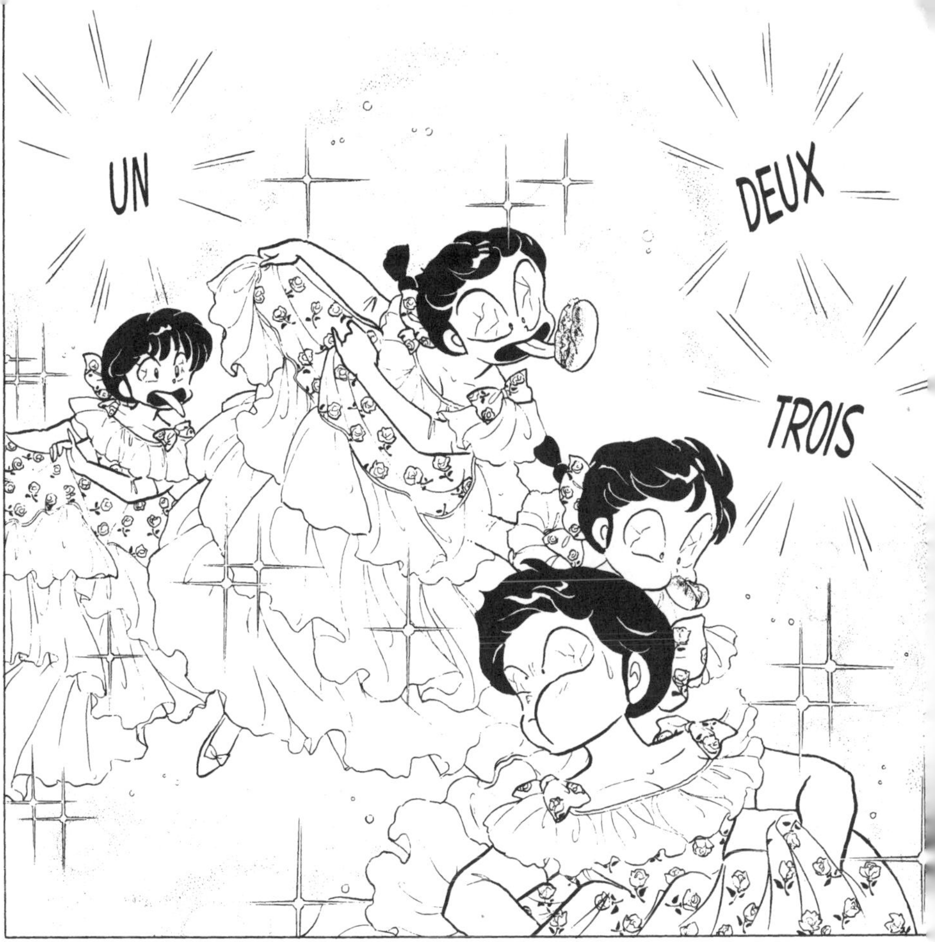
UN
DEUX
TROIS

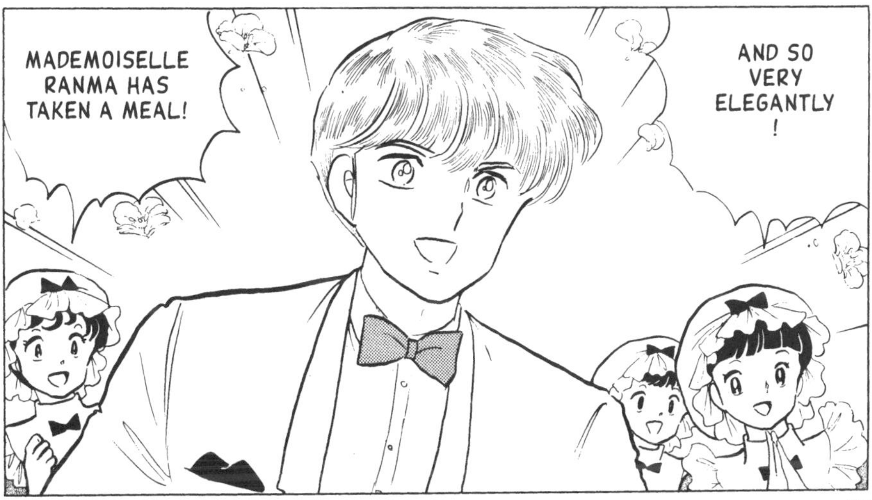
MADEMOISELLE RANMA HAS TAKEN A MEAL!
AND SO VERY ELEGANTLY !

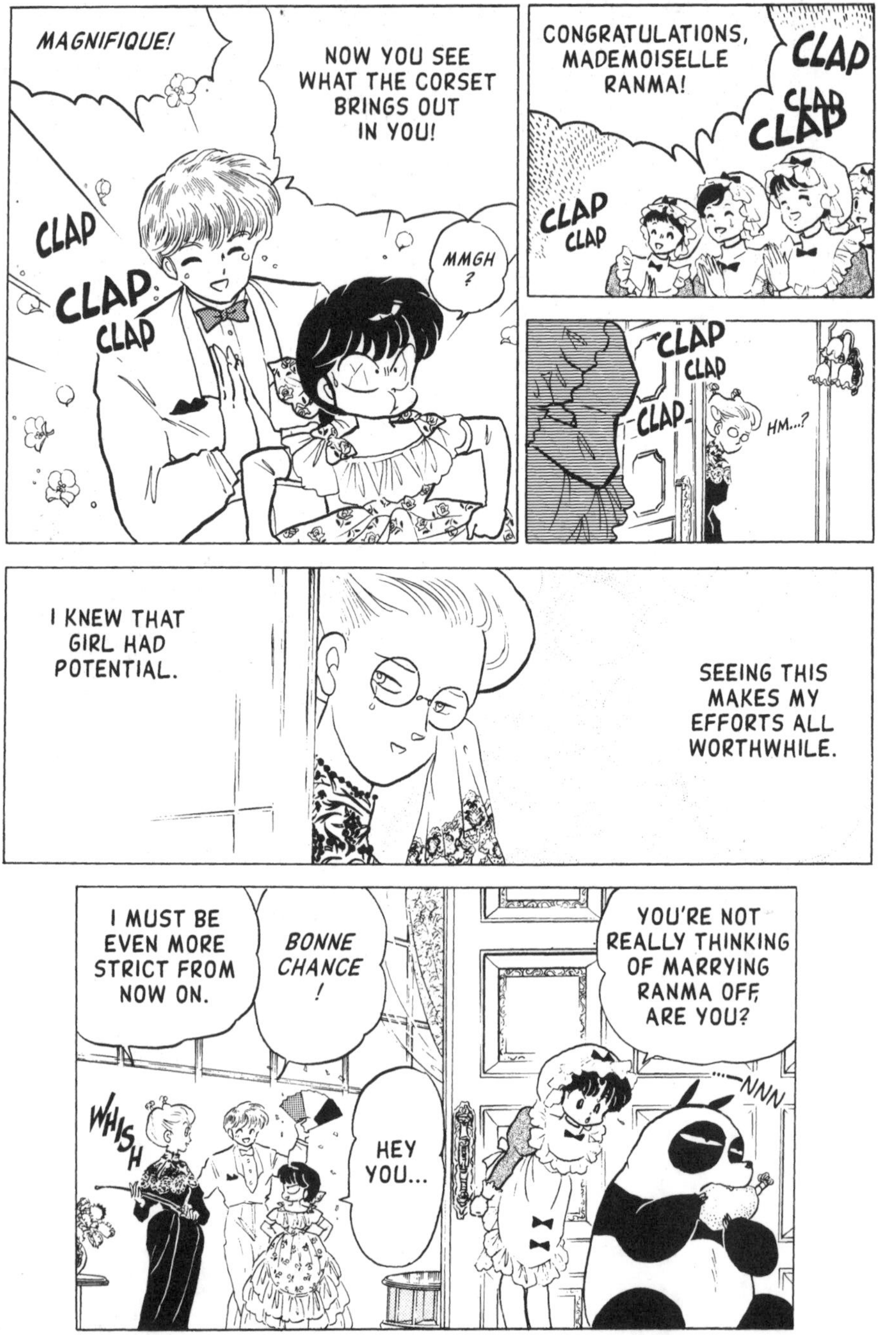
MAGNIFIQUE!
NOW YOU SEE WHAT THE CORSET BRINGS OUT IN YOU!
CLAP
CLAP
CLAP
MMGH ?
CONGRATULATIONS, MADEMOISELLE RANMA!
CLAP
CLAP
CLAP
CLAP
CLAP
CLAP
CLAP
CLAP
HM...?
I KNEW THAT GIRL HAD POTENTIAL.
SEEING THIS MAKES MY EFFORTS ALL WORTHWHILE.
I MUST BE EVEN MORE STRICT FROM NOW ON.
BONNE CHANCE!
WHISH
HEY YOU...
YOU'RE NOT REALLY THINKING OF MARRYING RANMA OFF, ARE YOU?
...NNN

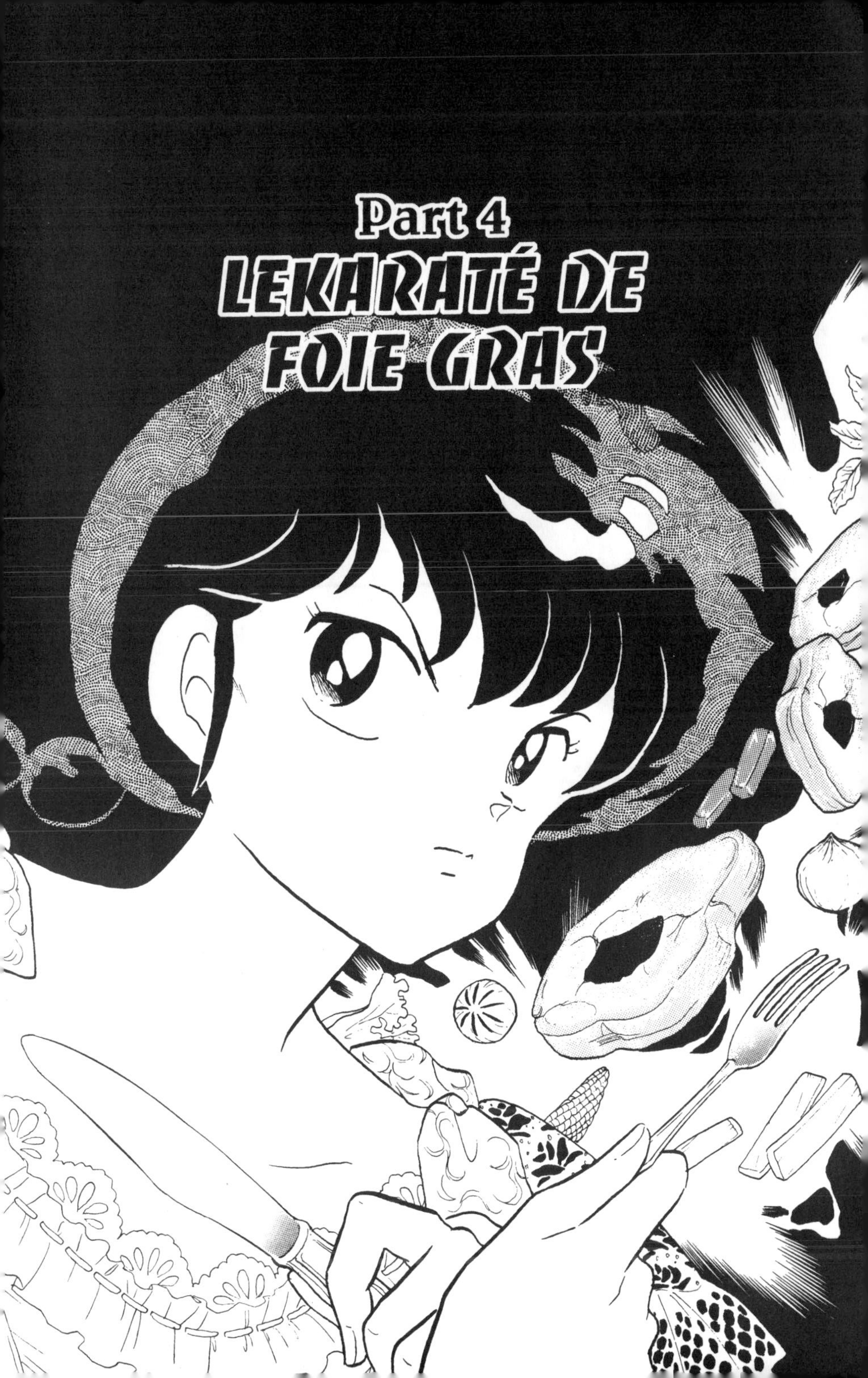
Part 4
LEKARATÉ DE FOIE GRAS

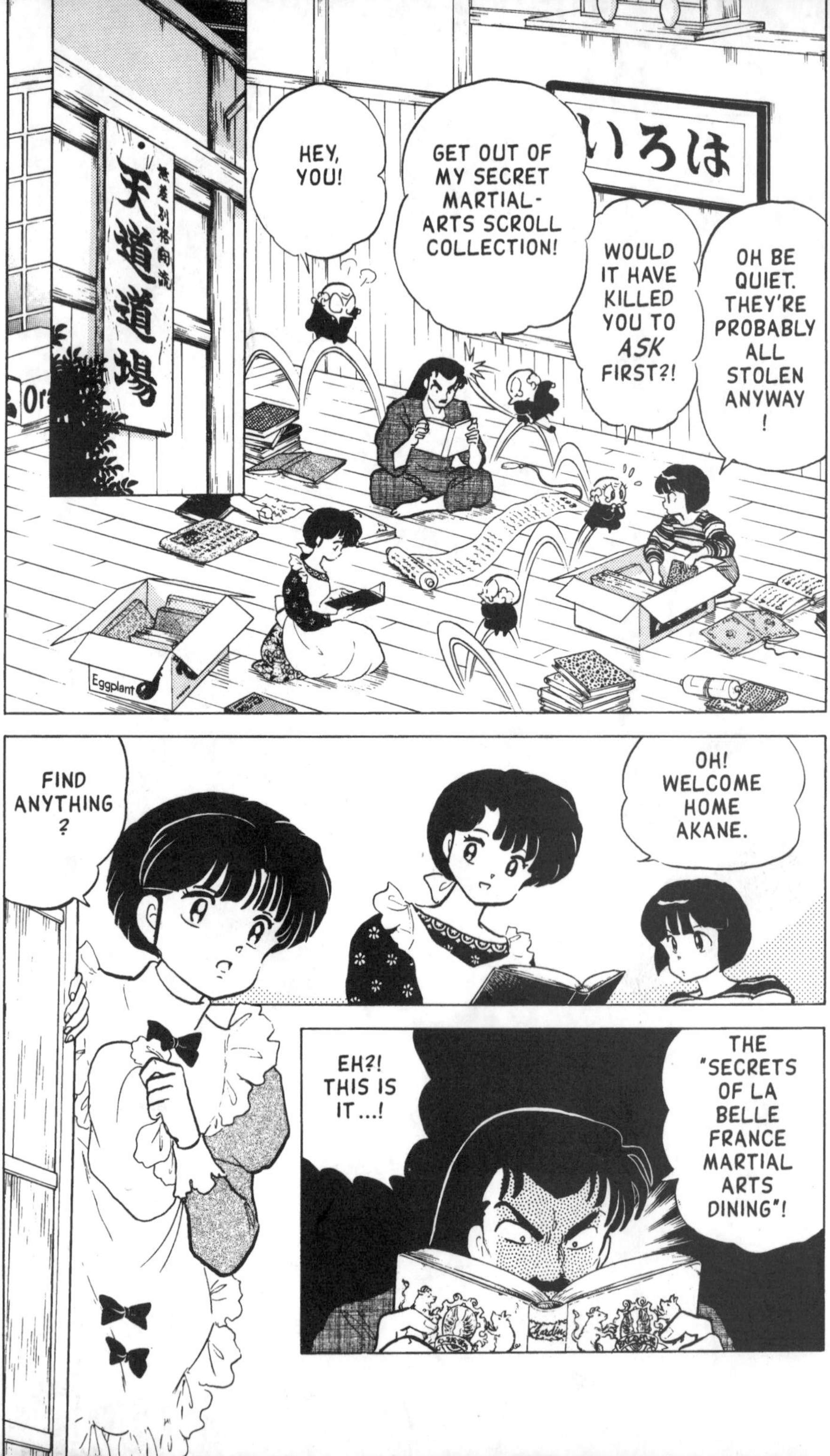
天道道場
いろは
HEY, YOU!
GET OUT OF MY SECRET MARTIAL-ARTS SCROLL COLLECTION!
WOULD IT HAVE KILLED YOU TO *ASK* FIRST?!
OH BE QUIET. THEY'RE PROBABLY ALL STOLEN ANYWAY!
Eggplant
FIND ANYTHING?
OH! WELCOME HOME AKANE.
EH?! THIS IS IT...!
THE "SECRETS OF LA BELLE FRANCE MARTIAL ARTS DINING"!

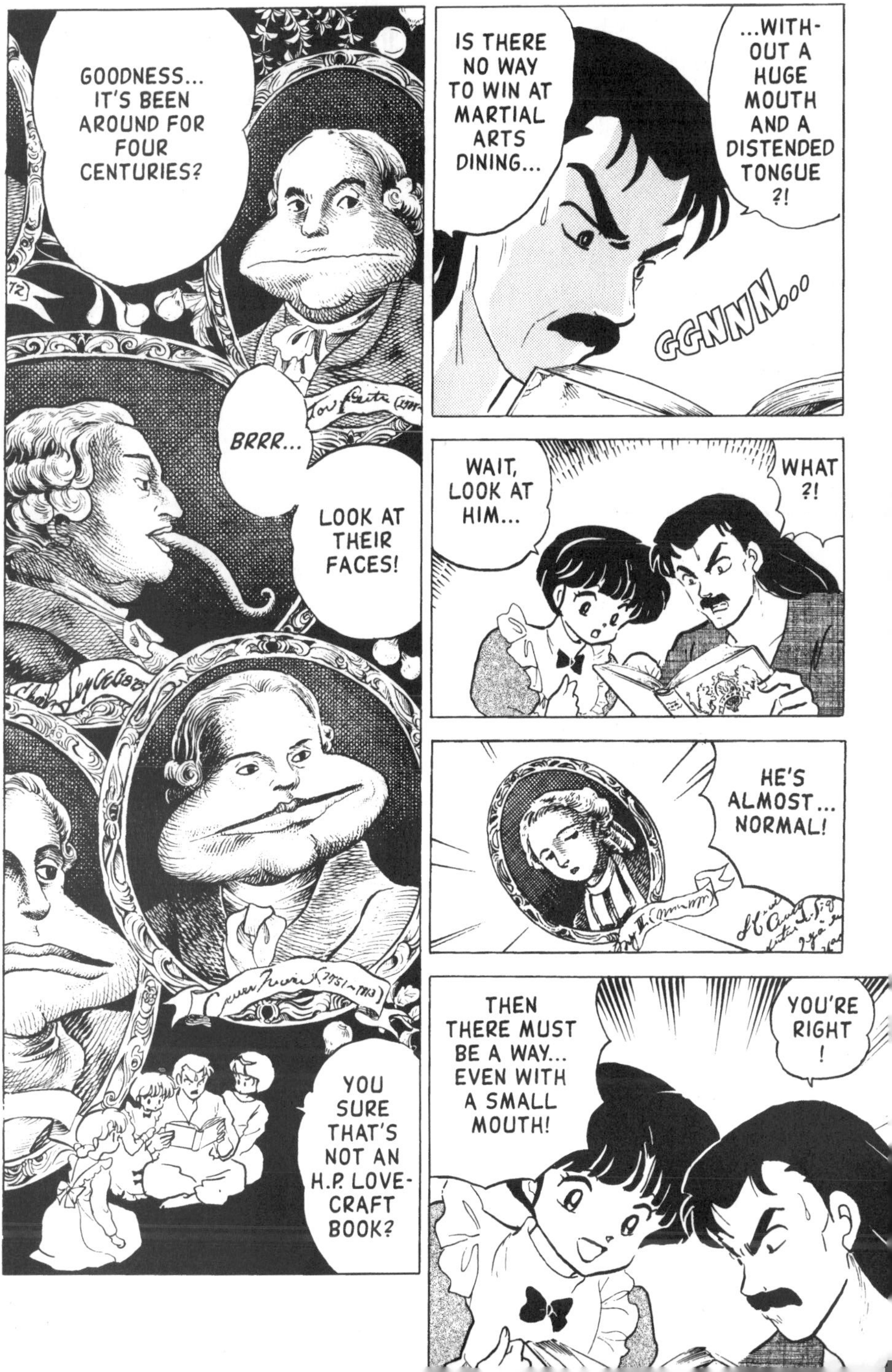
GOODNESS... IT'S BEEN AROUND FOR FOUR CENTURIES?
BRRR...
LOOK AT THEIR FACES!
YOU SURE THAT'S NOT AN H.P. LOVECRAFT BOOK?
IS THERE NO WAY TO WIN AT MARTIAL ARTS DINING...
...WITHOUT A HUGE MOUTH AND A DISTENDED TONGUE?!
GGNNNooo
WAIT, LOOK AT HIM...
WHAT?!
HE'S ALMOST... NORMAL!
THEN THERE MUST BE A WAY... EVEN WITH A SMALL MOUTH!
YOU'RE RIGHT!

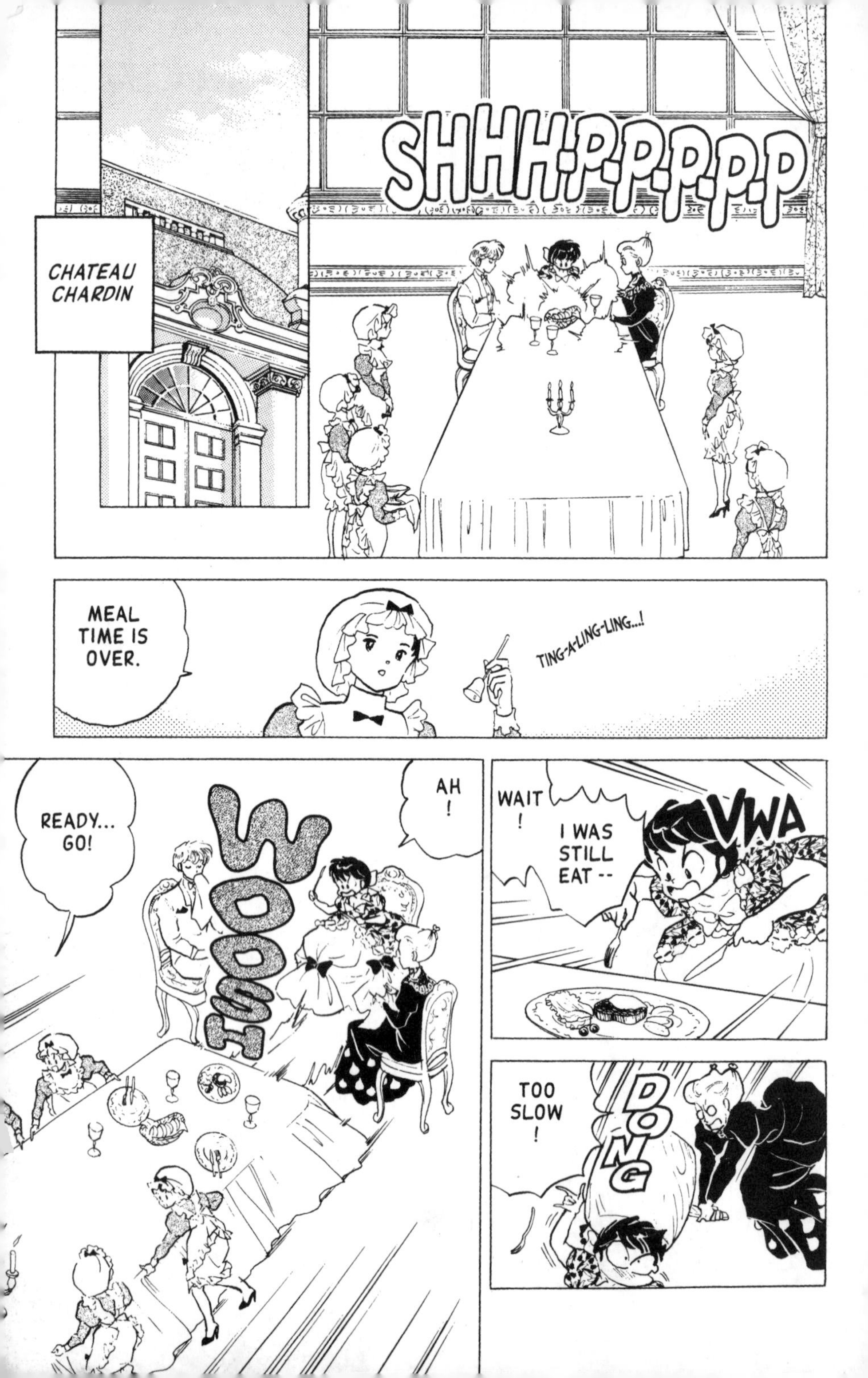
CHATEAU CHARDIN
SHHH-P-P-P-P-P
MEAL TIME IS OVER.
TING-A-LING-LING...!
READY... GO!
WOOSH
AH!
WAIT!
I WAS STILL EAT --
VWA
TOO SLOW!
DONG

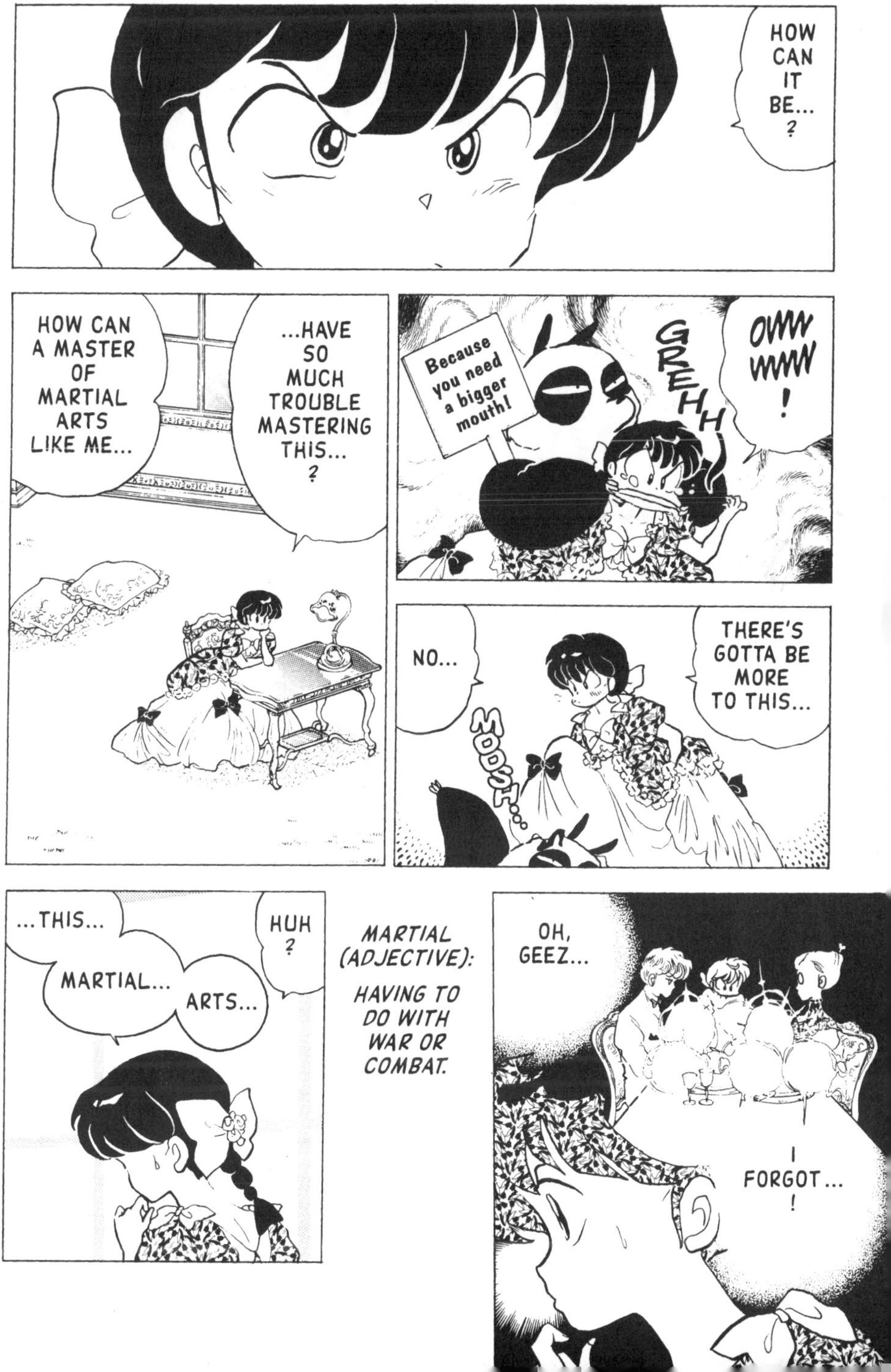
HOW CAN IT BE...?
HOW CAN A MASTER OF MARTIAL ARTS LIKE ME...
...HAVE SO MUCH TROUBLE MASTERING THIS...?
Because you need a bigger mouth!
GREHH
OWWWWW!
NO...
THERE'S GOTTA BE MORE TO THIS...
MOOSH...
...THIS...
MARTIAL...
ARTS...
HUH?
MARTIAL (ADJECTIVE): HAVING TO DO WITH WAR OR COMBAT.
OH, GEEZ...
I FORGOT...!

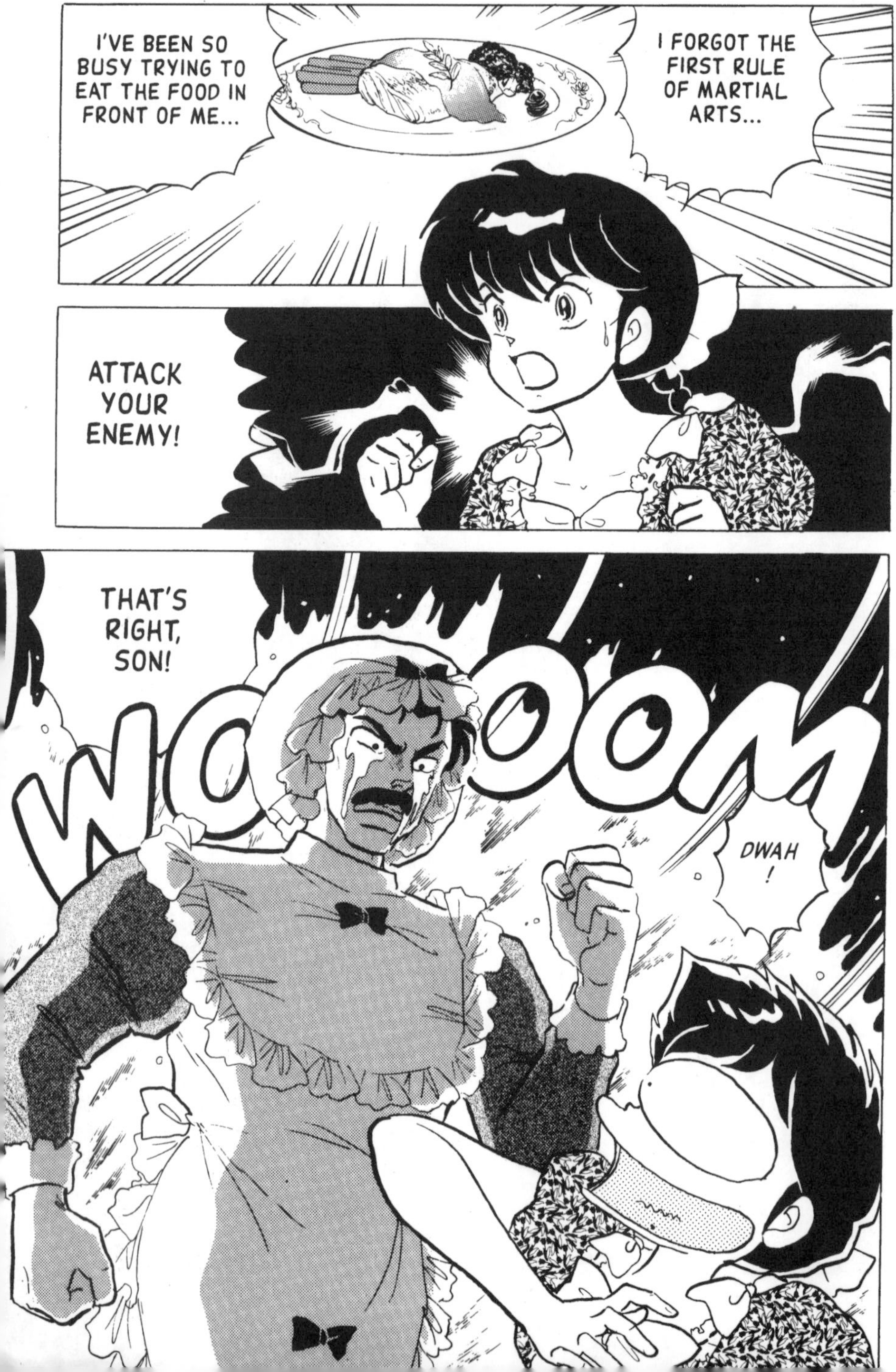
I'VE BEEN SO BUSY TRYING TO EAT THE FOOD IN FRONT OF ME...
I FORGOT THE FIRST RULE OF MARTIAL ARTS...
ATTACK YOUR ENEMY!
THAT'S RIGHT, SON!
WOOOOM
DWAH!

WH-WH-WHAT IN THE...?

WHAT.

YOU NEVER SAW A FRENCH MAID BEFORE?

DAAAD...!

B-BWUMP B-BWUMP

TAKE A LOOK AT THIS, RANMA.

FFP

SECRETS OF MARTIAL ARTS DINING...?

CORRECT. AND IN ITS 400-YEAR HISTORY...

...THERE WAS BUT ONE MAVERICK... ONE RADICAL...THE MAN CALLED "LE PETIT BOUCHE"...

..."LITTLE MOUTH"! WHO INGENIOUSLY PARLAYED HIS ORAL SHORTCOMINGS INTO A MASTERY OF A "CUISINE-FU"...

...WITH A TECHNIQUE BASED HEAVILY ON ATTACKING THE OPPONENT.

HE CALLED IT "PARLAY DU FOIE GRAS"!

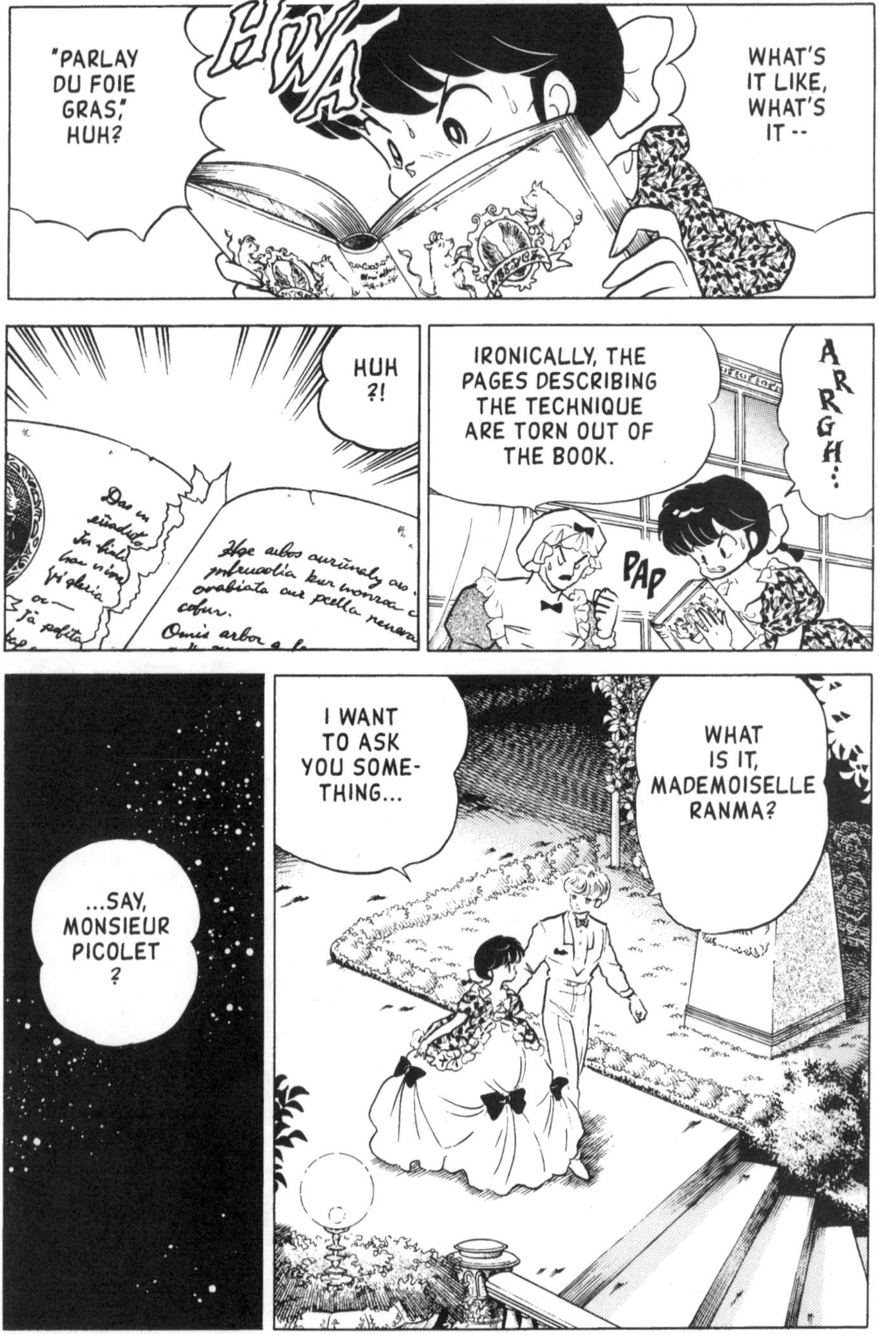
HWA
"PARLAY DU FOIE GRAS," HUH?
WHAT'S IT LIKE, WHAT'S IT --
HUH ?!
IRONICALLY, THE PAGES DESCRIBING THE TECHNIQUE ARE TORN OUT OF THE BOOK.
ARRGH...
PAP
...SAY, MONSIEUR PICOLET ?
I WANT TO ASK YOU SOMETHING...
WHAT IS IT, MADEMOISELLE RANMA?

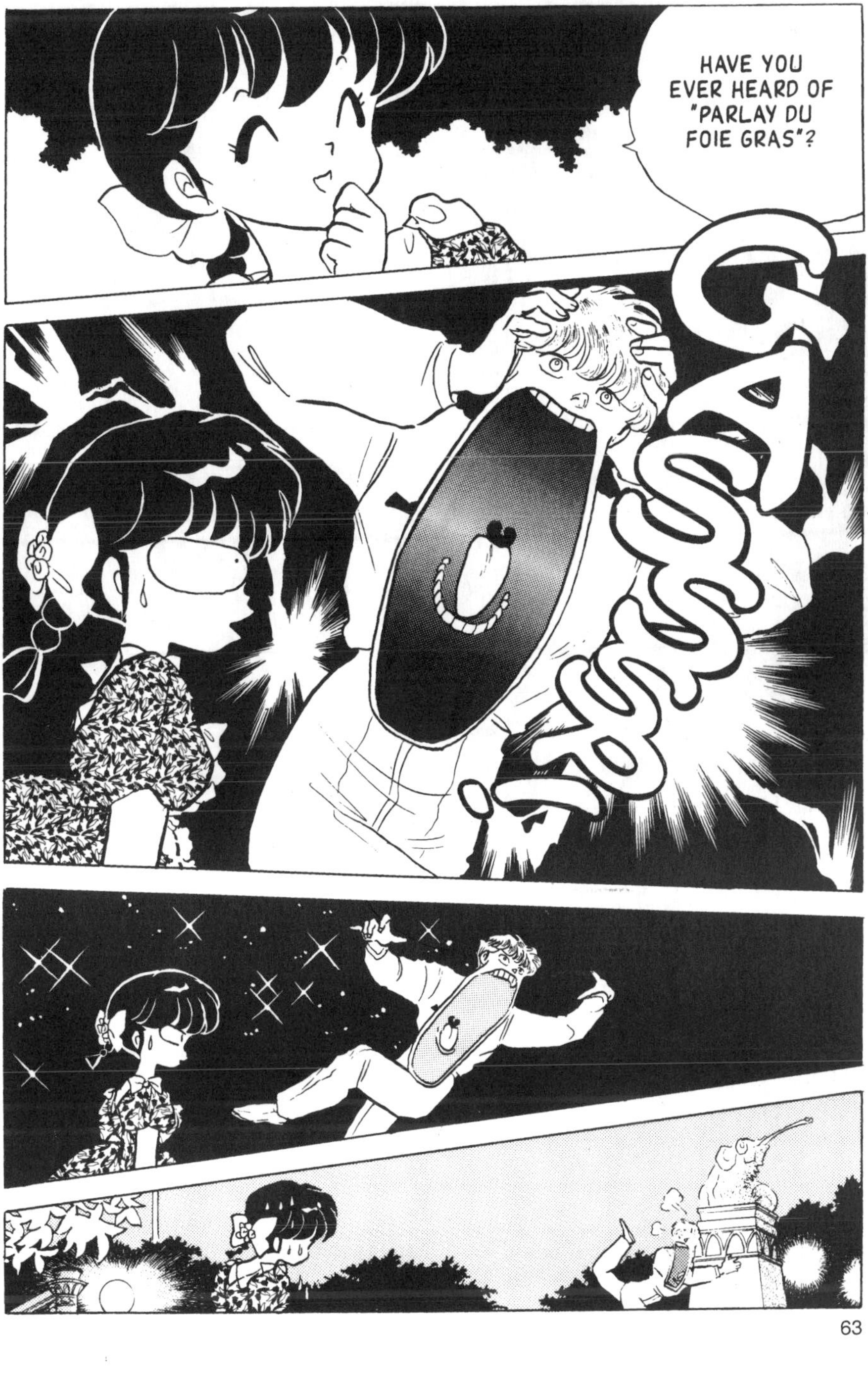
HAVE YOU EVER HEARD OF "PARLAY DU FOIE GRAS"?
GASHUNK!

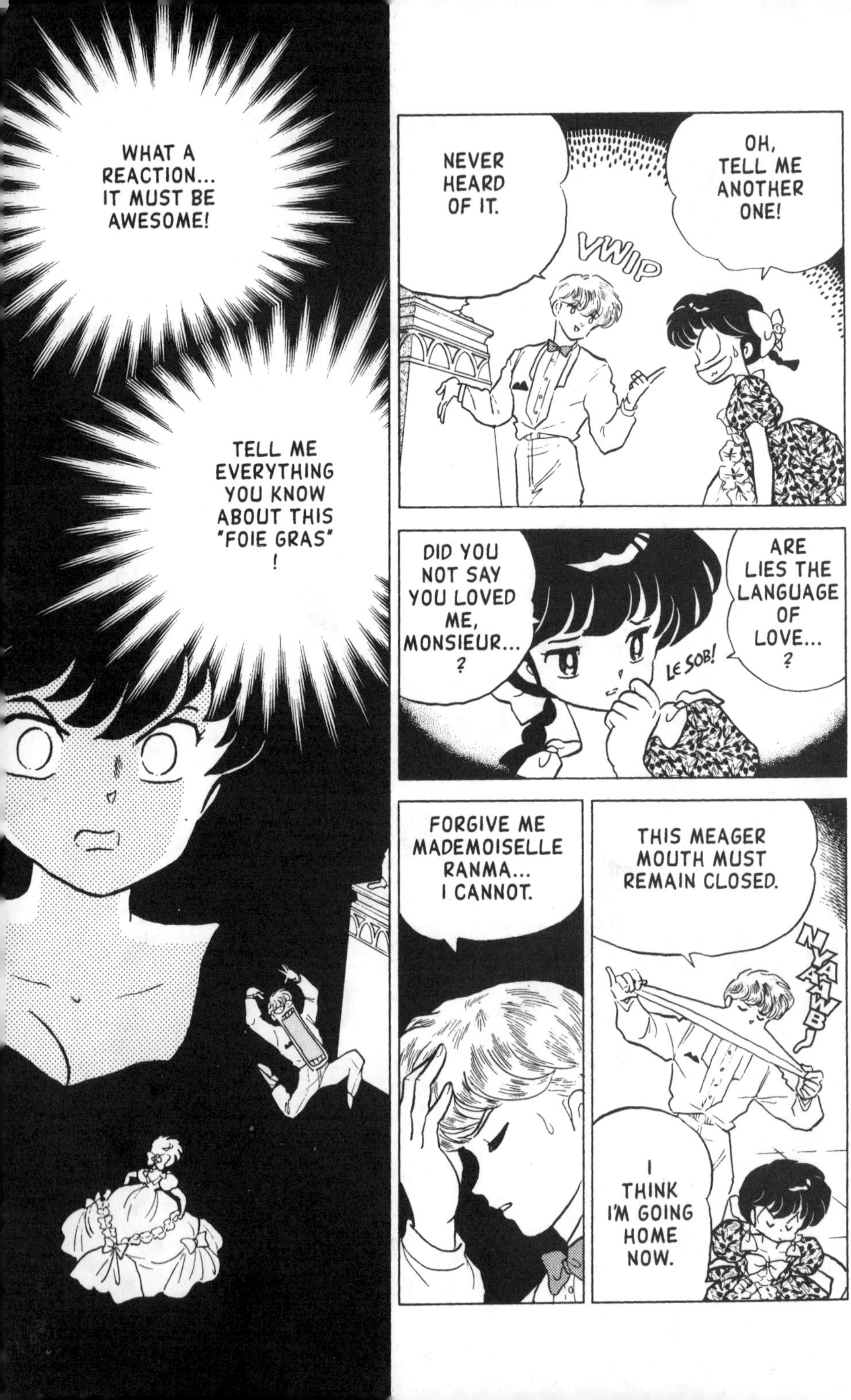
WHAT A REACTION... IT MUST BE AWESOME!
TELL ME EVERYTHING YOU KNOW ABOUT THIS "FOIE GRAS" !
NEVER HEARD OF IT.
OH, TELL ME ANOTHER ONE!
VWIP
DID YOU NOT SAY YOU LOVED ME, MONSIEUR... ?
LE SOB!
ARE LIES THE LANGUAGE OF LOVE... ?
FORGIVE ME MADEMOISELLE RANMA... I CANNOT.
THIS MEAGER MOUTH MUST REMAIN CLOSED.
NYAAWB
I THINK I'M GOING HOME NOW.

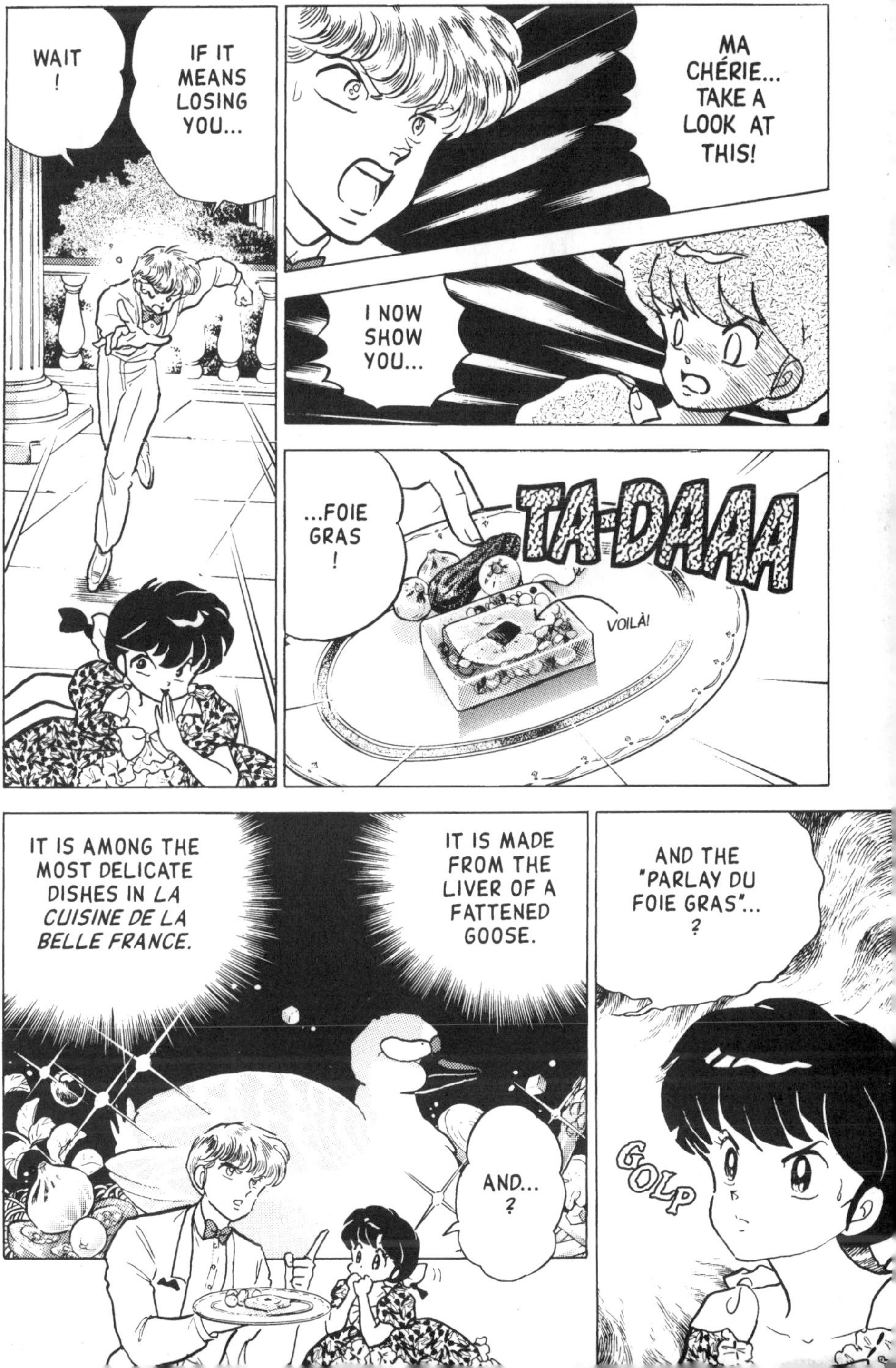
WAIT!
IF IT MEANS LOSING YOU...
MA CHÉRIE... TAKE A LOOK AT THIS!
I NOW SHOW YOU...
...FOIE GRAS!
TA-DAAA
VOILÀ!
IT IS AMONG THE MOST DELICATE DISHES IN *LA CUISINE DE LA BELLE FRANCE.*
IT IS MADE FROM THE LIVER OF A FATTENED GOOSE.
AND...?
AND THE "PARLAY DU FOIE GRAS"...?
GOLP

PLEMMF

A "PARLAY" IS A CLEVER MANEUVER.

AND...?

MMK MKK MMK

GGGG-

...AND THAT'S IT.

.....

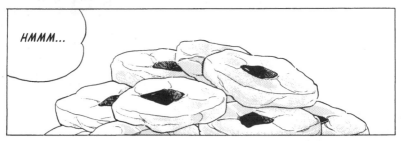

HMMM...

HOW DOES THIS FOIE GRAS TIE INTO THE SECRET TECHNIQUE...?

PICOLET'S STILL HIDING SOMETHING!

I'M GOING TO FIGURE OUT WHAT THIS "PARLAY DU FOIE GRAS" IS, NO MATTER WHAT IT TAKES!

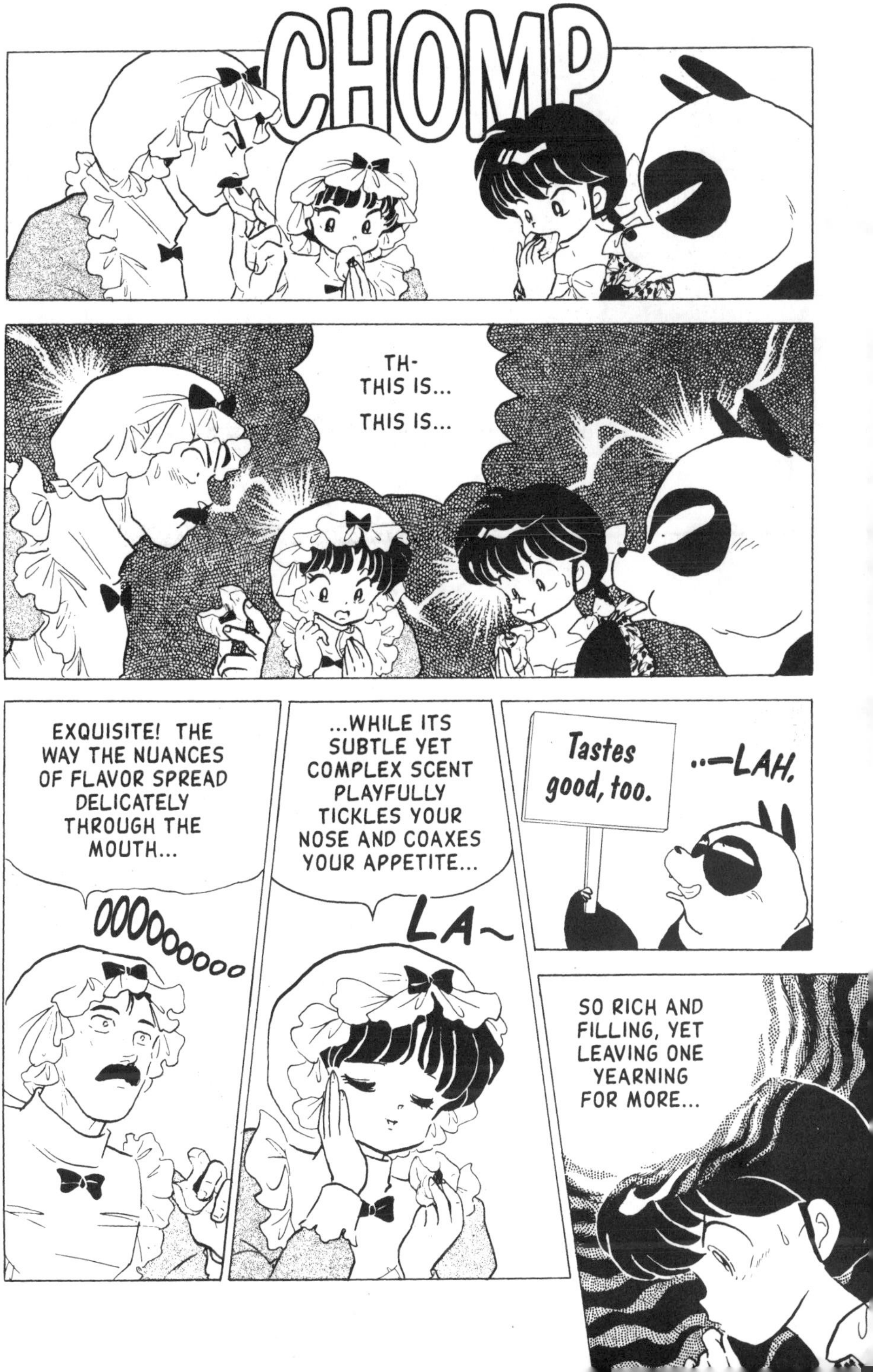
CHOMP
TH-
THIS IS...
THIS IS...
EXQUISITE! THE WAY THE NUANCES OF FLAVOR SPREAD DELICATELY THROUGH THE MOUTH...
OOOOOOOOOO
...WHILE ITS SUBTLE YET COMPLEX SCENT PLAYFULLY TICKLES YOUR NOSE AND COAXES YOUR APPETITE...
LA~
Tastes good, too.
...—LAH.
SO RICH AND FILLING, YET LEAVING ONE YEARNING FOR MORE...

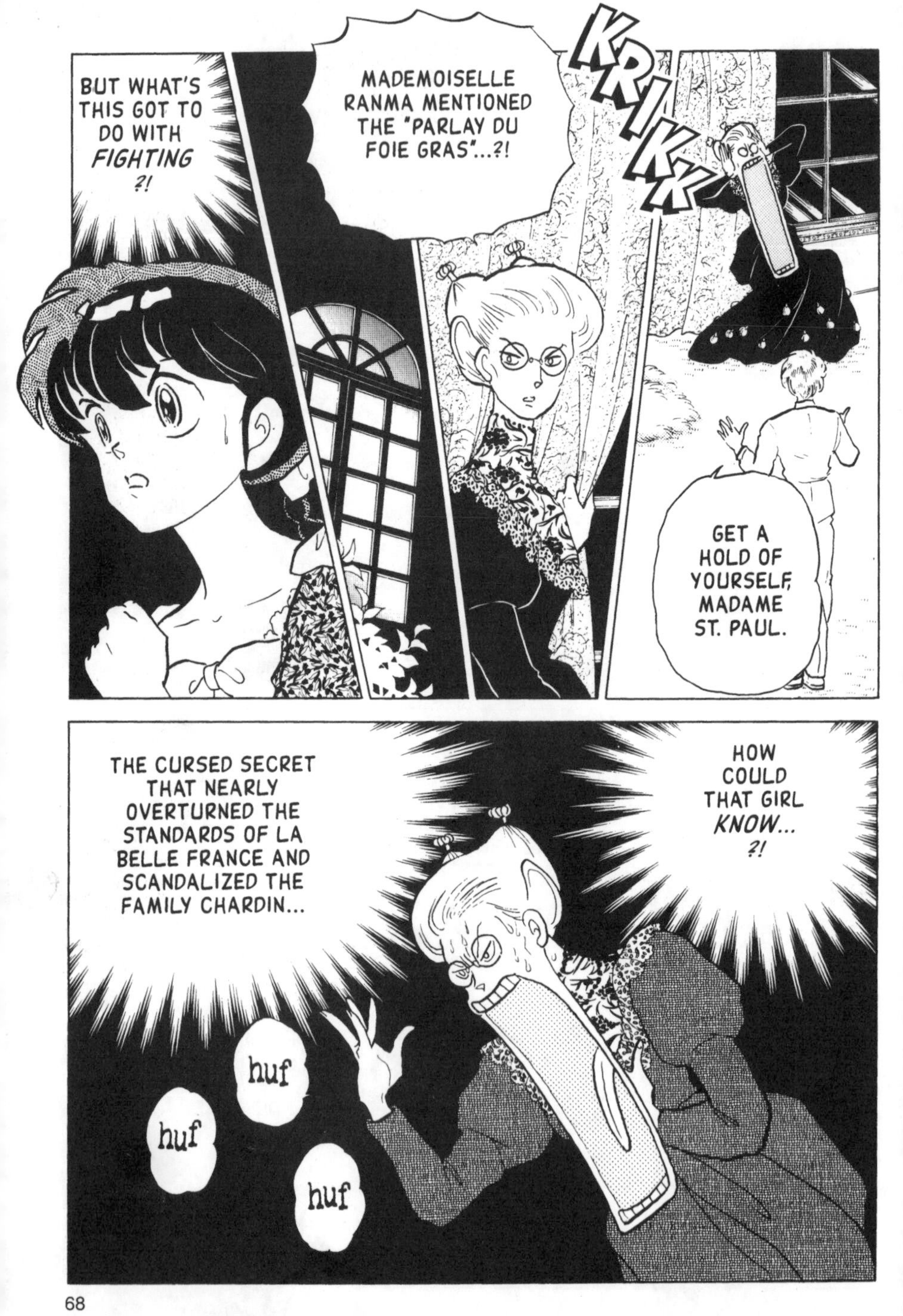
BUT WHAT'S THIS GOT TO DO WITH *FIGHTING* ?!
MADEMOISELLE RANMA MENTIONED THE "PARLAY DU FOIE GRAS"...?!
KRIKK
GET A HOLD OF YOURSELF, MADAME ST. PAUL.
THE CURSED SECRET THAT NEARLY OVERTURNED THE STANDARDS OF LA BELLE FRANCE AND SCANDALIZED THE FAMILY CHARDIN...
HOW COULD THAT GIRL *KNOW*... ?!
huf
huf
huf

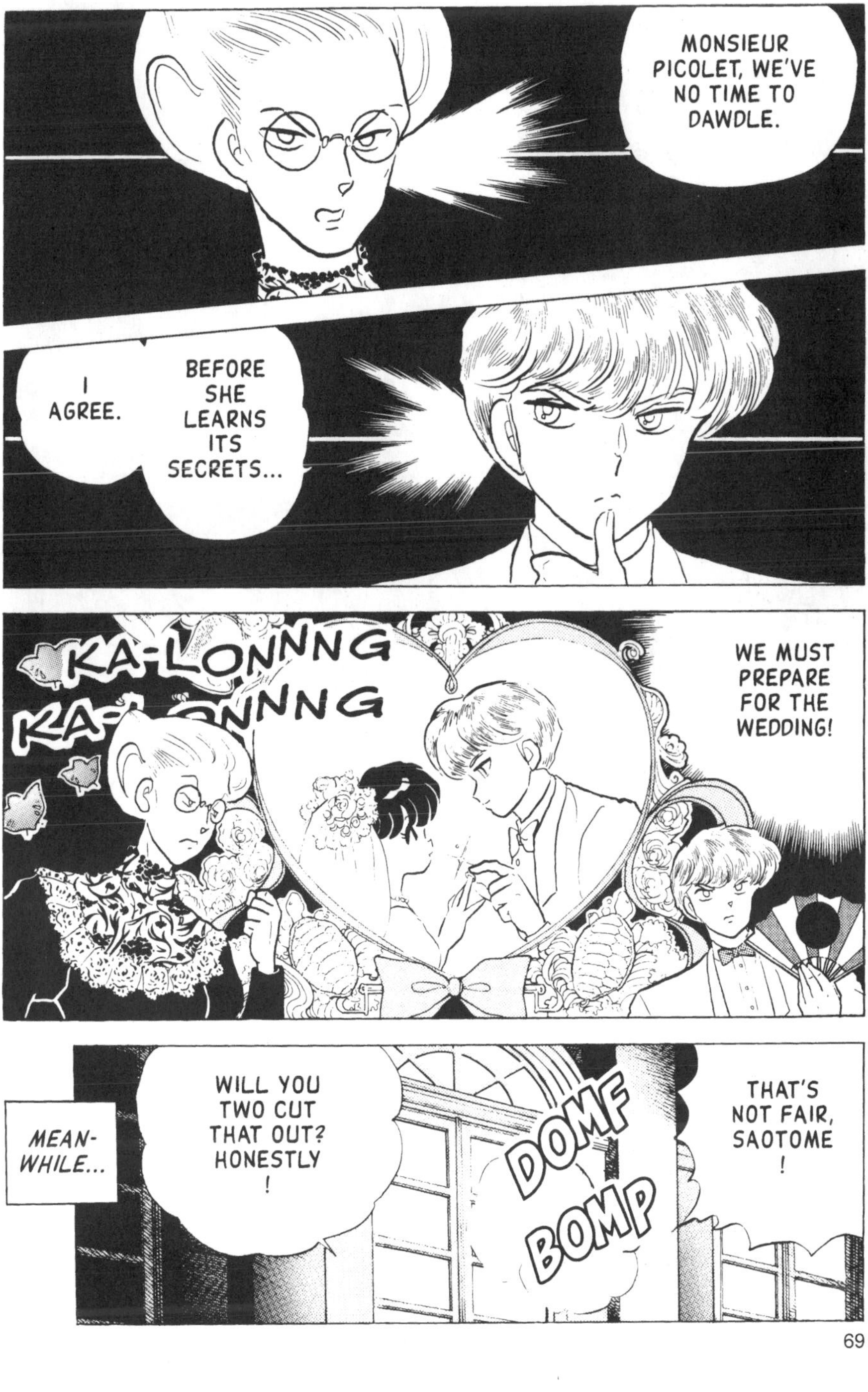
MONSIEUR PICOLET, WE'VE NO TIME TO DAWDLE.
I AGREE.
BEFORE SHE LEARNS ITS SECRETS...
KA-LONNNG
KA-LONNNG
WE MUST PREPARE FOR THE WEDDING!
MEAN-WHILE...
WILL YOU TWO CUT THAT OUT? HONESTLY!
DOMF
BOMP
THAT'S NOT FAIR, SAOTOME!

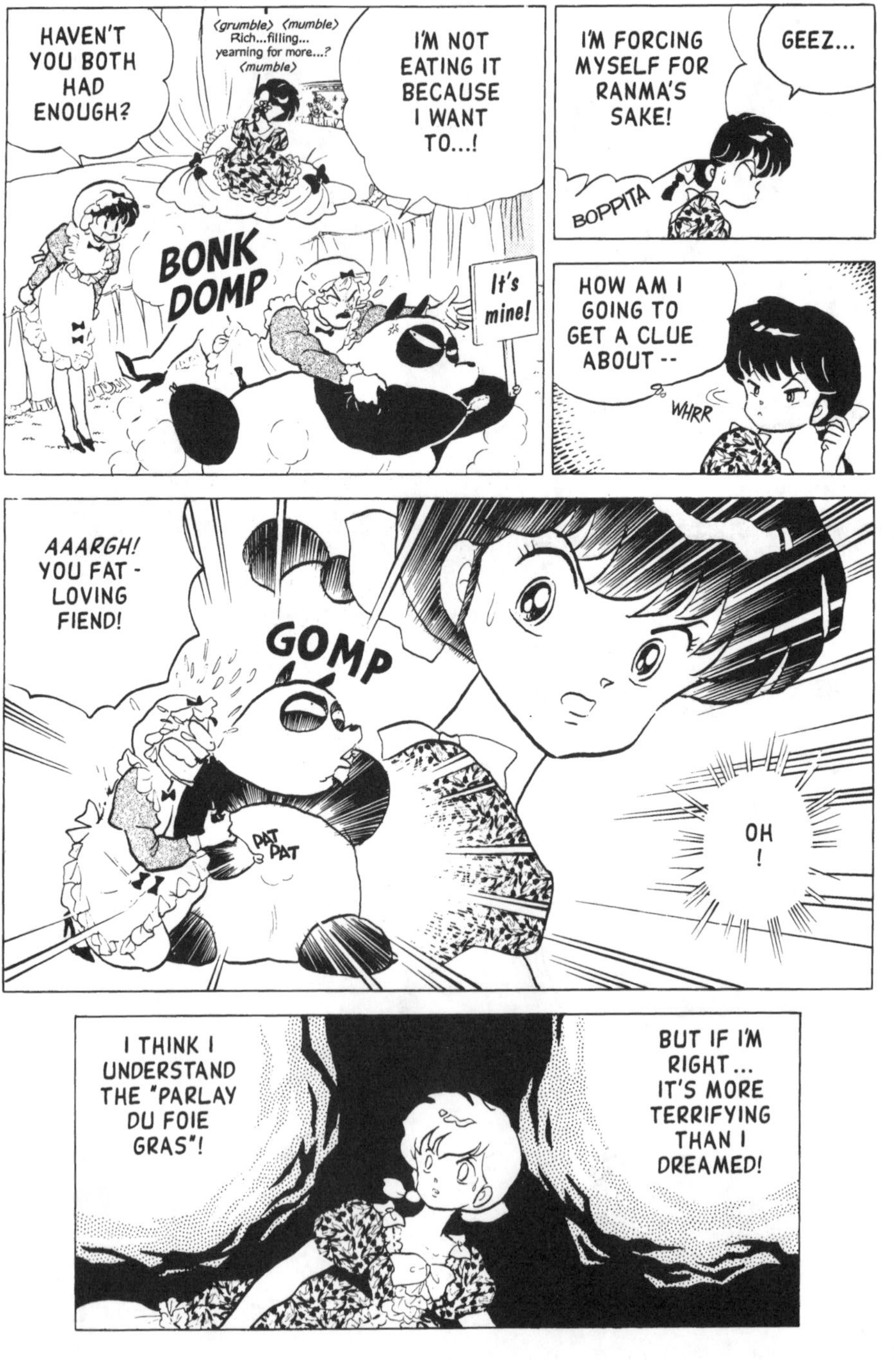
HAVEN'T YOU BOTH HAD ENOUGH?
<grumble> <mumble> Rich...filling... yearning for more...? <mumble>
I'M NOT EATING IT BECAUSE I WANT TO...!
BONK DOMP
It's mine!
I'M FORCING MYSELF FOR RANMA'S SAKE!
GEEZ...
BOPPITA
HOW AM I GOING TO GET A CLUE ABOUT --
WHRR
AAARGH! YOU FAT-LOVING FIEND!
GOMP
PAT PAT
OH !
I THINK I UNDERSTAND THE "PARLAY DU FOIE GRAS"!
BUT IF I'M RIGHT... IT'S MORE TERRIFYING THAN I DREAMED!

Part 5
BATHROOM TRAINING

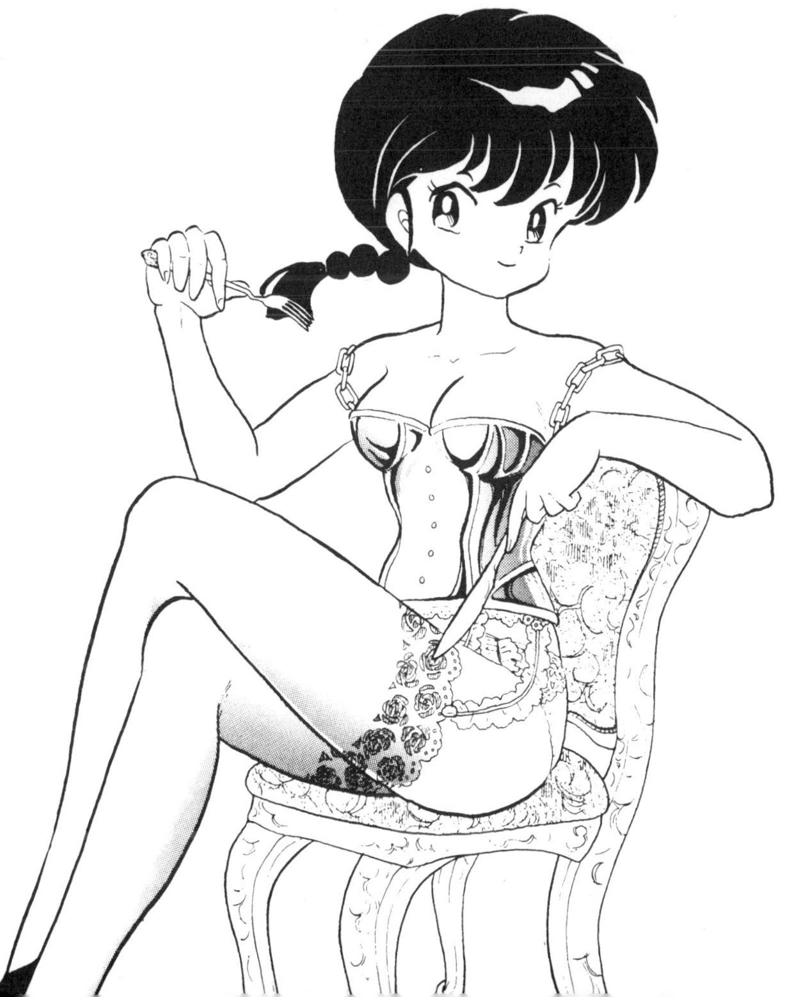

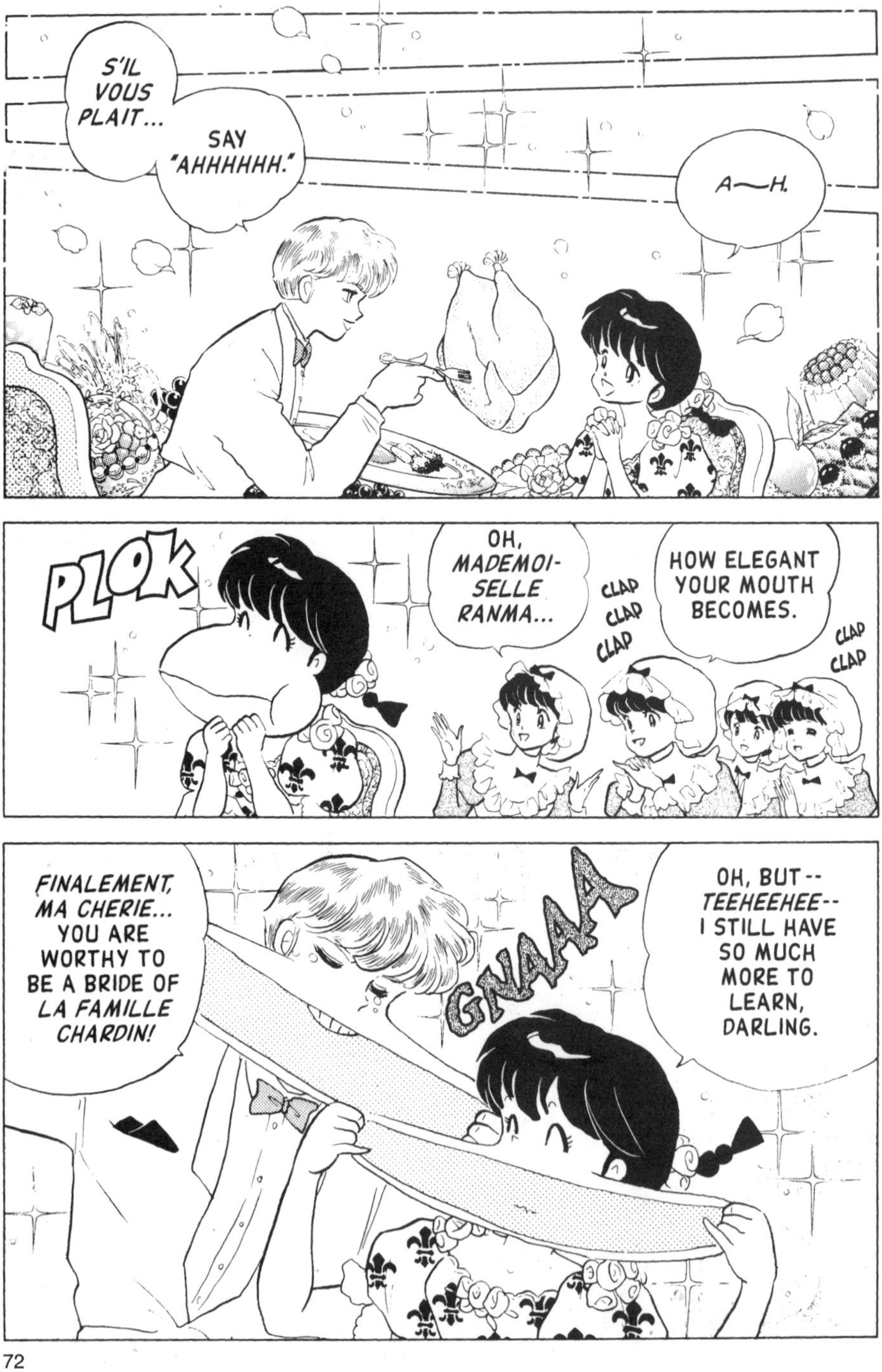
S'IL VOUS PLAIT...
SAY "AHHHHHH."
A—H.
PLOK
OH, MADEMOI-SELLE RANMA...
CLAP CLAP CLAP
HOW ELEGANT YOUR MOUTH BECOMES.
CLAP CLAP
FINALEMENT, MA CHERIE... YOU ARE WORTHY TO BE A BRIDE OF LA FAMILLE CHARDIN!
GNAAA
OH, BUT-- TEEHEEHEE-- I STILL HAVE SO MUCH MORE TO LEARN, DARLING.

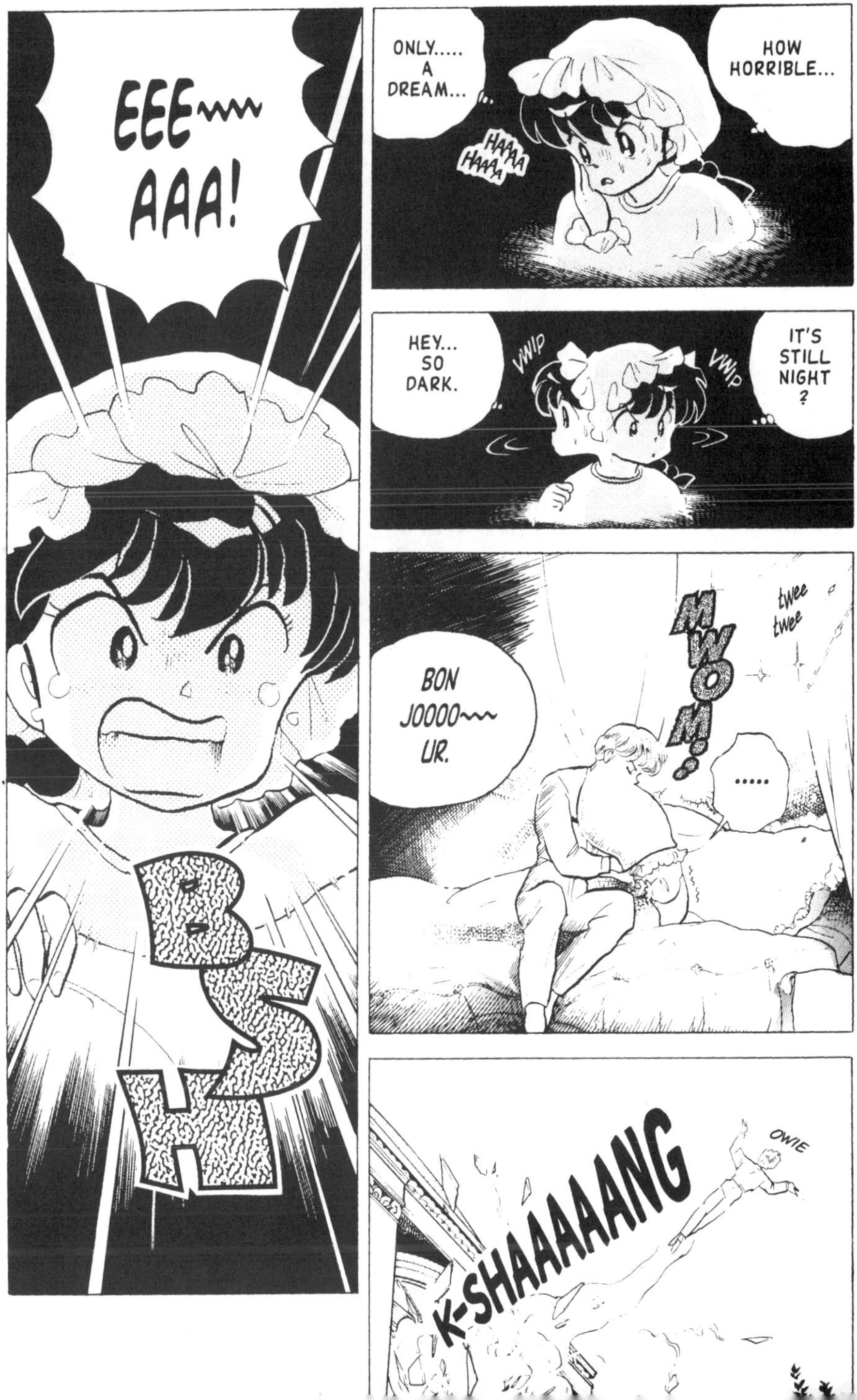
HOW HORRIBLE...
ONLY..... A DREAM...
HAAAA HAAAA
IT'S STILL NIGHT?
VWIP
VWIP
HEY... SO DARK.
EEE~~~ AAA!
BSH
twee twee
MWOM!
.....
BON JOOOO~~~ UR.
OWIE
K-SHAAAAANG

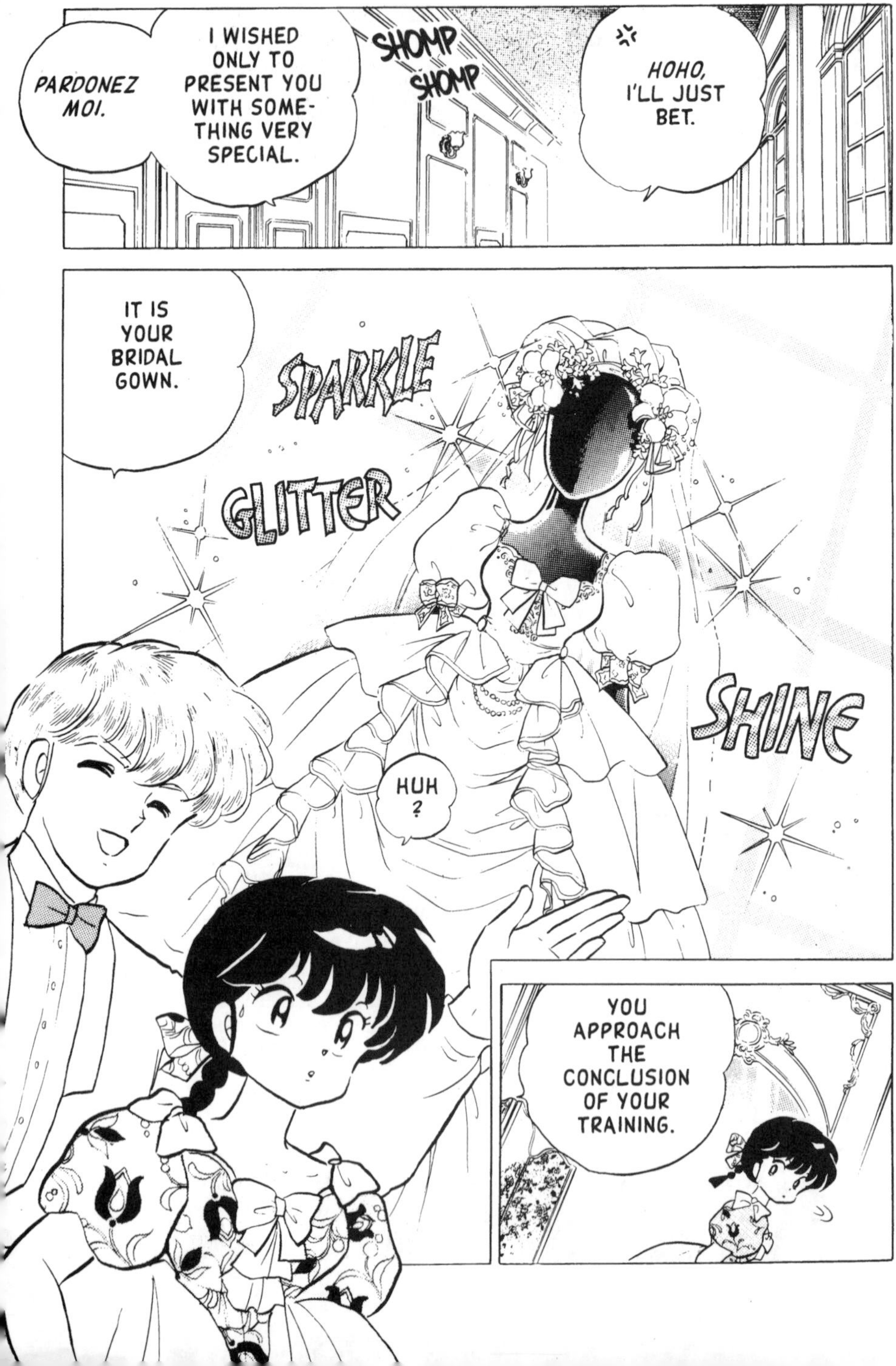
PARDONEZ MOI.
I WISHED ONLY TO PRESENT YOU WITH SOME-THING VERY SPECIAL.
SHOMP SHOMP
HOHO, I'LL JUST BET.
IT IS YOUR BRIDAL GOWN.
SPARKLE
GLITTER
SHINE
HUH ?
YOU APPROACH THE CONCLUSION OF YOUR TRAINING.

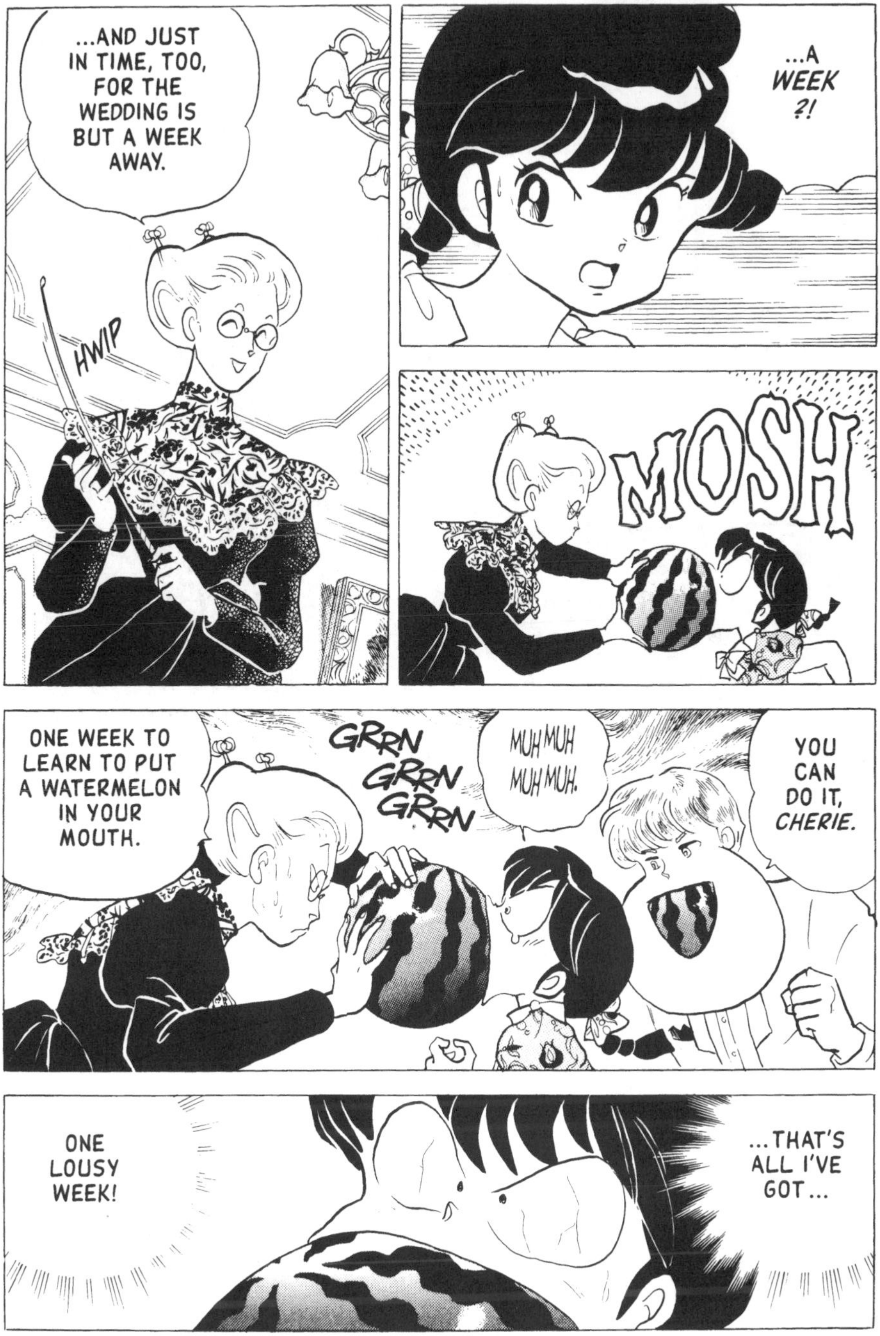
...AND JUST IN TIME, TOO, FOR THE WEDDING IS BUT A WEEK AWAY.
HWIP
...A WEEK ?!
MOSH
ONE WEEK TO LEARN TO PUT A WATERMELON IN YOUR MOUTH.
GRRN GRRN GRRN
MUH MUH MUH MUH.
YOU CAN DO IT, CHERIE.
ONE LOUSY WEEK!
...THAT'S ALL I'VE GOT...

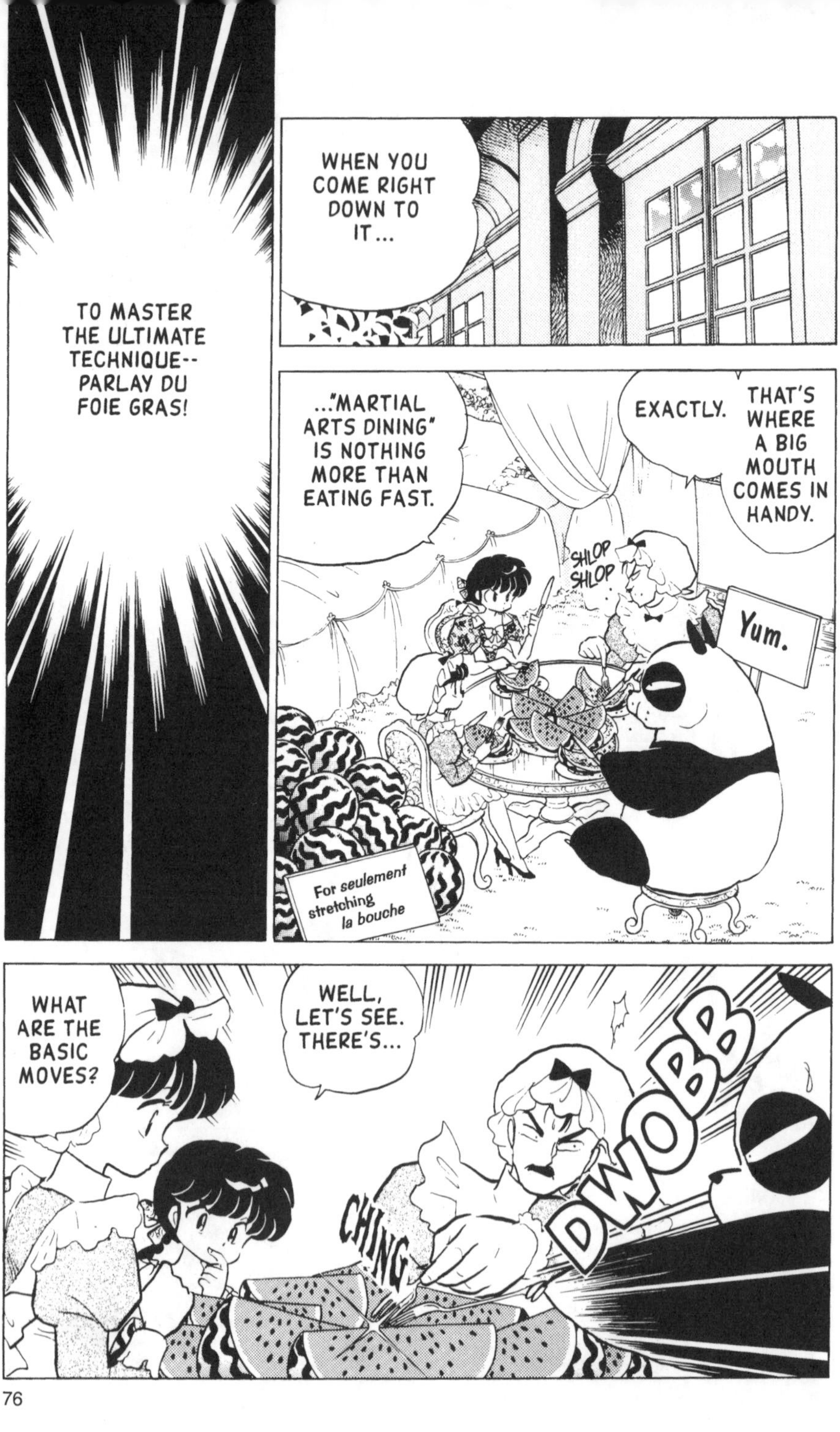
TO MASTER THE ULTIMATE TECHNIQUE-- PARLAY DU FOIE GRAS!
WHEN YOU COME RIGHT DOWN TO IT...
..."MARTIAL ARTS DINING" IS NOTHING MORE THAN EATING FAST.
EXACTLY.
THAT'S WHERE A BIG MOUTH COMES IN HANDY.
SHLOP SHLOP
Yum.
For seulement stretching la bouche
WHAT ARE THE BASIC MOVES?
WELL, LET'S SEE. THERE'S...
CHING
DWOBB

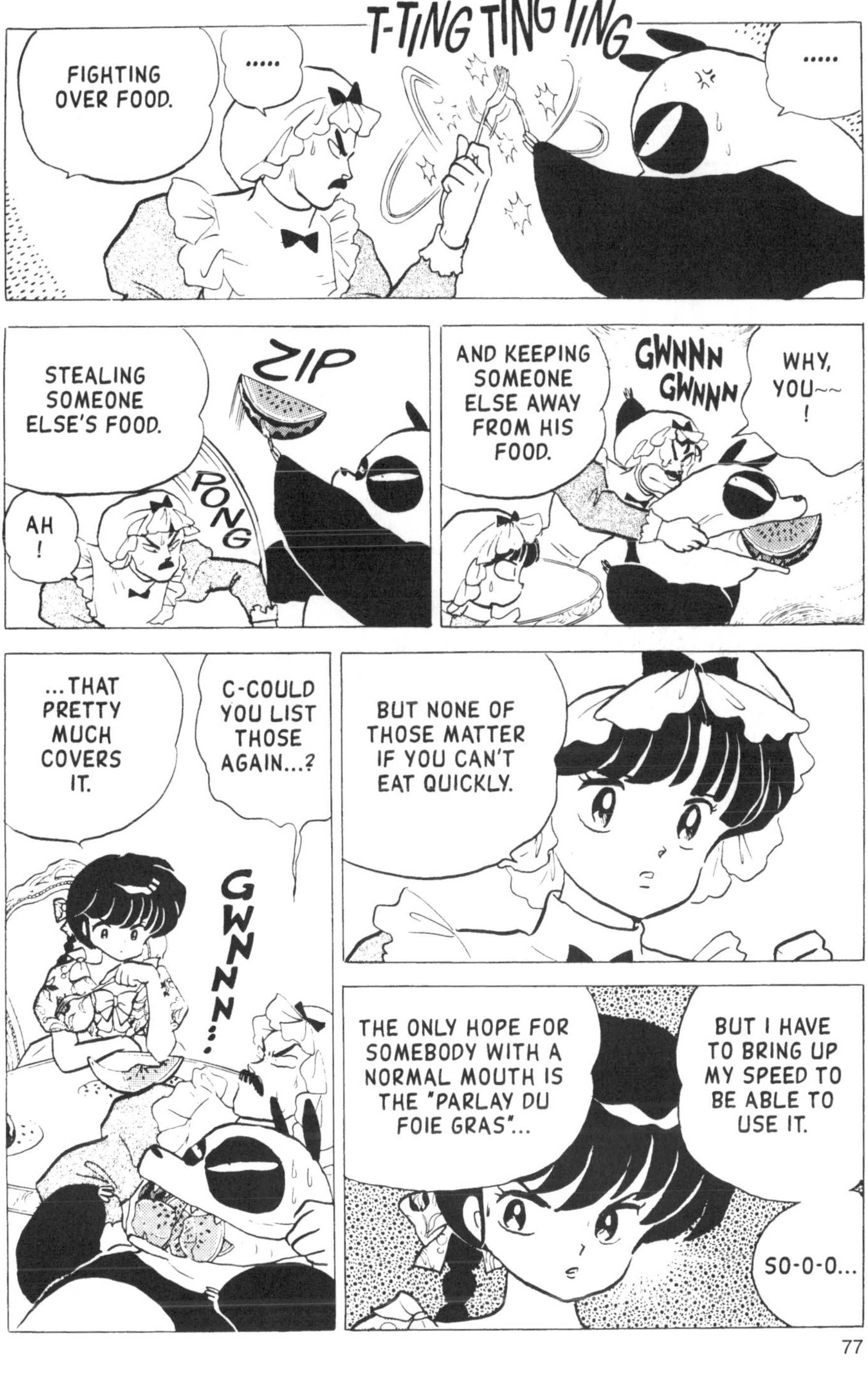

T-TING TING TING
FIGHTING OVER FOOD.
.....
.....
STEALING SOMEONE ELSE'S FOOD.
ZIP
PONG
AH !
AND KEEPING SOMEONE ELSE AWAY FROM HIS FOOD.
GWNNN GWNNN
WHY, YOU~~ !
...THAT PRETTY MUCH COVERS IT.
C-COULD YOU LIST THOSE AGAIN...?
GWNNN..
BUT NONE OF THOSE MATTER IF YOU CAN'T EAT QUICKLY.
THE ONLY HOPE FOR SOMEBODY WITH A NORMAL MOUTH IS THE "PARLAY DU FOIE GRAS"...
BUT I HAVE TO BRING UP MY SPEED TO BE ABLE TO USE IT.
SO-O-O...

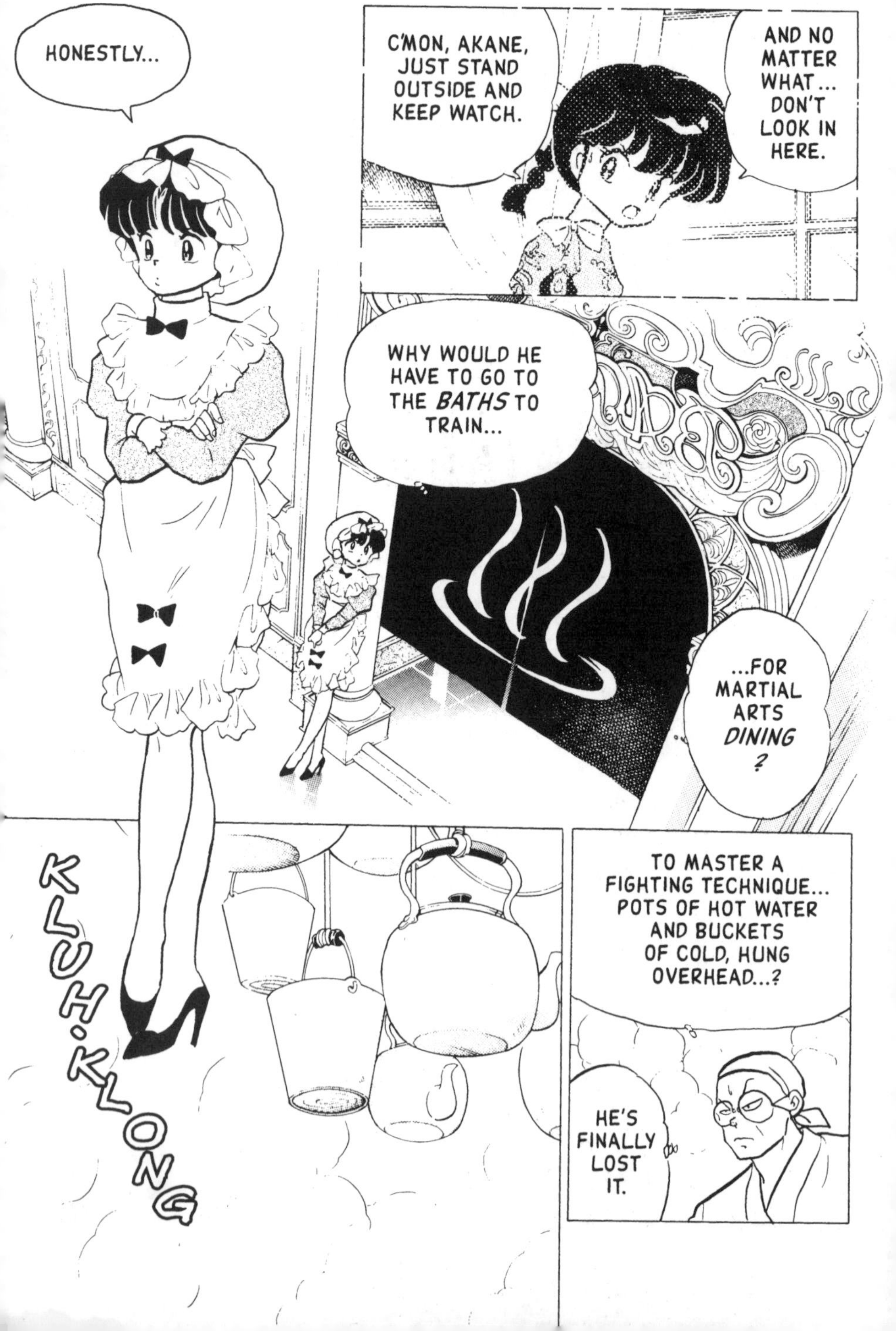
HONESTLY...
C'MON, AKANE, JUST STAND OUTSIDE AND KEEP WATCH.
AND NO MATTER WHAT... DON'T LOOK IN HERE.
WHY WOULD HE HAVE TO GO TO THE *BATHS* TO TRAIN...
...FOR MARTIAL ARTS *DINING*?
KLUH-KLONG
TO MASTER A FIGHTING TECHNIQUE... POTS OF HOT WATER AND BUCKETS OF COLD, HUNG OVERHEAD...?
HE'S FINALLY LOST IT.

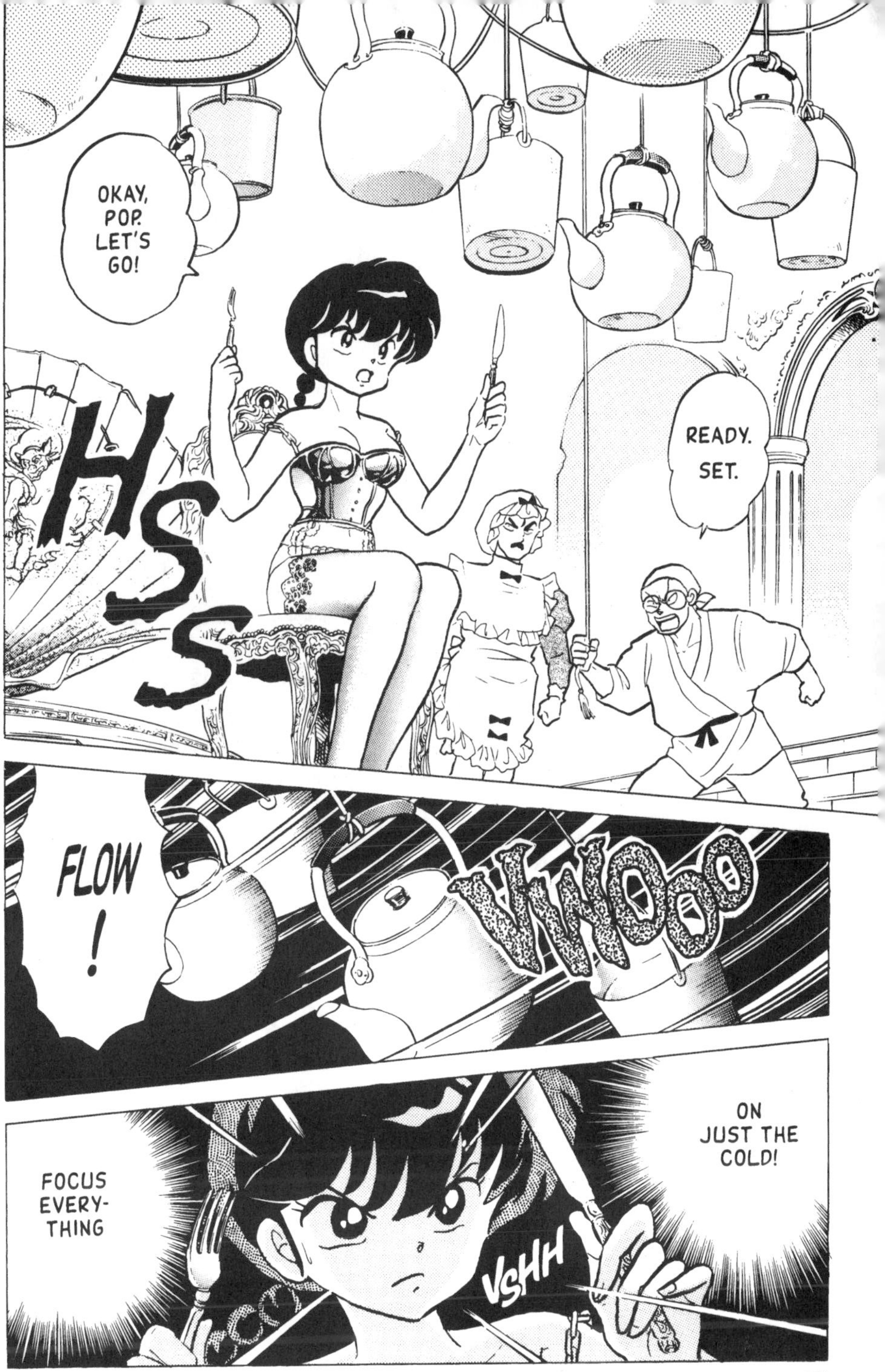
OKAY, POP. LET'S GO!
HSS
READY. SET.
FLOW!
VWOOO
FOCUS EVERY-THING
ON JUST THE COLD!
VSHH

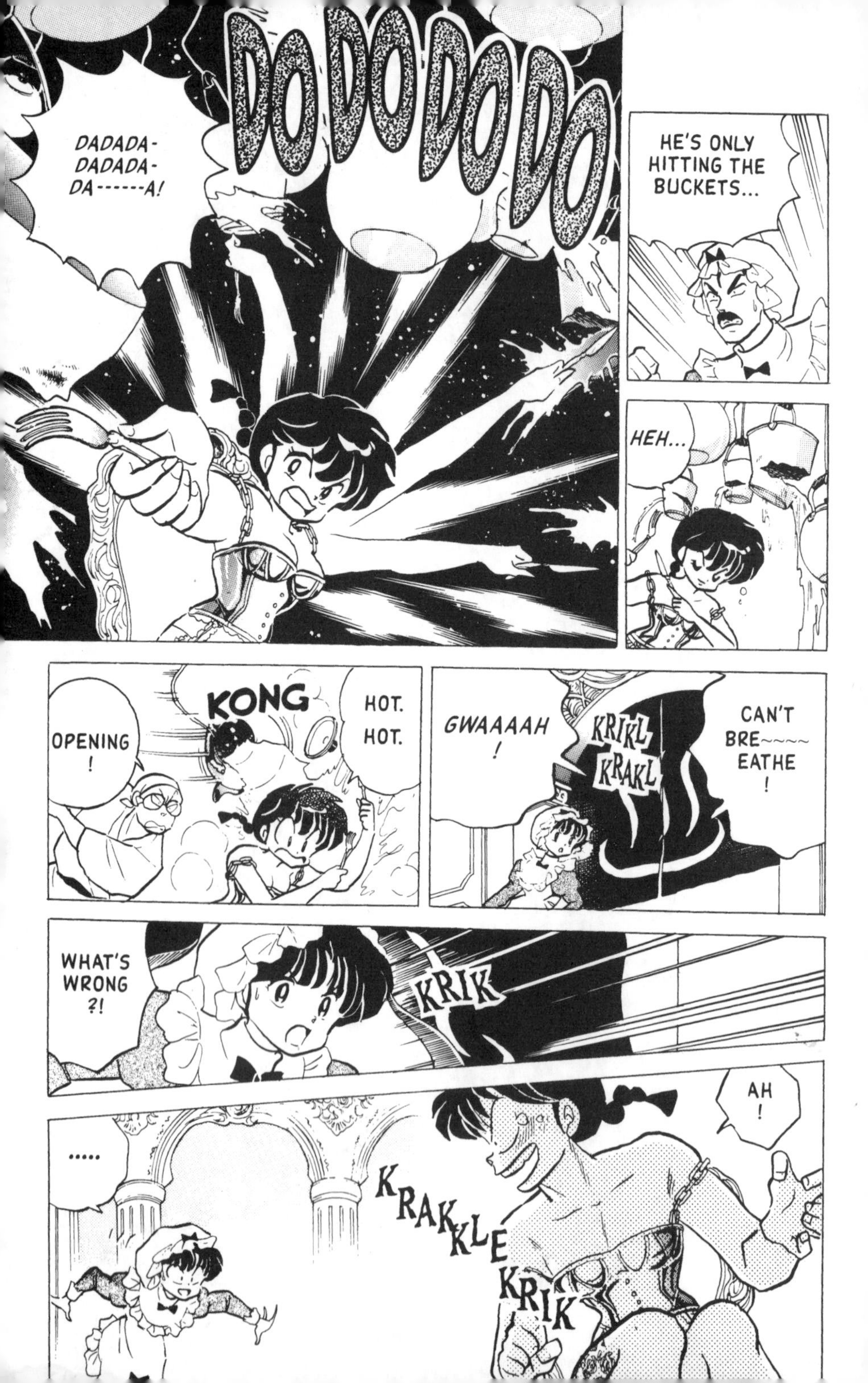
DADADA-
DADADA-
DA------A!
DODODODODO
HE'S ONLY HITTING THE BUCKETS...
HEH...
OPENING!
KONG
HOT. HOT.
GWAAAAH!
KRIKL KRAKL
CAN'T BRE~~~~EATHE!
WHAT'S WRONG?!
KRIK
.....
KRAKKLE
KRIK
AH!

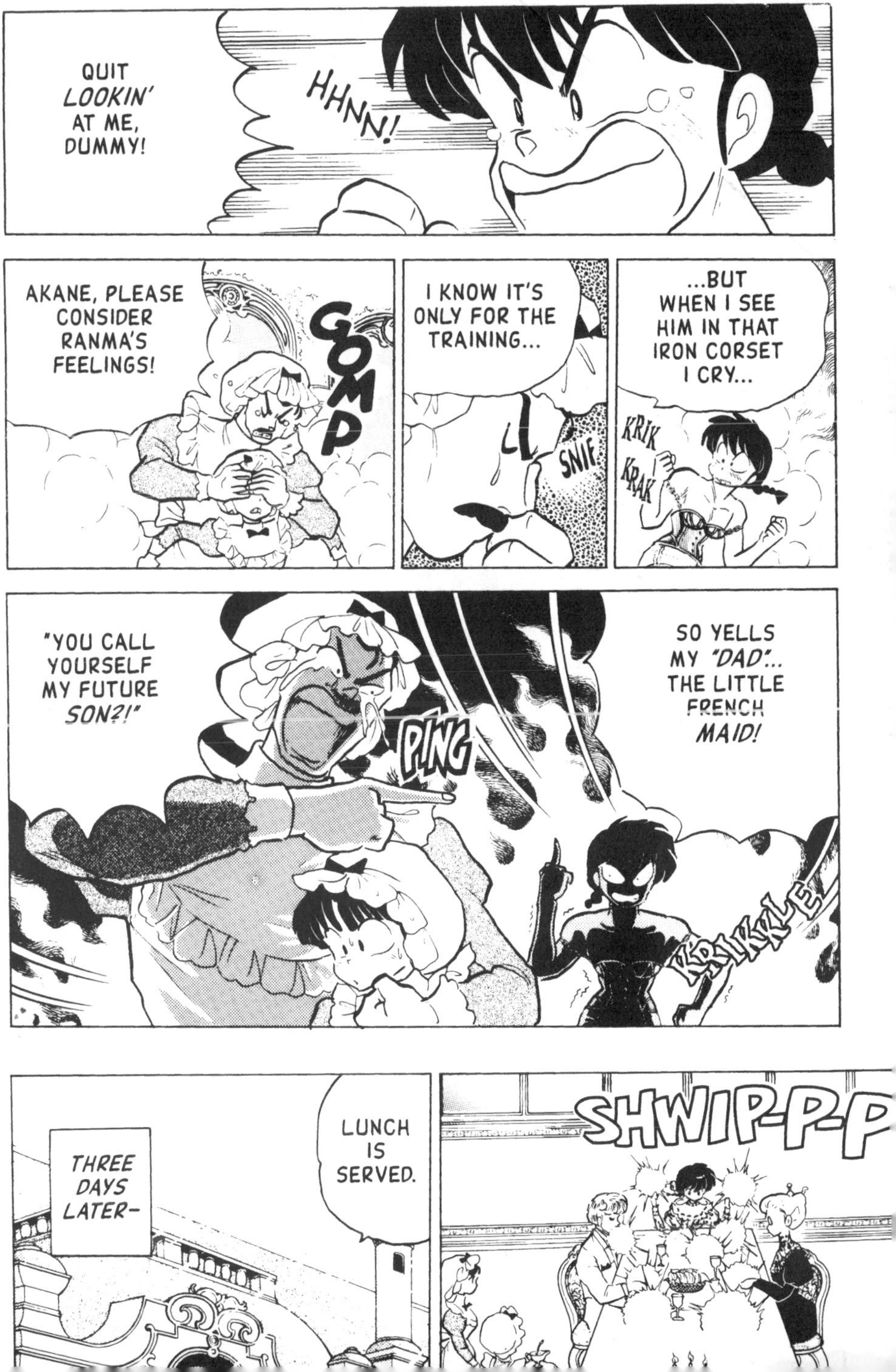
QUIT LOOKIN' AT ME, DUMMY!
HHNN!
AKANE, PLEASE CONSIDER RANMA'S FEELINGS!
GOMP
I KNOW IT'S ONLY FOR THE TRAINING...
SNIF
...BUT WHEN I SEE HIM IN THAT IRON CORSET I CRY...
KRIK
KRAK
"YOU CALL YOURSELF MY FUTURE SON?!"
PING
SO YELLS MY "DAD"... THE LITTLE FRENCH MAID!
KRIKKLE
THREE DAYS LATER—
LUNCH IS SERVED.
SHWIP-P-P

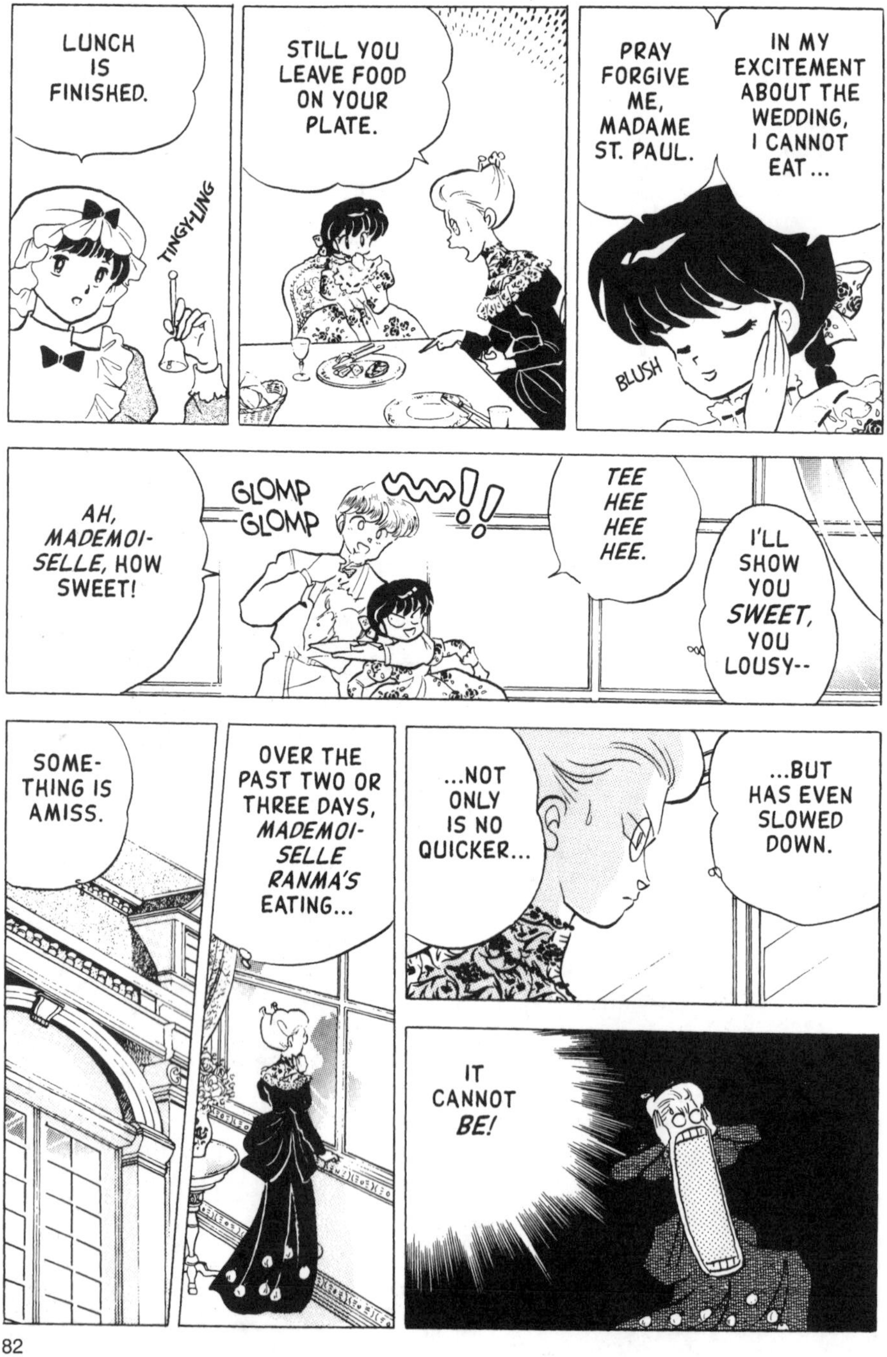
LUNCH IS FINISHED.
TINGY-LING
STILL YOU LEAVE FOOD ON YOUR PLATE.
PRAY FORGIVE ME, MADAME ST. PAUL.
IN MY EXCITEMENT ABOUT THE WEDDING, I CANNOT EAT...
BLUSH
AH, *MADEMOISELLE*, HOW SWEET!
GLOMP GLOMP
TEE HEE HEE HEE.
I'LL SHOW YOU *SWEET*, YOU LOUSY--
SOMETHING IS AMISS.
OVER THE PAST TWO OR THREE DAYS, *MADEMOISELLE RANMA'S* EATING...
...NOT ONLY IS NO QUICKER...
...BUT HAS EVEN SLOWED DOWN.
IT CANNOT *BE!*

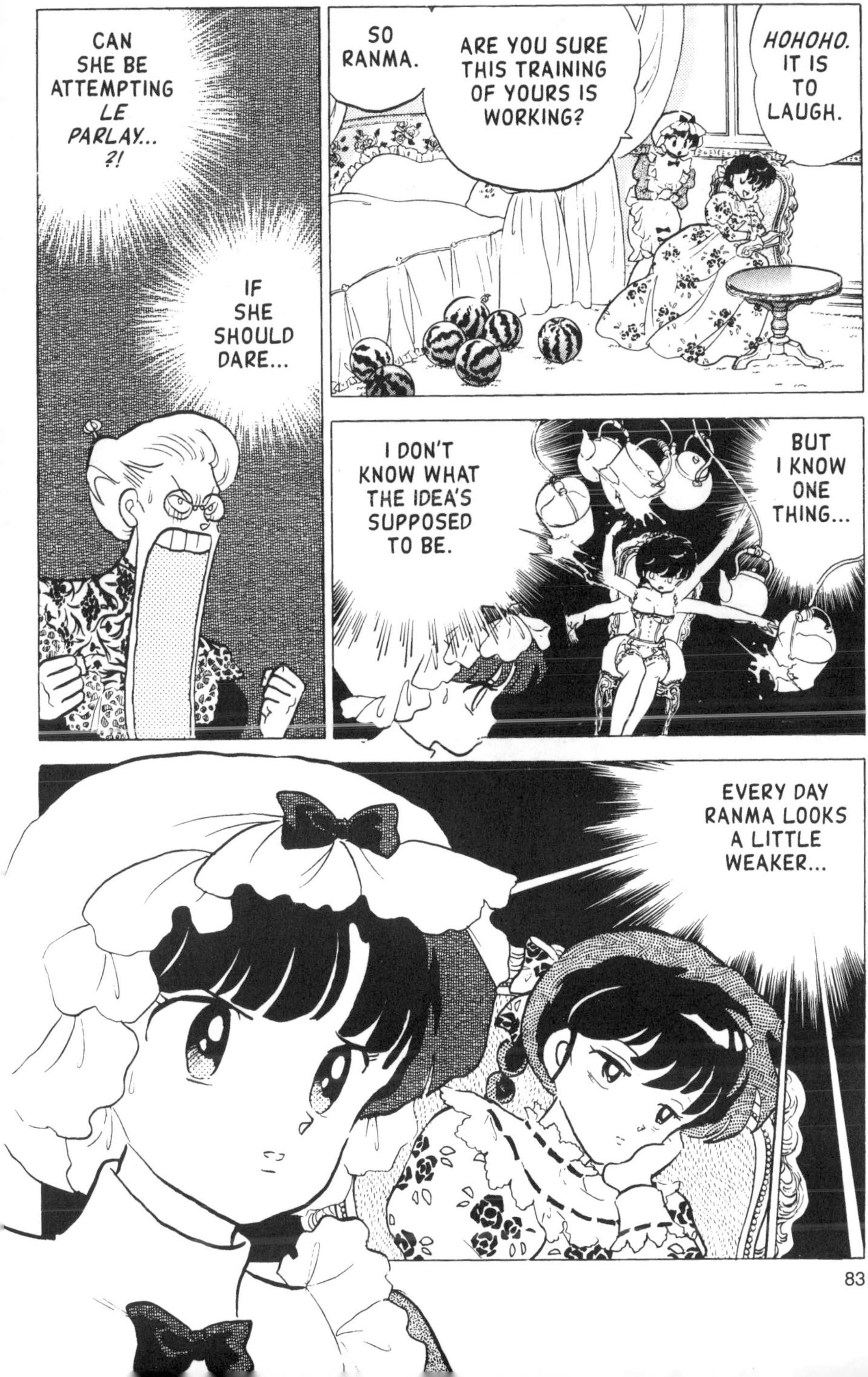
CAN SHE BE ATTEMPTING *LE PARLAY...* ?!
IF SHE SHOULD DARE...
SO RANMA.
ARE YOU SURE THIS TRAINING OF YOURS IS WORKING?
HOHOHO. IT IS TO LAUGH.
I DON'T KNOW WHAT THE IDEA'S SUPPOSED TO BE.
BUT I KNOW ONE THING...
EVERY DAY RANMA LOOKS A LITTLE WEAKER...

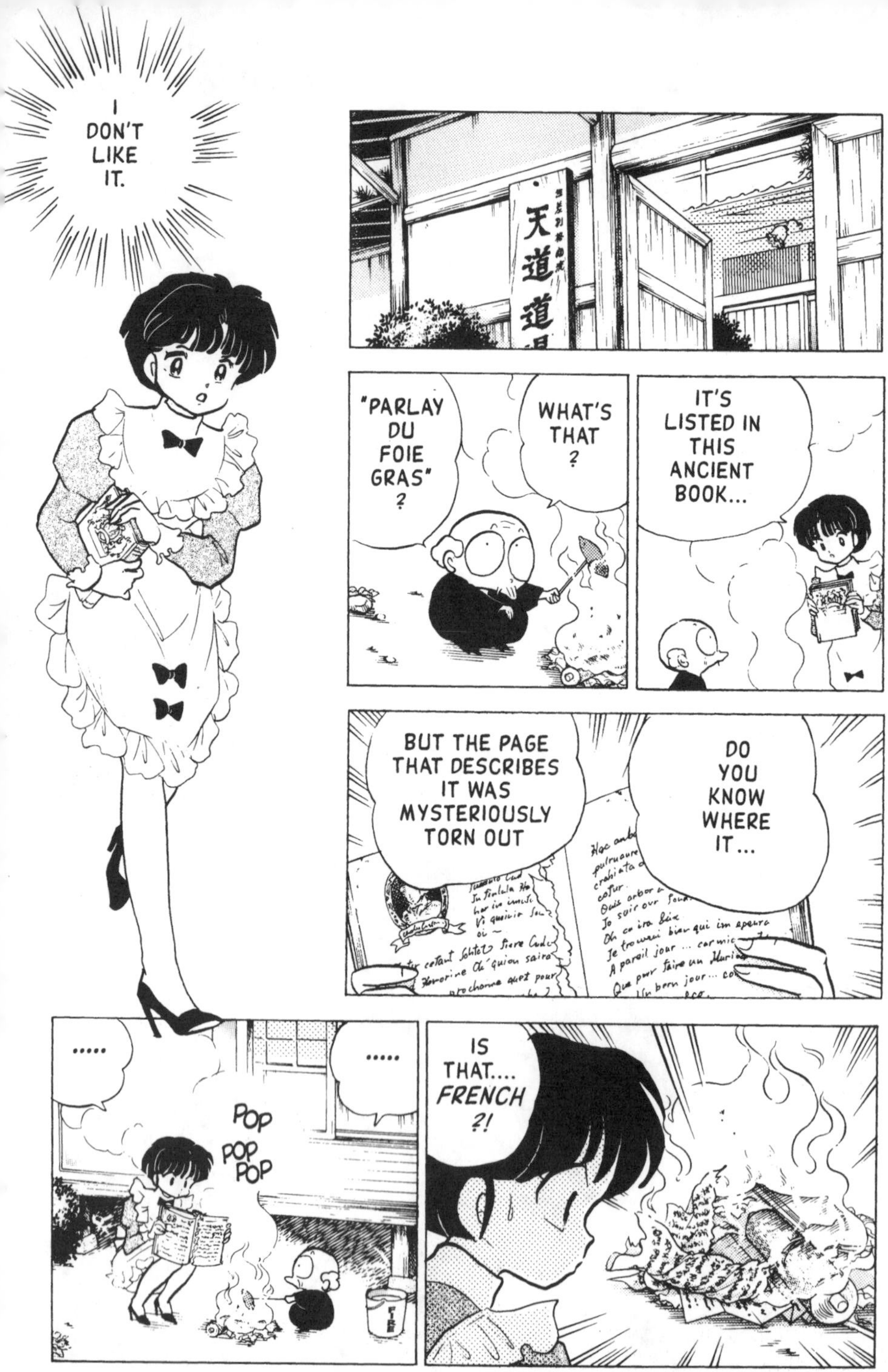
I DON'T LIKE IT.
"PARLAY DU FOIE GRAS"?
WHAT'S THAT?
IT'S LISTED IN THIS ANCIENT BOOK...
BUT THE PAGE THAT DESCRIBES IT WAS MYSTERIOUSLY TORN OUT
DO YOU KNOW WHERE IT...
.....
.....
POP
POP POP
IS THAT.... FRENCH?!
FIRE

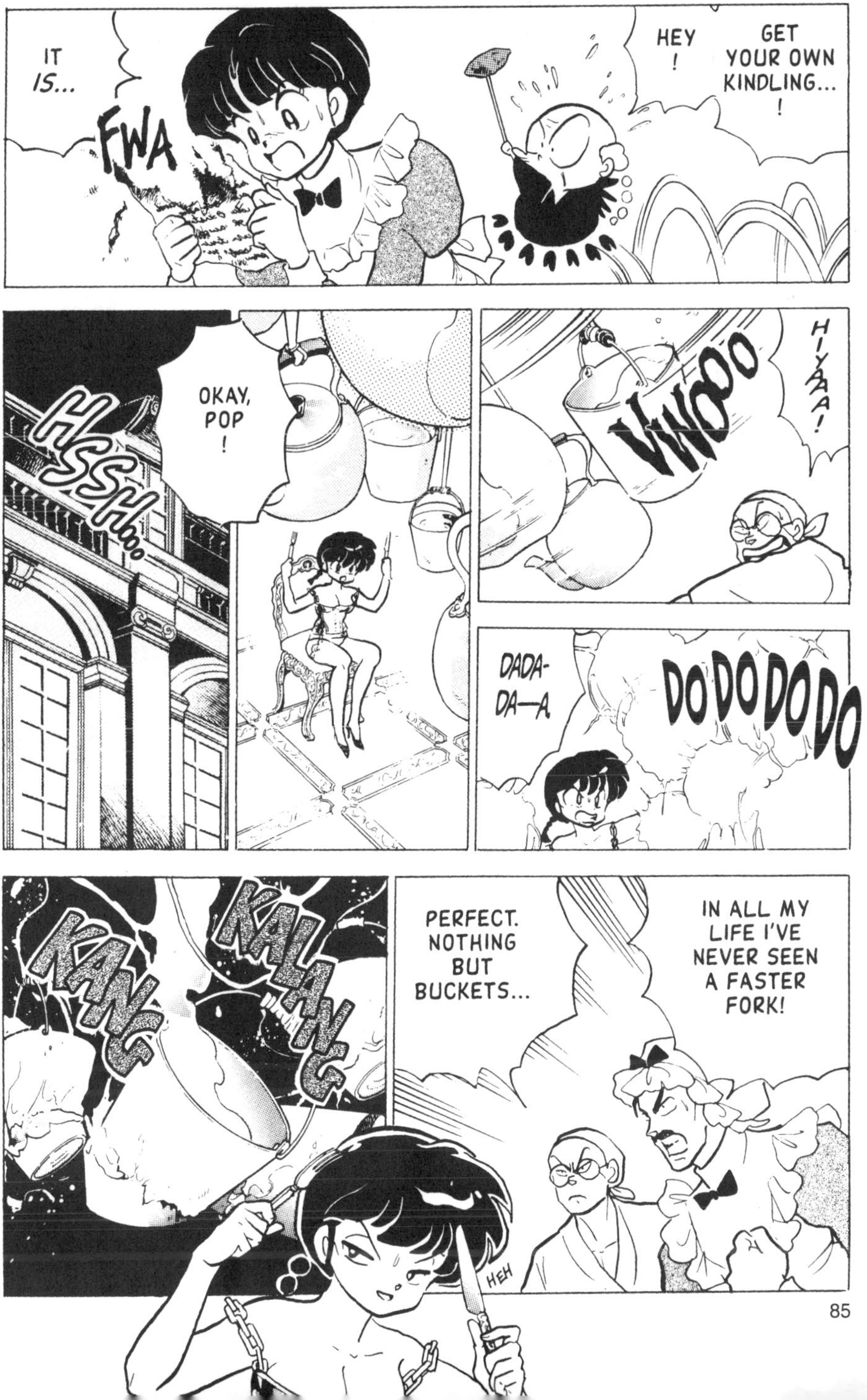
IT IS...
FWA
HEY!
GET YOUR OWN KINDLING...!
HSSH...
OKAY, POP!
VWOOO
HIYAAAA!
DADA-DA—A.
DODODODODO
KANG
KALANG
PERFECT. NOTHING BUT BUCKETS...
IN ALL MY LIFE I'VE NEVER SEEN A FASTER FORK!
HEH

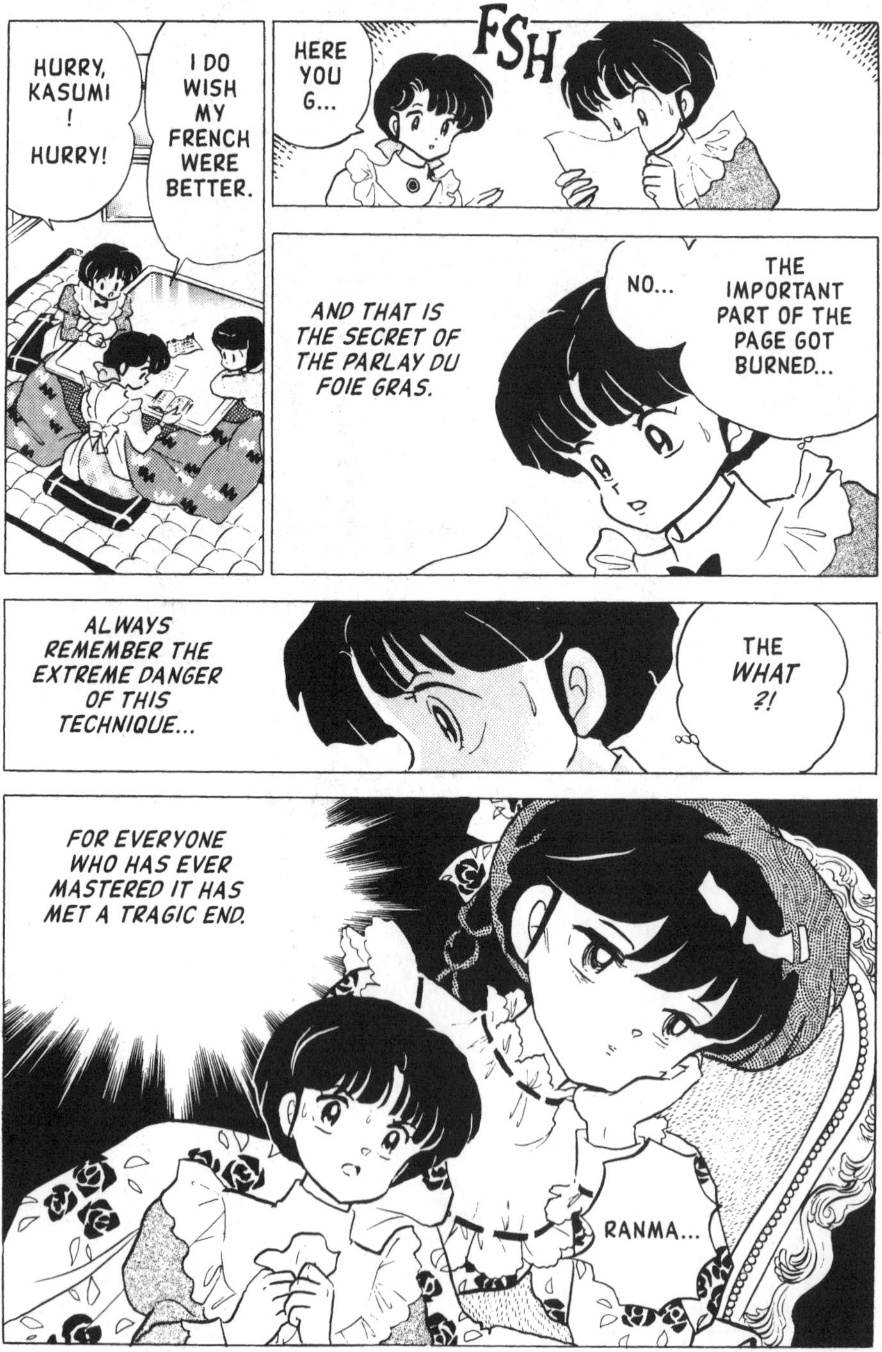
HURRY, KASUMI! HURRY!
I DO WISH MY FRENCH WERE BETTER.
HERE YOU G...
FSH
AND THAT IS THE SECRET OF THE PARLAY DU FOIE GRAS.
NO...
THE IMPORTANT PART OF THE PAGE GOT BURNED...
ALWAYS REMEMBER THE EXTREME DANGER OF THIS TECHNIQUE...
THE WHAT?!
FOR EVERYONE WHO HAS EVER MASTERED IT HAS MET A TRAGIC END.
RANMA...

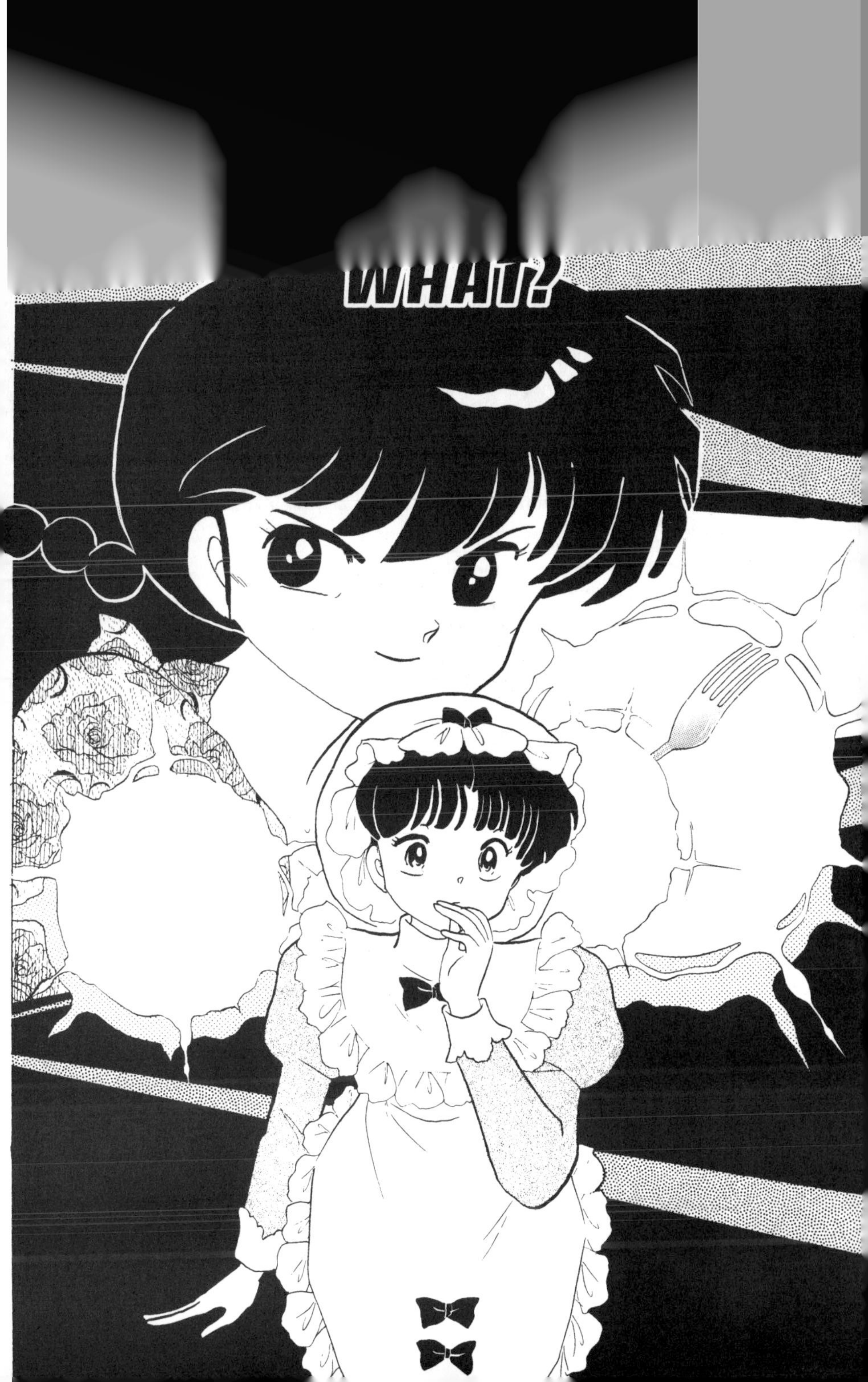
WHAT?

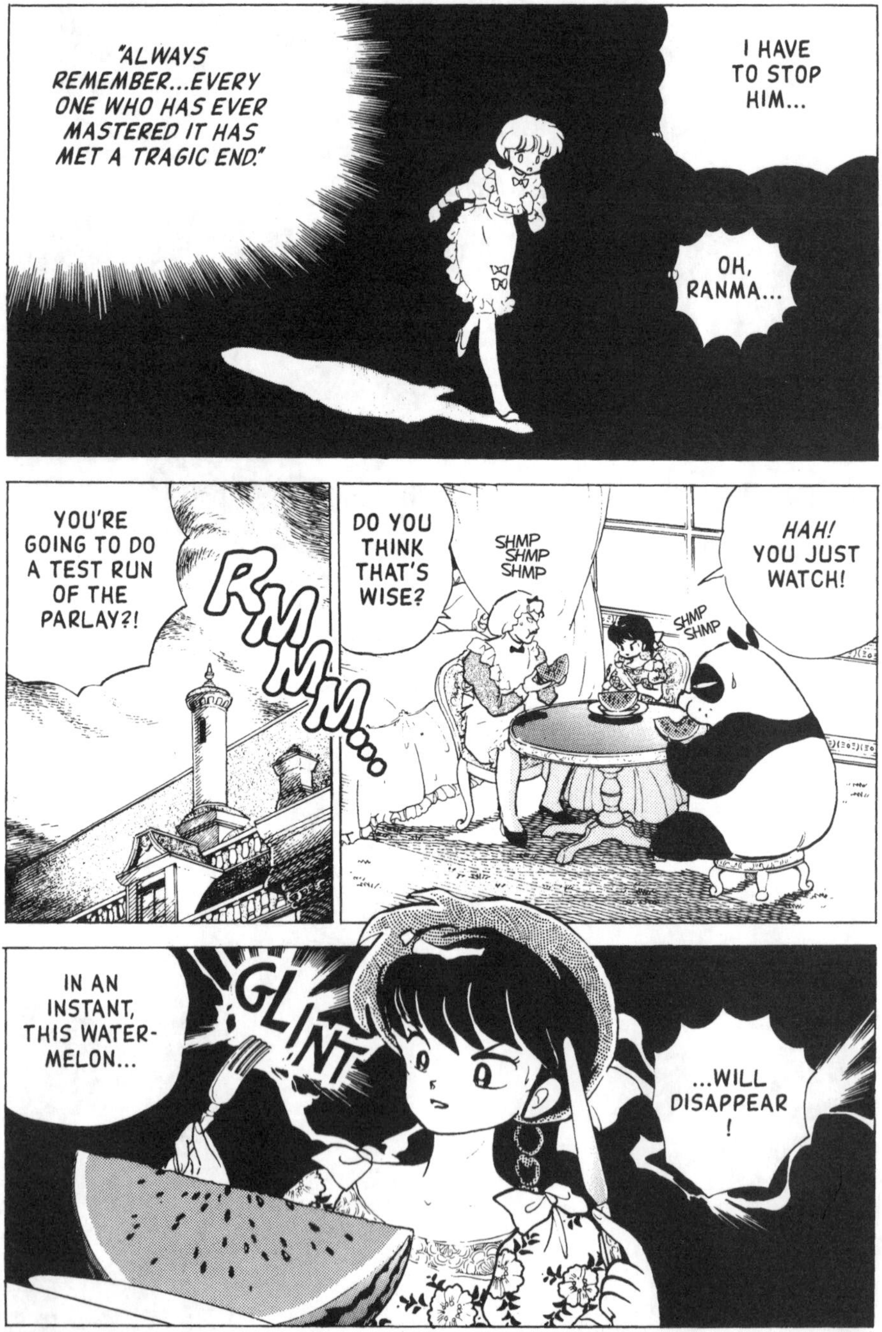
"ALWAYS REMEMBER...EVERY ONE WHO HAS EVER MASTERED IT HAS MET A TRAGIC END."
I HAVE TO STOP HIM...
OH, RANMA...
YOU'RE GOING TO DO A TEST RUN OF THE PARLAY?!
RMMM...
DO YOU THINK THAT'S WISE?
SHMP SHMP SHMP
SHMP SHMP
HAH! YOU JUST WATCH!
IN AN INSTANT, THIS WATER-MELON...
GLINT
...WILL DISAPPEAR!

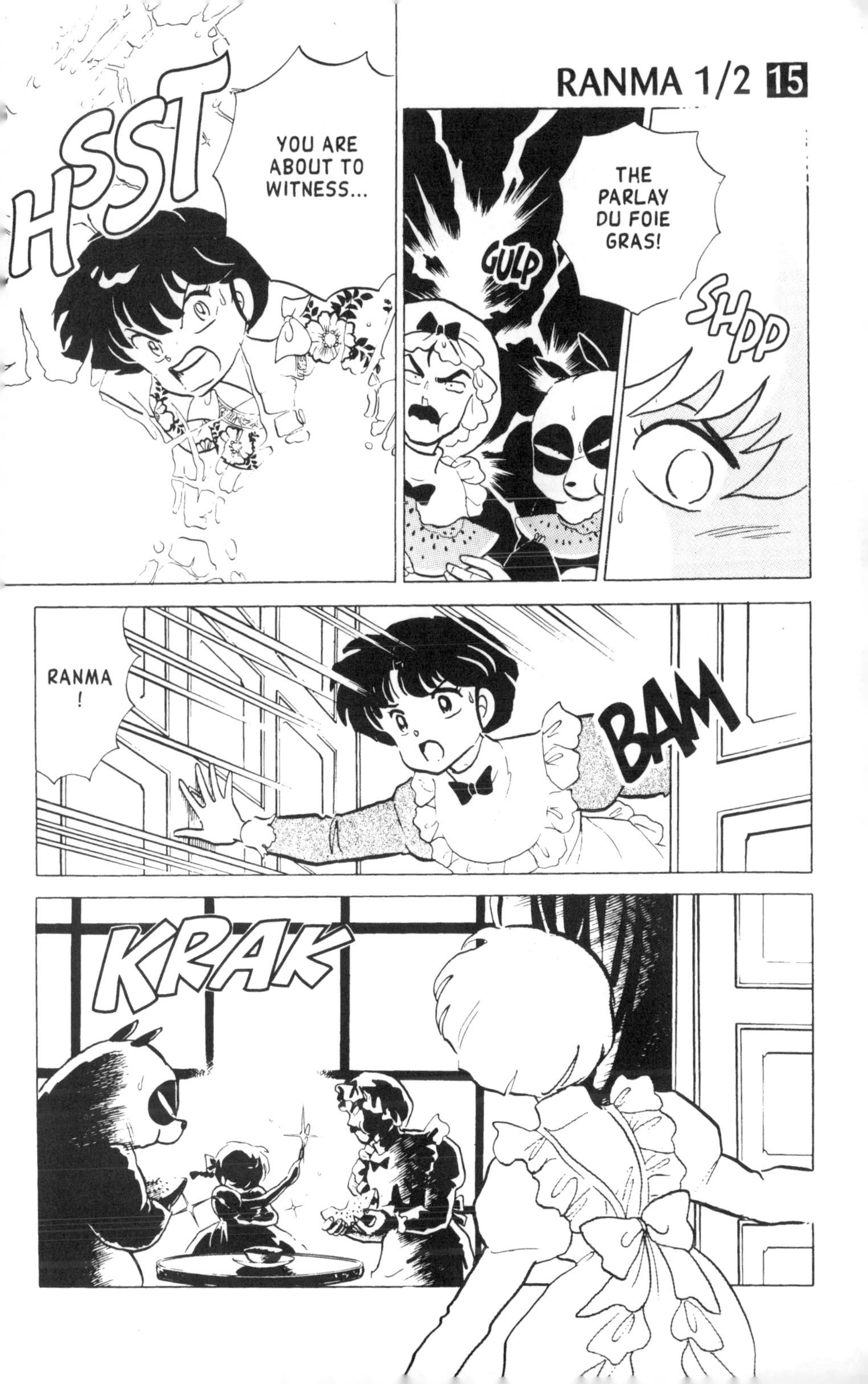
HSST
YOU ARE ABOUT TO WITNESS...
GULP
THE PARLAY DU FOIE GRAS!
SHPP
RANMA !
BAM
KRAK

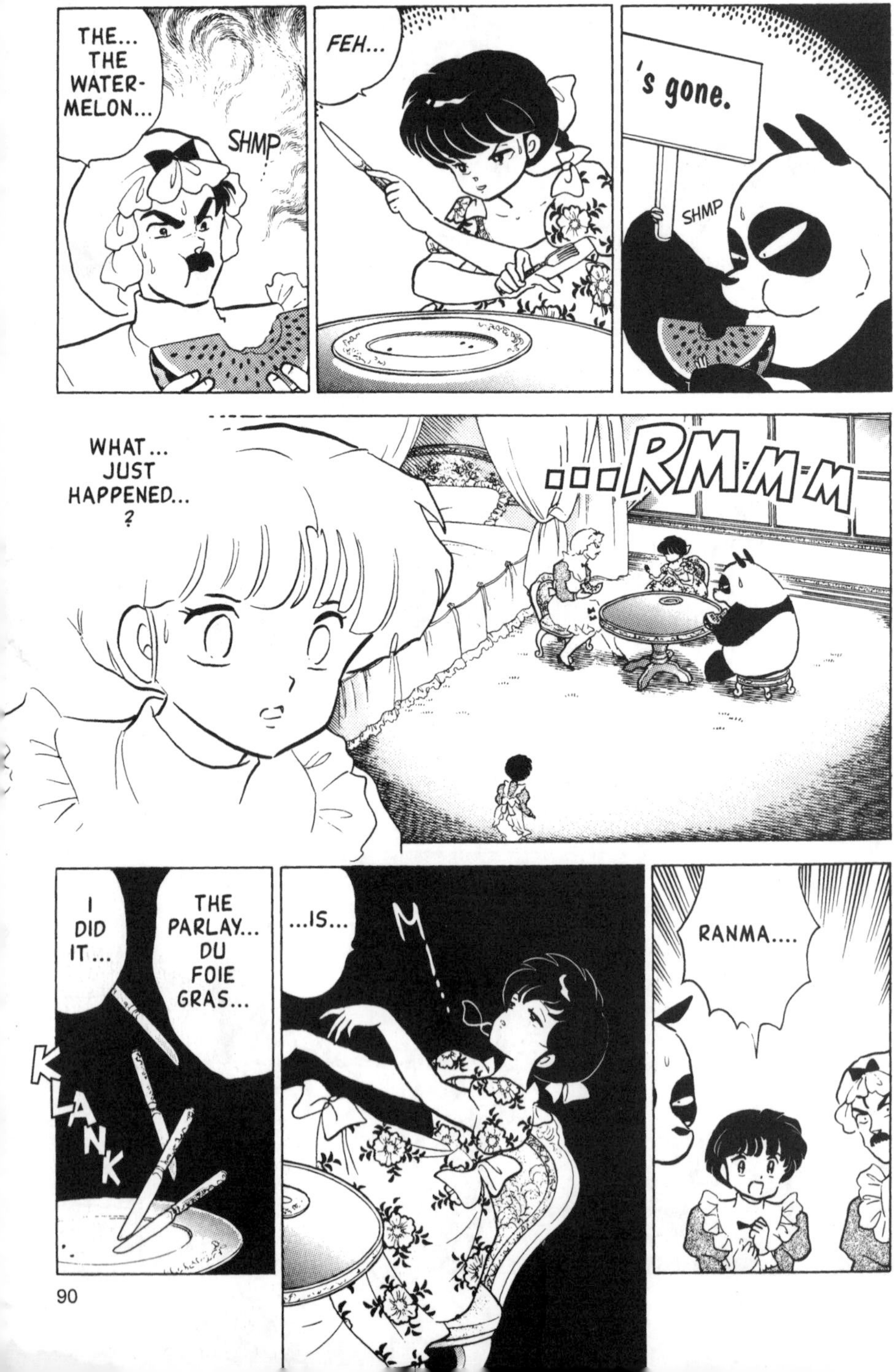
THE... THE WATER-MELON...
SHMP
FEH...
's gone.
SHMP
WHAT... JUST HAPPENED... ?
...RM-M-M
I DID IT...
THE PARLAY... DU FOIE GRAS...
KLANK
...IS...
M-...
RANMA....

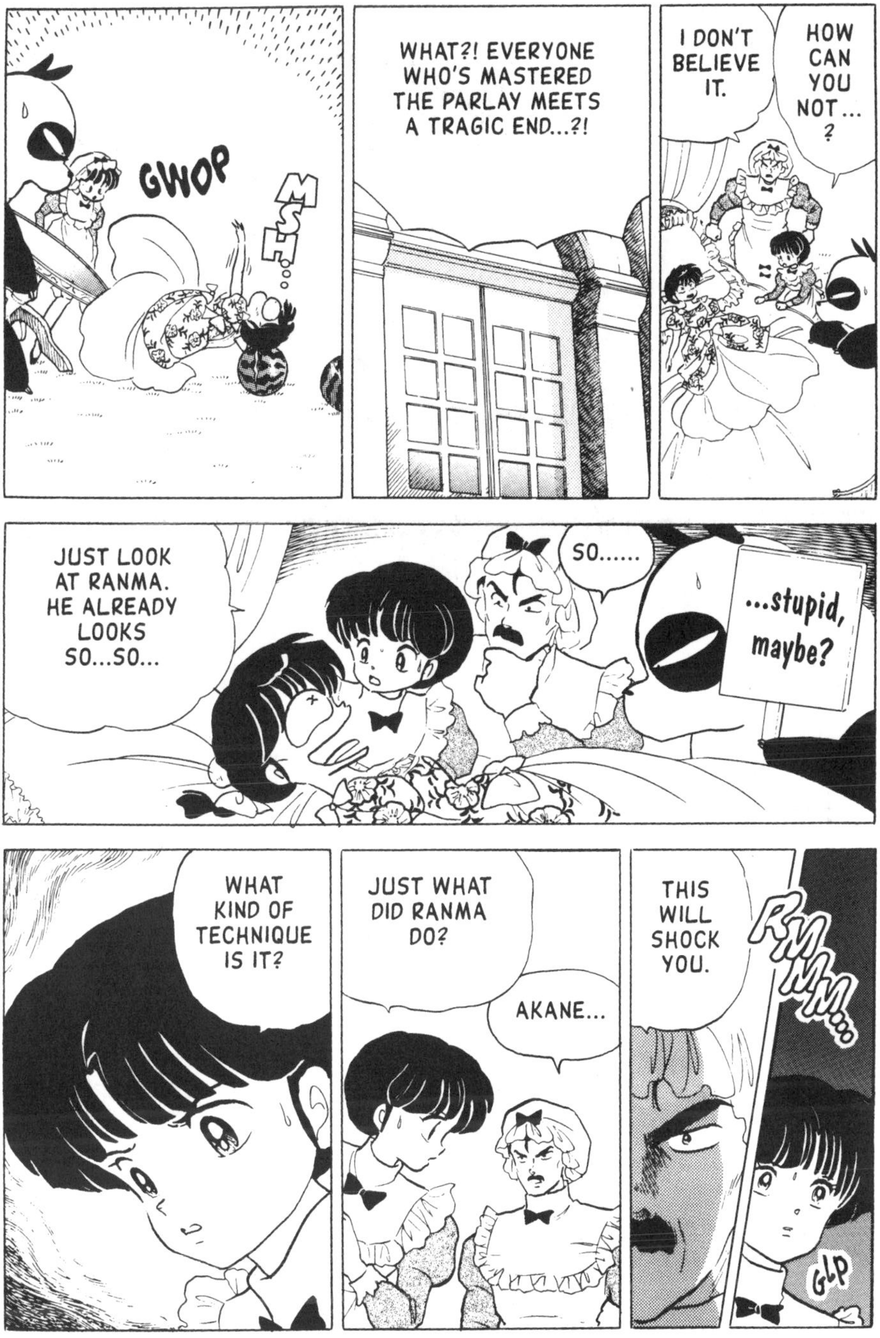
GWOP
MSH...
WHAT?! EVERYONE WHO'S MASTERED THE PARLAY MEETS A TRAGIC END...?!
I DON'T BELIEVE IT.
HOW CAN YOU NOT...?
JUST LOOK AT RANMA. HE ALREADY LOOKS SO...SO...
SO......
...stupid, maybe?
WHAT KIND OF TECHNIQUE IS IT?
JUST WHAT DID RANMA DO?
AKANE...
THIS WILL SHOCK YOU.
RMMM...
GLP

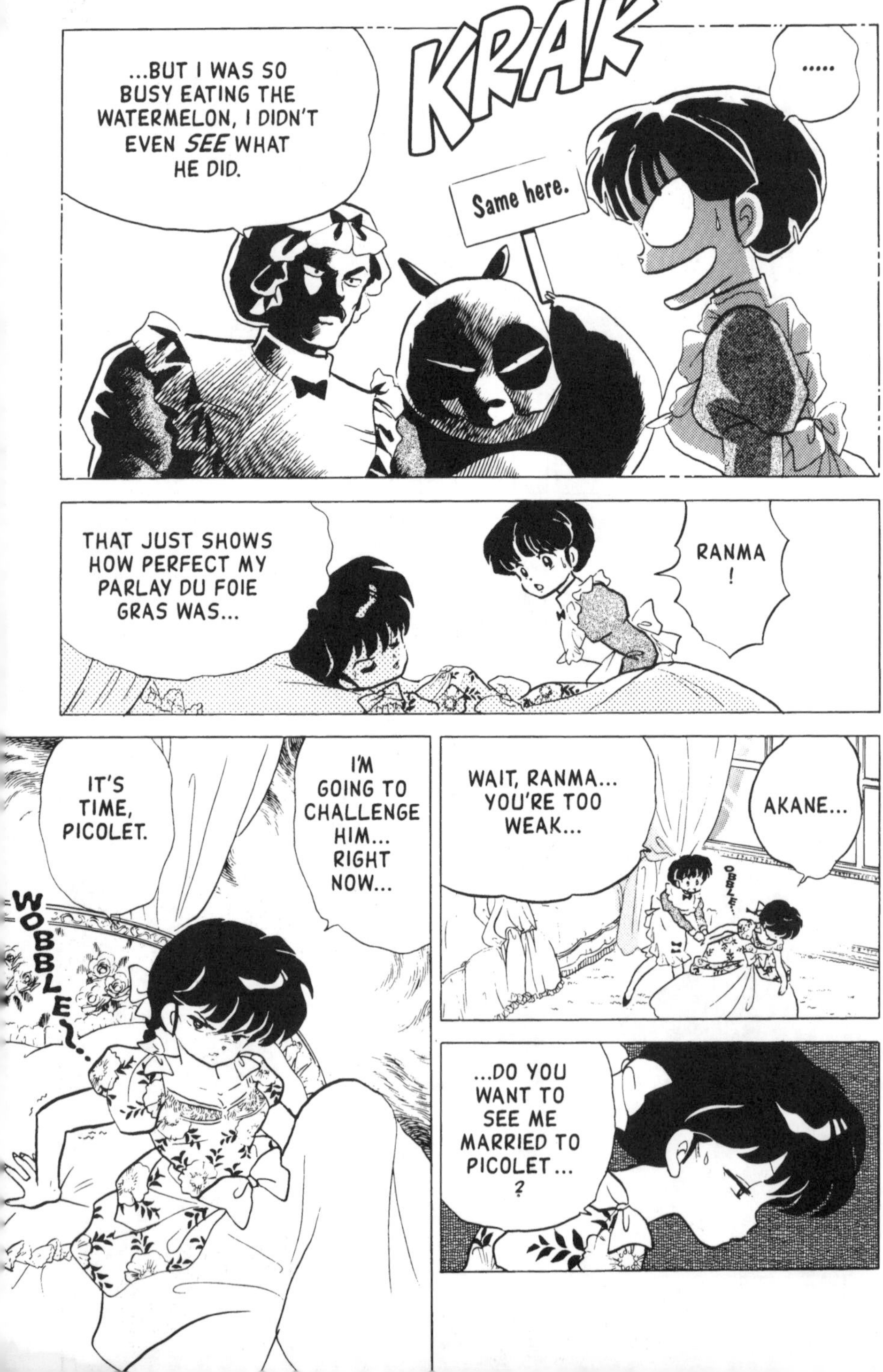

...BUT I WAS SO BUSY EATING THE WATERMELON, I DIDN'T EVEN *SEE* WHAT HE DID.
KRAK
Same here.
.....
THAT JUST SHOWS HOW PERFECT MY PARLAY DU FOIE GRAS WAS...
RANMA!
IT'S TIME, PICOLET.
I'M GOING TO CHALLENGE HIM... RIGHT NOW...
WOBBLE~...
WAIT, RANMA... YOU'RE TOO WEAK...
AKANE...
...DO YOU WANT TO SEE ME MARRIED TO PICOLET...?

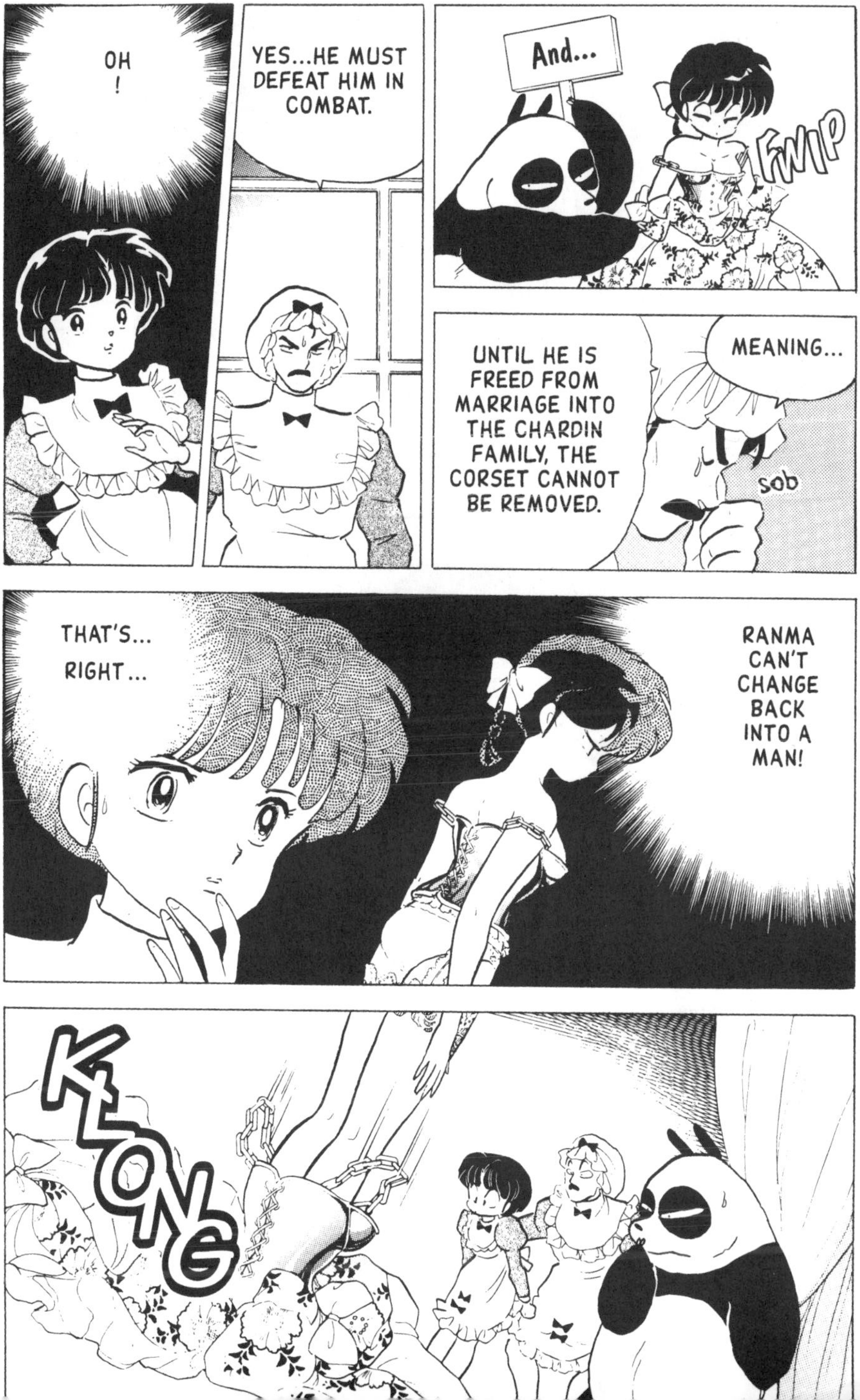
OH
!
YES...HE MUST DEFEAT HIM IN COMBAT.
And...
FWIP
UNTIL HE IS FREED FROM MARRIAGE INTO THE CHARDIN FAMILY, THE CORSET CANNOT BE REMOVED.
MEANING...
sob
THAT'S... RIGHT...
RANMA CAN'T CHANGE BACK INTO A MAN!
KLONG

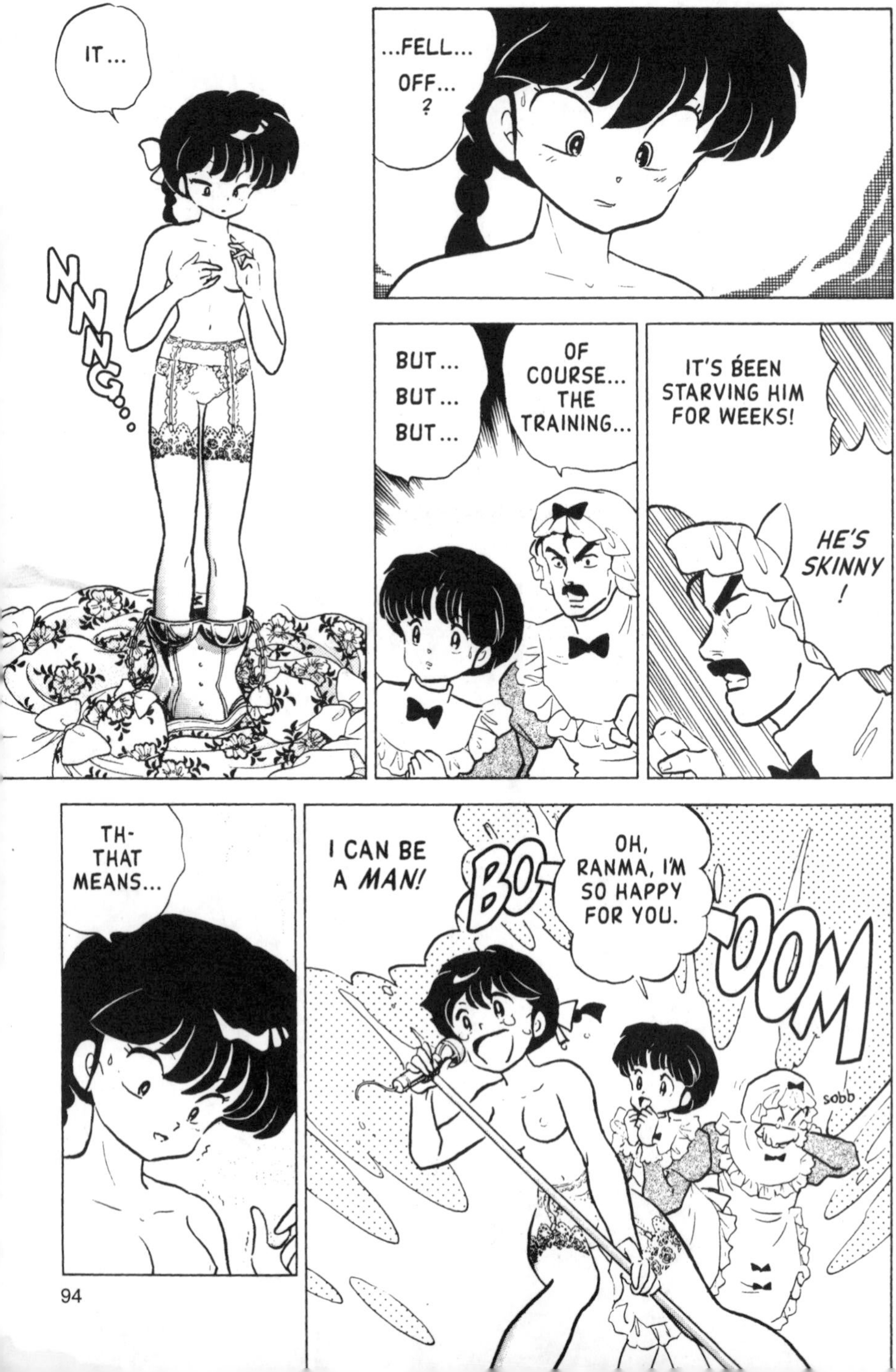
IT...
NNNG...
...FELL... OFF... ?
BUT... BUT... BUT...
OF COURSE... THE TRAINING...
IT'S BEEN STARVING HIM FOR WEEKS!
HE'S SKINNY!
TH-THAT MEANS...
I CAN BE A *MAN!*
BO-
OH, RANMA, I'M SO HAPPY FOR YOU.
OOM
sobb

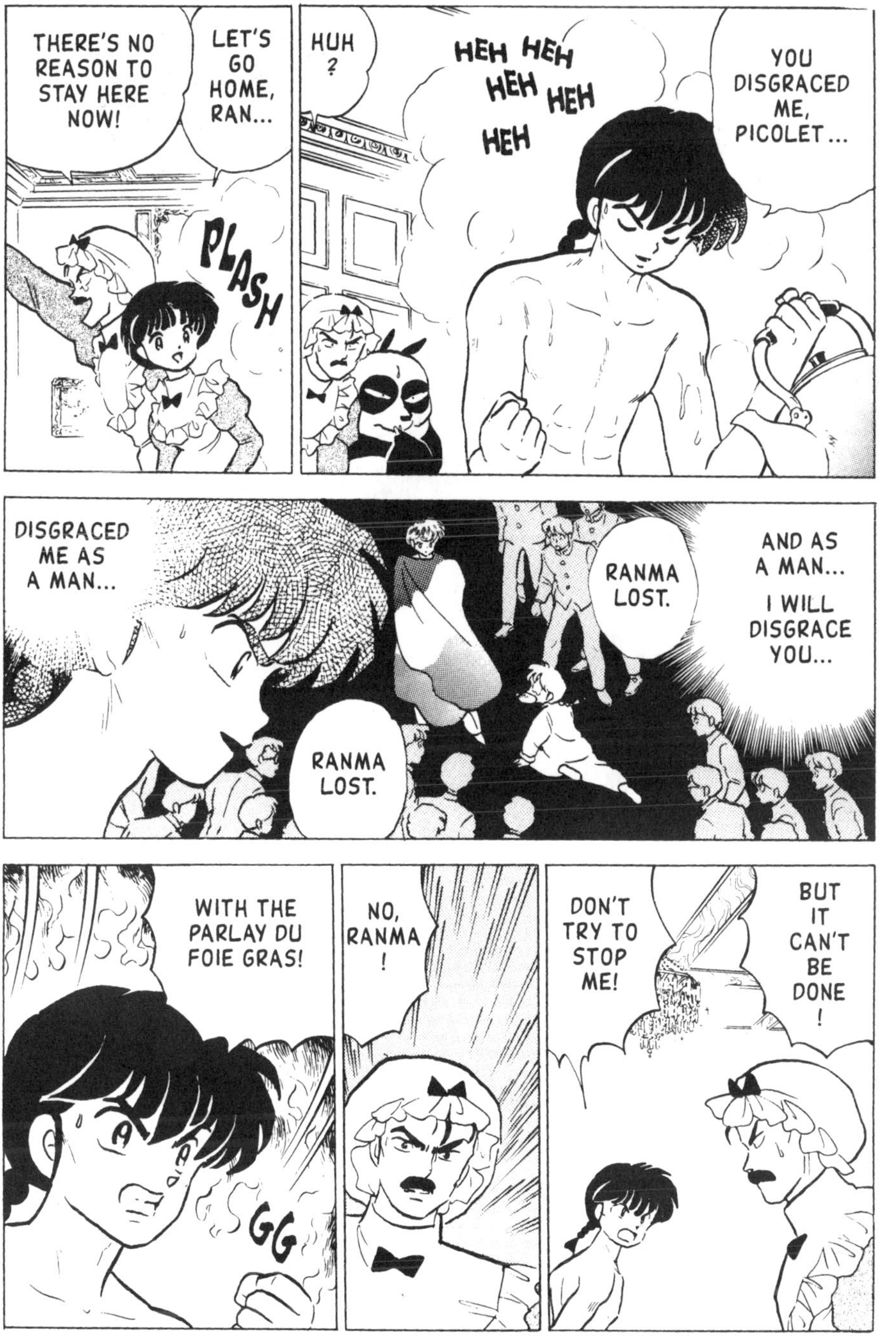
THERE'S NO REASON TO STAY HERE NOW!
LET'S GO HOME, RAN...
PLASH
HUH?
HEH HEH HEH HEH HEH
YOU DISGRACED ME, PICOLET...
DISGRACED ME AS A MAN...
RANMA LOST.
RANMA LOST.
AND AS A MAN... I WILL DISGRACE YOU...
WITH THE PARLAY DU FOIE GRAS!
GG
NO, RANMA!
DON'T TRY TO STOP ME!
BUT IT CAN'T BE DONE!

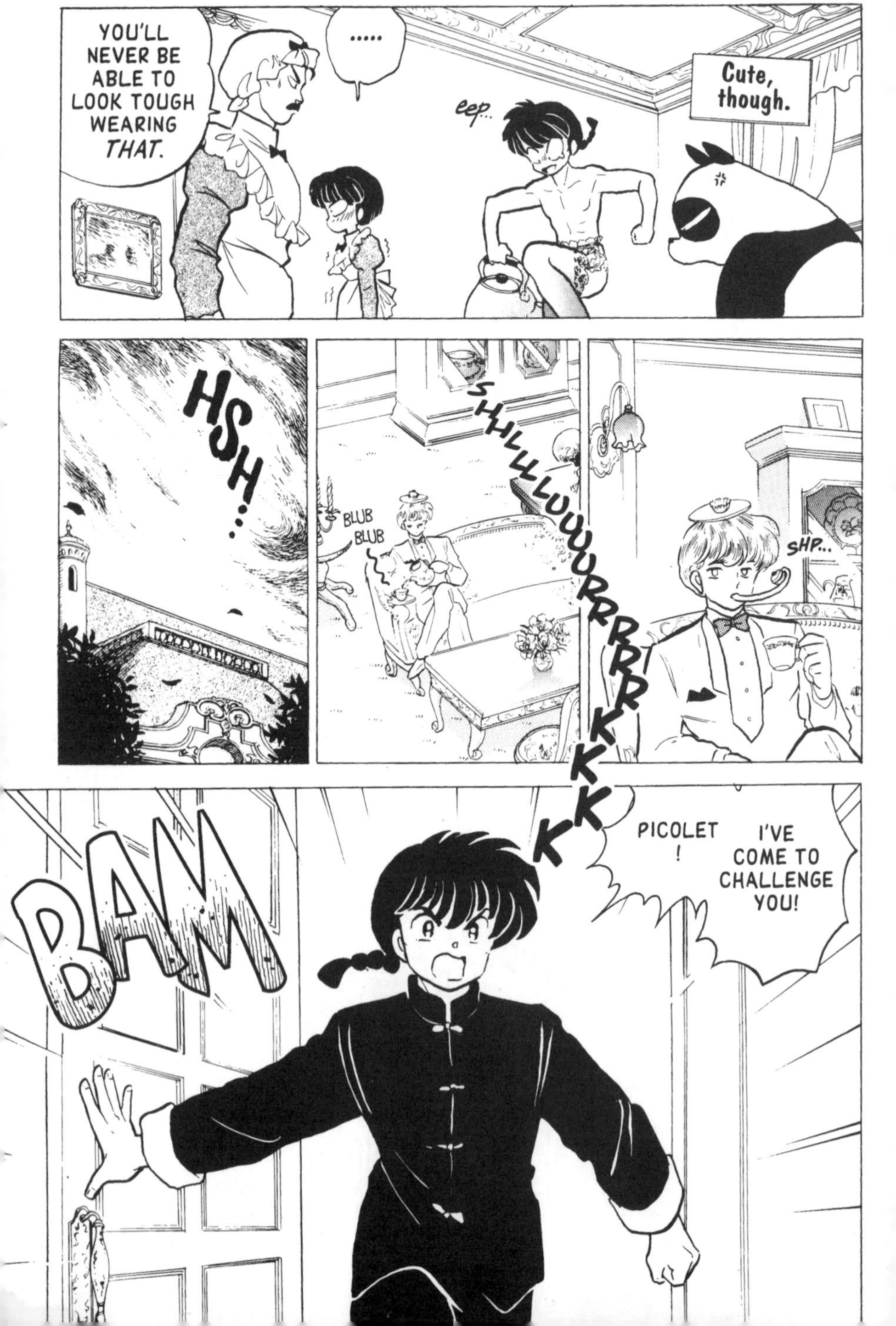
YOU'LL NEVER BE ABLE TO LOOK TOUGH WEARING *THAT*.
.....
eep...
Cute, though.
HSH...
BLUB BLUB
SHHLLLLUUUURRRRRKKKK
SHP...
BAM
PICOLET!
I'VE COME TO CHALLENGE YOU!

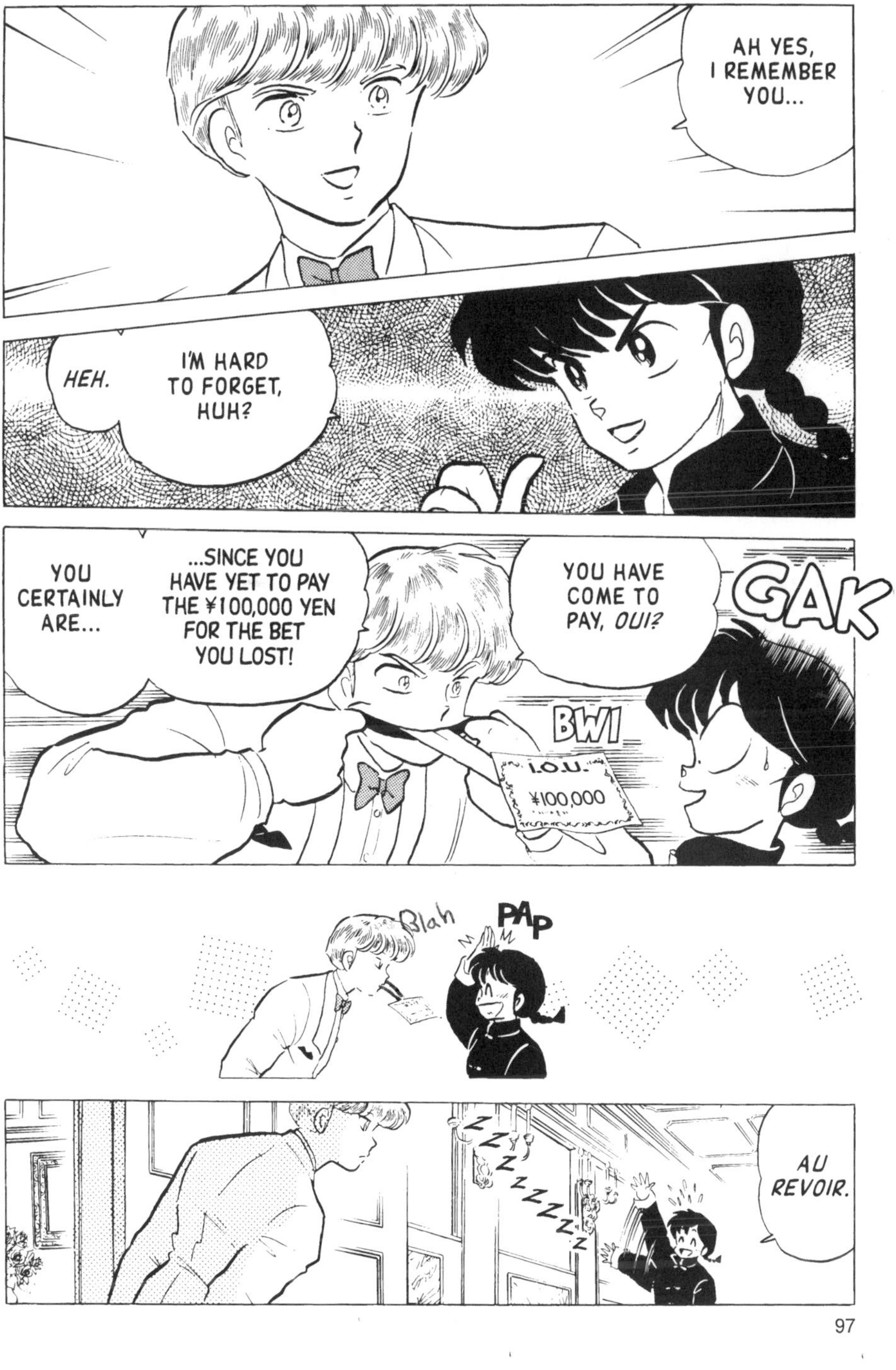
AH YES, I REMEMBER YOU...
HEH.
I'M HARD TO FORGET, HUH?
YOU CERTAINLY ARE...
...SINCE YOU HAVE YET TO PAY THE ¥100,000 YEN FOR THE BET YOU LOST!
YOU HAVE COME TO PAY, OUI?
GAK
BWI
I.O.U.
¥100,000
Blah
PAP
ZZZZZZZZZZ
AU REVOIR.

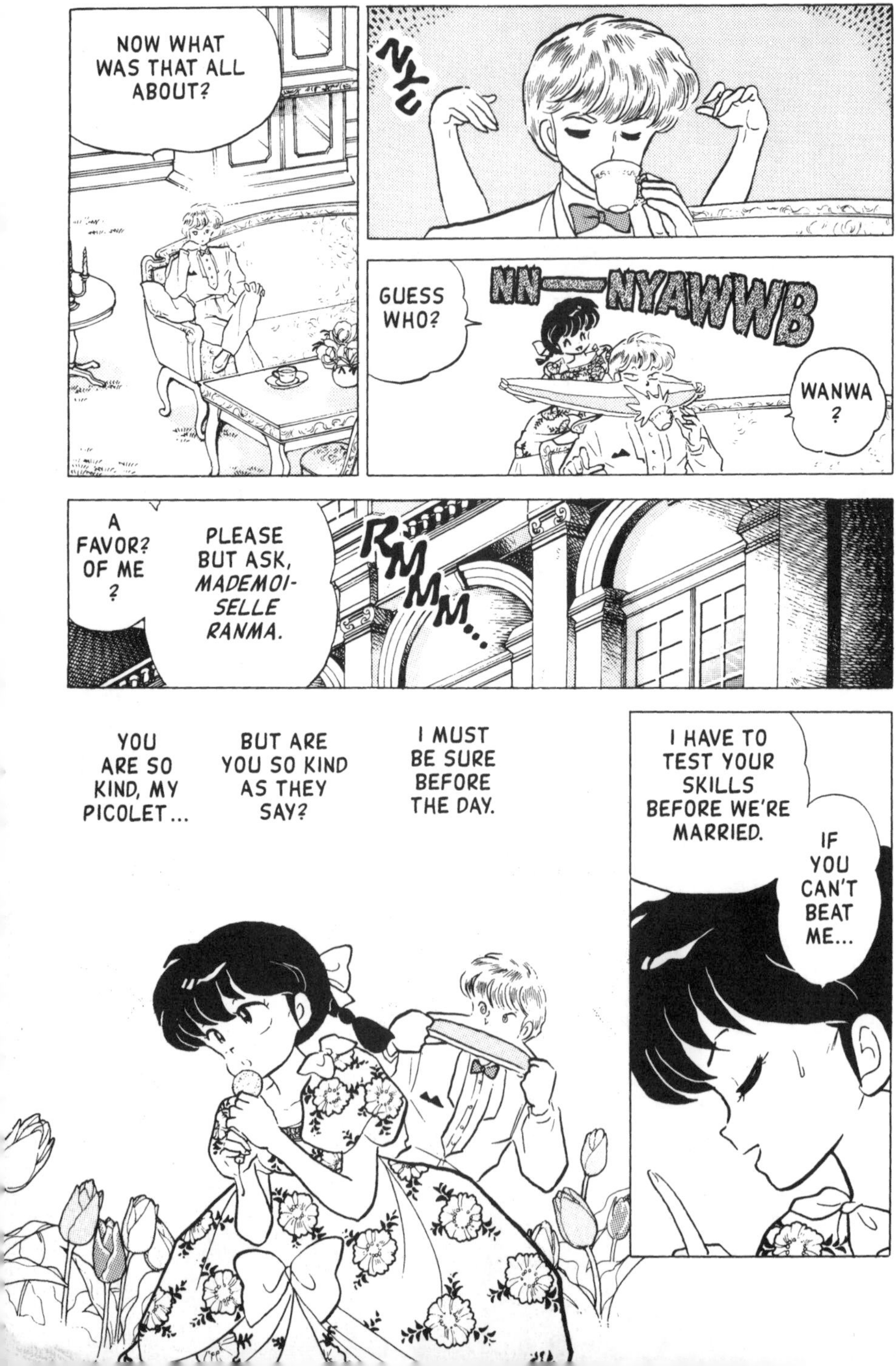
NOW WHAT WAS THAT ALL ABOUT?
NYU
GUESS WHO?
NN—NYAWWB
WANWA?
A FAVOR? OF ME?
PLEASE BUT ASK, *MADEMOISELLE* RANMA.
RMMM...
YOU ARE SO KIND, MY PICOLET...
BUT ARE YOU SO KIND AS THEY SAY?
I MUST BE SURE BEFORE THE DAY.
I HAVE TO TEST YOUR SKILLS BEFORE WE'RE MARRIED.
IF YOU CAN'T BEAT ME...

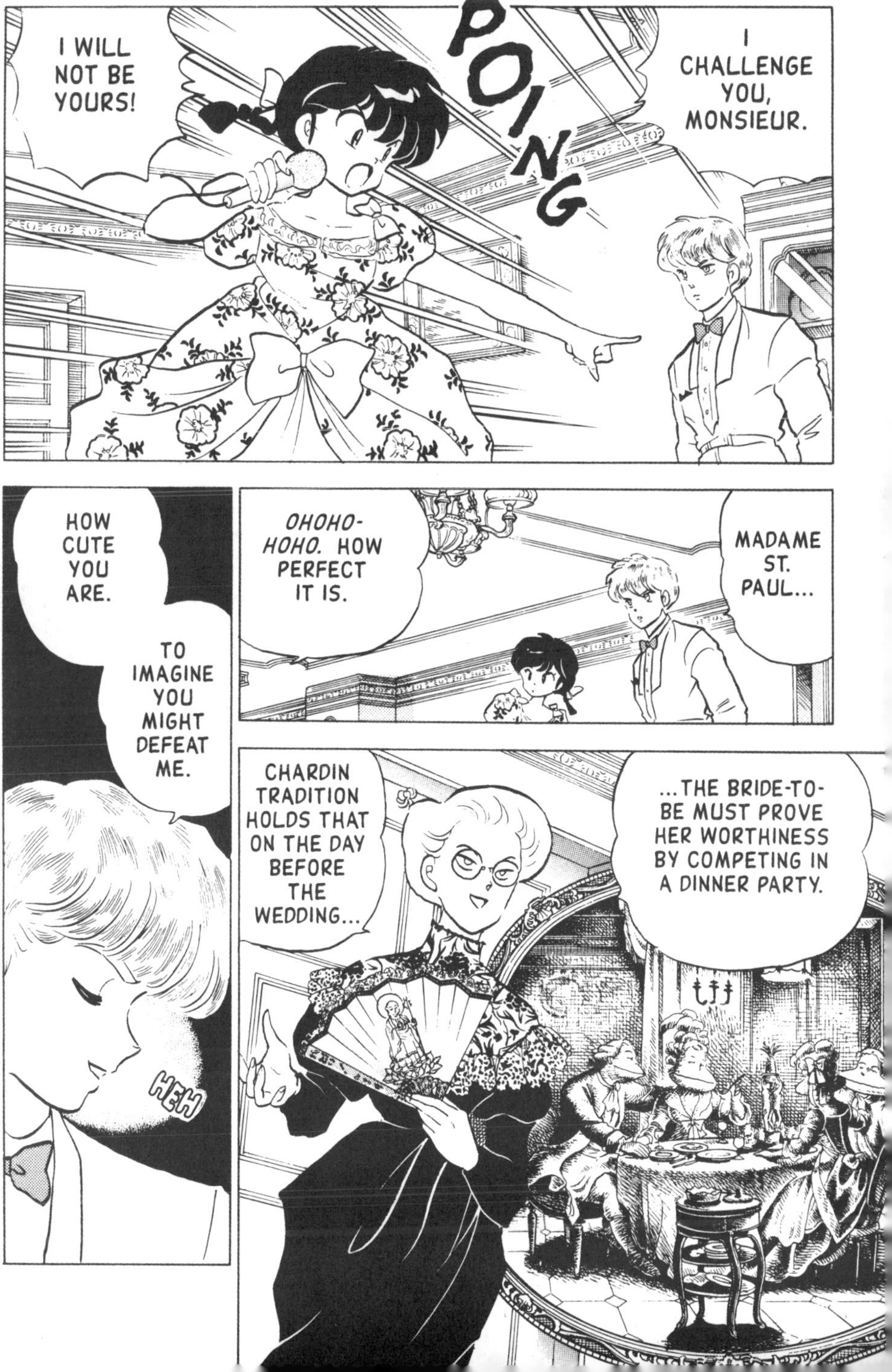
I WILL NOT BE YOURS!
POING
I CHALLENGE YOU, MONSIEUR.
HOW CUTE YOU ARE.
TO IMAGINE YOU MIGHT DEFEAT ME.
HEH
OHOHO-HOHO. HOW PERFECT IT IS.
MADAME ST. PAUL...
CHARDIN TRADITION HOLDS THAT ON THE DAY BEFORE THE WEDDING...
...THE BRIDE-TO-BE MUST PROVE HER WORTHINESS BY COMPETING IN A DINNER PARTY.

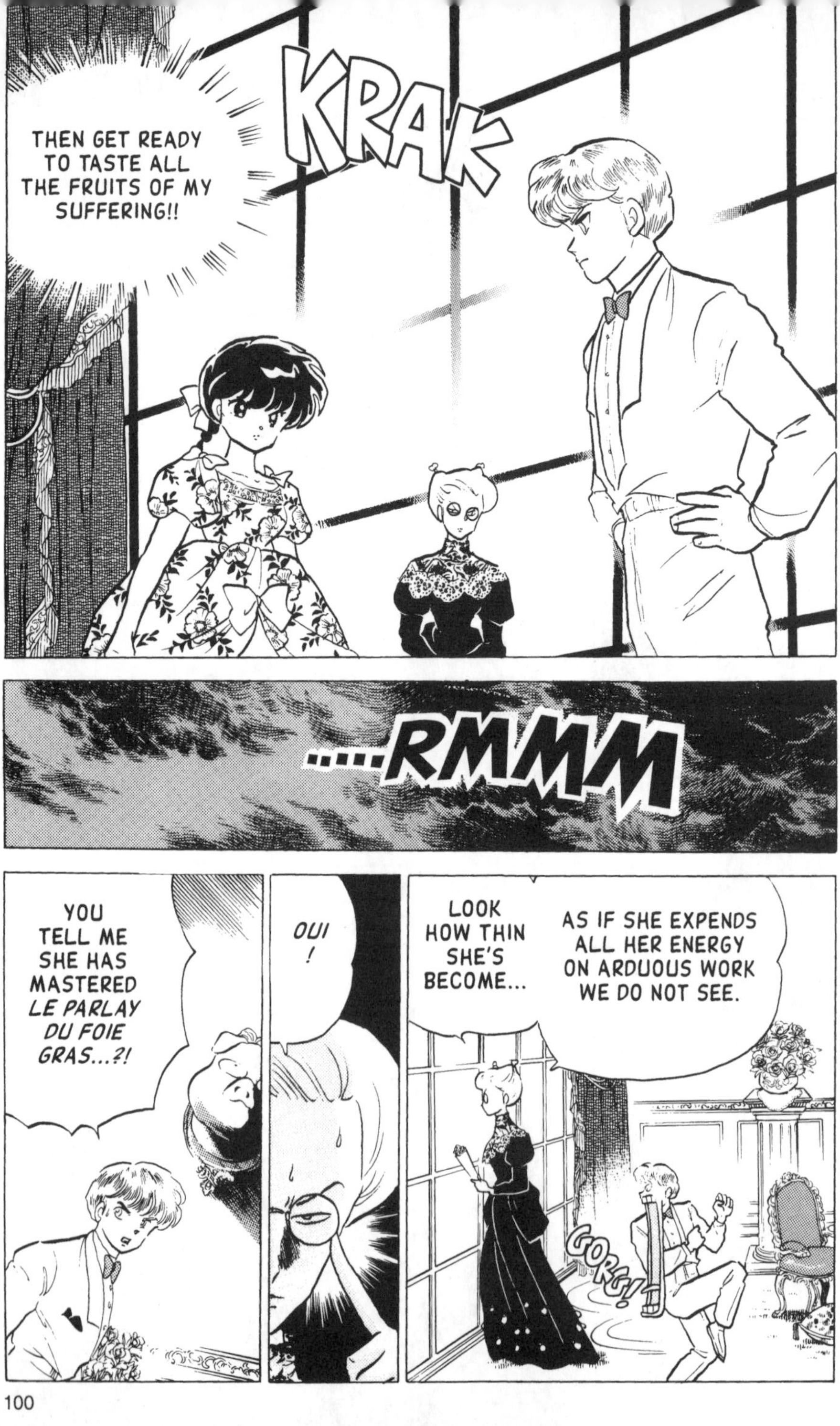
THEN GET READY TO TASTE ALL THE FRUITS OF MY SUFFERING!!
KRAK
.....RMMM
YOU TELL ME SHE HAS MASTERED *LE PARLAY DU FOIE GRAS*...?!
OUI !
LOOK HOW THIN SHE'S BECOME...
AS IF SHE EXPENDS ALL HER ENERGY ON ARDUOUS WORK WE DO NOT SEE.
GORG!

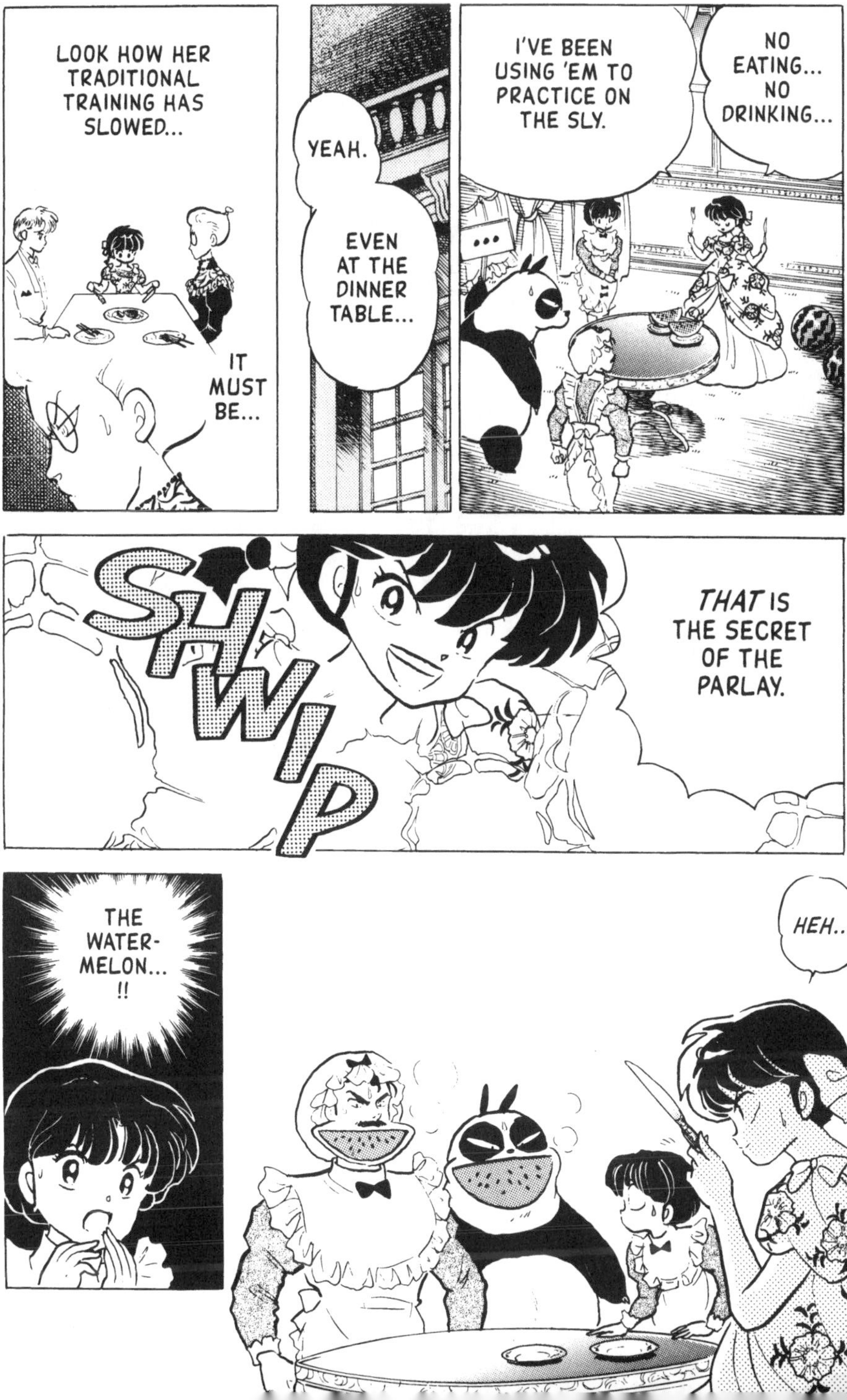
LOOK HOW HER TRADITIONAL TRAINING HAS SLOWED...
IT MUST BE...
YEAH.
EVEN AT THE DINNER TABLE...
I'VE BEEN USING 'EM TO PRACTICE ON THE SLY.
NO EATING... NO DRINKING...
...
SHWIP
THAT IS THE SECRET OF THE PARLAY.
THE WATER-MELON... !!
HEH...

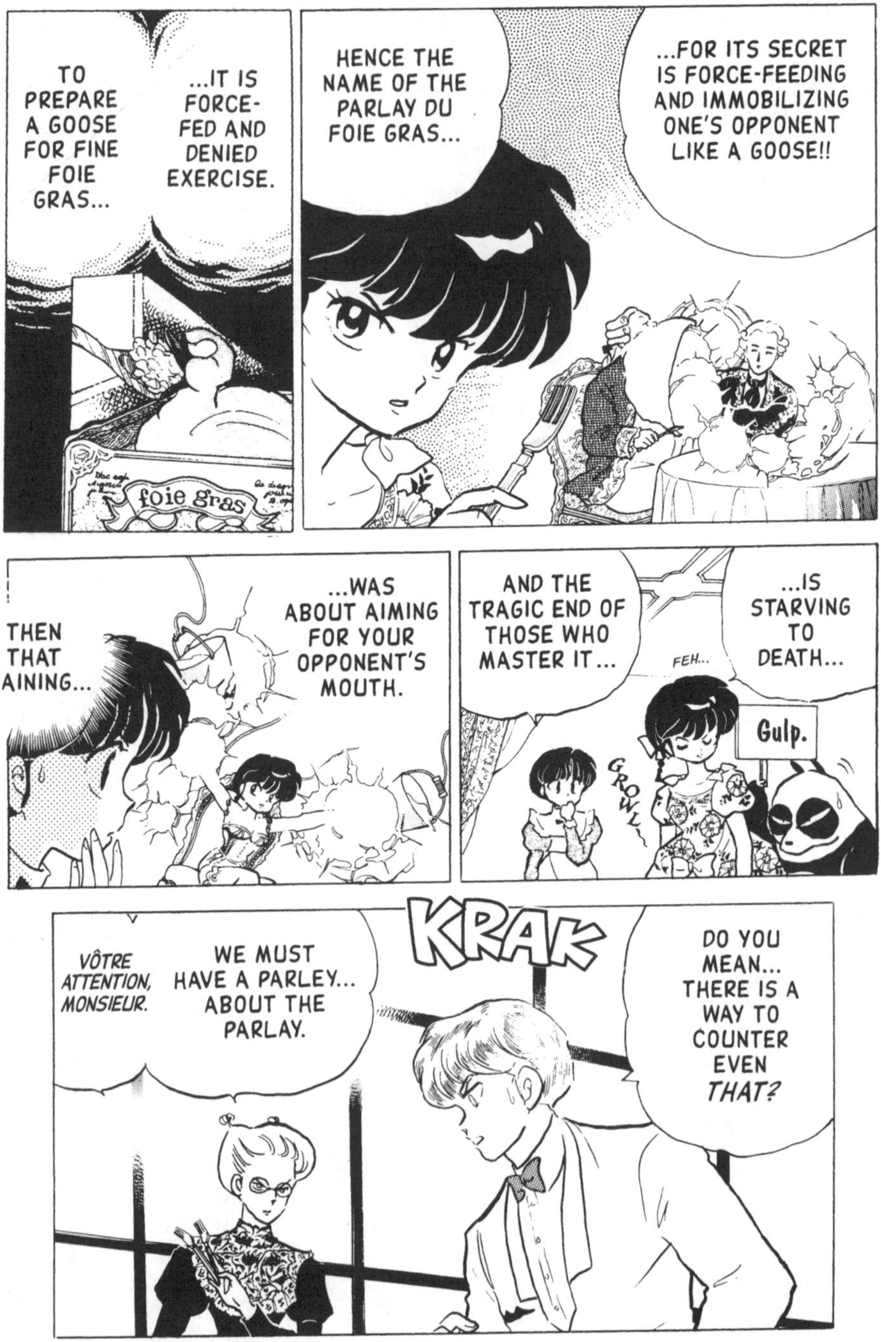

TO PREPARE A GOOSE FOR FINE FOIE GRAS...
...IT IS FORCE-FED AND DENIED EXERCISE.
foie gras
HENCE THE NAME OF THE PARLAY DU FOIE GRAS...
...FOR ITS SECRET IS FORCE-FEEDING AND IMMOBILIZING ONE'S OPPONENT LIKE A GOOSE!!
THEN THAT TRAINING...
...WAS ABOUT AIMING FOR YOUR OPPONENT'S MOUTH.
AND THE TRAGIC END OF THOSE WHO MASTER IT...
...IS STARVING TO DEATH...
FEH...
GROWL
Gulp.
KRAK
VÔTRE ATTENTION, MONSIEUR.
WE MUST HAVE A PARLEY... ABOUT THE PARLAY.
DO YOU MEAN... THERE IS A WAY TO COUNTER EVEN *THAT?*

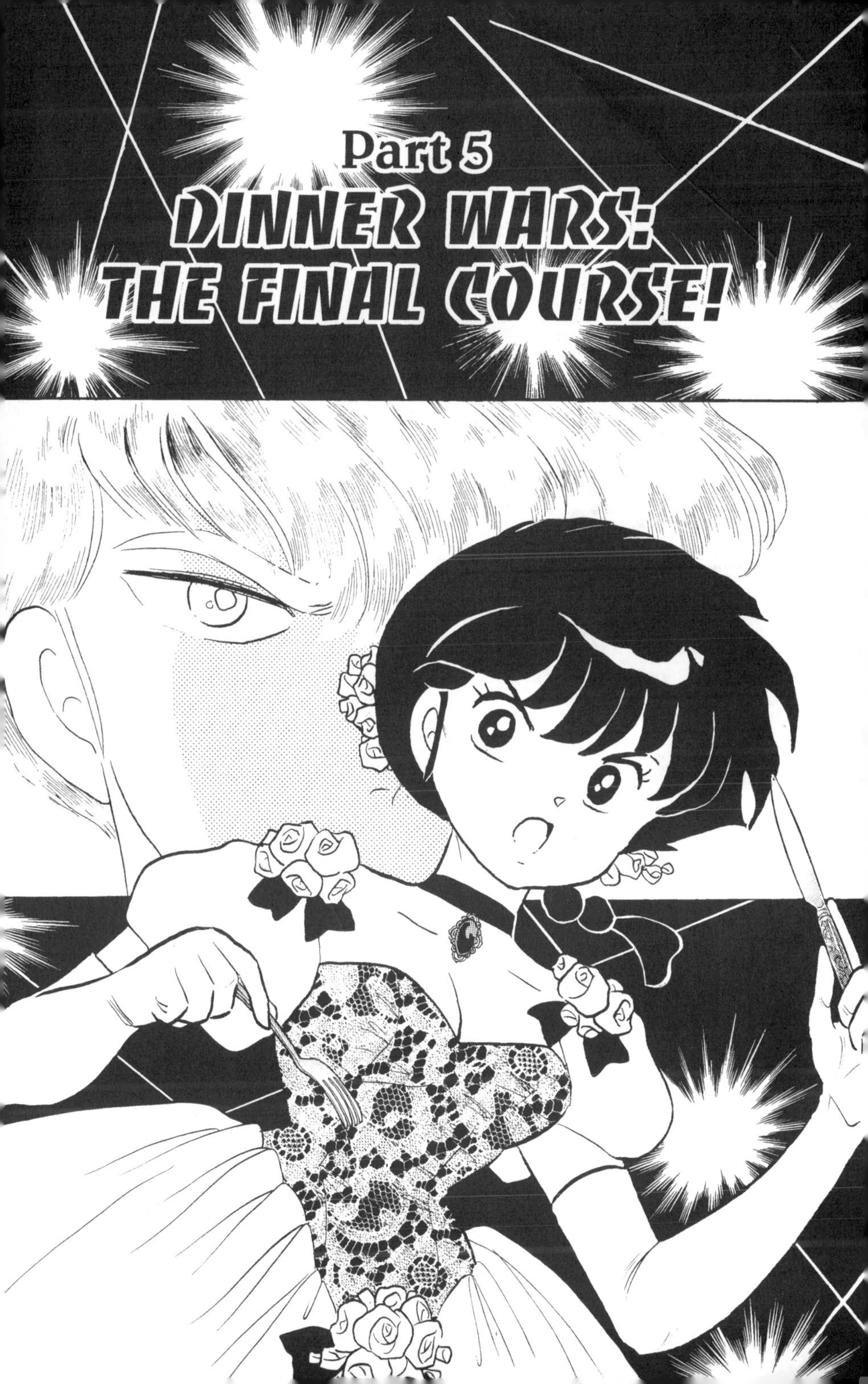
Part 5
DINNER WARS:
THE FINAL COURSE!

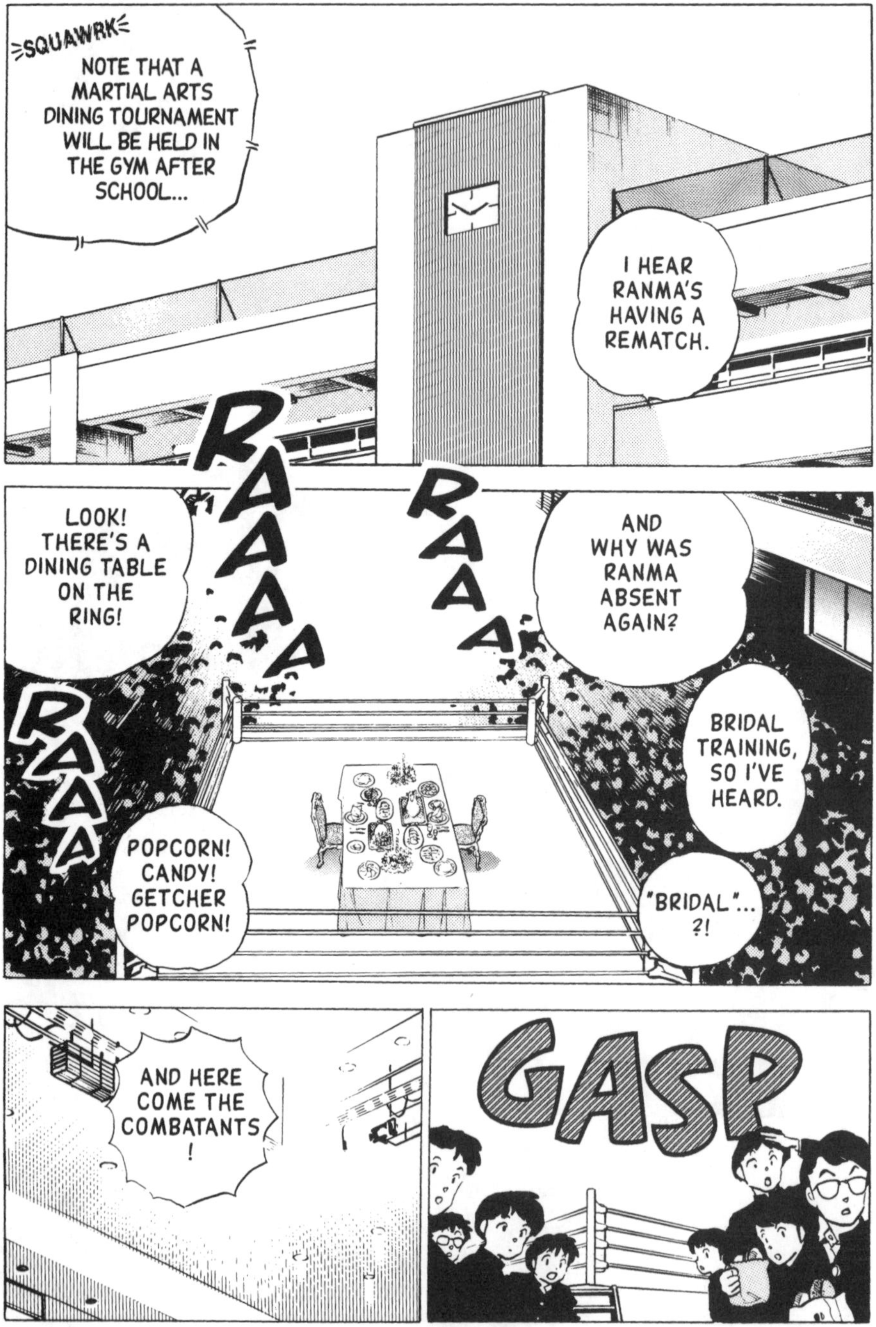
SQUAWRK
NOTE THAT A MARTIAL ARTS DINING TOURNAMENT WILL BE HELD IN THE GYM AFTER SCHOOL...
I HEAR RANMA'S HAVING A REMATCH.
RAAAAA
LOOK! THERE'S A DINING TABLE ON THE RING!
RAAAA
AND WHY WAS RANMA ABSENT AGAIN?
RAAAA
POPCORN! CANDY! GETCHER POPCORN!
BRIDAL TRAINING, SO I'VE HEARD.
"BRIDAL"... ?!
AND HERE COME THE COMBATANTS!
GASP

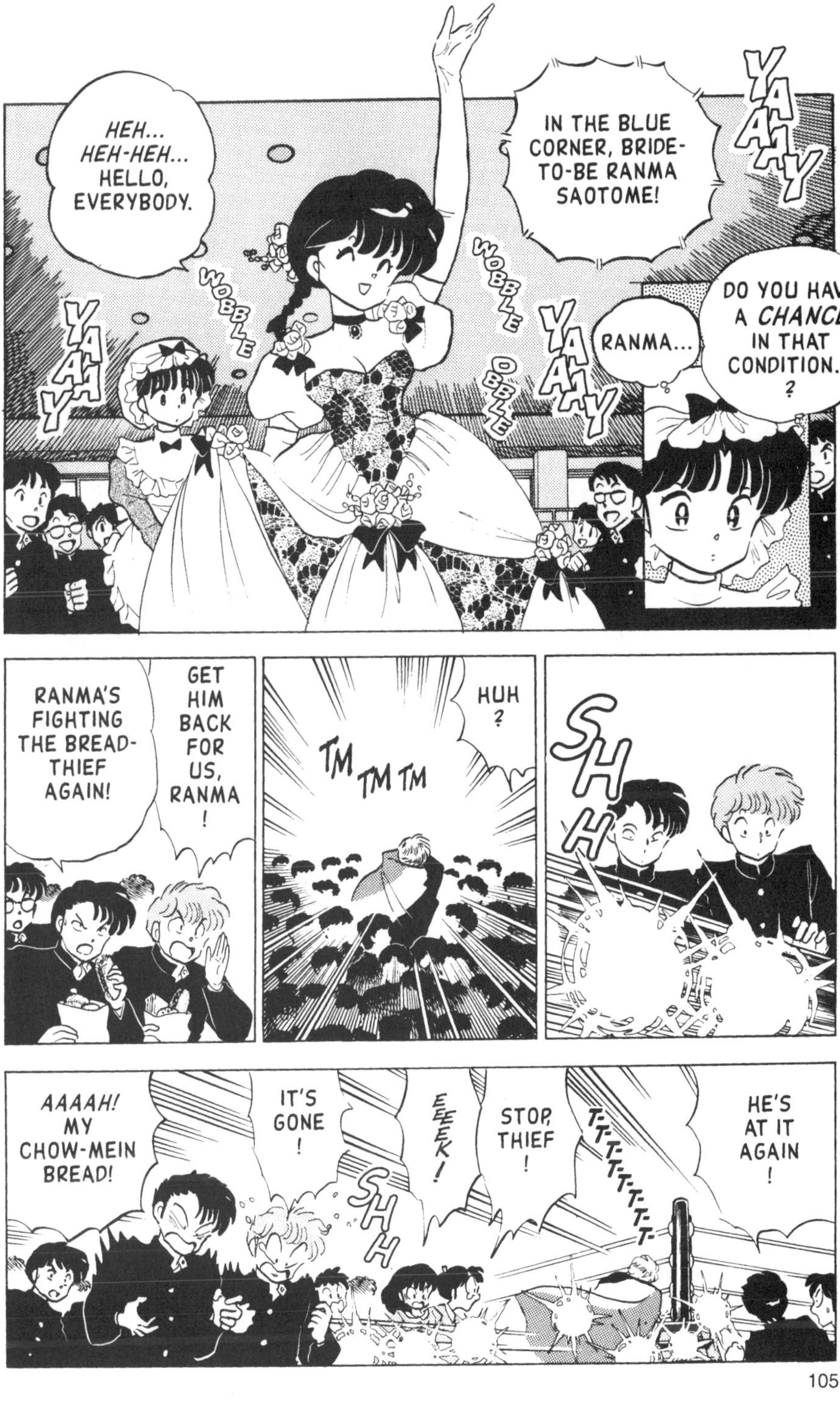
HEH... HEH-HEH... HELLO, EVERYBODY.
IN THE BLUE CORNER, BRIDE-TO-BE RANMA SAOTOME!
YAAAAY
WOBBLE
YAAAAY
WOBBLE OBBLE
YAAAAY
RANMA...
DO YOU HAVE A *CHANCE* IN THAT CONDITION...?
RANMA'S FIGHTING THE BREAD-THIEF AGAIN!
GET HIM BACK FOR US, RANMA!
HUH?
TM TM TM
SHH
AAAAH! MY CHOW-MEIN BREAD!
IT'S GONE!
EEEK!
SHH
STOP, THIEF!
T-T-T-T-T-T-T-T-T-
HE'S AT IT AGAIN!

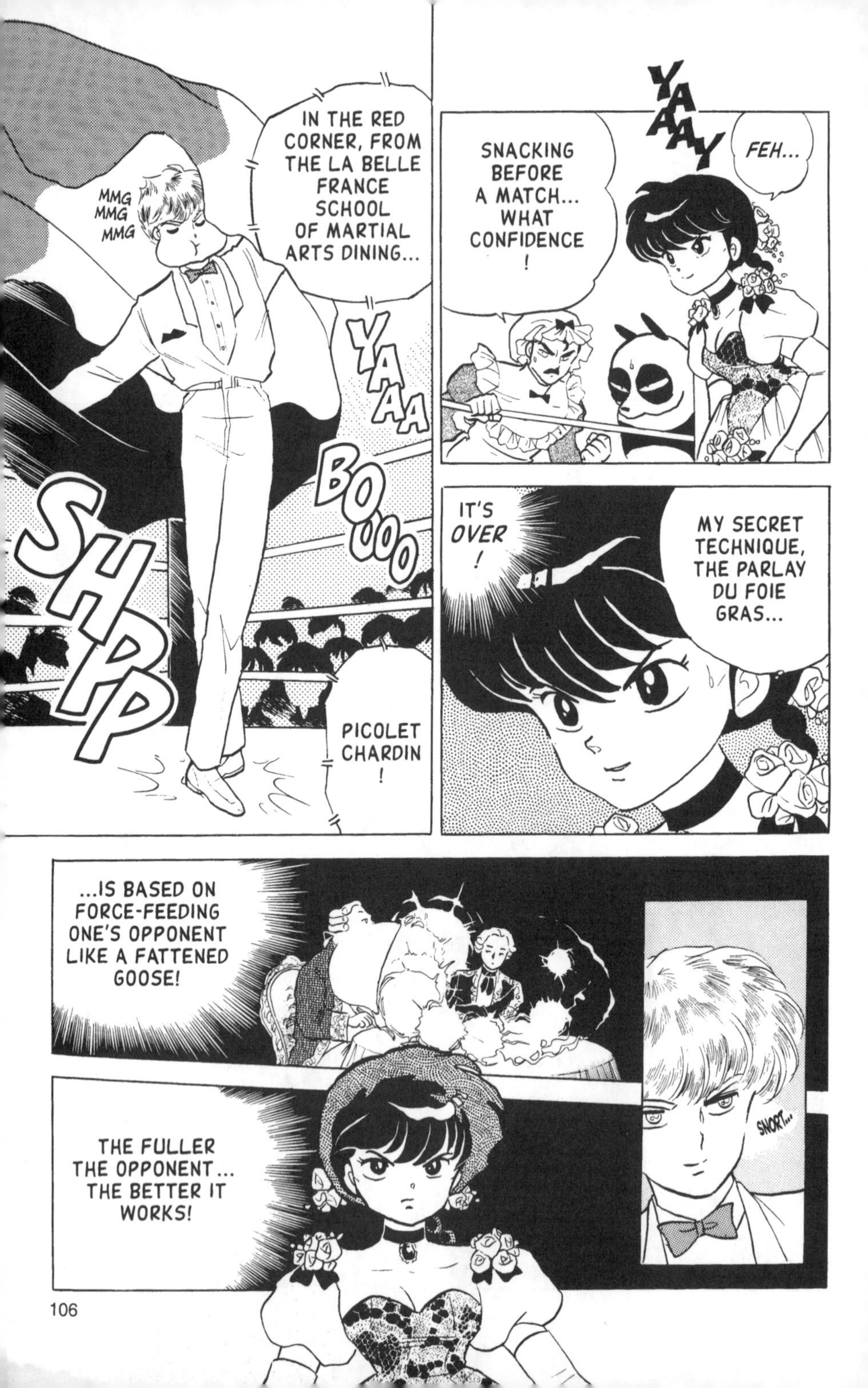
IN THE RED CORNER, FROM THE LA BELLE FRANCE SCHOOL OF MARTIAL ARTS DINING...
MMG MMG MMG
YAAAA
BOOOO
SHPP
PICOLET CHARDIN !
YAAAY
SNACKING BEFORE A MATCH... WHAT CONFIDENCE !
FEH...
IT'S OVER !
MY SECRET TECHNIQUE, THE PARLAY DU FOIE GRAS...
...IS BASED ON FORCE-FEEDING ONE'S OPPONENT LIKE A FATTENED GOOSE!
THE FULLER THE OPPONENT... THE BETTER IT WORKS!
SNORT...

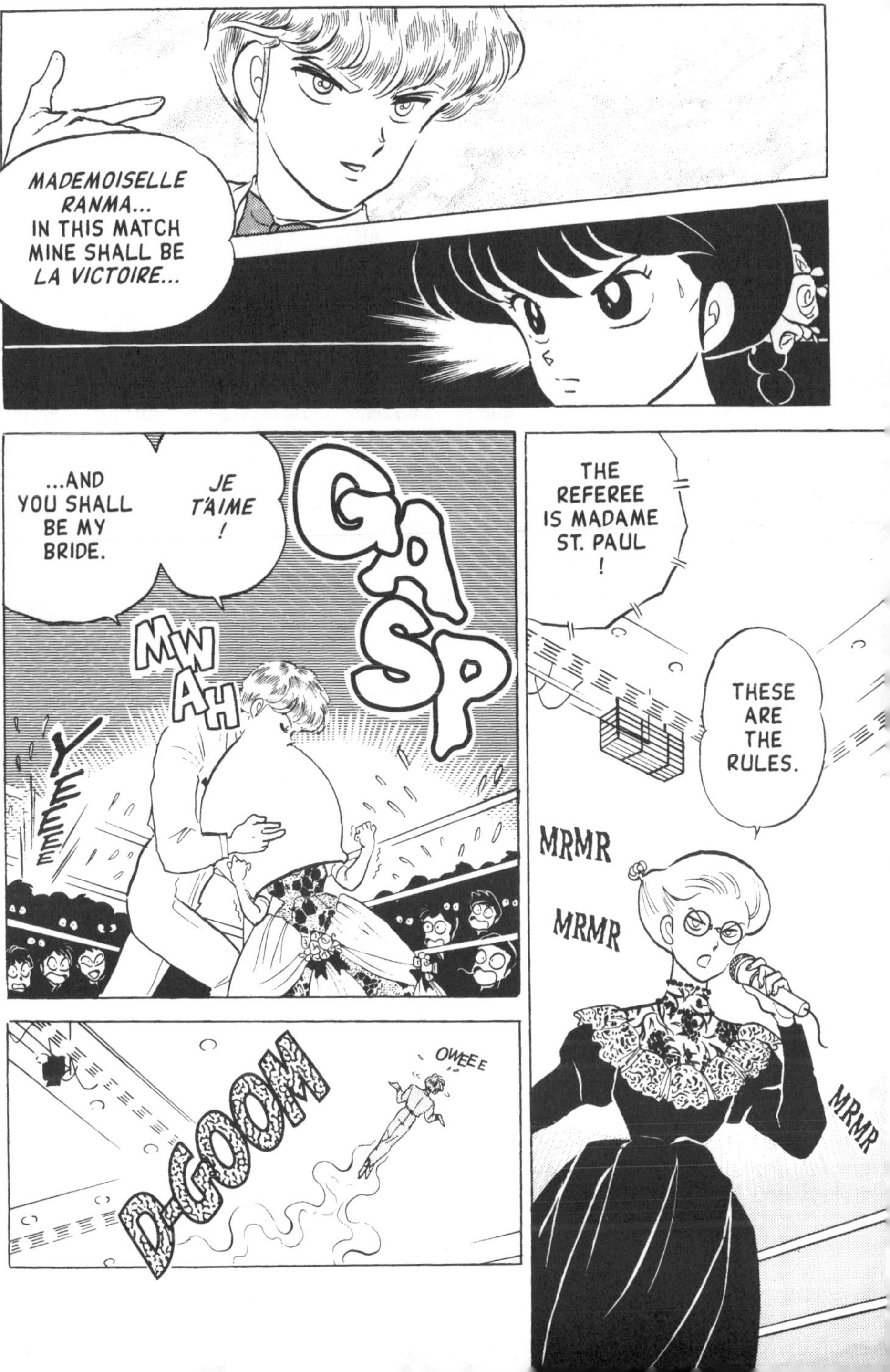
MADEMOISELLE RANMA... IN THIS MATCH MINE SHALL BE LA VICTOIRE...
...AND YOU SHALL BE MY BRIDE.
JE T'AIME !
GASP
MWAH
YEEEEE
OWEEE
D-GOOOM
THE REFEREE IS MADAME ST. PAUL !
THESE ARE THE RULES.
MRMR
MRMR
MRMR

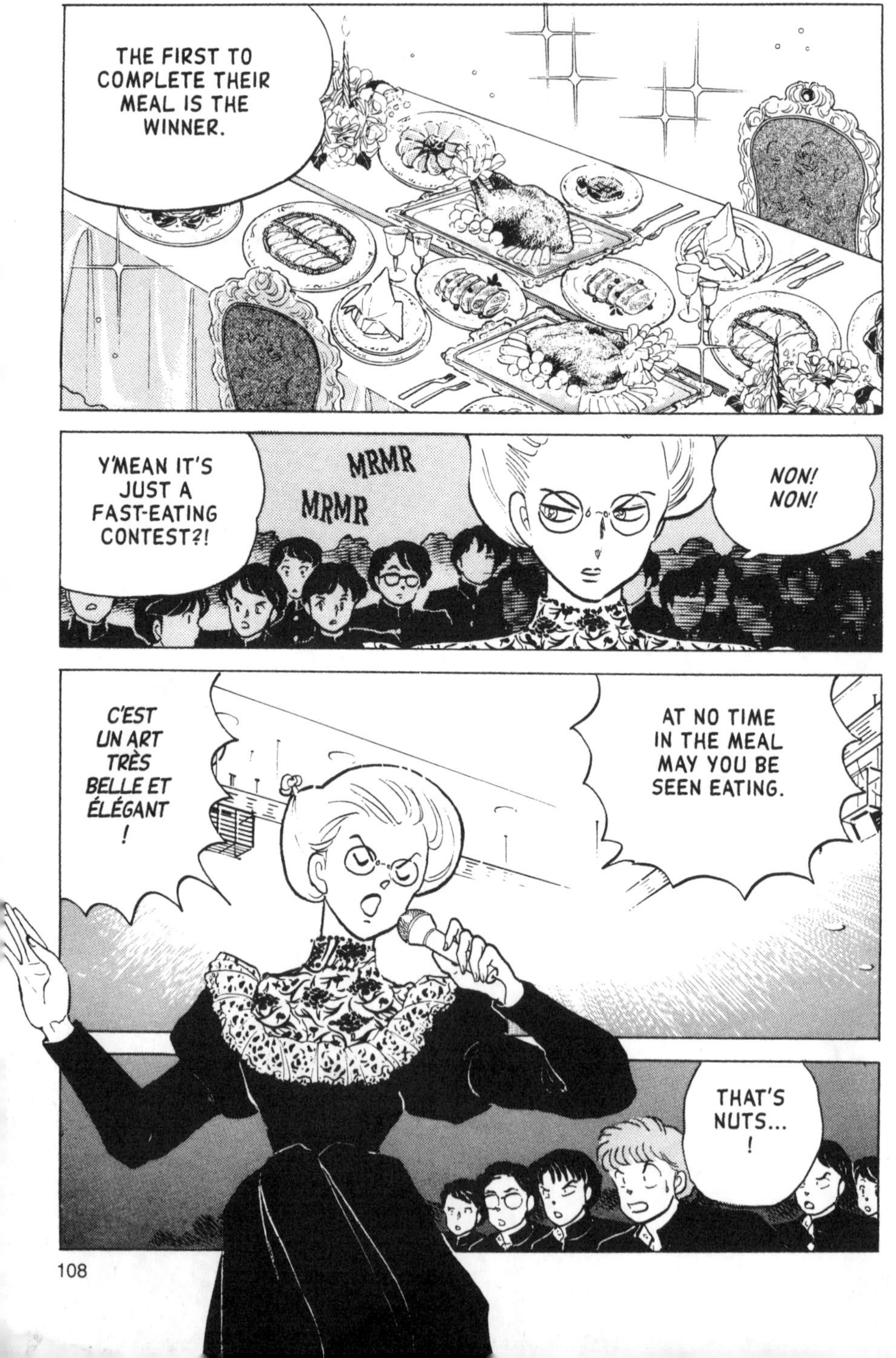
THE FIRST TO COMPLETE THEIR MEAL IS THE WINNER.
Y'MEAN IT'S JUST A FAST-EATING CONTEST?!
MRMR
MRMR
NON! NON!
C'EST UN ART TRÈS BELLE ET ÉLÉGANT !
AT NO TIME IN THE MEAL MAY YOU BE SEEN EATING.
THAT'S NUTS... !

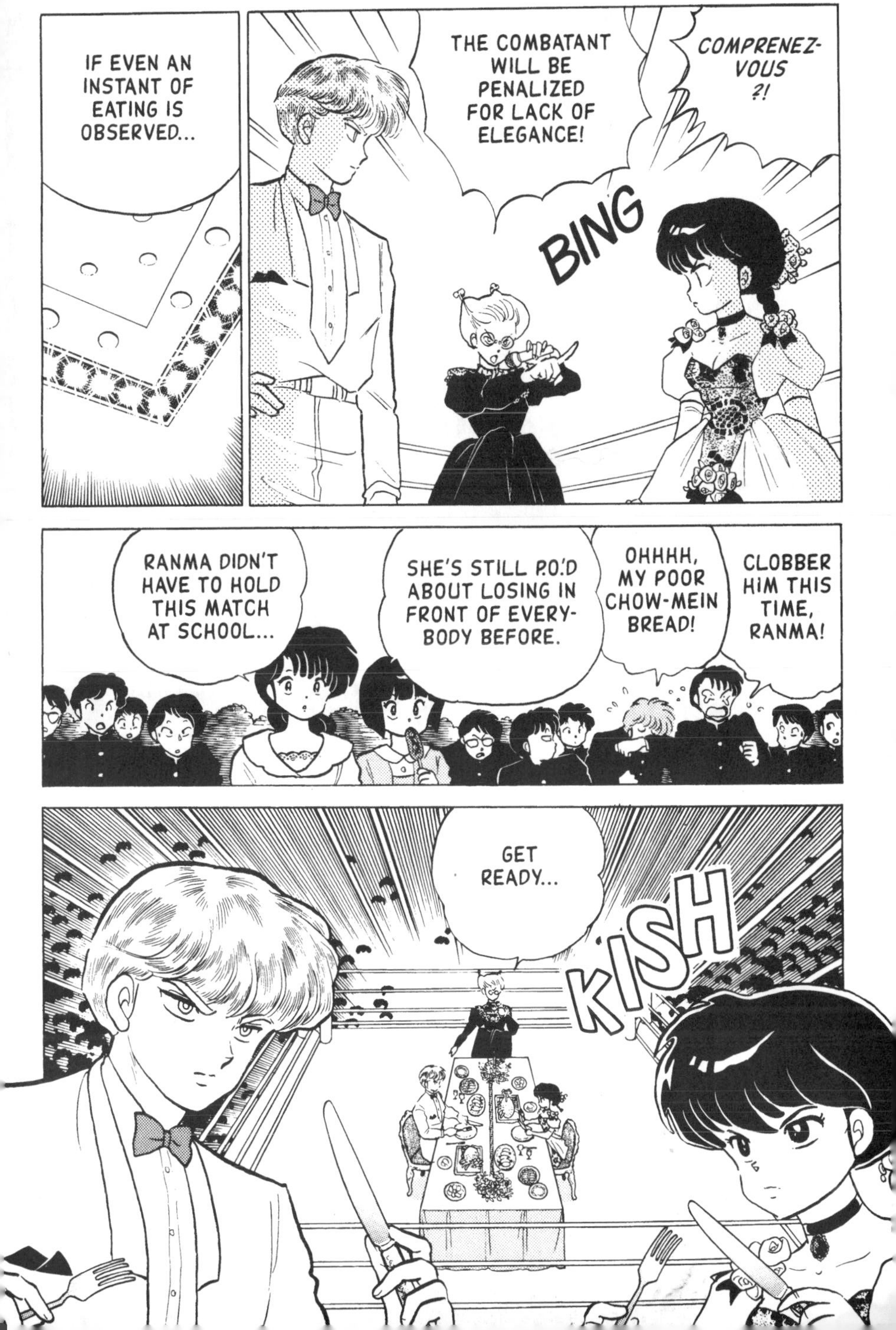
IF EVEN AN INSTANT OF EATING IS OBSERVED...
THE COMBATANT WILL BE PENALIZED FOR LACK OF ELEGANCE!
COMPRENEZ-VOUS ?!
BING
RANMA DIDN'T HAVE TO HOLD THIS MATCH AT SCHOOL...
SHE'S STILL P.O.'D ABOUT LOSING IN FRONT OF EVERY-BODY BEFORE.
OHHHH, MY POOR CHOW-MEIN BREAD!
CLOBBER HIM THIS TIME, RANMA!
GET READY...
KISH

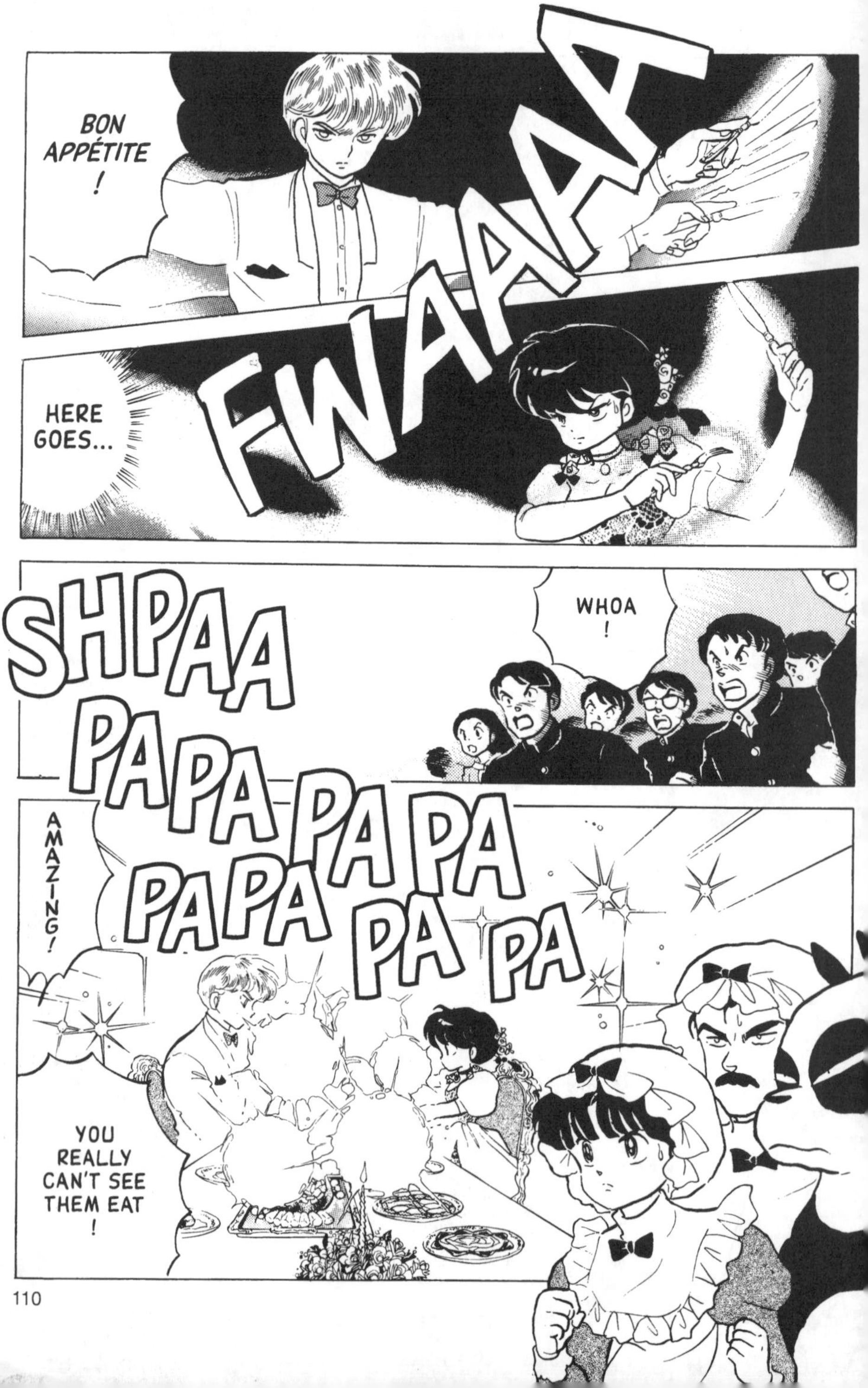
BON APPÉTITE !
FWAAAAA
HERE GOES...
SHPAA
WHOA !
PAPAPAPAPAPAPAPAPA
AMAZING!
YOU REALLY CAN'T SEE THEM EAT !

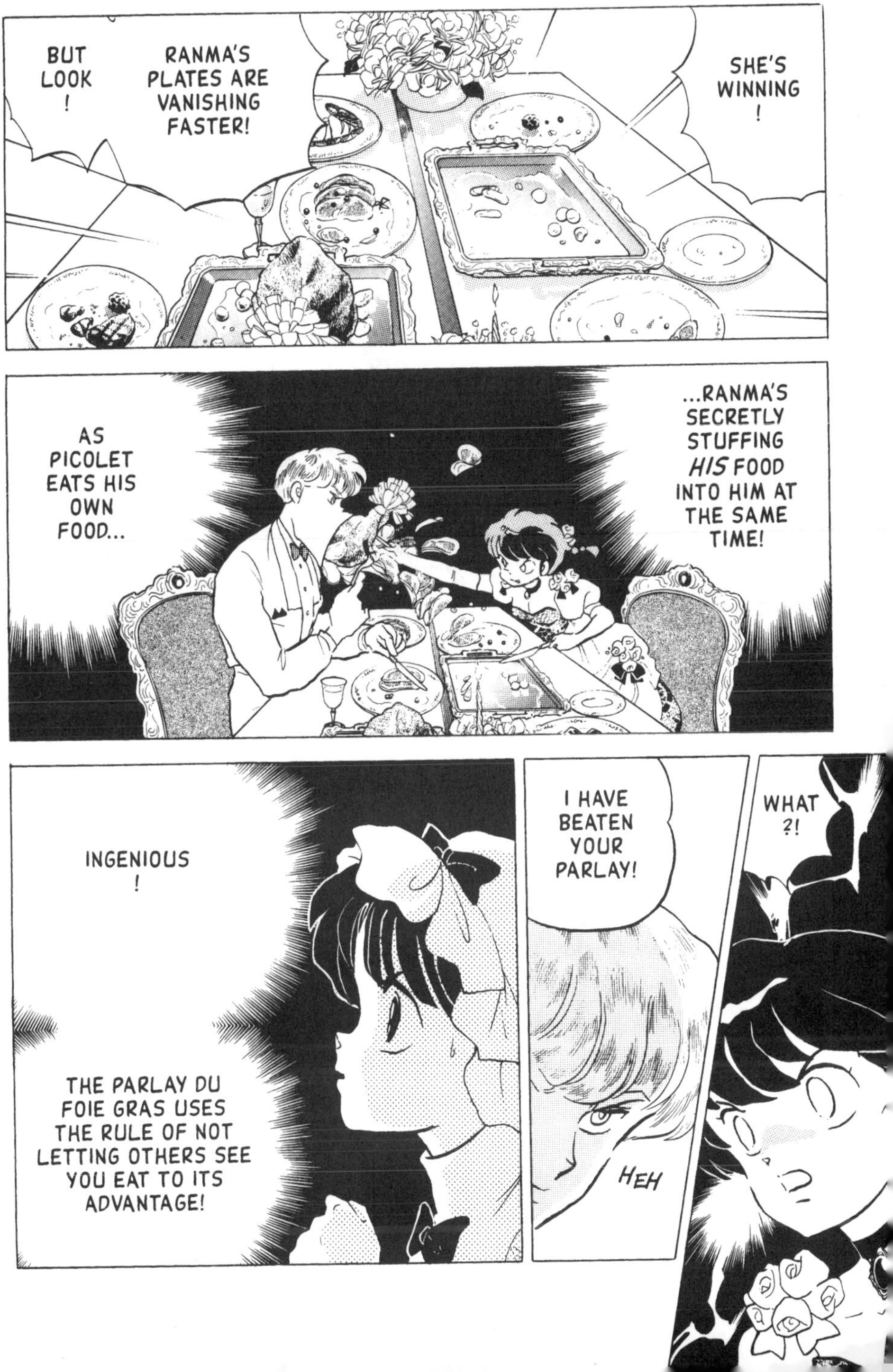
BUT LOOK !
RANMA'S PLATES ARE VANISHING FASTER!
SHE'S WINNING !
AS PICOLET EATS HIS OWN FOOD...
...RANMA'S SECRETLY STUFFING *HIS* FOOD INTO HIM AT THE SAME TIME!
INGENIOUS !
THE PARLAY DU FOIE GRAS USES THE RULE OF NOT LETTING OTHERS SEE YOU EAT TO ITS ADVANTAGE!
I HAVE BEATEN YOUR PARLAY!
HEH
WHAT ?!

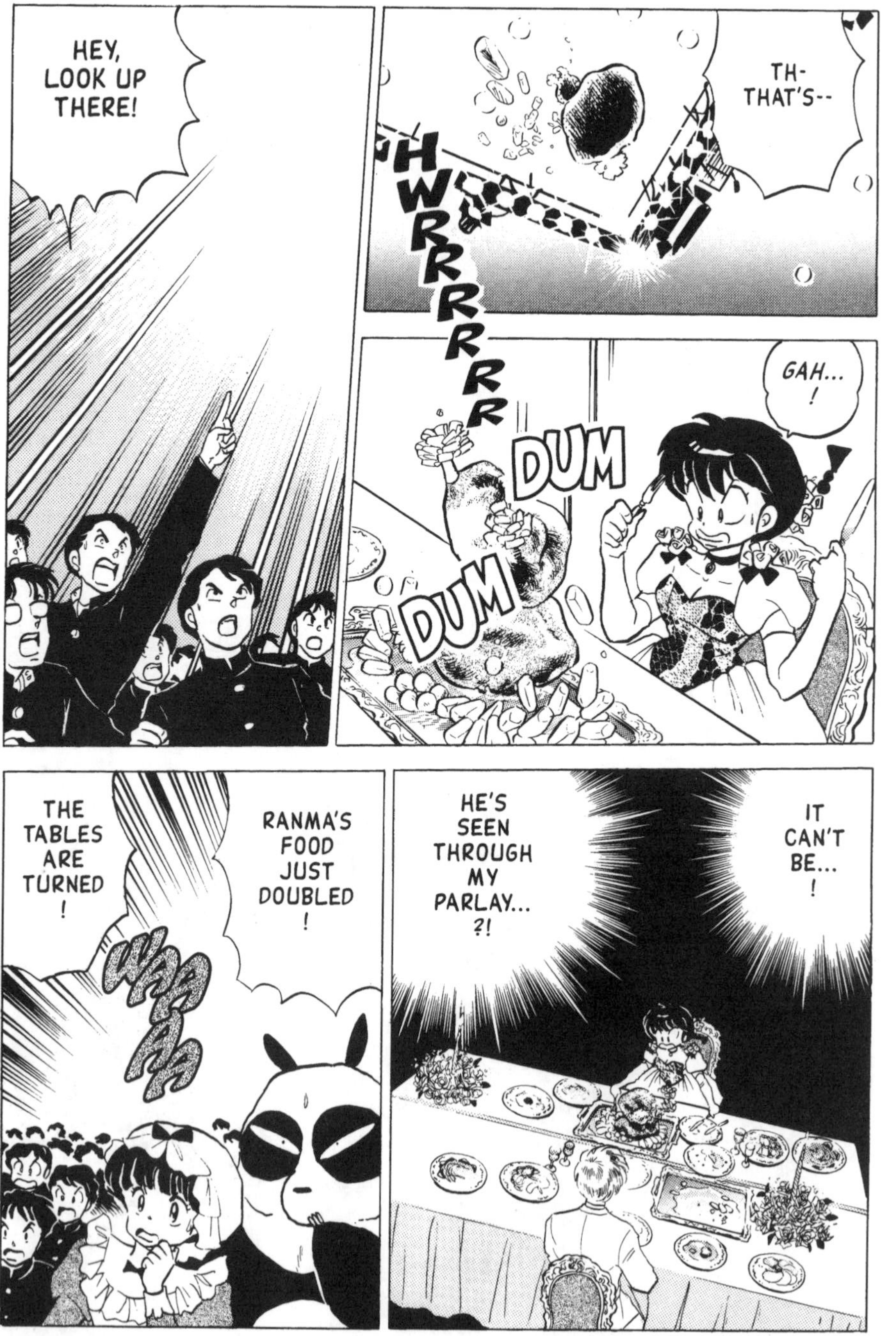
HEY, LOOK UP THERE!
TH- THAT'S--
HWRRRRRR
GAH...!
DUM
DUM
THE TABLES ARE TURNED!
RANMA'S FOOD JUST DOUBLED!
HE'S SEEN THROUGH MY PARLAY...?!
IT CAN'T BE...!

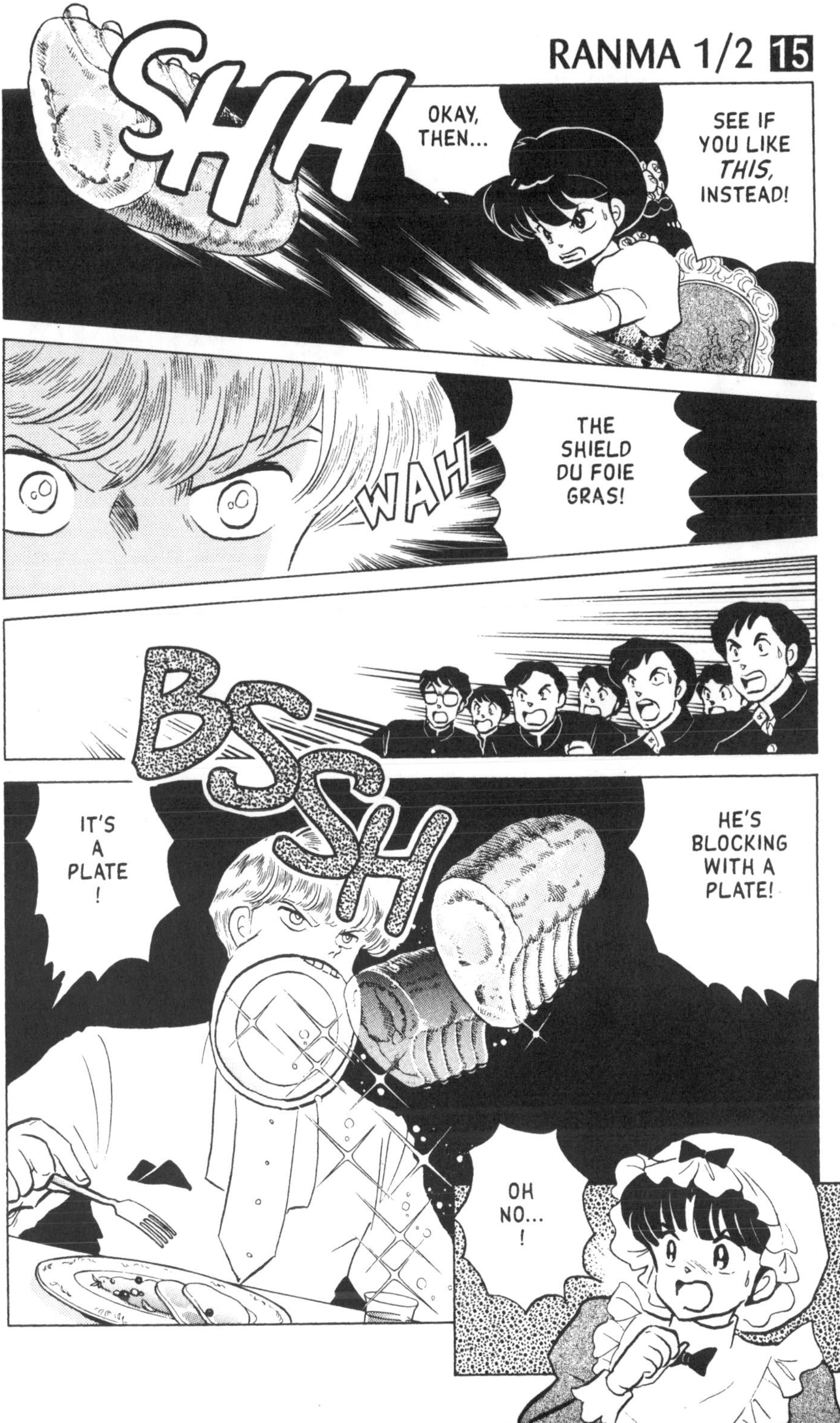
SHH
OKAY, THEN...
SEE IF YOU LIKE *THIS,* INSTEAD!
WAH
THE SHIELD DU FOIE GRAS!
BSSH
IT'S A PLATE!
HE'S BLOCKING WITH A PLATE!
OH NO...!

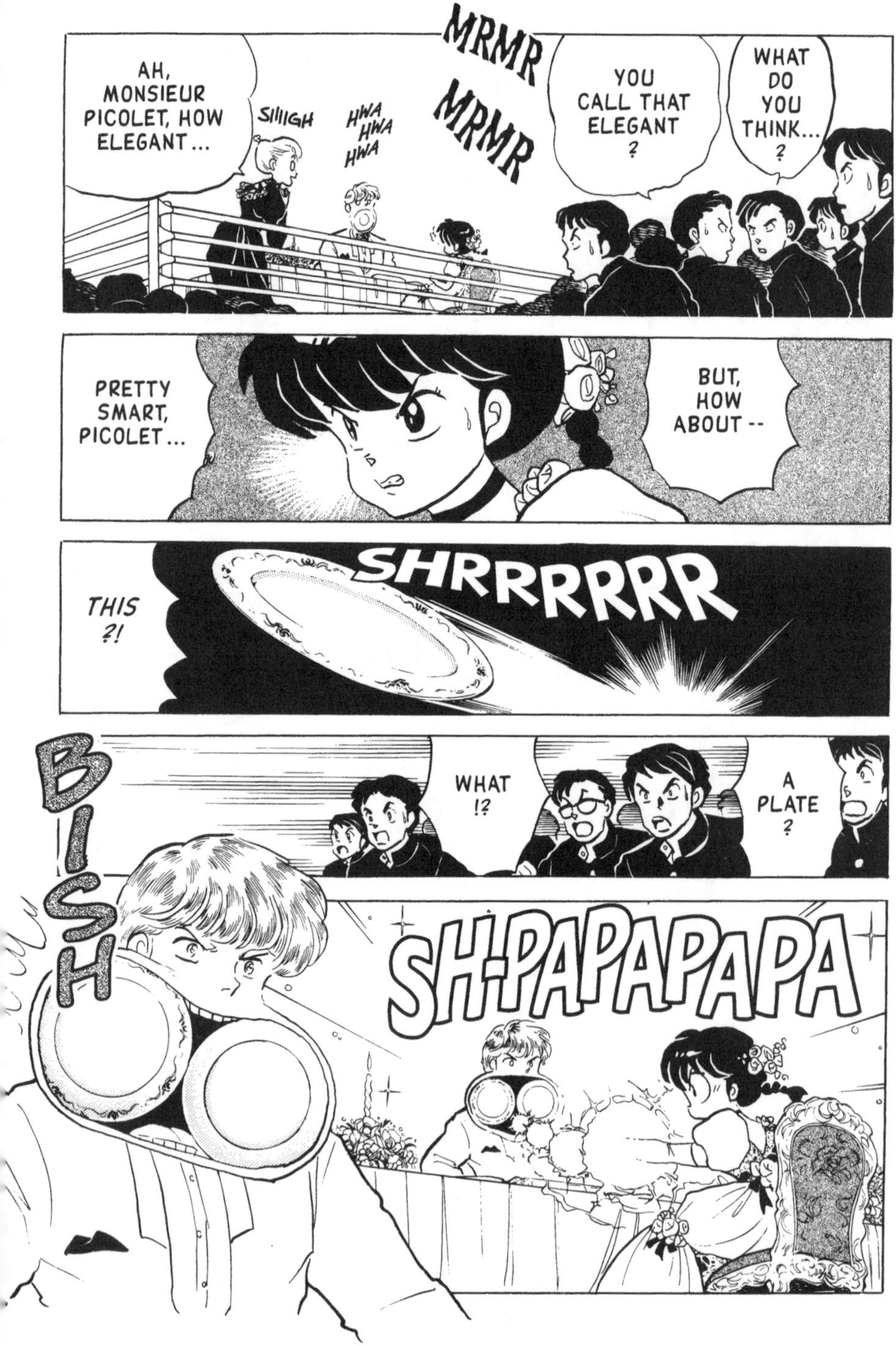
AH, MONSIEUR PICOLET, HOW ELEGANT...
SIIIIGH
HWA HWA HWA
MRMR MRMR
YOU CALL THAT ELEGANT?
WHAT DO YOU THINK...?
PRETTY SMART, PICOLET...
BUT, HOW ABOUT --
THIS?!
SHRRRRRR
WHAT!?
A PLATE?
BISH
SH-PAPAPAPA

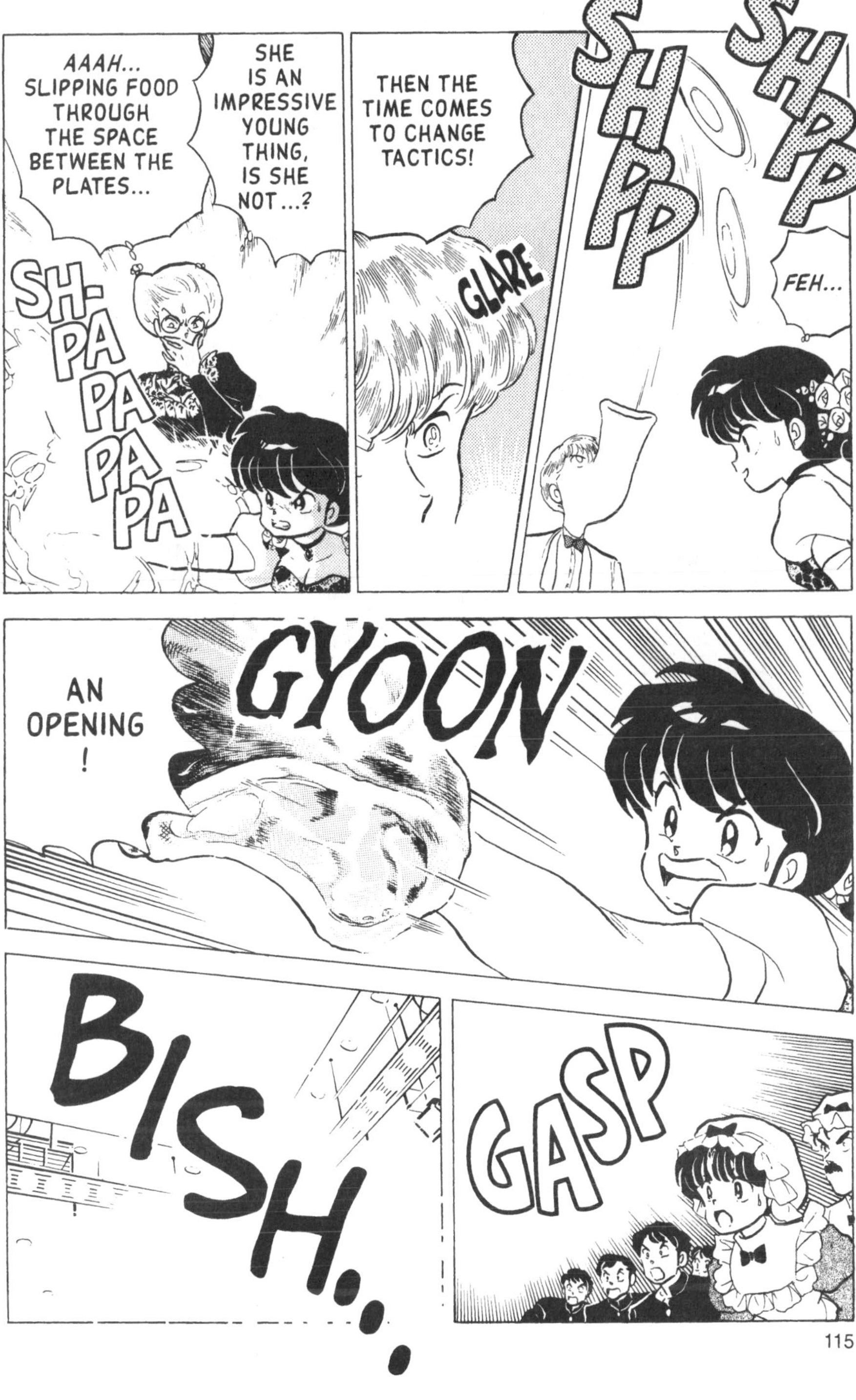
AAAH... SLIPPING FOOD THROUGH THE SPACE BETWEEN THE PLATES...
SHE IS AN IMPRESSIVE YOUNG THING, IS SHE NOT...?
SH-PA PA PA PA PA
THEN THE TIME COMES TO CHANGE TACTICS!
GLARE
SHPP SHPP
FEH...
AN OPENING!
GYOON
BISH...
GASP

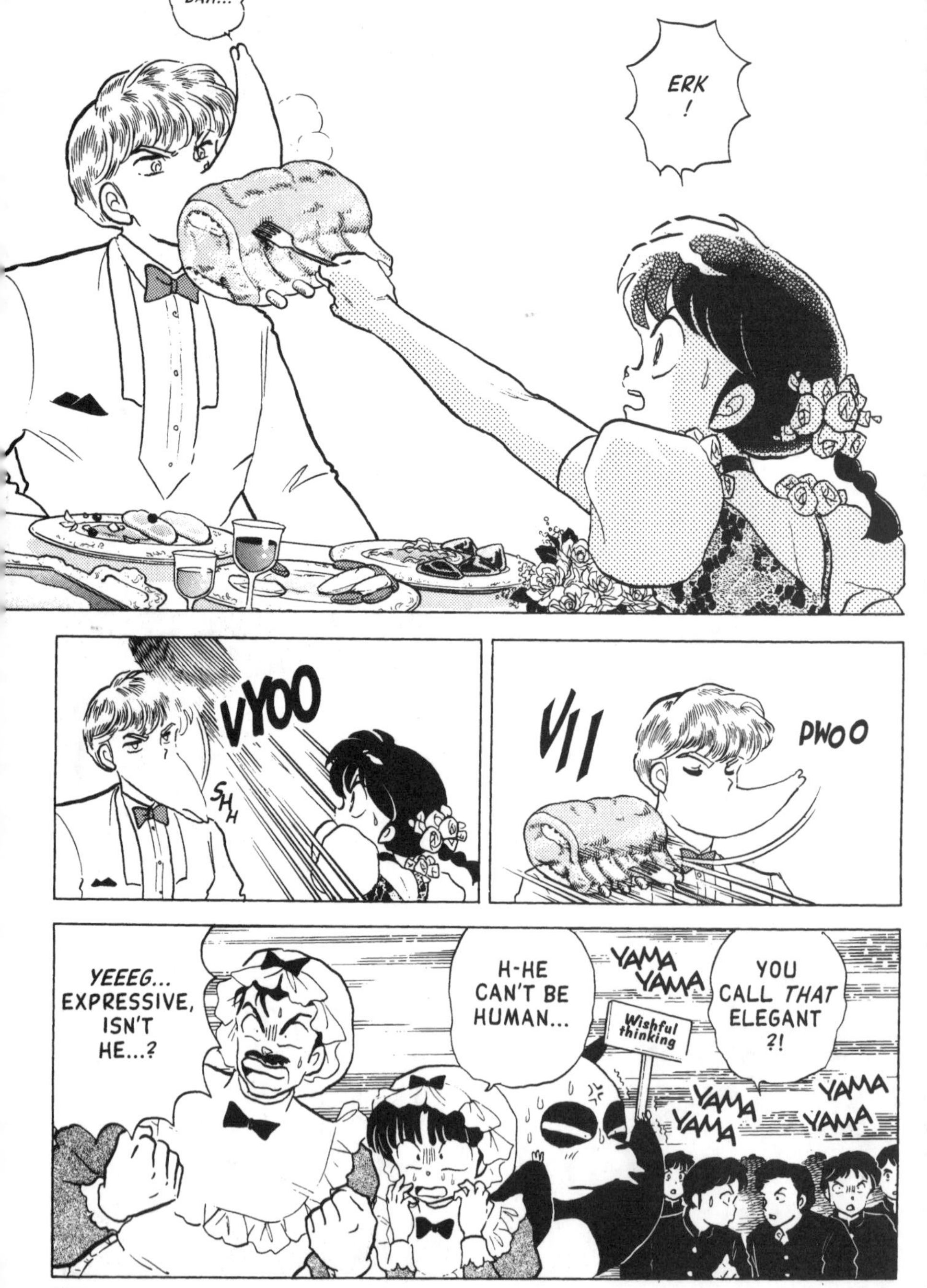

BAH...
ERK !
VYOO
SHH
VII
PWOO
YEEEG... EXPRESSIVE, ISN'T HE...?
H-HE CAN'T BE HUMAN...
YAMA YAMA
Wishful thinking
YOU CALL THAT ELEGANT ?!
YAMA YAMA
YAMA YAMA

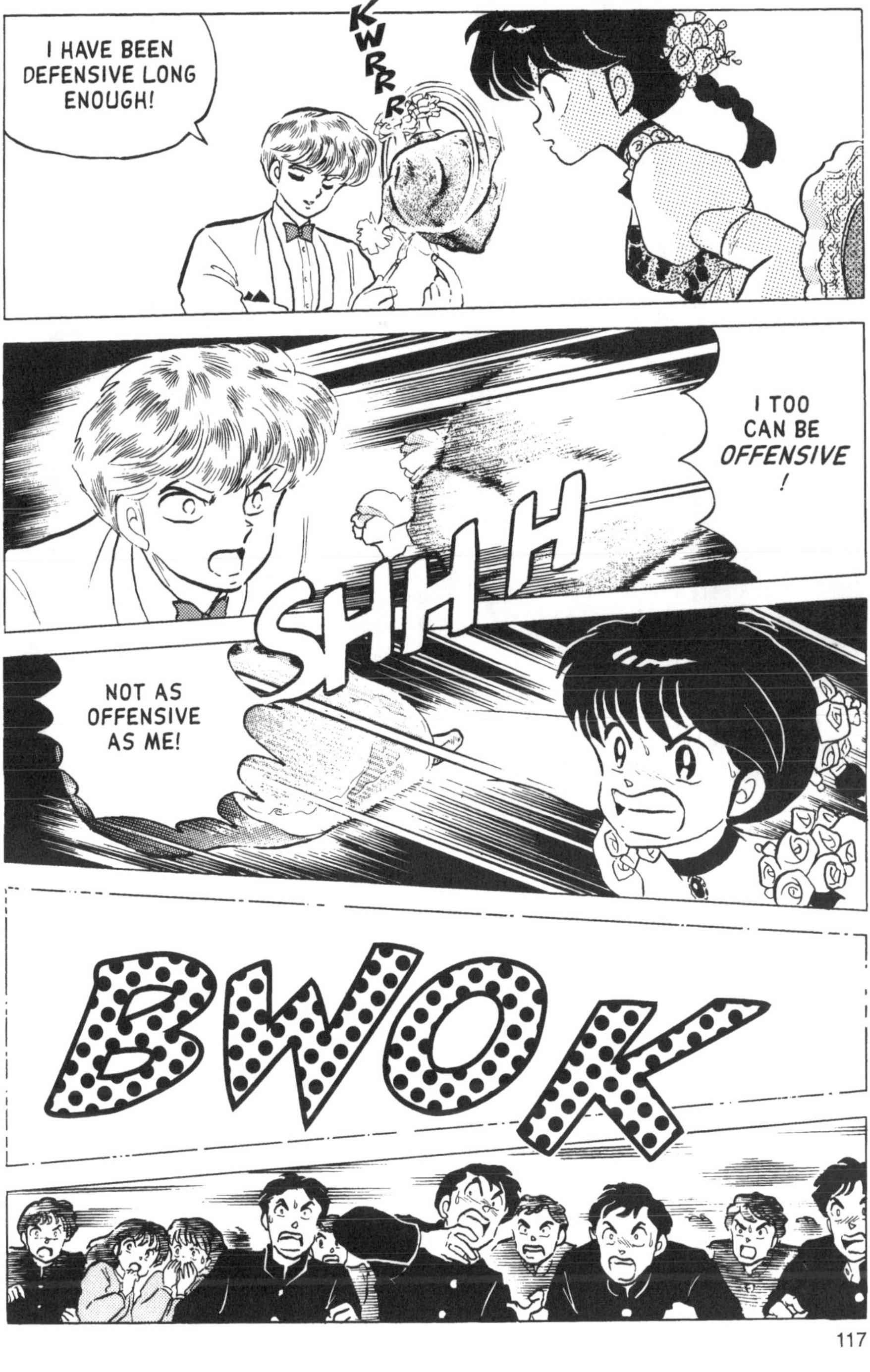
I HAVE BEEN DEFENSIVE LONG ENOUGH!
KWRRR
I TOO CAN BE OFFENSIVE!
SHHH
NOT AS OFFENSIVE AS ME!
BWOK

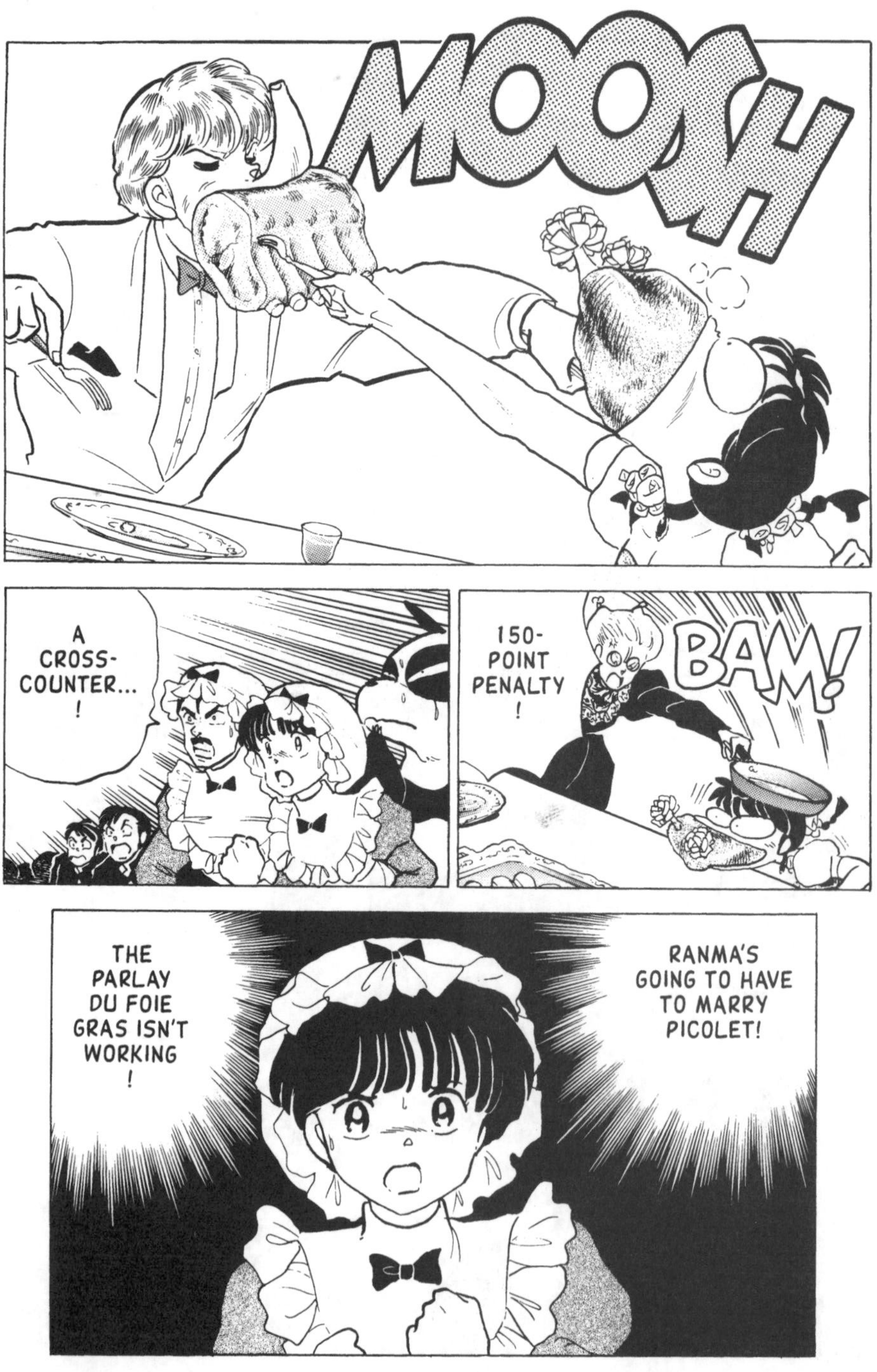
MOOSH
A CROSS-COUNTER... !
150-POINT PENALTY !
BAM!
THE PARLAY DU FOIE GRAS ISN'T WORKING !
RANMA'S GOING TO HAVE TO MARRY PICOLET!

Part 6

DO NOT DESSERT ME

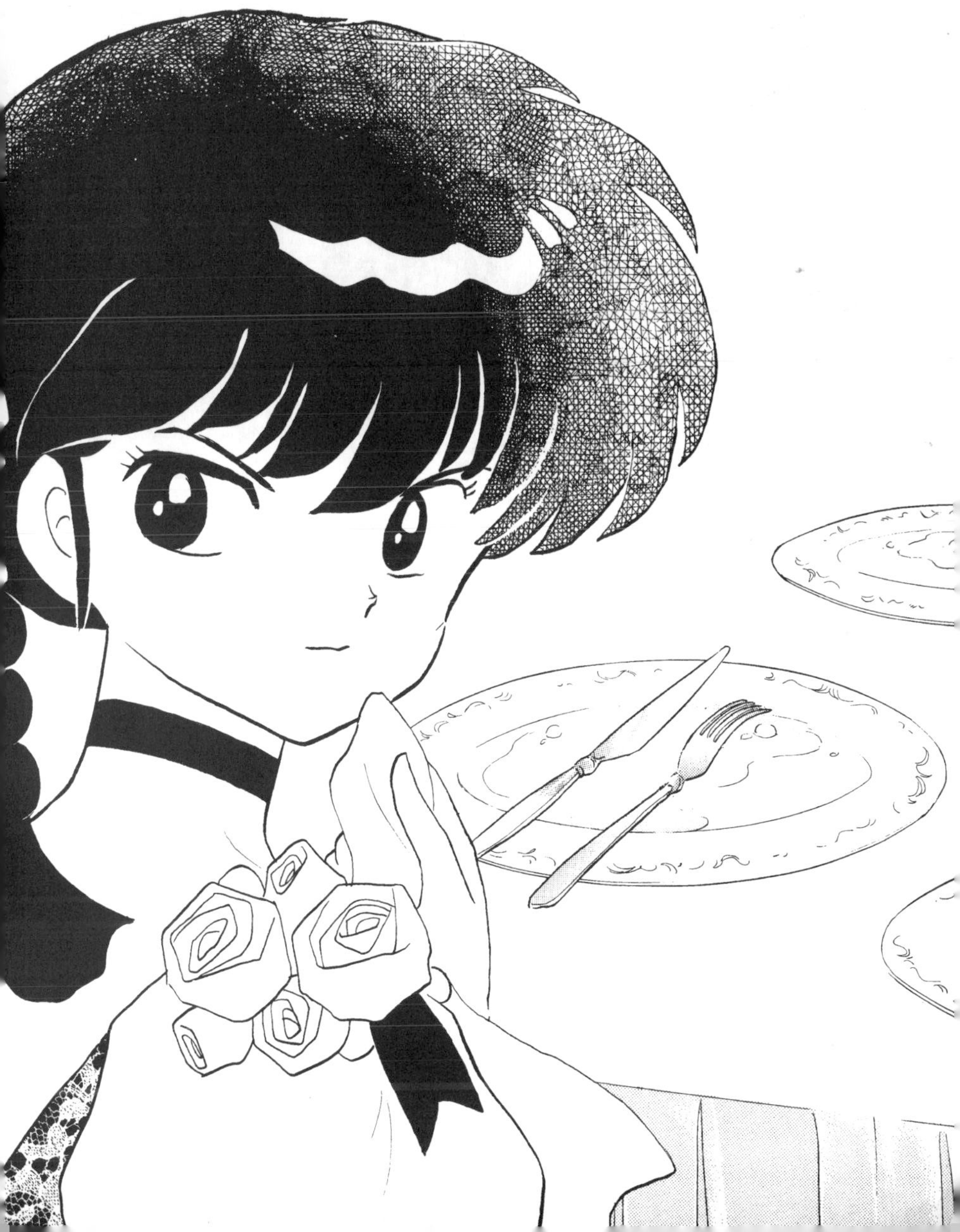

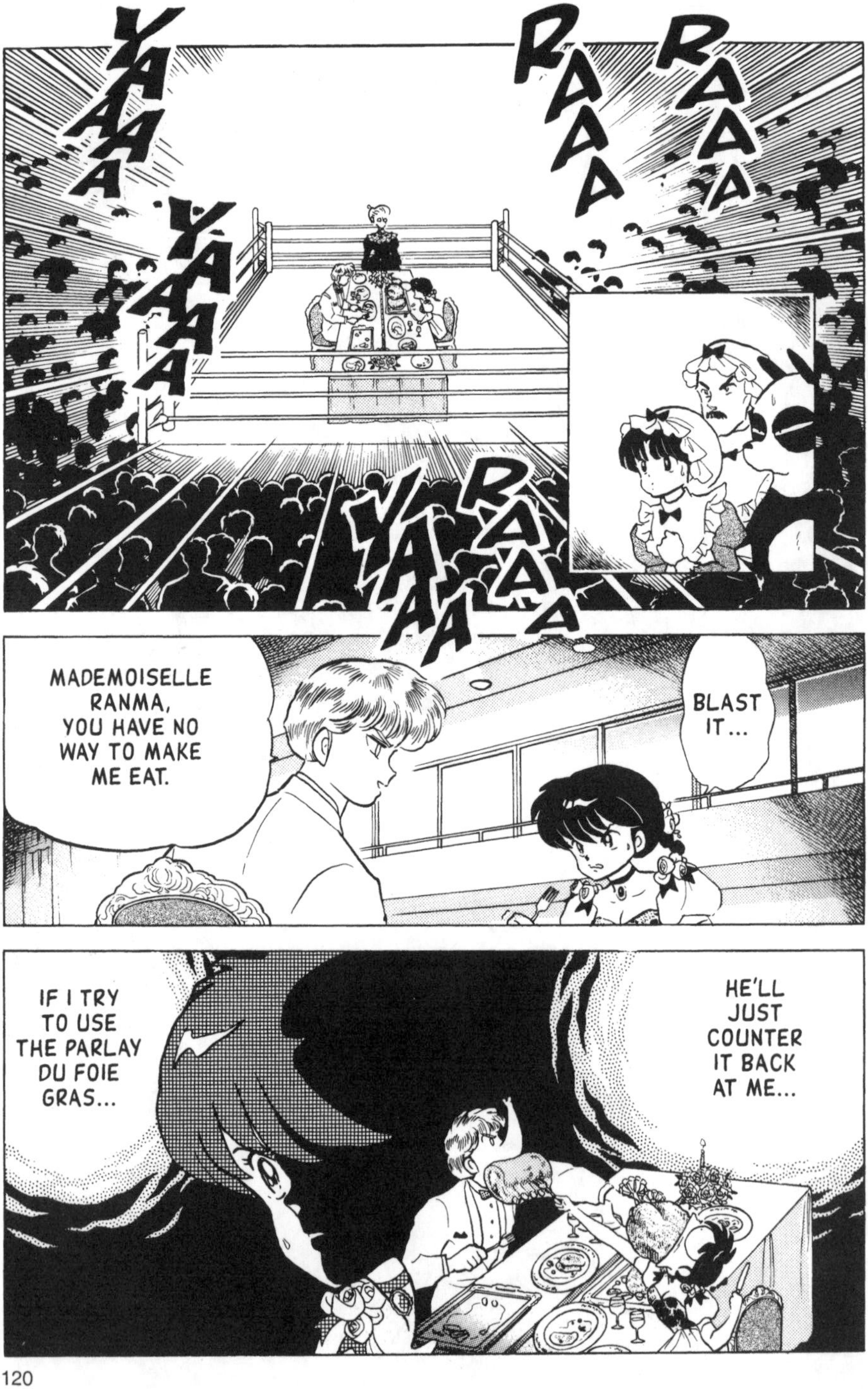

YAAAA
YAAAAA
RAAAA
RAAAA
YAAA
RAAAA
MADEMOISELLE RANMA, YOU HAVE NO WAY TO MAKE ME EAT.
BLAST IT...
IF I TRY TO USE THE PARLAY DU FOIE GRAS...
HE'LL JUST COUNTER IT BACK AT ME...

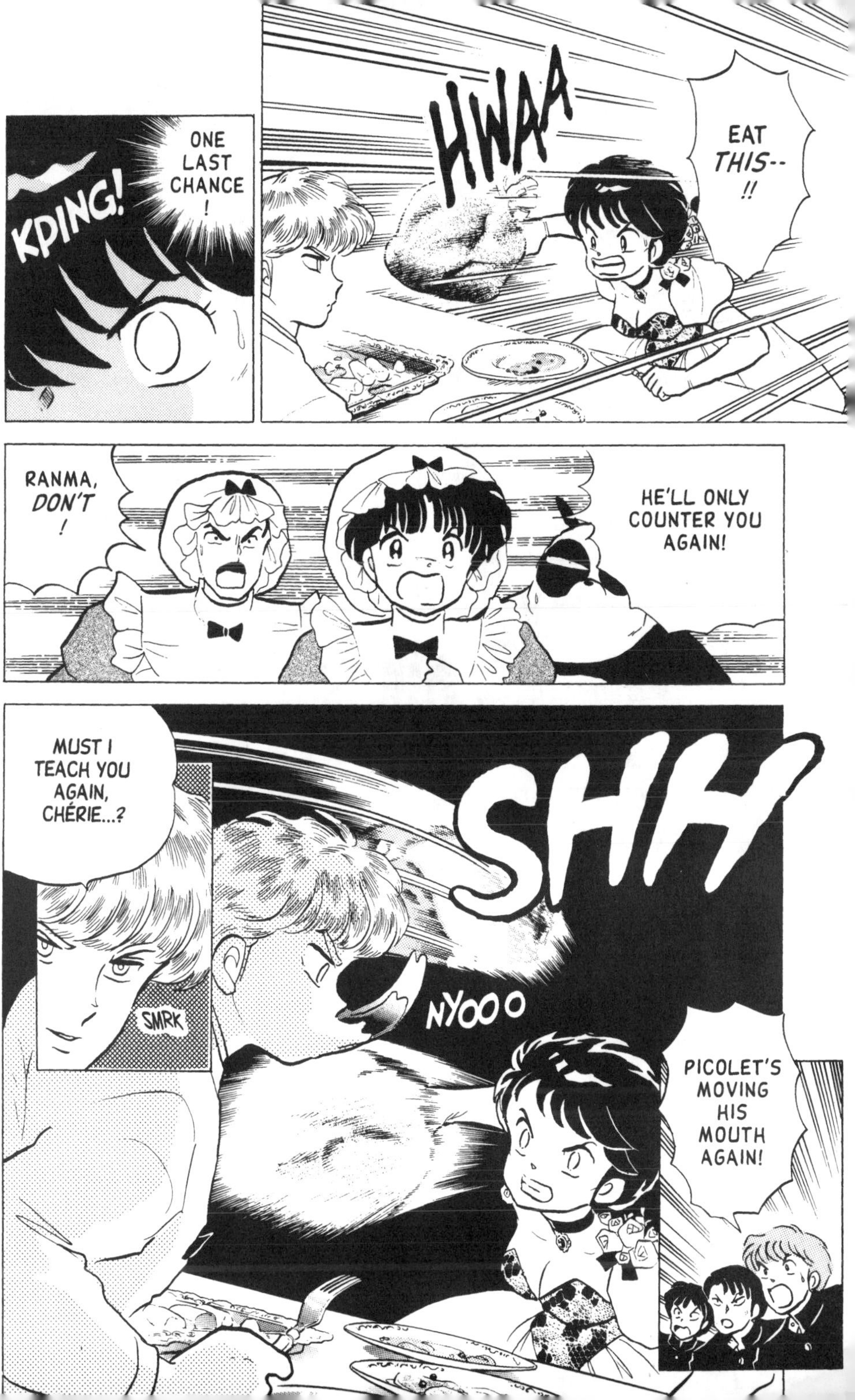
KPING!
ONE LAST CHANCE !
HWAA
EAT *THIS*-- !!
RANMA, *DON'T* !
HE'LL ONLY COUNTER YOU AGAIN!
MUST I TEACH YOU AGAIN, CHÉRIE...?
SHH
SMRK
NYOOO
PICOLET'S MOVING HIS MOUTH AGAIN!

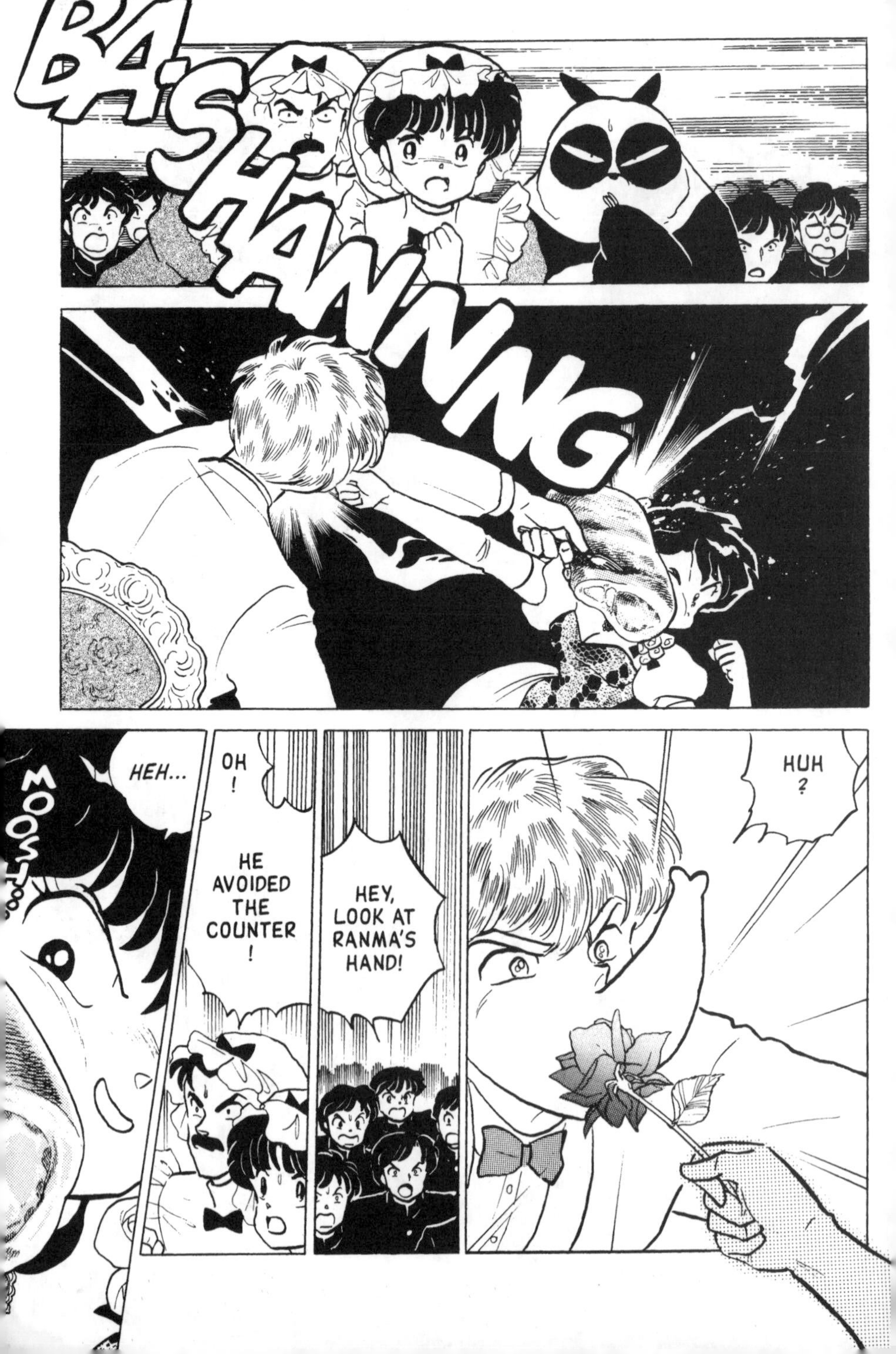
BA-SHANNNG
WOOSH...
HEH...
OH!
HE AVOIDED THE COUNTER!
HEY, LOOK AT RANMA'S HAND!
HUH?

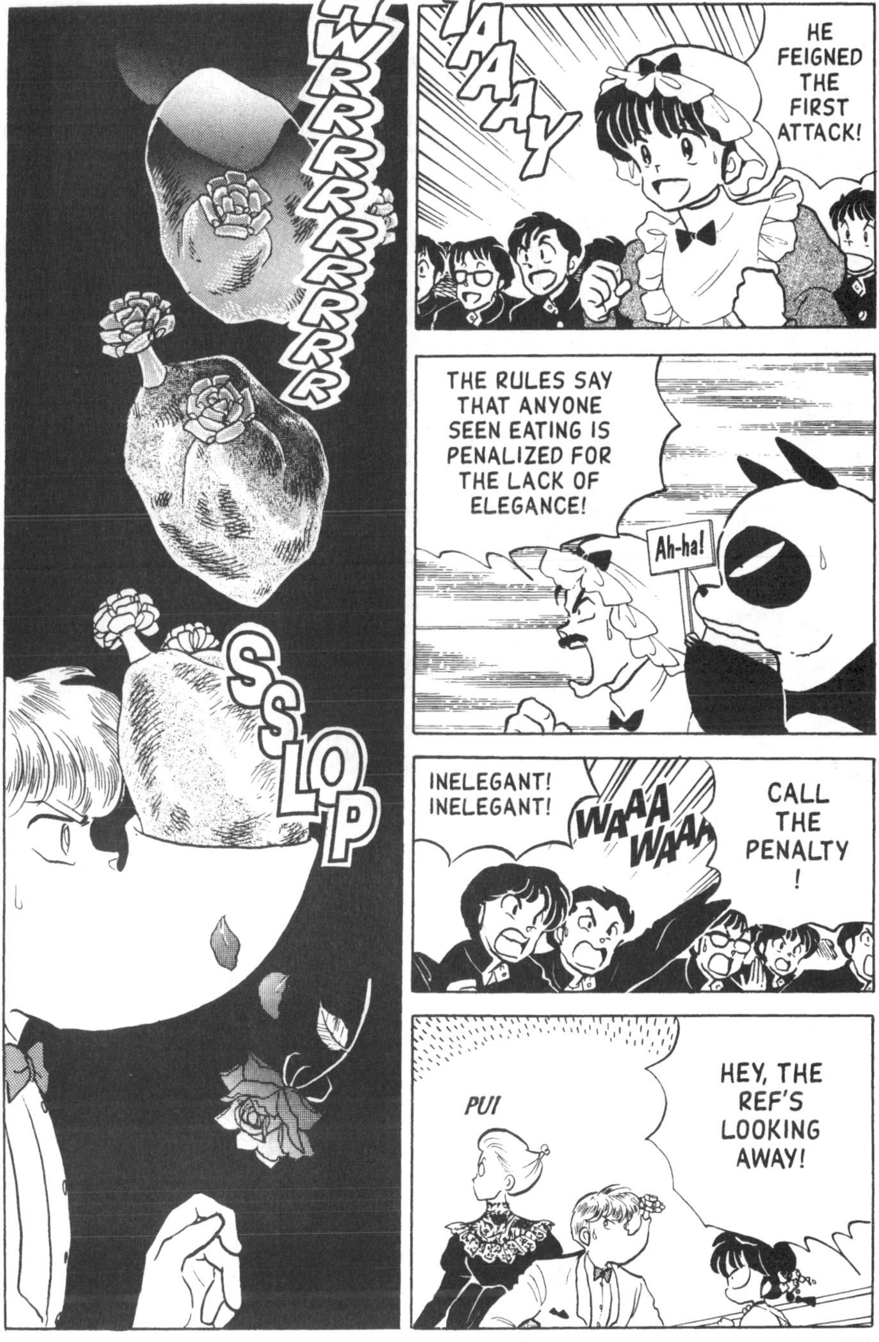
HWRRRRRRRRRR
SSLOP
YAAAY
HE FEIGNED THE FIRST ATTACK!
THE RULES SAY THAT ANYONE SEEN EATING IS PENALIZED FOR THE LACK OF ELEGANCE!
Ah-ha!
INELEGANT! INELEGANT!
WAAA WAAA
CALL THE PENALTY!
PUI
HEY, THE REF'S LOOKING AWAY!

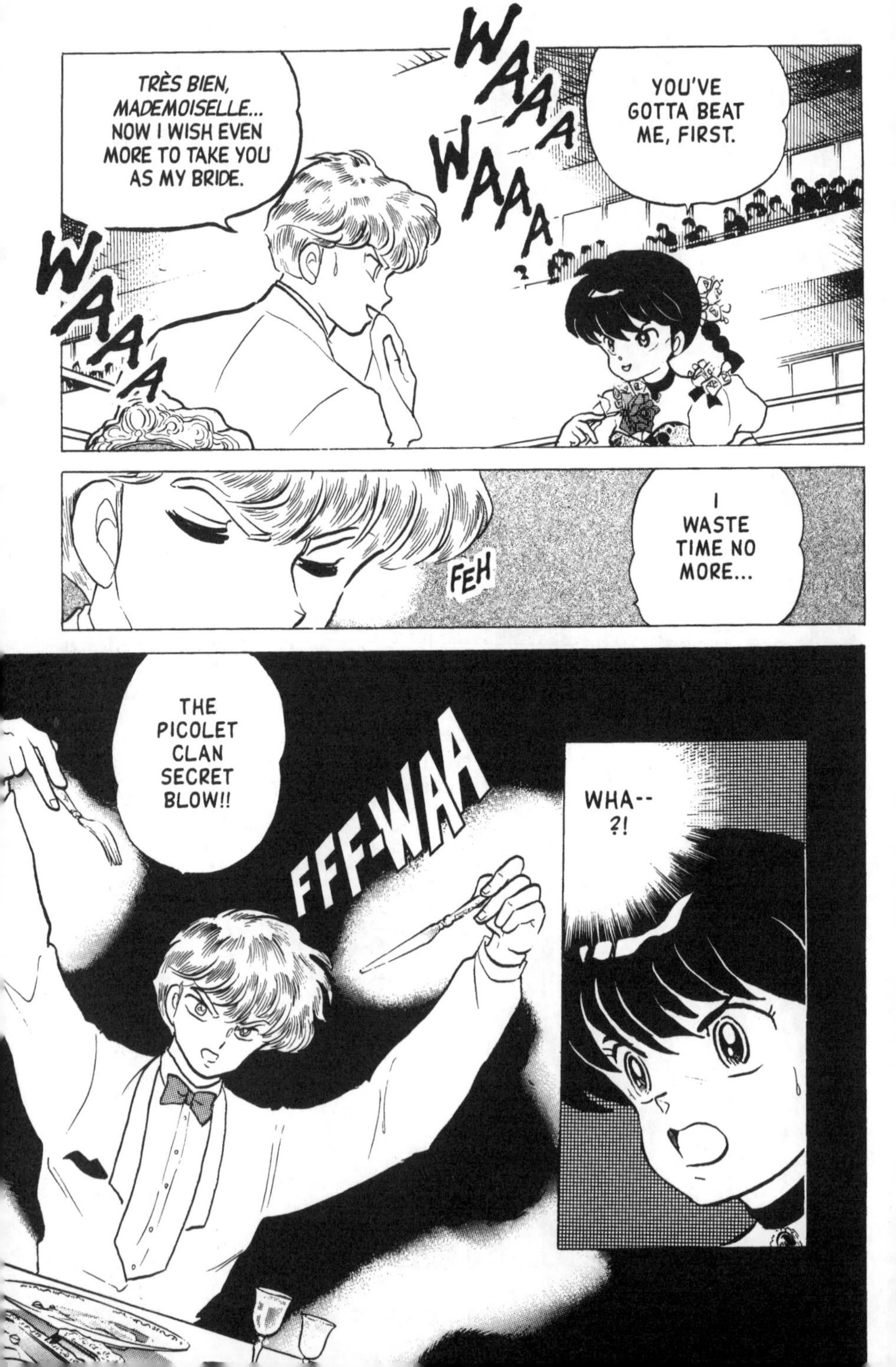
TRÈS BIEN, MADEMOISELLE... NOW I WISH EVEN MORE TO TAKE YOU AS MY BRIDE.
WAAAA
WAAAA
WAAAA
YOU'VE GOTTA BEAT ME, FIRST.
FEH
I WASTE TIME NO MORE...
THE PICOLET CLAN SECRET BLOW!!
FFF-WAA
WHA-- ?!

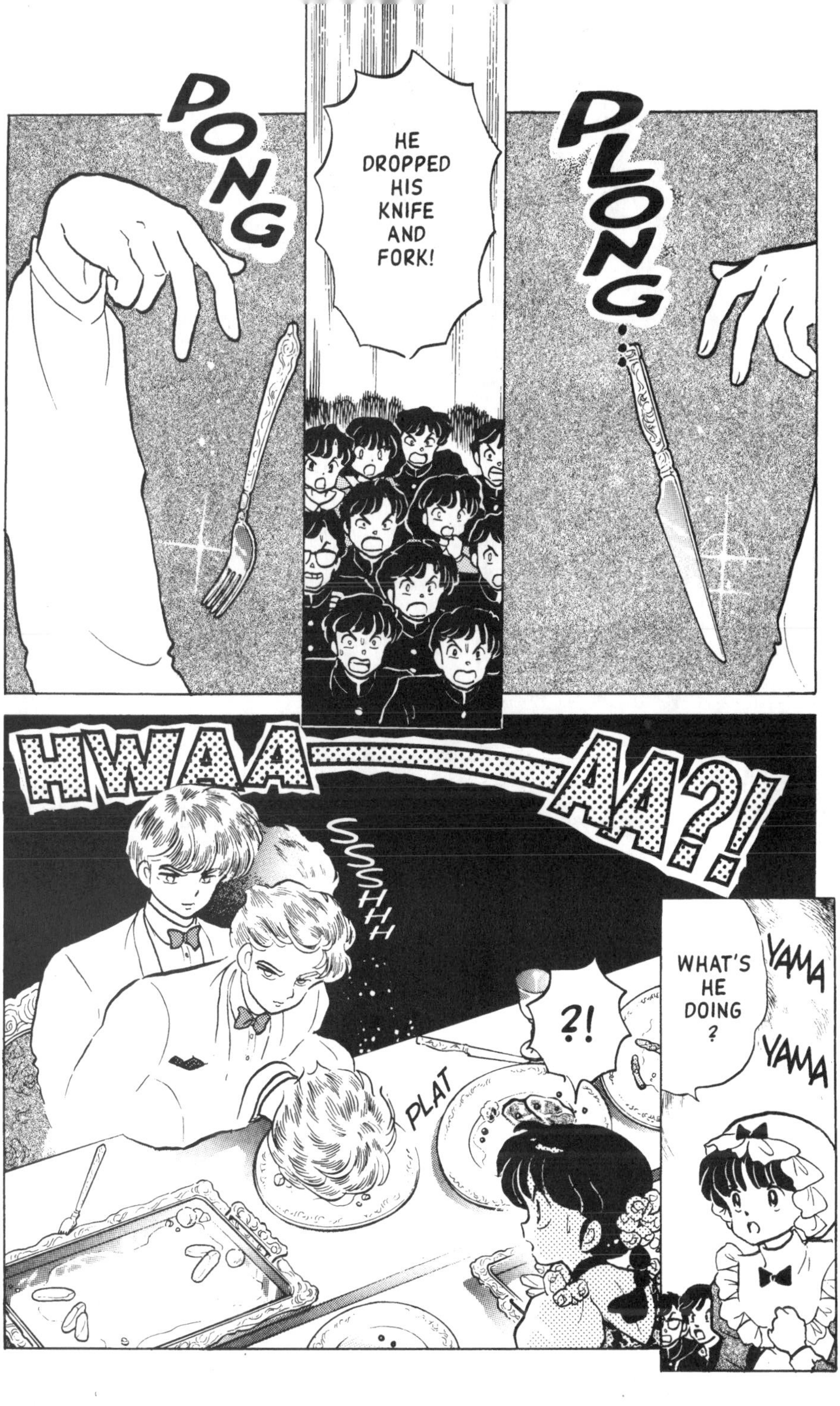
PONG
HE DROPPED HIS KNIFE AND FORK!
PLONG...
HWAA-AA?!
SSSSHHH
PLAT
?!
WHAT'S HE DOING?
YAMA
YAMA

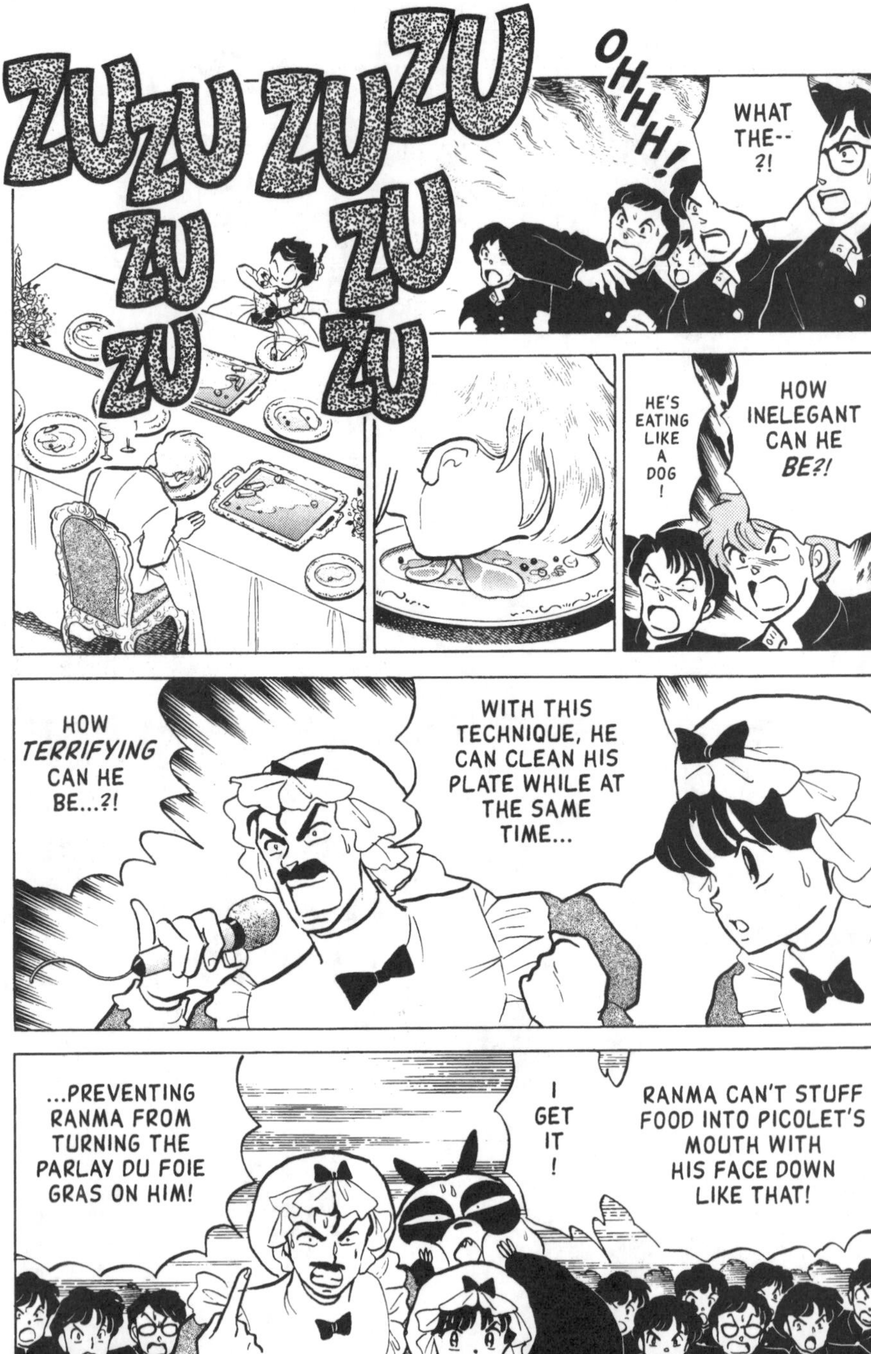

ZUZU ZUZU ZU ZU ZU ZU
OHHH!
WHAT THE--?!
HE'S EATING LIKE A DOG!
HOW INELEGANT CAN HE *BE?!*
HOW *TERRIFYING* CAN HE BE...?!
WITH THIS TECHNIQUE, HE CAN CLEAN HIS PLATE WHILE AT THE SAME TIME...
...PREVENTING RANMA FROM TURNING THE PARLAY DU FOIE GRAS ON HIM!
I GET IT!
RANMA CAN'T STUFF FOOD INTO PICOLET'S MOUTH WITH HIS FACE DOWN LIKE THAT!

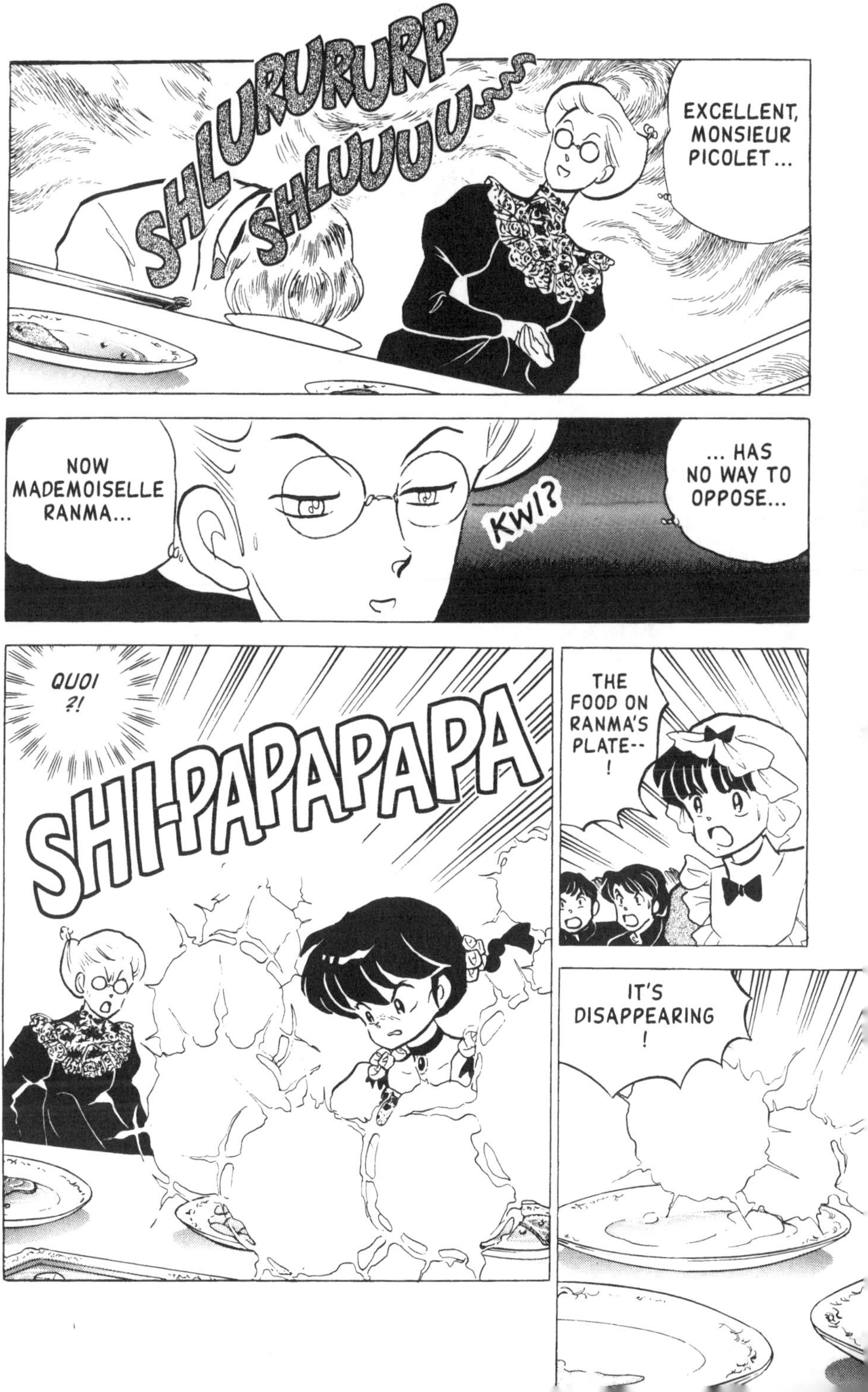
SHLURURURP
SHLUUUU...
EXCELLENT, MONSIEUR PICOLET...
NOW MADEMOISELLE RANMA...
KWI?
... HAS NO WAY TO OPPOSE...
QUOI ?!
SHI-PAPAPAPA
THE FOOD ON RANMA'S PLATE-- !
IT'S DISAPPEARING !

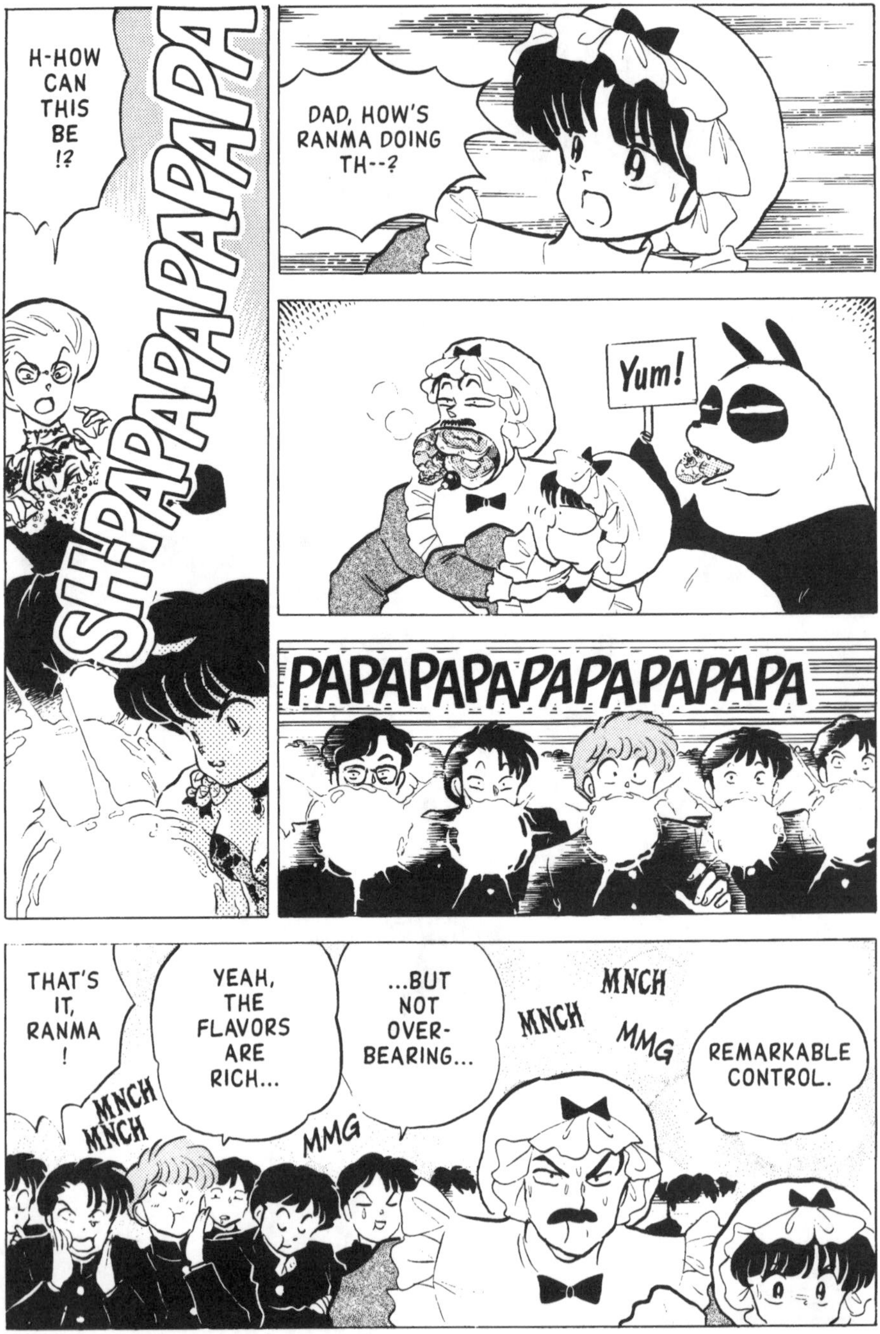

H-HOW CAN THIS BE !?
SHPAPAPAPAPAPA
DAD, HOW'S RANMA DOING TH--?
Yum!
PAPAPAPAPAPAPAPAPA
THAT'S IT, RANMA !
YEAH, THE FLAVORS ARE RICH...
...BUT NOT OVER-BEARING...
MNCH
MNCH
MMG
REMARKABLE CONTROL.
MNCH MNCH
MMG

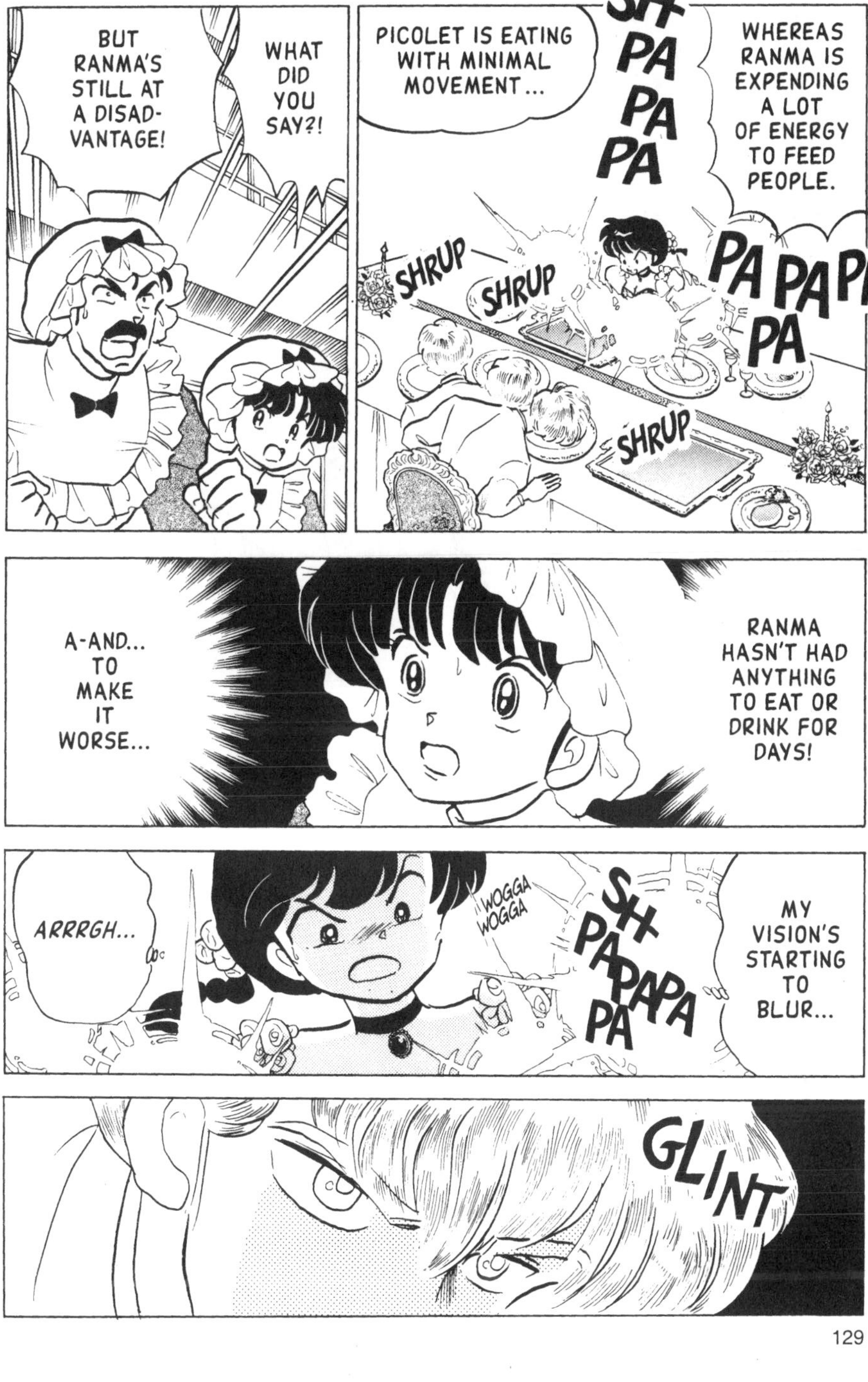
BUT RANMA'S STILL AT A DISAD-VANTAGE!
WHAT DID YOU SAY?!
PICOLET IS EATING WITH MINIMAL MOVEMENT...
SH PA PA PA
WHEREAS RANMA IS EXPENDING A LOT OF ENERGY TO FEED PEOPLE.
SHRUP
SHRUP
PA PA PA PA
SHRUP
A-AND... TO MAKE IT WORSE...
RANMA HASN'T HAD ANYTHING TO EAT OR DRINK FOR DAYS!
ARRRGH...
WOGGA WOGGA
SH PAPAPAPA
MY VISION'S STARTING TO BLUR...
GLINT

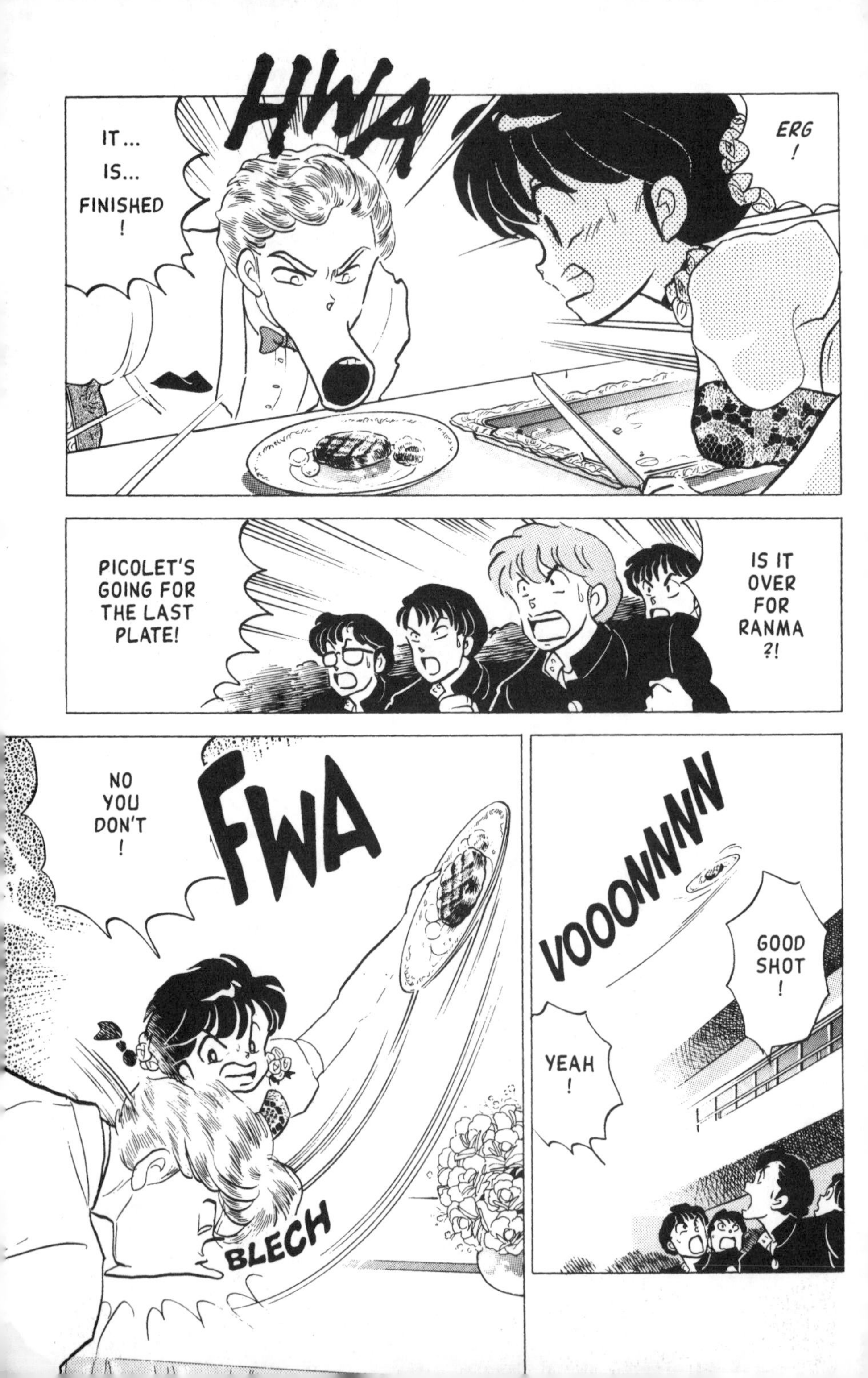
HWA
IT... IS... FINISHED!
ERG!
PICOLET'S GOING FOR THE LAST PLATE!
IS IT OVER FOR RANMA?!
NO YOU DON'T!
FWA
BLECH
VOOONNNN
GOOD SHOT!
YEAH!

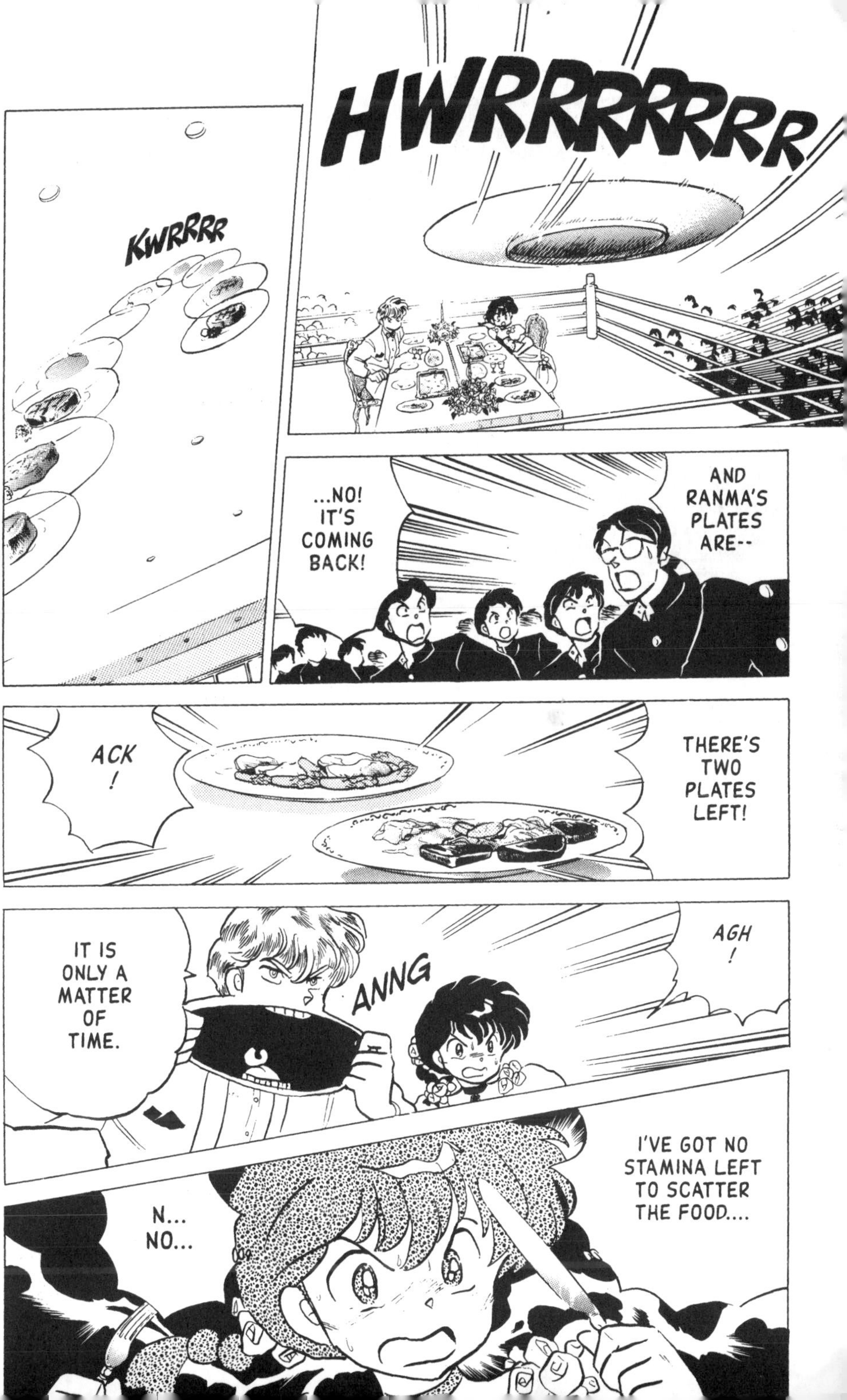
KWRRRR
HWRRRRRRRR
...NO! IT'S COMING BACK!
AND RANMA'S PLATES ARE--
ACK!
THERE'S TWO PLATES LEFT!
IT IS ONLY A MATTER OF TIME.
ANNG
AGH!
N... NO...
I'VE GOT NO STAMINA LEFT TO SCATTER THE FOOD....

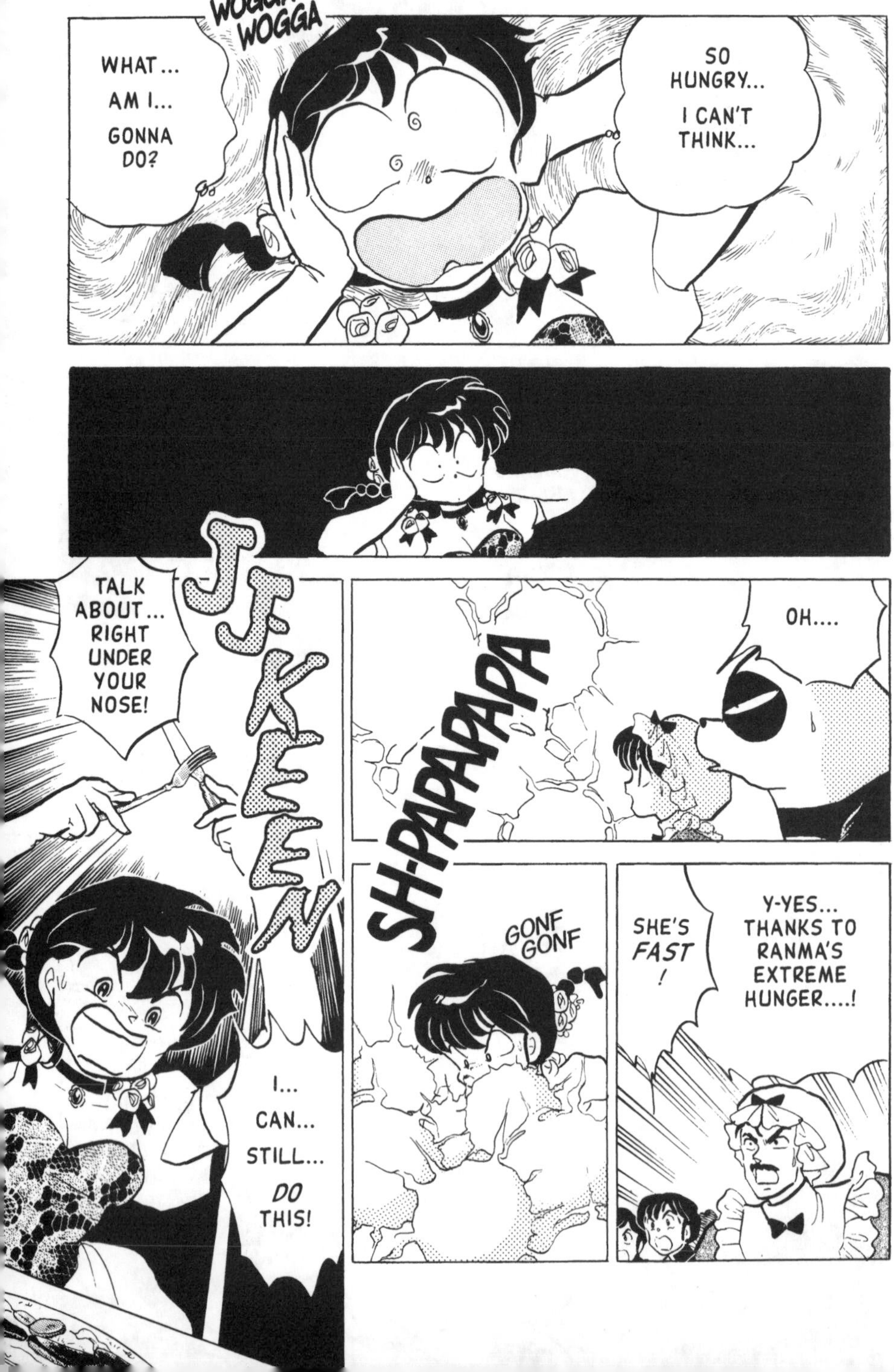

WOGGA WOGGA
WHAT... AM I... GONNA DO?
SO HUNGRY... I CAN'T THINK...
TALK ABOUT... RIGHT UNDER YOUR NOSE!
JJKEEN
I... CAN... STILL... *DO* THIS!
OH....
SH-PAPAPAPA
GONF GONF
SHE'S *FAST*!
Y-YES... THANKS TO RANMA'S EXTREME HUNGER....!

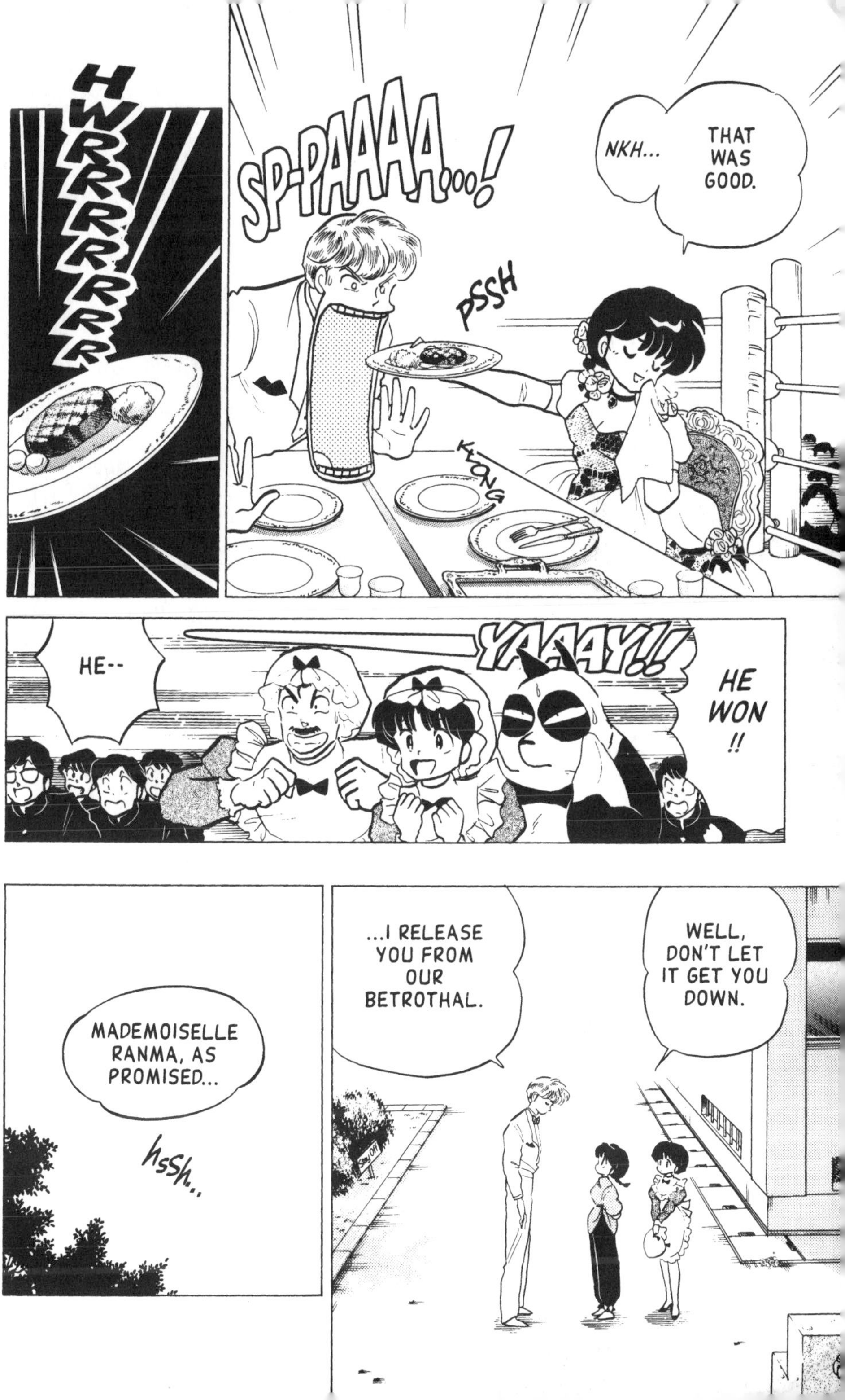
HWRRRRRRR
SP-PAAAA...!
NKH...
THAT WAS GOOD.
PSSH
KLONG
HE--
YAAAY!!
HE WON!!
MADEMOISELLE RANMA, AS PROMISED...
hssh..
...I RELEASE YOU FROM OUR BETROTHAL.
WELL, DON'T LET IT GET YOU DOWN.

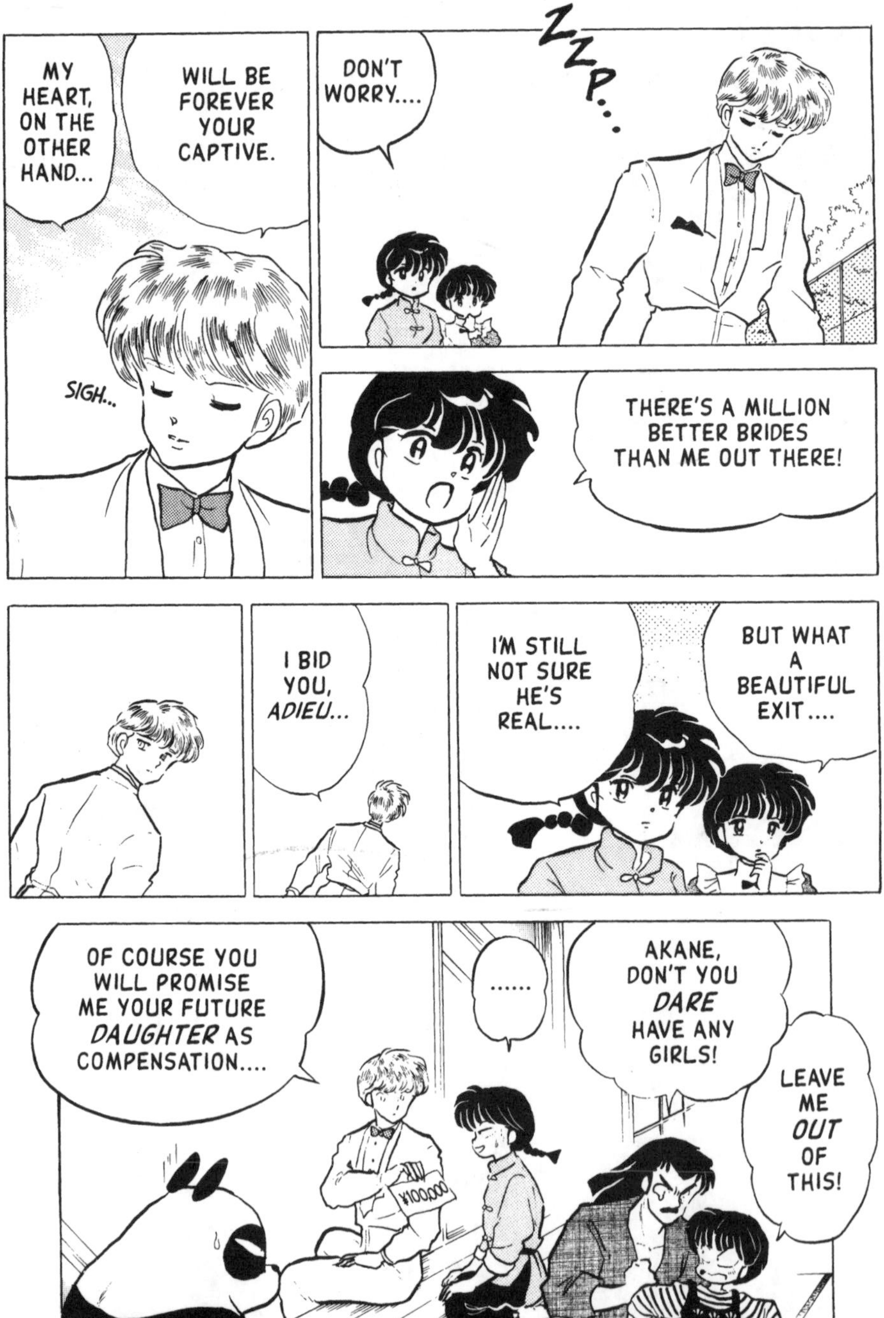
MY HEART, ON THE OTHER HAND...
WILL BE FOREVER YOUR CAPTIVE.
SIGH...
DON'T WORRY....
ZZZP...
THERE'S A MILLION BETTER BRIDES THAN ME OUT THERE!
I BID YOU, *ADIEU*...
I'M STILL NOT SURE HE'S REAL....
BUT WHAT A BEAUTIFUL EXIT....
OF COURSE YOU WILL PROMISE ME YOUR FUTURE *DAUGHTER* AS COMPENSATION....
¥100,000
......
AKANE, DON'T YOU *DARE* HAVE ANY GIRLS!
LEAVE ME *OUT* OF THIS!

Part 9
HAND-ME-DOWN RANMA

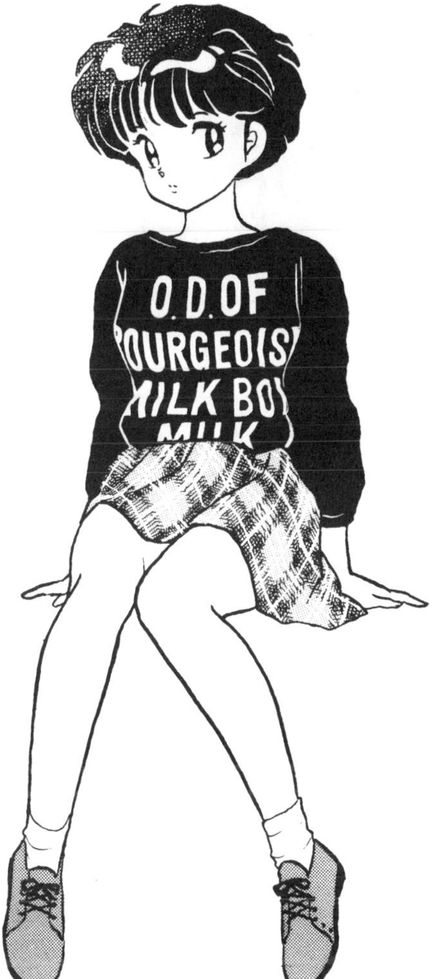
O.D.OF
OURGEOIS
MILK BO

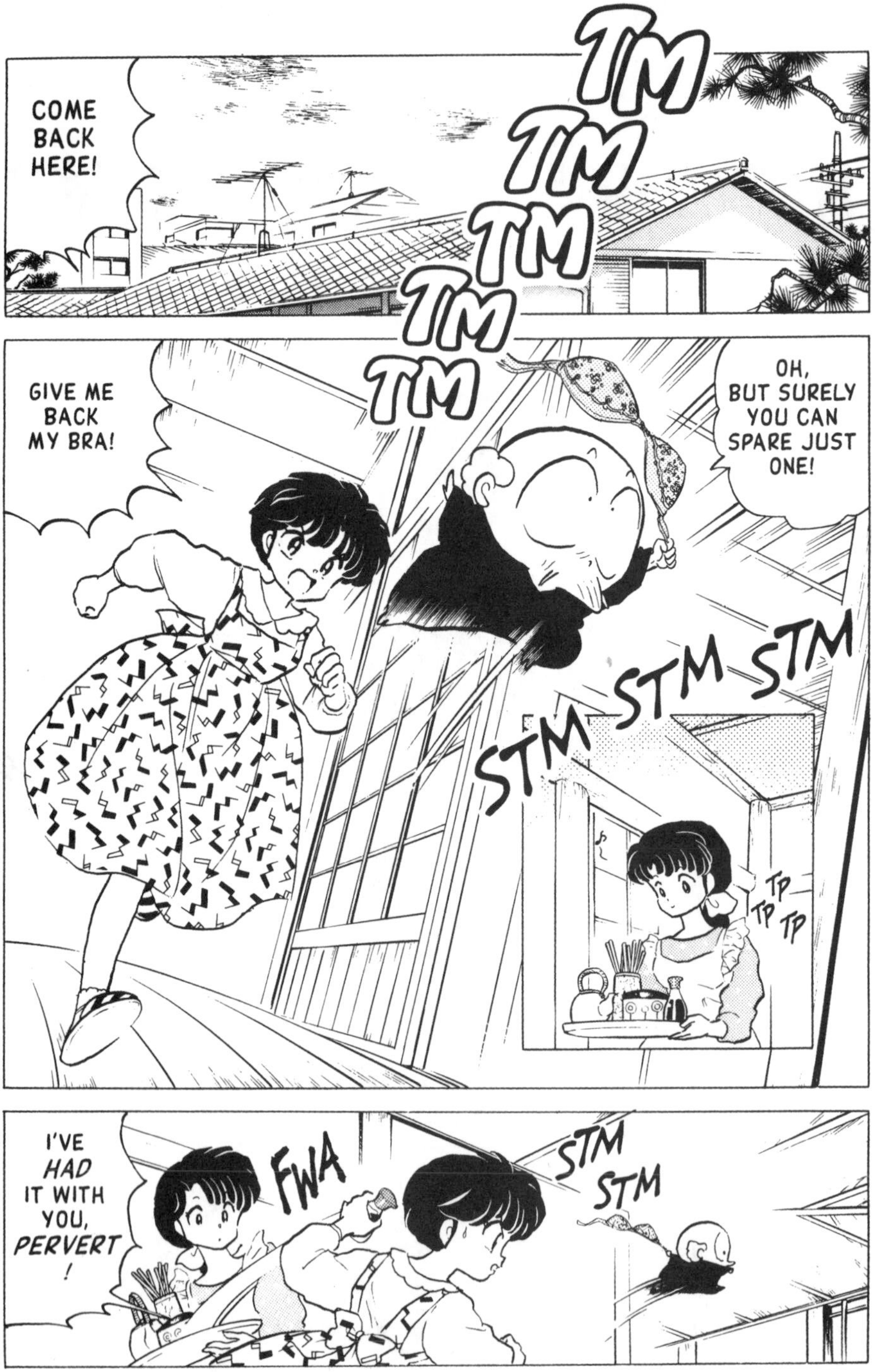
COME BACK HERE!
TM TM TM TM TM
GIVE ME BACK MY BRA!
OH, BUT SURELY YOU CAN SPARE JUST ONE!
STM STM STM STM
TP TP TP TP
I'VE *HAD* IT WITH YOU, *PERVERT*!
FWA
STM STM

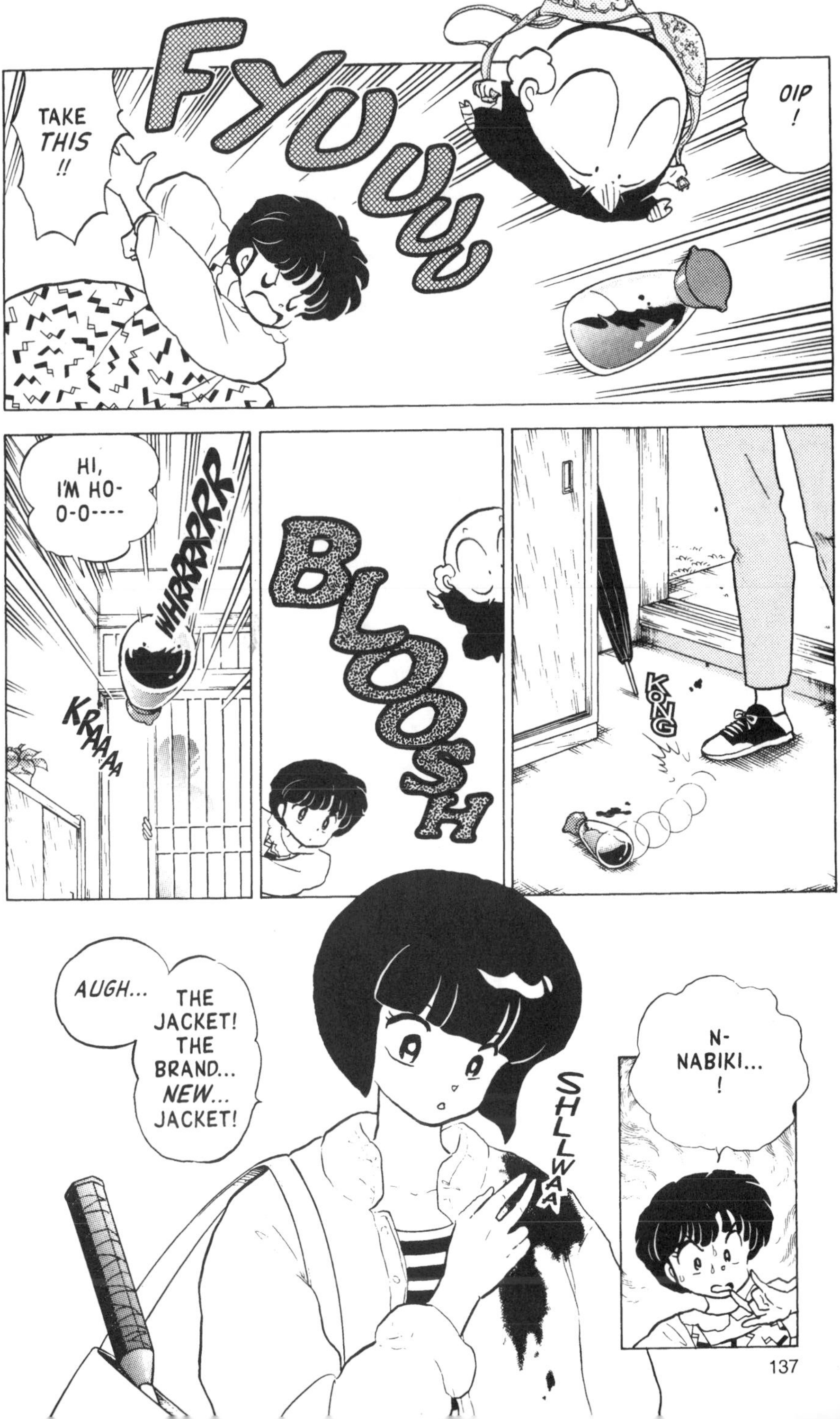
FYUUUU
TAKE THIS !!
OIP !
HI, I'M HO-O-O----
WHRRRRRRR
KRAAAAA
BLOOSH
KONG
AUGH...
THE JACKET! THE BRAND... NEW... JACKET!
SHLLWAA
N-NABIKI... !

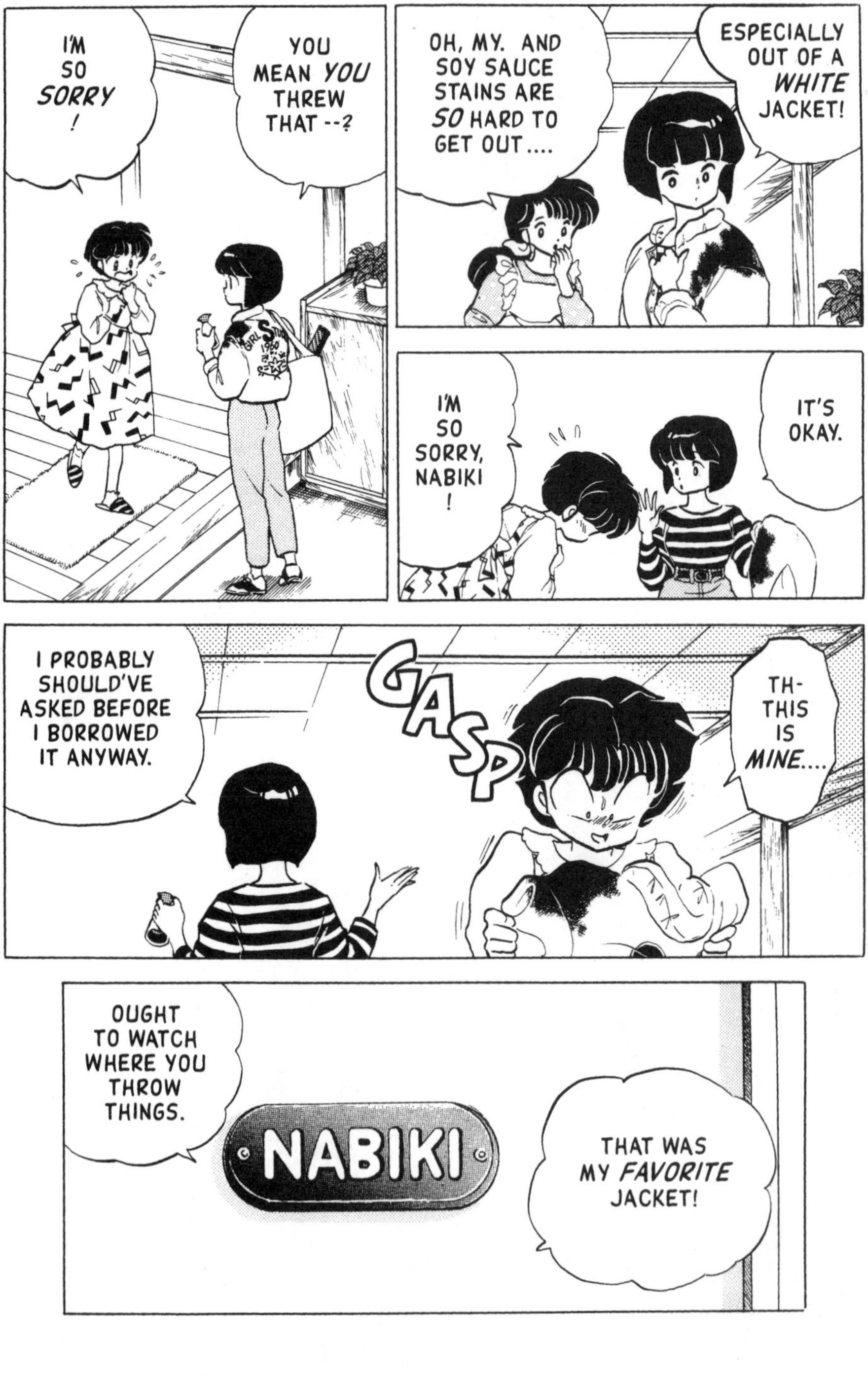
I'M SO SORRY!
YOU MEAN YOU THREW THAT --?
OH, MY. AND SOY SAUCE STAINS ARE SO HARD TO GET OUT....
ESPECIALLY OUT OF A WHITE JACKET!
I'M SO SORRY, NABIKI!
IT'S OKAY.
I PROBABLY SHOULD'VE ASKED BEFORE I BORROWED IT ANYWAY.
GASP
TH-THIS IS MINE....
OUGHT TO WATCH WHERE YOU THROW THINGS.
NABIKI
THAT WAS MY FAVORITE JACKET!

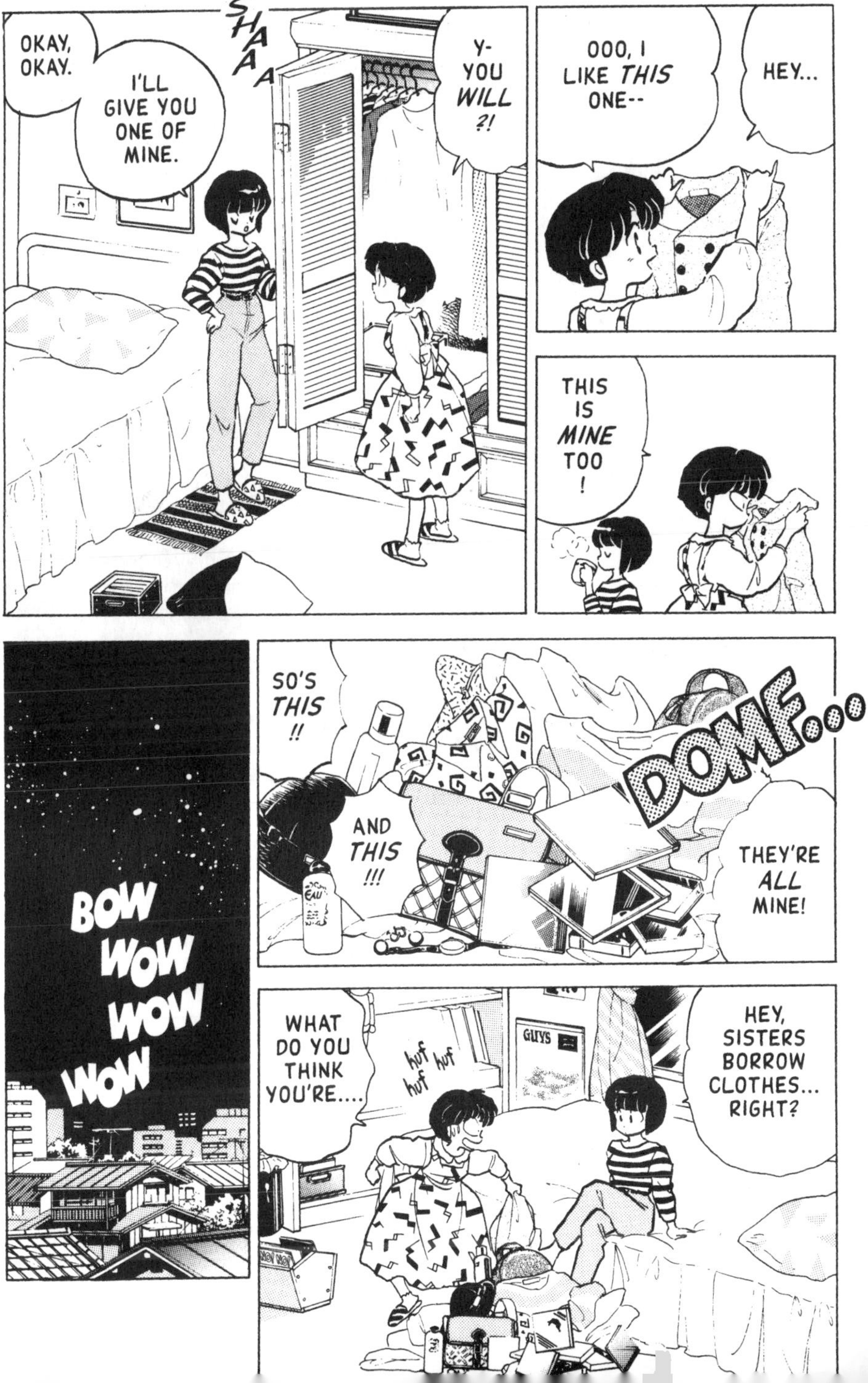
OKAY, OKAY.
I'LL GIVE YOU ONE OF MINE.
SHAAA
Y-YOU WILL ?!
OOO, I LIKE THIS ONE--
HEY...
THIS IS MINE TOO !
BOW WOW WOW WOW
SO'S THIS !!
AND THIS !!!
DOMF...
THEY'RE ALL MINE!
WHAT DO YOU THINK YOU'RE....
huf huf huf
GUYS
HEY, SISTERS BORROW CLOTHES... RIGHT?

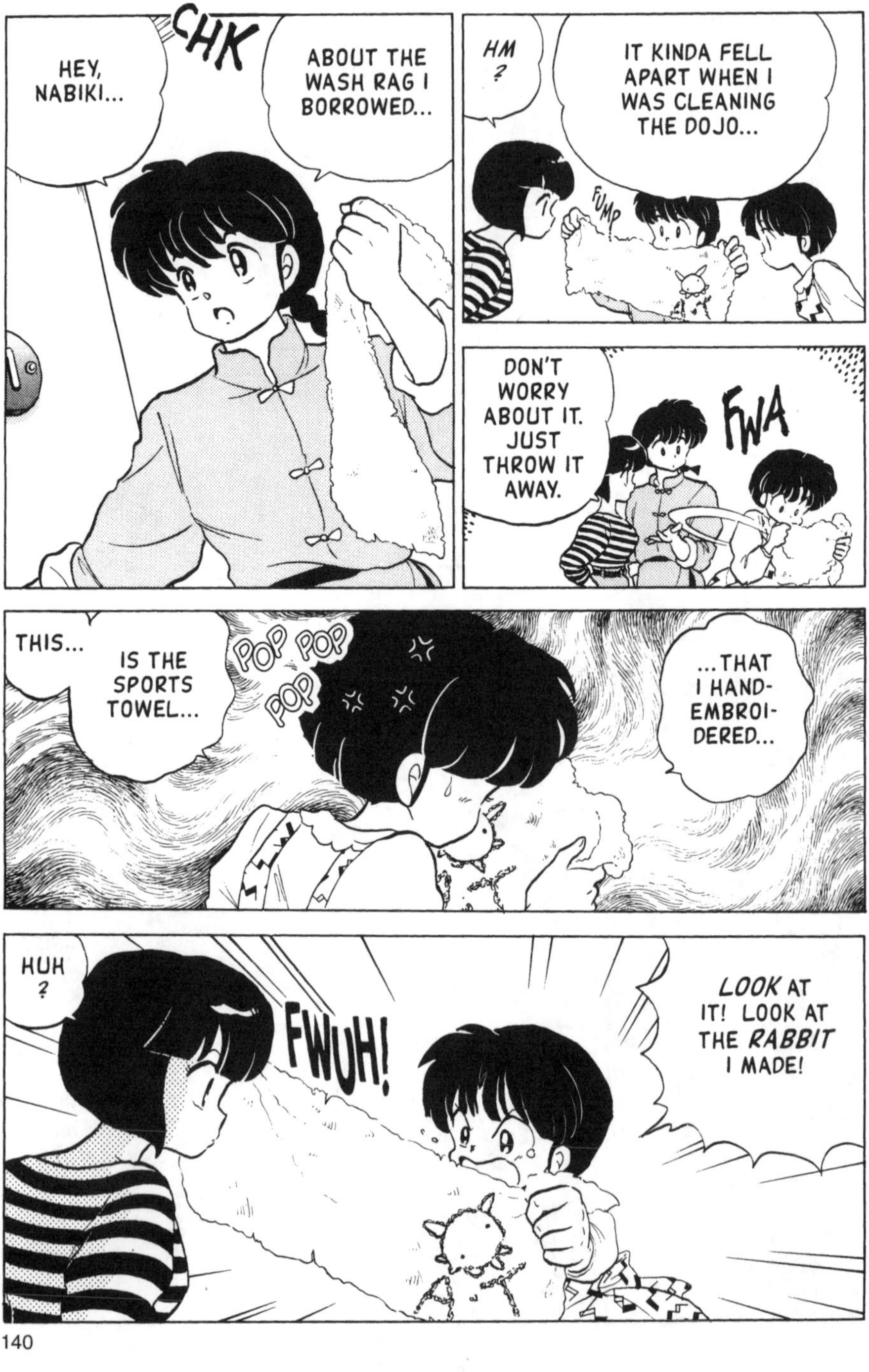
HEY, NABIKI...
CHK
ABOUT THE WASH RAG I BORROWED...
HM?
IT KINDA FELL APART WHEN I WAS CLEANING THE DOJO...
FUMP
DON'T WORRY ABOUT IT. JUST THROW IT AWAY.
FWA
THIS...
IS THE SPORTS TOWEL...
POP POP POP
...THAT I HAND-EMBROIDERED...
HUH?
FWUH!
LOOK AT IT! LOOK AT THE *RABBIT* I MADE!

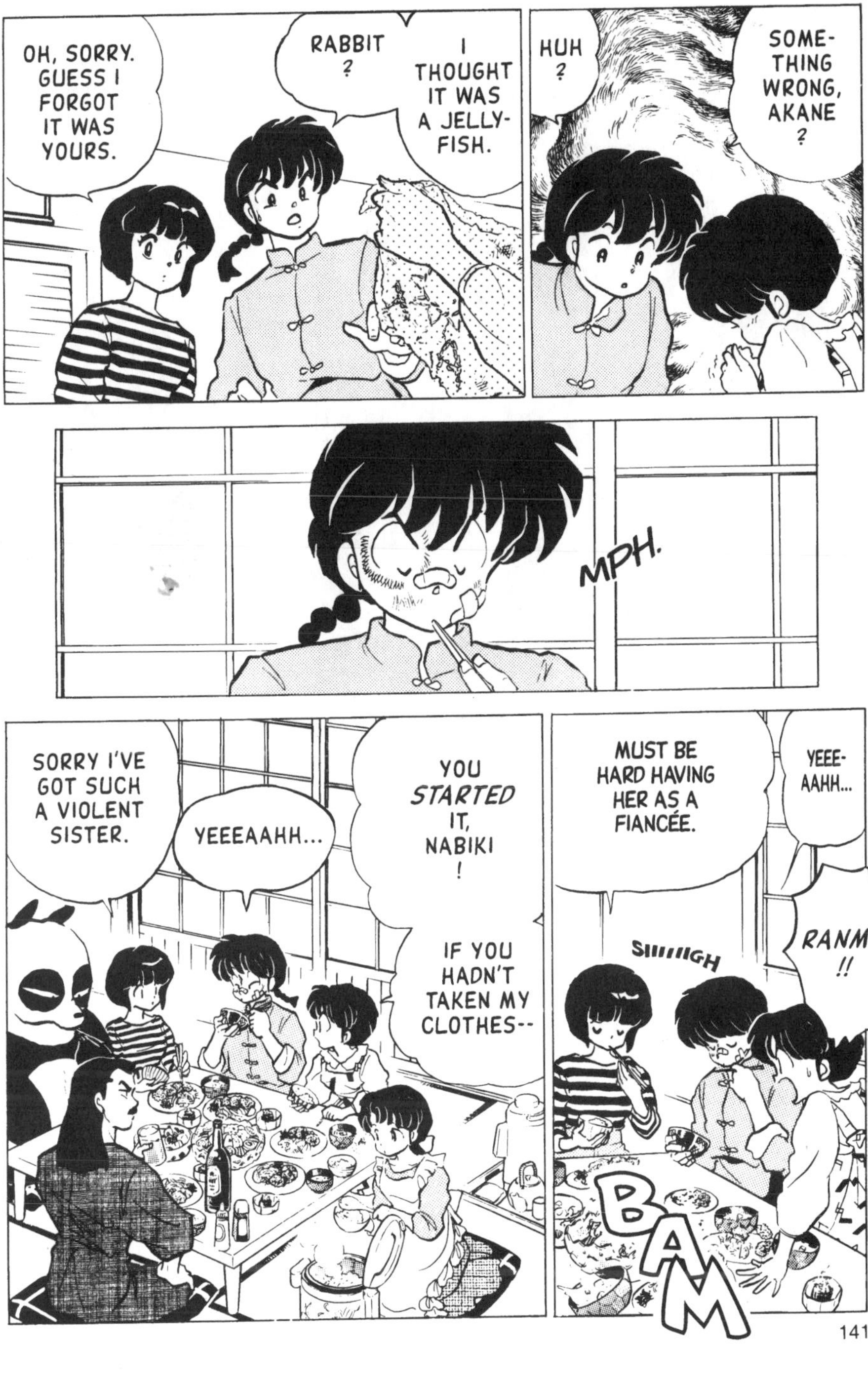
RABBIT ?
I THOUGHT IT WAS A JELLY-FISH.
OH, SORRY. GUESS I FORGOT IT WAS YOURS.
HUH ?
SOME-THING WRONG, AKANE ?
MPH.
SORRY I'VE GOT SUCH A VIOLENT SISTER.
YEEEAAHH...
YOU *STARTED* IT, NABIKI !
IF YOU HADN'T TAKEN MY CLOTHES--
YEEE-AAHH...
MUST BE HARD HAVING HER AS A FIANCÉE.
SIIIIIGH
RANMA !!
BAM

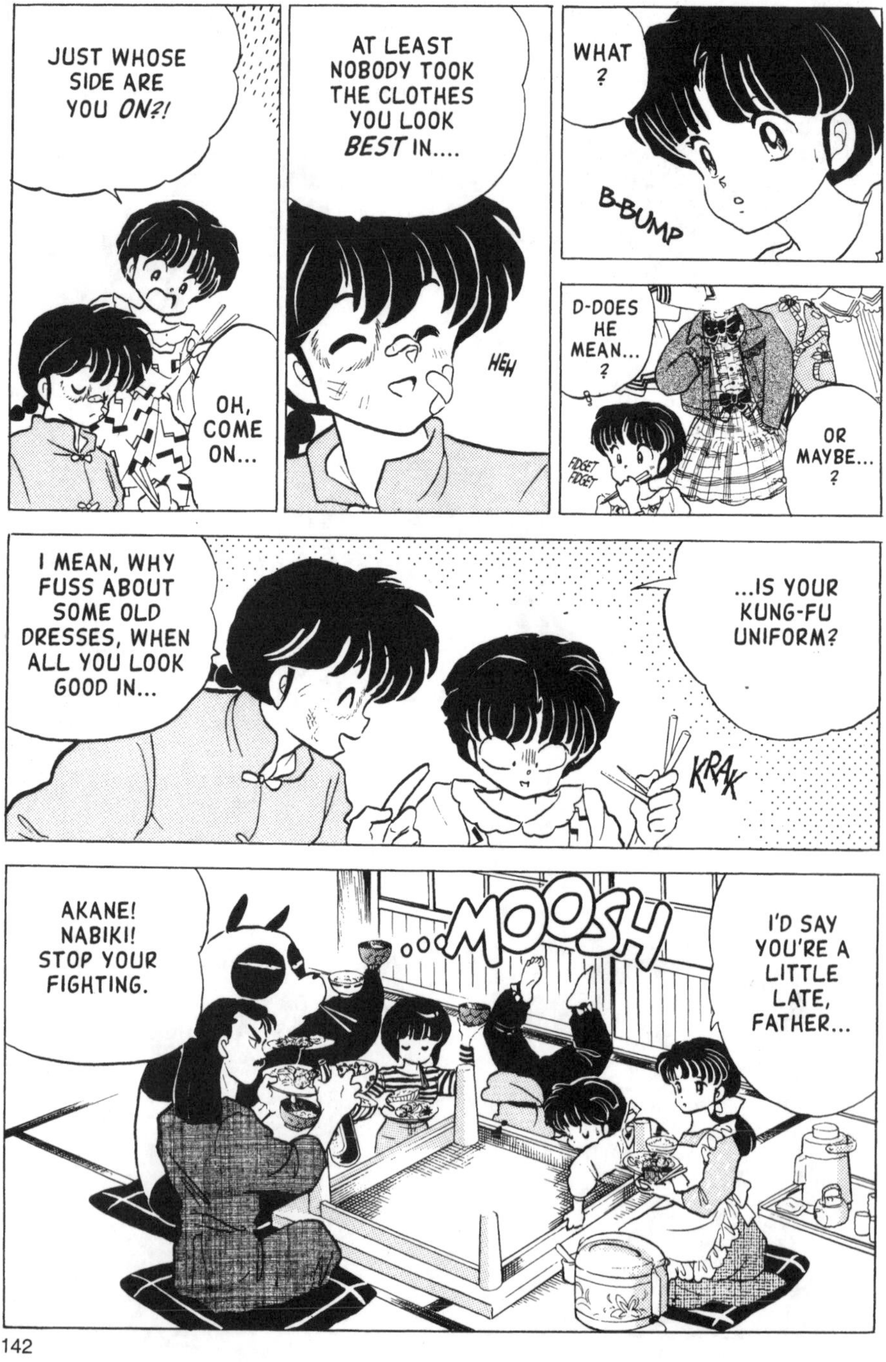
JUST WHOSE SIDE ARE YOU ON?!
OH, COME ON...
AT LEAST NOBODY TOOK THE CLOTHES YOU LOOK BEST IN....
HEH
WHAT?
B-BUMP
D-DOES HE MEAN...?
FIDGET FIDGET
OR MAYBE...?
I MEAN, WHY FUSS ABOUT SOME OLD DRESSES, WHEN ALL YOU LOOK GOOD IN...
...IS YOUR KUNG-FU UNIFORM?
KRAK
AKANE! NABIKI! STOP YOUR FIGHTING.
...MOOSH
I'D SAY YOU'RE A LITTLE LATE, FATHER...

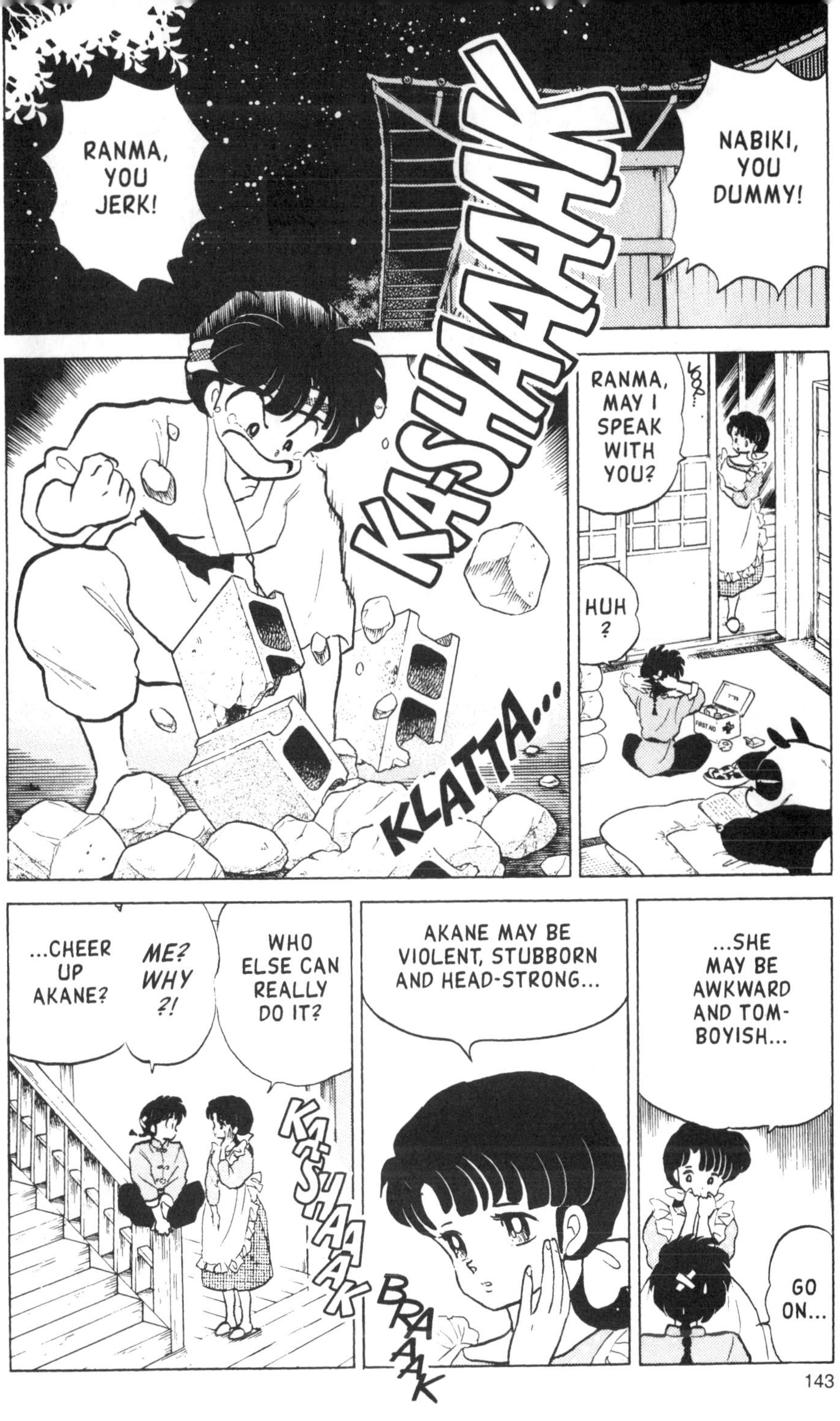

RANMA, YOU JERK!
NABIKI, YOU DUMMY!
KASHAAAK
KASHAAAK
KLATTA...
VOOP...
RANMA, MAY I SPEAK WITH YOU?
HUH?
...CHEER UP AKANE?
ME? WHY?!
WHO ELSE CAN REALLY DO IT?
KASHAAAK
BRAAAK
AKANE MAY BE VIOLENT, STUBBORN AND HEAD-STRONG...
...SHE MAY BE AWKWARD AND TOM-BOYISH...
GO ON...

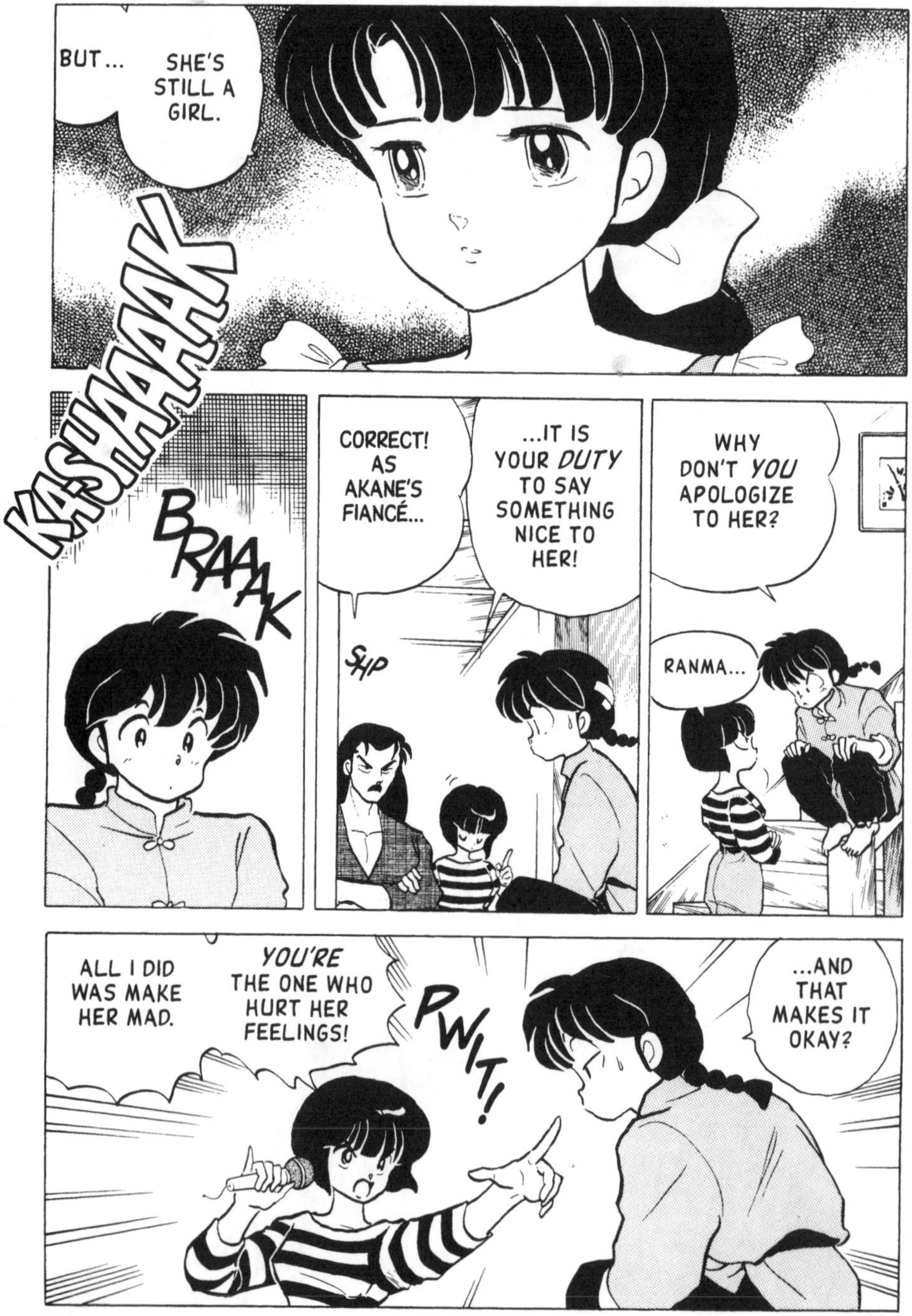
BUT...
SHE'S STILL A GIRL.
KASHAAAAK
BRAAAAK
CORRECT! AS AKANE'S FIANCÉ...
...IT IS YOUR *DUTY* TO SAY SOMETHING NICE TO HER!
SHP
WHY DON'T *YOU* APOLOGIZE TO HER?
RANMA...
ALL I DID WAS MAKE HER MAD.
YOU'RE THE ONE WHO HURT HER FEELINGS!
PWIT!!
...AND THAT MAKES IT OKAY?

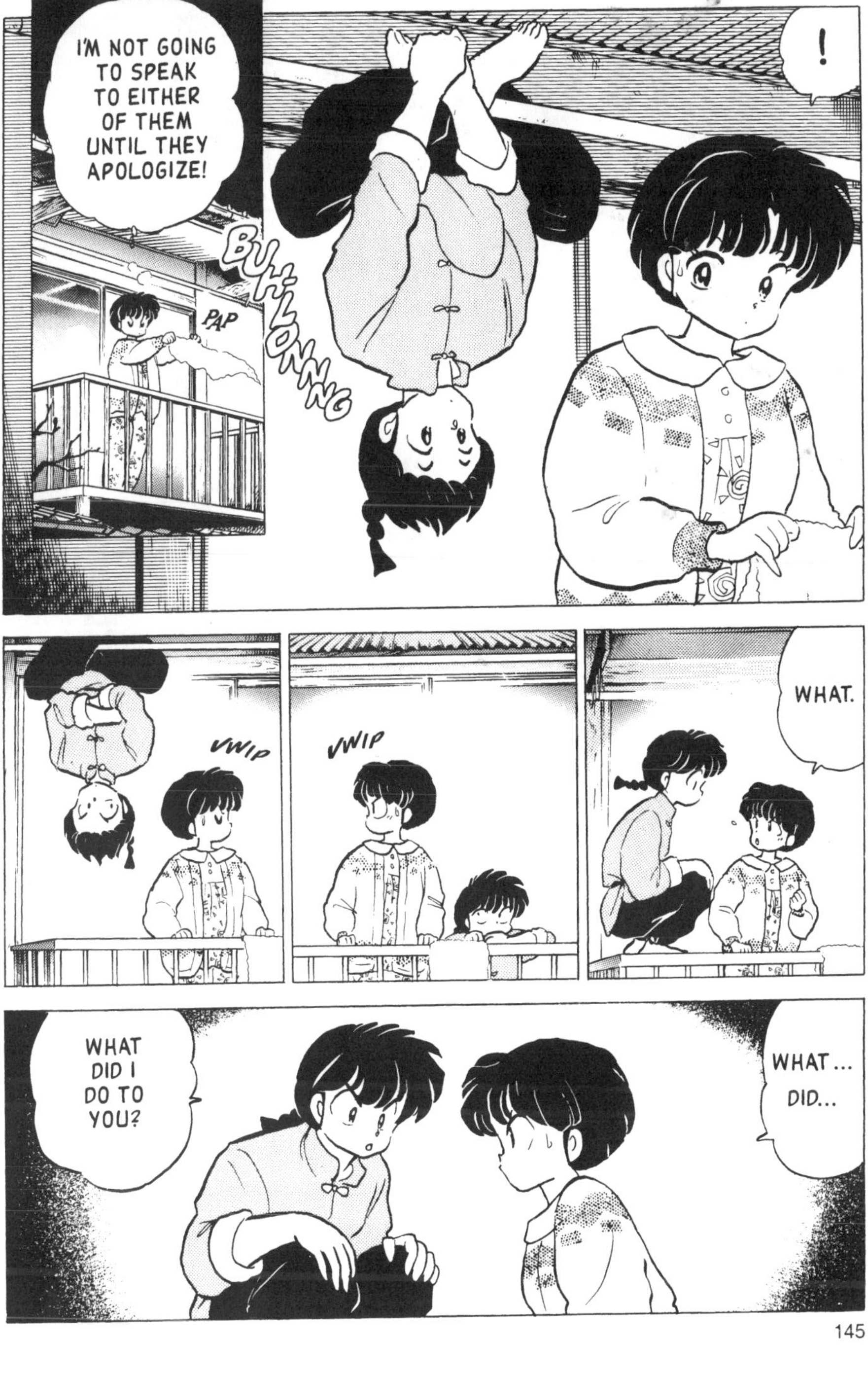
I'M NOT GOING TO SPEAK TO EITHER OF THEM UNTIL THEY APOLOGIZE!
PAP
BUHLONNNG
!
VWIP
VWIP
WHAT.
WHAT DID I DO TO YOU?
WHAT... DID...

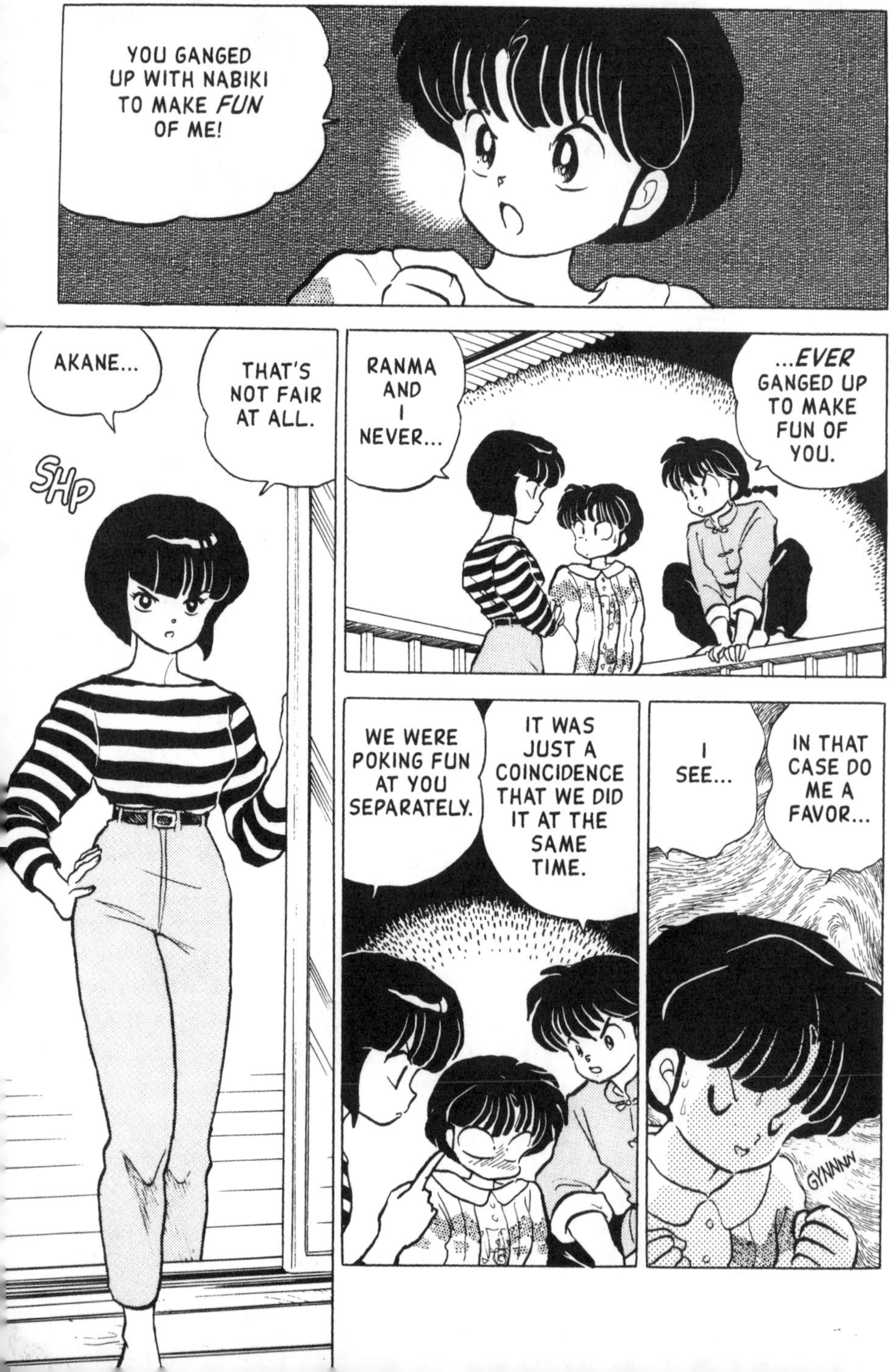
YOU GANGED UP WITH NABIKI TO MAKE *FUN* OF ME!
AKANE...
THAT'S NOT FAIR AT ALL.
SHP
RANMA AND I NEVER...
...*EVER* GANGED UP TO MAKE FUN OF YOU.
WE WERE POKING FUN AT YOU SEPARATELY.
IT WAS JUST A COINCIDENCE THAT WE DID IT AT THE SAME TIME.
I SEE...
IN THAT CASE DO ME A FAVOR...
GYNNNN

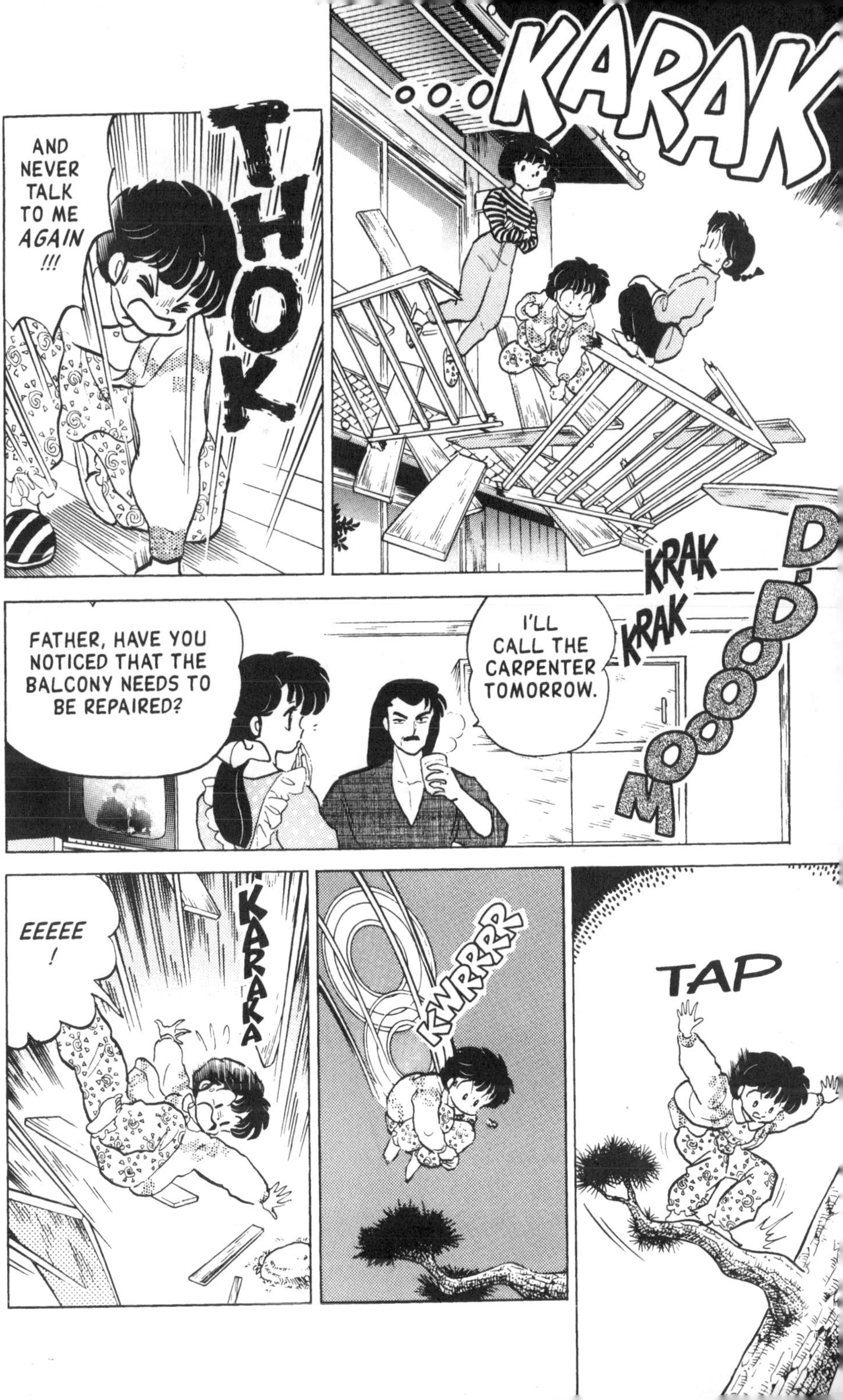
AND NEVER TALK TO ME AGAIN !!!
THOK
...KARAK
FATHER, HAVE YOU NOTICED THAT THE BALCONY NEEDS TO BE REPAIRED?
I'LL CALL THE CARPENTER TOMORROW.
KRAK KRAK
DOOOOOM
EEEEE !
KARAKA
KWRRRR
TAP

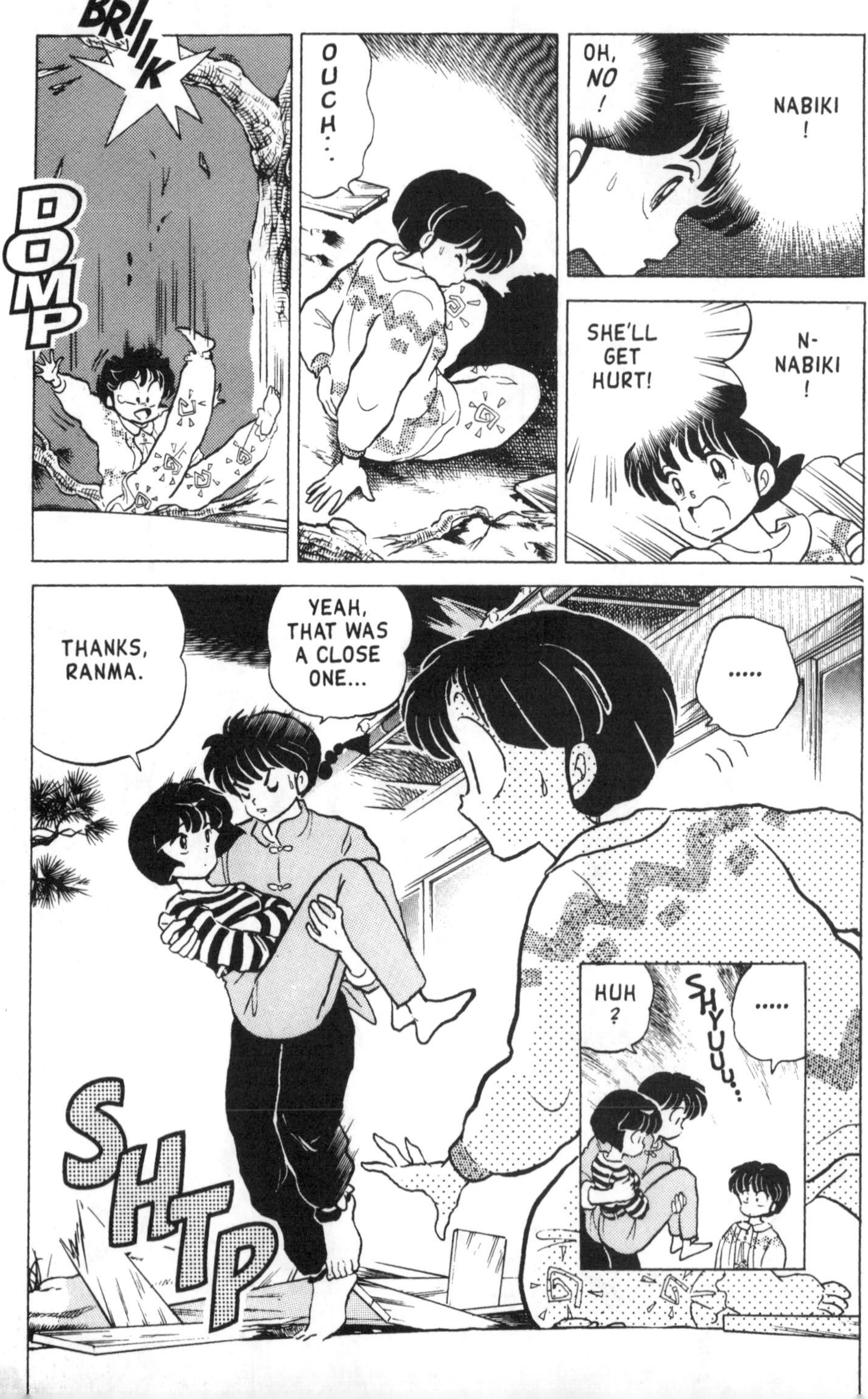
BRIIIK
DOMP
OUCH...
OH, NO!
NABIKI!
SHE'LL GET HURT!
N-NABIKI!
THANKS, RANMA.
YEAH, THAT WAS A CLOSE ONE...
.....
SHTP
HUH?
SHYUUU...
.....

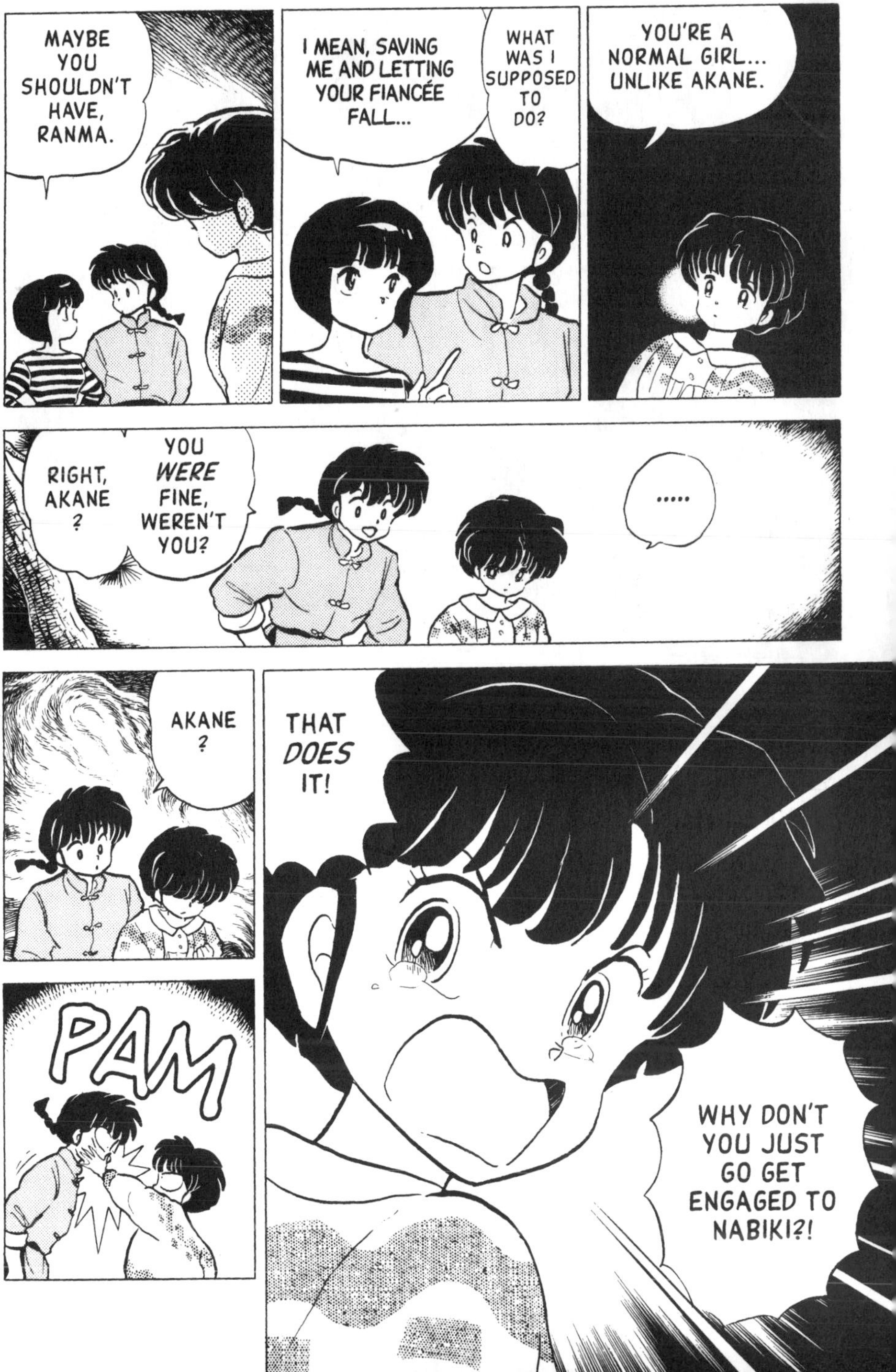
MAYBE YOU SHOULDN'T HAVE, RANMA.
I MEAN, SAVING ME AND LETTING YOUR FIANCÉE FALL...
WHAT WAS I SUPPOSED TO DO?
YOU'RE A NORMAL GIRL... UNLIKE AKANE.
RIGHT, AKANE?
YOU *WERE* FINE, WEREN'T YOU?
.....
AKANE?
THAT *DOES* IT!
PAM
WHY DON'T YOU JUST GO GET ENGAGED TO NABIKI?!

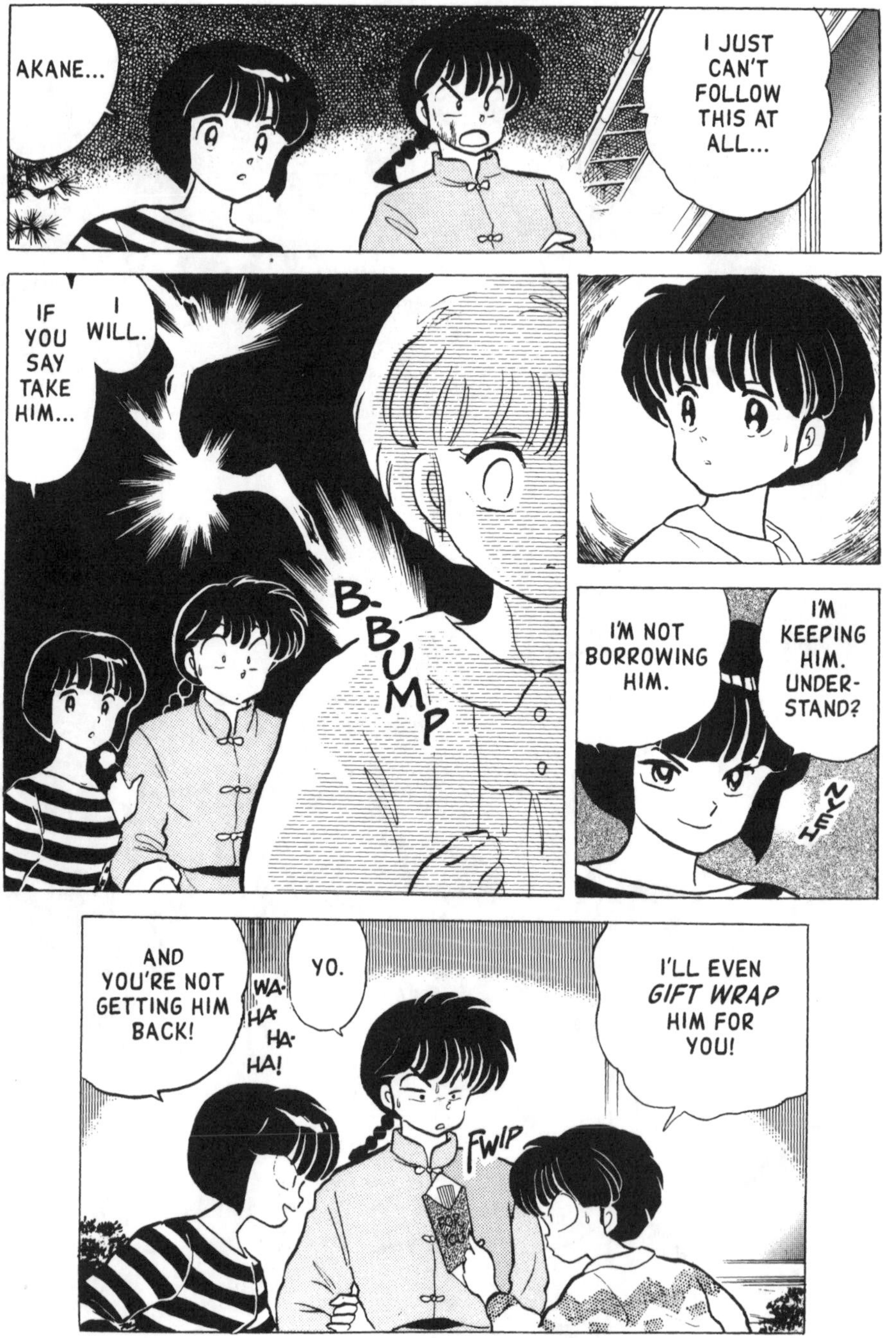
AKANE...
I JUST CAN'T FOLLOW THIS AT ALL...
IF YOU SAY TAKE HIM...
I WILL.
B-BUMP
I'M NOT BORROWING HIM.
I'M KEEPING HIM. UNDER-STAND?
NYEH
AND YOU'RE NOT GETTING HIM BACK!
WA-HA HA-HA!
YO.
I'LL EVEN *GIFT WRAP* HIM FOR YOU!
FWIP

Part 10
THE TERRIBLE TRUTH!

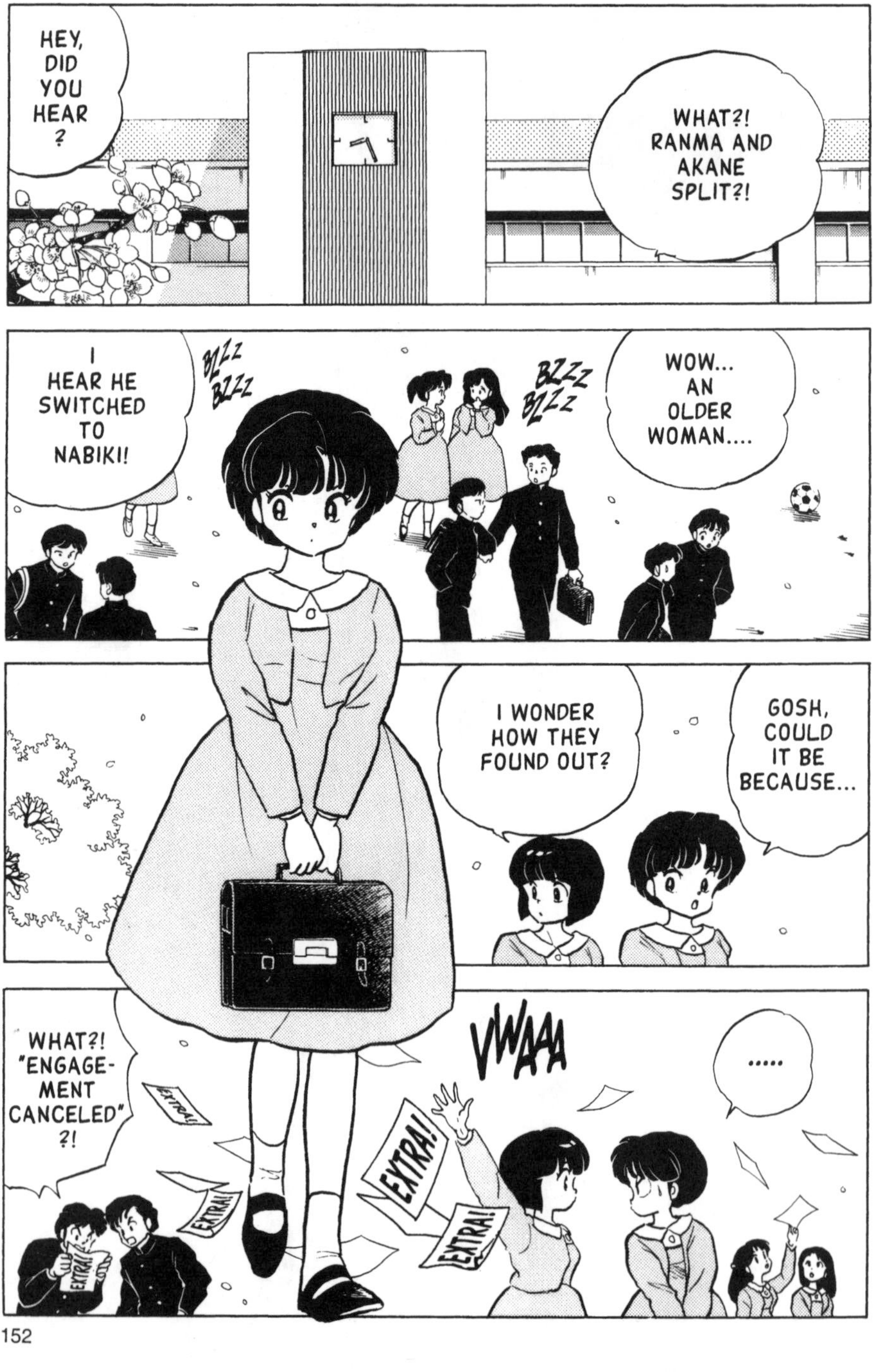
HEY, DID YOU HEAR?
WHAT?! RANMA AND AKANE SPLIT?!
I HEAR HE SWITCHED TO NABIKI!
BZZZ BZZZ
BZZZ BZZZ
WOW... AN OLDER WOMAN....
I WONDER HOW THEY FOUND OUT?
GOSH, COULD IT BE BECAUSE...
WHAT?! "ENGAGEMENT CANCELED"?!
EXTRA!
VWAAA
EXTRA!
EXTRA!
EXTRA!
EXTRA!
.....

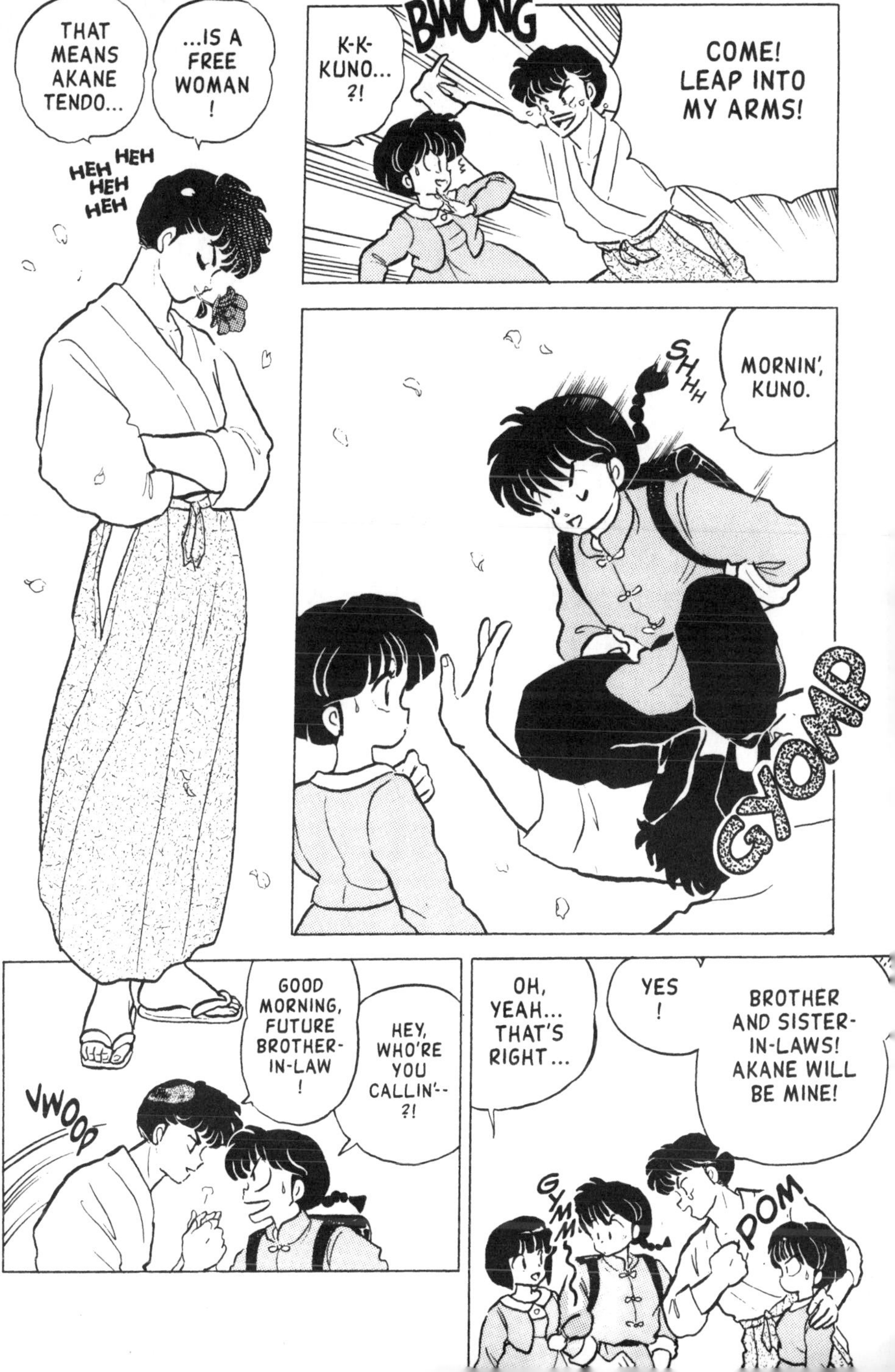
THAT MEANS AKANE TENDO...
...IS A FREE WOMAN!
HEH HEH HEH HEH
BWONG
K-K-KUNO...?!
COME! LEAP INTO MY ARMS!
SHHH
MORNIN', KUNO.
GYOMP
GOOD MORNING, FUTURE BROTHER-IN-LAW!
HEY, WHO'RE YOU CALLIN'--?!
VWOOP
OH, YEAH... THAT'S RIGHT...
YES!
BROTHER AND SISTER-IN-LAWS! AKANE WILL BE MINE!
GYMM
POM

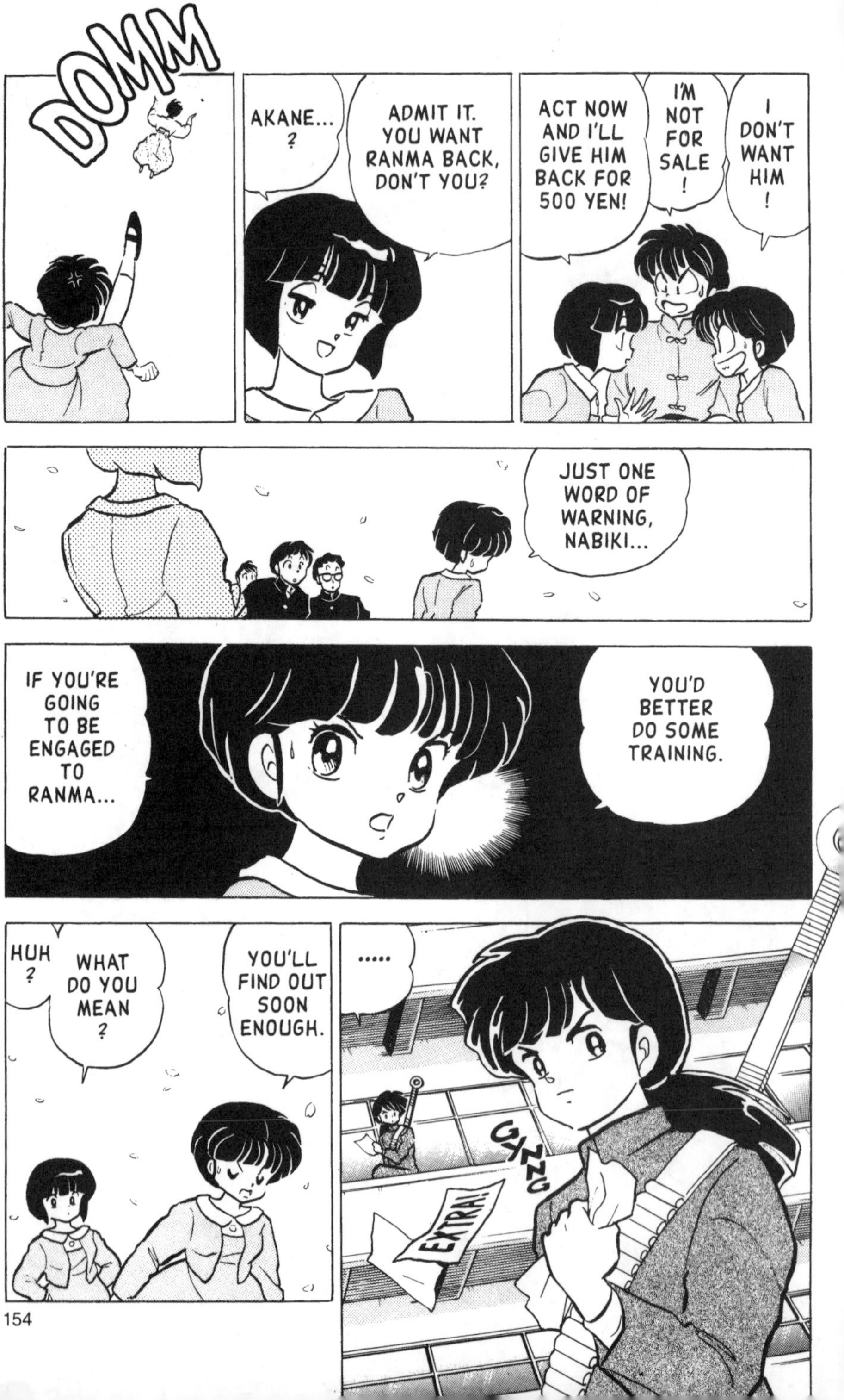
DOMM
AKANE...?
ADMIT IT. YOU WANT RANMA BACK, DON'T YOU?
ACT NOW AND I'LL GIVE HIM BACK FOR 500 YEN!
I'M NOT FOR SALE!
I DON'T WANT HIM!
JUST ONE WORD OF WARNING, NABIKI...
IF YOU'RE GOING TO BE ENGAGED TO RANMA...
YOU'D BETTER DO SOME TRAINING.
HUH?
WHAT DO YOU MEAN?
YOU'LL FIND OUT SOON ENOUGH.
.....
GYNNU
EXTRA!

E-2

SHHH

PAMP

Come to the back of the gymnasium. Ukyo.

OKONO-MIYAKI...

Come to the back of the gymnasium. Ukyo.

HYUUUU

WHAT'S WITH ALL THE FORMALITY, UCCHAN?

BEING RAN-CHAN'S FIANCÉE MYSELF...

I THOUGHT WE SHOULD GET RE-ACQUAINTED.

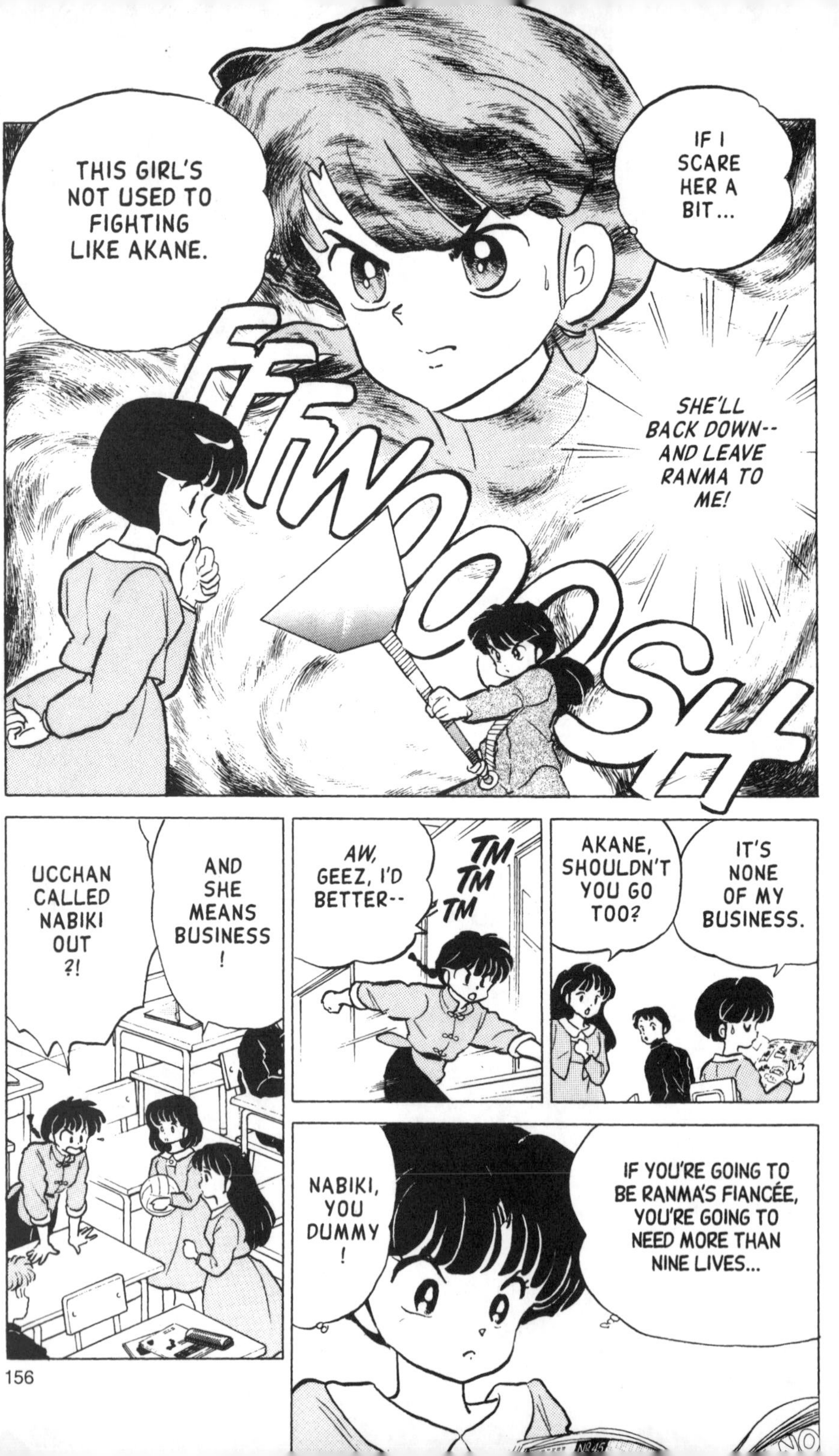
THIS GIRL'S NOT USED TO FIGHTING LIKE AKANE.
IF I SCARE HER A BIT...
SHE'LL BACK DOWN-- AND LEAVE RANMA TO ME!
FFWOOOSH
UCCHAN CALLED NABIKI OUT ?!
AND SHE MEANS BUSINESS !
AW, GEEZ, I'D BETTER--
TM TM TM
AKANE, SHOULDN'T YOU GO TOO?
IT'S NONE OF MY BUSINESS.
NABIKI, YOU DUMMY !
IF YOU'RE GOING TO BE RANMA'S FIANCÉE, YOU'RE GOING TO NEED MORE THAN NINE LIVES...

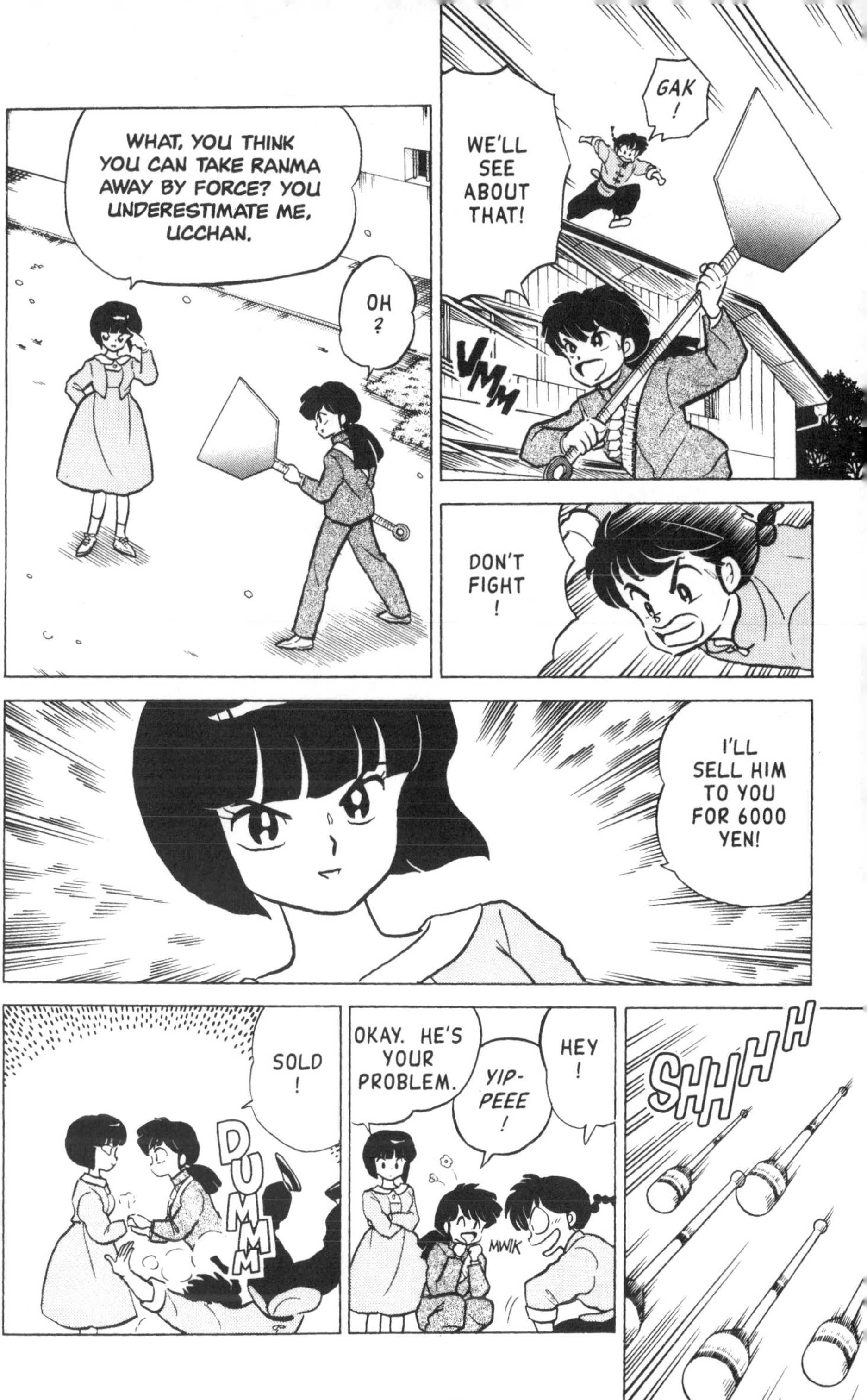
WHAT, YOU THINK YOU CAN TAKE RANMA AWAY BY FORCE? YOU UNDERESTIMATE ME, UCCHAN.
OH?
WE'LL SEE ABOUT THAT!
GAK!
VMM
DON'T FIGHT!
I'LL SELL HIM TO YOU FOR 6000 YEN!
SOLD!
DUMMM
OKAY. HE'S YOUR PROBLEM.
YIP-PEEE!
HEY!
MWIK
SHHHHH

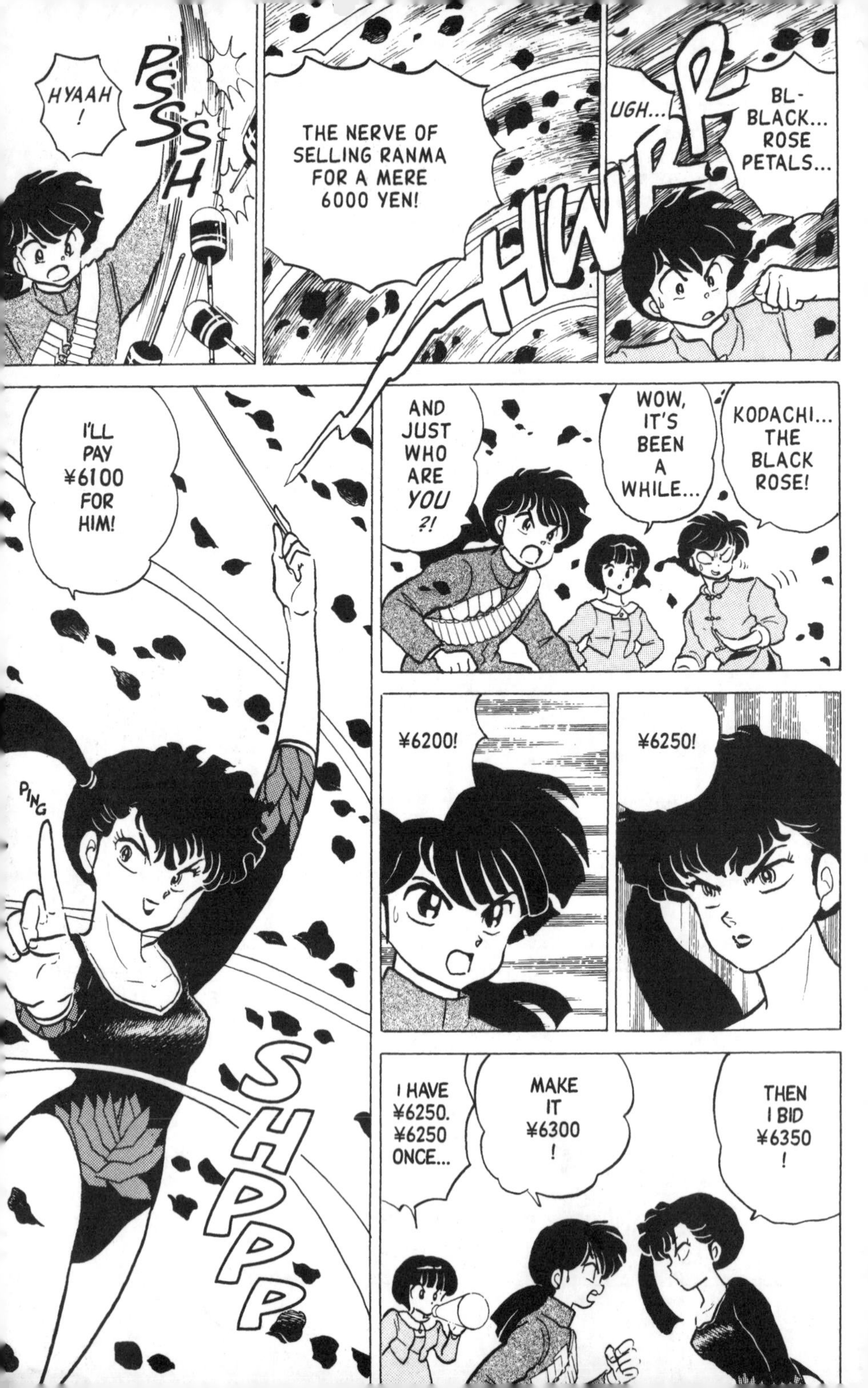
HYAAH!
PSSSH
THE NERVE OF SELLING RANMA FOR A MERE 6000 YEN!
UGH...
HWRP
BL- BLACK... ROSE PETALS...
I'LL PAY ¥6100 FOR HIM!
PING
SHPPP
AND JUST WHO ARE *YOU* ?!
WOW, IT'S BEEN A WHILE...
KODACHI... THE BLACK ROSE!
¥6200!
¥6250!
I HAVE ¥6250. ¥6250 ONCE...
MAKE IT ¥6300!
THEN I BID ¥6350!

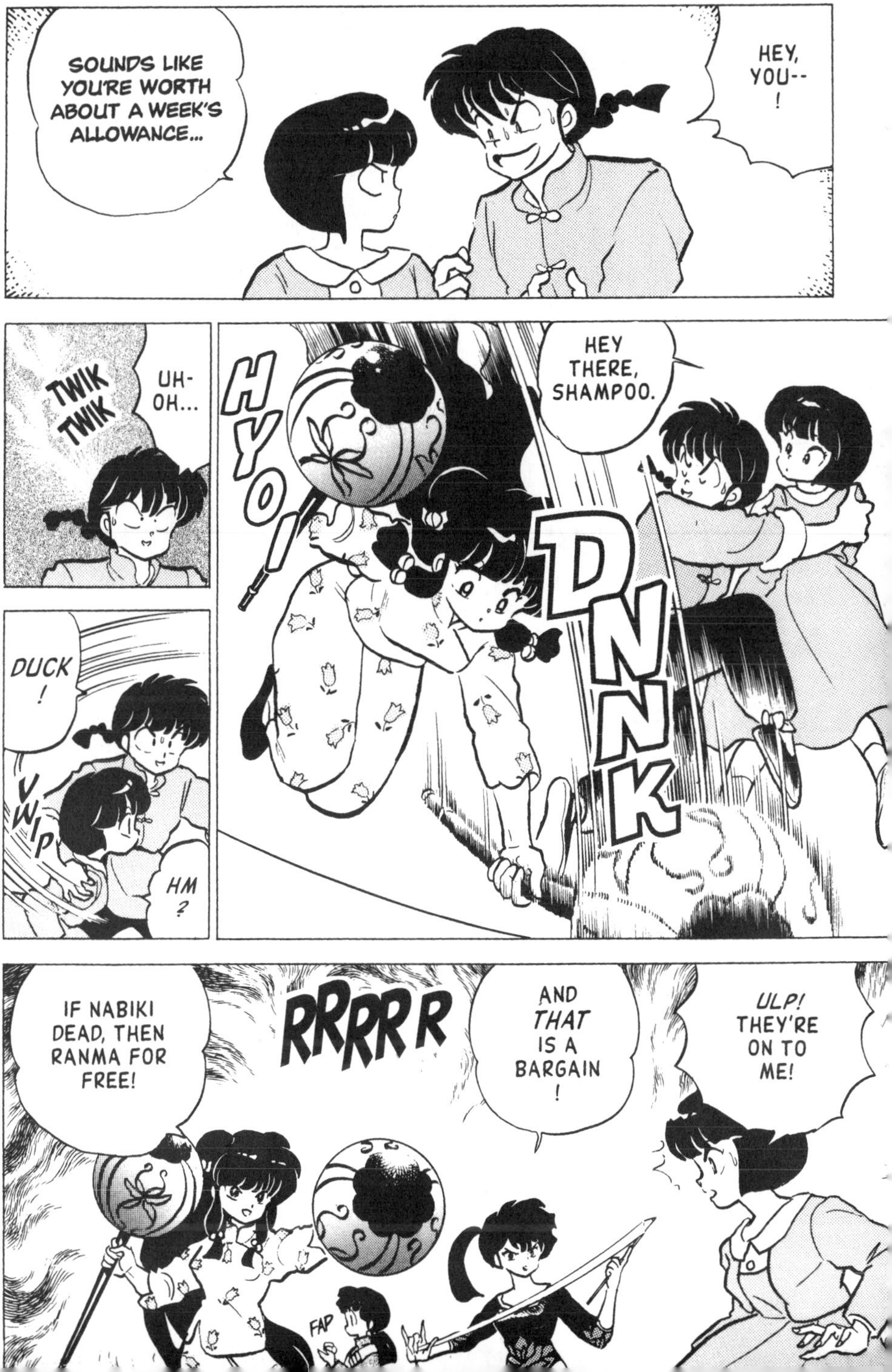
SOUNDS LIKE YOU'RE WORTH ABOUT A WEEK'S ALLOWANCE...
HEY, YOU-- !
TWIK TWIK
UH-OH...
DUCK !
VWIP
HM ?
HYO!
HEY THERE, SHAMPOO.
DNNK
IF NABIKI DEAD, THEN RANMA FOR FREE!
RRRRR
AND THAT IS A BARGAIN !
ULP! THEY'RE ON TO ME!
FAP

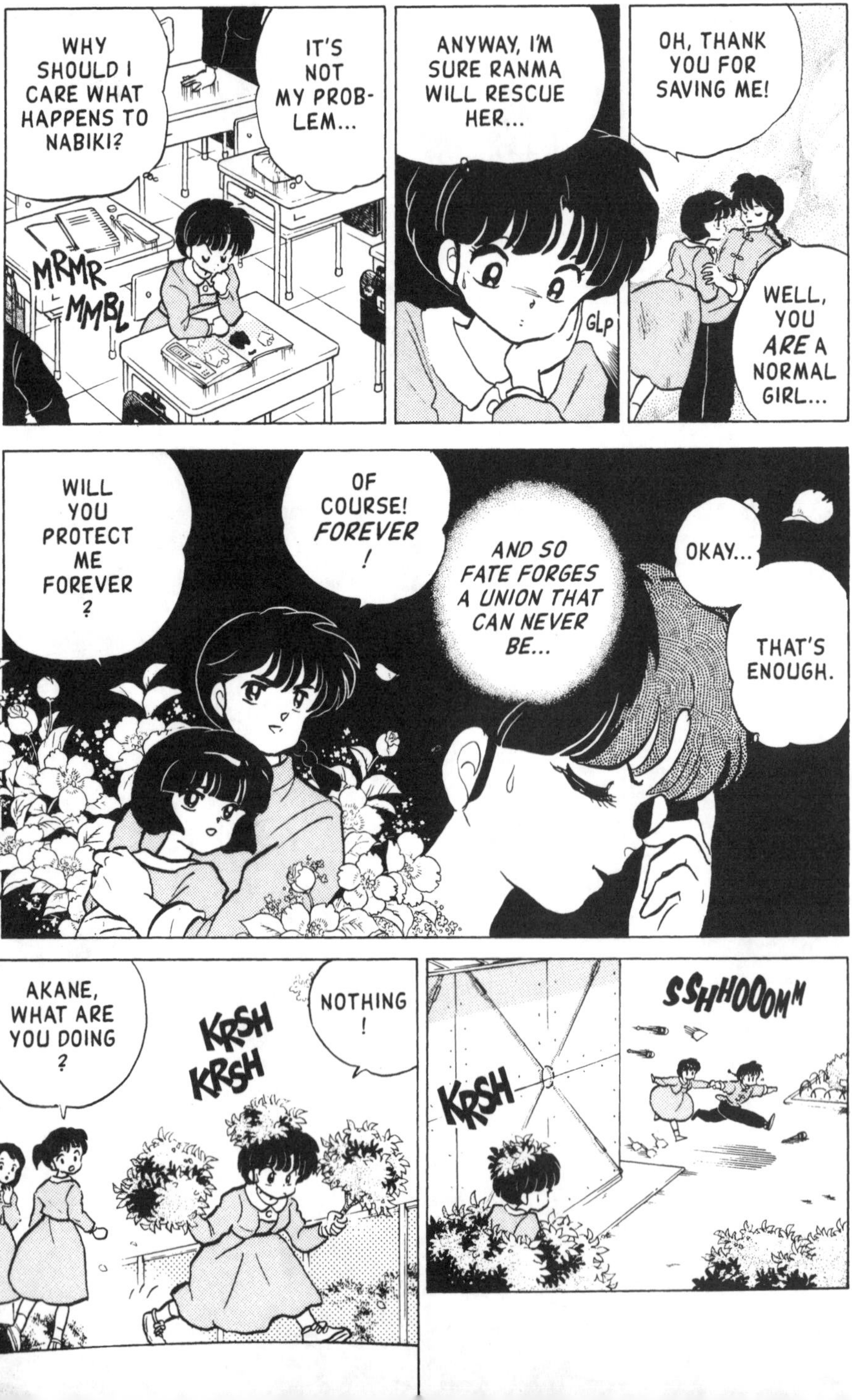
WHY SHOULD I CARE WHAT HAPPENS TO NABIKI?
MRMR MMBL
IT'S NOT MY PROB-LEM...
ANYWAY, I'M SURE RANMA WILL RESCUE HER...
GLP
OH, THANK YOU FOR SAVING ME!
WELL, YOU *ARE* A NORMAL GIRL...
WILL YOU PROTECT ME FOREVER?
OF COURSE! *FOREVER*!
AND SO FATE FORGES A UNION THAT CAN NEVER BE...
OKAY...
THAT'S ENOUGH.
AKANE, WHAT ARE YOU DOING?
KRSH KRSH
NOTHING!
SSHHOOOMM
KRSH

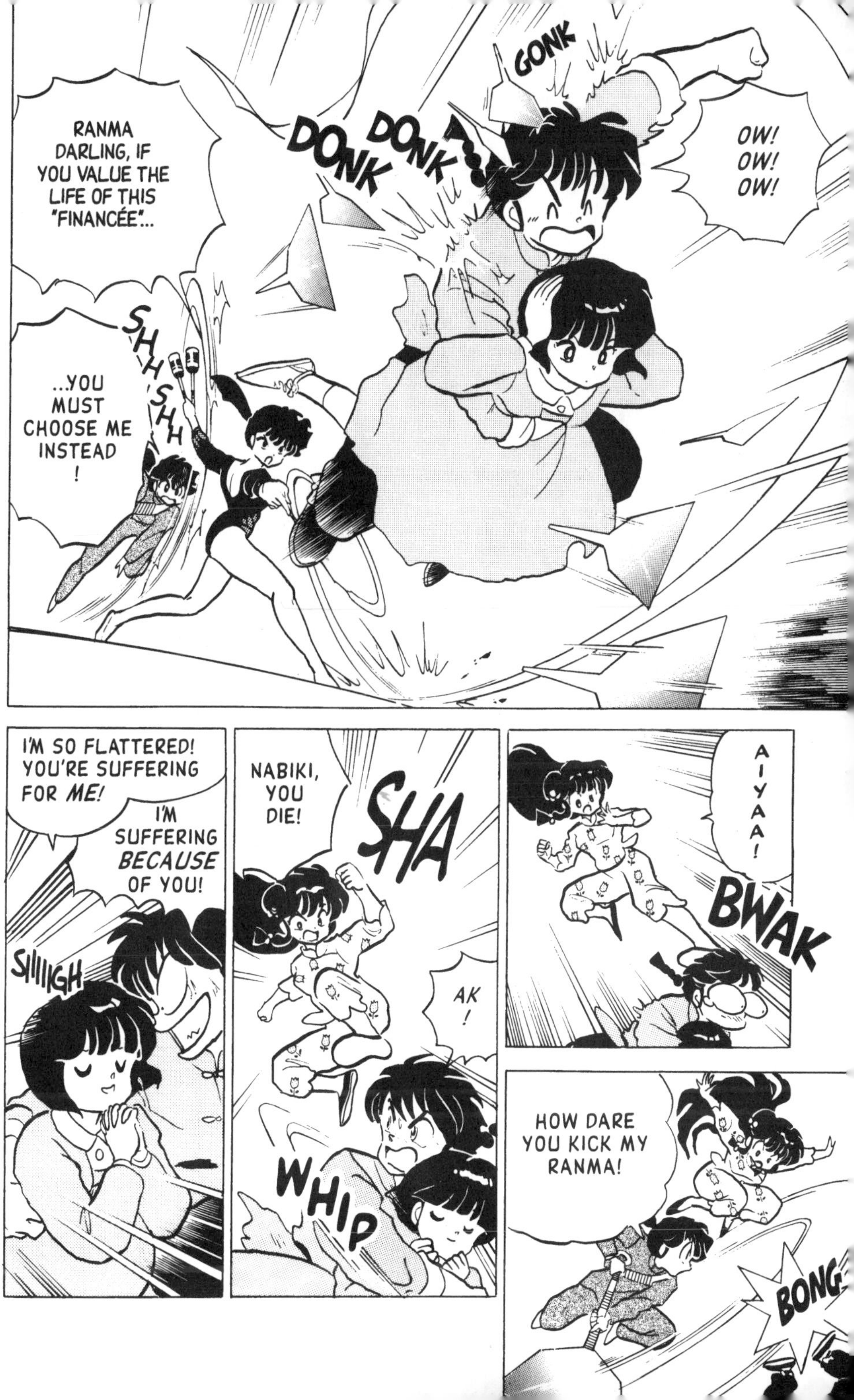
GONK
RANMA DARLING, IF YOU VALUE THE LIFE OF THIS "FINANCÉE"...
DONK DONK
OW! OW! OW!
SHHSHH
...YOU MUST CHOOSE ME INSTEAD !
I'M SO FLATTERED! YOU'RE SUFFERING FOR *ME!*
I'M SUFFERING *BECAUSE* OF YOU!
SHHGH
NABIKI, YOU DIE!
SHA
AK !
WHIP
AIYAA!
BWAK
HOW DARE YOU KICK MY RANMA!
BONG

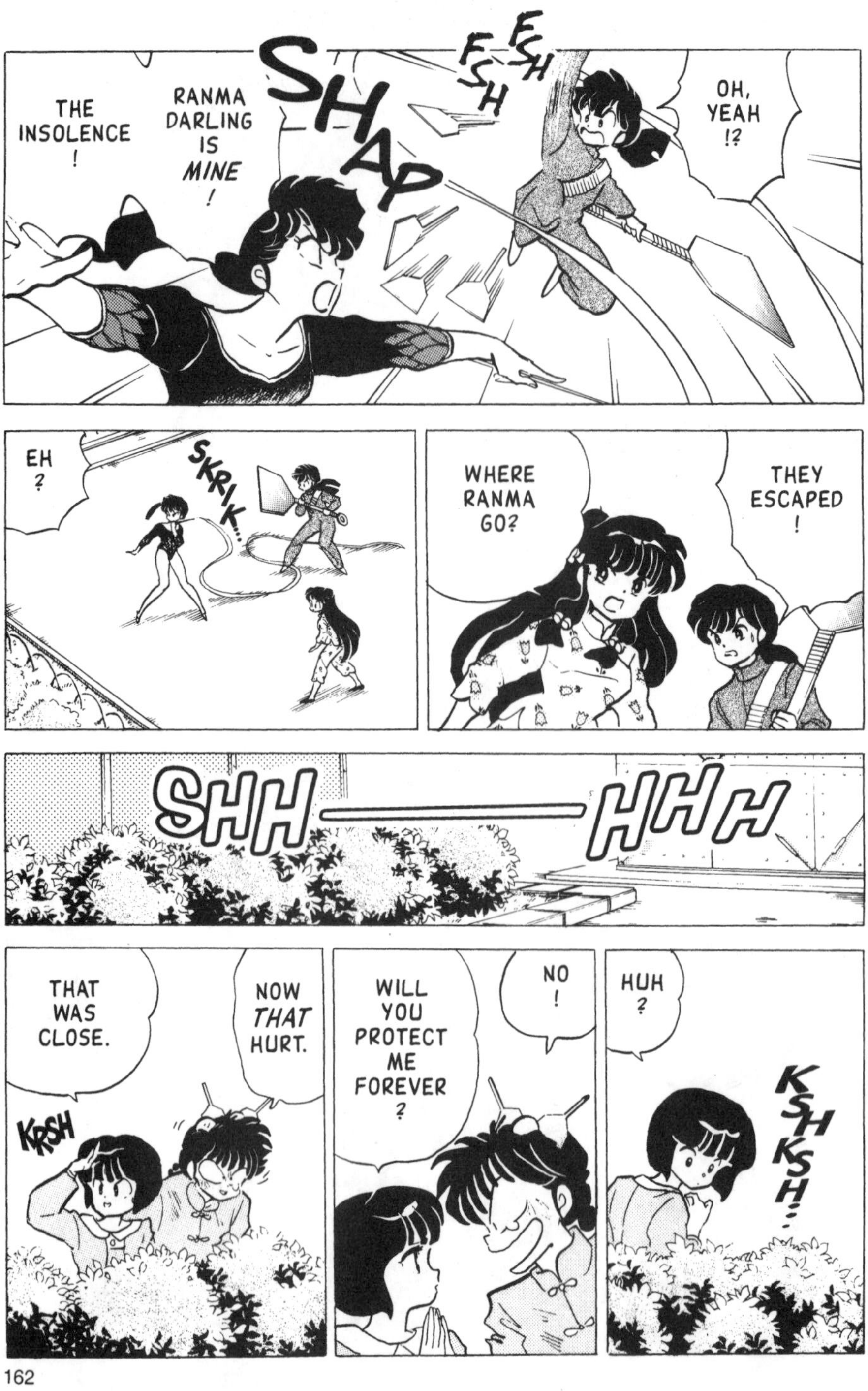
THE INSOLENCE!
RANMA DARLING IS *MINE*!
SHAP
FSH
FSH
OH, YEAH!?
EH?
SKRIK...
WHERE RANMA GO?
THEY ESCAPED!
SHH——HHH
THAT WAS CLOSE.
NOW *THAT* HURT.
KRSH
WILL YOU PROTECT ME FOREVER?
NO!
HUH?
KSH KSH!?

WHAT ARE YOU DOING THERE, AKANE?

ZOOOB

PEH

NOTHING...

AT LEAST MAKE UP WITH RANMA, AKANE...

B- BUT...

ARE YOU SURE ABOUT THIS, AKANE?

HM?

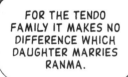

FOR THE TENDO FAMILY IT MAKES NO DIFFERENCE WHICH DAUGHTER MARRIES RANMA.

I RESPECT THE PERSONAL FEELINGS OF EACH OF MY--

NABIKI SAID SHE WANTS TO SELL THE DOJO AND LIVE OFF THE PROFITS.

YOU WILL MAKE UP WITH RANMA RIGHT NOW!!!

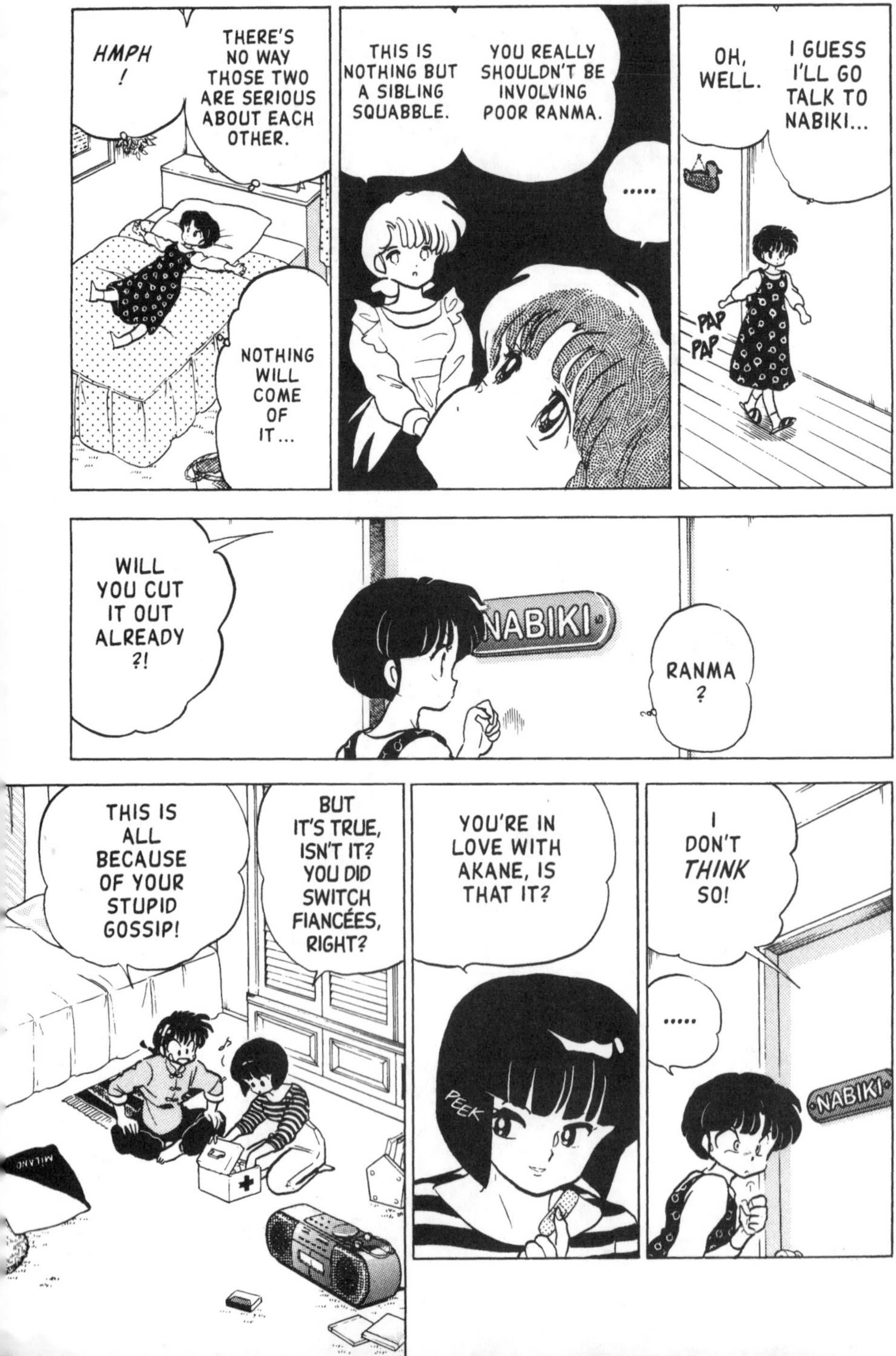
HMPH!
THERE'S NO WAY THOSE TWO ARE SERIOUS ABOUT EACH OTHER.
NOTHING WILL COME OF IT...
THIS IS NOTHING BUT A SIBLING SQUABBLE.
YOU REALLY SHOULDN'T BE INVOLVING POOR RANMA.
.....
OH, WELL.
I GUESS I'LL GO TALK TO NABIKI...
PAP PAP
WILL YOU CUT IT OUT ALREADY ?!
NABIKI
RANMA ?
THIS IS ALL BECAUSE OF YOUR STUPID GOSSIP!
BUT IT'S TRUE, ISN'T IT? YOU DID SWITCH FIANCÉES, RIGHT?
MILANO
YOU'RE IN LOVE WITH AKANE, IS THAT IT?
PEEK
I DON'T *THINK* SO!
.....
NABIKI

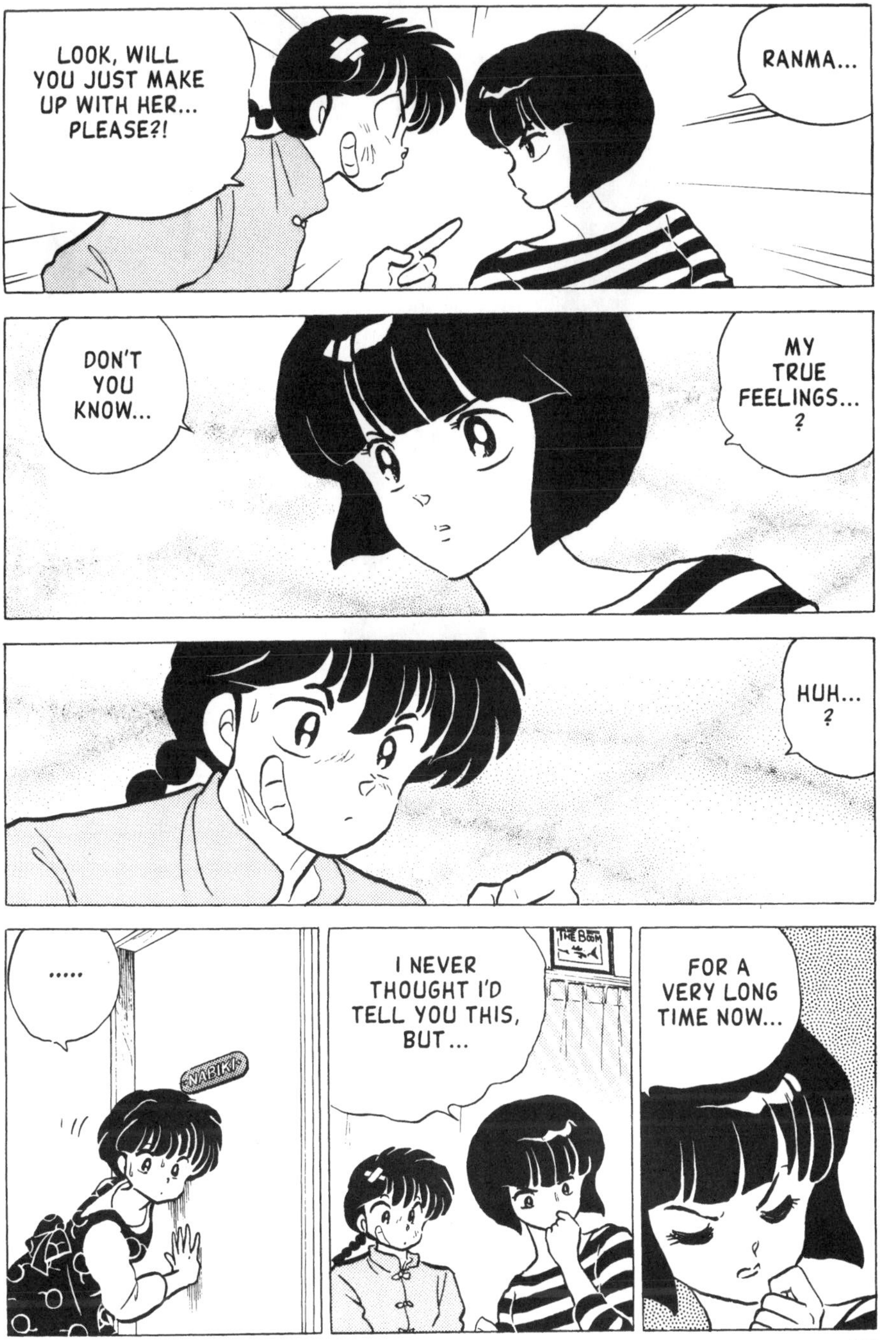
LOOK, WILL YOU JUST MAKE UP WITH HER... PLEASE?!
RANMA...
DON'T YOU KNOW...
MY TRUE FEELINGS...?
HUH...?
.....
NABIKI
I NEVER THOUGHT I'D TELL YOU THIS, BUT...
THE BOOM
FOR A VERY LONG TIME NOW...

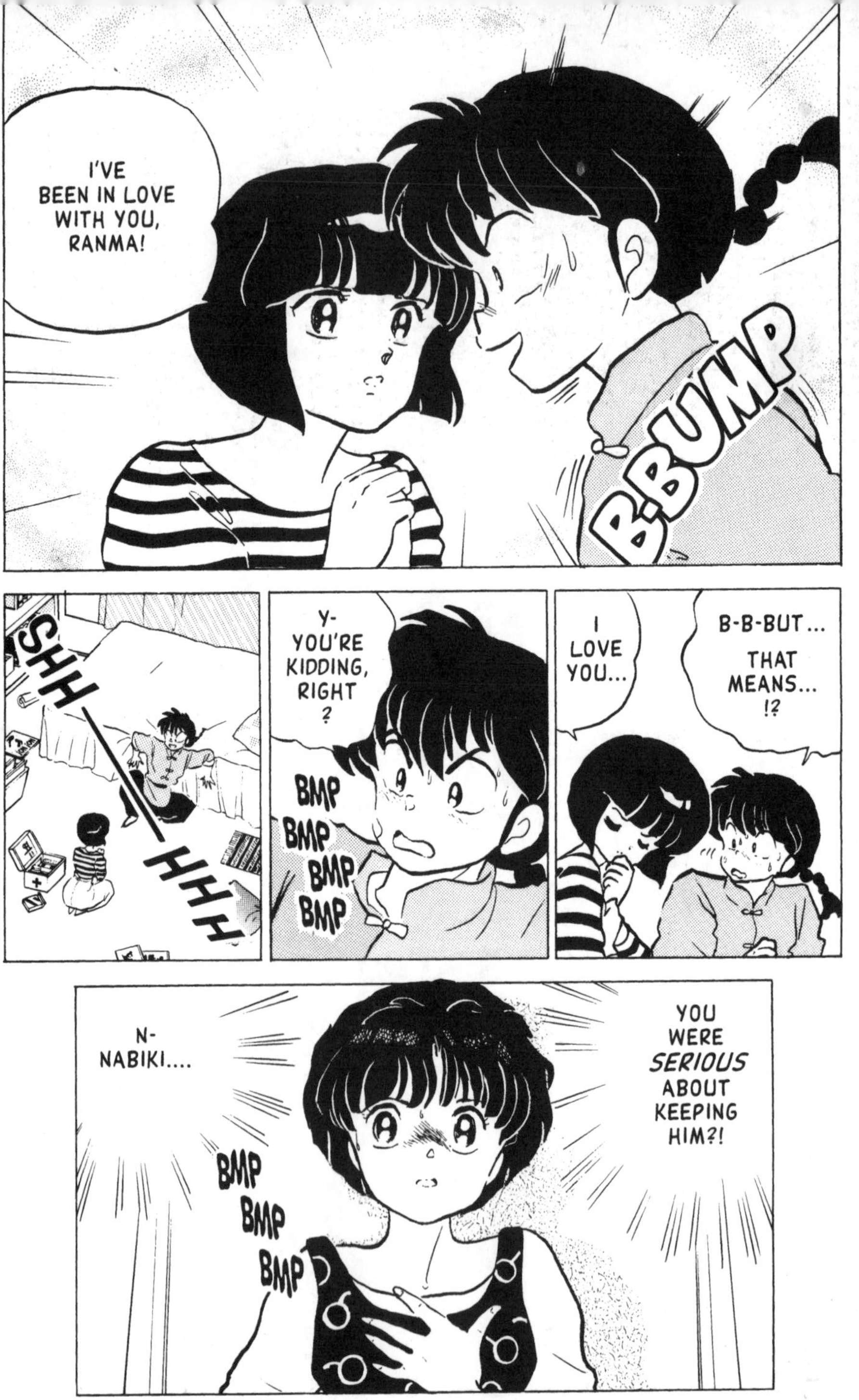
I'VE BEEN IN LOVE WITH YOU, RANMA!
B-BUMP
SHHHHHH
Y- YOU'RE KIDDING, RIGHT ?
BMP BMP BMP BMP
I LOVE YOU...
B-B-BUT... THAT MEANS... !?
N- NABIKI....
YOU WERE *SERIOUS* ABOUT KEEPING HIM?!
BMP BMP BMP

Part 11
NABIKI'S FEELINGS

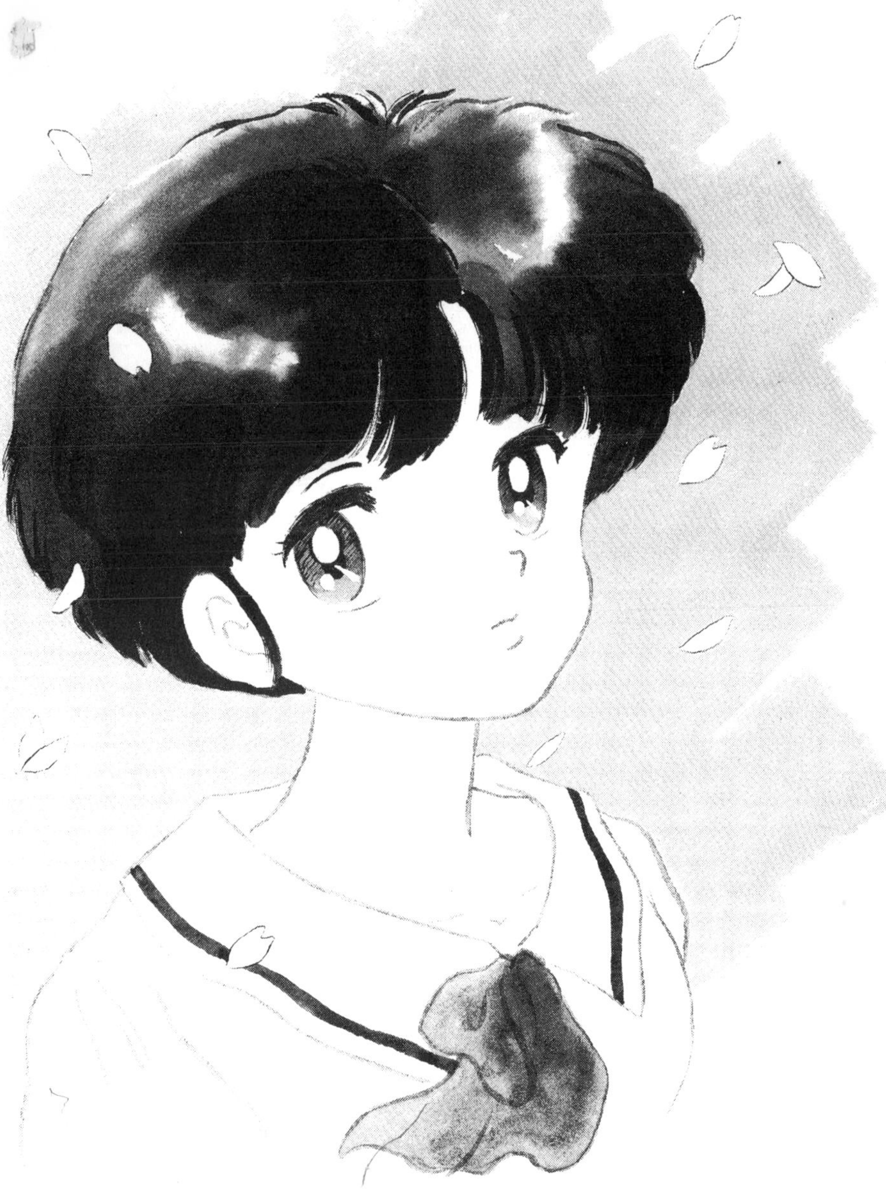

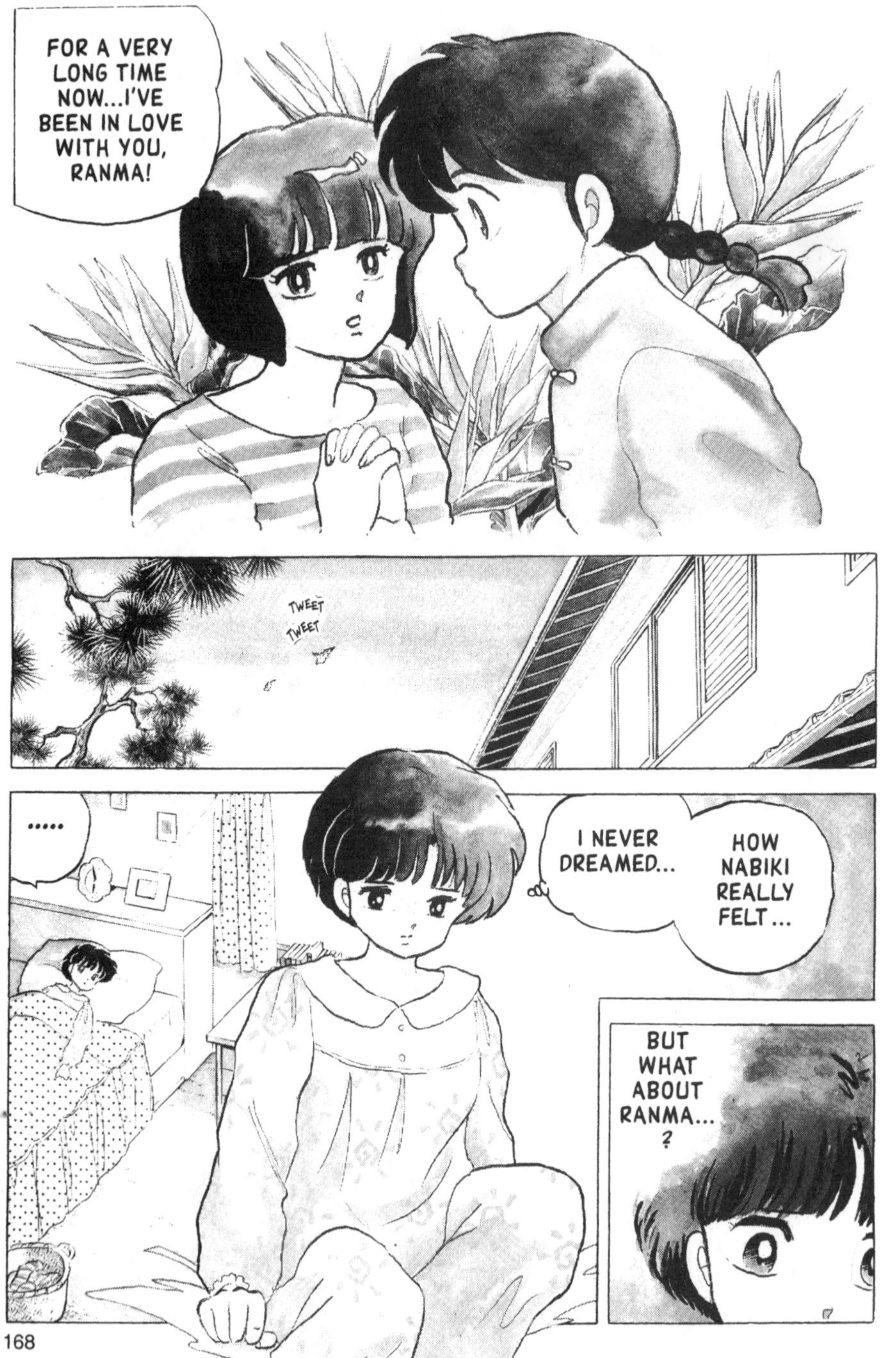
FOR A VERY LONG TIME NOW...I'VE BEEN IN LOVE WITH YOU, RANMA!
TWEET
TWEET
.....
I NEVER DREAMED...
HOW NABIKI REALLY FELT...
BUT WHAT ABOUT RANMA...?

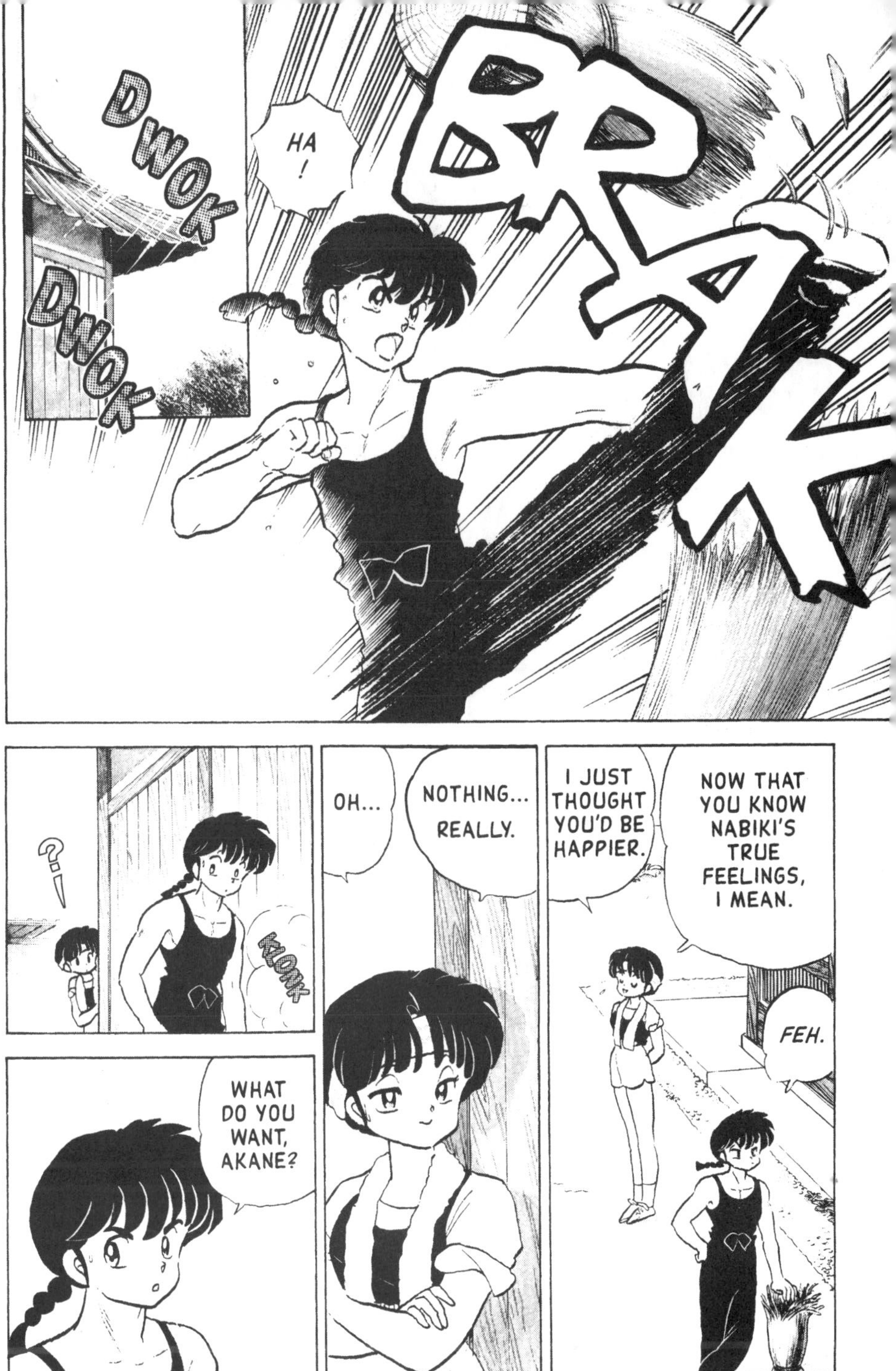

DWOK
DWOK
HA!
BRAK
?!
KLONK
WHAT DO YOU WANT, AKANE?
OH...
NOTHING... REALLY.
I JUST THOUGHT YOU'D BE HAPPIER.
NOW THAT YOU KNOW NABIKI'S TRUE FEELINGS, I MEAN.
FEH.

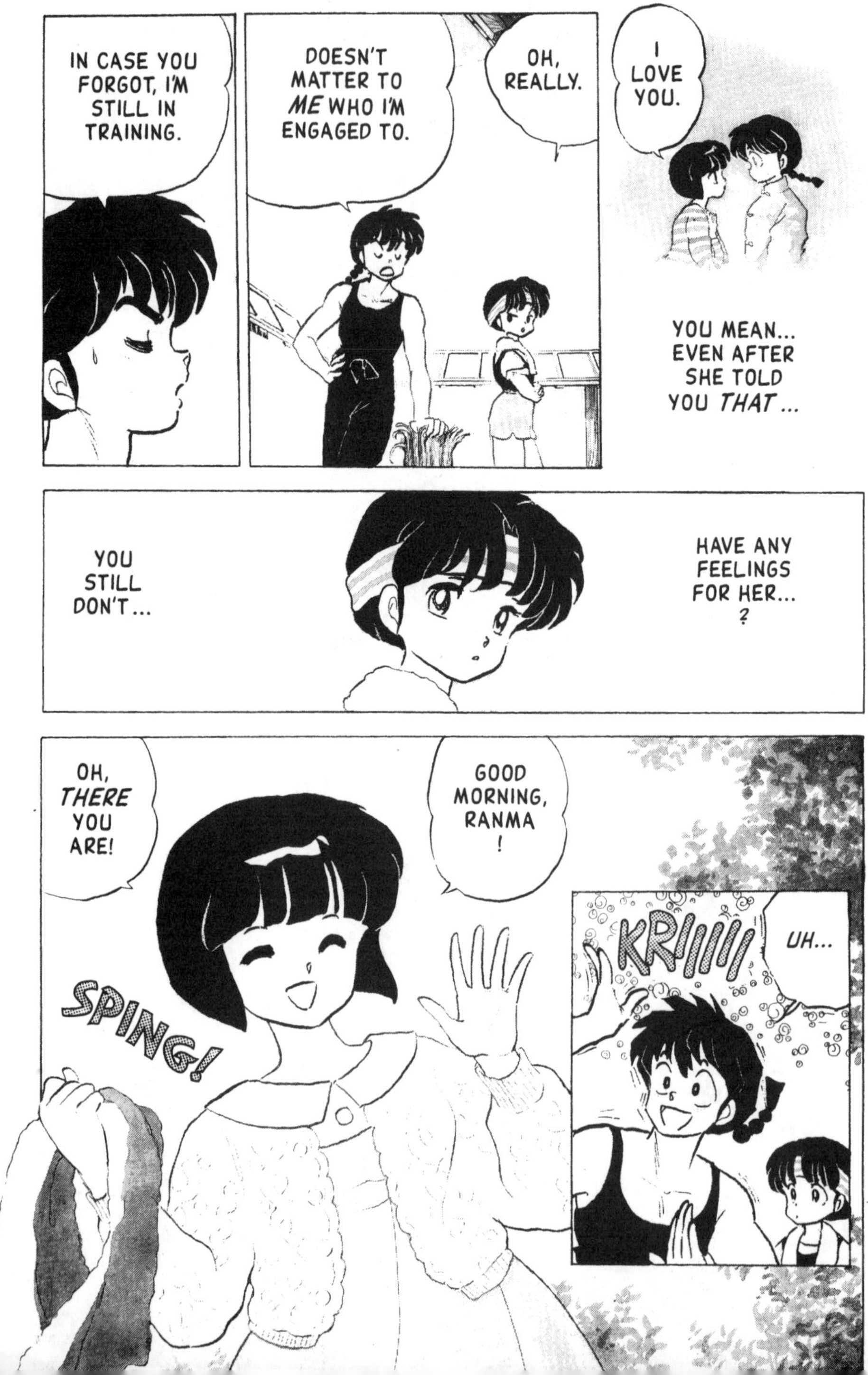
IN CASE YOU FORGOT, I'M STILL IN TRAINING.
DOESN'T MATTER TO *ME* WHO I'M ENGAGED TO.
OH, REALLY.
I LOVE YOU.
YOU MEAN... EVEN AFTER SHE TOLD YOU *THAT*...
YOU STILL DON'T...
HAVE ANY FEELINGS FOR HER... ?
OH, *THERE* YOU ARE!
GOOD MORNING, RANMA !
SPING!
KRIIIII
UH...

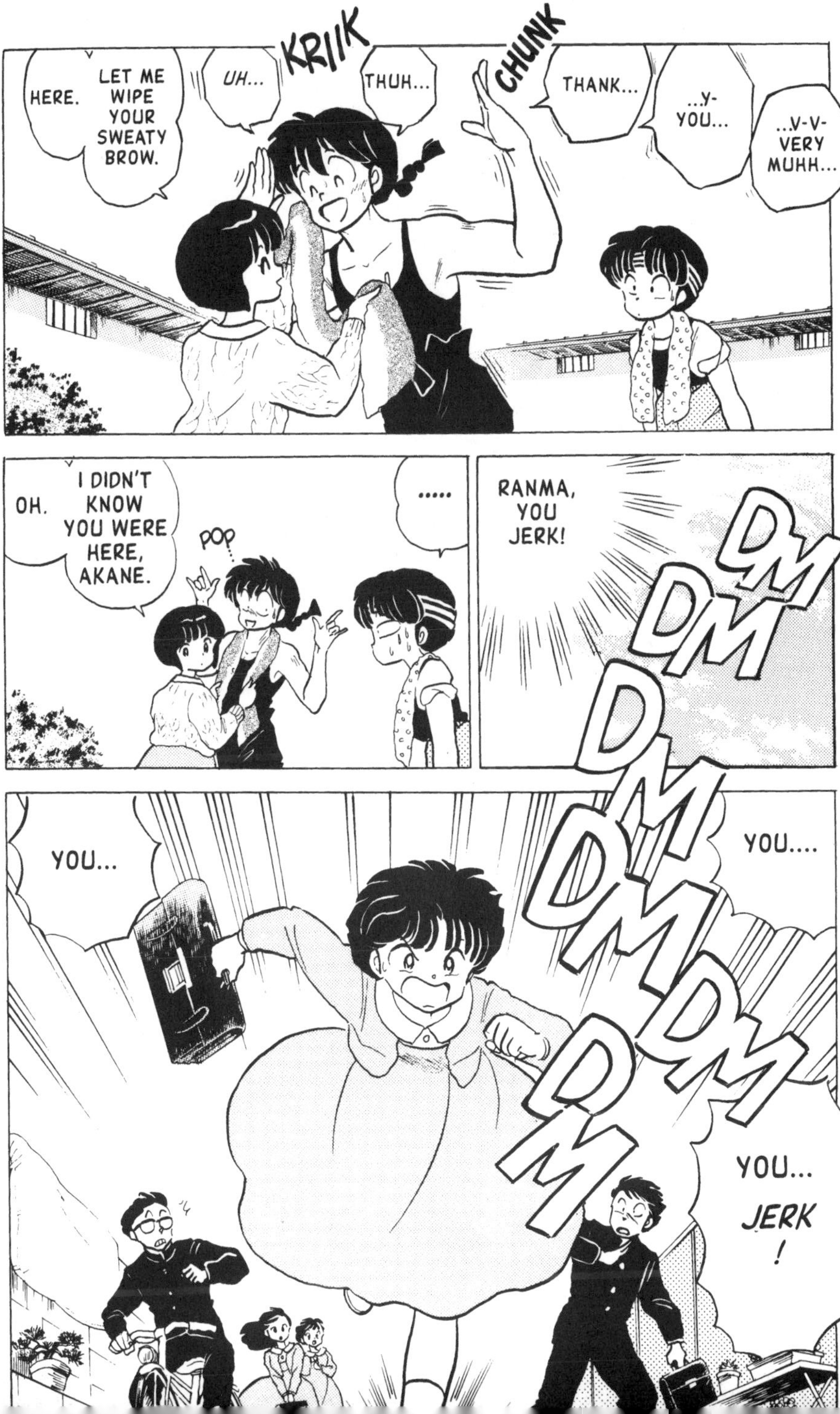
HERE.
LET ME WIPE YOUR SWEATY BROW.
UH...
KRIIK
THUH...
CHUNK
THANK...
...Y-YOU...
...V-V-VERY MUHH...
OH.
I DIDN'T KNOW YOU WERE HERE, AKANE.
POP
.....
RANMA, YOU JERK!
DM DM DM DM DM DM DM
YOU...
YOU....
YOU... JERK!

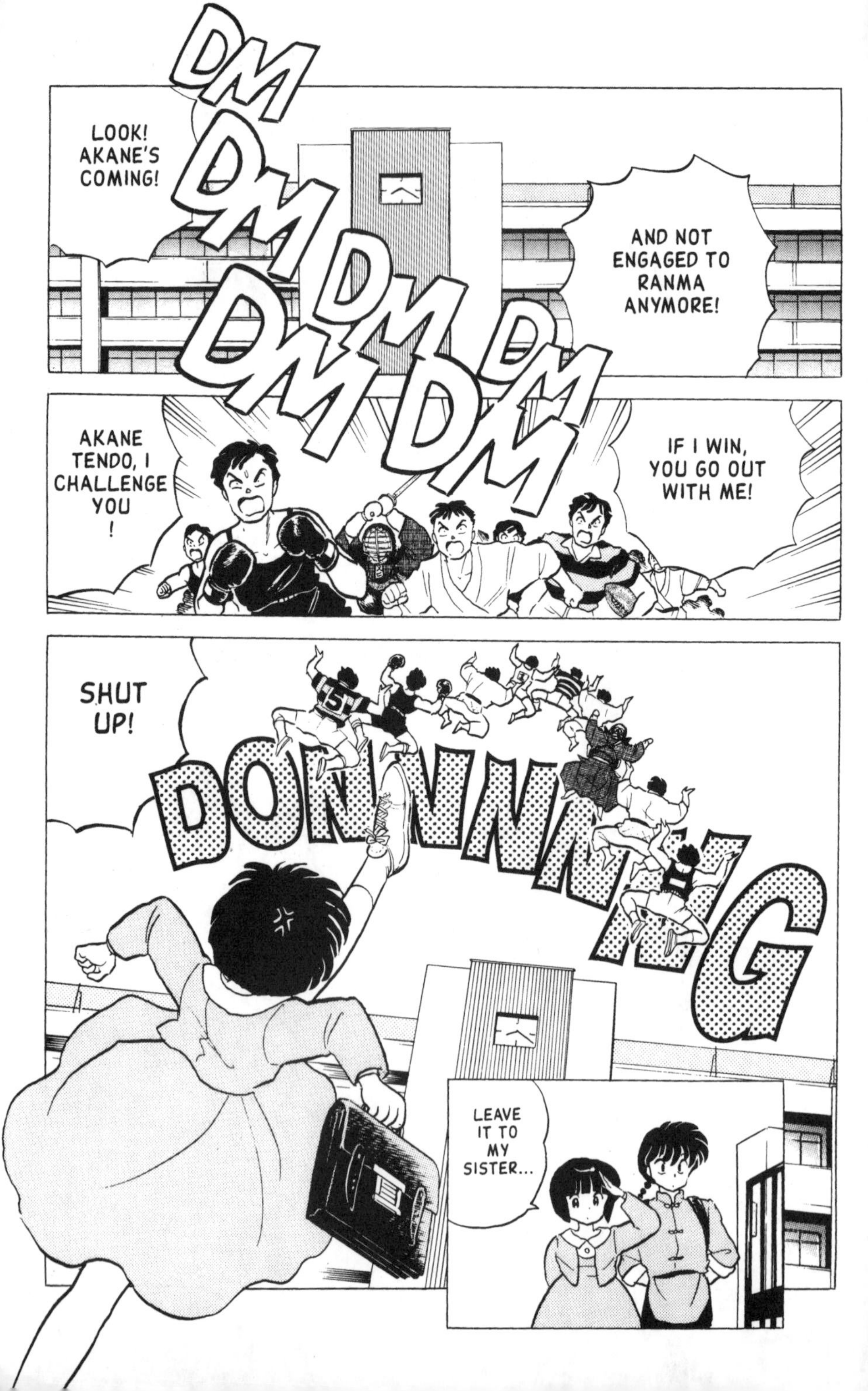
DM
DM DM DM DM DM DM DM
LOOK! AKANE'S COMING!
AND NOT ENGAGED TO RANMA ANYMORE!
AKANE TENDO, I CHALLENGE YOU!
IF I WIN, YOU GO OUT WITH ME!
SHUT UP!
DONNNNNNG
LEAVE IT TO MY SISTER...

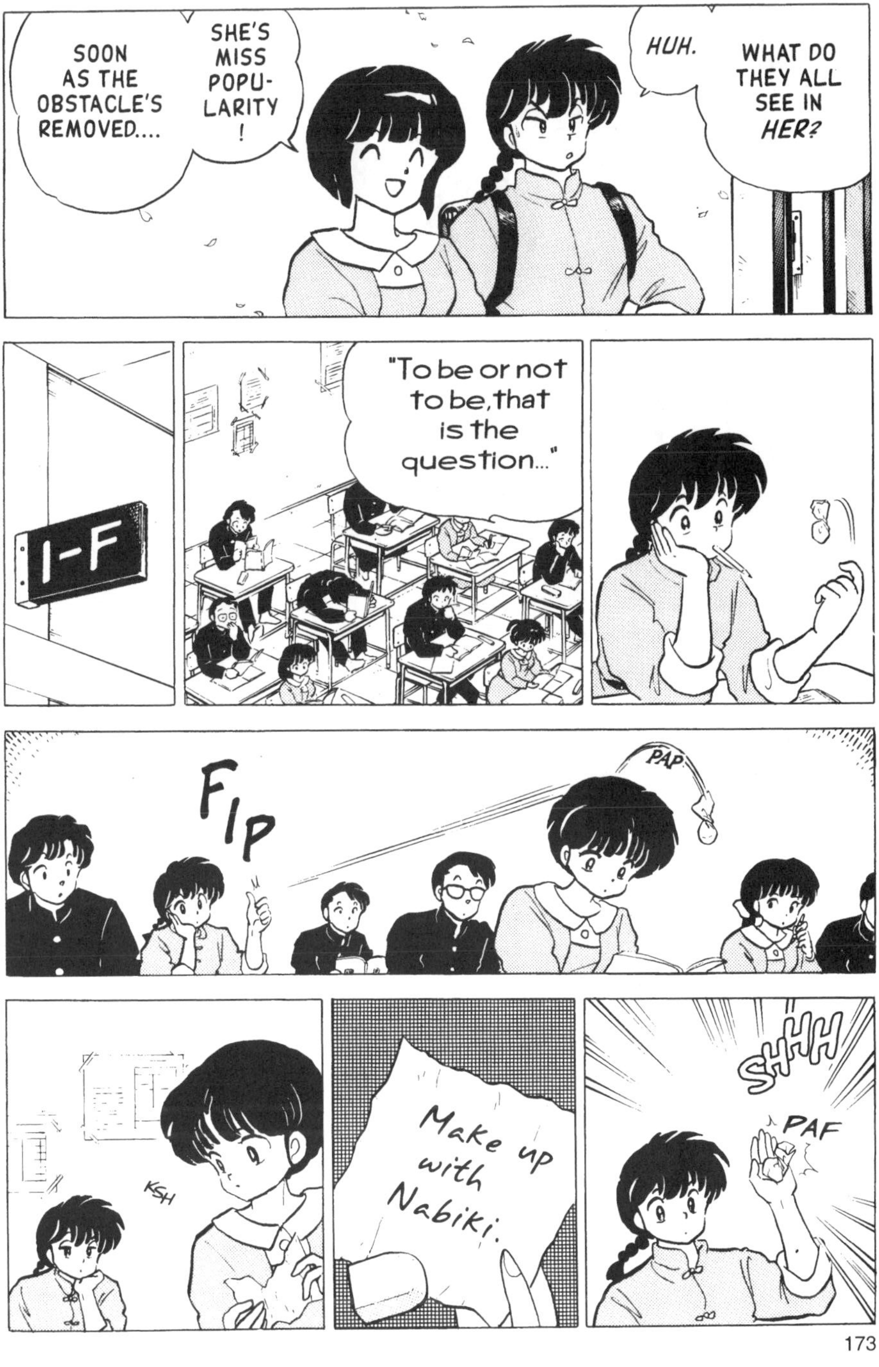
SOON AS THE OBSTACLE'S REMOVED....
SHE'S MISS POPULARITY!
HUH.
WHAT DO THEY ALL SEE IN HER?
1-F
"To be or not to be, that is the question..."
FLIP
PAP
KSH
Make up with Nabiki.
SHHH
PAF

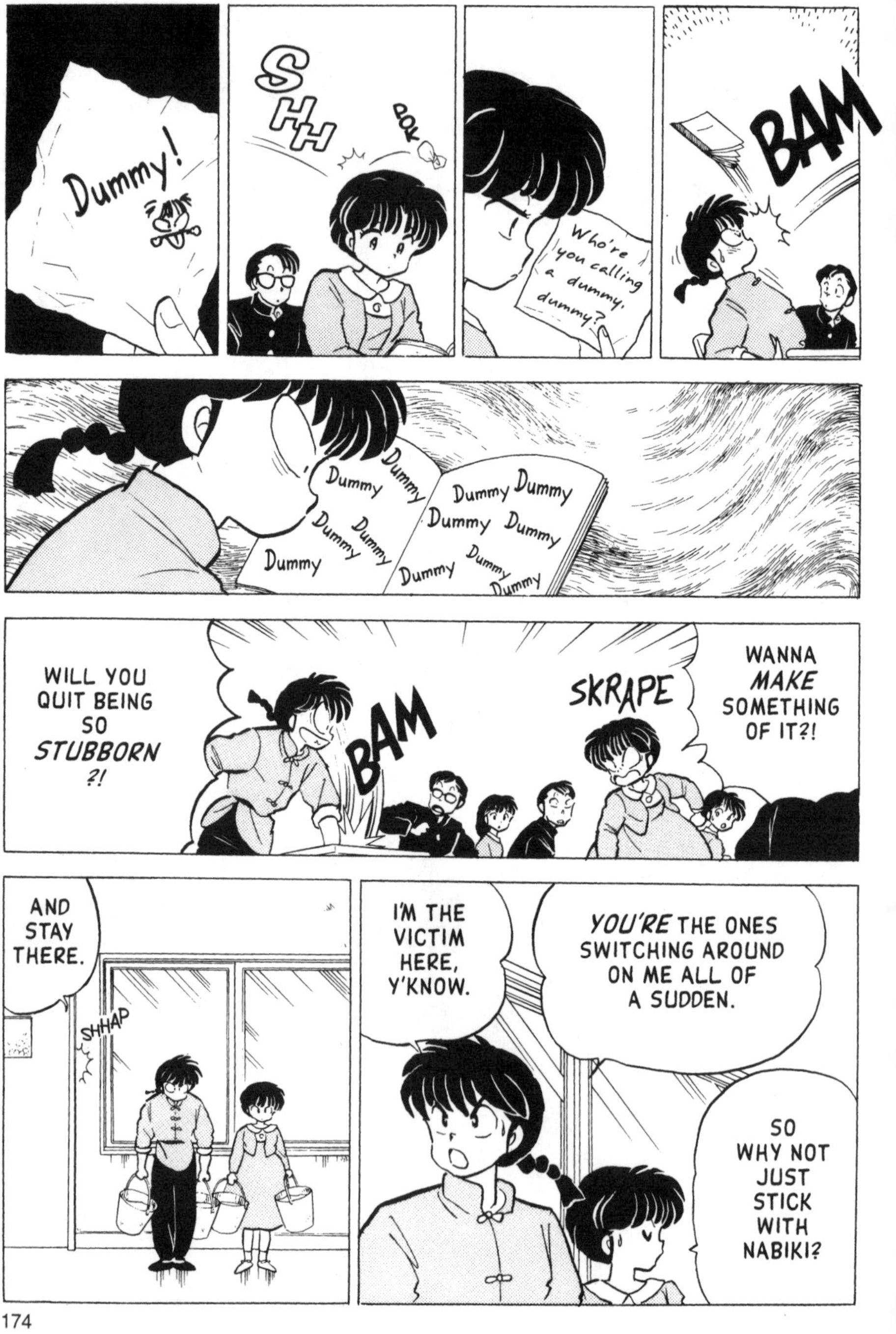
Dummy!
SHH
POK
Who're you calling a dummy, dummy?
BAM
Dummy Dummy Dummy Dummy Dummy
Dummy Dummy Dummy Dummy Dummy Dummy Dummy
WILL YOU QUIT BEING SO *STUBBORN* ?!
BAM
SKRAPE
WANNA *MAKE* SOMETHING OF IT?!
AND STAY THERE.
SHHAP
I'M THE VICTIM HERE, Y'KNOW.
YOU'RE THE ONES SWITCHING AROUND ON ME ALL OF A SUDDEN.
SO WHY NOT JUST STICK WITH NABIKI?

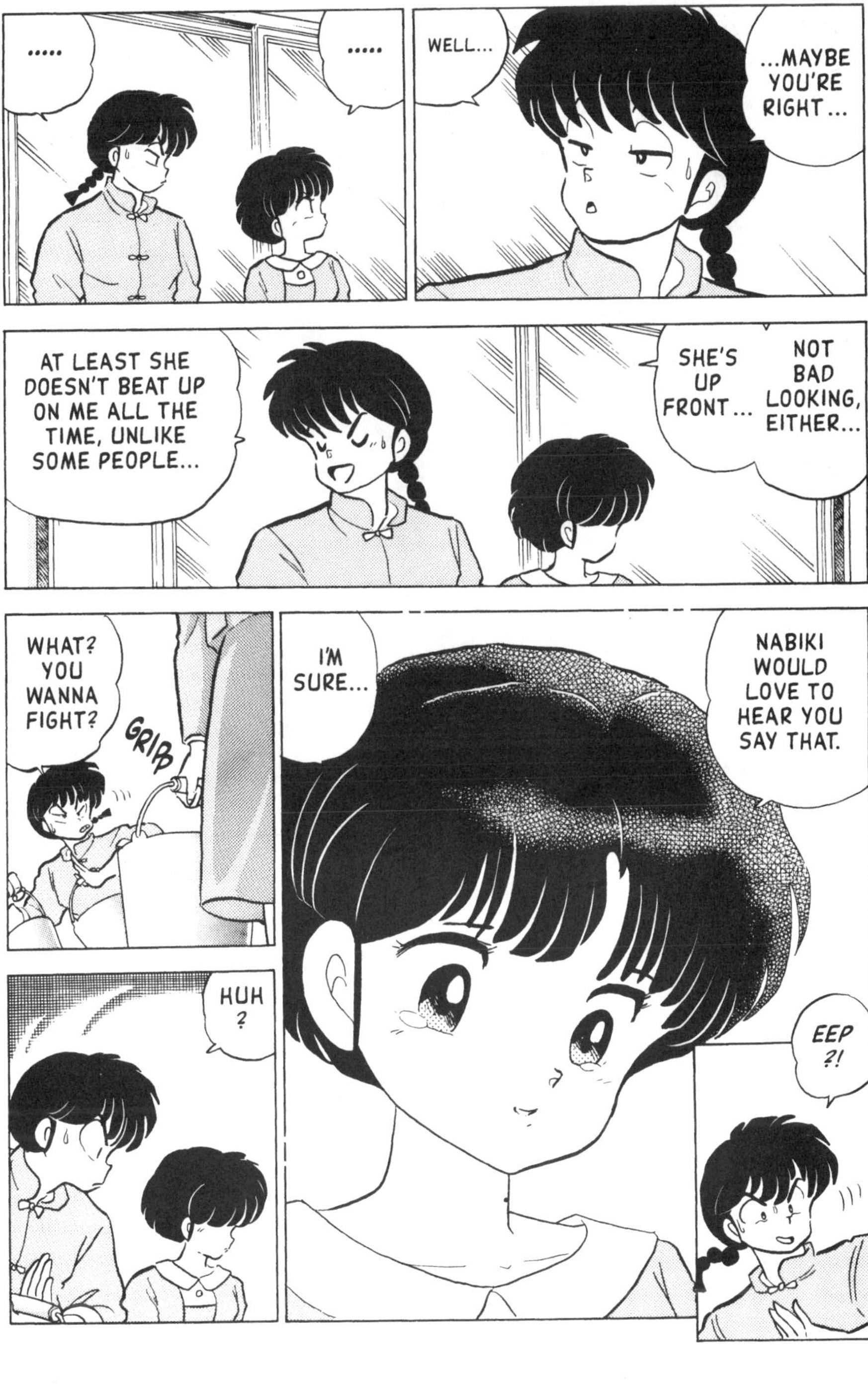
......
......
WELL...
...MAYBE YOU'RE RIGHT...
AT LEAST SHE DOESN'T BEAT UP ON ME ALL THE TIME, UNLIKE SOME PEOPLE...
SHE'S UP FRONT...
NOT BAD LOOKING, EITHER...
WHAT? YOU WANNA FIGHT?
GRIP
HUH ?
I'M SURE...
NABIKI WOULD LOVE TO HEAR YOU SAY THAT.
EEP ?!

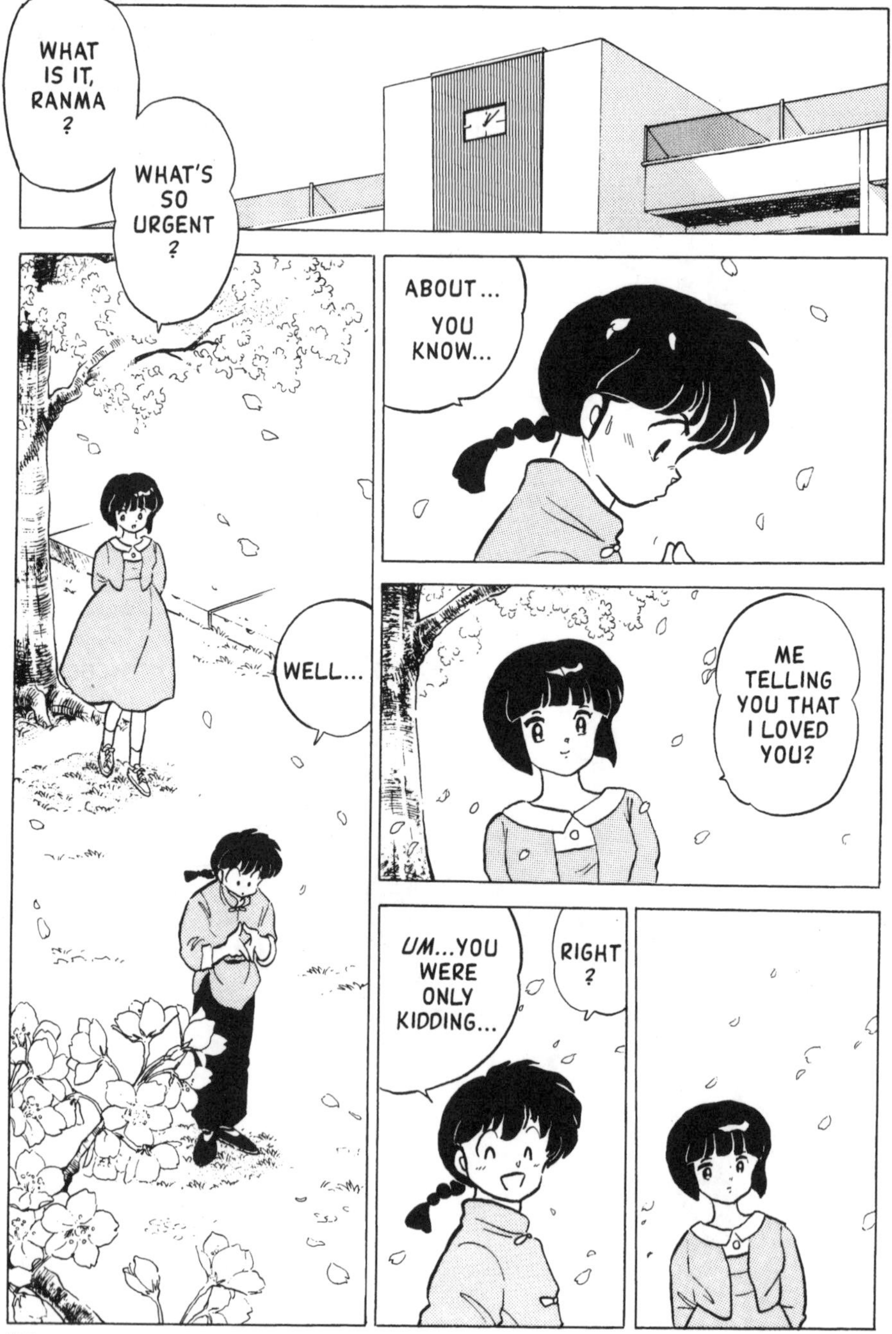
WHAT IS IT, RANMA?
WHAT'S SO URGENT?
WELL...
ABOUT... YOU KNOW...
ME TELLING YOU THAT I LOVED YOU?
UM...YOU WERE ONLY KIDDING...
RIGHT?

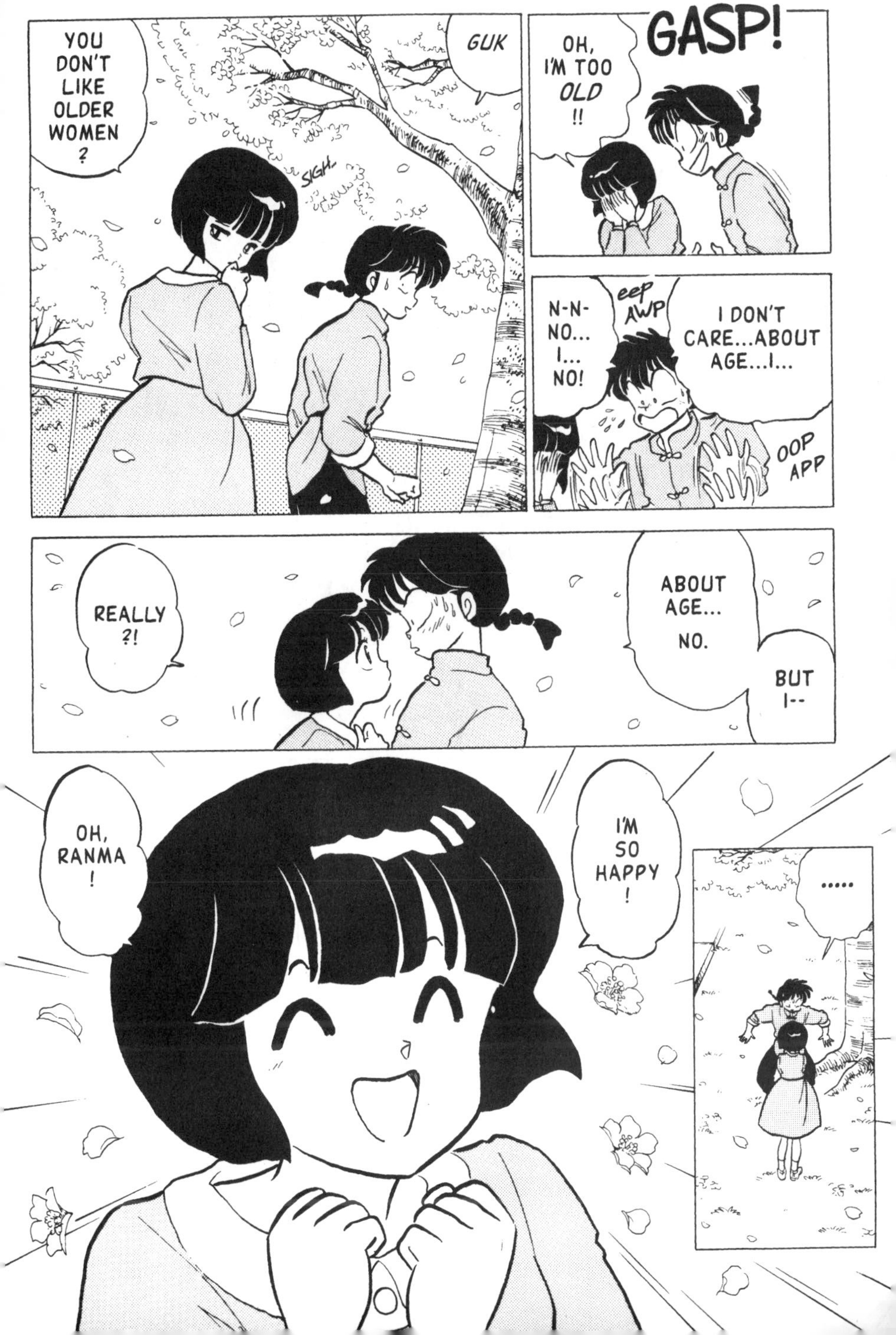
YOU DON'T LIKE OLDER WOMEN ?
SIGH
GUK
OH, I'M TOO OLD !!
GASP!
N-N-NO... I... NO!
eep AWP
I DON'T CARE...ABOUT AGE...I...
OOP APP
REALLY ?!
ABOUT AGE... NO.
BUT I--
OH, RANMA !
I'M SO HAPPY !
.....

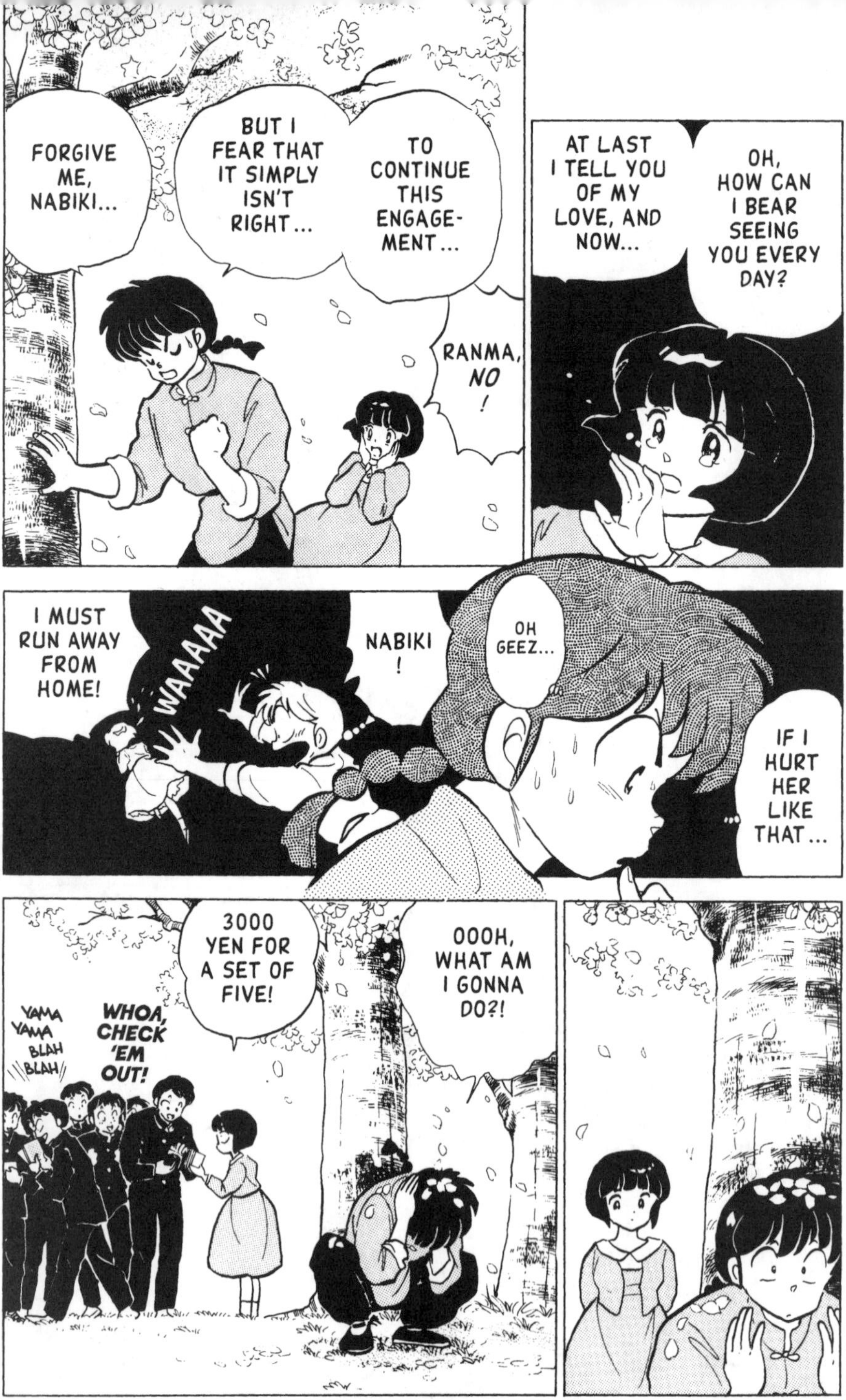
FORGIVE ME, NABIKI...
BUT I FEAR THAT IT SIMPLY ISN'T RIGHT...
TO CONTINUE THIS ENGAGEMENT...
RANMA, NO!
AT LAST I TELL YOU OF MY LOVE, AND NOW...
OH, HOW CAN I BEAR SEEING YOU EVERY DAY?
I MUST RUN AWAY FROM HOME!
WAAAAA
NABIKI!
OH GEEZ...
IF I HURT HER LIKE THAT...
YAMA YAMA BLAH BLAH
WHOA, CHECK 'EM OUT!
3000 YEN FOR A SET OF FIVE!
OOOH, WHAT AM I GONNA DO?!

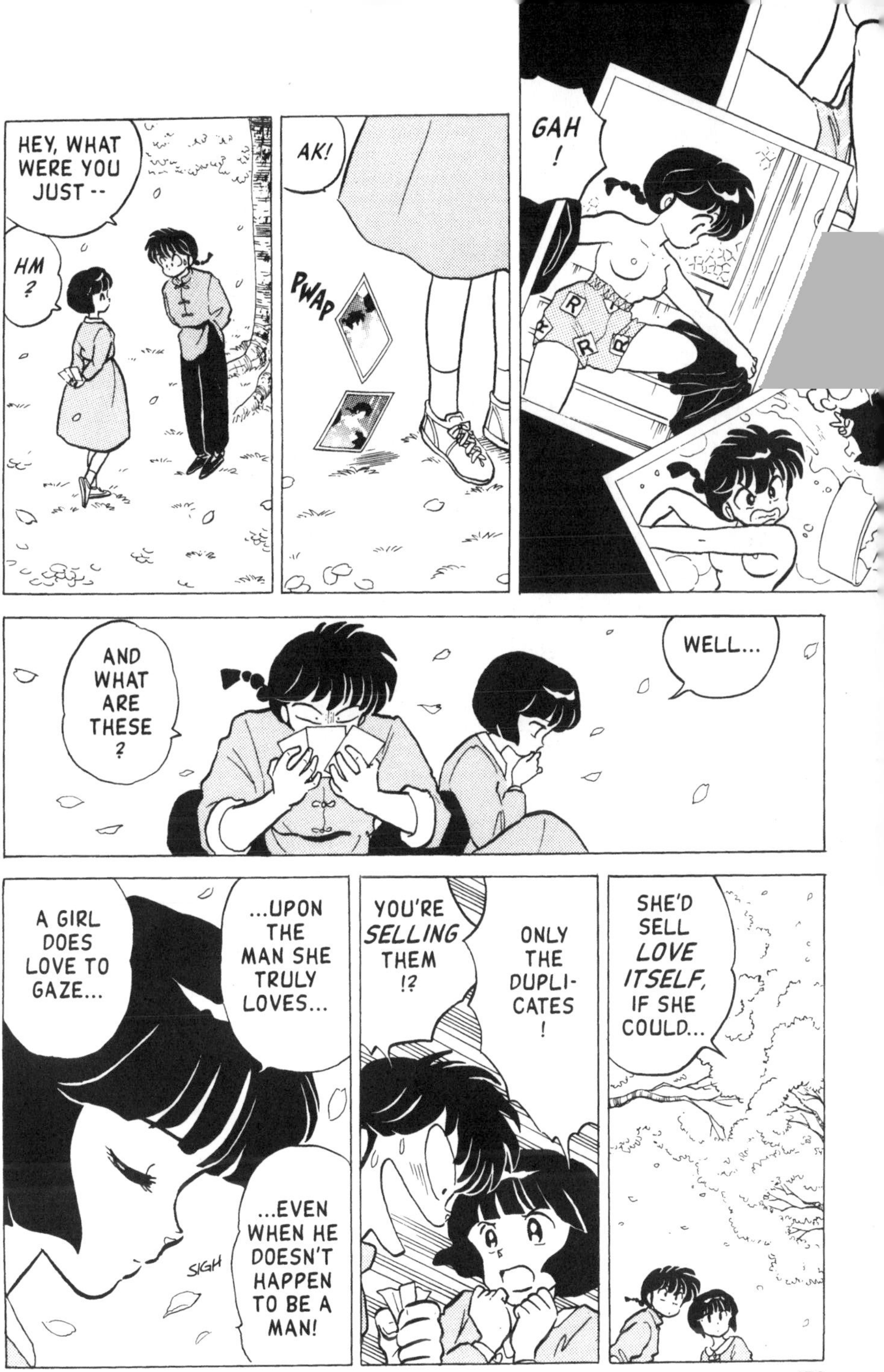
HEY, WHAT WERE YOU JUST --
HM ?
AK!
PWAP
GAH !
AND WHAT ARE THESE ?
WELL...
A GIRL DOES LOVE TO GAZE...
...UPON THE MAN SHE TRULY LOVES...
...EVEN WHEN HE DOESN'T HAPPEN TO BE A MAN!
SIGH
YOU'RE *SELLING* THEM !?
ONLY THE DUPLICATES !
SHE'D SELL *LOVE ITSELF,* IF SHE COULD...

NABIKI TENDO, TAKE THIS!

SHHH

UKYO, NO!

PASH

I WON'T LET YOU HURT --

HUH?

WHAT?!

1000

日本銀行券 千円 日本銀行

10

THE RENTAL FEE FOR RANMA.

FEE?

1000 YEN AN HOUR.

DID YOU SAY YOU'RE RENTING OUT RANMA?!

WE WANT HIM FOR OUR COMPE-TITIONS!

STEP RIGHT UP!

HOLD *ON*!

UH-UH! YOU'RE *MINE* FOR THE NEXT HOUR!

BLAH BLAH

CHATTER CHATTER

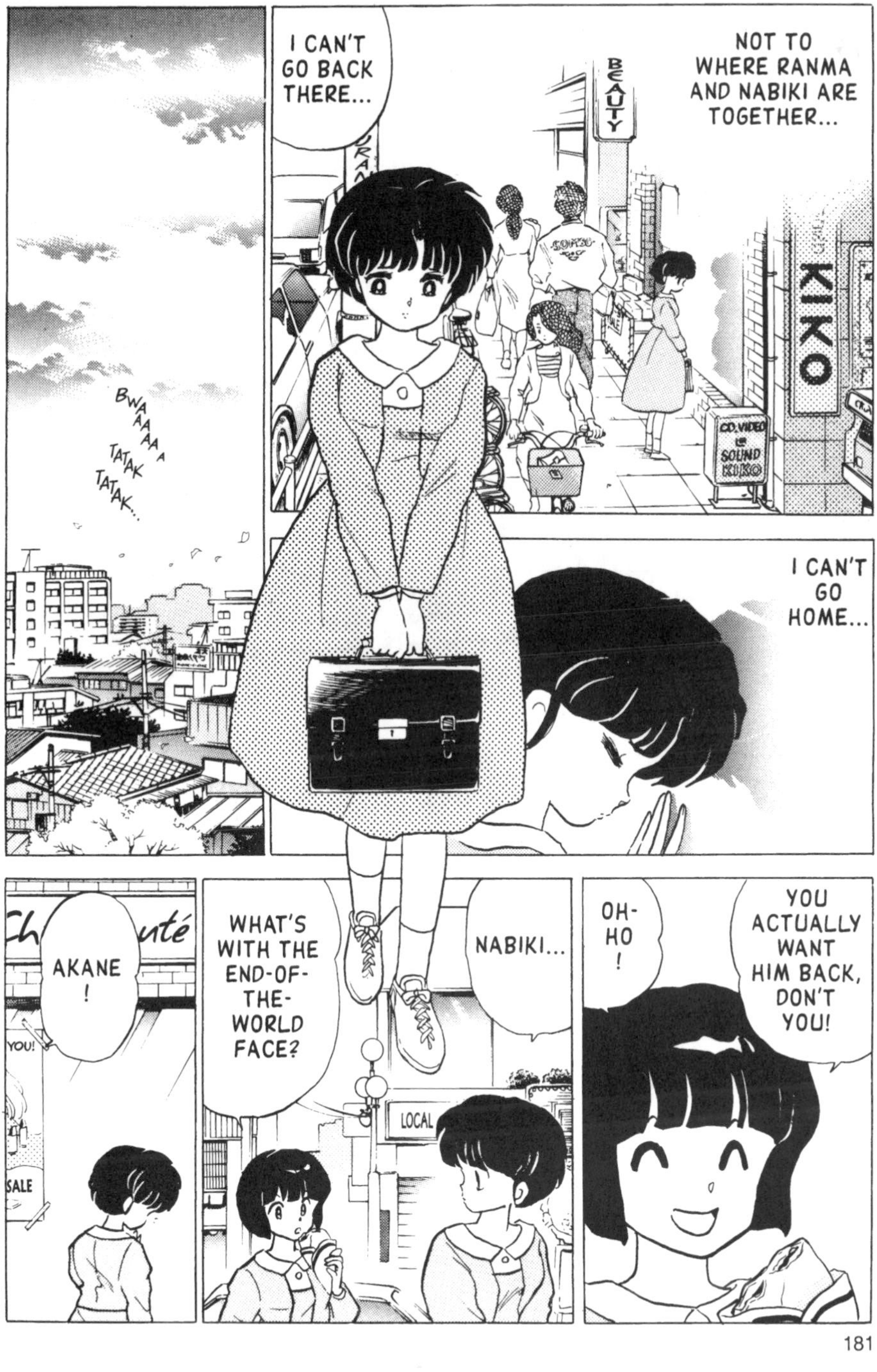
BWAAAAAAA
TATAK TATAK...
I CAN'T GO BACK THERE...
BEAUTY
NOT TO WHERE RANMA AND NABIKI ARE TOGETHER...
KIKO
CD,VIDEO SOUND KIKO
I CAN'T GO HOME...
AKANE!
YOU!
SALE
WHAT'S WITH THE END-OF-THE-WORLD FACE?
NABIKI...
LOCAL
OH-HO!
YOU ACTUALLY WANT HIM BACK, DON'T YOU!

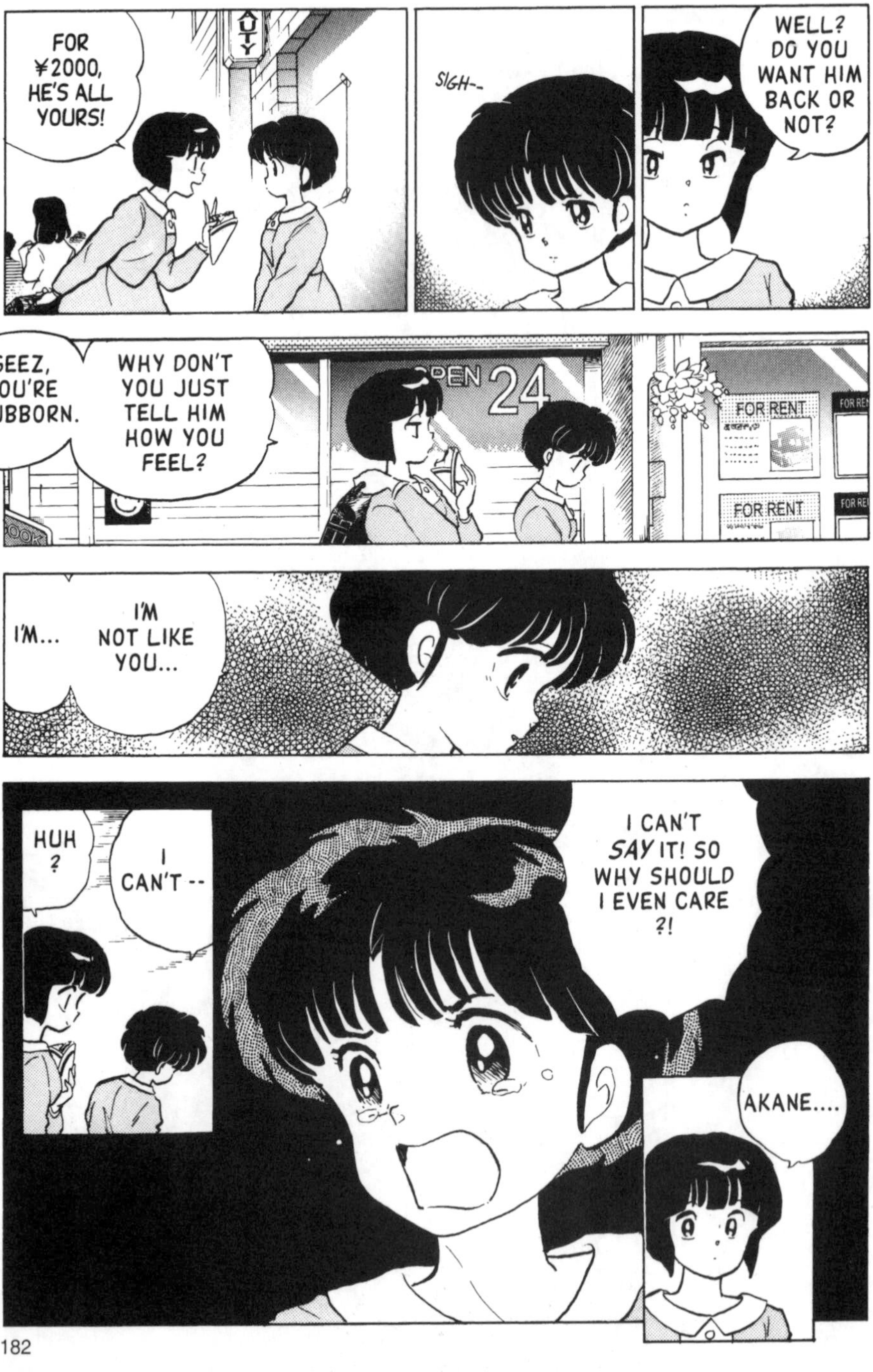
FOR ¥2000, HE'S ALL YOURS!
SIGH--
WELL? DO YOU WANT HIM BACK OR NOT?
GEEZ, YOU'RE STUBBORN.
WHY DON'T YOU JUST TELL HIM HOW YOU FEEL?
OPEN 24
FOR RENT
FOR RENT
I'M...
I'M NOT LIKE YOU...
HUH?
I CAN'T --
I CAN'T SAY IT! SO WHY SHOULD I EVEN CARE?!
AKANE....

Part 12
I'M THE VICTIM HERE!

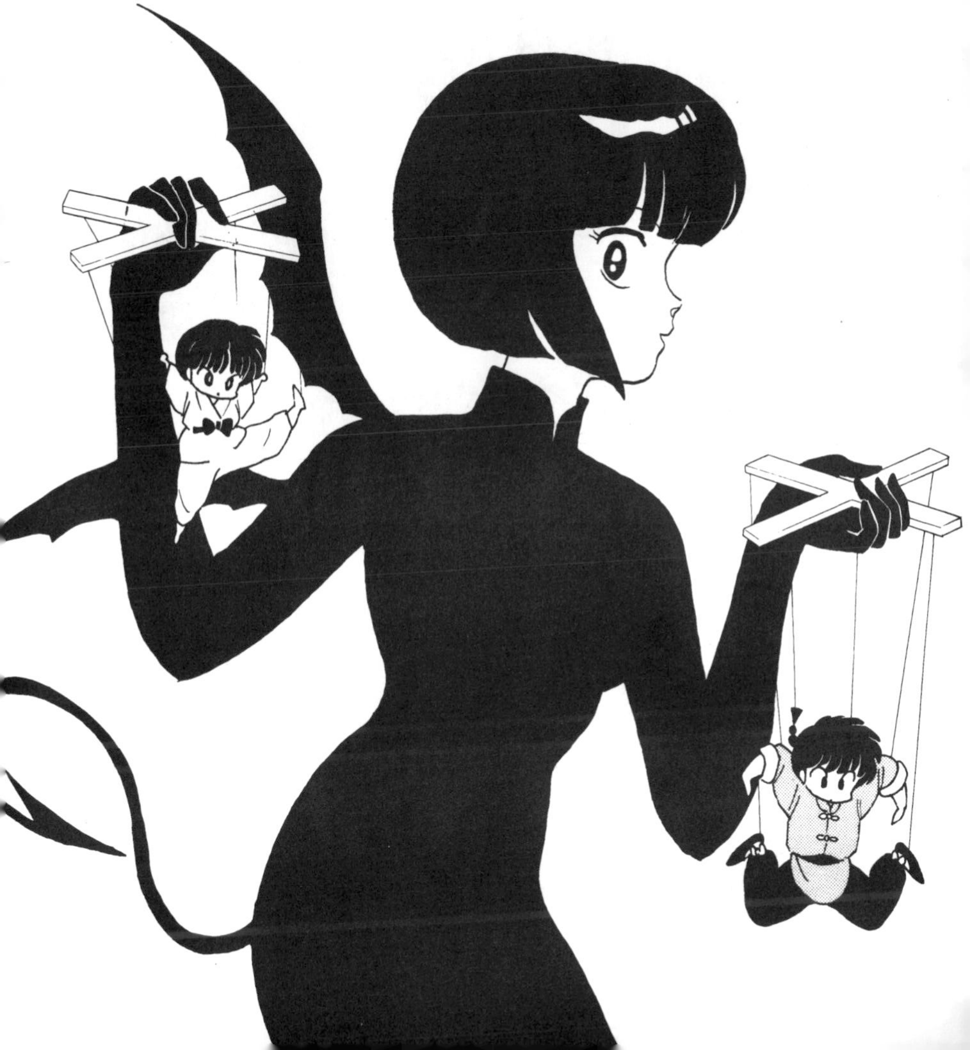

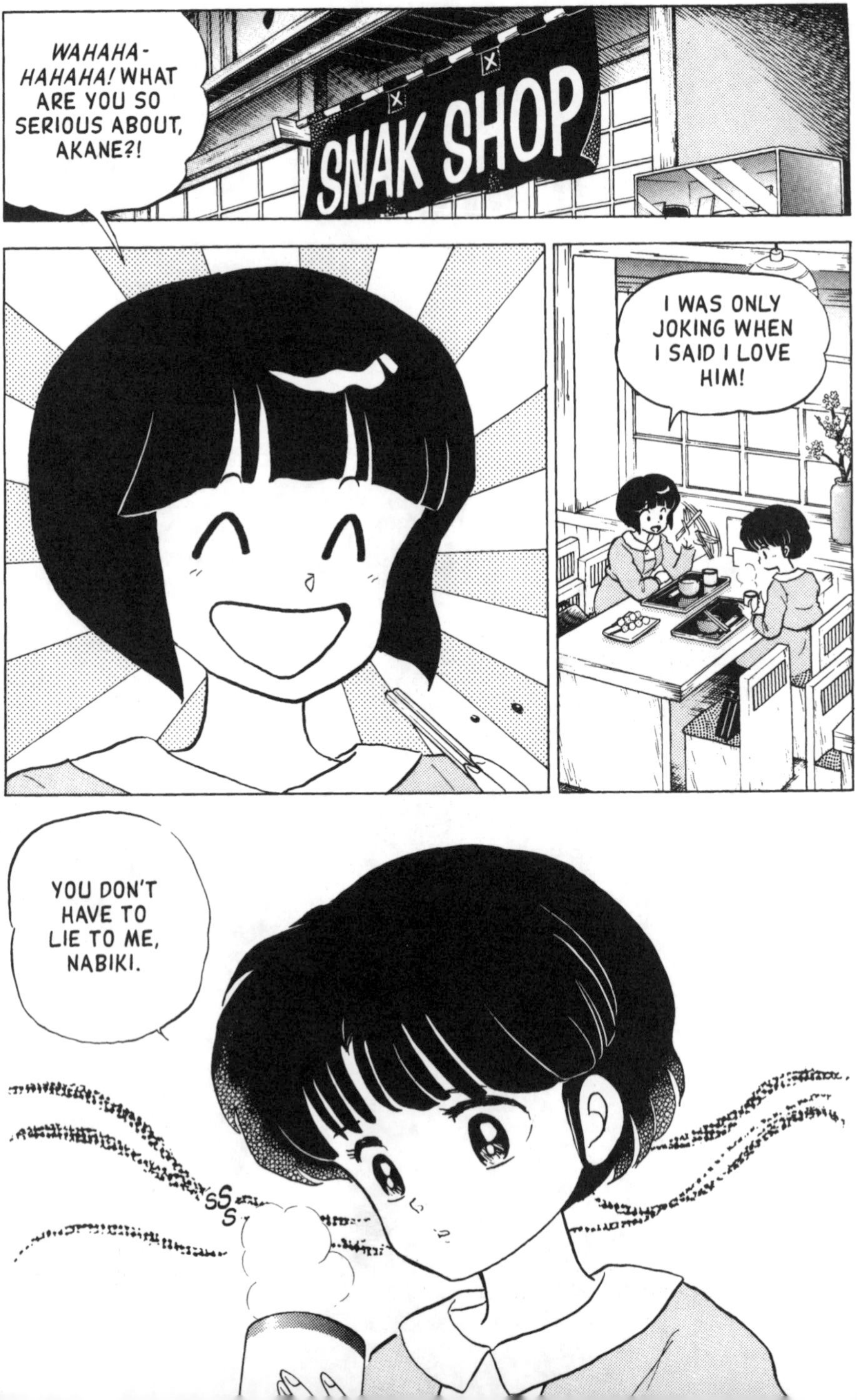
SNAK SHOP
WAHAHA-HAHAHA! WHAT ARE YOU SO SERIOUS ABOUT, AKANE?!
I WAS ONLY JOKING WHEN I SAID I LOVE HIM!
YOU DON'T HAVE TO LIE TO ME, NABIKI.
SSS

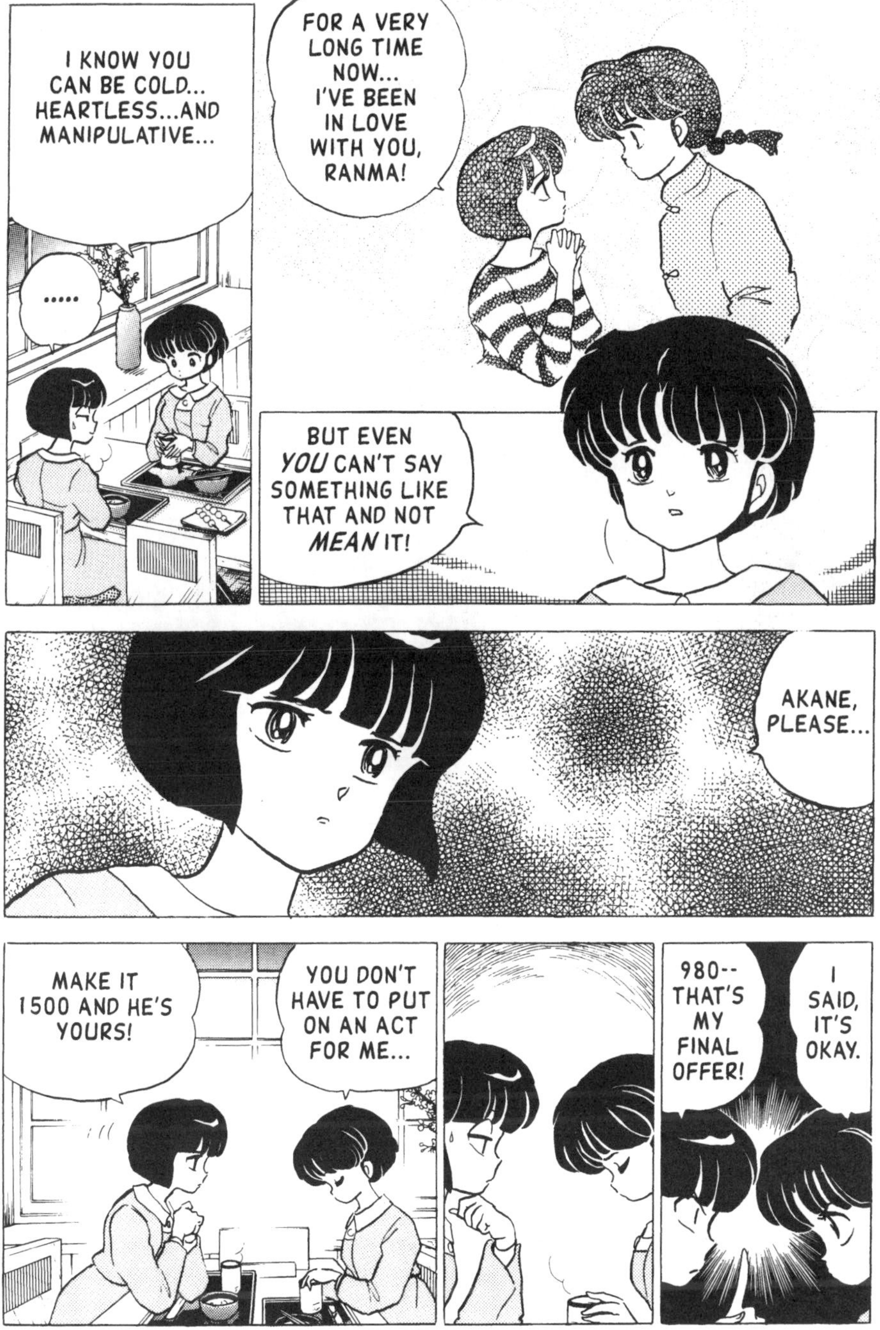
I KNOW YOU CAN BE COLD... HEARTLESS...AND MANIPULATIVE...
.....
FOR A VERY LONG TIME NOW... I'VE BEEN IN LOVE WITH YOU, RANMA!
BUT EVEN *YOU* CAN'T SAY SOMETHING LIKE THAT AND NOT *MEAN* IT!
AKANE, PLEASE...
MAKE IT 1500 AND HE'S YOURS!
YOU DON'T HAVE TO PUT ON AN ACT FOR ME...
980-- THAT'S MY FINAL OFFER!
I SAID, IT'S OKAY.

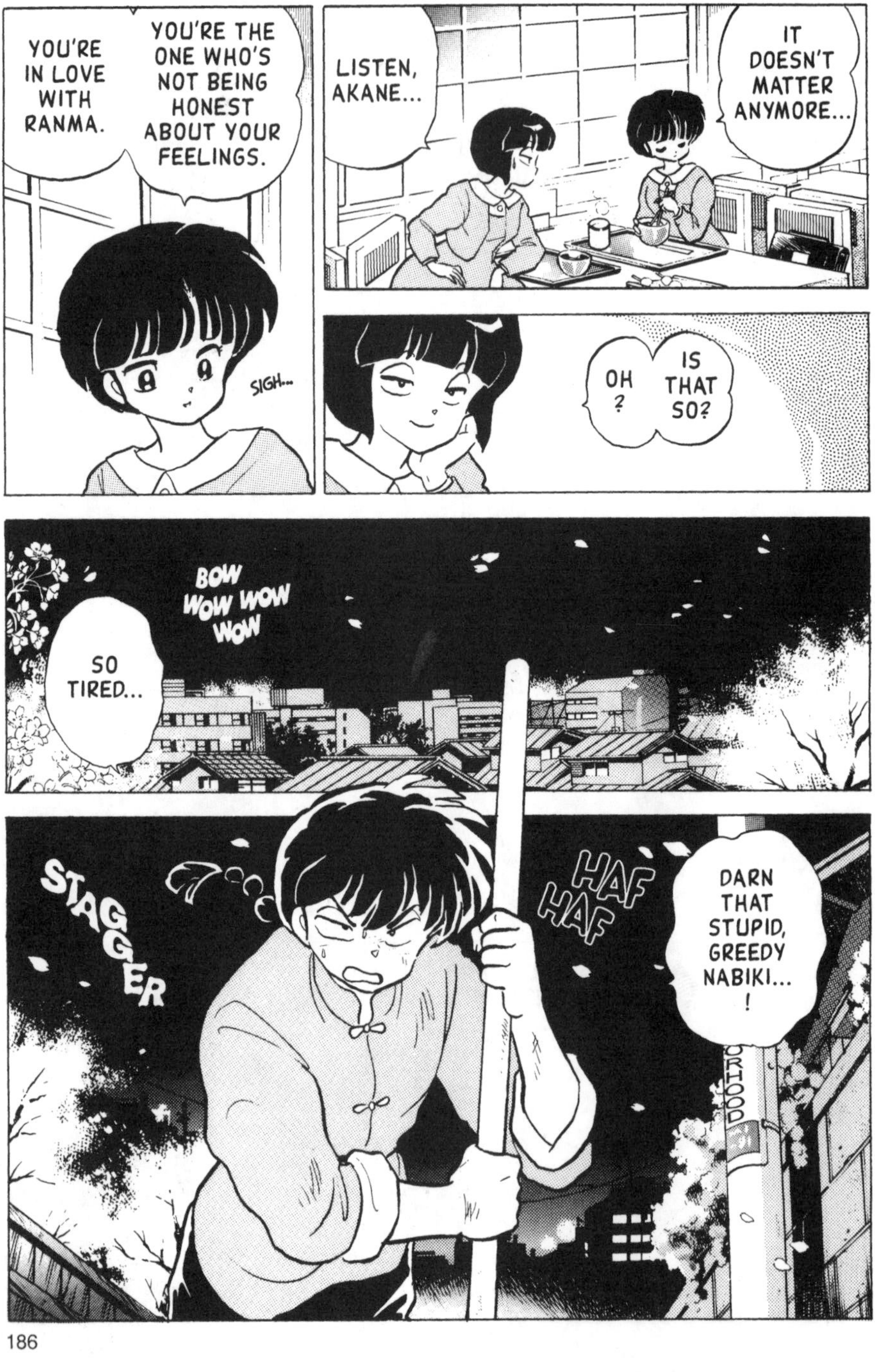
YOU'RE IN LOVE WITH RANMA.
YOU'RE THE ONE WHO'S NOT BEING HONEST ABOUT YOUR FEELINGS.
SIGH...
LISTEN, AKANE...
IT DOESN'T MATTER ANYMORE...
OH?
IS THAT SO?
BOW WOW WOW WOW
SO TIRED...
STAGGER
HAF HAF
DARN THAT STUPID, GREEDY NABIKI...!

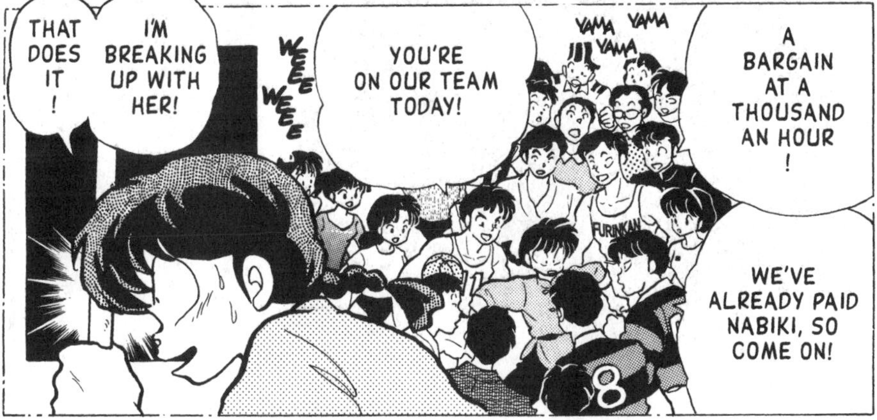
THAT DOES IT !
I'M BREAKING UP WITH HER!
WEEE WEEE
YOU'RE ON OUR TEAM TODAY!
YAMA YAMA YAMA
A BARGAIN AT A THOUSAND AN HOUR !
FURINKAN
WE'VE ALREADY PAID NABIKI, SO COME ON!

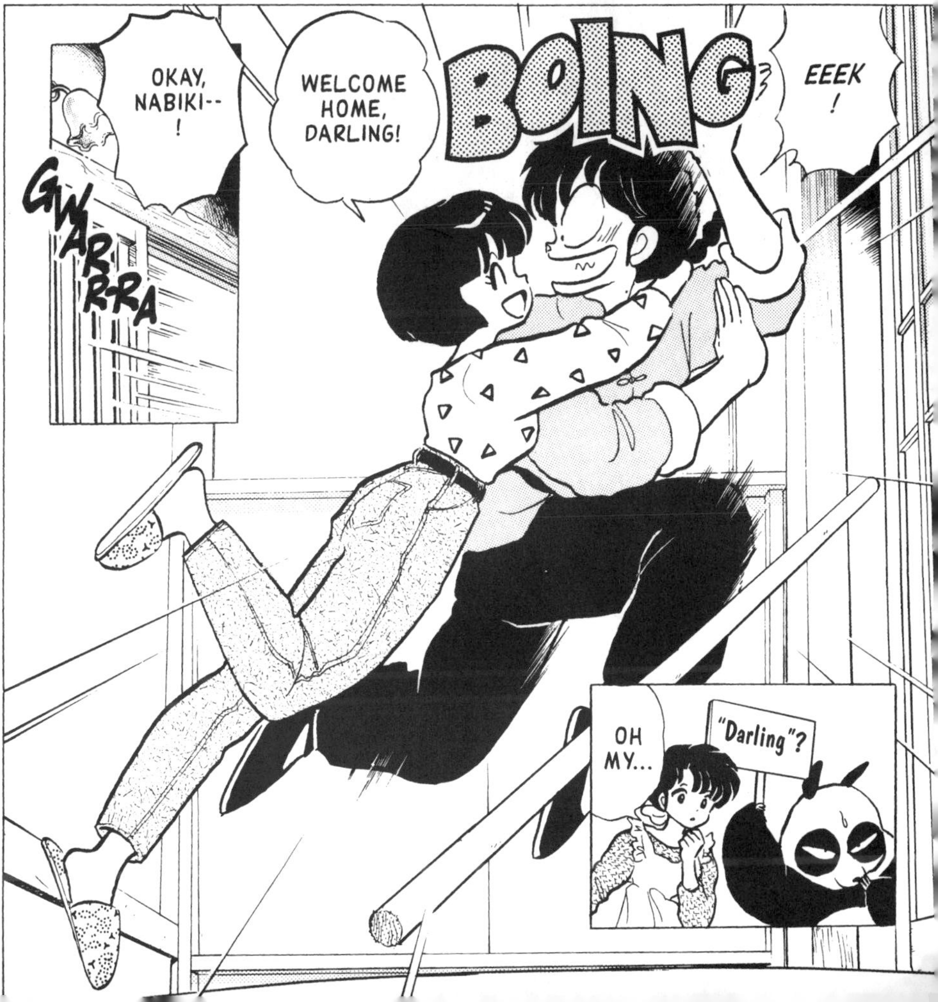
OKAY, NABIKI-- !
GWARRRA
WELCOME HOME, DARLING!
BOING
EEEK !
OH MY...
"Darling"?

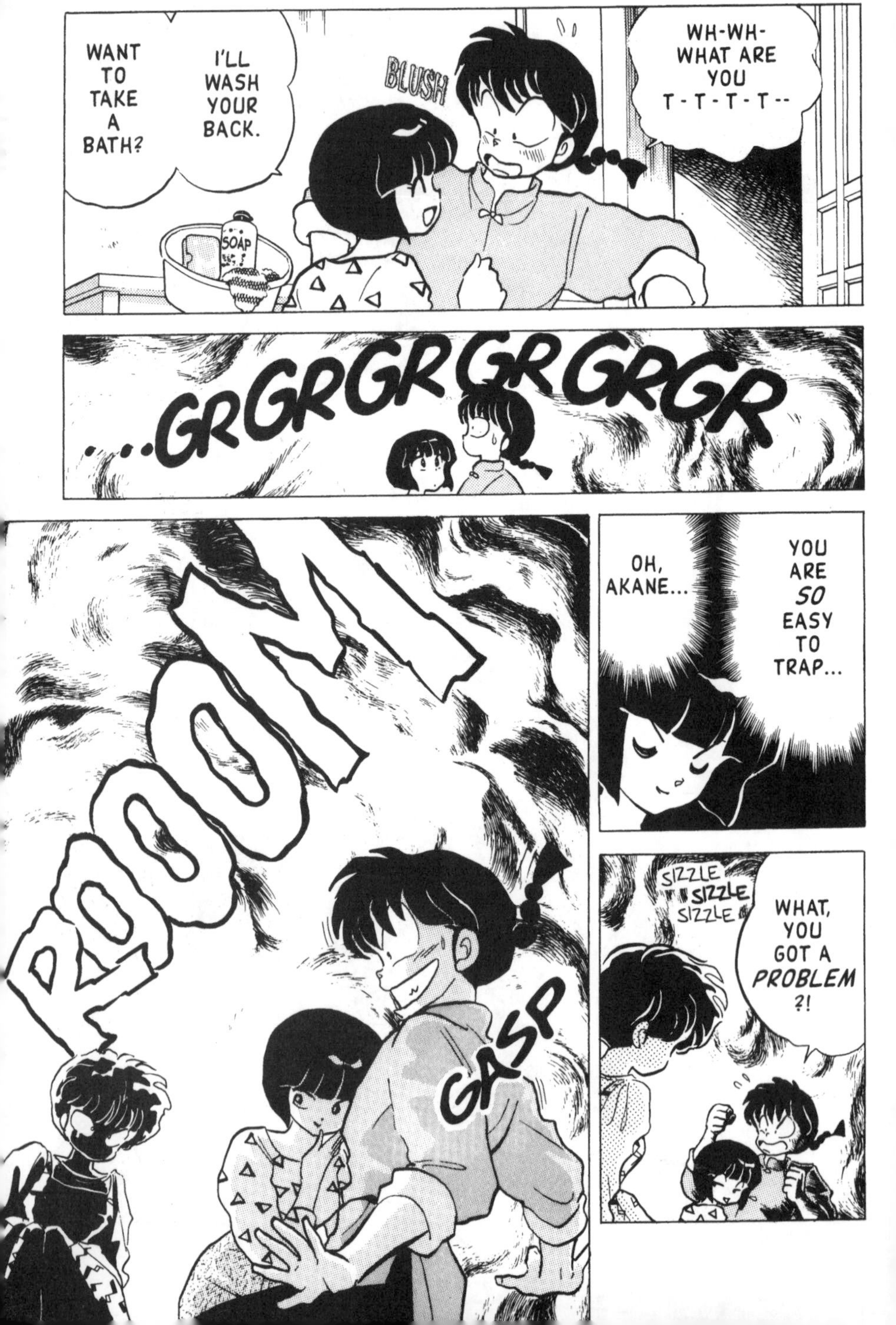
WANT TO TAKE A BATH?
I'LL WASH YOUR BACK.
BLUSH
WH-WH-WHAT ARE YOU T-T-T-T--
...GRGRGRGRGRGRGR
BOOM!
GASP
OH, AKANE...
YOU ARE SO EASY TO TRAP...
SIZZLE SIZZLE SIZZLE
WHAT, YOU GOT A PROBLEM ?!

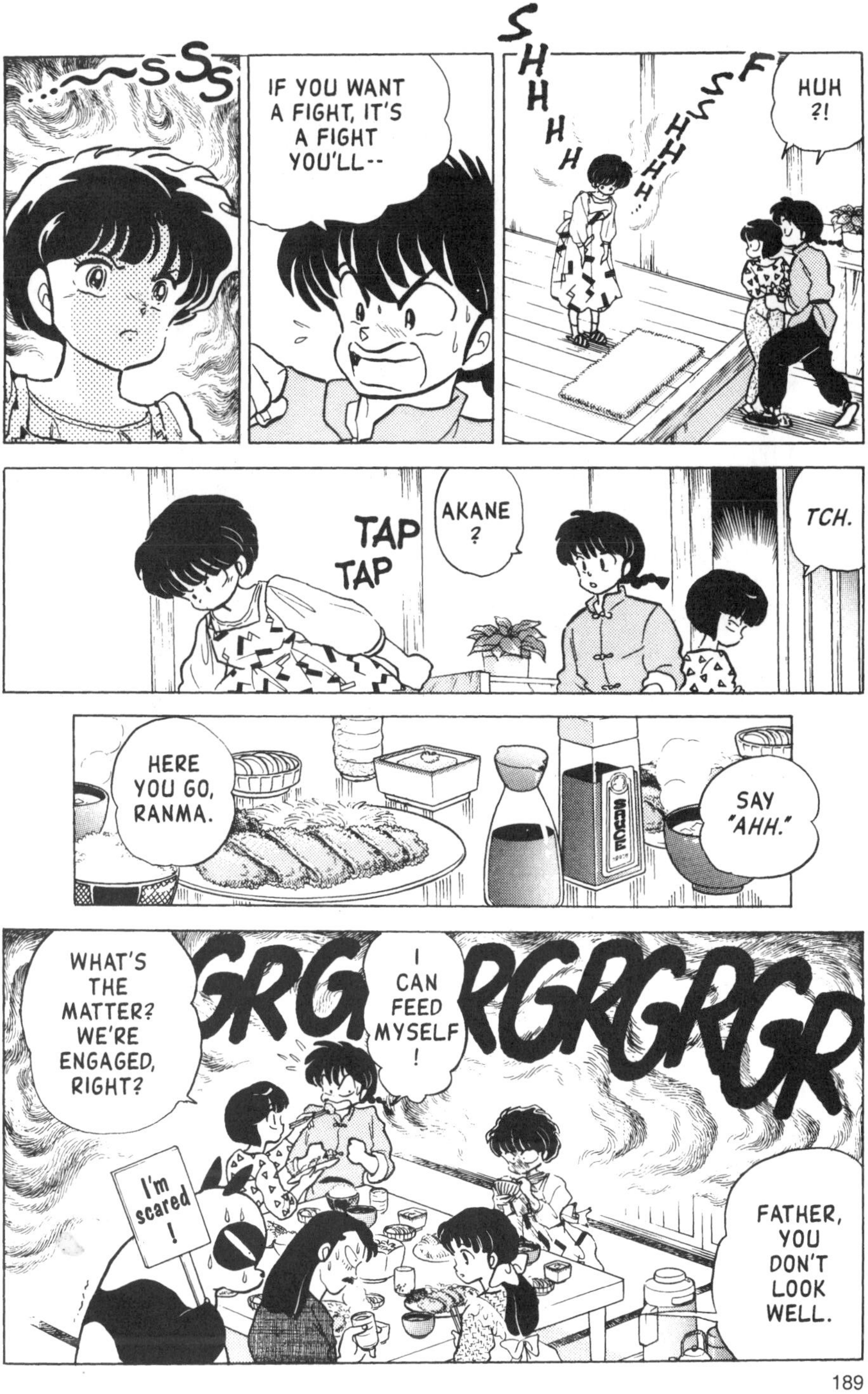

...~~sSS
IF YOU WANT A FIGHT, IT'S A FIGHT YOU'LL--
SHHHH
SHHHHH...
F
HUH ?!
TAP TAP
AKANE ?
TCH.
HERE YOU GO, RANMA.
SAUCE
SAY "AHH."
WHAT'S THE MATTER? WE'RE ENGAGED, RIGHT?
GRG
I CAN FEED MYSELF !
RGRGRGRGR
I'm scared !
FATHER, YOU DON'T LOOK WELL.

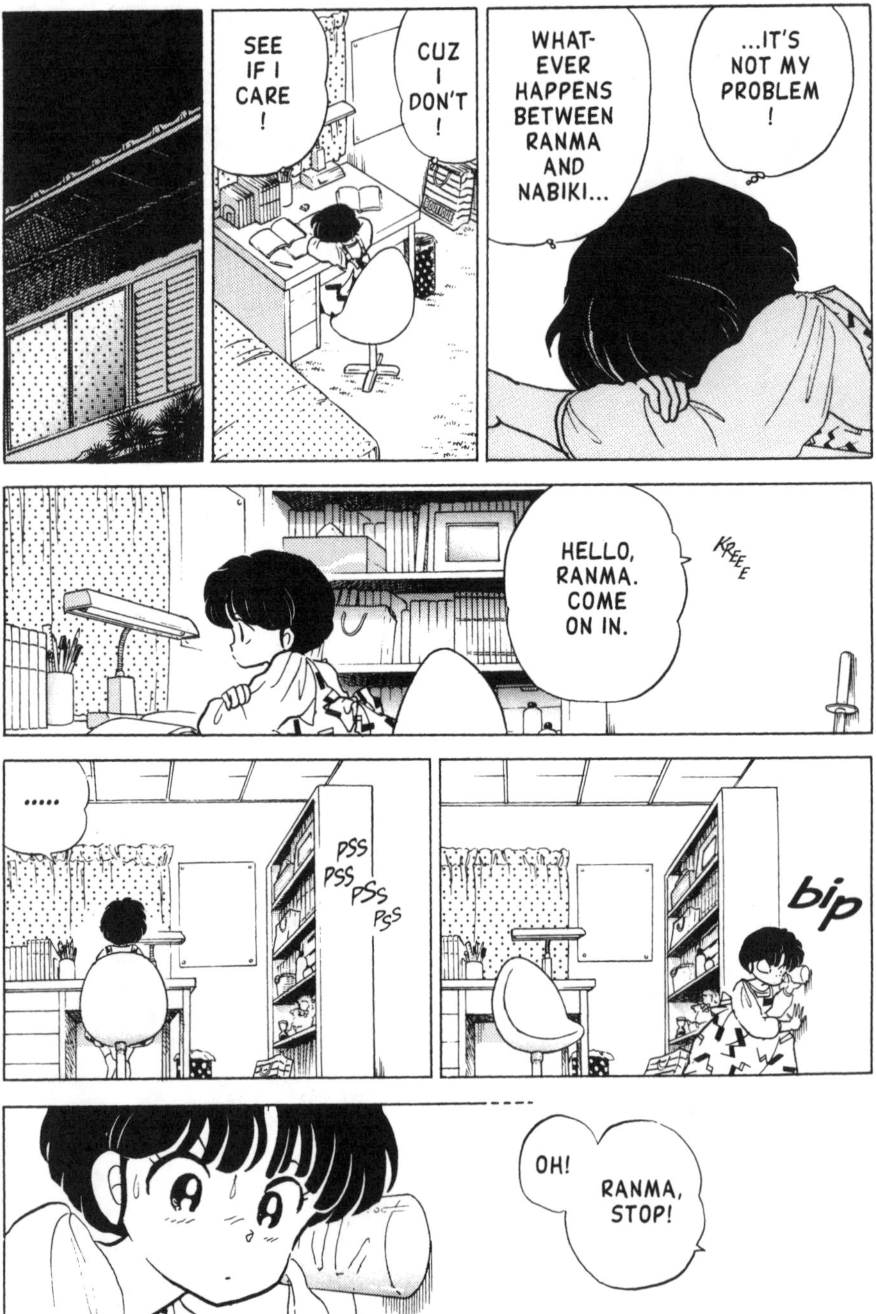
SEE IF I CARE!
CUZ I DON'T!
WHAT-EVER HAPPENS BETWEEN RANMA AND NABIKI...
...IT'S NOT MY PROBLEM!
HELLO, RANMA. COME ON IN.
KREEE
......
PSS PSS PSS PSS
bip
OH!
RANMA, STOP!

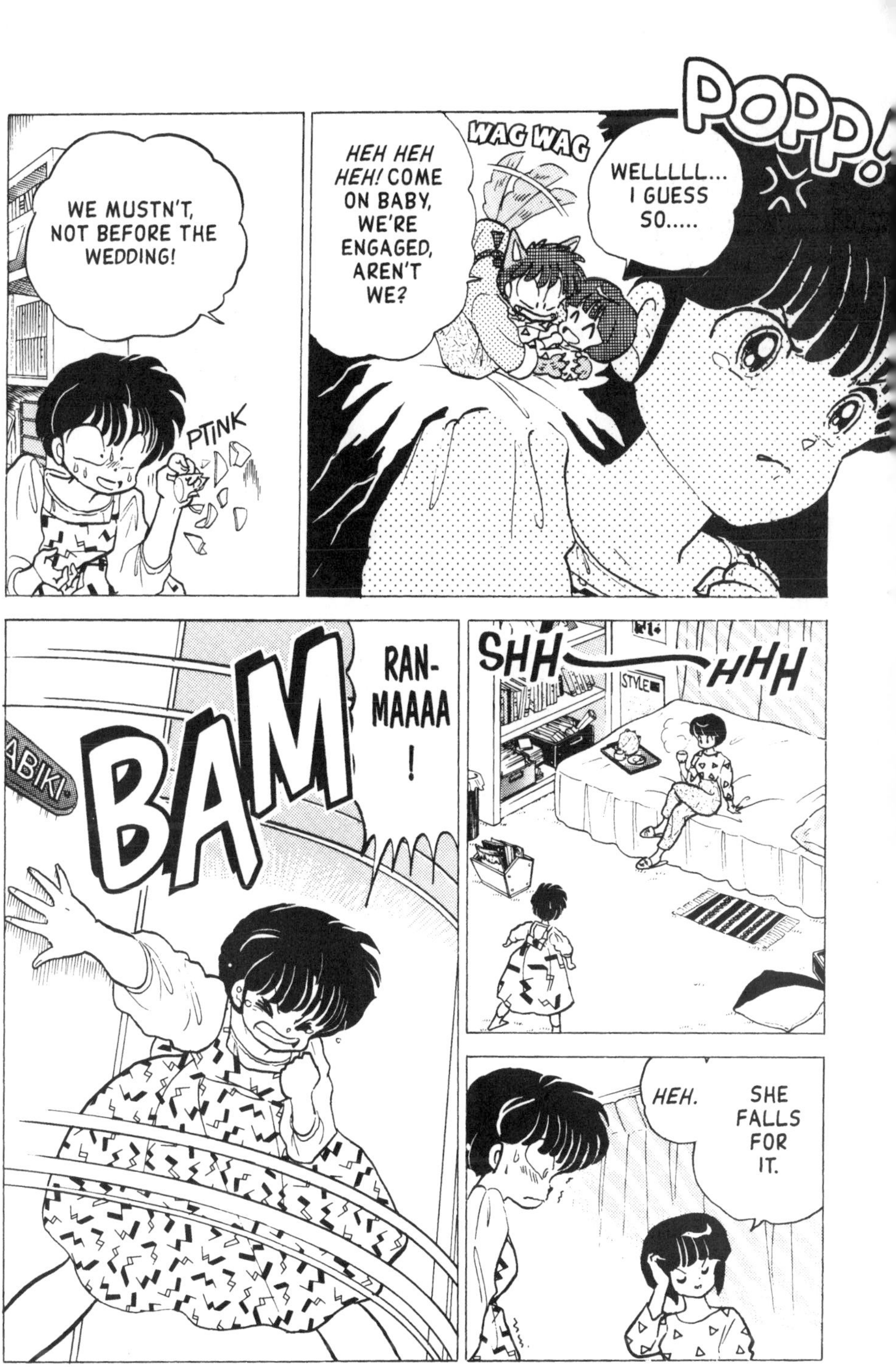
WE MUSTN'T, NOT BEFORE THE WEDDING!
PTINK
HEH HEH HEH! COME ON BABY, WE'RE ENGAGED, AREN'T WE?
WAG WAG
WELLLLL... I GUESS SO.....
POPP!
ABIKI
BAM
RAN-MAAAA!
SHH——HHH
STYLE
HEH.
SHE FALLS FOR IT.

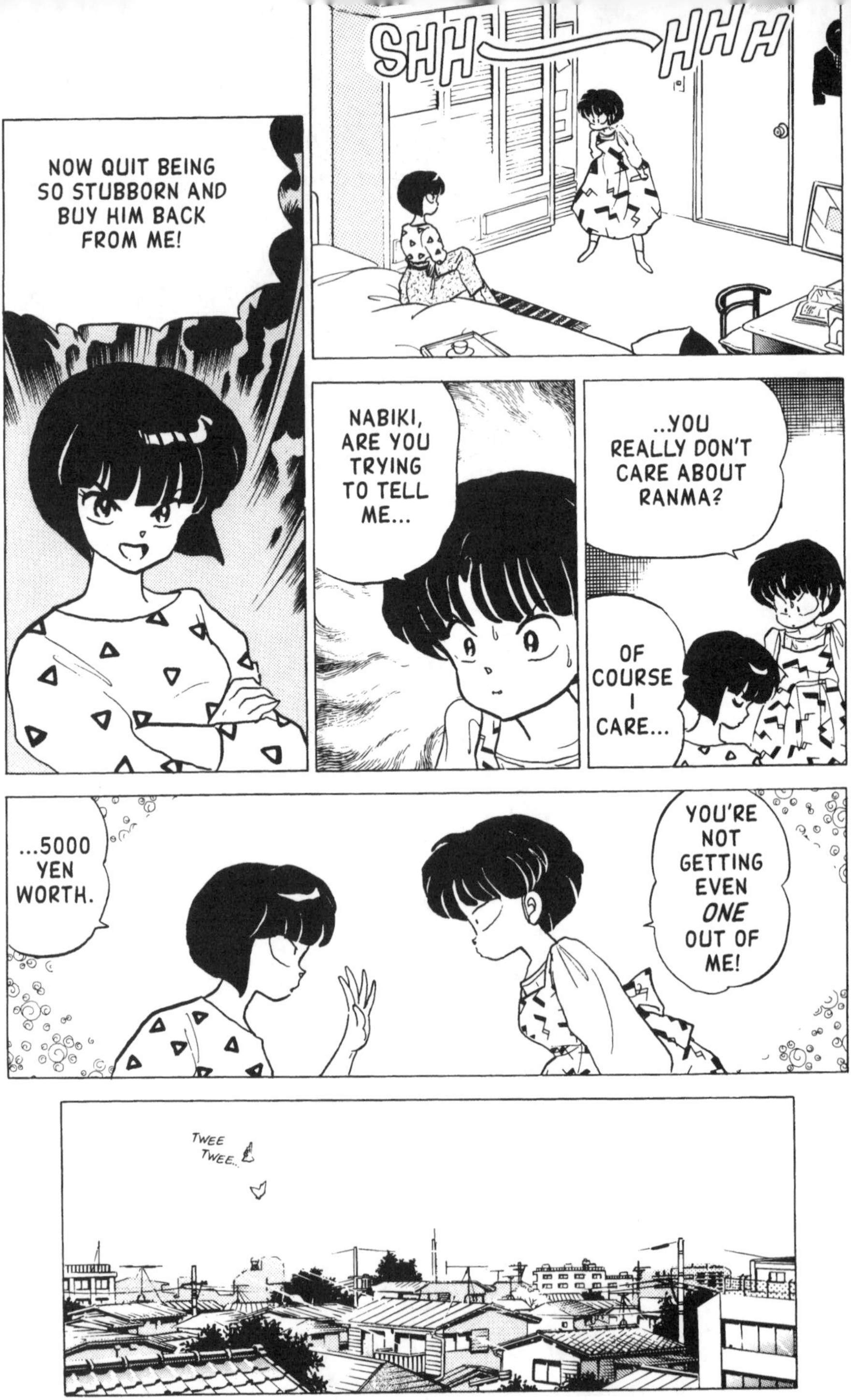
NOW QUIT BEING SO STUBBORN AND BUY HIM BACK FROM ME!
SHH—HHH
NABIKI, ARE YOU TRYING TO TELL ME...
...YOU REALLY DON'T CARE ABOUT RANMA?
OF COURSE I CARE...
...5000 YEN WORTH.
YOU'RE NOT GETTING EVEN *ONE* OUT OF ME!
TWEE TWEE...

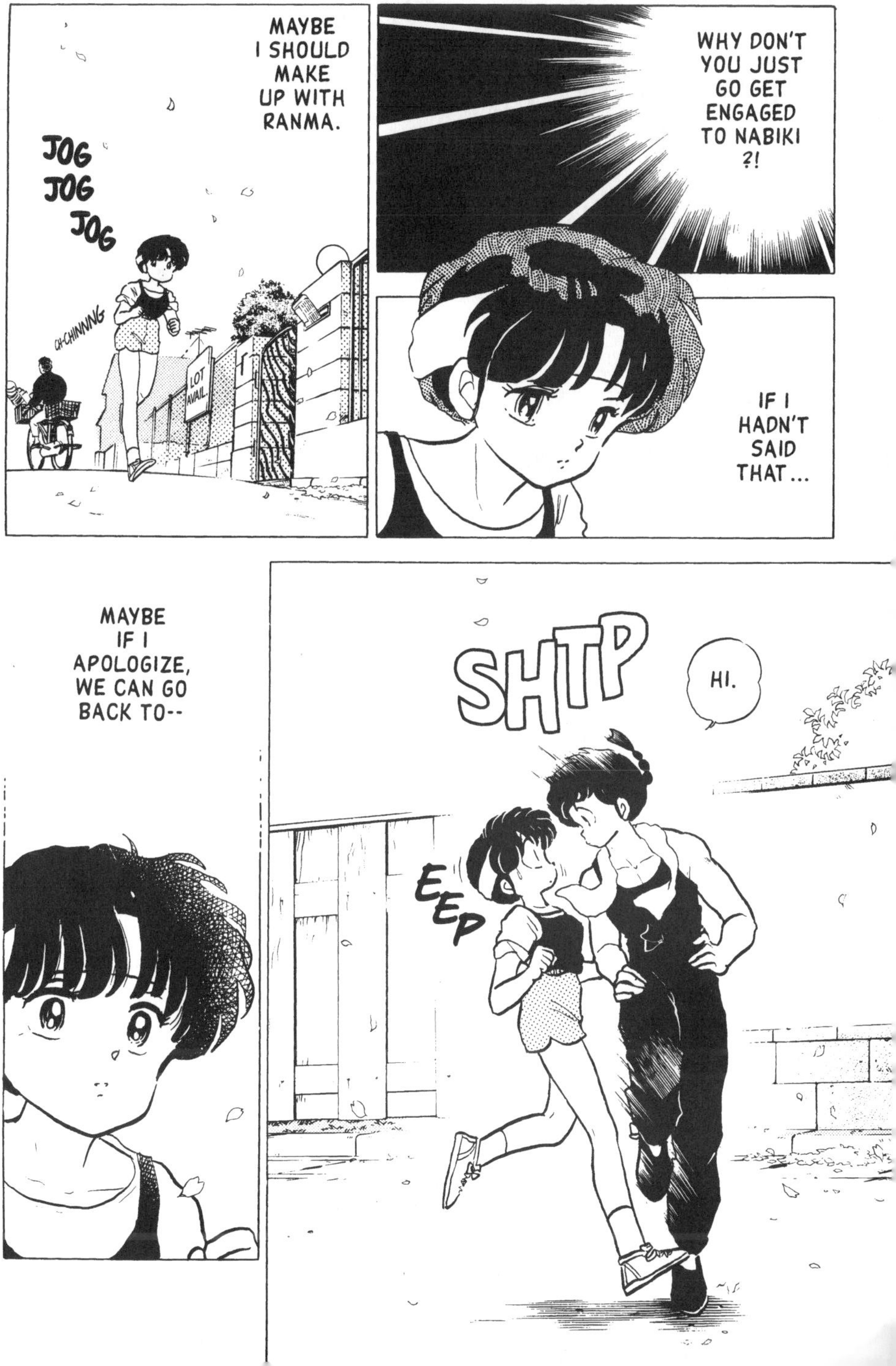

MAYBE I SHOULD MAKE UP WITH RANMA.
JOG JOG JOG
CH-CHINNNG
LOT AVAIL.
WHY DON'T YOU JUST GO GET ENGAGED TO NABIKI ?!
IF I HADN'T SAID THAT...
MAYBE IF I APOLOGIZE, WE CAN GO BACK TO--
SHTP
HI.
EEEP

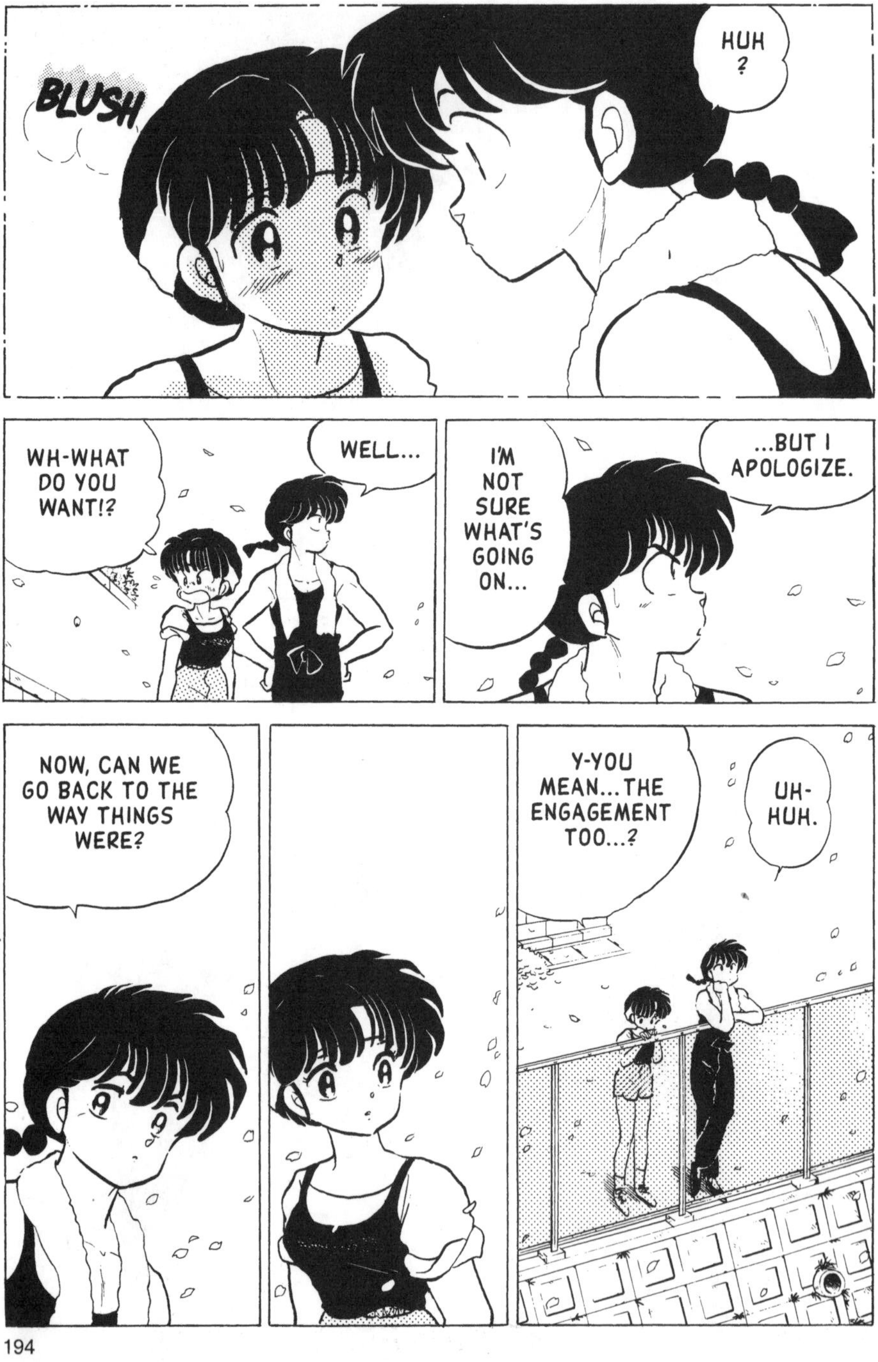
BLUSH
HUH?
WH-WHAT DO YOU WANT!?
WELL...
I'M NOT SURE WHAT'S GOING ON...
...BUT I APOLOGIZE.
NOW, CAN WE GO BACK TO THE WAY THINGS WERE?
Y-YOU MEAN...THE ENGAGEMENT TOO...?
UH-HUH.

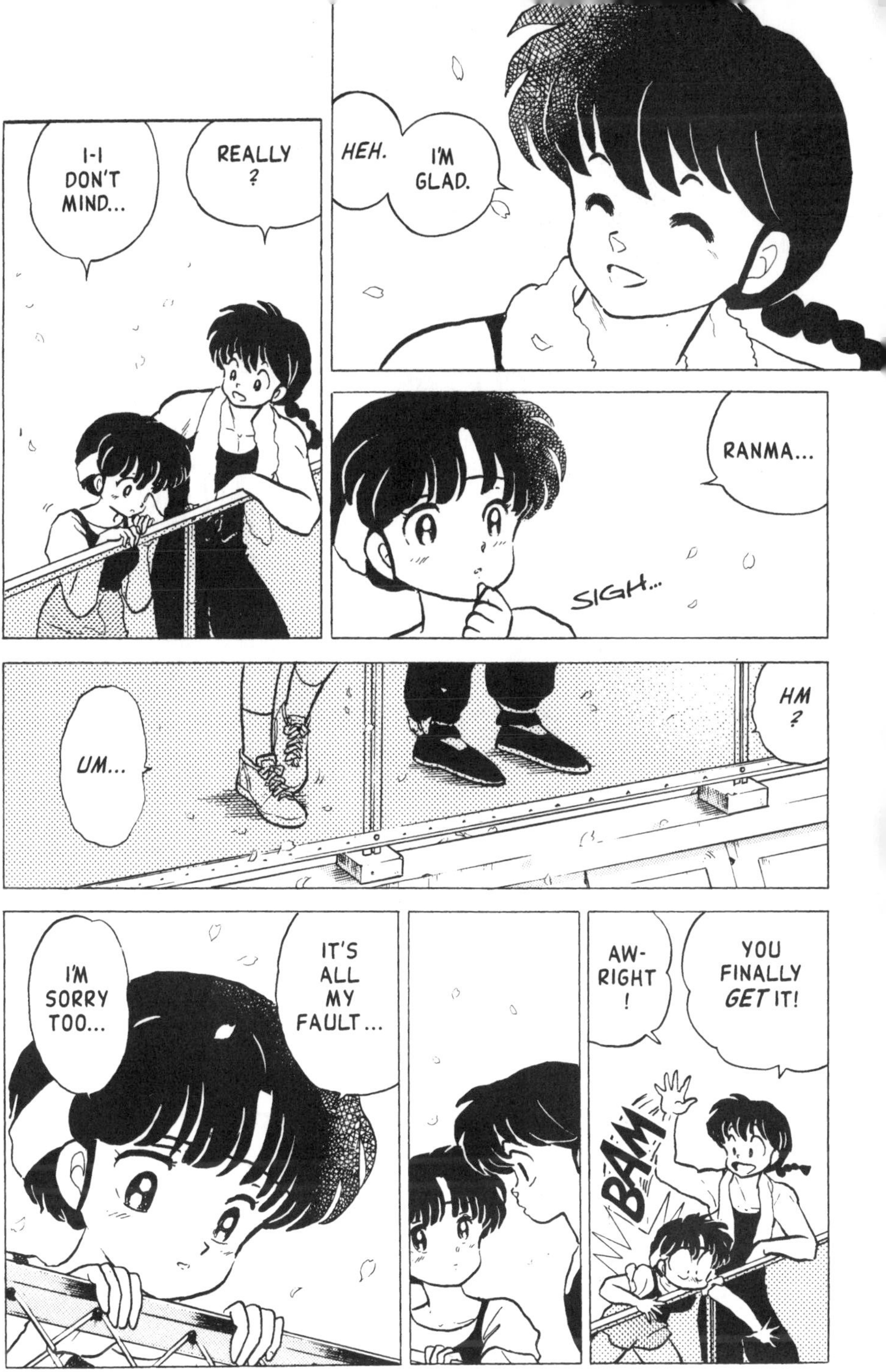
I-I DON'T MIND...
REALLY ?
HEH.
I'M GLAD.
RANMA...
SIGH...
UM...
HM ?
I'M SORRY TOO...
IT'S ALL MY FAULT...
AW- RIGHT !
YOU FINALLY *GET* IT!
BAM

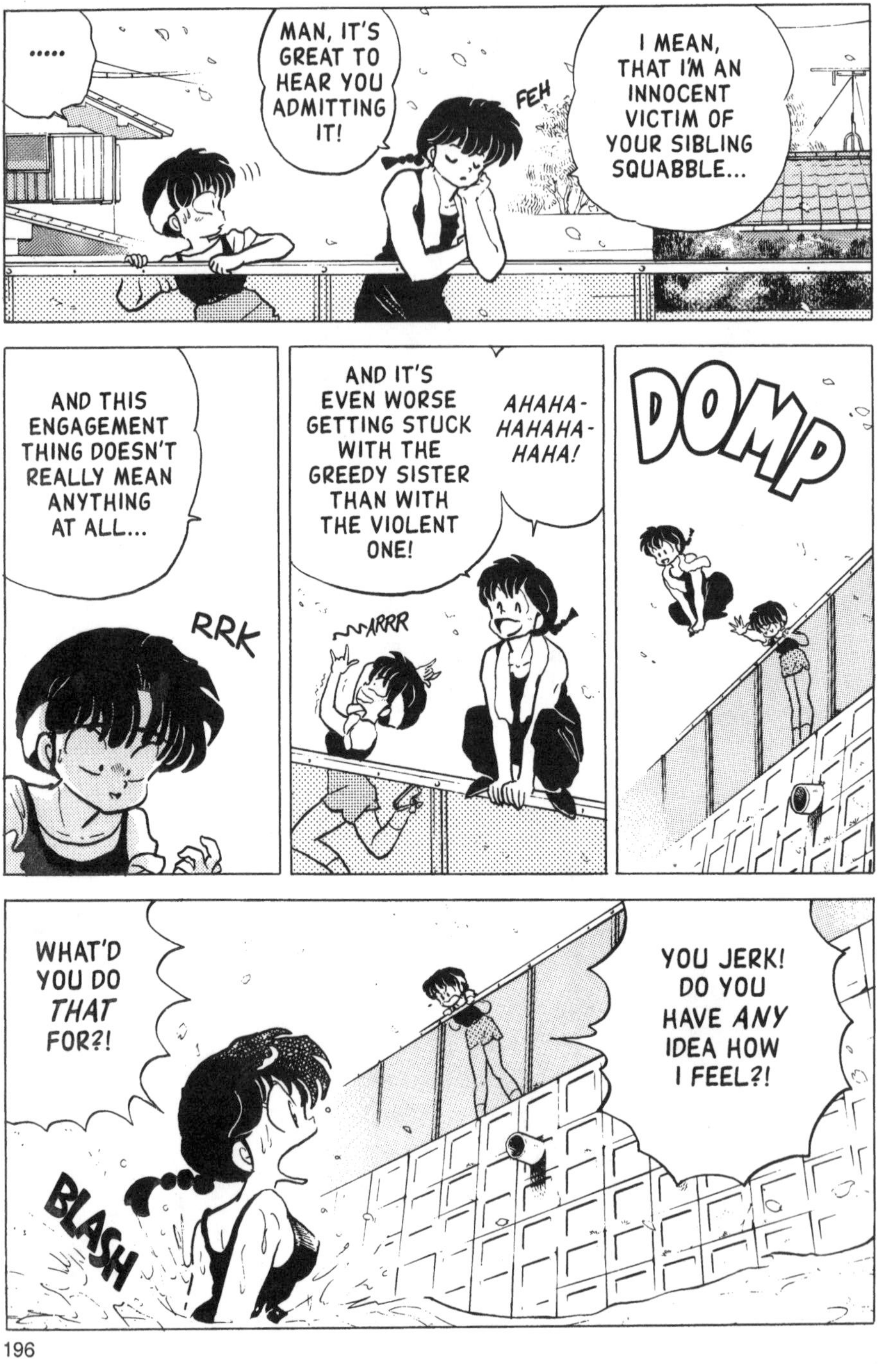
......
MAN, IT'S GREAT TO HEAR YOU ADMITTING IT!
FEH
I MEAN, THAT I'M AN INNOCENT VICTIM OF YOUR SIBLING SQUABBLE...
AND THIS ENGAGEMENT THING DOESN'T REALLY MEAN ANYTHING AT ALL...
RRK
AND IT'S EVEN WORSE GETTING STUCK WITH THE GREEDY SISTER THAN WITH THE VIOLENT ONE!
AHAHA-HAHAHA-HAHA!
ARRR
DOMP
WHAT'D YOU DO *THAT* FOR?!
BLASH
YOU JERK! DO YOU HAVE *ANY* IDEA HOW I FEEL?!

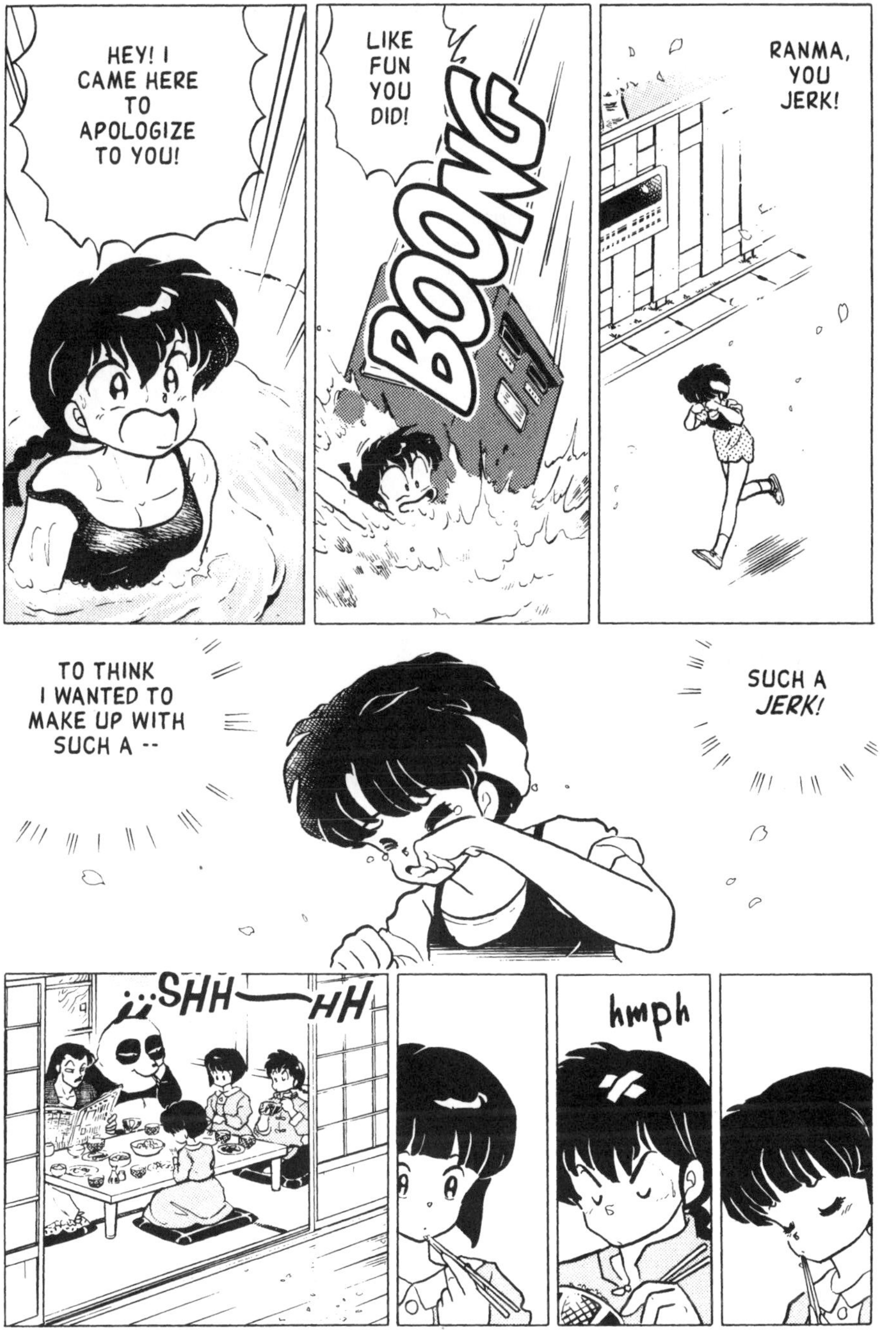
HEY! I CAME HERE TO APOLOGIZE TO YOU!
LIKE FUN YOU DID!
BOONG
RANMA, YOU JERK!
TO THINK I WANTED TO MAKE UP WITH SUCH A --
SUCH A JERK!
SHH——HH
hmph

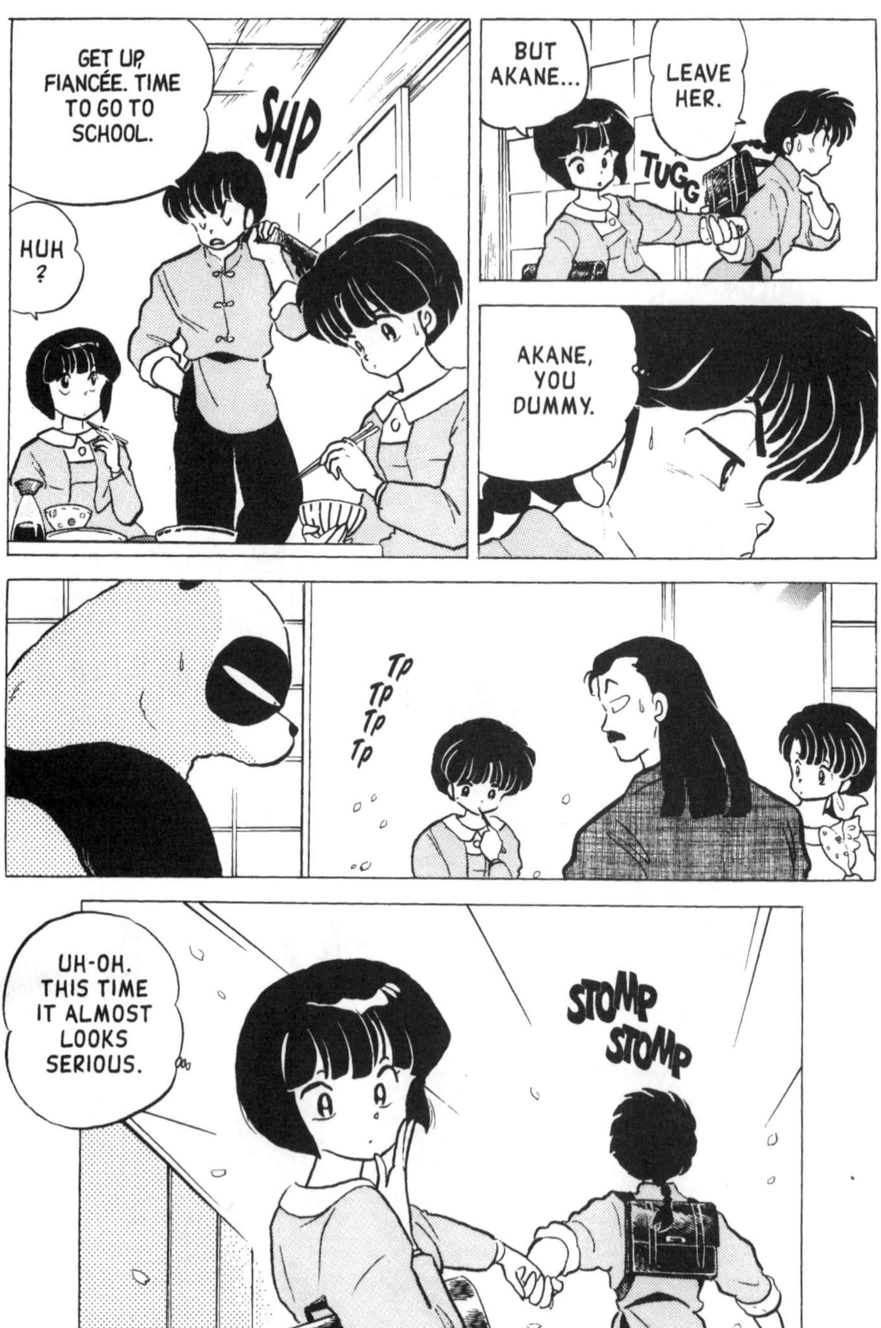
GET UP, FIANCÉE. TIME TO GO TO SCHOOL.
SHP
HUH ?
BUT AKANE...
LEAVE HER.
TUGG
AKANE, YOU DUMMY.
Tp Tp Tp Tp
UH-OH. THIS TIME IT ALMOST LOOKS SERIOUS.
STOMP STOMP

Part 13
I'M SORRY, AKANE

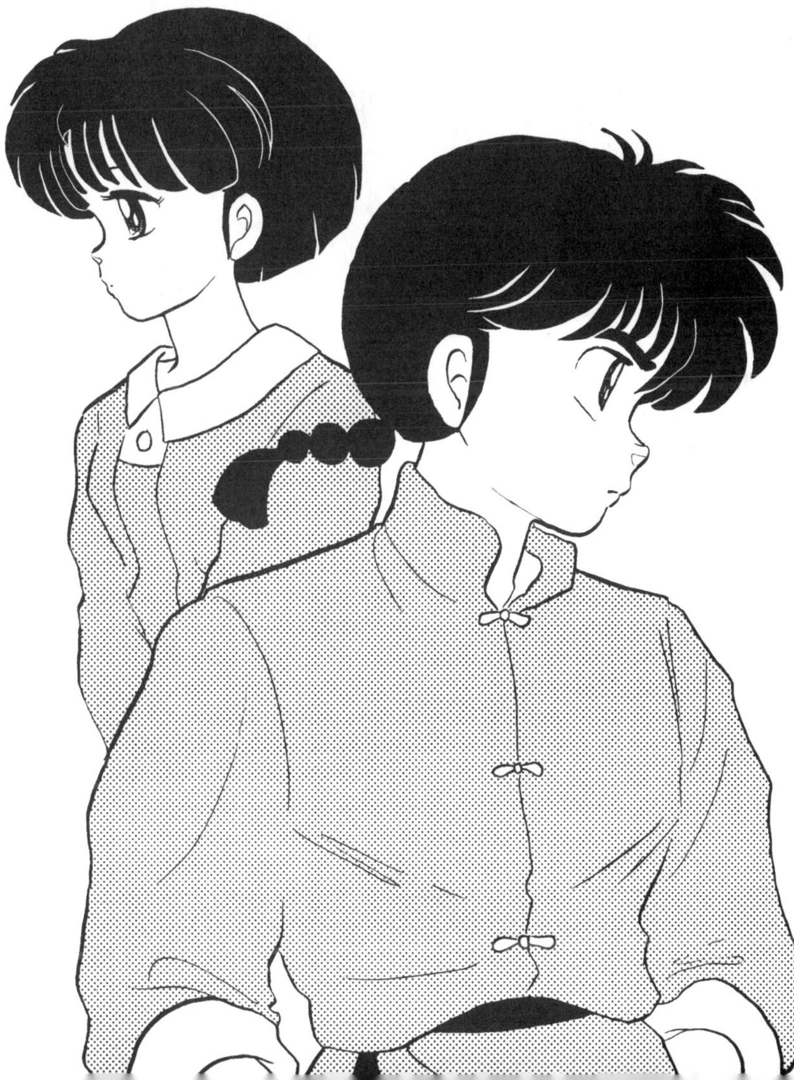

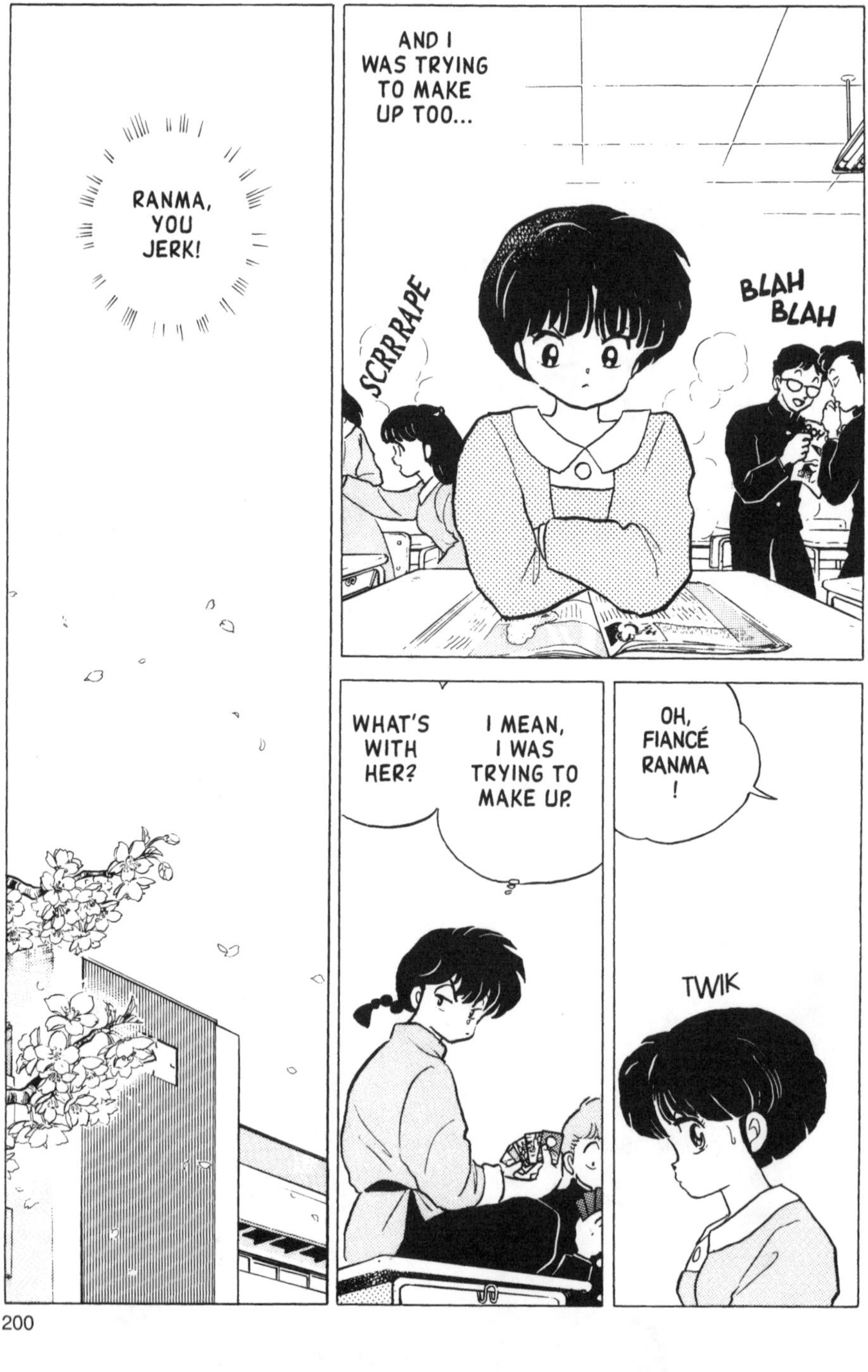
RANMA, YOU JERK!
AND I WAS TRYING TO MAKE UP TOO...
SCRRRAPE
BLAH BLAH
WHAT'S WITH HER?
I MEAN, I WAS TRYING TO MAKE UP.
OH, FIANCÉ RANMA!
TWIK

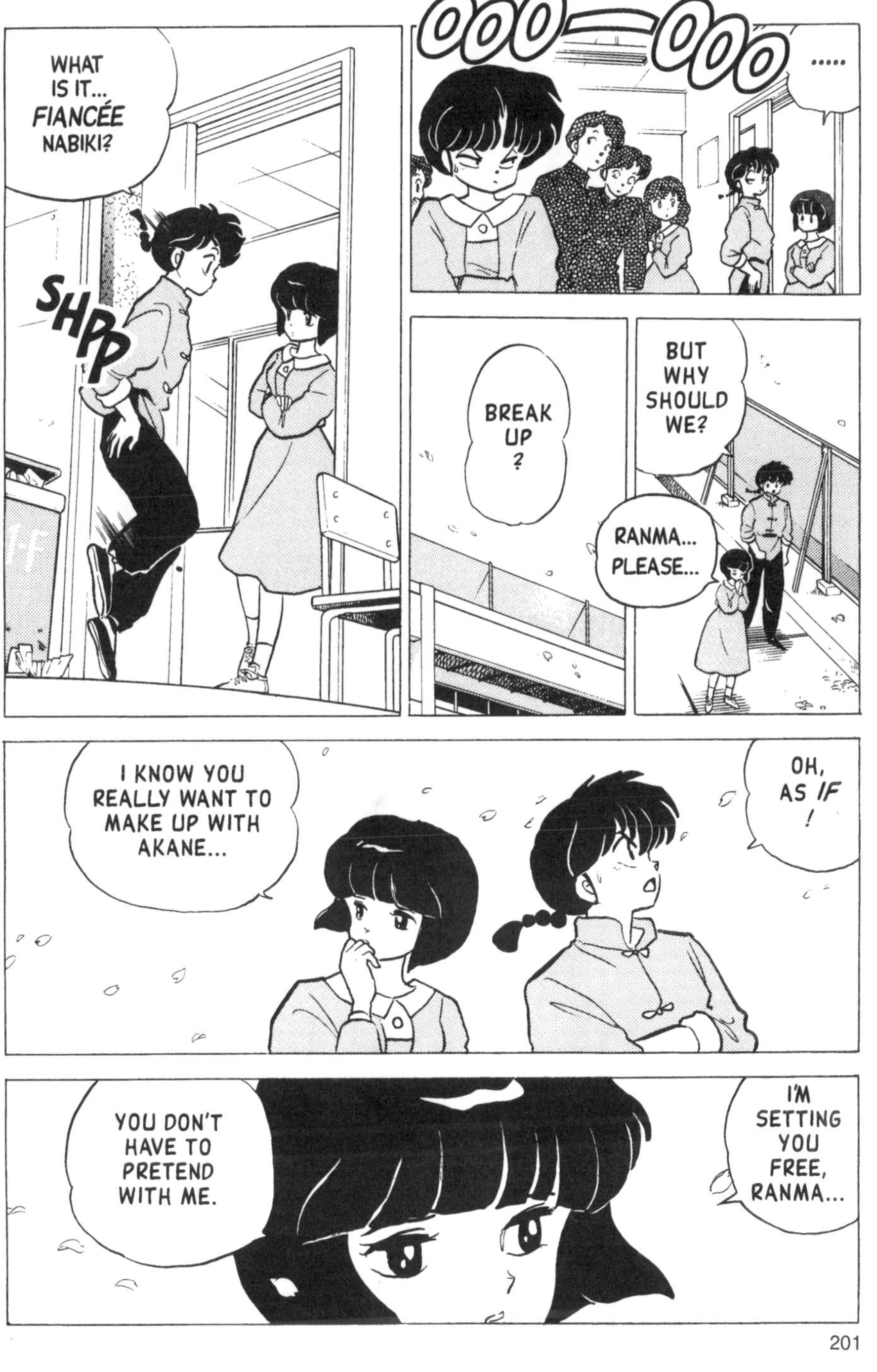
WHAT IS IT... FIANCÉE NABIKI?
SHPP
OOO—OOO
.....
BREAK UP?
BUT WHY SHOULD WE?
RANMA... PLEASE...
I KNOW YOU REALLY WANT TO MAKE UP WITH AKANE...
OH, AS IF!
YOU DON'T HAVE TO PRETEND WITH ME.
I'M SETTING YOU FREE, RANMA...

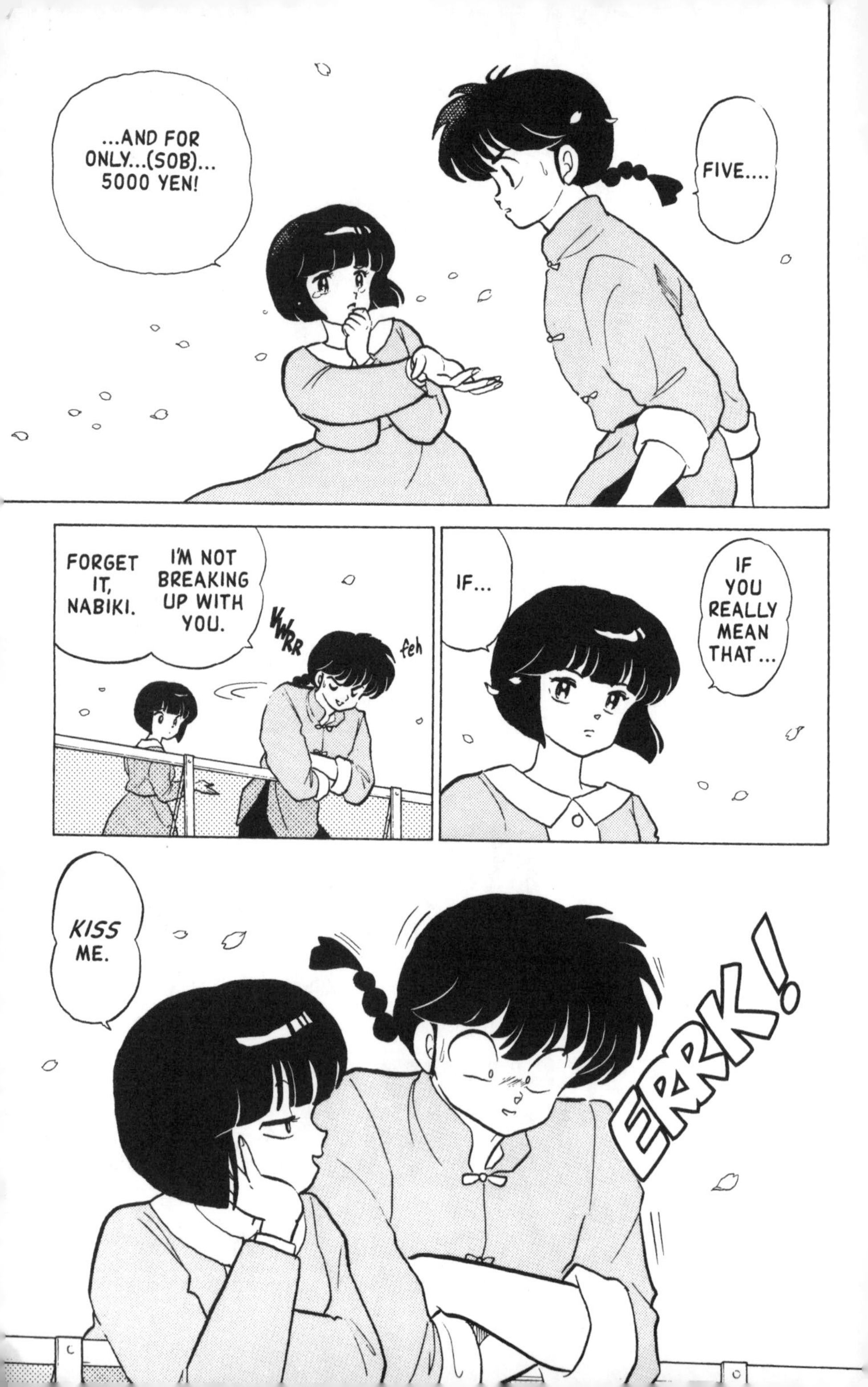
...AND FOR ONLY...(SOB)... 5000 YEN!
FIVE....
FORGET IT, NABIKI.
I'M NOT BREAKING UP WITH YOU.
KWRR
feh
IF...
IF YOU REALLY MEAN THAT...
KISS ME.
ERRK!

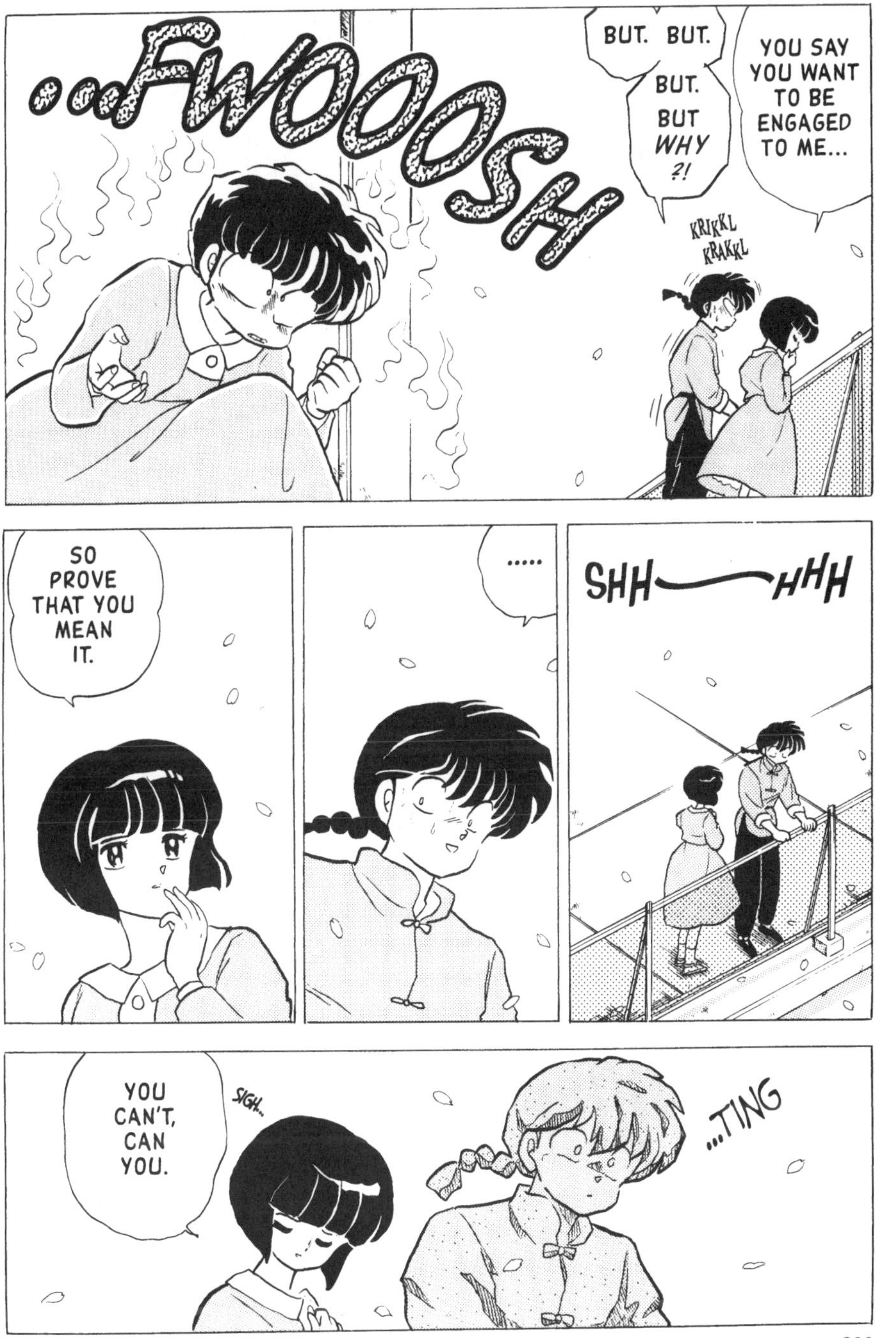
...FWOOOSH
BUT. BUT.
BUT. BUT WHY ?!
YOU SAY YOU WANT TO BE ENGAGED TO ME...
KRIKKL KRAKKL
SO PROVE THAT YOU MEAN IT.
.....
SHH——HHH
YOU CAN'T, CAN YOU.
SIGH..
...TING

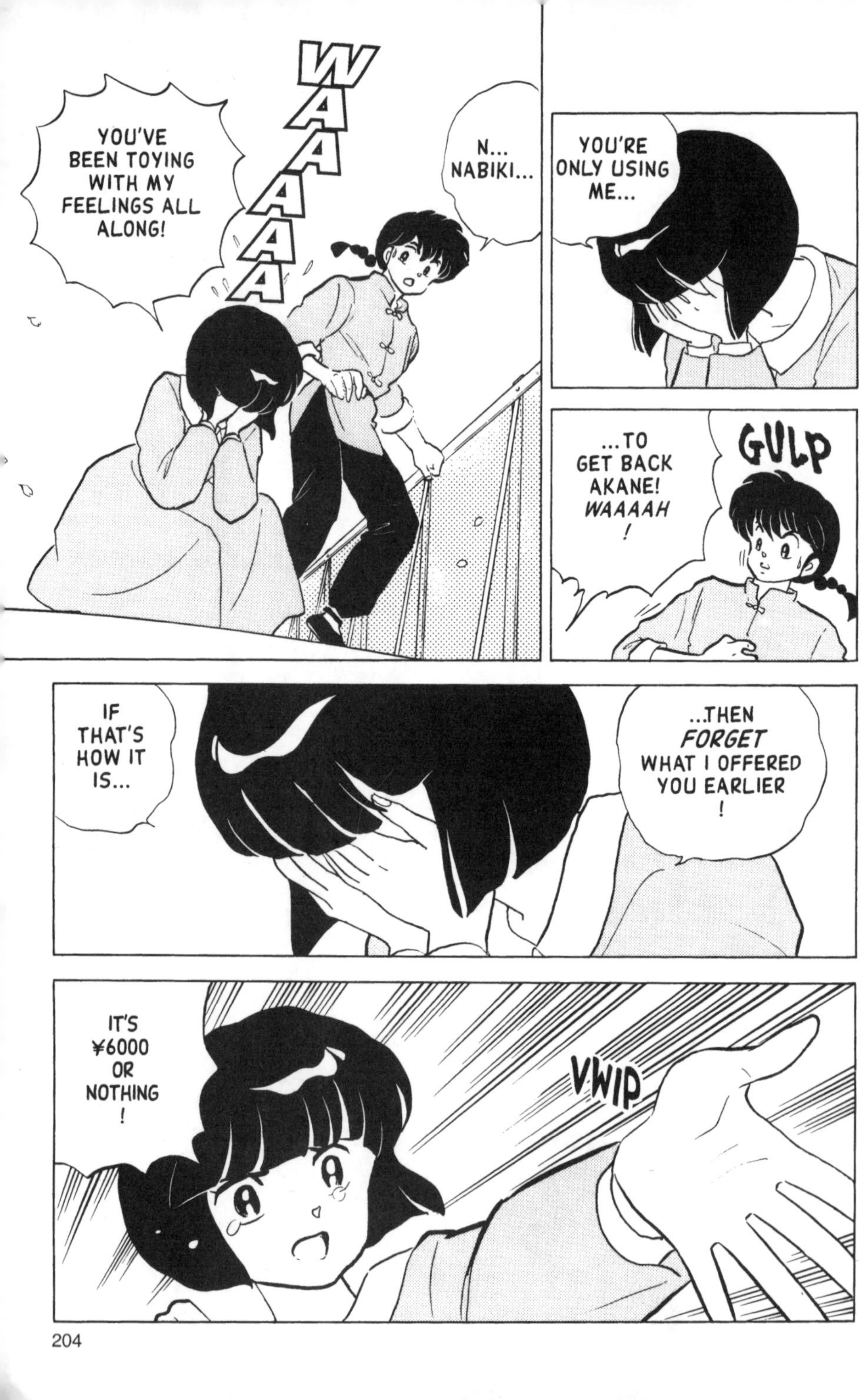
YOU'VE BEEN TOYING WITH MY FEELINGS ALL ALONG!
WAAAAAA
N... NABIKI...
YOU'RE ONLY USING ME...
...TO GET BACK AKANE! *WAAAAH*!
GULP
IF THAT'S HOW IT IS...
...THEN *FORGET* WHAT I OFFERED YOU EARLIER!
IT'S ¥6000 OR NOTHING!
VWIP

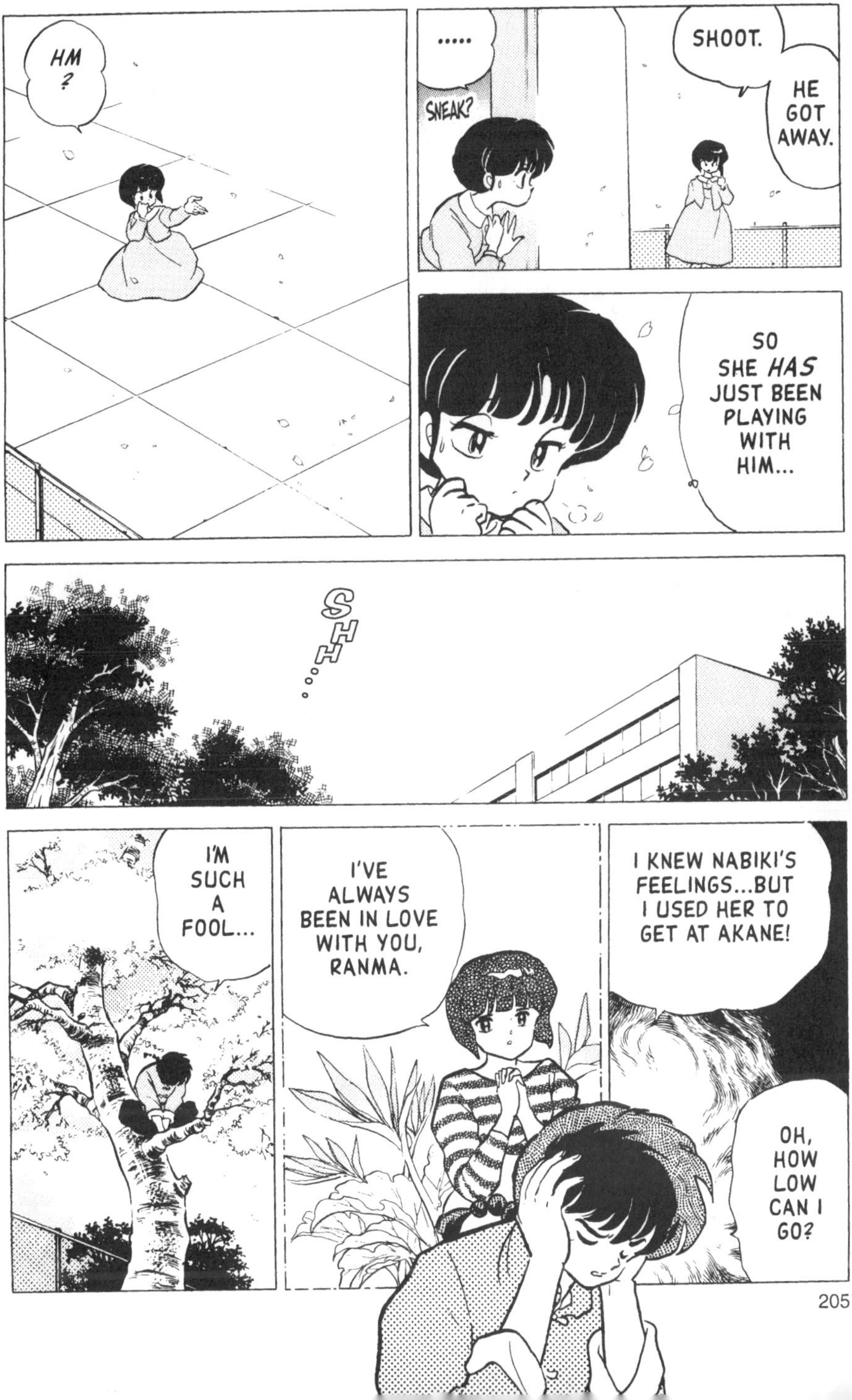
HM ?
......
SNEAK?
SHOOT.
HE GOT AWAY.
SO SHE HAS JUST BEEN PLAYING WITH HIM...
SHHH...
I'M SUCH A FOOL...
I'VE ALWAYS BEEN IN LOVE WITH YOU, RANMA.
I KNEW NABIKI'S FEELINGS...BUT I USED HER TO GET AT AKANE!
OH, HOW LOW CAN I GO?

IT'S THE ONLY HONORABLE THING TO DO!

I'M GOING TO MAKE UP WITH AKANE!

SHAA

I'M SORRY, AKANE. I WAS WRONG.

LET'S MAKE UP.

I'M SORRY.

I WAS WRONG.

WHAT COULD HE HAVE DONE TO THAT TREE?

DON'T ASK.

PSS PSS

ENOUGH TRAINING.

I'VE MASTERED MY MOVES!

HEH!

I'M SORRY, AKANE.

I'M SORRY, AKANE.

TOOM

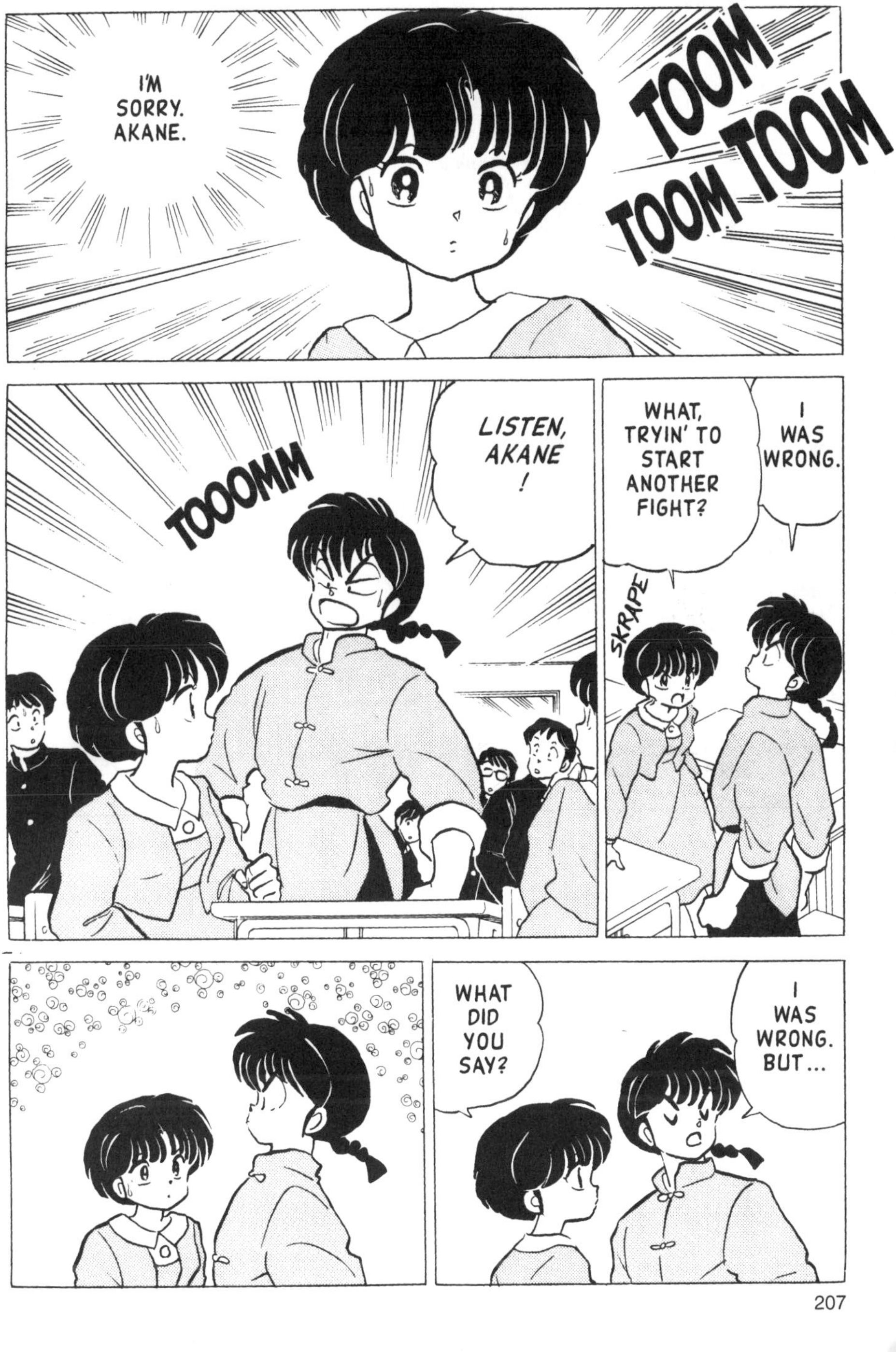
I'M SORRY. AKANE.
TOOM TOOM TOOM
TOOOMM
LISTEN, AKANE!
I WAS WRONG.
WHAT, TRYIN' TO START ANOTHER FIGHT?
SKRAPE
WHAT DID YOU SAY?
I WAS WRONG. BUT...

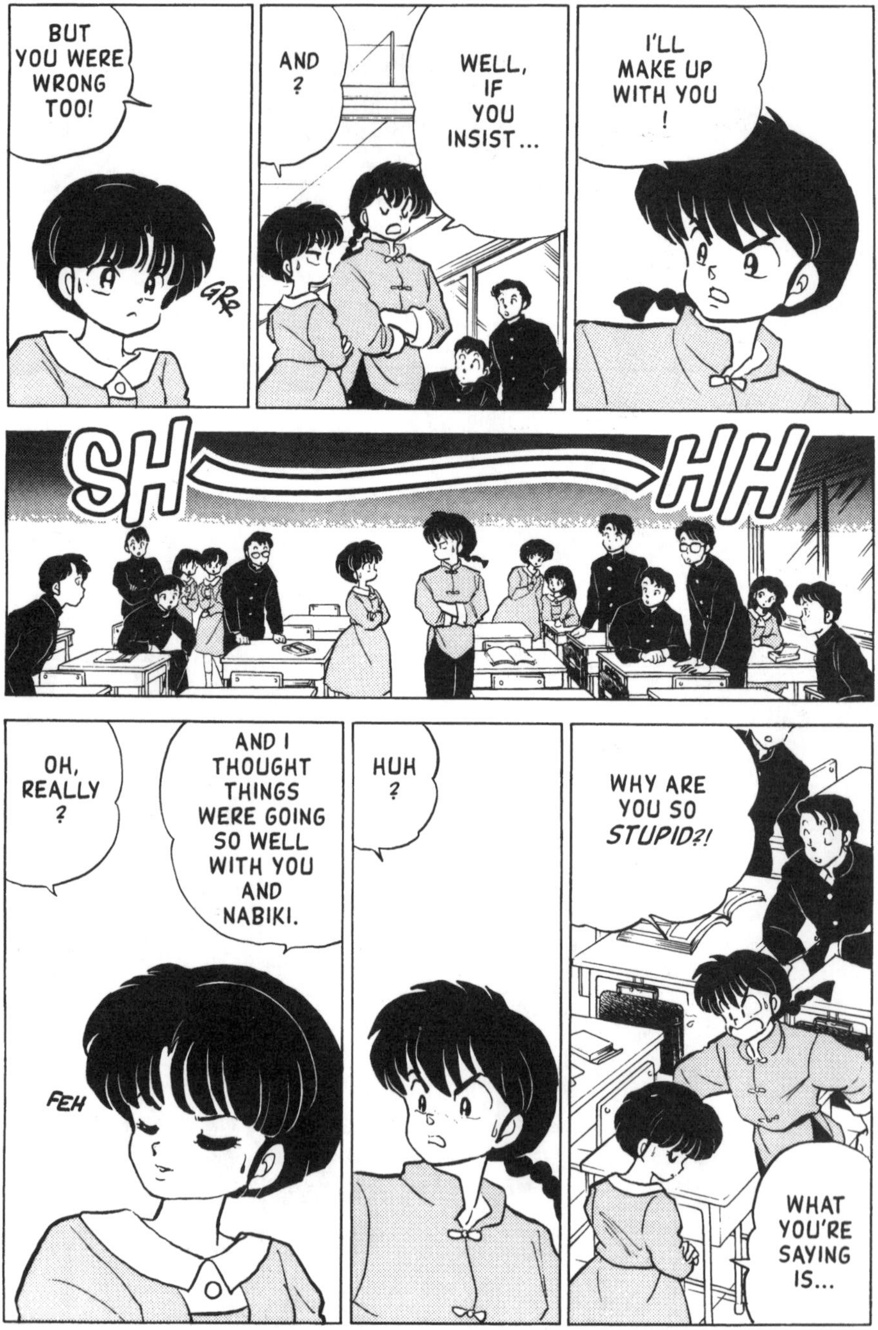
BUT YOU WERE WRONG TOO!
GRR
AND ?
WELL, IF YOU INSIST...
I'LL MAKE UP WITH YOU !
SH——HH
OH, REALLY ?
AND I THOUGHT THINGS WERE GOING SO WELL WITH YOU AND NABIKI.
FEH
HUH ?
WHY ARE YOU SO *STUPID*?!
WHAT YOU'RE SAYING IS...

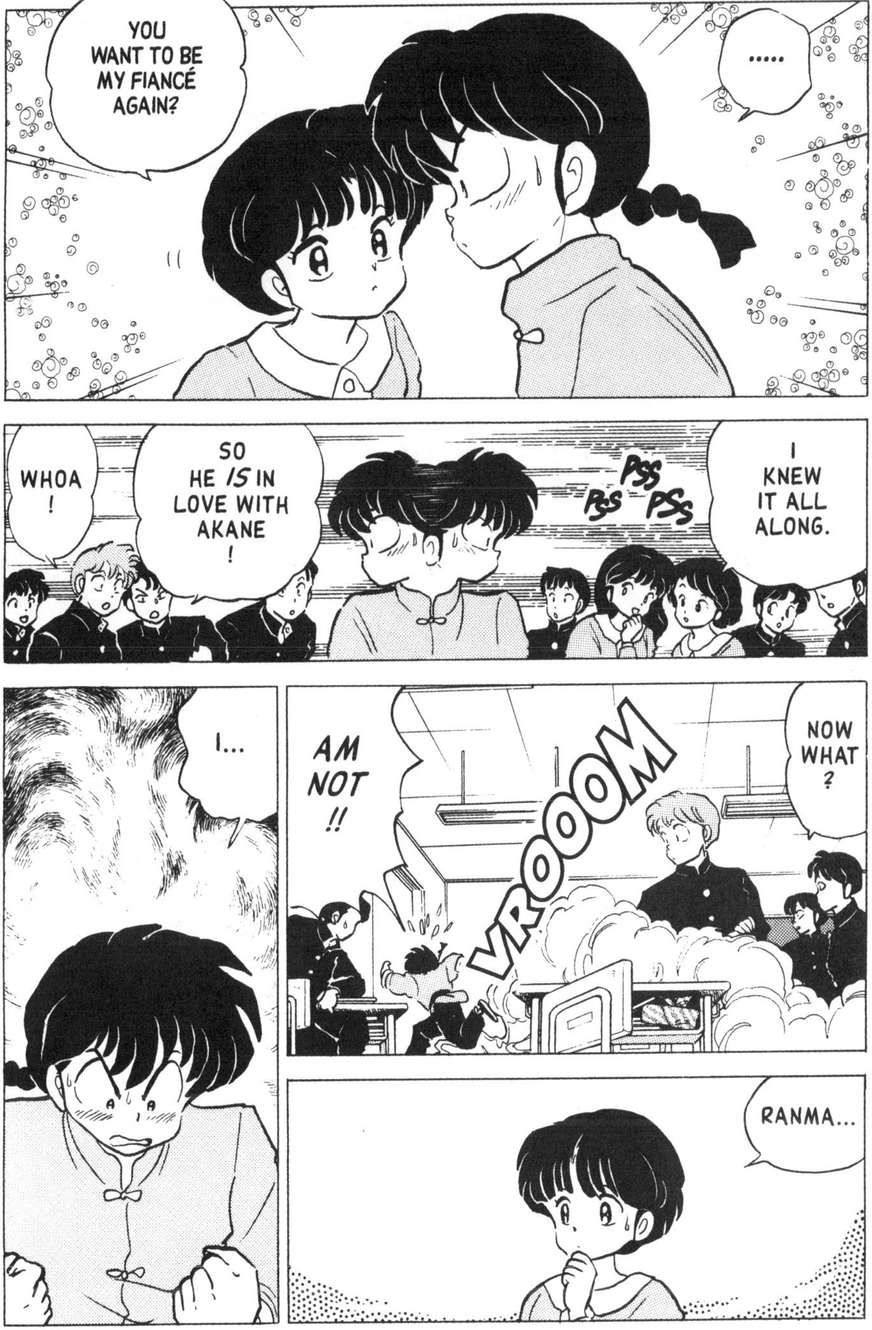
YOU WANT TO BE MY FIANCÉ AGAIN?
.....
WHOA !
SO HE *IS* IN LOVE WITH AKANE !
PSS PSS PSS
I KNEW IT ALL ALONG.
I...
AM NOT !!
VROOOM
NOW WHAT ?
RANMA...

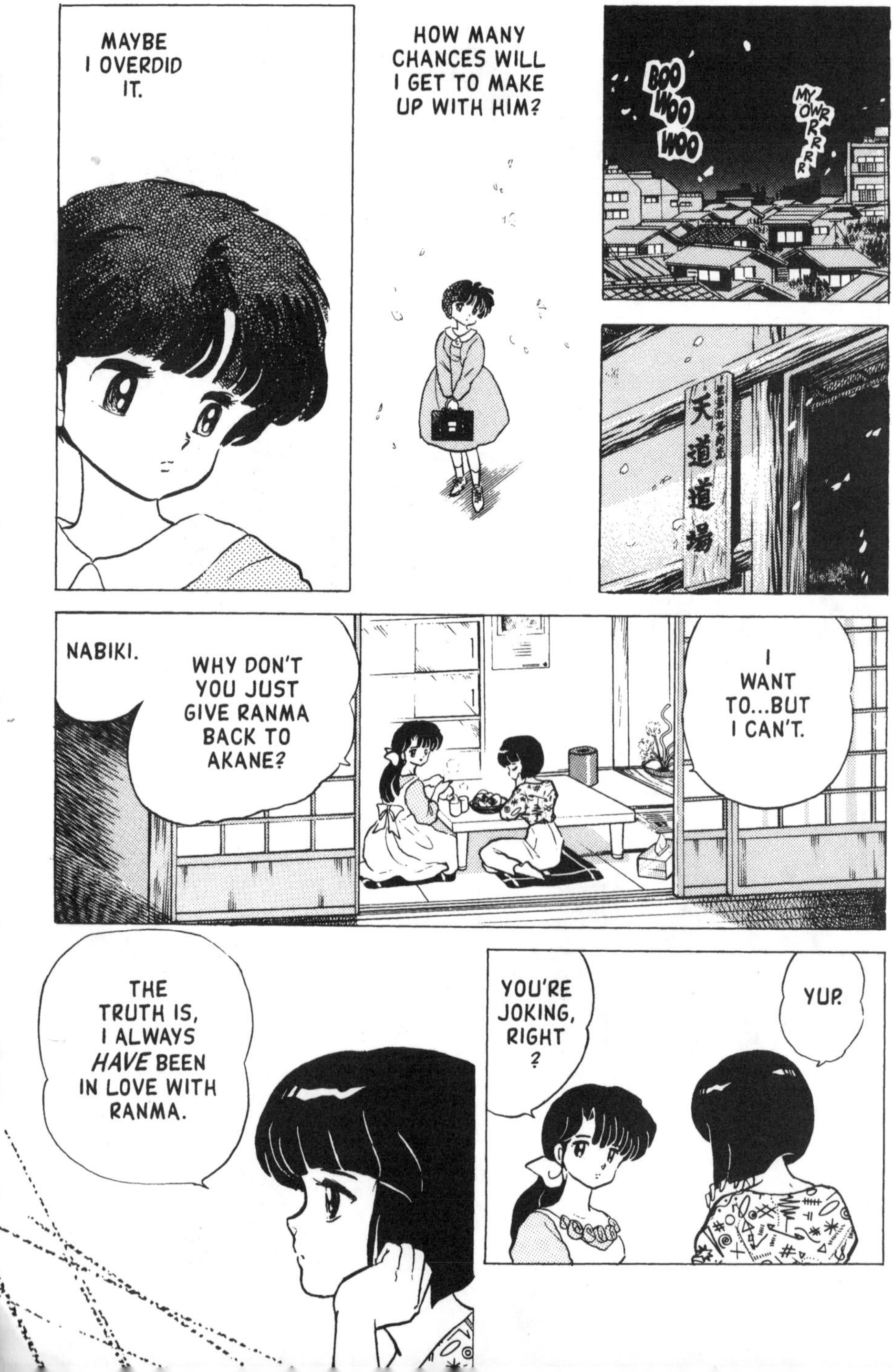
MAYBE I OVERDID IT.
HOW MANY CHANCES WILL I GET TO MAKE UP WITH HIM?
BOO WOO WOO
MYOWRRRRR
天道道場
NABIKI.
WHY DON'T YOU JUST GIVE RANMA BACK TO AKANE?
I WANT TO...BUT I CAN'T.
THE TRUTH IS, I ALWAYS *HAVE* BEEN IN LOVE WITH RANMA.
YOU'RE JOKING, RIGHT?
YUP.

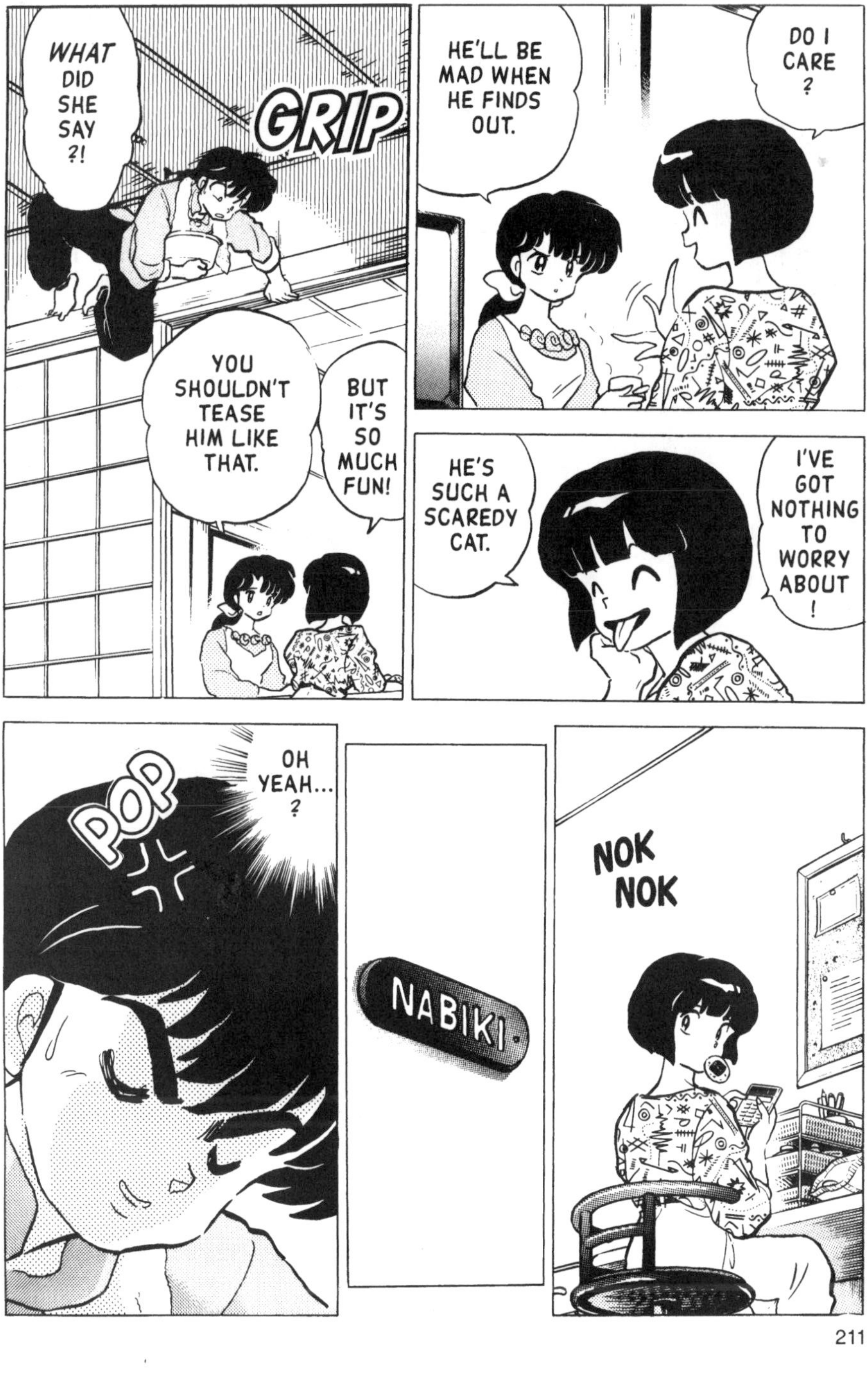
WHAT DID SHE SAY ?!
GRIP
YOU SHOULDN'T TEASE HIM LIKE THAT.
BUT IT'S SO MUCH FUN!
HE'LL BE MAD WHEN HE FINDS OUT.
DO I CARE ?
HE'S SUCH A SCAREDY CAT.
I'VE GOT NOTHING TO WORRY ABOUT !
POP
OH YEAH... ?
NABIKI
NOK NOK

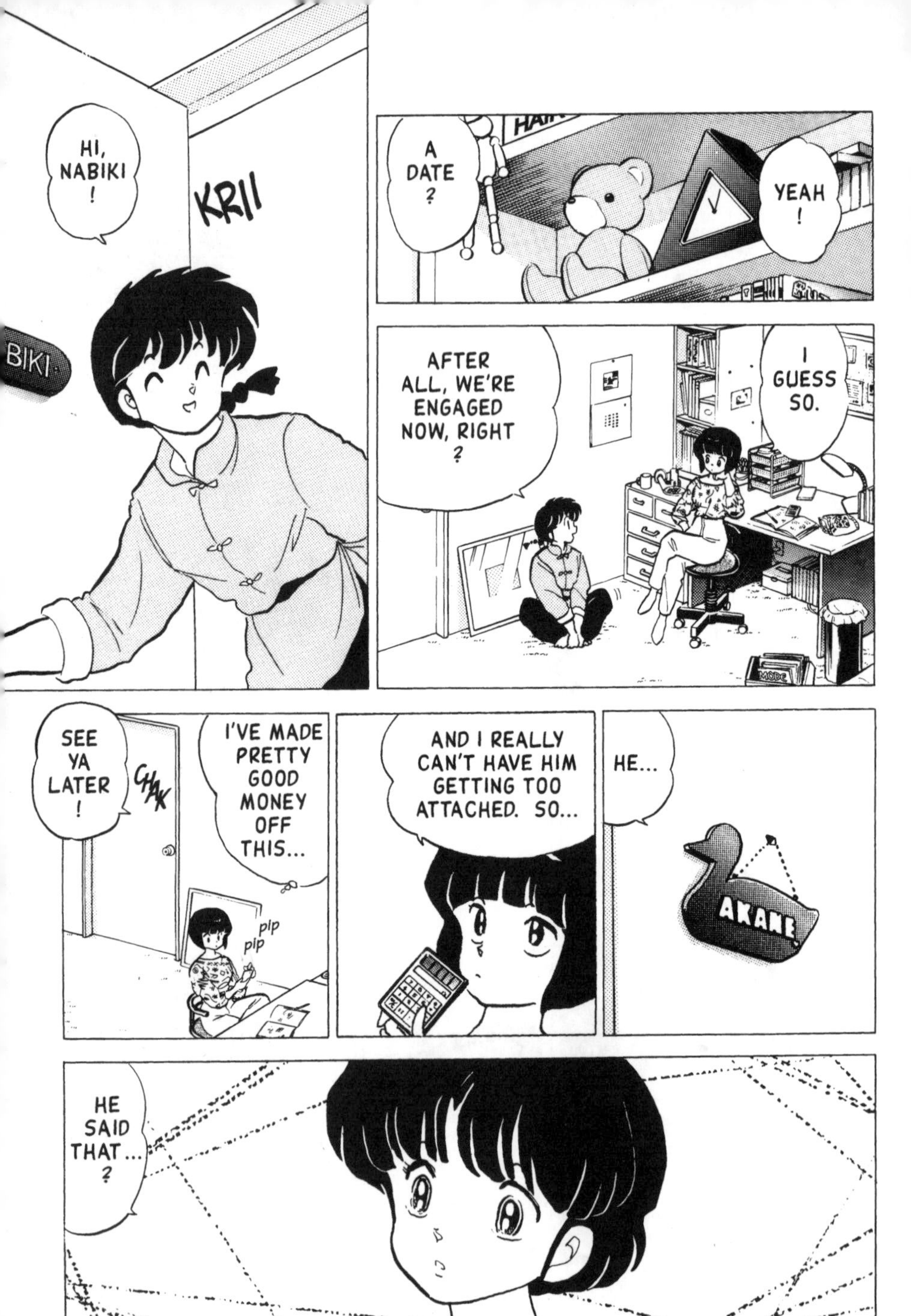
HI, NABIKI!
KRII
BIKI
A DATE?
YEAH!
AFTER ALL, WE'RE ENGAGED NOW, RIGHT?
I GUESS SO.
SEE YA LATER!
CHAK
I'VE MADE PRETTY GOOD MONEY OFF THIS...
pip pip
AND I REALLY CAN'T HAVE HIM GETTING TOO ATTACHED. SO...
HE...
AKANE
HE SAID THAT...?

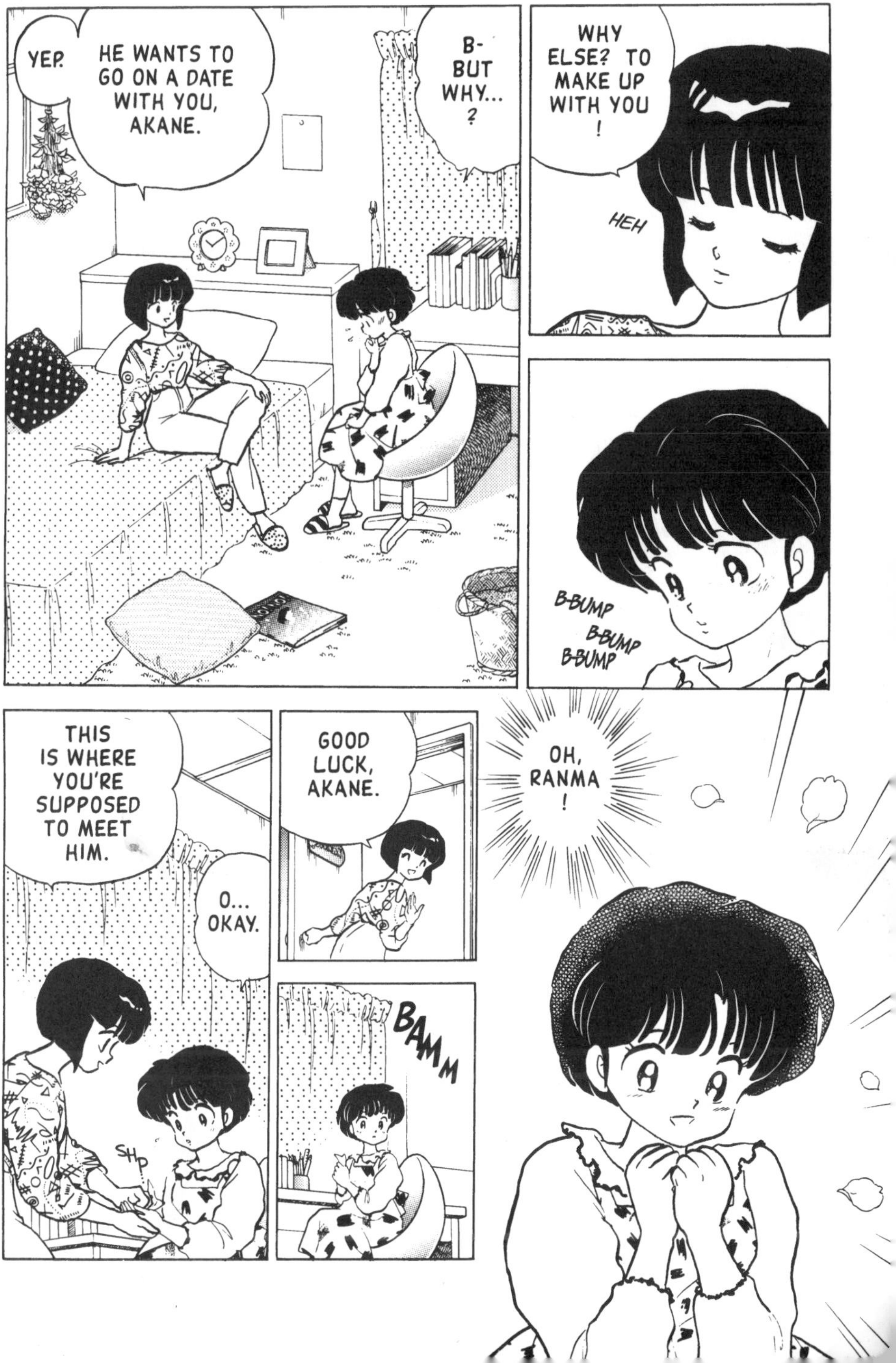
YEP.
HE WANTS TO GO ON A DATE WITH YOU, AKANE.
B- BUT WHY...?
WHY ELSE? TO MAKE UP WITH YOU!
HEH
B-BUMP
B-BUMP
B-BUMP
THIS IS WHERE YOU'RE SUPPOSED TO MEET HIM.
O... OKAY.
SHP
GOOD LUCK, AKANE.
BAMM
OH, RANMA!

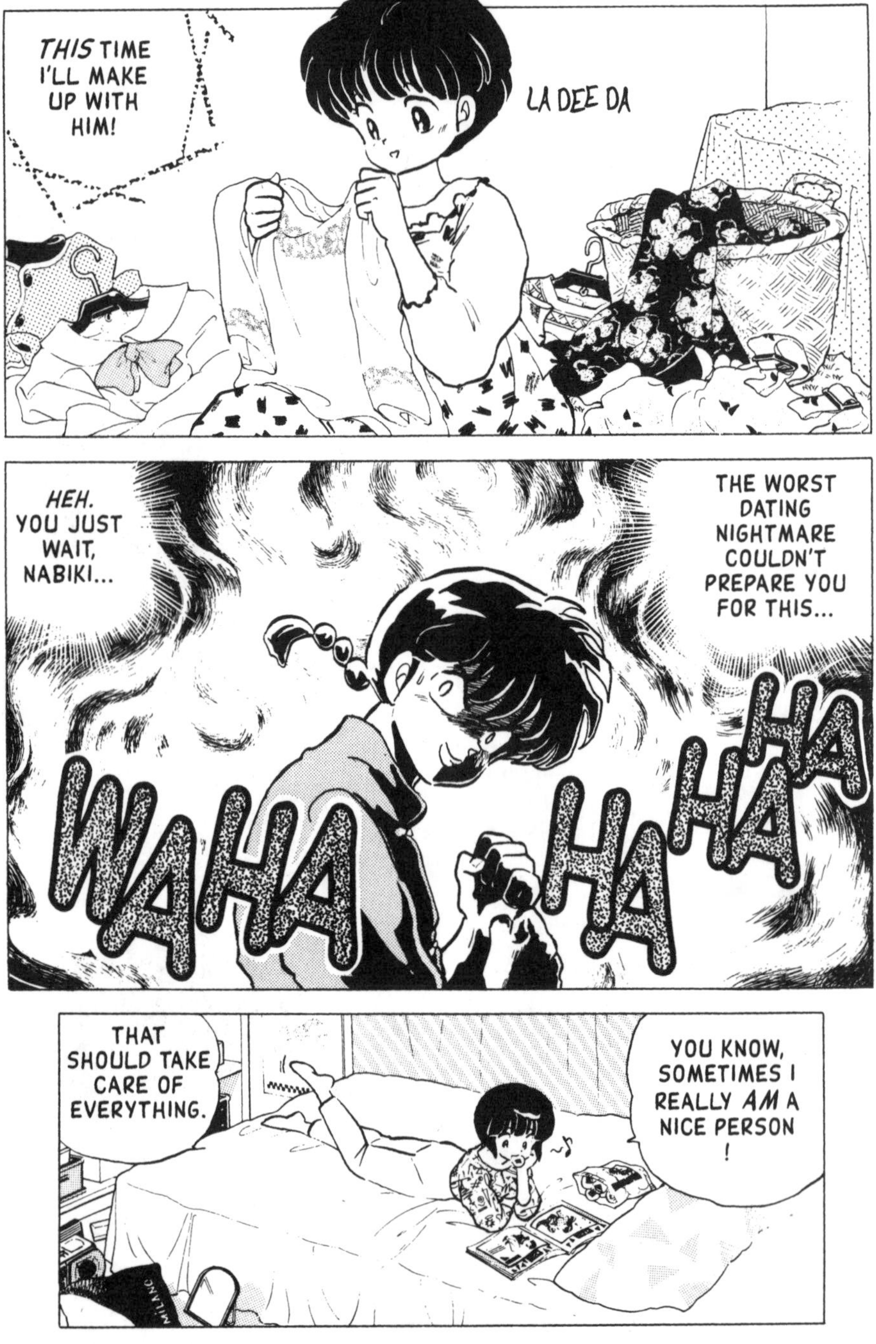
THIS TIME I'LL MAKE UP WITH HIM!
LA DEE DA
HEH. YOU JUST WAIT, NABIKI...
THE WORST DATING NIGHTMARE COULDN'T PREPARE YOU FOR THIS...
WAHAHA HAHAHAHA
THAT SHOULD TAKE CARE OF EVERYTHING.
YOU KNOW, SOMETIMES I REALLY AM A NICE PERSON!

Part 14
MAZE OF LOVE

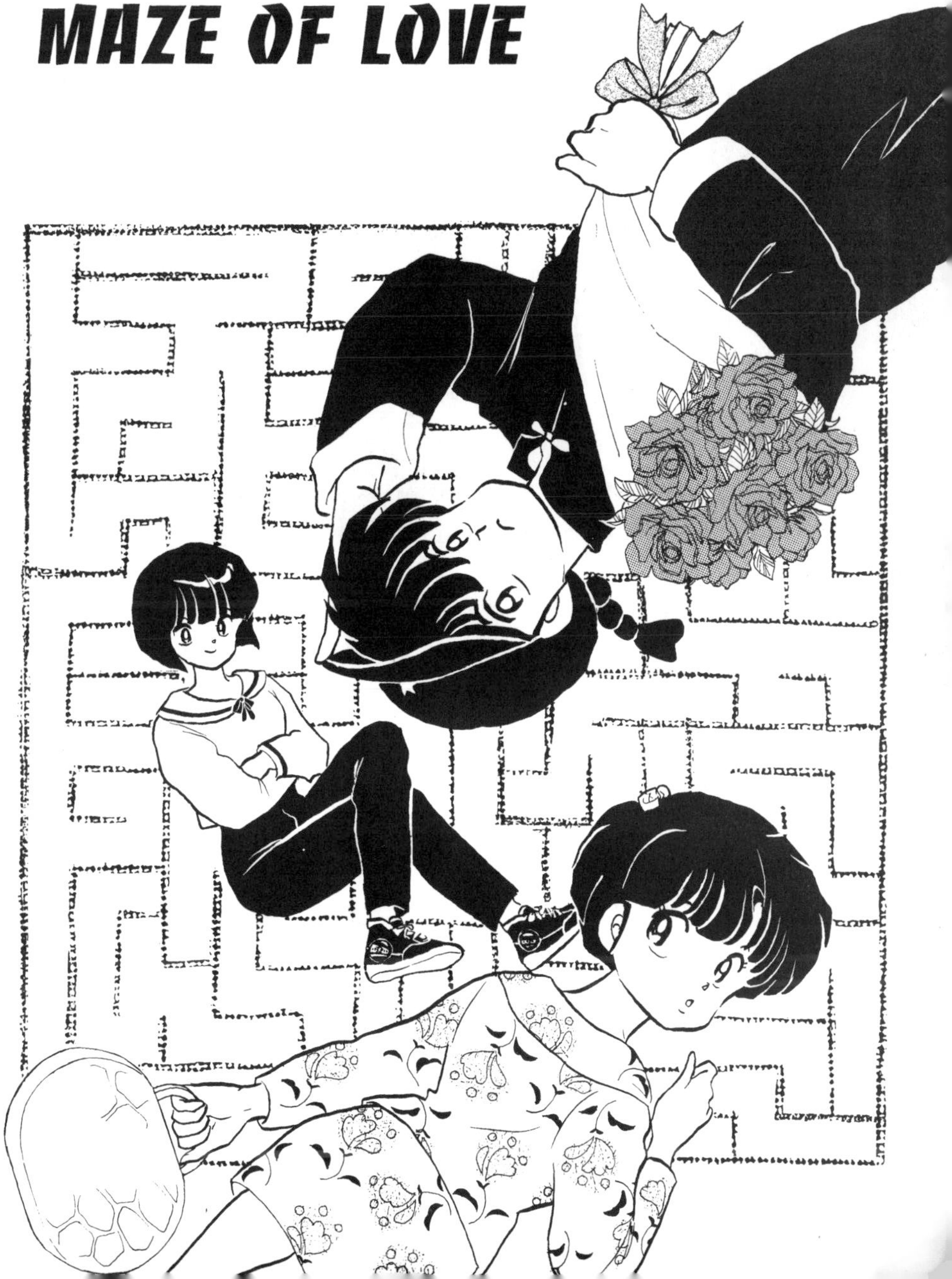

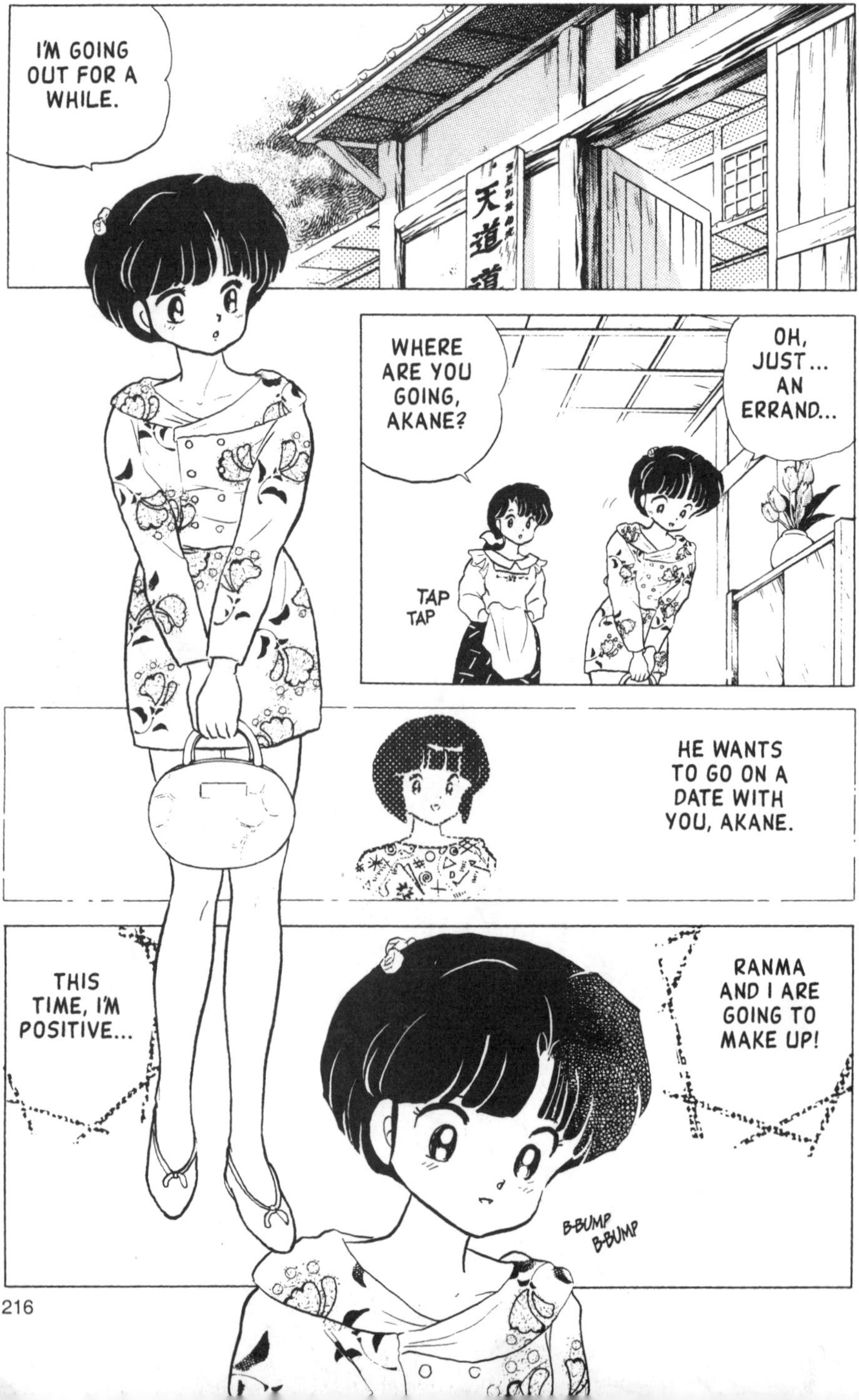

I'M GOING OUT FOR A WHILE.
WHERE ARE YOU GOING, AKANE?
TAP TAP
OH, JUST... AN ERRAND...
HE WANTS TO GO ON A DATE WITH YOU, AKANE.
THIS TIME, I'M POSITIVE...
RANMA AND I ARE GOING TO MAKE UP!
B-BUMP B-BUMP

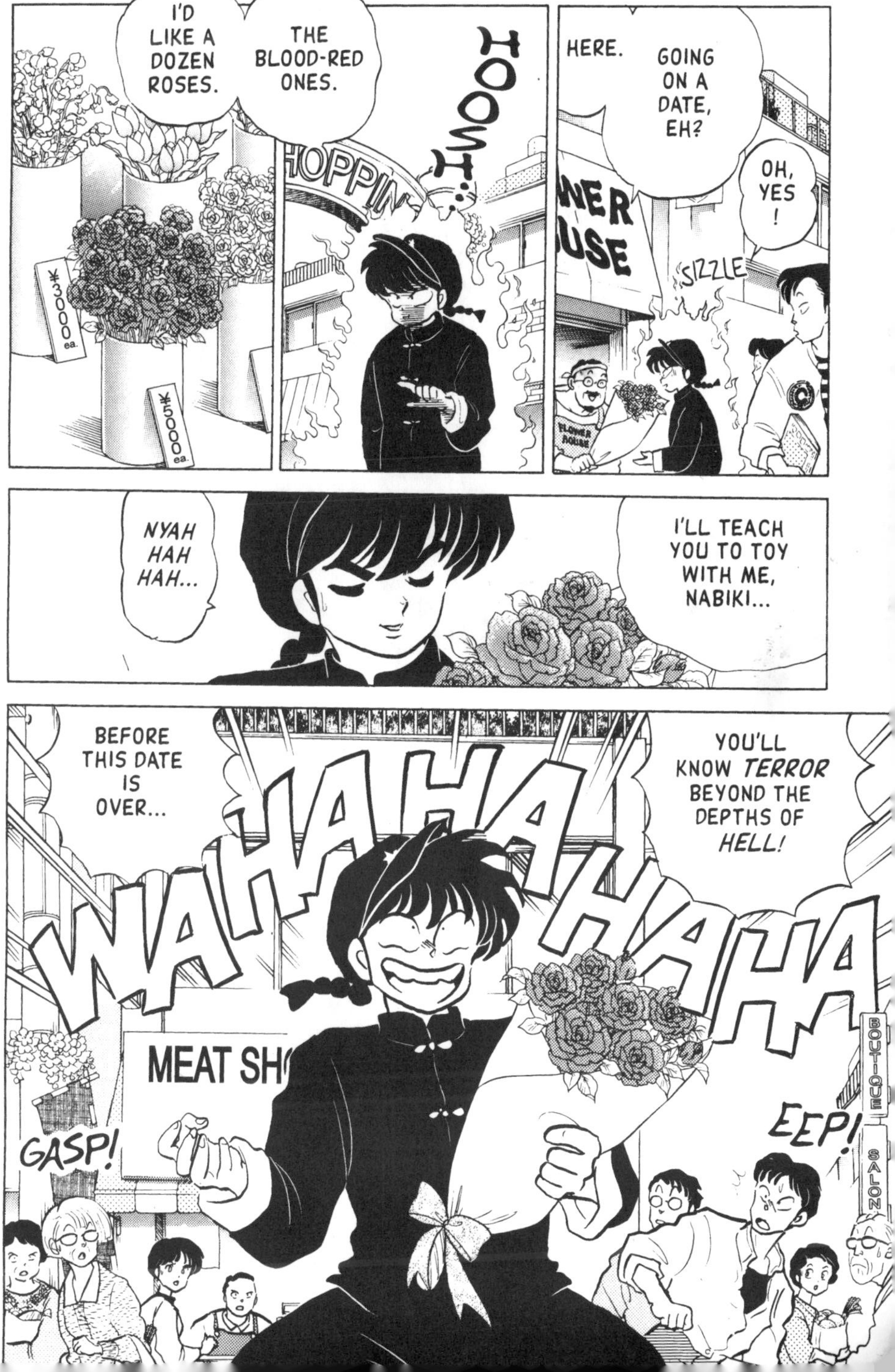
I'D LIKE A DOZEN ROSES.
THE BLOOD-RED ONES.
¥3000 ea.
¥5000 ea.
HOOOSH...
HOPPIN
HERE.
GOING ON A DATE, EH?
OH, YES!
SIZZLE
NER USE
FLOWER HOUSE
NYAH HAH HAH...
I'LL TEACH YOU TO TOY WITH ME, NABIKI...
BEFORE THIS DATE IS OVER...
YOU'LL KNOW TERROR BEYOND THE DEPTHS OF HELL!
WAHAHAHAHAHAHA
MEAT SH
BOUTIQUE
SALON
GASP!
EEP!

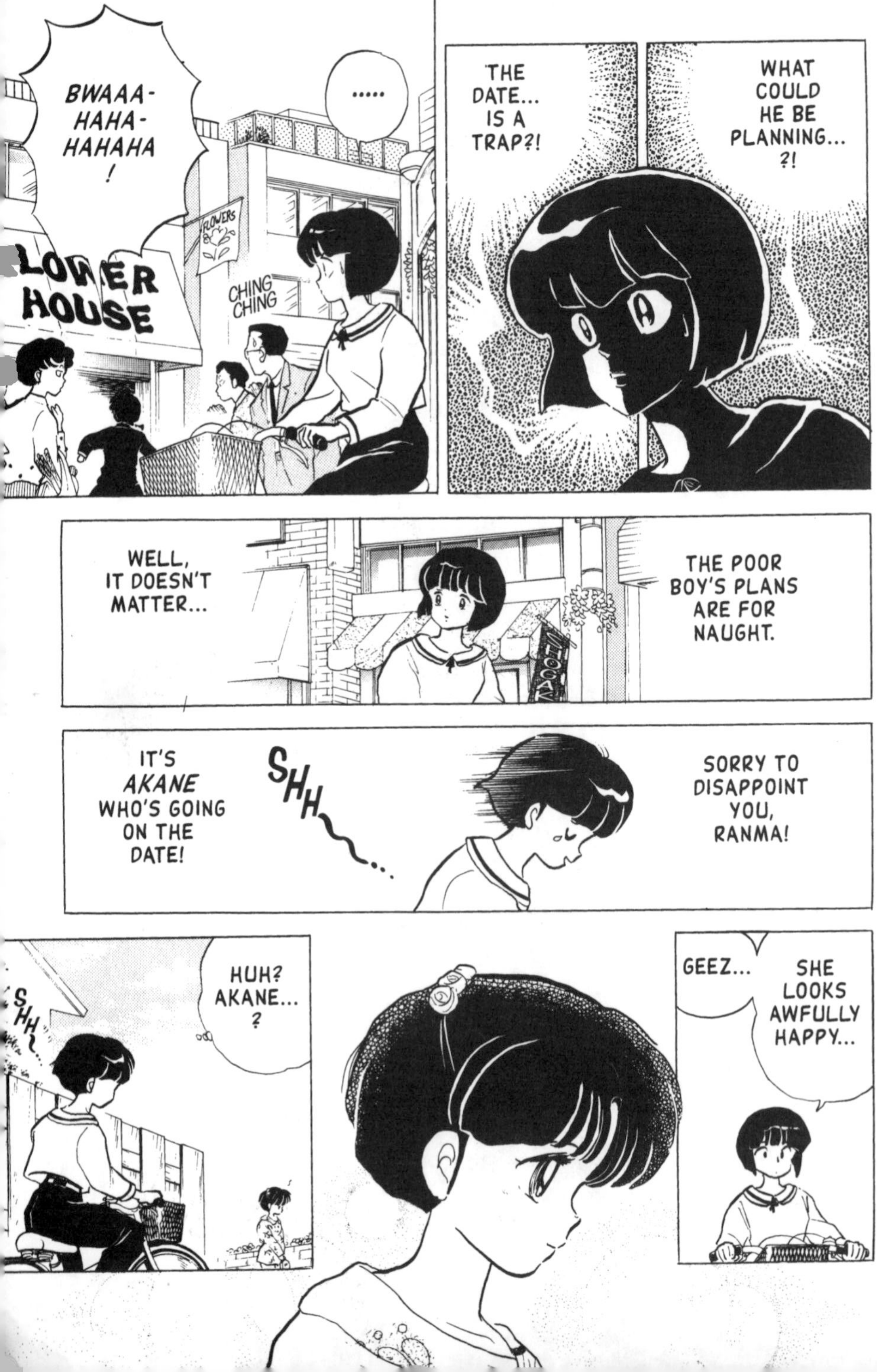
BWAAA-HAHA-HAHAHA!
.....
LOWER HOUSE
FLOWERS
CHING CHING
THE DATE... IS A TRAP?!
WHAT COULD HE BE PLANNING...?!
WELL, IT DOESN'T MATTER...
THE POOR BOY'S PLANS ARE FOR NAUGHT.
IT'S *AKANE* WHO'S GOING ON THE DATE!
SHH~...
SORRY TO DISAPPOINT YOU, RANMA!
SHH~
HUH? AKANE...?
GEEZ...
SHE LOOKS AWFULLY HAPPY...

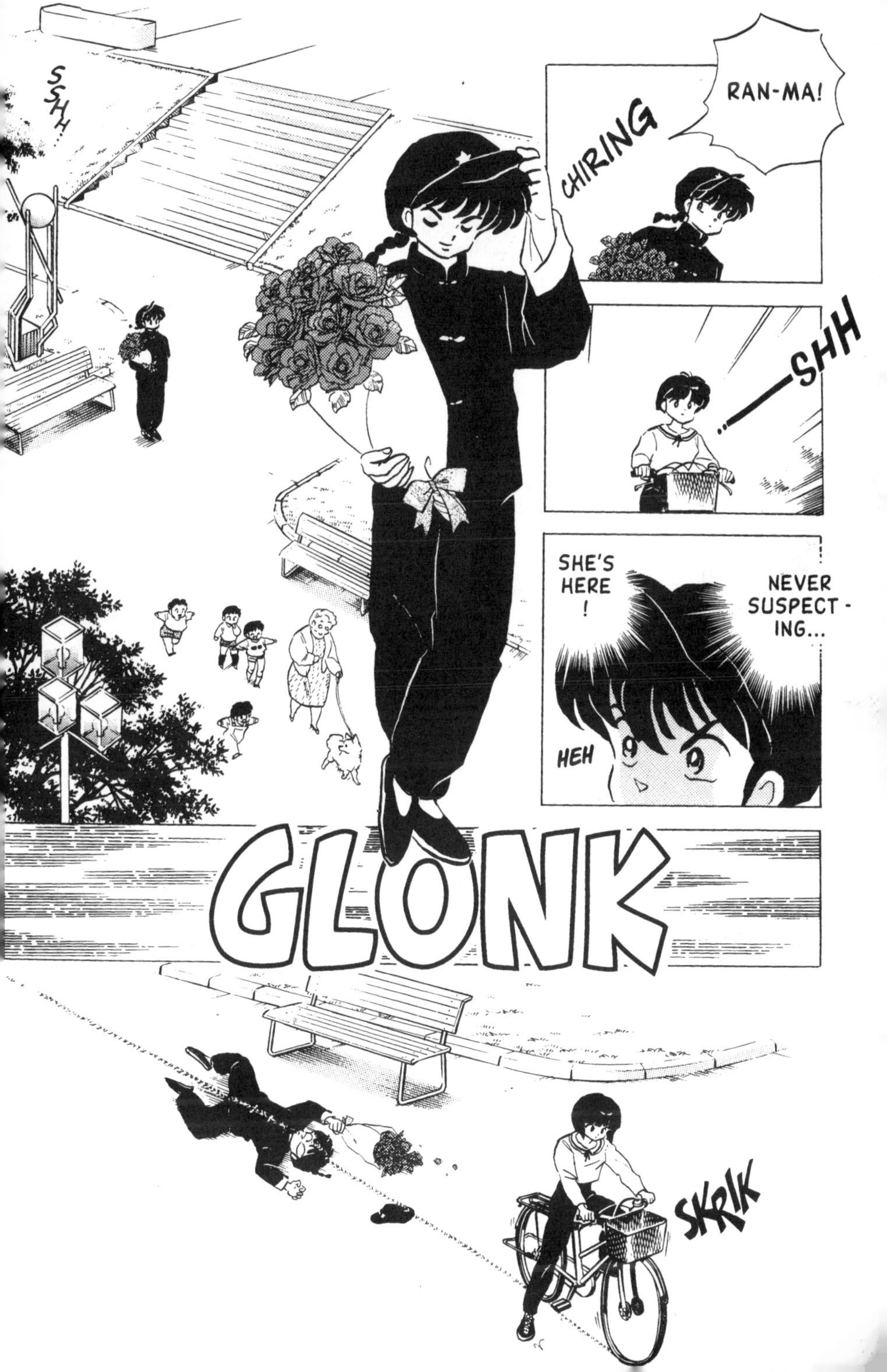

SSHH...
CHIRING
RAN-MA!
SHH
SHE'S HERE!
NEVER SUSPECT-ING...
HEH
GLONK
SKRIK

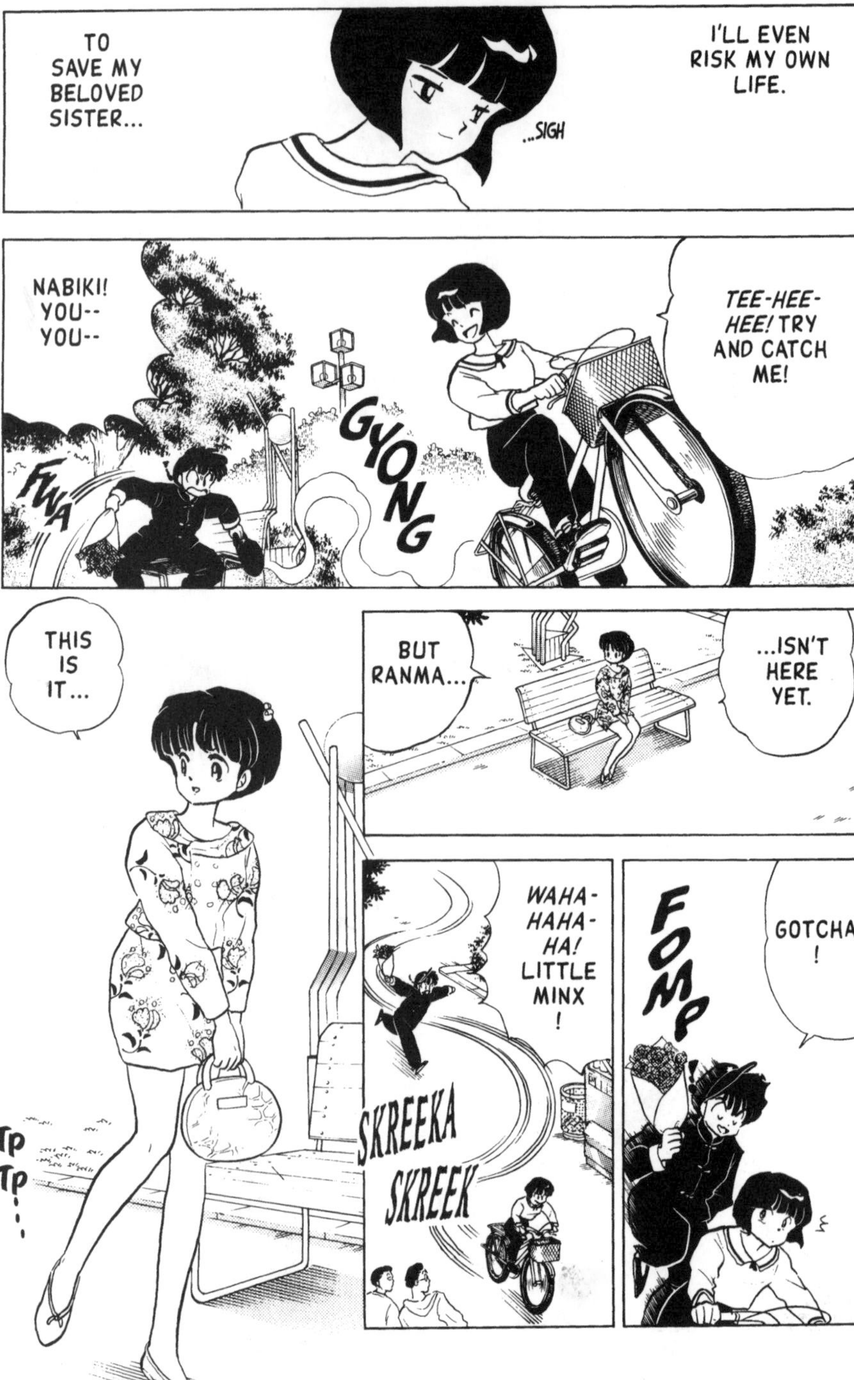

TO SAVE MY BELOVED SISTER...
...SIGH
I'LL EVEN RISK MY OWN LIFE.
NABIKI! YOU-- YOU--
FWA
GYONG
TEE-HEE-HEE! TRY AND CATCH ME!
THIS IS IT...
Tp Tp...
BUT RANMA...
...ISN'T HERE YET.
WAHA-HAHA-HA! LITTLE MINX!
SKREEKA SKREEK
FOMP
GOTCHA!

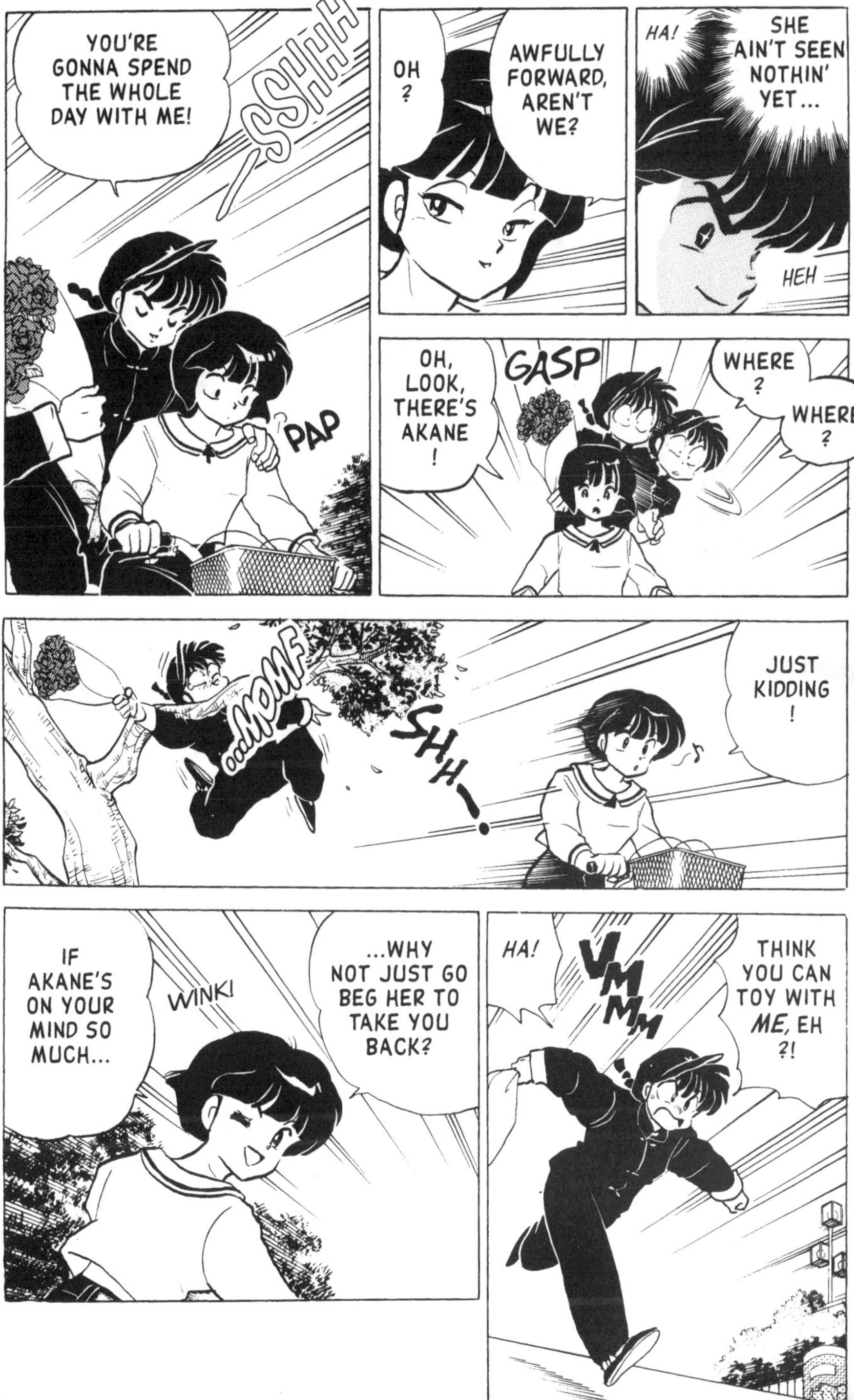
YOU'RE GONNA SPEND THE WHOLE DAY WITH ME!
SSHHH
PAP
OH ?
AWFULLY FORWARD, AREN'T WE?
HA!
SHE AIN'T SEEN NOTHIN' YET...
HEH
OH, LOOK, THERE'S AKANE !
GASP
WHERE ?
WHERE ?
MOMF
SHH-!
JUST KIDDING !
IF AKANE'S ON YOUR MIND SO MUCH...
WINK!
...WHY NOT JUST GO BEG HER TO TAKE YOU BACK?
HA!
VMMM
THINK YOU CAN TOY WITH ME, EH ?!

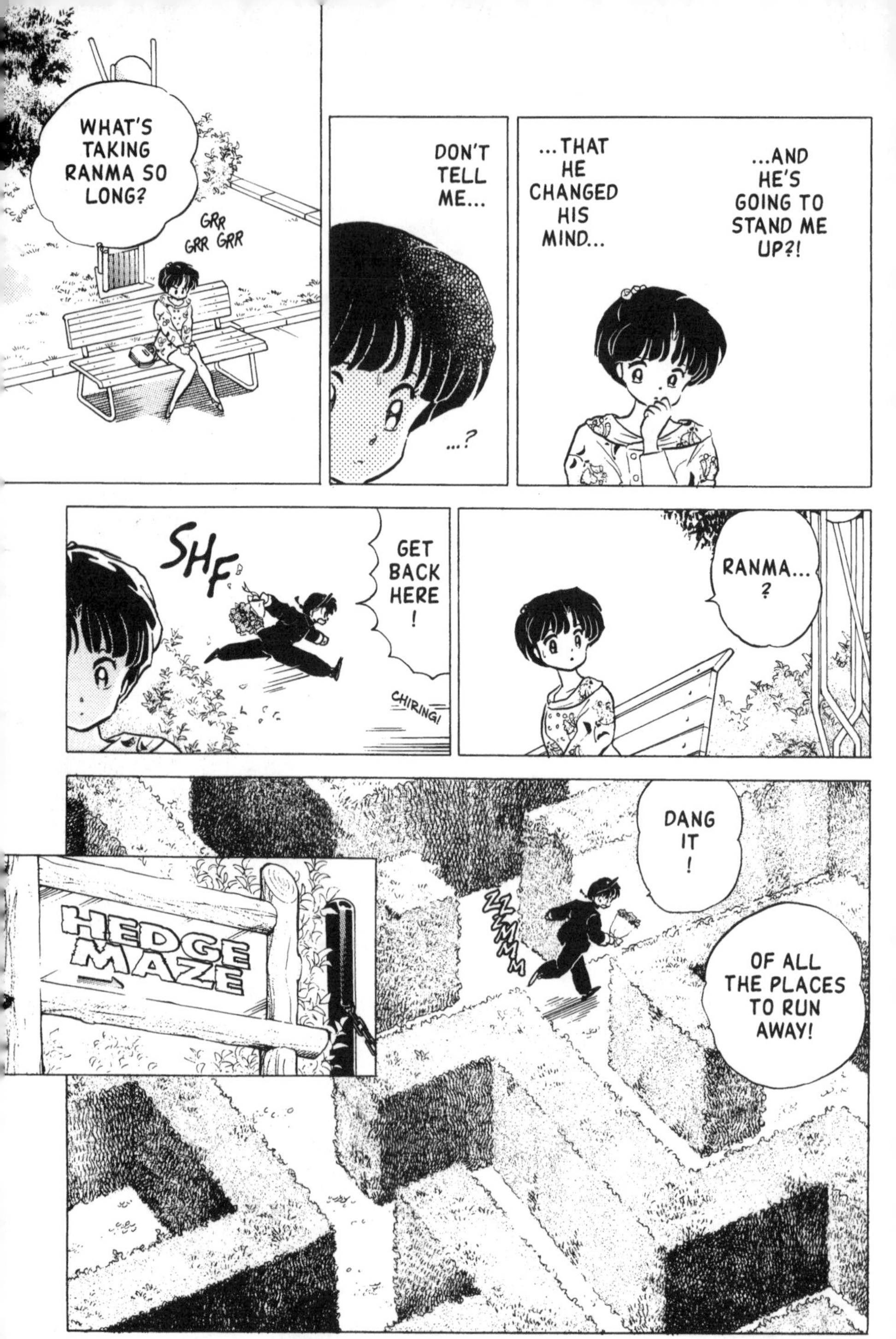
WHAT'S TAKING RANMA SO LONG?
GRR GRR GRR
DON'T TELL ME...
...?
...THAT HE CHANGED HIS MIND...
...AND HE'S GOING TO STAND ME UP?!
SHF
GET BACK HERE!
CHIRING!
RANMA...?
HEDGE MAZE
DANG IT!
ZZMMM
OF ALL THE PLACES TO RUN AWAY!

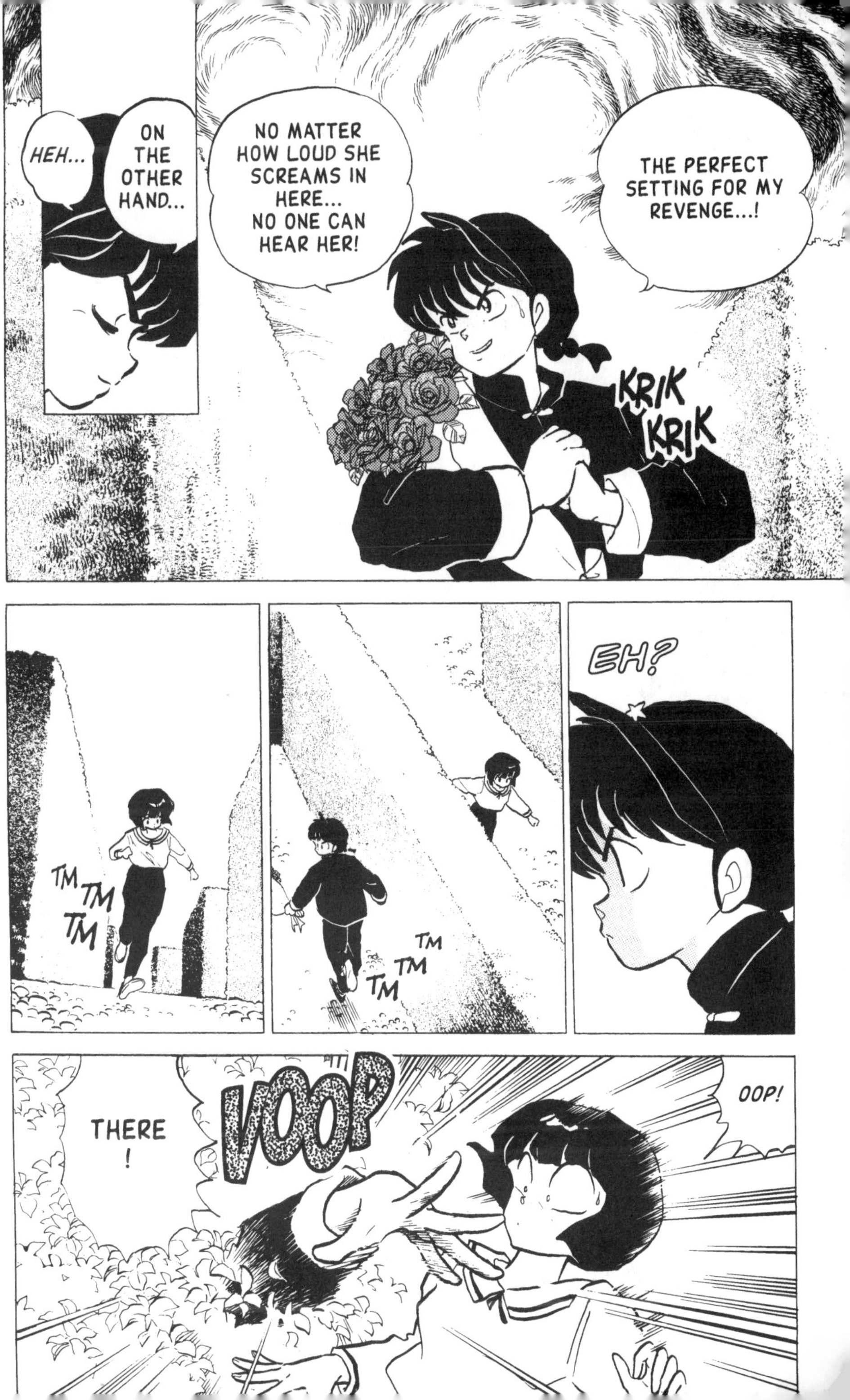
HEH...
ON THE OTHER HAND...
NO MATTER HOW LOUD SHE SCREAMS IN HERE... NO ONE CAN HEAR HER!
THE PERFECT SETTING FOR MY REVENGE...!
KRIK KRIK
TM TM TM
TM TM TM
EH?
THERE !
VOOP
OOP!

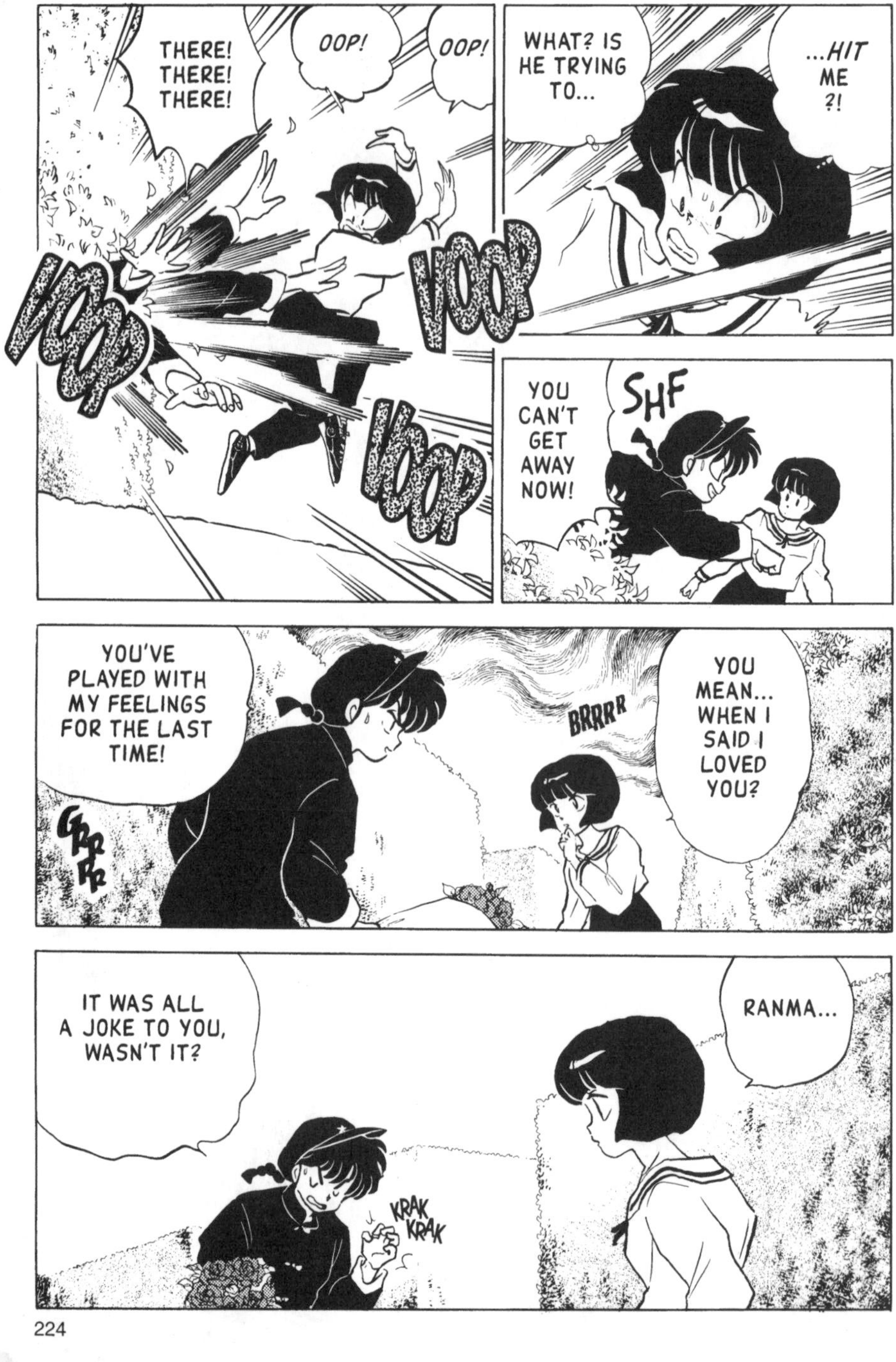

THERE! THERE! THERE!
OOP!
OOP!
VOOP
VOOP
VOOP
WHAT? IS HE TRYING TO...
...HIT ME ?!
YOU CAN'T GET AWAY NOW!
SHF
YOU'VE PLAYED WITH MY FEELINGS FOR THE LAST TIME!
GRRRR
BRRRR
YOU MEAN... WHEN I SAID I LOVED YOU?
IT WAS ALL A JOKE TO YOU, WASN'T IT?
KRAK KRAK
RANMA...

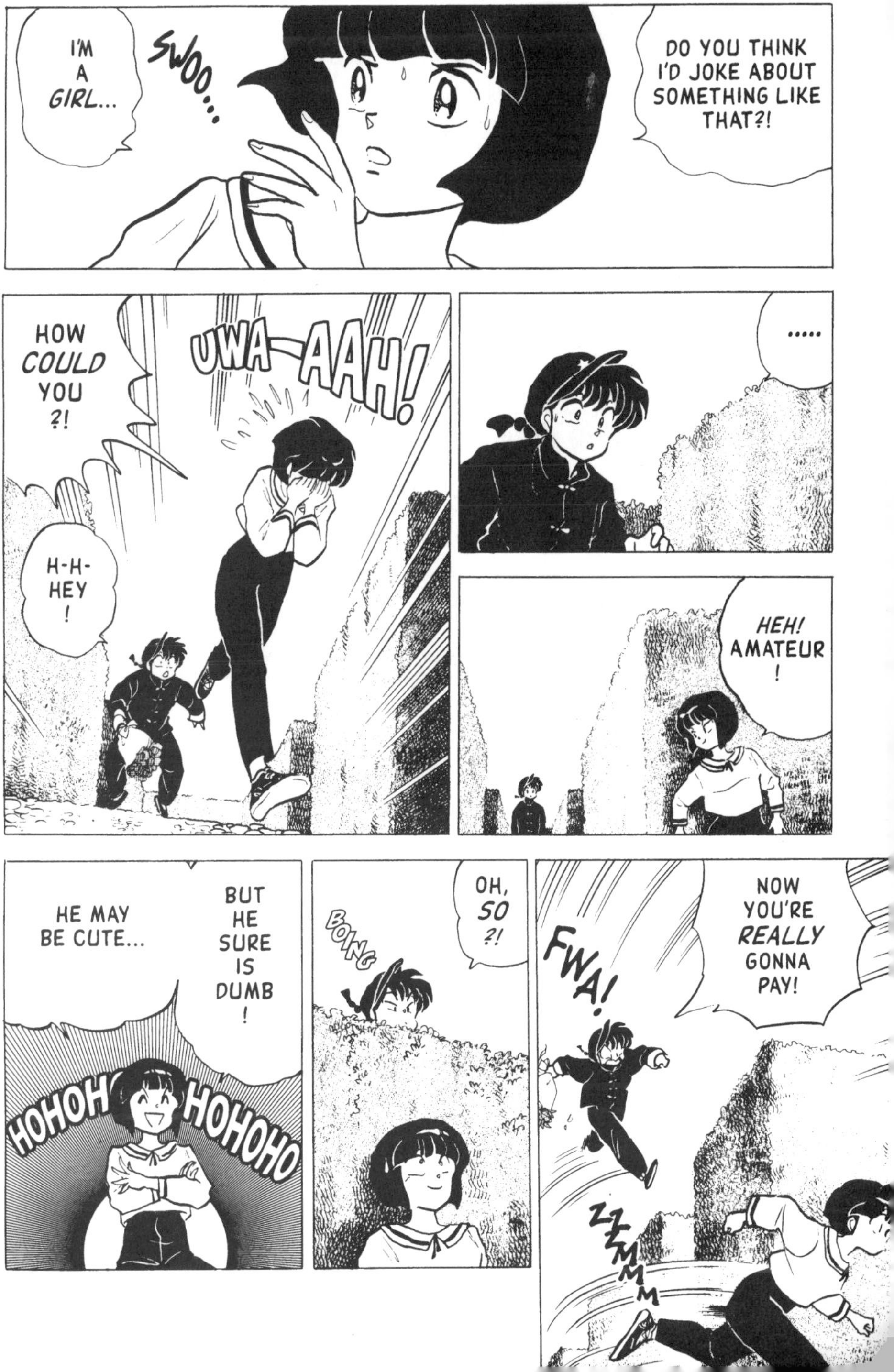
I'M A GIRL...
SWOO...
DO YOU THINK I'D JOKE ABOUT SOMETHING LIKE THAT?!
HOW COULD YOU ?!
UWA-AAH!
H-H-HEY !
.....
HEH! AMATEUR !
HE MAY BE CUTE...
BUT HE SURE IS DUMB !
HOHOHO HOHOHO
BOING
OH, SO ?!
NOW YOU'RE REALLY GONNA PAY!
FWA!
ZZZMMM

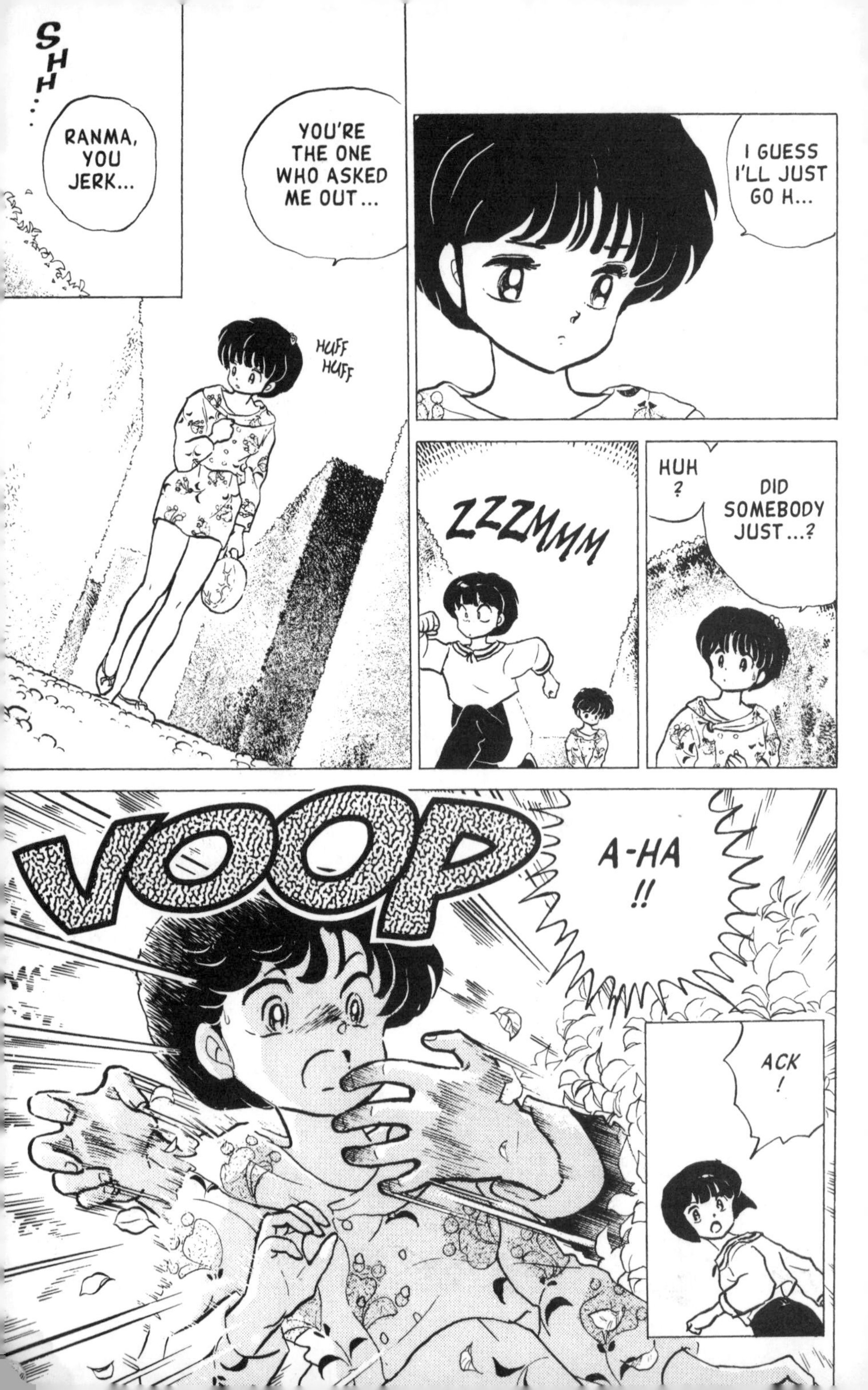
SHH...
RANMA, YOU JERK...
YOU'RE THE ONE WHO ASKED ME OUT...
HUFF HUFF
I GUESS I'LL JUST GO H...
ZZZMMM
HUH?
DID SOMEBODY JUST...?
VOOP
A-HA!!
ACK!

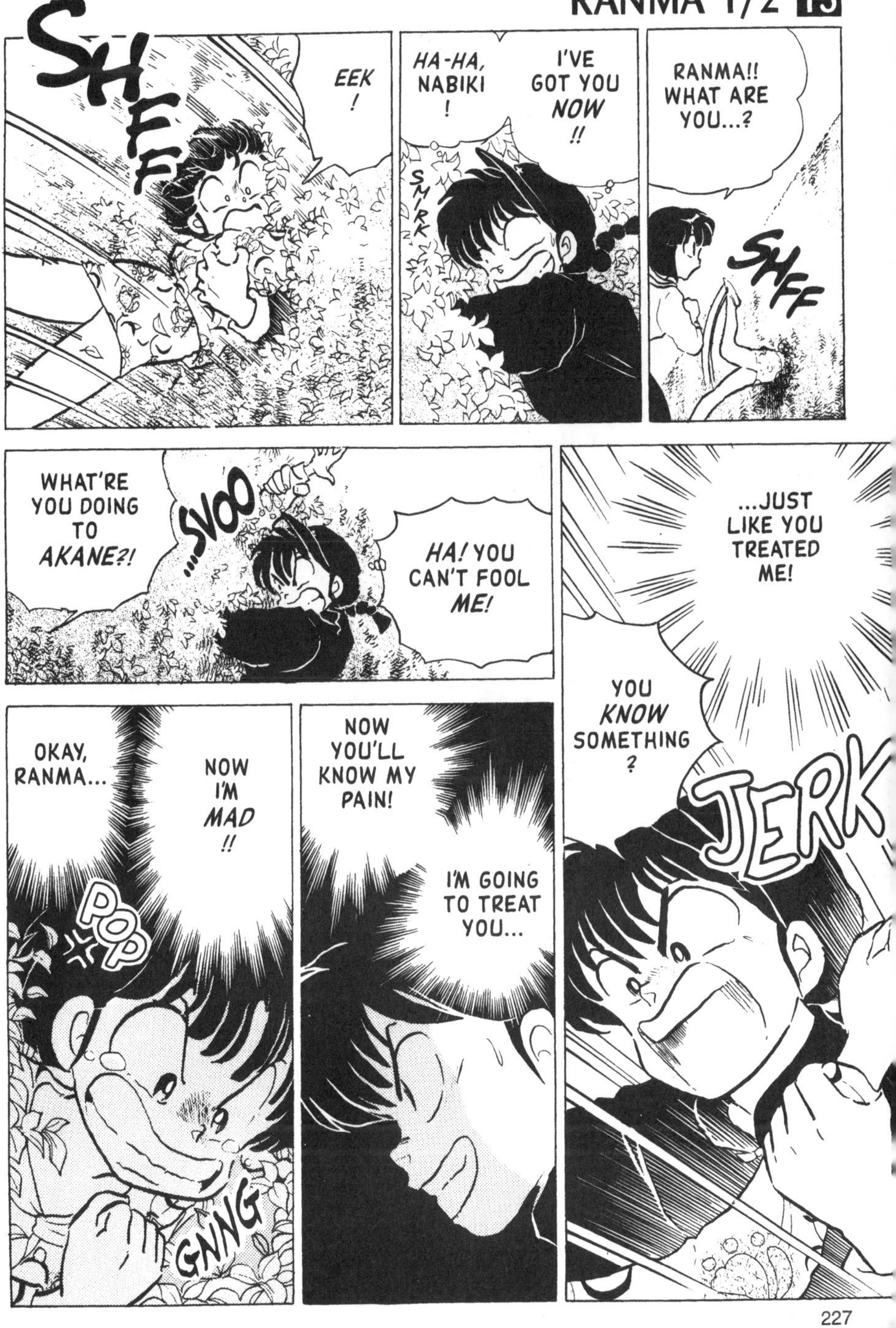
SHEFF
EEK!
HA-HA, NABIKI!
I'VE GOT YOU NOW!!
SMIRK
RANMA!! WHAT ARE YOU...?
SHFF
WHAT'RE YOU DOING TO AKANE?!
...SVOO
HA! YOU CAN'T FOOL ME!
OKAY, RANMA...
NOW I'M MAD!!
POP
GNNG
NOW YOU'LL KNOW MY PAIN!
I'M GOING TO TREAT YOU...
...JUST LIKE YOU TREATED ME!
YOU KNOW SOMETHING?
JERK

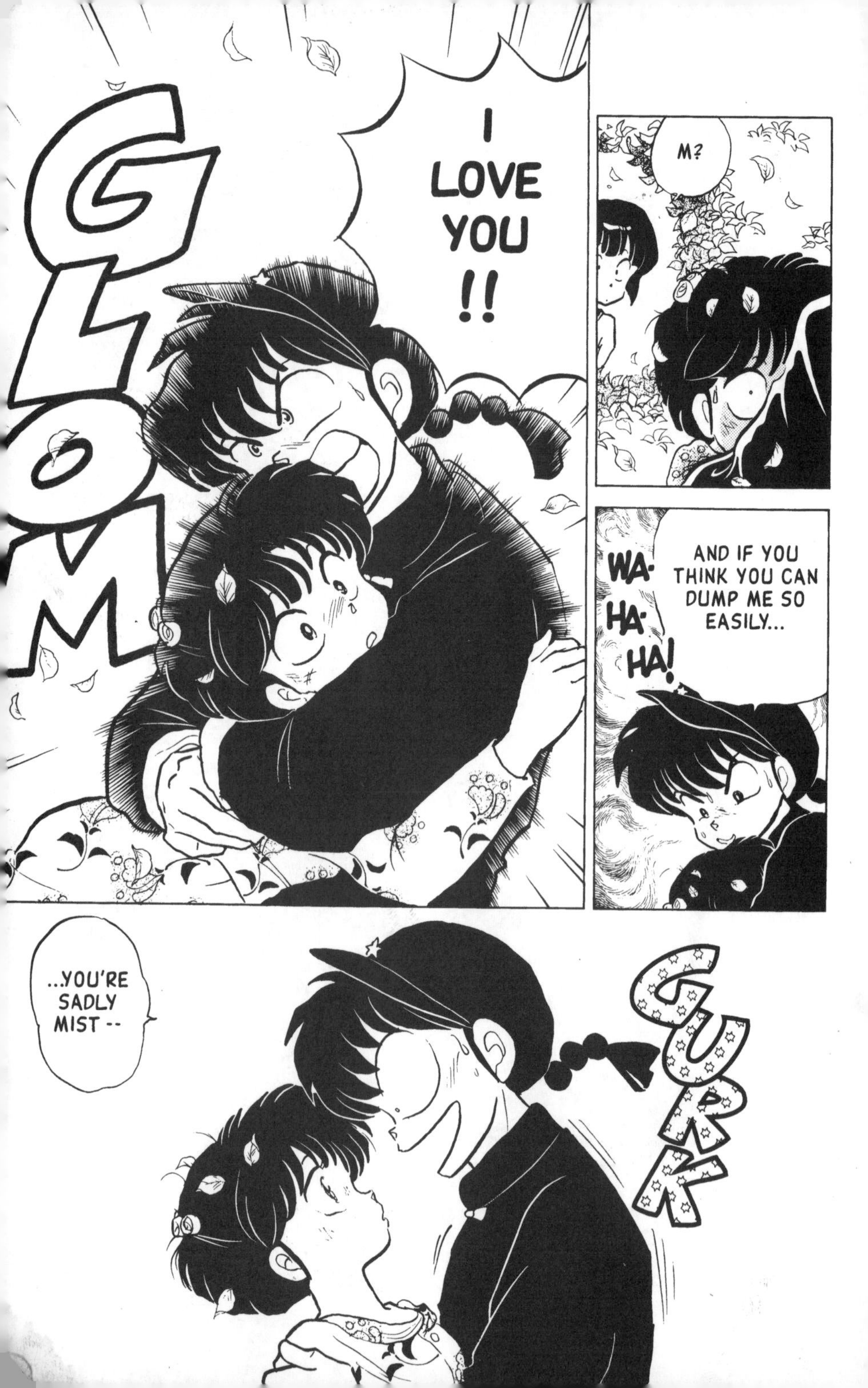
GLOMM
I LOVE YOU !!
M?
WA-HA-HA!
AND IF YOU THINK YOU CAN DUMP ME SO EASILY...
...YOU'RE SADLY MIST --
GURK

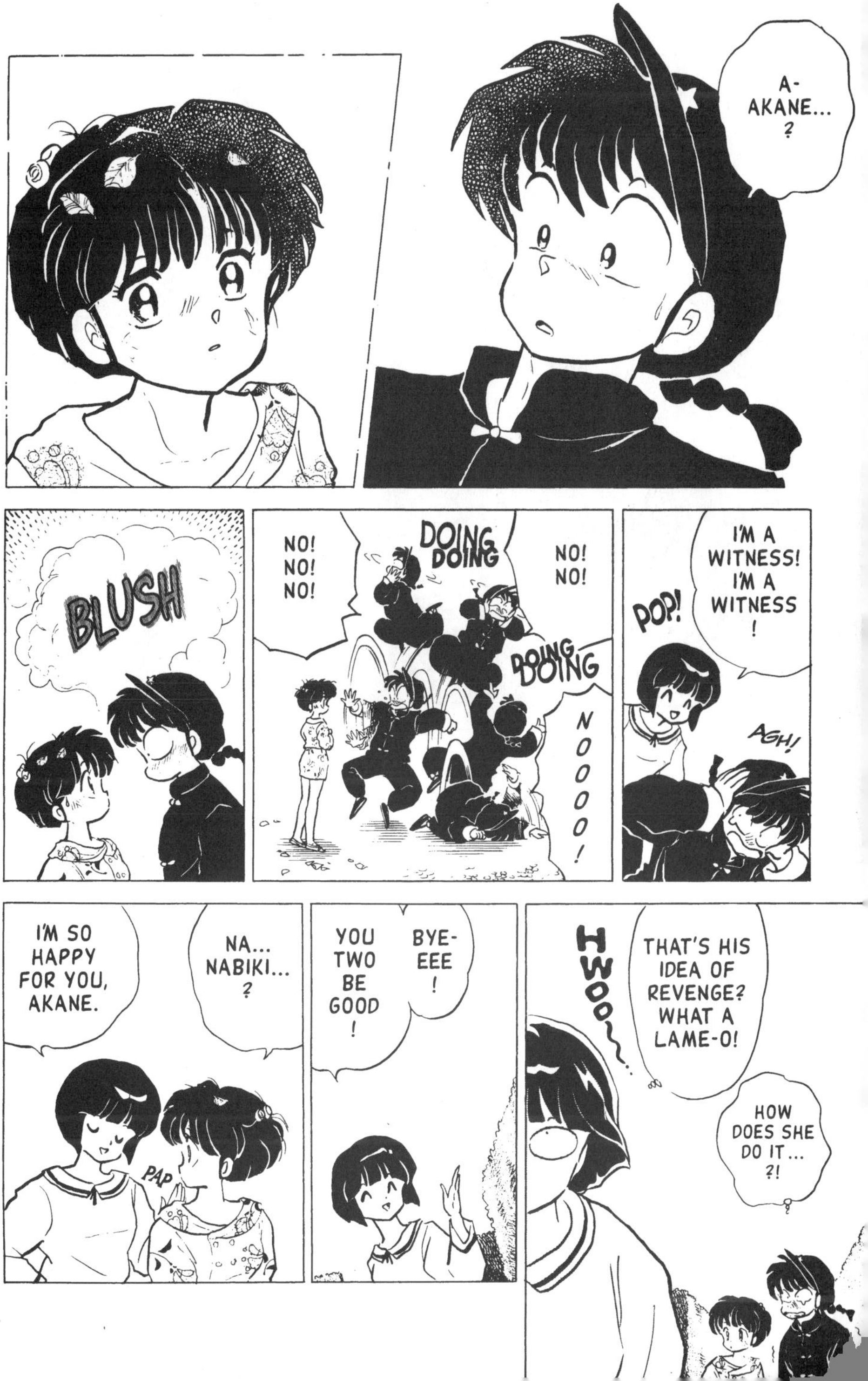
A-
AKANE...
?
BLUSH
NO!
NO!
NO!
DOING
DOING
NO!
NO!
DOING
DOING
NOOOOO!
POP!
I'M A
WITNESS!
I'M A
WITNESS
!
AGH!
I'M SO
HAPPY
FOR YOU,
AKANE.
NA...
NABIKI...
?
PAP
YOU
TWO
BE
GOOD
!
BYE-
EEE
!
HWOO~~
THAT'S HIS
IDEA OF
REVENGE?
WHAT A
LAME-O!
HOW
DOES SHE
DO IT...
?!

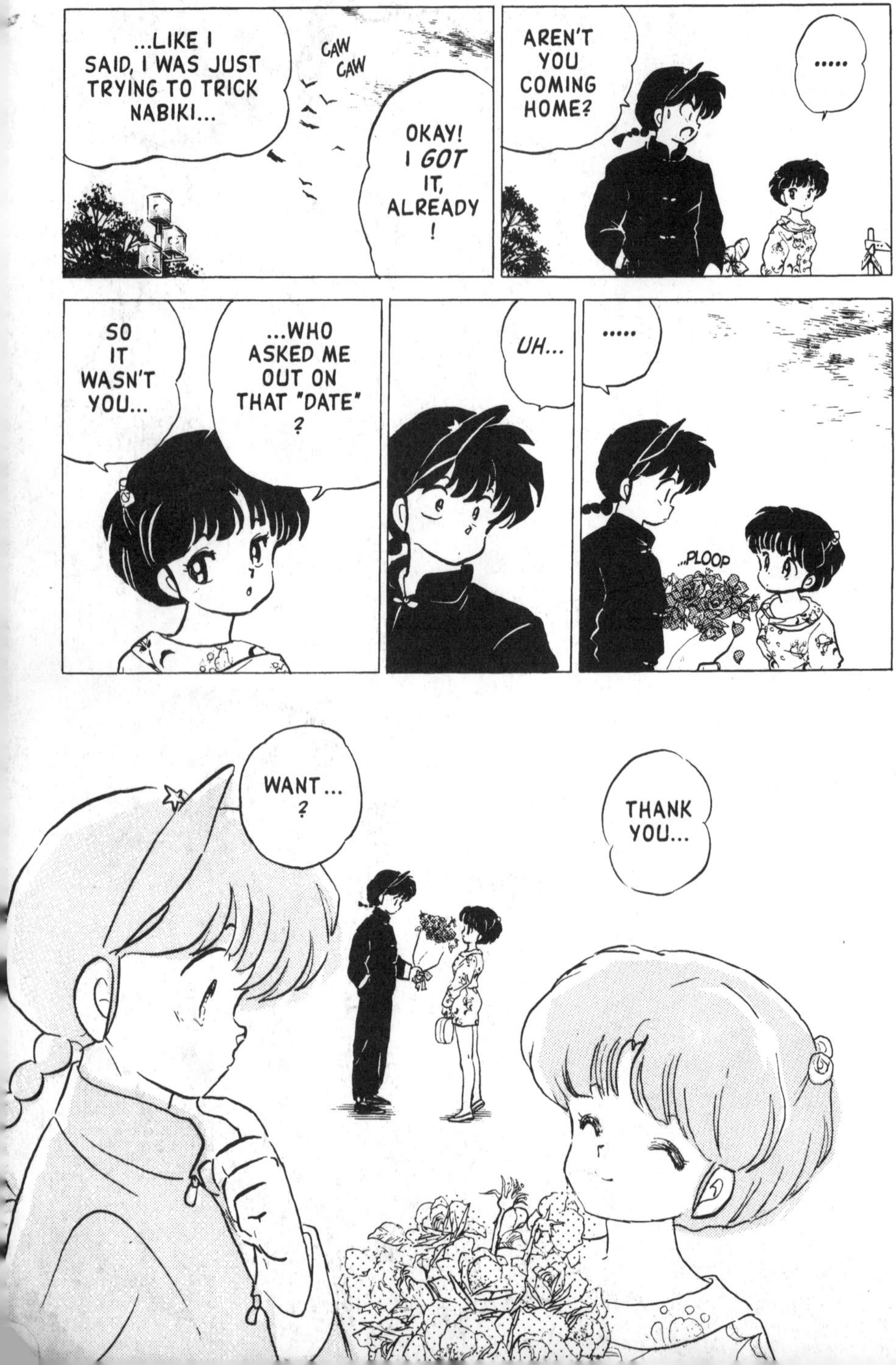
...LIKE I SAID, I WAS JUST TRYING TO TRICK NABIKI...
CAW CAW
OKAY! I GOT IT, ALREADY!
AREN'T YOU COMING HOME?
.....
SO IT WASN'T YOU...
...WHO ASKED ME OUT ON THAT "DATE"?
UH...
.....
...PLOOP
WANT...?
THANK YOU...

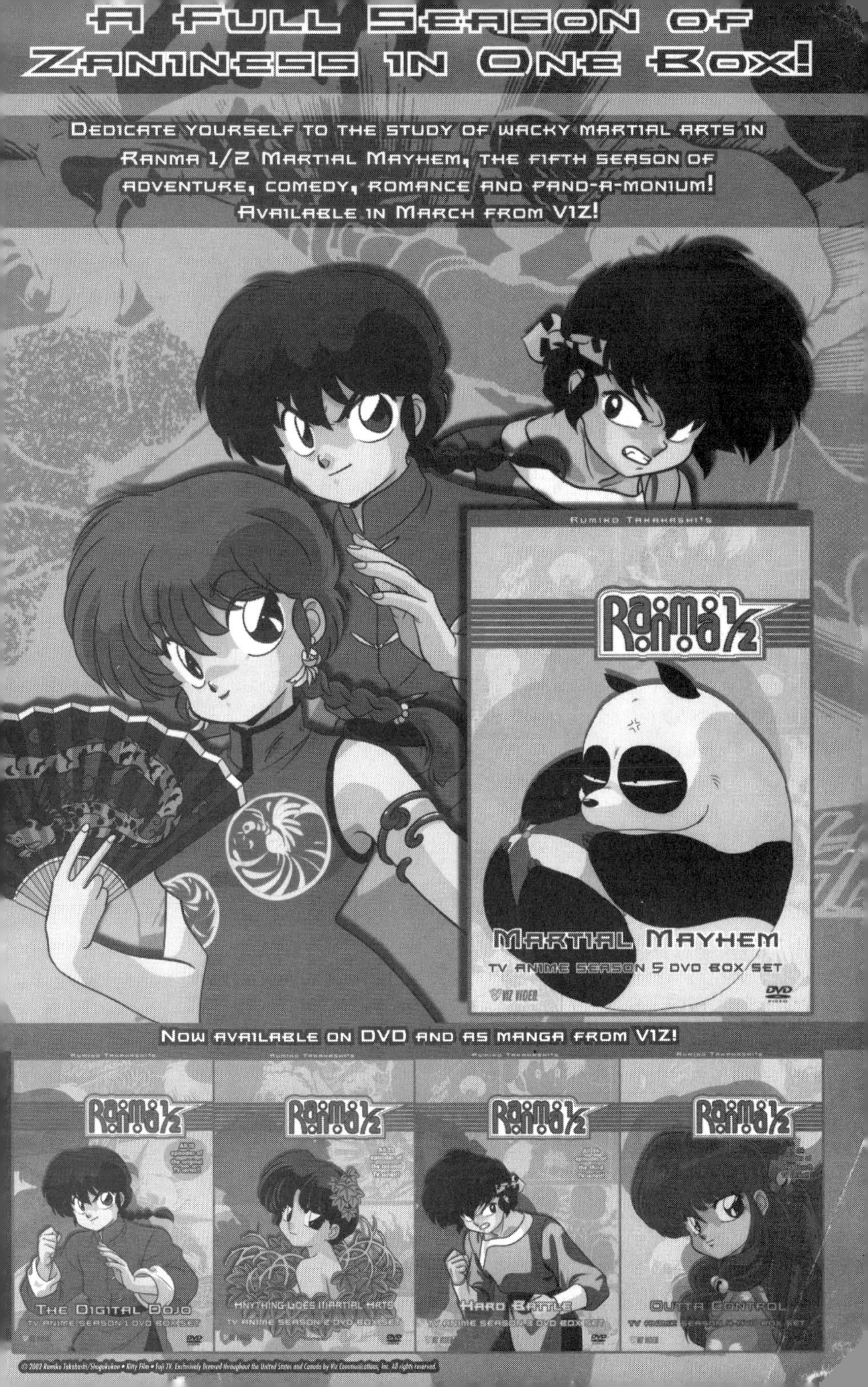
A FULL SEASON OF ZANINESS IN ONE BOX!
DEDICATE YOURSELF TO THE STUDY OF WACKY MARTIAL ARTS IN RANMA 1/2 MARTIAL MAYHEM, THE FIFTH SEASON OF ADVENTURE, COMEDY, ROMANCE AND PAND-A-MONIUM! AVAILABLE IN MARCH FROM VIZ!
RUMIKO TAKAHASHI'S
Ranma 1/2
MARTIAL MAYHEM
TV ANIME SEASON 5 DVD BOX SET
VIZ VIDEO
DVD
NOW AVAILABLE ON DVD AND AS MANGA FROM VIZ!
Ranma 1/2
THE DIGITAL DOJO
TV ANIME SEASON 1 DVD BOX SET
Ranma 1/2
ANYTHING-GOES MARTIAL ARTS
TV ANIME SEASON 2 DVD BOX SET
Ranma 1/2
HARD BATTLE
TV ANIME SEASON 3 DVD BOX SET
Ranma 1/2
OUTTA CONTROL
TV ANIME SEASON 4 DVD BOX SET
© 2002 Rumiko Takahashi/Shogakukan • Kitty Film • Fuji TV. Exclusively licensed throughout the United States and Canada by Viz Communications, Inc. All rights reserved.